To my wife, Robin, my partner in life and in the adventure of making this series, whose hard work and dedication made it all possible

To my daughter Sarah, who would not read the story until it was published

To Steve Gillick for his feedback, and Pete DeBrule, who started this whole thing

And to the members of Dragonchow, my original fan club

Contents

Book I

The Crown Conspiracy
1

Book II

Avempartha
313

Known Regions of the World of Elan

Estrendor: Northern wastes
Erivan Empire: Elvenlands
Apeladorn: Nations of man
Ba Ran Archipelago: Islands of goblins
Westerlands: Western wastes
Dacca: Isle of south men

Nations of Apeladorn

Avryn: Central wealthy kingdoms
Trent: Northern mountainous kingdoms
Calis: Southeastern tropical region ruled by warlords
Delgos: Southern republic

Kingdoms of Avryn

Ghent: Ecclesiastical holding of the Nyphron Church
Melengar: Small but old and respected kingdom
Warric: Most powerful of the kingdoms of Avryn
Dunmore: Youngest and least sophisticated kingdom
Alburn: Forested kingdom
Rhenydd: Poor kingdom
Maranon: Producer of food. Once part of Delgos, which was lost when Delgos became a republic
Galeannon: Lawless kingdom of barren hills, the site of several great battles

THEFT
OF
SWORDS

DeWitt had told Hadrian he had left the sword behind the altar, and they headed toward it. As they approached the first set of pews, both men froze in mid-step. Lying there, facedown in a pool of freshly spilled blood, was the body of a man. The rounded handle of a dagger protruded from his back. While Royce made a quick survey for Pickering's sword, Hadrian checked the man for signs of life. The man was dead, and the sword was nowhere to be found. Royce tapped Hadrian on the shoulder and pointed at the gold crown that had rolled to the far side of a pillar. The full weight of the situation registered with both of them—it was time to leave.

They headed for the door. Royce paused only momentarily to listen to ensure the hall was clear. They slipped out of the chapel, closed the door, and moved down the hall toward the bedroom.

"*Murderers!*"

The shout was so close and so terrifying that they both spun with weapons drawn. Hadrian had his bastard sword in one hand, his short sword in the other. Royce held a brilliant white-bladed dagger.

Standing before the open chapel door was a bearded dwarf.

"*Murderers!*" the dwarf cried again, but it was not necessary. Footfalls could already be heard, and an instant later, soldiers, with weapons drawn, poured into the hallway from both sides.

BY MICHAEL J. SULLIVAN

The Riyria Revelations

Theft of Swords

Rise of Empire

Heir of Novron

THEFT OF SWORDS

Volume One of the Riyria Revelations

MICHAEL J. SULLIVAN

www.orbitbooks.net

ORBIT

First published in Great Britain in 2011 by Orbit

A CIP catalogue record for this book is available from the British Library.

ISBN 978-0-356-50106-2

Printed and bound in Great Britain by
Clays Ltd, St Ives plc.

Papers used by Orbit are from well-managed forests
and other responsible sources.

MIX
Paper from
responsible sources
FSC® C104740

Orbit
An imprint of
Little, Brown Book Group
100 Victoria Embankment
London EC4Y 0DY

An Hachette UK Company
www.hachette.co.uk

www.orbitbooks.net

The Gods

Erebus: Father of the gods
Ferrol: Eldest son, god of elves
Drome: Second son, god of dwarves
Maribor: Third son, god of men
Muriel: Only daughter, goddess of nature
Uberlin: Son of Muriel and Erebus, god of darkness

Political Parties

Imperialists: Those wishing to unite mankind under a single leader who is the direct descendant of the demigod Novron
Nationalists: Those wishing to be ruled by a leader chosen by the people
Royalists: Those wishing to continue rule by individual, independent monarchs

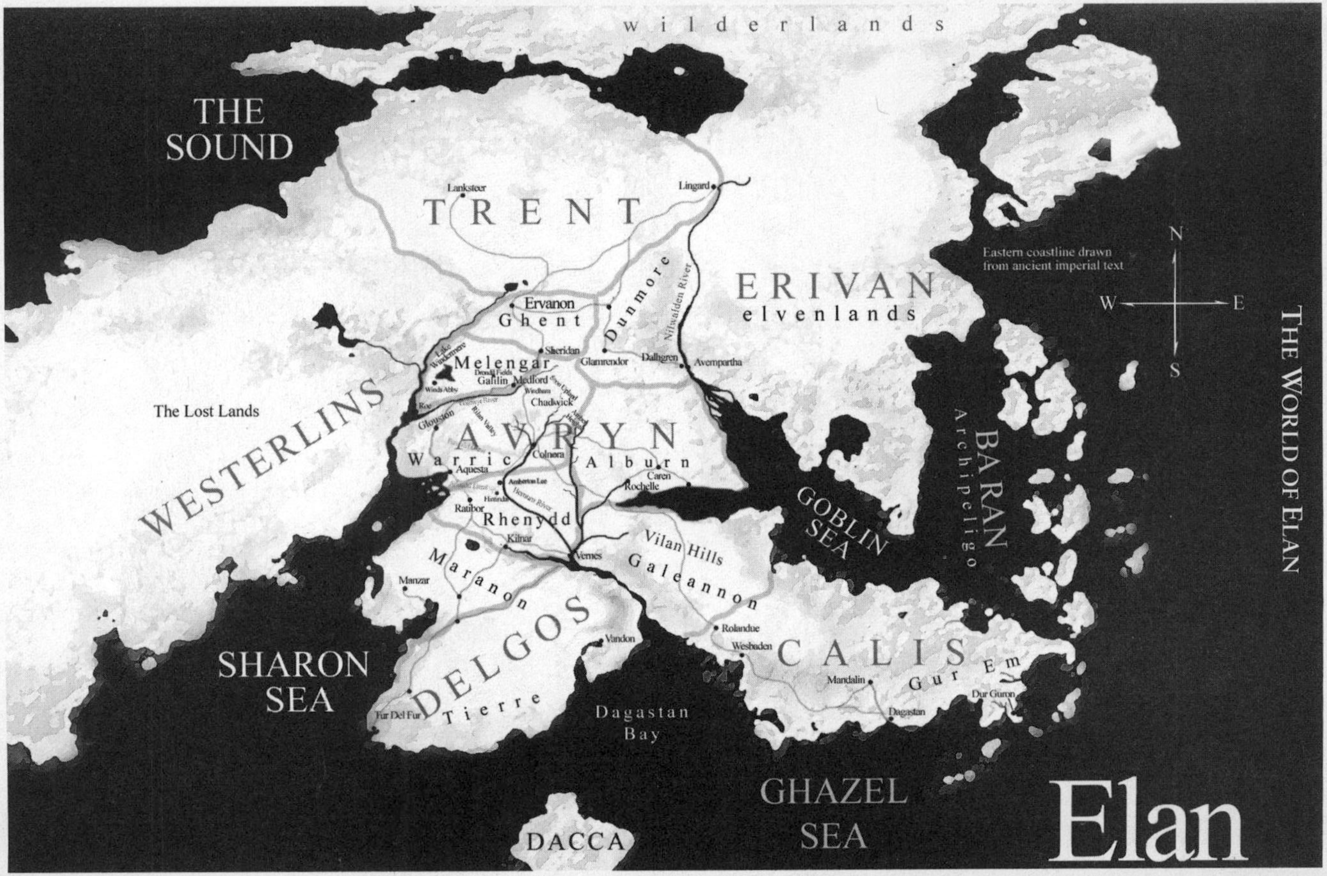

THE WORLD OF ELAN
Elan
wilderlands
THE SOUND
TRENT
ERIVAN
elvenlands
Eastern coastline drawn from ancient imperial text
N
S
E
W
BA RAN
Archipeligo
GOBLIN SEA
The Lost Lands
WESTERLINS
Lanksteer
Lingard
Dunmore
Nilwalden River
Ervanon
Ghent
Melengar
Glamrendor
Dalhgren
Avempartha
Sheridan
Medford
Chadwick
AVRYN
Alburn
Colnora
Warric
Aquesta
Rhenydd
Ratibor
Kilnar
Vernes
Caren
Rochelle
Vilan Hills
Galeannon
Rolandue
Wesbaden
CALIS
Mandalin
Dagastan
Gur Em
Dur Guron
SHARON SEA
Maranon
Manzar
DELGOS
Tierre
Tur Del Fur
Vandon
Dagastan Bay
GHAZEL SEA
DACCA

Detail of Avryn

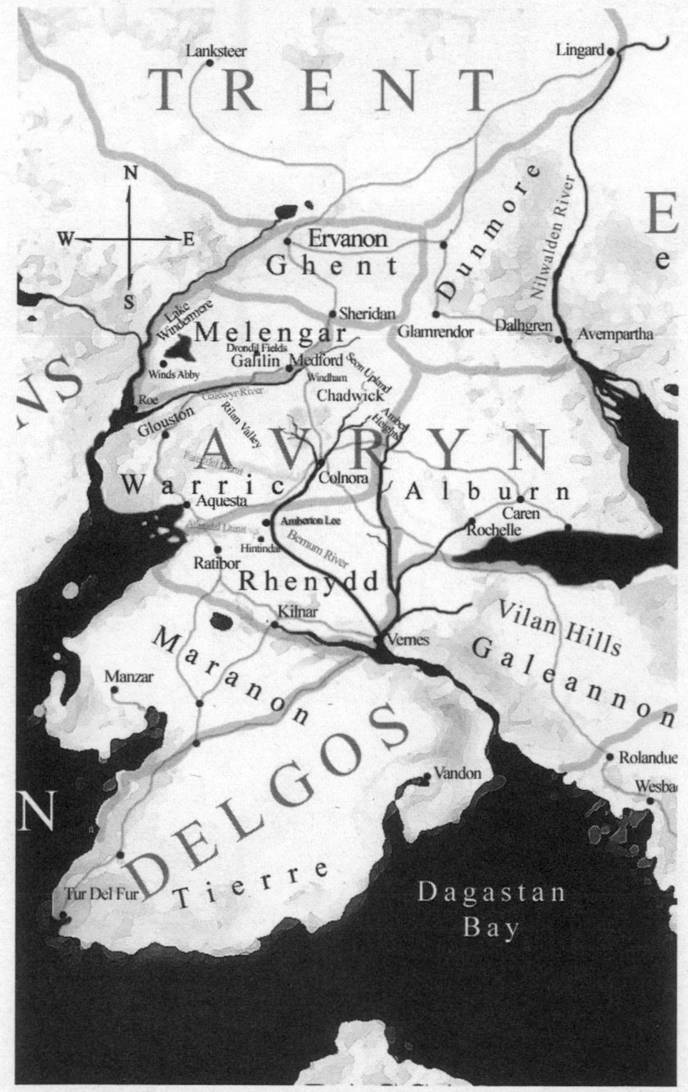

BOOK I

THE CROWN CONSPIRACY

Chapter 1

Stolen Letters

Hadrian could see little in the darkness, but he could hear them—the snapping of twigs, the crush of leaves, and the brush of grass. There were more than one, more than three, and they were closing in.

"Don't neither of you move," a harsh voice ordered from the shadows. "We've got arrows aimed at your backs, and we'll drop you in your saddles if you try to run." The speaker was still in the dark eaves of the forest, just a vague movement among the naked branches. "We're just gonna lighten your load a bit. No one needs to get hurt. Do as I say and you'll keep your lives. Don't—and we'll take those, too."

Hadrian felt his stomach sink, knowing this was his fault. He glanced over at Royce, who sat beside him on his dirty gray mare with his hood up, his face hidden. His friend's head was bowed and shook slightly. Hadrian did not need to see his expression to know what it looked like.

"Sorry," he offered.

Royce said nothing and just continued to shake his head.

Before them stood a wall of fresh-cut brush blocking their way. Behind lay the long moonlit corridor of empty road. Mist pooled in the dips and gullies, and somewhere an unseen stream trickled over rocks. They were deep in the forest on the old southern road, engulfed in a long tunnel of oaks and ash whose slender branches reached out over the road, quivering and clacking in the cold autumn wind. Almost a day's ride from any town, Hadrian could not recall passing so much as a farmhouse in hours. They were on their own, in the middle of nowhere—the kind of place people never found bodies.

The crush of leaves grew louder until at last the thieves stepped into the narrow band of moonlight. Hadrian counted four men with unshaven faces and drawn swords. They wore rough clothes, leather and wool, stained, worn, and filthy. With them was a girl wielding a bow, an arrow notched and aimed. She was dressed like the rest in pants and boots, her hair a tangled mess. Each was covered in mud, a ground-in grime, as if the whole lot slept in a dirt burrow.

"They don't look like they got much money," a man with a flat nose said. An inch or two taller than Hadrian, he was the largest of the party, a stocky brute with a thick neck and large hands. His lower lip looked to have been split about the same time his nose was broken.

"But they've got bags of gear," the girl said. Her voice surprised him. She was young, and—despite the dirt—cute, and almost childlike, but her tone was aggressive, even vicious. "Look at all this stuff they're carrying. What's with all the rope?"

Hadrian was uncertain if she was asking him or her fellows. Either way, he was not about to answer. He considered making a joke, but she did not look like the type he could charm with a compliment and a smile. On top of that, she was pointing the arrow at him and it looked like her arm might be growing tired.

"I claim the big sword that fella has on his back," flat-nose said. "Looks right about my size."

"I'll take the other two he's carrying." This came from one with a scar that divided his face at a slight angle, crossing the bridge of his nose just high enough to save his eye.

The girl aimed the point of her arrow at Royce. "I want the little one's cloak. I'd look good in a fine black hood like that."

With deep-set eyes and sunbaked skin, the man closest to Hadrian appeared to be the oldest. He took a step closer and grabbed hold of Hadrian's horse by the bit. "Be real careful now. We've killed plenty of folks along this road. Stupid folks who didn't listen. You don't want to be stupid, do you?"

Hadrian shook his head.

"Good. Now drop them weapons," the thief said. "And then climb down."

"What do you say, Royce?" Hadrian asked. "We give them a bit of coin so nobody gets hurt."

Royce looked over. Two eyes peered out from the hood with a withering glare.

"I'm just saying, we don't want any trouble, am I right?"

"You don't want my opinion," Royce said.

"So you're going to be stubborn."

Silence.

Hadrian shook his head and sighed. "Why do you have to make everything so difficult? They're probably not bad people—just poor. You know, taking what they need to buy a loaf of bread to feed their family. Can you begrudge them that? Winter is coming and times are hard." He nodded his head in the direction of the thieves. "Right?"

"I ain't got no family," flat-nose replied. "I spend most of my coin on drink."

"You're not helping," Hadrian said.

"I'm not trying to. Either you two do as you're told, or we'll gut you right here." He emphasized this by pulling a long dagger from his belt and scraping it loudly against the blade of his sword.

A cold wind howled through the trees, bobbing the branches and stripping away more foliage. Red and gold leaves flew, swirling in circles, buffeted by the gusts along the narrow road. Somewhere in the dark an owl hooted.

"Look, how about we give you half our money? *My half.* That way this won't be a total loss for you."

"We ain't asking for half," the man holding his mount said. "We want it all, right down to these here horses."

"Now wait a second. Our horses? Taking a little coin is fine but horse thieving? If you get caught, you'll hang. And you know we'll report this at the first town we come to."

"You're from up north, ain't you?"

"Yeah, left Medford yesterday."

The man holding his horse nodded and Hadrian noticed a small red tattoo on his neck. "See, that's your problem." His face softened to a sympathetic expression that appeared more threatening by its intimacy. "You're probably on your way to Colnora—nice city. Lots of shops. Lots of fancy rich folk. Lots of trading going on down there, and we get lots of people along this road carrying all kinds of stuff to sell to them fancy folk. But I'm guessing you ain't been south before, have you? Up in Melengar, King Amrath goes to the trouble of having soldiers patrol the roads. But here in Warric, things are done a bit differently."

Flat-nose came closer, licking his split lip as he studied the spadone sword on his back.

"Are you saying theft is legal?"

"Naw, but King Ethelred lives in Aquesta and that's awfully far from here."

"And the Earl of Chadwick? Doesn't he administer these lands on the king's behalf?"

"Archie Ballentyne?" The mention of his name brought

chuckles from the other thieves. "Archie don't give a rat's ass what goes on with the common folk. He's too busy picking out what to wear." The man grinned, showing yellowed teeth that grew at odd angles. "So now drop them swords and climb down. Afterward, you can walk on up to Ballentyne Castle, knock on old Archie's door, and see what he does." Another round of laughter. "Now unless you think this is the perfect place to die—you're gonna do as I say."

"You were right, Royce," Hadrian said in resignation. He unclasped his cloak and laid it across the rear of his saddle. "We should have left the road, but honestly—I mean, we are in the middle of nowhere. What were the odds?"

"Judging from the fact that we're being robbed—pretty good, I think."

"Kinda ironic—Riyria being robbed. Almost funny even."

"It's not funny."

"Did you say Riyria?" the man holding Hadrian's horse asked.

Hadrian nodded and pulled his gloves off, tucking them into his belt.

The man let go of his horse and took a step away.

"What's going on, Will?" the girl asked. "What's Riyria?"

"There's a pair of fellas in Melengar that call themselves that." He looked toward the others and lowered his voice a bit. "I got connections up that way, remember? They say two guys calling themselves Riyria work out of Medford and I was told to keep my distance if I was ever to run across them."

"So what you thinking, Will?" scar-face asked.

"I'm thinking maybe we should clear the brush and let them ride through."

"What? Why? There's five of us and just two of them," flat-nose pointed out.

"But they're Riyria."

"So what?"

"So, my *associates* up north—they ain't stupid, and they told everyone never to touch these two. And my associates ain't exactly the squeamish types. If they say to avoid them, there's a good reason."

Flat-nose looked at them again with a critical eye. "Okay, but how do you know these two guys are them? You just gonna take their word for it?"

Will nodded toward Hadrian. "Look at the swords he's carrying. A man wearing one—maybe he knows how to use it, maybe not. A man carries two—he probably don't know nothing about swords, but he wants you to think he does. But a man carrying three swords—that's a lot of weight. No one's gonna haul that much steel around unless he makes a living using them."

Hadrian drew two swords from his sides in a single elegant motion. He flipped one around, letting it spin against his palm once. "Need to get a new grip on this one. It's starting to fray again." He looked at Will. "Shall we get on with this? I believe you were about to rob us."

The thieves shot uncertain glances to each other.

"Will?" the girl asked. She was still holding the bow taut but looked decidedly less confident.

"Let's clear the brush out of their way and let them pass," Will said.

"You sure?" Hadrian asked. "This nice man with the busted nose seems to have his heart set on getting a sword."

"That's okay," flat-nose said, looking up at Hadrian's blades as the moonlight glinted off the mirrored steel.

"Well, if you're sure."

All five nodded and Hadrian sheathed his weapons.

Will planted his sword in the dirt and waved the others

over as he hurried to clear the barricade of branches blocking the roadway.

"You know, you're doing this all wrong," Royce told them.

The thieves stopped and looked up, concerned.

Royce shook his head. "Not clearing the brush—the robbery. You picked a nice spot. I'll give you that. But you should have come at us from both sides."

"And, William—it is William, isn't it?" Hadrian asked.

The man winced and nodded.

"Yeah, William, most people are right-handed, so those coming in close should approach from the left. That would've put us at a disadvantage, having to swing across our bodies at you. Those with bows should be on our right."

"And why just one bow?" Royce asked. "She could have only hit one of us."

"Couldn't even have done that," Hadrian said. "Did you notice how long she held the bow bent? Either she's incredibly strong—which I doubt—or that's a homemade greenwood bow with barely enough power to toss the arrow a few feet. Her part was just for show. I doubt she's ever launched an arrow."

"Have too," the girl said. "I'm a fine marksman."

Hadrian shook his head at her with a smile. "You had your forefinger on top of the shaft, dear. If you had released, the feathers on the arrow would have brushed your finger and the shot would have gone anywhere but where you wanted it to."

Royce nodded. "Invest in crossbows. Next time stay hidden and just put a couple bolts into each of your targets' chests. All this talking is just stupid."

"Royce!" Hadrian admonished.

"What? You're always saying I should be nicer to people. I'm trying to be helpful."

"Don't listen to him. If you do want some advice, try building a better barricade."

"Yeah, drop a tree across the road next time," Royce said. Waving a hand toward the branches, he added, "This is just pathetic. And cover your faces for Maribor's sake. Warric isn't that big of a kingdom and people might remember you. Sure Ballentyne isn't likely to bother tracking you down for a few petty highway robberies, but you're gonna walk into a tavern one day and get a knife in your back." Royce turned to William. "You were in the Crimson Hand, right?"

Will looked startled. "No one said nothing about that." He stopped pulling on the branch he was working on.

"Didn't need to. The Hand requires all guild members to get that stupid tattoo on their necks." Royce turned to Hadrian. "It's supposed to make them look tough, but all it really does is make it easy to identify them as thieves for the rest of their lives. Painting a red hand on everyone is pretty stupid when you think about it."

"That tattoo is supposed to be a hand?" Hadrian asked. "I thought it was a little red chicken. But now that you mention it, a hand does make more sense."

Royce looked back at Will and tilted his head to one side. "Does kinda look like a chicken."

Will clamped a palm over his neck.

After the last of the brush was cleared, William asked, "Who are you, really? What exactly is Riyria? The Hand never told me. They just said to keep clear."

"We're nobody special," Hadrian replied. "Just a couple of travelers enjoying a ride on a cool autumn's night."

"But seriously," Royce said. "You need to listen to us if you're going to keep doing this. After all, we're going to take your advice."

"What advice?"

Royce gave a gentle kick to his horse and started forward

on the road again. "We're going to visit the Earl of Chadwick, but don't worry—we won't mention you."

❧

In his hands Archibald Ballentyne held the world, conveniently contained within fifteen stolen letters. Each parchment had been penned with meticulous care in a fine, elegant script. He could tell the writer believed that the words were profound and that their meaning conveyed a beautiful truth. Archibald felt the writing was drivel, yet he agreed with the author that they held a value beyond measure. He took a sip of brandy, closed his eyes, and smiled.

"Milord?"

Reluctantly Archibald opened his eyes and scowled at his master-at-arms. "What is it, Bruce?"

"The marquis has arrived, sir."

Archibald's smile returned. He carefully refolded the letters, tied them in a stack with a blue ribbon, and returned them to his safe. He closed its heavy iron door, snapped the lock in place, and tested the seal with two sharp tugs on the unyielding bolt. Then he headed downstairs to greet his guest.

When Archibald reached the foyer, he spied Victor Lanaklin waiting in the anteroom. He paused for a moment and watched the old man pacing back and forth. Watching him brought Archibald a sense of satisfaction. While the marquis enjoyed a superior title, the man had never impressed the earl. Perhaps Victor had once been lofty, intimidating, or even gallant, but all his glory had been lost long before, shrouded under a mat of gray hair and a hunched back.

"May I offer you something to drink, Your Lordship?" a mousy steward asked the marquis with a formal bow.

"No, but you can get me your earl," he commanded. "Or shall I hunt for him myself?"

The steward cringed. "I'm certain my master will be with you presently, sir." The servant bowed again and hastily retreated through a door on the far side of the room.

"Marquis!" Archibald called out graciously as he made his entrance. "I'm so pleased you have arrived—and so quickly."

"You sound surprised," Victor replied with a sharp voice. Shaking a wrinkled parchment clasped in his fist, he continued, "You send a message like this and expect me to delay? Archie, I demand to know what is going on."

Archibald concealed his disdain at the use of his childhood nickname, *Archie*. This was the moniker his dead mother had given him and one of the reasons he would never forgive her. When he was a youth, everyone from the knights to the servants had used it, and Archibald had always felt demeaned by its familiarity. Once he became earl, he made it law in Chadwick that anyone referring to him by the name would suffer the lash. Archibald did not have the power to enforce the edict on the marquis, and he was certain Victor used it intentionally.

"Please do try to calm down, Victor."

"Don't tell me to calm down!" The marquis's voice echoed off the stone walls. He moved closer, his face mere inches from the younger man's, and glared into his eyes. "You wrote that my daughter Alenda's future was at stake and spoke of evidence. Now I must know—is she, or is she not, in danger?"

"She is most certainly," the earl replied calmly, "but nothing imminent, to be sure. There is no kidnapping plot nor is anyone planning to murder her, if that's what you fear."

"Then why send me this message? If you've caused me to run my carriage team to near collapse while I worried myself sick for nothing, you'll regret—"

Holding up his hand, Archibald cut the threat short. "I

assure you, Victor, it's not for nothing. Nevertheless, before we discuss this further, let us retire to the comfort of my study, where I can show you the evidence I mentioned."

Victor glowered at him but nodded in agreement.

The two men crossed the foyer, passed through the large reception hall, and veered off through a door that led to the living quarters of the castle. As they traversed various hallways and stairways, the atmosphere of their surroundings changed dramatically. In the main entry, fine tapestries and etched stonework adorned the walls, and the floors were made of finely crafted marble. Yet beyond the entry, no displays of grandeur were found, leaving barren walls of stone the predominate feature.

By architectural standards, or any other measures, Ballentyne Castle was unremarkable and ordinary in every respect. No great king or hero had ever called the castle home. Nor was it the site of any legend, ghost story, or battle. Instead, it was the perfect example of mediocrity and the mundane.

After several minutes navigating the various hallways, Archibald stopped at a formidable cast-iron door. Impressive oversized bolts secured the door at its hinges, but no latch or knob was visible. Flanking either side of it stood two large well-armored guards bearing halberds. Upon Archibald's approach, one rapped three times. A tiny viewing window opened, and a moment later, the hall echoed with the sharp sound of a bolt snapping back. As the door opened, the metal hinges screamed with a deafening noise.

Victor's hands moved to defend his ears. "By Mar! Have one of your servants tend to that!"

"Never," Archibald replied. "This is the entrance to the Gray Tower—my private study. This is my safe haven and I want to hear this door's opening from anywhere in the castle, which I can."

Behind the door, Bruce greeted the pair with a deep and

stately bow. Holding a lantern before him, he escorted the men up a wide spiral staircase. Halfway up the tower, Victor's pace slowed and his breathing appeared labored.

Archibald paused courteously. "I must apologize for the long ascent. I really don't notice it anymore. I must have climbed these stairs a thousand times. When my father was the earl, this was the one place I could go to be alone. No one ever bothered to take the time or effort to reach the top. While it may not reach the majestic height of the Crown Tower at Ervanon, it's the tallest tower in my castle."

"Don't some people come merely to see the view?" Victor speculated.

The earl chuckled. "You would think so, but this tower has no windows, which is what makes it the perfect location for my private study. I added the doors to protect the things dear to me."

Reaching the top of the stairs, they encountered another door. Archibald removed a large key from his pocket, unlocked it, and gestured for the marquis to enter. Bruce resumed his normal post outside the study and closed the door.

The room was large and circular with an expansive ceiling. The furnishings were sparse: a large disheveled desk, two cushioned chairs near a small fireplace, and a delicate table between them. A fire burned in the hearth behind a simple brass screen, illuminating most of the study. Candles, which lined the walls, provided light to the remaining areas and filled the chamber with a pleasant, heady aroma of honey and salifan.

Archibald smiled when he noticed Victor eyeing the cluttered desk overflowing with various scrolls and maps. "Don't worry, sir. I hid all the truly incriminating plans for world domination prior to your visit. Please, do sit down." Archibald indicated the pair of chairs near the hearth. "Rest yourself from your long journey while I pour us a drink."

The older man scowled and grumbled, "Enough of the tour and formalities. Now that we are here, let's get on with it. Explain what this is all about."

Archibald ignored the marquis's tone. He could afford to be gracious now that he was about to claim his prize. He waited while the marquis took his seat.

"You are aware, are you not, that I have shown an interest in your daughter, Alenda?" Archibald asked, walking to the desk to pour two glasses of brandy.

"Yes, she's mentioned it to me."

"Has she mentioned why she refuses my advances?"

"She doesn't like you."

"She hardly knows me," countered Archibald with a raised finger.

"Archie, is this why you asked me here?"

"Marquis, I would appreciate your addressing me by my proper name. It's inappropriate to call me *that*, since my father is dead and I now hold title. In any case, your question does have a bearing on the subject. As you know, I'm the twelfth Earl of Chadwick. Granted, it's not a huge estate, and Ballentyne isn't the most influential of families, but I'm not without merit. I control five villages and twelve hamlets, as well as the strategic Senon Uplands. I currently command more than sixty professional men-at-arms, and twenty knights are loyal to me—including Sir Enden and Sir Breckton, perhaps the two greatest living knights. Chadwick's wool and leather exports are the envy of all of Warric. There is even talk of the Summersrule Games being held here—on the very lawn you crossed to enter my castle."

"Yes, Archie—I mean, *Archibald*—I'm well aware of Chadwick's status in the world. I don't need a commerce lesson from you."

"Are you also aware that King Ethelred's nephew has dined here on more than one occasion? Or that the Duke and Duchess of Rochelle have asked to dine with me at Wintertide this year?"

"Archibald, this is quite tiresome. What exactly is your point?"

Archibald frowned at the marquis's lack of awe. Carrying over the glasses of brandy, he handed one to Victor and took the remaining seat. He paused a moment to sip his liquor.

"My point is this. Given my position, my stature, and my promising future, it makes no sense for Alenda to reject me. Certainly, it's not because of my appearance. I'm young, handsome, and wear only the finest imported fashions made from the most expensive silks to be found. The rest of her suitors are old, fat, or bald—in several cases all three."

"Perhaps looks and wealth are not her only concerns," replied Victor. "Women don't always think about politics and power. Alenda is the kind of girl who follows her heart."

"But she will also follow her father's wishes. Am I correct?"

"I don't understand your meaning."

"If you told her to marry me, she would. You could *order* her."

"So, this is why you coerced me into coming here? I'm sorry, Archibald, but you have wasted your time and mine. I have no intention of forcing her to marry anyone, least of all you. She would hate me for the rest of her life. I care more about my daughter's feelings than the political implications of her marriage. I happen to cherish Alenda. Of all my children, she is my greatest joy."

Archibald took another sip of brandy and considered Victor's remarks. He decided to approach the subject from a different direction. "What if it were for her own good? To save her from what would be certain disaster."

"You warned me of danger to get me here. Are you finally ready to explain, or do you prefer to see if this old man can still handle a blade?"

Archibald disregarded what he knew was an idle threat. "When Alenda repeatedly declined my advances, I reasoned something must be amiss. There was no logic to her rebuffs. I have connections and my star is rising. Then I discovered the real reason for your daughter's refusal—she is already involved with someone else. Alenda is having an affair, a secret affair."

"I find that difficult to believe," Victor declared. "She has not mentioned anyone to me. If someone caught her eye, she would tell me."

"It's little wonder she's kept his identity from you. She's ashamed. She knows that their relationship will bring disgrace to your family. The man she is entertaining is a mere commoner without a single drop of noble blood in his veins."

"You're lying!"

"I assure you, I'm not. The problem goes further than that, I'm afraid. His name is Degan Gaunt. You've heard of him, haven't you? He's quite famous. He's the leader of that Nationalist movement out of Delgos. You know that down south he has stirred up all kinds of emotions with his fellow commoners. They are all intoxicated with the idea of butchering the nobility and establishing self-rule. He and your daughter have been rendezvousing at Windermere near the monastery. They meet when you are away and occupied with matters of state."

"That is ridiculous. My daughter would never—"

"Don't you have a son there?" Archibald inquired. "At the abbey, I mean. He's a monk, isn't he?"

Victor nodded. "My third son, Myron."

"Perhaps he has been helping them. I've made inquiries and it seems that your son is a very intelligent fellow. Perhaps he is masterminding liaisons for his beloved sister and carrying their correspondences. This looks very bad, Victor. Here you are, the marquis of a staunchly Imperialist king, and your daughter is involved with a revolutionary and meeting him in the Royalist kingdom of Melengar while your son sets the whole thing up. Many could assume it's a family plot. What would King Ethelred say if he knew? We both know you're loyal, but others may have their doubts. While I realize this is nothing more than the misguided affections of an innocent girl, her escapades could ruin your family's honor."

"You *are* insane," Victor shot back. "Myron went to the abbey when he was barely four years old. Alenda has never even spoken to him. This whole fabrication is an obvious attempt to have me pressure Alenda into marrying you and I know why. You don't care about her. You want her dowry, the Rilan Valley. That piece of land borders ever so nicely against your own and that's what you are really after. Well, that and the opportunity to raise your own standing by marrying into a family that's above yours both socially and politically. You are pathetic."

"Pathetic, am I?" Archibald set down his glass and produced a key on a silver chain from inside his shirt. He rose and crossed the room to a tapestry depicting a Calian prince on horseback abducting a fair-haired noblewoman. He drew it back, revealing a hidden safe. Inserting the key, he opened the small metal door.

"I have a stack of letters written in your precious daughter's own hand that proves what I've been saying. They tell of her undying love for her disgusting revolutionary peasant."

"How did you get these letters?"

"I stole them. When I was trying to determine who my rival was, I had her watched. She was sending letters that led a path to the abbey and I arranged to have them intercepted." From the safe, Archibald brought forth a stack of parchments and dropped them in Victor's lap. "There!" he declared triumphantly. "Read what your daughter has been up to and decide for yourself whether or not she would be better off marrying me instead."

Archibald returned to his seat and lifted his brandy glass victoriously. He had won. In order to avoid political ruin, Victor Lanaklin, the great Marquis of Glouston, would order his daughter to marry him. The marquis had no choice. If word of this reached Ethelred, it was even possible Victor could face charges for treason. Imperialist kings demand that their nobles mirror their political attitudes and devotion to the church. While Archibald doubted that Victor was really a Royalist or Nationalist sympathizer, any appearance of impropriety would be enough reason for their king to express his displeasure. At the very least, Victor faced crippling embarrassment from which the House of Lanaklin might never recover. The only sensible course for the marquis was to agree to the marriage.

Finally, Archibald would have the borderland, and perhaps in time, he would control the whole of the marchland. With Chadwick in his right hand and Glouston in his left, he would have power at court that would rival that of the Duke of Rochelle.

Looking down at the old, gray-haired man in his fine traveling clothes, Archibald almost felt sorry for him. Once, long ago, the marquis had enjoyed a reputation for cleverness and fortitude. Such distinction came with his title. The marquis was no mere noble, nor was he a simple sheriff of the land, like an earl or a count. Victor had been responsible for guarding the king's borders. This was a serious duty, which required a capable leader, an ever-vigilant man tested in battle. However, times had changed, and peaceful neighbors now bordered Warric, such that the great guard had become complacent, and his strength had withered from lack of use.

As Victor opened the letters, Archibald contemplated his future. The marquis was right. He was after the land that came with his daughter. Still, Alenda was attractive, and the thought of forcing her to his bed was more than a little appealing.

"Archibald, is this a joke?" Victor questioned.

Startled from his thoughts, Archibald set down his drink. "What do you mean?"

"These parchments are blank."

"What? Are you blind? They're—" Archibald stopped when he saw the empty pages in the marquis's hand. He grabbed a handful of letters and tore them open, only to find still more blank parchments. "This is impossible!"

"Perhaps they were written in disappearing ink?" Victor smirked.

"No...I don't understand...These aren't even the same parchments!" He rechecked the safe but found it empty. His confusion turned to panic and he tore open the door, calling anxiously for Bruce. The master-at-arms rushed in, his sword at the ready. "What happened to the letters I had in this safe?" Archibald shouted at the soldier.

"I—I don't know, my lord," Bruce replied. He sheathed his weapon and stood at attention before the earl.

"What do you mean, you don't know? Have you left your post at all this evening?"

"No, sir, of course not."

"Did anyone, anyone at all, enter my study during my absence?"

"No, my lord, that's impossible. You hold the only key."

"Then where in Maribor's name are those letters? I put

them there myself. I was reading them when the marquis arrived. I was only gone a few minutes. How could they disappear like that?"

Archibald's mind raced. He had held them in his hands only moments ago. He had locked them in the safe. He was convinced of that fact.

Where had they gone?

Victor drained his glass and stood. "If you don't mind, *Archie*, I'll be leaving now. This has been a tremendous waste of my time."

"Victor, wait. Don't go. The letters are real. I assure you I had them!"

"But of course you did, Archie. The next time you plan to blackmail me, I suggest you provide a better bluff." He crossed the room, passed through the door, and disappeared down the stairs.

"You had better consider what I said, Victor," Archibald yelled after him. "I'll find those letters. I will! I'll bring them to Aquesta! I'll present them at court!"

"What do you want me to do, my lord?" Bruce asked.

"Just wait, you fool. I have to think." Archibald ran his trembling fingers through his hair as he began to pace around the room. He reexamined the letters closely. They were indeed a different grade of parchment than the ones he had read so many times before.

Despite his certainty he had placed the letters in the safe, he began pulling out the drawers and riffling through the parchments on his desk. Archibald poured himself another drink and crossed the room. Ripping the screen from the fireplace, he probed the ashes with a poker to search for any telltale signs of parchment remains. In frustration, Archibald threw the blank letters into the fire. He drained his drink in one long swallow and collapsed into one of the chairs.

"They were just here," Archibald said, puzzled. Slowly, a solution began to form in his mind. "Bruce, the letters must have been stolen. The thief could not have gotten far. I want you to search the entire castle. Seal every exit. Don't let anyone out. Not the staff or any of the guards—no one leaves. Search everyone!"

"Right away, my lord," Bruce responded, and then paused. "What about the marquis, my lord? Shall I stop him as well?"

"Of course not, you idiot, he doesn't have the letters."

Archibald stared into the fire, listening to Bruce's footsteps fade away as he ran down the tower stairs. Alone, he had only the sound of the crackling flames and a hundred unanswered questions. He racked his brain but could not determine exactly how the thief had managed it.

"Your Lordship?" The timid voice of the steward roused him from his thoughts. Archibald glared up at the man who poked his head through the open door, causing the steward to take an extra breath before speaking. "My lord, I hate to disturb you, but there seems to be a problem down in the courtyard that requires your attention."

"What kind of problem?" Archibald snarled.

"Well, my lord, I was not actually informed of the details, but it has something to do with the marquis, sir. I have been sent to request your presence—respectfully request it, that is."

Archibald descended the stairs, wondering if perhaps the old man had dropped dead on his doorstep, which would not be such a terrible thing. When he reached the courtyard, he found the marquis alive but in a furious temper.

"There you are, Ballentyne! What have you done with my carriage?"

"Your what?"

Bruce approached Archibald and motioned him aside. "Your

Lordship," he whispered in the earl's ear. "It seems the marquis's carriage and horses are missing, sir."

Archibald held up a finger in the direction of the marquis. With a raised voice, he replied, "I'll be with you in a moment, Victor." Then he returned his attention to Bruce and whispered, "Did you say *missing*? How is that possible?"

"I don't know exactly, sir, but you see, the gate warden reports that the marquis and his driver, or rather two people he thought were them, have already passed through the front gate."

Suddenly feeling quite ill, Archibald turned back to address the red-faced marquis.

Chapter 2

Meetings

Several hours after nightfall, Alenda Lanaklin arrived by carriage at the impoverished Lower Quarter of Medford. The Rose and Thorn Tavern lay hidden among crooked-roofed hovels on an unnamed street, which to Alenda appeared to be little more than an alley. A recent storm had left the cobblestones wet, and puddles littered the street. Passing carriages splashed filthy water on the pub's front entrance, leaving streaks of grime on the dull stone and weathered timbers.

From a nearby doorway, a sweaty, shirtless man with a bald head emerged carrying a large copper pot. He unceremoniously cast the pot's contents, the bony remains of several stewed animals, into the street. Immediately, half a dozen dogs set upon the scraps. Wretched-looking figures, dimly lit by the flickering light from the tavern's windows, shouted angrily at the canines in a language that Alenda did not recognize. Several of them threw rocks at the scrawny animals, which yelped and darted away. They rushed to what the animals had left behind and stuffed the remnants into their mouths and pockets.

"Are you *sure* this is the right place, my lady?" Emily asked, taking in the scene. "Viscount Winslow couldn't have meant for us to come here."

Alenda reexamined the curled thorny branch with a single bloom painted on the warped signboard above the door. The red rose had faded to gray, and the weathered stem looked like a coiled snake. "This has to be it. I don't think there's more than one tavern called The Rose and Thorn in Medford."

"I just can't believe he'd send us to such a—a place!"

"I don't like it any more than you do, but this is what was arranged. I don't see how we have a choice," Alenda replied, surprised by how brave she sounded.

"I know you're tired of hearing this, but I still think this is a mistake. We shouldn't be dealing with *thieves.* You can't trust them, my lady. Mark my words: these people you hired will steal from you just like they steal from everyone else."

"Nevertheless, we're here now, so we might as well get on with it." Alenda opened the door of the carriage and stepped out onto the street. As she did, she noticed with concern that several of those loitering nearby were watching her intently.

"That'll be a silver tenent," the driver told her. He was a gruff, elderly man who had not shaved in days. His narrow eyes were framed with so many wrinkles that Alenda wondered how he could see to drive the carriage.

"Oh, well, you see, I was expecting to pay you at the end of our journey," Alenda explained. "We're only stopping here for a short while."

"If you want me to wait, it'll cost ya extra. And I want the money ya owe me now, in case ya decide not ta come back."

"Don't be absurd. I can assure you we will be coming back."

The man's expression was as pliable as granite. He spit over the side of the carriage at Alenda's feet.

"Oh! Well, really!" Alenda pulled a coin from her bag and handed it to the driver. "Here, take the silver, but don't wander off. I'm not exactly sure how long we'll be, but as I told you, we *will* return."

Emily exited the carriage and took a moment to adjust Alenda's hood and to ensure her ladyship's buttons were secure. She brushed the wrinkles out of Alenda's cloak and then repeated the procedure on herself.

"I wish I could tell that stupid driver who I am," Alenda whispered. "Then I'd tell him a few more things."

The two women were dressed in matching woolen cloaks, and with their hoods up, little more than their noses were visible. Alenda scowled at Emily and brushed her fidgeting hands away.

"You're being such a mother hen, Emmy. I'm sure women have come into this establishment before."

"Women, yes, but I doubt any ladies have."

As they entered the narrow wooden doorway of the tavern, the pungent odor of smoke, alcohol, and a scent that Alenda had previously smelled only in a privy assaulted them. The din of twenty conversations fighting each other for supremacy filled the room while a fiddler worked a lively tune. Before a bar, a small crowd danced, hammering their heels loudly on the warped wooden floor, keeping time to the jig. Glasses clinked, fists pounded on tables, and people laughed and sang far louder than Alenda thought dignified.

"What do we do now?" Emily's voice emanated from the depths of her woolen hood.

"I suppose we look for the viscount. Stay close to me."

Alenda took Emily's hand and led the way, weaving through the tables and dodging the dancers and a dog that was gleefully licking up spilled beer. Never in her life had Alenda been in such a place. Vile-looking men surrounded her. Most were dressed in rags, and more than a few were shoeless. She spotted only four women in the place; all were barmaids dressed indecently in tattered gowns with plunging necklines. Alenda thought their manner of dress invited men to paw at them. A toothless, hairy beast grabbed one of the barmaids around her waist. Dragging her to his lap, he ran his hands along the length of her body. Alenda was shocked to see the girl giggle instead of scream.

At last, Alenda spotted him. Viscount Albert Winslow was dressed not in his typical doublet and hose but in a simple cloth shirt, wool pants, and a neatly tailored suede vest. His apparel was not entirely without noble adornment; he was sporting a lovely, if not ostentatious, plumed hat. He sat at a small table with a stocky, black-bearded man dressed in cheap work clothes.

On their approach, Winslow stood and pulled out chairs for them. "Welcome, ladies," he said with a cheerful smile. "So glad you were able to meet me this evening. Please sit down. May I order you both something to drink?"

"No, thank you," Alenda replied. "I was hoping not to stay very long. My driver is not a considerate man, and I would like to conclude our business before he decides to strand us here."

"I understand and, might I say, very wise of you, Your Ladyship. But I'm sad to say your delivery has not yet arrived."

"It hasn't?" Alenda felt Emily give her hand a squeeze of support. "Is there something wrong?"

"Unfortunately, I don't know. You see, I'm not privy to the inner workings of this operation. I don't concern myself with such trifles. You should understand, however, this wasn't an easy assignment. Any number of things could have transpired that might create delays. Are you sure there's nothing I may order for you?"

"Thank you, no," Alenda replied.

"At least take a seat, won't you?"

Alenda glanced at Emily, whose eyes were awash with concern. They sat down, and as they did, she whispered to Emily, "I know, I know. I shouldn't deal with thieves."

"Make no mistake, Your Ladyship," the viscount said in reassurance. "I would not waste your time, money, or risk your station if I didn't have the utmost confidence in the outcome."

The bearded man seated at the table chuckled softly. He was dark and seedy with skin as tan as leather. His huge hands were calloused and dirty. Alenda watched as he tipped his mug to his lips. When he withdrew the cup, droplets of ale ran unchecked through his whiskers and dripped onto the tabletop. Alenda decided she did not like him.

"This is Mason Grumon," Winslow explained. "Forgive me for not introducing him sooner. Mason is a blacksmith here in Medford's Lower Quarter. He's... a friend."

"Those chaps you hired are very good," Mason told them. His voice reminded Alenda of the sound her carriage wheels made traveling over crushed stone.

"Are they?" Emily asked. "Could they steal the ancient treasures of Glenmorgan from the Crown Tower of Ervanon?"

"What's that?" Winslow asked.

"I once heard a rumor about thieves who stole treasure from the Crown Tower of Ervanon and replaced it the very next night," Emily explained.

"Why would anyone do such a thing?" Alenda asked.

The viscount chuckled softly. "I'm sure that's merely a legend. No sensible thief would behave in such a way. Most people don't understand the workings of thieves. The reality is that most of them steal to line their pockets. They break into homes or waylay travelers on the open road. Your bolder variety might kidnap nobles and hold them for ransom. Sometimes, they even cut off a finger of their victim and send it to a loved one. It helps to prove how dangerous they are and reinforces that the family should take their demands seriously. In general, they are an unsavory lot to be sure. They care only about making a profit with as little effort as possible."

Alenda felt another squeeze on her hand. This one was so tight it caused her to wince.

"Now, your better class of thief, they form guilds, sort of like masons' or woodworkers' guilds, although far more hush-hush, you understand. They are very organized and make a business out of thievery. They stake out territories where they maintain a monopoly on pilfering. Oftentimes, they have arrangements with the local militia or potentate that allow them to work relatively unmolested for a fee, as long as they avoid certain targets and abide by accepted rules."

"What kind of rules could be acceptable between officers of a province and known criminals?" Alenda asked skeptically.

"Oh, I think you'd be quite surprised to discover the number of compromises made to maintain a smoothly functioning kingdom. There is, however, one more type of malefactor—the freelance contractor or, to put it bluntly, thief-for-hire. These rogues are employed for a particular purpose, such as obtaining an item in the possession of a fellow noble. Codes of honor, or *fear of embarrassment*," he said with a wink, "force some nobles and wealthy merchants to seek out just such a professional."

"So, they'll steal anything for anyone?" Alenda asked. "The ones you hired for me, I mean."

"No, not anyone—only those who are willing to pay the number of tenents equal to the job."

"Then it doesn't matter if the client is a criminal or a king?" Emily chimed in.

Mason snorted. "Criminal or king, what's the difference?" For the first time during their meeting, he produced a wide grin that revealed several missing teeth.

Disgusted, Alenda turned her attention back to Winslow. He was looking in the direction of the door, straining to see above the tavern patrons. "You'll have to excuse me, ladies," he said, abruptly standing up. “I need another drink, and the waitstaff seems preoccupied. Look after the ladies, won’t you, Mason?”

“I’m not a bloody wet nurse, you daffy old sod!” Mason shouted after the viscount as he left the table and moved off through the crowd.

“I’ll—I’ll not have you referring to Her Ladyship in such a way,” Emily declared boldly to the smith. “She’s no infant. She’s a noblewoman of title, and *you* had best remember your place.”

Mason’s expression darkened. “This *is* my place. I live five bloody doors down. My pa helped build this infernal pub. My brother works here as a ruddy cook. My mother used ta work here as a cook too, up until she died being hit by one of yer fancy noble carriages. This is *my* place. *You’re* the one who needs to be remembering yours.” Mason slammed his fist down on the table, causing the candle, and the ladies, to jump.

Alenda pulled Emily close. *What have I gotten myself into?* She was starting to think Emily was right. She should never have trusted that no-account Winslow. She really did not know anything about him except that he attended the Aquesta Autumn Gala as a guest of Lord Daref. Of all people, she should have learned by now that not all nobles are noble.

They sat in silence until Winslow returned without a drink.

“Ladies, if you’ll please follow me?” The viscount beckoned.

“What is it?” Alenda asked, concerned.

“Just, please, come with me, this way.”

Alenda and Emily left the table and followed Winslow through the haze of pipe smoke and the obstacle course of dancers, dogs, and drunks to the back door. The scene behind the tavern made everything they had endured so far appear virtuous. They entered an alley that was almost beyond comprehension. Trash lay scattered everywhere, and excrement, discarded from the windows above, mixed with mud in a wide-open trench. Wooden planks, serving as bridges, criss-crossed the foul river of slime, causing the ladies to hold their gowns above their ankles as they shuffled forward.

A large rat darted from a woodpile to join two more in the sewage trough.

"Why are we in an alley?" Emily whispered in a quavering voice to Alenda.

"I don't know," Alenda answered, trying desperately to control her own fear. "I think you were right, Emmy. I should never have dealt with these people. I don't care what the viscount says. People like *us* simply shouldn't do business with people like *them*."

The viscount led them through a wooden fence and around a pair of shanties to a poor excuse for a stable. The shelter was little more than a shack with four stalls, each filled with straw and a bucket of water.

"So good to see you again, Your Ladyship." A man out front addressed her.

Alenda could tell it was the big one of the pair, but she could not remember his name. She had seen them only briefly through an arranged meeting by the viscount, which had been on a lonely road on a night darker than this. Now, with the moon more than half-full and his hood thrown back, she could make out his face. He was tall, rugged in feature and dress but not unkind or threatening in appearance. Wrinkles, which might have come from laughter, tugged at the edges of his eyes. Alenda thought his demeanor was remarkably cheerful, even friendly. She could not help thinking he was handsome, which was not the reaction she had expected to have about anyone she might meet in such a place. He was dressed in dirt-stained leather and wool and was well armed. On his left side, he had a short sword with an unadorned hilt.

On his right was a similarly plain, longer, wider sword. Finally, slung on his back was a massive blade, nearly as tall as he was.

"My name is Hadrian, in case you have forgotten," he said, and followed the introduction with a suitable bow. "And who is this lovely lady with you?"

"This is Emily, my maid."

"A maid?" Hadrian feigned surprise. "For one so fair, I would have guessed her to be a duchess."

Emily inclined her head, and for the first time on this trip, Alenda saw her smile.

"I hope we didn't keep you waiting too long. The viscount tells me he and Mason were keeping you company?"

"Yes, they were."

"Did Mr. Grumon tell you the tragic tale of his mother being run down by an insensitive royal carriage?"

"Why, yes, he did. And I must say—"

Hadrian held up his hands in mock defense. "Mason's mother is alive and well. She lives on Artisan Row in a home considerably nicer than the hovel where Mason resides. She has never been a cook at The Rose and Thorn. He tells that story to every gentleman or lady he meets to put them on the defensive and make them feel guilty. You have my apologies."

"Well, thank you. He was rather rude and I found his comments more than a little disturbing, but now..." Alenda paused. "Did you—I mean, do you have...Were you able to get them?"

Hadrian smiled warmly; then, turning, he called over his shoulder in the direction of the stable.

"Royce?"

"If you knew how to tie a proper knot, I wouldn't be taking so long," said a voice from inside. A moment later, the other half of the pair emerged and joined them.

Alenda's memory of him was easier to recall, because he

was the more disturbing of the two. He was smaller than Hadrian and possessed elegant features, dark hair, and dark eyes. He was dressed in layers of black with a knee-length tunic and a long flowing cloak that gathered about him like a shadow. Not a single weapon was visible. Despite his smaller size and apparent unarmed state, Alenda feared this man. His cold eyes, expressionless face, and curt manner had all the warmth of a predator.

From his tunic, Royce drew forth a bundle of letters bound with a blue ribbon. Handing them to her, he said, "Getting to those letters before Ballentyne presented them to your father wasn't easy. As far as races go, it was very close but ultimately successful. You might want to burn those before something like this happens again."

She stared at the package as a smile of relief crossed her face. "I—I can't believe it! I don't know how you did it, or how to thank you!"

"Payment would be nice," Royce replied.

"Oh, yes, of course." She handed the bundle to Emily, untied the purse from her waist, and handed it to the thief. He quickly scanned the contents, snapped the purse closed, and tossed it to Hadrian, who slipped it in his vest as he headed for the stables.

"You'd better be careful. It's a dangerous game you and Gaunt are playing," Royce told her.

"You read my letters?" she asked fearfully.

"No. I'm afraid you didn't pay us that much."

"Then how did you know—"

"We overheard your father and Archibald Ballentyne talking. The marquis appeared not to believe the earl's accusations, but I'm certain he did. Letters or no letters, your father will be watching you closely now. Still, the marquis is a good man. He'll do the right thing. My guess is he's so relieved

Ballentyne doesn't have proof to take to court that your affair won't bother him much. However, as I said, you'd better be more careful in the future."

"How would the likes of *you* know anything about my father?"

"Oh, I'm sorry. Did I say your father? I meant the other marquis, the one with the appreciative daughter."

Alenda felt as though Royce had slapped her.

"Making friends again, Royce?" Hadrian asked as he led two horses from the stable. "You'll have to forgive my friend. He was raised by wolves."

"Those are my father's horses!"

Hadrian nodded. "We left the carriage behind a bramble patch by the river bridge. By the way, I think I might have stretched out one of your father's doublets. I put it and the rest of his things back in the carriage."

"You were wearing my father's clothes?"

"I told you," Royce repeated, "it was close, very close."

⁂

They called it the Dark Room because of the business conducted in it, but the little back room at The Rose and Thorn was anything but gloomy. Several candles set in sconces on the walls and on the meeting table, along with a nice-sized fire burning in the hearth, gave off a warm, friendly light. A row of copper pots, reminders of the days when the Dark Room doubled as kitchen storage, hung from an exposed wooden beam. There was room for only one table and a handful of chairs, but it was more than enough for their purposes.

The door opened, and a small party filed in. Royce poured himself a glass of wine, took a seat near the fire, removed his boots, and wriggled his toes before the hearth. Hadrian, Viscount Albert Winslow, Mason Grumon, and a pretty young woman opted for chairs at the meeting table. Gwen, the owner of the tavern, always prepared a fine feast when they returned from a job, and that night was no exception. The evening's selections included a pitcher of ale, a large roast, a loaf of freshly baked sweet bread, boiled potatoes, a cloth-wrapped cask of white cheese, carrots, onions, and the big pickles from the barrel normally kept behind the bar. For Royce and Hadrian, she spared no expense, which included the black bottle of Montemorcey wine she had imported all the way from Vandon. Gwen always kept it on hand because it was Royce's favorite. Despite how appealing everything looked, Hadrian showed no interest in any of it. He focused his attention on the woman.

"So, how did it go last night?" Emerald asked, sitting atop Hadrian's lap and pouring him a frothy stein of the inn's home brew. Her real name was Falina Brockton, but all the girls who worked at the tavern, or Medford House next door, went by monikers for their own safety. Emerald, a bright and cheery waif, was the senior barmaid at The Rose and Thorn and one of only two women allowed in the Dark Room when a meeting was in session.

"It was cold," he told her, encircling her waist with his arms. "As was the ride here, so I desperately need warming." He pulled her to him and began kissing her neck as a sea of brunette waves engulfed him.

"We did get paid, didn't we?" Mason asked.

The blacksmith had started to prepare a heaping plate almost the instant he sat down. Mason was the son of the former preeminent Medford metalworker. He had inherited his father's shop but had lost it through a gambling habit coupled with bad luck. Forced out of Artisan Row, he landed in the Lower Quarter, where he fashioned horseshoes and nails, making enough to pay for his forge, drinks, and the occasional meal. For Royce and Hadrian, he offered three benefits: he was cheap, he was local, and he was solitary.

"We did indeed. Alenda Lanaklin paid us the full fifteen gold tenents," Royce said.

"Quite the haul," Winslow declared, happily clapping his hands.

"And my arrows? How'd they work?" Mason asked. "Did they anchor in the tiles?"

"They anchored just fine," Royce said. "Getting them out was the problem."

"The release failed?" Mason asked, concerned. "But I thought—well, I'm no fletcher. Ya shoulda gone to a fletcher. Told ya that, didn't I? I'm a smith. I work with steel, not wood. That fine-toothed saw I made—that worked, didn't it? That's a smithing product, by Mar! But not the arrows and, for sure, not ones like you wanted. No, sir. I done said ya shoulda gotten a fletcher and ya shoulda."

"Relax, Mason," Hadrian said, emerging from Emerald's mane. "Of the two, the anchor was the most important, and it worked perfectly."

"A'course it did. The arrow tips are metal, and I know metal. I'm just disappointed the rope release didn't work. How did ya get the rope down? Ya didn't leave it there, did ya?"

"Couldn't, the guard would have spotted it on his next pass," Royce said.

"So, how'd ya do it?"

"Personally, I would like to know how you did the whole thing," Winslow said. Like Royce, he was sitting back with his feet up and mug in hand. "You never let me in on the details of these operations."

The Viscount Albert Winslow came from a long line of

landless gentry. Years ago, one of his ancestors had lost the family fief. Now all that remained was his title. This was enough to open doors closed to the peasantry or merchant class and was a step better than the common baronage. When Royce and Hadrian had first met him, he was living in a barn in Colnora. The pair invested a little money on clothes and a carriage, and he aptly performed the delicate duties of liaison to the nobles. With an allowance funded by them, the viscount attended every ball, gala, and ceremony, patrolling the political landscape for business opportunities.

"You're too visible, Albert," Hadrian explained. "Can't afford to have our favorite noble hauled to some dungeon where they cut off your eyelids or pull off your fingernails until you tell them what we're up to."

"But if they torture me, and I don't know the plan, how will I save myself?"

"I'm sure they'll believe you after the fourth nail or so," Royce said with a wicked grin.

Albert grimaced and took another long drink of his ale. "But you can tell me now, can't you? How did you get past the iron door? When I met with Ballentyne, I had the impression a dwarf with a full set of tools couldn't get it open. It didn't even have a lock to pick, or a latch to lift."

"Well, your information was very helpful," Royce said. "That's why we avoided it completely."

The viscount looked confused. He started to speak but instead remained silent and cut himself a piece of the roast beef.

Royce took a sip of his wine, and when he did, Hadrian took over the tale. "We scaled the exterior of the east tower, or rather Royce did, and he dropped me a rope. It wasn't as tall but it was the closest to the one we were interested in. We used Mason's arrows to connect the two towers and, with our knees wrapped around the rope, inched our way across the length hand over hand."

"But there are no windows in the tower," Albert protested.

"Who said anything about using a window?" Royce interjected. "The arrows anchored in the taller tower's roof."

"Yep, like I said, that was quality craftsmanship," Mason said proudly.

"So, that gets you to the tower, but how did you get in? Through the chimney?" Albert inquired.

"No, it was too small, and last night there was a fire burning," Hadrian said. "So we used Mason's second little tool, a small saw, and cut the roof on a bevel. All in all, the night was going pretty much according to plan, until Archibald decided to visit his study. We figured he'd have to leave eventually, so we waited."

"We should have just slipped down, cut his throat, and taken the letters," Royce insisted.

"But we weren't being paid for that, were we?" Hadrian reminded him. Royce rolled his eyes in response. Ignoring him, Hadrian continued. "As I was saying, we lay there waiting and the wind on the top of that tower was bitter. The bastard must have sat in that room for two hours."

"You poor thing," Emerald purred, and nuzzled him like a cat.

"The good news was he actually looked at the letters while we were watching him through the cuts, so we knew right where the safe was. Then a carriage came into the courtyard, and you'll never guess who it was."

"The marquis arrived while you were on the roof?" Albert asked with his mouth full of roast beef.

"Yep—that's when our timetable got really tricky. Archibald left the tower to meet the marquis, and we made our move."

"So," Emerald said, guessing, "you opened the roof like the top of a pumpkin."

"Exactly. I lowered Royce into the study. He picked the safe, dumped the dummy letters, and I hauled him back up. Just as we replaced the roof section, Archibald and Victor walked in. We waited to make sure they did not hear us. Incredibly, he presented the letters right there and then. I must say, it was hilarious watching Archibald's reaction when he discovered the blank replacements. Things got pretty loud at this point, so we decided we better take the chance and rappelled down the tower to the courtyard below."

"That's amazing. I was telling Alenda sometimes problems occur during a job, but I had no idea I was telling the truth. We should have charged her extra," Albert interjected.

"It crossed my mind," Royce replied, "but you know Hadrian. Still, we've made a nice profit on both sides of this one."

"But wait, you didn't explain how you got the rope off the side of the tower if my releases didn't work."

Royce sighed. "Don't ask."

"Why not?" The smith looked from one to the other. "Is it a secret?"

"They want to know, Royce," Hadrian said with a wide grin.

Royce frowned. "He shot it off."

"He did what?" Albert asked, sitting up so abruptly his feet hit the floor with a clap.

"Hadrian used another arrow to cut the rope at the roofline."

"But that's impossible," Albert declared. "No man can shoot the width of a rope at—what was it?—two hundred feet maybe, in total darkness!"

"There *was* a moon," Royce said, correcting him. "Let's not make more out of this than it already is. You forget I have to work with him. Besides, it's not like he did it in a single shot."

"How many arrows?" Emerald inquired.

"What's that, sweetie?" Hadrian asked, wiping foam from his mouth with his sleeve.

"How many arrows did it take for you to cut the rope, silly?"

"Be honest," Royce told him.

Hadrian scowled. "Four."

"Four?" Albert said. "It was much more impressive when I imagined it as one lone shot, but still—"

"Do you think the earl will ever figure it out?" Emerald asked.

"The first time it rains, I imagine," Mason said.

There was a triple tap on the door and the stocky smith pushed back his chair and crossed the room. "Who is it?" he asked.

"Gwen."

Sliding the dead bolt free, he opened the door, and an exotic-looking woman with long, thick black hair and dazzling green eyes entered.

"A fine thing when a woman can't get access to her own back room."

"Sorry, gal," Mason said, closing the door behind her, "but Royce would skin me alive if I ever opened the door without asking first."

Gwen DeLancy was an enigma of the Lower Quarter. An immigrant to Avryn from the distant nation of Calis, she survived in the city as a prostitute and fortune-teller. Her dark skin, almond-shaped eyes, and high cheekbones were uniquely foreign. Her talent for eye makeup and an eastern accent made her an alluring mystery that the nobles found irresistible. Yet Gwen was no simple whore. In three short years, she turned her fortunes around, buying up shop rights in the district. Only nobles could own land, but merchants traded the rights to operate a business. Before long, she owned or possessed an interest in a sizable section of Artisan Row and most of the Lower Quarter. Medford House, commonly known as the House, was her most lucrative establishment. Despite its back-alley location, gentry from far and near frequented this expensive brothel. Gwen had a reputation for being discreet, especially with the identities of men who could not afford to be seen frequenting a brothel.

"Royce," Gwen said, "a potential customer visited the House earlier this evening. He was quite anxious to speak to one of you. I set up a meeting for tomorrow evening."

"Know him?"

"I asked the girls. None of them have ever seen him before."

"Was he serviced?"

Gwen shook her head. "No, he was just after information about thieves for hire. Funny how a man always expects prostitutes to know everything when he is looking for answers, but assumes a girl will take *his* secrets to her grave."

"Who talked to him?"

"Tulip. She said he was foreign, dark-skinned, and she mentioned an accent. He might be from Calis, but I didn't bump into him, so I can't tell you for sure."

"Was he alone?"

"Tulip didn't mention any companions."

"Want me to talk to him?" Albert asked.

"Nah, I'll do it," Hadrian said. "If he's poking around these parts, he'll probably be looking for someone more like me than you."

"If you like, Albert, you can be here tomorrow and watch the door for strangers," Royce added. "I'll keep an eye on the street. Has there been anyone new hanging around?"

"It has been pretty busy, and there are a few people I don't recognize. There are four right now in the main bar," Gwen mentioned, "and there was a different party of five a few hours ago."

"She's right," Emerald confirmed. "I waited on the five."

"What were they like? Travelers?"

Gwen shook her head. "Soldiers, I think. They weren't dressed like it but I could tell."

"Mercs?" Hadrian asked.

"I don't think so. Mercenaries are usually troublesome, grabbing the girls, shouting, picking fights—you know the type. These guys were quiet, and one was a noble, I think. At least, some of the others referred to him as Baron something—Trumbul, I think it was."

"I saw some like that up on Wayward Street yesterday," Mason said. "Mighta been as many as twelve."

"Anything going on in town?" Royce asked.

They looked at one another doubtfully.

"Do you think it has anything to do with those rumors about killings out near the Nidwalden River?" Hadrian asked. "Maybe the king is calling up support from other nobles."

"Are you talking about the elves?" Mason asked. "I heard about that."

"Me too," Emerald said. "They say elves attacked a village or something. I heard they slaughtered everyone—some even while they slept."

"Who said that? That doesn't sound right," Albert commented. "I've never known an elf to look a man in the eye, much less attack one."

Royce grabbed his boots and cloak and headed for the door. "You've never known an elf, Albert," he said as he abruptly left.

"What'd I say?" Albert asked, staring at everyone with an innocent expression.

Emerald shrugged.

Hadrian took out Alenda's purse and tossed it at the viscount. "I wouldn't worry about it. Royce can be moody at times. Here, divvy out the profits."

"Royce is right, though," Emerald said. She appeared pleased that she knew something they did not. "The elves that attacked the village were *wild* elves, full-bloods. The half-breeds from around here are nothing but a bunch of lazy drunks."

"A thousand years of slavery can do that to a person," Gwen pointed out. "Can I have my cut, Albert? I have to get back to work. We've got a bishop, the magistrate, and the Brotherhood of Barons visiting the House tonight."

Hadrian was still sore from the previous day's exertion when he took a seat at an empty table near the bar and observed the patrons of the Diamond Room. The name came from its odd, stretched rectangle shape, caused by how the addition fit into the space at the end of Wayward Street. Hadrian knew or was familiar with almost everyone in the room. Lamplighters, carriage drivers, tinkers, they were the usual late crowd who came in after work for a meal. They all had the same tired, worn-out, dirty look about them as they sat with their heads bowed over their plates. Each was dressed in a coarse work shirt and poor-fitting britches gathered at the waist like the mouth of a sack. They chose this room because it was quieter, and they could eat in peace. One individual, however, stood out.

He sat alone at the far end of the room, his back to the wall. His table remained bare except for the standard tavern candle. He had not bought a drink or a plate. He wore a wide-brimmed felt hat with one side pinned up by a lavish blue plume. His doublet, worn over a brilliant gold satin waist shirt, was made of rich black and red brocade with stuffed shoulders. At his side was a saber attached to a fine studded-leather girdle matching his high black riding boots. Whoever he was, he was not hiding. Hadrian noted beneath the table a bundle on which he rested one boot at all times.

Once Royce sent Emerald over with the news that the street was clear of associates, Hadrian got up and walked the length of the room, stopping before the empty chair in front of the stranger.

"Care for some company?" he asked.

"That depends," the man replied, and Hadrian noted the slight saucy accent of a Calian native. "I'm looking for a representative of an organization called Riyria. Do you speak for that group?"

"That depends on what you want," Hadrian replied with a small grin.

"In that case, please sit down."

Hadrian took the seat and waited.

"My name is Baron Delano DeWitt, and I'm looking to hire men of talent. I was told there were a few in the area that could be had for a price."

"What kind of talents are you looking to buy?"

"Procurement skills," DeWitt said simply. "I have an item I need to make disappear. If at all possible, I would prefer it to disappear completely. But it has to happen tonight."

Hadrian smiled. "Sorry, I'm quite certain Riyria won't work under such tight constraints. Too dangerous. I hope you understand."

"I'm sorry about the timing. I tried to reach your organization last night, but I was told you were unavailable. I'm in a position to make it worth the risk."

"Sorry, but they have very strict rules." Hadrian started to get up.

"Please, listen. I have asked around. Those who know the

pulse of this city tell me there is a pair of independent professionals who take on such jobs if thc pricc is right. How they manage to work with impunity outside of the organized guilds is a matter of speculation, but the fact remains that they do. This is a testament to their reputation, is it not? If you know these men, the members of this Riyria, I beg you, implore them to assist me."

Hadrian considered the man. Initially, he had thought him to be another of the many self-absorbed nobles looking for a chuckle at some royal banquet. Now, however, the man's demeanor changed. There was a hint of desperation in his voice.

"What's so important about this item?" Hadrian asked as he eased back into his seat. "And why does it have to disappear tonight?"

"Have you heard of Count Pickering?"

"Master swordsman, winner of the Silver Shield and the Golden Laurel? He has an incredibly beautiful wife named... Belinda, I think. I've heard he has killed at least eight men in duels because of how they have looked at her, or so the legend goes."

"You're unusually well informed."

"Part of the job," Hadrian admitted.

"In a contest of swords, the count has only been beaten by Braga, the Archduke of Melengar, and that was in an exhibition tournament on the one day he didn't have his sword. He was forced to use a replacement."

"Oh, right," Hadrian said as much to himself as to DeWitt. "He's the one with the special rapier he won't duel without, at least not in a real fight."

"Yes! The count is very superstitious about it." DeWitt said nothing more for a moment and looked uncomfortable.

"Did you stare at the count's wife too long?" Hadrian inquired.

The man nodded and bowed his head. "I've been challenged to a duel tomorrow at noon."

"And you want Riyria to steal the count's sword." It was a statement, not a question, but DeWitt nodded again.

"I'm with the retinue of Duke DeLorkan of Dagastan. We arrived in Medford two days ago, part of a trade negotiation hosted by King Amrath. They held a feast for our arrival and Pickering was there." The baron wiped his face nervously. "I've never been to Avryn before—for Maribor's sake, I didn't know who he was! I didn't even know she was his wife until I was slapped in the face with a glove."

Hadrian sighed. "That is not an easy job. Taking a prized sword from the bedside of—"

"Ah—but I have made it easier," DeWitt told him. "The count, like me, is staying with the king for the negotiations. His quarters are very near my duke's. Earlier this evening, I slipped into his room and took his sword. There were so many people around I panicked and dropped it in the first open door I found. It must be removed from the castle before he notices it's missing, since a search will surely find it."

"So, where is it now?"

"The royal chapel," he said. "It's not guarded and is just down the hall from an empty bedroom with a window. I can make certain the window will be open tonight. There are also ivy vines just outside the wall below the window. It should be a simple thing really."

"Then why don't *you* do it?"

"If thieves are caught with the sword, all that will happen is the loss of their hands, but if *I* am caught, my reputation will be destroyed!"

"I can see the reason for your concern," Hadrian said sardonically, but DeWitt appeared oblivious.

"Exactly! Now, seeing as how I have done most of the work, it doesn't sound so bad, does it? Before you answer, let me add this to the proposal."

With some strain, the baron pulled the bundle from beneath his foot and placed it on the table. A metallic jingle rustled when the saddlebag settled on the wood. "Inside you'll find one hundred gold tenents."

"I see," Hadrian responded, staring at the bag and trying to breathe at an even pace. "And you are paying up front?"

"Of course, I'm not a fool. I know how these things work. I'll pay you half now and half when I get the sword."

Hadrian took another controlled breath, nodding and reminding himself to stay calm. "So, you're offering *two hundred* gold tenents?"

"Yes," DeWitt said with a look of concern. "As you can see, this is very important to me."

"Apparently, if the job is as easy as you say."

"Then you think they will do it?" he asked eagerly.

Hadrian sat back in his chair just as DeWitt leaned forward anxiously. DeWitt looked like a man set before a judge, awaiting sentencing on a murder charge.

Royce would kill him if he agreed. One of the basic rules they had established for Riyria was that they would not take jobs on short notice. They needed time to do background checks, verify stories, and case potential targets. Still, DeWitt's only crime was choosing the wrong moment to look at a beautiful woman, and Hadrian knew he held the man's life in his hands. There was no chance he could hire anyone else. As DeWitt had mentioned, no independent thieves other than them would dare take a job in a guild city. The officers of the Crimson Hand would not allow any of their boys to do it, for the same reason Hadrian felt he ought to turn it down. On the other hand, Hadrian was not really a thief and was not familiar with all their various deliberations. Royce was the one who had grown up on the streets of Ratibor, picking pockets to survive. He was the professional burglar, the ex-member of the infamous Black Diamond Guild. Hadrian was a warrior, a soldier who preferred his battles to be fair and in the daylight.

Hadrian was never completely comfortable with most of the tasks they did for nobles. They wanted to embarrass a rival, to hurt an ex-lover, or to increase their standing in the strange and twisted world of high-stakes politics. The gentry hired them because they possessed fortunes and could afford to pay for their games. To them, that was what life was—one big chess match with real knights, kings, and pawns. There was no good or evil, no right or wrong. It was all just politics. A game within a game with its own set of rules and no values. Their squabbles, however, did provide a fertile field for them to harvest profits. Not only were the nobles rich and petty, they were also dim-witted. How else could Royce and Hadrian receive payment from the Earl of Chadwick to intercept letters Alenda Lanaklin sent to Degan Gaunt only to turn around and double their profit by stealing them back? They had simply asked Albert to contact Alenda with the news Ballentyne had her letters and an offer to help get them back. Their business was profitable but ugly. Just another game he played in a world where heroes were legends and honor was a myth.

He tried to rationalize that what he and Royce did was not that horrible. After all, Alenda could certainly afford it. People like Mason and Emerald needed the money more than a wealthy marquis's daughter. Besides, perhaps it taught her a valuable lesson that might save her father's reputation and lands. Yet it was still just a way of lying to himself. Trying to convince his conscience that what he was doing was right, or at least not wrong. He desired to do a job with merit, one with which he could actually save a man's life, one with intentions that resembled what he remembered as virtuous.

"Sure," he said.

❧

When Hadrian finished speaking, the silence in the Dark Room was thick with anticipation. Only three men were present and when Hadrian stopped, both he and Albert turned their attention to Royce. As expected, the thief did not look pleased and began slowly shaking his head even before he spoke. "I can't believe you took this job," he scolded.

"Look, I know it's short notice, but his story checks out, right?" Hadrian asked. "You followed him back to the castle. He is a guest of King Amrath. He didn't make any side trips. I can verify he appears to be from Calis, and none of Gwen's girls heard anything to contradict his claims. The job looks clean."

"*Two hundred gold tenents* to slip a sword out an open window—you don't find that suspicious?" Royce asked with a tone of amazed disbelief.

"Personally, I would call it a dream come true," Albert mentioned.

"Maybe they do things differently in Calis. It's pretty far away," Hadrian argued.

"It's not *that* far," Royce shot back. "And how is it this DeWitt is walking around with that much coin? Does he always travel to international trade meetings carrying bags bursting with gold? Why did he bring it?"

"Maybe he didn't. Maybe he sold a valuable ring tonight, or perhaps he obtained a loan using the good name of the Duke DeLorkan. It's even possible that he got it from the duke himself. I'm certain the two of them didn't ride up here on a couple of ponies. The duke likely travels in a huge caravan of wagons. To them, several hundred gold coins might not be unusual."

Hadrian's voice became more serious. "You weren't there. You didn't see this guy. He's facing a virtual execution tomorrow. How much is gold worth if you're dead?"

"We just got done with a job. I was hoping to take a few days off, and now you've signed us up for a new one." Royce sighed. "You say DeWitt was scared?"

"He was sweating."

"So, that's what this is really about. You want to take the job because it's for a good cause. You think risking our necks is worth it so long as we can pat ourselves on the back afterward."

"Pickering will kill him—you know it. And he's not the first."

"He won't be the last either."

Hadrian sighed and, folding his arms across his chest, sat back in his chair. "You're right; there will be others. So imagine we pinch the sword and get rid of the damn thing. The count never sees it again. Think of all the happy men who could finally look at Belinda without fear."

Royce chuckled. "So now it's a public service?"

"And there is the two hundred gold tenents," Hadrian added. "That's more money than we've made all year. Cold weather is coming, and with that coin, we could sit out the winter."

"Well, at least now you are talking some sense. That would be nice," Royce admitted.

"And it's only a couple hours of work, just a quick climb and grab. You're the one always telling me how poorly guarded Essendon Castle is. We'll be done and in bed before dawn."

Royce bit his lower lip and grimaced, refusing to look at his partner.

Hadrian saw his opening and pressed his advantage. "You remember how cold it was on top of that tower. Just think how cold it will be in a few months. You can spend the winter safe and warm, eating richly and drinking your favorite wine. Then of course"—Hadrian leaned closer—"there's the snow. You know how you hate the snow."

"All right, all right. Grab the gear. I'll meet you in the alley."

Hadrian smiled. "I knew there was a heart in there somewhere."

❧

Outside, the night was even colder than it had been. A slick frost formed on the roads. Winter snows would indeed be falling soon. Despite what Hadrian thought, Royce did not actually hate snow. He liked the way it blanketed the Lower Quarter, dressing it up in an elegant white gown. Nevertheless, its beauty came with a cost; tracks remained in snow and made his job much harder. Hadrian was right: after that night they would have enough cash set aside to spend the whole winter in quiet hibernation. With that much money, they could even consider opening a legitimate business. He thought about it every time they scored big, and he and Hadrian had discussed it on more than one occasion. A year ago, they had talked seriously about opening a winery, but it did not suit them. That was always the problem. Neither could think of any lawful business that was right for them.

He stopped in front of Medford House at the end of Wayward Street and across the street from The Rose and Thorn Tavern. The House was nearly as large as the tavern, which Gwen considered linking with by building extensions so customers could move back and forth freely without exposing themselves to the elements, or public scrutiny. Gwen DeLancy was a genius. Royce had never known anyone like her. She was clever and intelligent beyond reason, and she was more open and sincere than anyone he had ever met. She was a paradox to him, an impossible mystery he could not solve—she was an honest person.

"I thought you might stop by," Gwen said, stepping out onto the porch of the House and wrapping a cape about her shoulders. "I was watching for you through the doorway."

"You have good eyes. Most people never see me when I walk a dark street."

"You must have wanted to be seen, then. You were coming to visit me, weren't you?"

"I just wanted to be sure you received your portion of the payment last night."

Gwen smiled. As she did, Royce could not help noticing how beautifully her hair shimmered in the moonlight.

"Royce, you know you don't have to pay me. I'd give you anything you asked for."

"No," Royce insisted. "We use your place as a base. It's dangerous, and for that, you get a part of the profit. We've been over this."

She stepped closer and took his hand. Her touch was soothingly warm amidst the chilling air. "I also wouldn't own The Rose and Thorn if it wasn't for you. There's a very good chance I wouldn't even be alive."

"I have no idea what you speak of, Your Ladyship," Royce said as he performed a formal bow. "I can prove I wasn't even in town that night."

She stared at him with the same smile. He loved to see her happy, but now her brilliant green eyes searched for something, and Royce turned away, letting go of her hand.

"Listen, Hadrian and I are taking that job. We have to do it tonight, so I need to—"

"You're a strange man, Royce Melborn. I wonder if I'll ever really know you."

Royce paused and then softly said, "You already know me better than any woman should, more than is safe for either of us."

Gwen stepped toward him again, her heeled shoes crunching on the frosty ground, her eyes intense with pleading. "Be careful, won't you?"

"I always am."

With his cloak billowing in the wind, he walked away. She watched him until he entered a shadow and was gone.

Chapter 3

Conspiracies

The crowned falcon standard flew from the highest tower of Essendon Castle, marking the presence of the king. The castle was the royal seat of the kingdom of Melengar, and although not especially large or powerful, it was nevertheless an old and respected realm. The castle, an imposing structure of elaborate gray walls and towers, stood at the center of the capital city of Medford, forming the hub of the four distinct quarters of Gentry Square, Artisan Row, the Common Quarter, and the Lower Quarter. Like most cities in Avryn, Medford lay behind the protection of a strong outer wall. Nevertheless, the castle also had its own fortifications partitioning it from the general city. This inner wall, crowned with crenellated parapets where skilled archers kept watch from behind stone merlons, did not completely encircle the castle. Instead, it connected to a large, imposing keep that served as its rear barrier. The height of the keep and the wide moat surrounding its base kept the king's home well protected.

During the day, merchants wheeled carts to the castle wall and positioned themselves on either side of the gate, forming a tent city of bustling vendors, entertainers, and lenders who sought to do business with the castle inhabitants. This wave of local commerce receded at sunset, as citizens could not pass within fifty feet of the walls from dusk until dawn. This restriction was enforced by royal archers, who were trained to fire at those who ventured too close at night. Pairs of guards, dressed in chain mail with steel helms bearing the falcon standard of Melengar, patrolled the perimeter of the castle. They walked casually, with thumbs in their sword belts, often discussing events of the day or their off-duty plans.

Royce and Hadrian watched the pace of the guard's routine for an hour before moving toward the rear of the keep. Just as DeWitt had explained, negligent gardeners had ignored a spider-work of thick-stemmed vines tracing their way up the stone. Unfortunately, the vines did not reach as high as the windows. On this frosty late-autumn night, the swim across the moat was bone-chillingly cold. The ivy, however, proved to be quite reliable, and the climb was as easy as ascending a ladder.

"I now know why DeWitt didn't want to do this himself," Hadrian whispered to Royce as they hung from the ivy. "After being frozen in that water, I think if I fell right now, I would shatter on impact."

"Just imagine how many chamber pots are dumped into it each day," Royce mentioned as he drove a small ringed spike into the seam between two stone blocks.

Hadrian looked up at the many windows he presumed led to bedrooms, and cringed at the implications. "I could have lived without that bit of insight." He pulled a strap harness from his satchel and fastened it to the eyelet of the spike's ring.

"Just trying to take your mind off the cold," Royce said, tapping in another spike.

Although tedious and tense, the process was surprisingly

fast, and they reached the lowest window before the guards completed their circuit. Royce tested the shutter, which was open, as promised. He pulled it gently back, just a hair, and peered inside. A moment later, he climbed in and waved Hadrian up.

A small bed draped in a burgundy canopy took up the center of one wall. A dresser with a washbasin stood beside it. The only other piece of furniture was a simple wooden chair. A modest tapestry of hounds hunting deer covered much of the opposite wall. Everything was neat but sterile. There were no boots near the door and no cloak thrown across the chair, and the bedcovers showed no wrinkles. The room was unused.

Hadrian remained silent near the window as Royce moved across the room to the door. He watched as the thief's feet tested the surface of the floor before committing his weight. Royce mentioned once how he had been in an attic on a job when he hit a weak board and fell through the bedroom ceiling. This floor was stone, but even stones sometimes had loose mortar or contained hidden traps or alarms. Royce made it to the door, where he crouched and paused to listen. He motioned a sign for walking with his hand and then began counting on his fingers for Hadrian to see. There was a pause, and then he repeated the signal. Hadrian crossed the room to join his friend and the two sat waiting for several minutes in silence.

Eventually Royce lifted the latch with gloved hands but did not open the door. Outside they could hear the heavy footfalls of hard boots on stone, first one set, and then a second. As the steps faded, Royce opened the door slightly and peered out. The hall was empty.

Before them lay a narrow hallway lit by widely spaced torches, whose flames cast flickering shadows, which created an illusion of movement on the walls. They entered the hall, quietly closed the door behind them, and quickly moved approximately fifty feet to a set of double doors, adorned with gilded hinges and a metal lock. Royce tried the doors and then shook his head. He knelt and pulled a small kit of tools from his belt pouch while Hadrian moved to the far side of the hall. From where Hadrian stood, he could see the length of the corridor in both directions as well as a portion of the stairs that entered from the right. He stood ready for any trouble, which came sooner than he had expected.

A noise echoed in the corridor and Hadrian could hear the faint sound of hard heels on stone coming in their direction. Still on his knees, Royce worked the lock as the steps grew closer. Hadrian moved his hand to the hilt of his sword when at last the thief quickly opened the door. Trusting to luck that the room was empty, the two slipped inside. Royce softly closed the door behind them, and the footsteps passed without pause.

They were in the royal chapel. Banks of candles burned on either side of the large room. Supporting a glorious vaulted ceiling, marble columns rose near the chamber's center. Four rows of wooden pews lined either side of the main aisle. Cinquefoil-shaped adornments and blind-tracery moldings common to the Nyphron Church decorated the walls. Alabaster statues of Maribor and Novron stood behind the altar. Novron, depicted as a strong, handsome man in the prime of his youth, was kneeling, sword in hand. The god Maribor, sculpted as a powerful, larger-than-life figure with a long beard and flowing robes, loomed over Novron, placing a crown upon the young man's head. The altar itself consisted of a wooden cabinet with three broad doors and a rose-colored marble top. Upon it, two more candles burned and a large gilded tome lay open.

DeWitt had told Hadrian he had left the sword behind the

altar, and they headed toward it. As they approached the first set of pews, both men froze in mid-step. Lying there, face-down in a pool of freshly spilled blood, was the body of a man. The rounded handle of a dagger protruded from his back. While Royce made a quick survey for Pickering's sword, Hadrian checked the man for signs of life. The man was dead, and the sword was nowhere to be found. Royce tapped Hadrian on the shoulder and pointed at the gold crown that had rolled to the far side of a pillar. The full weight of the situation registered with both of them—it was time to leave.

They headed for the door. Royce paused only momentarily to listen to ensure the hall was clear. They slipped out of the chapel, closed the door, and moved down the hall toward the bedroom.

"*Murderers!*"

The shout was so close and so terrifying that they both spun with weapons drawn. Hadrian had his bastard sword in one hand, his short sword in the other. Royce held a brilliant white-bladed dagger.

Standing before the open chapel door was a bearded dwarf.

"*Murderers!*" the dwarf cried again, but it was not necessary. Footfalls could already be heard, and an instant later, soldiers, with weapons drawn, poured into the hallway from both sides.

"*Murderers!*" The dwarf continued pointing at them. "They've killed the king!"

Royce lifted the latch to the bedroom door and pushed, but the door failed to give way. He pulled and then pushed again, but the door would not budge.

"Drop your weapons, or we'll butcher you where you stand!" a soldier ordered. He was a tall man with a bushy mustache that bristled as he gritted his teeth.

"How many do you think there are?" whispered Hadrian.

The walls echoed with the sounds of more soldiers about to arrive.

"Too many," Royce replied.

"Be a lot less in a minute," Hadrian assured him.

"We won't make it. I can't get the door open; we have no exit. I think someone spiked it from the inside. We can't fight the entire castle guard."

"Put them down now!" the soldier in charge shouted, and took a step closer while raising the level of his sword.

"Damn." Hadrian let his blades drop. Royce followed suit.

"Take them," the soldier barked.

~

Alric Essendon awoke, startled by the commotion. He was not in his room. The bed he was lying in was a fraction of the size and lacked the familiar velvet canopy. The walls were bare stone, and only a small dresser and wash table decorated the space. He sat up, rubbing his eyes, and soon realized where he was. He had accidentally fallen asleep, apparently several hours ago.

He looked over at Tillie, her bare back and shoulder exposed above the quilt. Alric wondered how she could sleep with all the shouting going on. He rolled out of bed and felt around for his nightshirt. Determining his clothing from hers was easy to do even in the dark. Hers was linen; his was silk.

Awakened by his movement, Tillie groggily asked, "What's wrong?"

"Nothing, go back to sleep," Alric replied.

She could sleep through a hurricane, but his leaving always woke her. That he had fallen asleep was not her fault, but he blamed her just the same. Alric hated waking up here. He hated Tillie even more and was conscious of the paradox.

Throughout the day, her need for him attracted Alric, but in the morning, it repulsed him. Of all the castle servants, however, she was by far the prettiest. Alric did not care for the noble ladies his father invited to court. They were haughty and considered their virginity more valuable than the crown. He found them dull and irritating. His father thought differently. Alric was only nineteen, but already his father was pressuring him to pick a bride.

"You'll be king someday," Amrath told him. "Your first duty to the kingdom is to sire an heir." His father spoke of marriage as if it were a profession, and that was how Alric saw it as well. For him, this, or any other form of work, was best avoided—or at least postponed as long as possible.

"I wish you could spend the whole night with me, my lord," Tillie babbled at him as he pulled his nightshirt over his head.

"Then you should be grateful I dozed as long as I did." With his toes he felt along the floor for his slippers, and finding them, he slid his feet into the warm fleece lining.

"I am, my lord."

"Good night, Tillie," Alric said as he reached the door and stepped outside.

"Good—" Alric closed the door before she finished.

Tillie usually slept with the other maids, in a dorm near the kitchens. Alric brought her to the little vacant bedroom on the third floor of the castle for privacy. He did not like taking girls to his room—his father's bedroom was right next door. The vacant room was on the north side of the castle, and because it received less sunlight, it was always cooler than the royal chambers. He pulled his nightshirt tight and shuffled down the corridor toward the stairs.

"I've checked all the upper floors, Captain. He's not there," Alric heard someone say from just up the steps. By the speaker's curt tone, Alric guessed him to be a sentry. He spoke to them rarely, but when he did, they were always abrupt, as if words were a commodity in short supply.

"Continue the search, down to the prisons if necessary. I want every room examined, each pantry, cabinet, and wardrobe. Do you understand?"

Alric knew that voice well; it was Wylin, the captain of the guard.

"Yes, sir, right away!"

Alric heard the sentry trotting down the steps, and he saw the soldier stop abruptly the moment he met Alric's gaze. "I found him, sir!" the soldier shouted with a hint of relief.

"What's going on, Captain?" Alric called out even as Wylin and three other castle guards rushed down the steps.

"Your Royal Highness!" The captain knelt briefly, bowing his head, and then rose abruptly. "Benton!" he snapped at the solider. "I want five more men here protecting the prince *right now.* Move!"

"Yes, sir!" The soldier snapped a salute and ran back up the stairs.

"Protecting me?" Alric said. "What's going on?"

"Your father's been murdered."

"My father? What?"

"His Majesty, the king—we found him in the royal chapel stabbed in the back. Two intruders are in custody. The dwarf Magnus confirmed it. He saw them murder your father, but he was powerless to stop them."

Alric heard Wylin's voice, but he could not understand the words. They did not make sense. *My father is dead?* He had just spoken with him before he had gone to Tillie's room, not more than a few hours ago. *How could he be dead?*

"I must insist that you remain here, Your Highness, under heavy guard until I finish sweeping the castle. They may not be alone. I'm presently conducting a—"

"Insist what you like, Wylin, but get out of my way. I want to see my father!" Alric demanded, pushing past him.

"King Amrath's body has been taken to his bedroom, Your Highness."

His body!

Alric did not want to hear any more. He ran up the steps, his slippers flying off his feet.

"Stay with the prince!" Wylin shouted after him.

Alric reached the royal wing. In the corridor there was a crowd, which moved aside at his approach. As he reached the chapel, its door lay open with several of the chief ministers gathered inside.

"My prince!" he heard his uncle Percy call, but he did not stop. He was determined to reach his father.

He couldn't be dead!

He rounded the corner, passed his own room, and rushed into the royal suite. Here the double doors were open as well. Several ladies in nightgowns and robes stood just outside weeping loudly. Inside, a pair of older women busied themselves wringing out pink-stained linens in a washbasin.

To the side of the bed stood his sister, Arista, dressed in a burgundy and gold gown. Her arms wrapped around the bedpost, which she gripped so tightly that her fingers were white. She stared at the figure on the mattress with eyes that were dry but wide with horror.

On the pale white sheets of the royal bed lay King Amrath Essendon. He still wore the same clothes Alric had seen him in before he had retired for the night. His face was pale and his eyes were closed. Near the corner of his lips, there was a tiny tear of dried blood.

"My prince—I mean, Your Royal Majesty." His uncle corrected himself as he followed Alric into the bedchamber. His uncle Percy had always looked older than his father had—his hair was very gray, his face wrinkled and drooping; however, he possessed the trim, elegant build of a swordsman. He was still in the process of tying up his robe as he entered. "Thank Maribor you are safe. We thought you might have met a similar fate."

Alric was at a loss for words. He just stood staring at the still body of his father.

"Your Majesty, do not worry. I'll take care of everything. I know how hard this must be. You're still a young man and—"

"What are you talking about?" Alric looked at him. "Take care of what? What are you taking care of?"

"A number of things, Your Majesty. There is the securing of the castle, the investigation as to how this happened, the apprehension of those responsible, arrangements for the funeral and, of course, the eventual coronation."

"Coronation?"

"You are king now, Sire. We will need to arrange your crowning ceremony, but that, of course, can wait until we have everything else settled."

"But I thought—Wylin told me the murderers have been captured."

"He captured two of them. I'm just making certain there aren't any more."

"What will happen to them?" He looked back at the still form of his father. "The killers, what will happen to them?"

"That is up to you, Your Royal Majesty. Their fate is yours to decide, unless you would prefer I handle the matter for you, since it can be quite unpleasant."

Alric turned to his uncle. "I want them to die, Uncle Percy. I want them to suffer horribly and then die."

"Of course, Your Majesty, of course. I assure you they will."

&

The dungeons of Essendon Castle lay buried two stories beneath the earth. Groundwater seeped through cracks in the walls and wet the face of the stone. Fungus grew in the mortar between stone blocks, and mold coated the wood of doors, stools, and buckets. The foul, musty smell mixed with the stench of decay, and the corridors echoed with the mournful cries of doomed men. Despite the rumors told in Medford's taverns, the castle dungeons had a limited capacity. Needless to say, the prison staff found room for the king-killers. They moved prisoners to provide Royce and Hadrian with their own private cell.

News of the king's death did not take long to spread, and for the first time in years, the prisoners had something exciting to talk about.

"Who woulda thought I'd outlast old Amrath," a gravelly voice muttered. He laughed, but the laughter quickly broke into a series of coughs and sputters.

"Any chance the prince might review our sentences on account of all this?" a weaker, younger voice asked. "I mean, it's possible, isn't it?"

This question was met with a lengthy silence, more coughing, and a sneeze.

"The guard said they stabbed the bastard in the back right in his own chapel. What does that say about his piety?" a new, bitter voice questioned. "Seems to me he was asking for a bit too much from the man upstairs."

"The ones that done it are in our old cell. They moved me and Danny out to make room. I saw them when they shifted us—two of them, one big, the other little."

"Anyone know them? Maybe they was trying to break some of us out and got sidetracked, eh?"

"Gotta have some pretty big brass ones to kill a king in his own castle. They won't get a trial, not even one for show. I'm surprised they've lived this long."

"Gonna want a public torture before the execution. Things been quiet a long time. Haven't had a good torture in years."

"So why ya think they did it?"

"Why don't you ask 'em?"

"Hey, over there? You conscious in that cell of yours? Or did they beat you stupid?"

"Maybe they're dead."

They were not dead but neither were they talking. Royce and Hadrian stood chained to the far wall of their cell, their ankles locked in stocks, and their mouths gagged with leather muzzles. They had been there only for the better part of an hour, but already the strain on Hadrian's muscles was painful. The soldiers had removed their gear, cloaks, boots, and tunics, leaving them with nothing but their britches to fight the damp chill of the dungeon.

They hung listening to the rambling conversations of the other inmates. The conversation halted at heavy approaching footfalls. The door to the cellblock opened and banged against the interior wall.

"Right this way, Your Royal Highness—I mean, Your Royal Majesty," the voice of the dungeon warden said rapidly.

A metal key twisted in the lock, and the door to their cell creaked open. Four royal bodyguards led the prince and his uncle, Percy Braga, inside. Hadrian recognized Braga, the Archduke and Lord Chancellor of Melengar, but he had never seen Alric before. The prince was young, perhaps no more than twenty. He was short, thin, and delicate in appearance with light brown hair that reached to his shoulders and only the ghost of a beard. His stature and features must have come from his mother, because the former king had been a bear of a man. He wore only a silk nightshirt with a massive sword strapped comically to his side by an oversized leather belt.

"These are the ones?"

"Yes, Your Majesty," Braga replied.

"Torch," Alric commanded, snapping his fingers impatiently as a soldier pulled one from the wall bracket and held it out for him. Alric scowled at the offer. "Hold it near their heads. I wish to see their faces." Alric peered at them. "No marks? They haven't been whipped?"

"No, Your Majesty," Braga said. "They surrendered without a fight and Captain Wylin thought it best to lock them up while he searched the rest of the castle. I approved his decision. We can't be certain these two acted alone in this."

"No, of course not. Who gave the order to gag them?"

"I don't know, Your Majesty," Braga replied. "Do you wish their gags removed?"

"No, Uncle Percy—oh, I can't call you that anymore, can I?"

"You're the king now, Your Majesty. You can call me whatever you wish."

"But it isn't dignified, not for a ruler, but *Archduke* is so formal—I'll call you Percy, is that all right?"

"It's not my place to approve of your decisions any longer, Sire."

"Percy it is, then, and no, leave their gags on. I have no desire to hear their lies. What will they say except that they didn't do it? Captured killers always deny their crimes. What choice do they have? Unless they wish to take their last few moments of life to spit in the face of their king. I won't give them the satisfaction of that."

"They could tell us if they were working alone or for someone else. They could even tell us who that person or persons might be."

Alric continued to study them. His eyes focused on a twisted mark in the shape of an M on Royce's left shoulder. He squinted and then, out of frustration, snatched the torch from a guard and held it so close to Royce's face that he winced. "What is this here? Like a tattoo but not quite."

"A brand, Your Majesty," Braga replied. "It's the Mark of Manzant. It would seem this creature was once an inmate of Manzant Prison."

Alric looked puzzled. "I didn't think inmates were released from Manzant, and I wasn't aware anyone has ever escaped."

Braga appeared puzzled as well.

Alric then moved to inspect Hadrian. When he observed the small silver medallion that hung around Hadrian's neck, the prince lifted it, turned it over with mild curiosity, and then let it go with disdain.

"It doesn't matter," Alric said. "I really don't think they look like the type to volunteer information. In the morning have them hauled out to the square and tortured. If they say anything of merit, have them beheaded."

"If not?"

"If not, quarter them slowly. Draw their bowels into the sun and have the royal surgeon keep them alive as long as possible. Oh, and before you do, make certain heralds have time to make several announcements. I want a crowd for this. People need to know the penalty for treason."

"As you wish, Sire."

Alric started for the door and then stopped. He turned and struck Royce across the face with the back of his hand. "He was my father, you worthless piece of filth!" The prince walked out, leaving the two hanging helplessly awaiting the dawn.

⁂

Hadrian could only guess how long they had been hanging against the wall; perhaps two or three hours had passed. The faceless voices of the other inmates grew less frequent until they stopped entirely, silenced with boredom or sleep. The muzzle covering Hadrian's mouth became soaked with spit and he found it difficult to breathe. His wrists were sore where the shackles rubbed and his back and his legs ached. To make matters worse, the cold tightened his muscles, making the strain even more painful. Not wanting to look at Royce, he alternated between closing his eyes and staring at the far wall. He did his best to avoid thinking about what would happen when daylight came. Instead, his mind was full of thoughts of self-incrimination—this was his fault. His insistence on breaking rules landed them where they were. Their death was on his hands.

The door opened, and once more, a royal guard, this time accompanied by a woman, entered the cell. She was tall, slender, and dressed in a gown of burgundy and gold silk, which shimmered like fire in the torchlight. She was pretty, with auburn hair and fair skin.

"Remove their gags," she ordered briskly.

The jailers rushed to unbuckle the straps and pull off the muzzles. "Now leave us, all of you."

The jailers promptly exited.

"You too, Hilfred."

"Your Highness, I'm your bodyguard. I need to stay to—"

"They are chained to the wall, Hilfred," she snapped, and then took a breath to calm herself. "I'm fine. Now please leave and guard the door. I want no interruptions by anyone. Do you understand?"

"As you wish, Your Highness." The guard bowed and stepped out, closing the door behind him.

She moved forward, carefully studying the two of them. On her belt was a jeweled kris dagger. Hadrian recognized the long wavy blade as the type used by eastern occultists for magical enchantments. Presently he was more concerned with its other use—as a deadly weapon. She toyed with the dragon-shaped hilt as if she might draw it forth and stab them at any moment.

"Do you know who I am?" she asked Hadrian.

"Princess Arista Essendon," Hadrian replied.

"Very good." She smiled at him. "Now, who are you? And don't bother lying. You'll be dead in less than four hours, so what is the point?"

"Hadrian Blackwater."

"And you?"

"Royce Melborn."

"Who sent you here?"

"A man by the name of DeWitt," Hadrian replied. "He's a member of Duke DeLorkan's group from Dagastan, but we weren't sent to kill your father."

"What were you sent to do?" Her painted nails clicked along the silver handle of the dagger, her eyes intent on them.

"To steal Count Pickering's sword. DeWitt said the count challenged him to a duel here last night at a dinner party."

"And what were you doing in the chapel?"

"That's where DeWitt said he hid the sword."

"I see..." She paused a moment as her mask of stone wavered. Her lips began to tremble, and tears welled in her eyes. She turned away from them, trying to compose herself. Her head was bowed and Hadrian could see her small body lurching.

"Listen," Hadrian said, "for what it's worth, we didn't kill your father."

"I know," she said, still facing away from them.

Royce and Hadrian exchanged glances.

"You were sent here tonight to take the blame for the murder. Both of you are innocent."

"Are you—" Hadrian began, but stopped. For the first time since their capture, he felt hopeful but thought better of it. He turned to Royce. "Is she being sarcastic? You can usually tell better than I."

"Not this time," Royce said, his face tense.

"I just can't believe he's really gone," Arista muttered. "I kissed him good night—it was only a few hours ago." She took a deep breath and straightened before turning to face them. "My brother has set plans for the two of you. You'll be tortured to death this morning. They're building a platform where you'll be drawn and quartered."

"We have already heard the details from your brother," Royce said dismally.

"He is the king now. I can't stop him. He is determined to see you punished."

"You could talk to him," Hadrian offered hopefully. "You could explain that we're innocent. You could tell him about DeWitt."

Arista wiped her eyes with the insides of her wrists. "There is no DeWitt. There was no dinner party here last night, no duke from Calis, and Count Pickering hasn't visited this castle in months. Even if any of that were true, Alric wouldn't believe me. Not a person in this castle will believe me. I'm just an emotional girl. They'll say, 'She's distraught. She's upset.' I can do no more to stop your execution today than I could do to save my own father's life last night."

"You knew he was going to die?" Royce asked.

She nodded, fighting the tears again. "I knew. I was told he would be killed, but I didn't believe it." She paused for a moment to study their faces. "Tell me, what would you do to get out of this castle alive before morning?"

The two glanced at each other in stunned silence.

"I'm thinking anything," Hadrian said. "How about you, Royce?"

His partner nodded. "I'd have to say I'm good with that."

"I can't stop the execution," Arista explained, "but I can see to it that you get out of this dungeon. I can return your clothes and weapons, and I can tell you a way to reach the sewers that run under this castle. I think they will take you out of the city. You should know that I have never personally explored them."

"I—I wouldn't think so," Hadrian said, not really certain he was hearing everything correctly.

"It's imperative that when you escape, you leave the city."

"I don't think that will be a problem," Hadrian explained. "We'd probably do that anyway."

"And one more thing, you must kidnap my brother."

There was a pause as they both stared at her.

"Wait, wait, hold on. You want us to *kidnap* the Prince of Melengar?"

"Technically, he's the King of Melengar now," Royce said, correcting him.

"Oh, yeah. I forgot," Hadrian muttered.

Arista walked back to the cell door, peeked out the window, and then returned.

"Why do you want us to kidnap your brother?" Royce asked.

"Because whoever killed my father will kill Alric next, and before his coronation, I imagine."

"Why?"

"To destroy the Essendon line."

Royce stared at her. "Wouldn't that place you at risk as well?"

"Yes, but the threat to me will not be serious as long as Alric is thought to be alive. He is the crown prince. I'm only the silly daughter. Besides, one of us has to stay here in order to run the kingdom and find my father's murderer."

"And your brother couldn't do that?" Hadrian asked.

"My brother is convinced *you* killed him."

"Oh, right—you have to forgive me. A minute ago I was about to be executed, and now I'm going to kidnap a king. Things are changing a bit fast for me."

"What are we supposed to do with your brother once we've gotten him out of the city?" Royce asked.

"I need you to take him to Gutaria Prison."

"I've never heard of the place," Royce said. He looked at Hadrian, who shook his head.

"I'm not surprised; few people have," Arista explained. "It's a secret ecclesiastical prison maintained exclusively by the Church of Nyphron. It lies on the north side of Windermere Lake. You know where that is?"

They both nodded.

"Travel around the edge of the lake; there is an old road that rises up between some hills; just follow it. I need you to take my brother to see a prisoner named Esrahaddon."

"And then what?"

"That's it," she said. "Hopefully, he will be able to explain everything to Alric well enough to convince him of what is going on."

"So," Royce said, "you want us to escape from this prison, kidnap the king, cross the countryside with him in tow while dodging soldiers who I assume might not accept our side of the story, and go to another secret prison so that he can visit an inmate?"

Arista did not appear amused. "Either that, or you can be tortured to death in four hours."

"Sounds like a really good plan to me," Hadrian declared. "Royce?"

"I like any plan where I don't die a horrible death."

"Good. I'll have two monks come in to give you last rites. I'll have your chains removed and the stocks opened so you can kneel. You'll take their frocks, lock them in your place, and silence them with the gags. Your things are right outside in the prison office. I'll tell the warden that you're taking them for the poor. I'll have my personal bodyguard, Hilfred, escort you to the lower kitchens. They won't be active for another hour or so. You should have the place to yourselves. A grate near the basin lifts out for sweeping debris into the sewer. I'll speak to my brother and convince him to meet me at the kitchens alone. I assume you are capable fighters?"

"He is." Royce bobbed his head toward Hadrian.

"My brother isn't, so you should be able to subdue him easily. Be certain not to hurt him."

"This is likely a really stupid question for me to ask," Royce said, "but what makes you think we won't just kill your brother, leave his body in the sewer to rot, and then just disappear?"

"Nothing," she replied. "Like you, I simply don't have a choice."

❧

The monks posed little problem, and once dressed in their frocks, with hoods carefully drawn, Hadrian and Royce slipped out of their cell. Hilfred stood waiting just outside and quickly escorted them as far as the entrance to the kitchens, where, without a word, he left them alone. Royce, who had always had better night vision, led the way through the dark labyrinth of massive pots and piled plates. Dressed as they were with loose sleeves and long, disabling robes, they navigated this sea of potential disaster, where one wrong move could topple a ceramic stack and cause alarm.

So far Arista's plan was a success. The kitchen was empty. They shed their clerical garb in favor of their own clothes and gear. They located the central basin, under which was a massive iron grating. Although it was heavy, they were able to move it out of position without making too much noise. They were pleasantly surprised to find some iron rungs leading into the void. In the depths below, they could hear the trickle of water. Hadrian found a pantry filled with vegetables and felt around until he located a burlap sack filled with potatoes. He quietly dumped out the spuds, shook the sack as clean as he could, and then rooted around for twine.

They were still a long way from free, but the future was looking considerably better than it had only minutes before. Although Royce had not said a word, the fact that Hadrian was responsible bothered him. As he and Royce waited there together, the guilt and silence became overpowering.

"Aren't you going to say, *I told you so*?" Hadrian whispered.

"What would be the point in that?"

"Oh, so you're saying that you're going to hang on to this and throw it at me at some future, more personally beneficial moment?"

"I don't see the point in wasting it now, do you?"

They left the door to the kitchen slightly ajar, and before long, the distant glow of a torch appeared and Hadrian could hear approaching voices. At this signal, they took their positions. Royce took a seat at the table with his back to the entryway. He put the hood of his cloak up and pretended to hunch over a plate of food. Hadrian stood to one side of the door, holding his short sword by the blade.

"For Maribor's sake, why here?"

"Because I'm offering the old man a plate of food and a place to wash."

Hadrian recognized the voices of Alric and Arista and surmised they were now just outside the kitchen door.

"I don't see why we had to leave the guards, Arista. We don't know we—there might be other assassins."

"That's why you need to talk to him. He says he knows who hired the killers, but he refuses to talk to a woman. He said he will only deal with you, and only if you are alone. Listen, I'm not sure who to trust at this point, and you don't know either. We can't be sure who's responsible and some of the guards could be involved. Don't worry, he's an old man and you're a skilled swordsman. We have to find out what he has to say. Don't you want to know?"

"Of course, but what makes you think he has any clue?"

"I don't know anything for certain. But he's not asking for money, just a fresh start. That reminds me, here are some clothes to give him." There was a brief pause. "Look, he seems trustworthy to me. I think if he was lying, he would request gold or land."

"It's just so... strange. Hilfred's not even with you. It's as if you're walking around without a shadow. It's unnerving is what it is. Just coming down here with you, it's—well, you and I, we—you know. We're brother and sister, yet we hardly see each other. In the last few years, I think I've only spoken to you a dozen times, and then only when we visit Drondil Fields on holiday. You always lock yourself up in that tower, doing who knows what, but now—"

"I know, it's strange," Arista replied. "I agree. It's like the night of the fire all over again. I still have nightmares about that evening. I wonder if I'll have nightmares about tonight."

Alric's voice softened. "That's not really my point. It's just that we've never gotten along, not really. But now, well, you're the only family I have left. It seems strange to be saying it, but I suddenly find that matters to me."

"Are you saying you want to be friends?"

"Let's just say I want to stop being enemies."

"I didn't know we were."

"You've been jealous of me ever since Mother told you elder daughters don't get to be queen as long as little brothers are around to be king."

"I have not!"

"I don't want to fight. Maybe I do want to be friends. I'm the king now, and I'll need your help. You're smarter than most of the ministers, anyway. Father always said so. And you've had university training; that's more than I've had."

"Trust me, Alric, I'm more than your friend. I'm your big sister, and I'll look out for you. Now go in there and see what this man has to say."

As Alric entered the kitchen, Hadrian brought the hilt of his sword down on the back of his head. The prince collapsed to the floor with a dull thud. Arista rushed in.

"I said not to hurt him!" she scolded.

"He would be screaming for the guard right now otherwise," Hadrian explained. He tied a gag around the prince's mouth and placed the sack over his head. Royce was already up from his seat and securing Alric's ankles with twine.

"He's all right, though?"

"He'll live," Hadrian told her as he secured the hands and arms of the unconscious prince.

"Which is a whole lot more than he had in store for us," Royce added, pulling tight the noose around the prince's ankles.

"Keep in mind he was certain you killed his father," the princess said. "How would you react?"

"I never knew my father," Royce replied indifferently.

"Your mother, then."

"Royce is an orphan," Hadrian explained as they continued to wrap the prince in twine. "He never knew either of his parents."

"I suppose that explains a lot. Well then, imagine how you'll treat the person who sent you to the chapel tonight, once you find him. I doubt you'll be very charitable when coming face to face with him. In any case, you gave your word. Please do as I ask, and take good care of my brother. Don't forget I spared your lives tonight. I'm hoping that fact will keep you to your word."

She held out the bundle dropped by her brother. "Here is a set of clothes that should fit him. They used to belong to the steward's son, and I always thought he looked about the same size as Alric. Oh, and remove his ring but keep it safe. It bears the royal seal of Melengar and is proof of his identity. Without it, unless you encounter someone who knows his face, Alric is just another peasant. Return it to him when you reach the prison. He'll need it to get in."

"We'll hold up our end of the bargain," Hadrian told her as he and Royce moved the bundled body of the prince toward the open basin. Royce pulled the opulent dark blue ring from Alric's finger and stuffed it in his breast pocket. He then climbed to the bottom of the cistern. Using the rope tied around Alric's ankles, Hadrian lowered him headfirst to Royce. Once the prince was down, Hadrian grabbed the torch and dropped it to Royce. Then he entered the hole and dragged the grating back into position. At the bottom of the ladder was a five-foot-wide, four-foot-high arched tunnel in which a shallow river of filth flowed.

"Remember," the princess whispered through the metal grid. "Go to Gutaria Prison and speak to Esrahaddon. And please, keep my brother safe."

An incomprehensible series of mumbles emitted from the prince under the potato sack. While they were not certain exactly what he was saying, Royce and Hadrian could tell the prince was doing his best to shout and was decidedly displeased with his situation.

The cold water backing up from the Galewyr River into the sewer had woken him. They were waist deep in it now and while the smell was better, the temperature was not. As they looked out through the end of the cistern, the first pale light of dawn revealed the difference between the forested horizon and the sky. Night was melting away fast, and they could hear the Mares Cathedral bell ringing for early service. The whole city would be waking soon.

Hadrian calculated they were below Gentry Square, not far from Artisan Row, where the city met the river. Determining their location was an easy guess, because it was the only section of town with covered sewers. A metal grate blocked their exit, and Hadrian was relieved to find hinges and a lock sealing it instead of bolts. Royce made quick work of the lock, and the rusted hinges surrendered to a few solid kicks from Hadrian. With the way clear, Royce went out to scout while Hadrian sat at the mouth of the sewer with Alric.

The prince had worked his gag loose, and Hadrian could recognize his words now. "I'll have you flailed to death! Release me this instant."

"You'll be quiet," Hadrian replied, "or I'll let you go into the river and we'll see how well you tread water with your hands and feet tied."

"You wouldn't dare! I'm the King of Melengar, you swine!"

Hadrian kicked Alric's legs out from under him, and the

prince fell facedown. After allowing him to struggle for a few moments, Hadrian pulled him up. "Now keep your mouth shut or I might leave you to drown next time." Alric coughed and sputtered but did not speak another word.

Royce returned, having slipped into the sewer soundlessly. "We are right on the river. I found a small boat by a fisherman's dock and took the liberty of commandeering it in His Majesty's name. It's just down the slope in a stand of reeds."

"No!" the prince protested, and shook his shoulders violently. "You must release me. I'm the king!"

Hadrian gripped him by the throat and into his ear whispered, "What did I tell you about talking? Not a sound or you swim."

"But—"

Hadrian dunked the prince again, pulled him up for a short breath, and dunked him once more. "Not another sound," Hadrian growled.

Alric sputtered, and Hadrian, dragging the prince with him, followed Royce down the slope.

The craft was little more than an oversized rowboat, bleached by the sun and filled with nets and small painted buoys. The heavy smell of fish from the boat helped mask the stench of sewage. A tarp, stretched to form a little tent used to store gear or to serve as a shelter, covered the bow. They stuffed the prince underneath, pinning him there with the nets and buoys.

Hadrian pushed off the bank with a long pole he found in the boat. Royce used the wooden rudder to steer the small craft as the river did the work of propelling them downstream. Near the headwaters, the current of the Galewyr was strong, and forward momentum was no problem. They found themselves working to keep the boat in the center of the river as they moved swiftly westward. Just as the sky was turning from a charcoal gray to dull steel, they passed under the shadow of the city of Medford. From the river, they could see the great tower of Essendon Castle, its falcon standard flying at half-mast for the dead king. The flag was a good sign, but how long would it be before they discovered the prince was missing and they removed it?

The river marked the southern edge of the city, skirting along Artisan Row. Large two-story warehouses of gray brick lined the bank, and great wooden wheels jutted out into the river, catching the current to power the millstones and lumberyards. Because the shallow waters of the Galewyr prevented the passage of deep-keeled ships, numerous docks serviced flat-bottomed barges that brought goods from the small seaport village of Roe. There were also piers built by the fishing industry, which led directly to fish markets, where pulleys raised large nets and dumped them onto the cutting floor. In the early morning light, the gulls had already begun to circle the docks where fishermen had started to clear the lines on their skiffs. No one paid particular attention to the two men in a small boat drifting down the river. Nevertheless, they stayed low in the boat until the last signs of the city disappeared behind the rising banks of the river.

The day's light grew strong, as did the pull of the current. Rocks appeared and the river trench deepened. Neither Royce nor Hadrian was an expert boatman, but they did their best dodging the rocks and shallows. Royce remained at the tiller while Hadrian, on his knees, used the long wooden pole to push the bow clear of obstacles. A few times, they glanced off unseen boulders, and the hull lurched abruptly with a deep unpleasant thud. When it did, they could hear the prince whimper, but otherwise he remained quiet and their trip was a smooth one.

In time, the full face of the sun rose overhead, and the river widened considerably and settled into a gentle flow with sandy banks and rich green fields beyond. The Galewyr divided two kingdoms. To the south lay Glouston, the northern marchland of the kingdom of Warric. To the north was Galilin, the largest province in Melengar, administered by Count Pickering. At one time, the river had been a hotly disputed division between two uneasy warlords, but those days were gone. Now it was a peaceful fence between good neighbors and both banks remained lovely, untroubled pastoral scenes of the late season, filled with hay mounds and grazing cows.

The day became unusually warm. Because it was so late in the year, there were few insects about. The cicadas' drone had disappeared, and even the frogs were quiet. The only sound that remained was that of the soft gentle breeze through the dry grasses. Hadrian reclined across the boat with his head on the bundle of the steward's son's old clothes and his feet on the gunwale. His cloak and boots were off and his shirt was open. Similarly, Royce lay with his legs up, idly guiding the boat. The sweet scent of wild salifan was strong in the air, the fragrance more pungent after the plants' surviving the year's first frost. Except for the lack of food, the day was turning out to be quite wonderful and would have been even if they had not just escaped a horrible death hours before.

Hadrian tilted his head back to catch the full light of the sun on his face. "Maybe we should be fishermen."

"Fishermen?" Royce asked dubiously.

"This is pretty nice, isn't it? I never realized how much I like the sound of water lapping against a boat before. I'm enjoying this: the buzzing of a dragonfly, the sight of the cattails, and the bank drifting lazily by."

"Fish don't just jump into the boat, you know?" Royce

pointed out. "You have to cast nets, haul them in, gut the fish, cut off their heads, and scale them. You don't just get to drift."

"Putting it that way makes it sound oddly more like work." Hadrian scooped a handful of water from the river and splashed it on his warm face. He ran his wet fingers through his hair and sighed contentedly.

"You think he's still alive?" Royce asked, nodding his head toward Alric.

"Sure," Hadrian replied without bothering to look. "He's probably sleeping. Why do you ask?"

"I was just pondering something. Do you think a person could smother in a wet potato bag?"

Hadrian lifted his head and looked over at the motionless prince. "I really hadn't thought about it until now." He got up and shook Alric, but the prince did not stir. "Why didn't you mention something earlier!" he said, drawing his dagger. He cut through the ropes and pulled the bag clear.

Alric lay still. Hadrian bent down to check if he was breathing. Just then, the prince kicked Hadrian hard, knocking him back toward Royce. Alric began feverishly untying his feet, but Hadrian was back on him before he cleared the first knot. He slammed Alric to the deck, pinning his hands over his head.

"Hand me the twine," Hadrian barked to Royce, who was watching the wrestling match with quiet amusement. Royce casually tossed him a small coil, and when Hadrian at last had the prince secured, he sat back down to rest.

"See," Royce said, "*that's* more like fishing; only fish don't kick, of course."

"Okay, so it was a bad idea." Hadrian rubbed his side where the prince had hit him.

"By brutalizing me, the two of you have sentenced yourselves to death! You know that, don't you?"

"That's a bit redundant, don't you think, Your Majesty?"

Royce inquired. "Seeing as how you already sentenced us to death once today."

The prince rolled onto his side, tilting his head back, squinted against the brilliant sunlight.

"You!" he shouted, amazed. "But how did you—Arista!" His eyes narrowed in anger. "Not jealous, is she! My dear sister is behind all this! She hired you to kill my father, and now she plans to eliminate me so she can rule!"

"The king was *her* father as well. Besides, if we wanted to kill you, don't you think you'd already be dead?" Royce asked. "Why would we go to all the trouble of hauling you down this river? We could have slit your throat, weighed you down with rocks, and dumped you hours ago. I might add that such a fate would still be considerably better than what you had planned for us."

The prince considered this for a moment. "So it's ransom, then. Do you intend to sell me to the highest bidder? Did she promise you a profit from my sale? You're both fools if you believe that. Arista will never allow it. She'll see me dead. She has to in order to secure her seat on the throne. You won't get a copper!"

"Listen, you little royal pain in the ass, we didn't kill your father. In fact, for what it's worth, I thought old Amrath was a fair king, as far as they go. We also aren't ransoming or selling you."

"Well, you certainly aren't trussing me up like a pig to get in my good graces. Now exactly what *are* you doing with me?" The prince struggled against his bonds but eventually settled down.

"If you really want to know, we are trying to save your life. As strange as that may seem," Hadrian said.

"You're what?" Alric asked, stunned.

"Your sister seems to think someone residing in the

castle—the same lot that killed your father—is plotting to kill everyone in the royal family. Because you would be the next likely target, she freed us to smuggle you out for your own safety."

Alric pulled his legs up under him and worked his way to a sitting position with his back resting up against the pile of white-and-red striped buoys. He stared at the two of them for a moment. "If Arista didn't hire you to kill my father, then exactly what were you doing in the castle tonight?"

Hadrian provided a quick summary of his meeting with DeWitt, to which the prince listened without interruption.

"And then Arista came to you in the dungeon with this story, asking you to abduct me to keep me safe?"

"Trust me," Hadrian said. "If there was another way to get out of there, we would have left you."

"So you actually believe her? You're dumber than I thought," Alric said, shaking his head. "Don't you see what she's doing? She's out to have the kingdom for herself."

"If that were so, why would she have us kidnap you?" Royce asked. "Why not just have you killed like your father?"

Alric thought a moment, his eyes drifting to the floor of the boat, and then he nodded. "She most likely tried." He looked back at them. "I wasn't in my room last night. I slipped out for a rendezvous and fell asleep until I heard the noise. It's very likely an assassin was sent for me but I wasn't there. After that, I had a guard with me at all times until Arista convinced me I had to come alone to the kitchen. I should have known she was betraying me."

He swung his bound legs into the mound of nets. "I just never thought she could be so cold as to kill our father, but that's how she is, you see. She's extremely clever. She told you this story about a traitor, and it was believable because it was true. She only lied about not knowing who it was. Once her assassin missed me, she used you. It was more likely that you'd agree to a kidnapping rather than murder, so she set you up."

Royce did not answer but glanced at Hadrian.

"There was this boat," the prince went on, looking around him, "perfect for your needs waiting at the river's edge."

Alric dipped his head at the tarp next to him. "How nice to have a boat with a cover like this to hide me under. With a nice boat, and a river, you wouldn't be tempted to stray off the water. You can't go upstream from the city. The headwaters are too rough. You have to go toward the sea. She knows exactly where we are, and where we'll be. Did she say where to take me? Is it somewhere down this river?"

"Lake Windermere."

"Ah, the Winds Abbey? It's not far from Roe, and this river travels toward it. How convenient! Of course, we'll never make it," the prince told them. "She'll have killers waiting along the bank. They will murder us. She'll say you two killed me, just as you killed my father. And, of course, her guards killed you when you tried to flee. She'll have a wonderful burial for me and my father. The next day she will call Bishop Saldur to perform her coronation."

Royce and Hadrian sat in silence.

"Do you need more proof?" the prince went on. "You say this fellow that hired you was called DeWitt? You said he was from Calis? Arista returned from a visit there only two months ago. Perhaps she made some new friends. Perhaps she promised them land in Melengar in return for help with a troublesome father and brother who stood between her and the crown."

"We need to get off this river," Royce told Hadrian.

"You think he's right?" Hadrian asked.

"Doesn't matter at this point. Even if he's wrong, the owner of this boat will report it stolen. When news leaks out that the prince is missing, they will connect the two."

Hadrian stood up and looked downstream. "If I were them, I would send a group of riders down the riverbank in case we stopped and another set of riders running fast down the Westfield road to catch us at Wicend Ford. It would only take them three or four hours."

"Which means they could already be there," Royce concluded.

"We need to get off this river," Hadrian said.

The boat came into view of Wicend Ford, a flat, rocky area where the river widened abruptly and became shallow enough to cross. Farmer Wicend had built a small stock shelter of split rails close to the water, allowing his animals to graze and drink unattended; it was a pretty spot. Thick hedges of heldaberry bushes lined the bank, and a handful of yellowing willows bent so low toward the river that their branches touched the water and created ripples and whimsical whirlpools along the surface.

The moment the boat entered the shallows, hidden archers launched a rain of arrows from the bank. One struck the gunwale with a thud. A second and third found their target in the royal falcon insignia emblazoned on the back of the prince's robe. The figure in the robe fell from view into the bottom of the boat. More arrows found their marks in the chest of the tillerman, who dropped into the water, and the pole man, who merely slumped to one side.

From behind the screen of bushes and willows, six men emerged, dressed in browns, dirty greens, and autumn golds. They entered the river, waded out, and caught the still drifting boat.

"It's official, we're dead," Royce declared comically. "Interestingly enough, the first arrows hit Alric."

The three of them were lying concealed in the tall field grass atop the eastern hill overlooking the river upstream of the ford. Less than a hundred yards to their right lay the Westfield road. From there, the road ran along the riverbank all the way to Roe, where the river joined the sea.

"Now do you believe me?" the prince asked.

"It only proves that someone is indeed trying to kill you and that they are not us. They're not soldiers either, or at least they aren't in uniform, so they could be anyone," Royce told them.

"How can he see so much—the arrows, their clothing? I can only see movement and color from this distance," Alric said.

Hadrian shrugged.

The prince was now dressed in the clothes of the steward's son: a loose-fitting gray tunic, worn and faded wool knee-length britches, brown stockings, and a tattered, stained wool cloak, which was too long. He wore on his feet a pair of shoes that were little more than soft leather bags tied at his ankles. Although the prince was no longer bound, Hadrian kept hold of a rope tethered around his waist. Hadrian also carried the prince's sword for him.

"They're moving in on the boat," Royce announced.

All Hadrian could really see were shadowy movements under the trees until one of the men stepped out into the sunlight to grab the bow of the boat.

"It won't be long before they discover they've only killed three bushels of thickets wrapped in old clothes," Hadrian told Royce. "So I'd be quick."

Royce nodded and promptly trotted down the slope.

“What’s he doing?” Alric asked in shock. “He’ll get himself killed and us as well!”

“That’s one opinion,” Hadrian said. “Just sit tight.”

Royce slipped into the shade of the trees, and Hadrian immediately lost sight of him. “Where’d he go?” the prince asked with a puzzled look on his face.

Once more Hadrian shrugged.

Below them, the men converged on the boat, and Hadrian heard a distant shout. He could not make out the words, but he saw someone holding up the Alric-bush complete with arrows. Two of the men remained with the boat while the others waded toward the bank. Just then, Hadrian caught sight of movement in the trees, a train of tethered horses trotting up the slope toward him and Alric. From the bank came shouts of alarm and cursing as the distant figures struggled to race across the field and up the hill.

When the horses drew nearer, Hadrian spotted Royce crouched down, hanging between the two foremost animals. He caught two of the horses, pulled the bridle off one, and quickly tied a lead line to the other horse’s halter. He ordered Alric to mount. Angry shouts erupted as the archers spotted them. Two or three stopped to fit arrows but their uphill shots fell short. Before they could close the distance, the three mounted and galloped toward the road.

Royce led them a mile northwest to where the Westfield and Stonemill roads intersected. Here Hadrian, and by default Alric, rode west. Royce, leading the train of captured horses, stayed behind to cloud their tracks and then rode north. An hour later he caught up with them with only the horse he rode. They turned off the road into an open field and headed away from the river but still moved generally westward.

The horses had built up a solid sweat and were puffing for air. When the men reached the hedgerow lands, they slowed their pace. Eventually they reached the thickets, and there they stopped and dismounted. Alric found a spot clear of thornbushes and sat down, fussing with his tunic, which did not hang on him quite right. Royce and Hadrian took the opportunity to search the animals. There were no markings, symbols, parchments, or emblems of any kind to identify the attackers. Moreover, except for a spare crossbow and a handful of bolts left on Hadrian's mount, they wore only saddles.

"You'd think they would have some bread at least. Who travels without water?" Hadrian complained.

"They clearly didn't expect to be out long."

"Why do you still have me tethered?" the prince asked, irritated. "This is extremely humiliating."

"I don't want you getting lost," Hadrian replied with a grin.

"There's no reason to drag me around any further. I accept that you did not kill my father. My cunning sister merely fooled you. It's quite understandable. She's very intelligent. She even fooled me. Now, if you don't mind, I would like to return to my castle so I can deal with her before she consolidates her power and has the whole army turned out to hunt me down. As for you two, you can go wherever Maribor dictates. I really don't care."

"But your sister said—" Hadrian began.

"My sister just tried to have us all killed back there, or weren't you paying attention?"

"We have no proof it was her. If we let you return to Essendon, and she is right, you'll be walking to your death."

"And what proof do we have it wasn't her? Do you still intend to escort me to wherever she told you to take me? Don't you think she'll have another trap waiting? I see my death far more probable on the road there than on any other road. Look, this is my life; I think it's fair for me to decide. Besides, what do you care if I live or die? I was about to have you two tortured to death. Remember?"

"You know"—Royce paused a moment—"he's got a point there."

"We promised her," Hadrian reminded him, "and she saved our lives. Let's not forget that."

Alric threw his hands up and rolled his eyes. "By Mar! You *are* thieves, aren't you? It's not as if you have a sense of honor to contend with. Besides, she was also the one who betrayed you and put your lives in danger in the first place. Let's not forget *that*!"

Hadrian ignored the prince. "We don't know she is responsible, and we *did* promise."

"Another good deed?" Royce asked. "You'll remember where the last one ended us?"

Hadrian sighed. "There it is! Didn't have to save it too long, did you? Yes, I did screw up, but that isn't to say I'm wrong this time. Windermere is only, what, ten miles from here? We could be there by nightfall. We could stop at the abbey. Monks have to help wayward travelers. It's in their doctrine or code or whatever. We could really use some food, don't you think?"

"They also might know something about the prison," Royce speculated.

"What prison?" Alric asked, nervously getting to his feet.

"Gutaria Prison—it's where your sister told us to take you."

"To lock me up?" the prince asked fearfully.

"No, no. She wants you to talk to someone there, some guy called...Esra—oh, what was it?"

"Haddon, I think," Hadrian said.

"Whatever. Do you know anything about this prison?"

"No, I've never heard of it," Alric replied. "Although it sounds like the kind of place unwanted royals go to disappear when a conniving sister steals her brother's throne."

Royce's horse butted against his shoulder, prompting him to rub its head while contemplating the situation. "I'm too tired to think clearly. I doubt any of us can make an intelligent decision at this point, and given the stakes, we don't want to be hasty. We'll go as far as the abbey at least. We'll talk to them and see what they can tell us about the prison. Then we'll decide what to do from there. Does that sound fair?"

Alric sighed heavily. "If I must go, can I at least be given the dignity of controlling my own horse?" There was a pause before he added, "I give you my word as king. I'll not try to escape until we reach this abbey."

Hadrian looked at Royce, who nodded. He then pulled the crossbow from behind his saddle. He braced it against the ground, pulled the string to the first notch, and loaded a bolt.

"It's not that we don't trust you," Royce said as Hadrian prepared the bow. "It's just that we've learned over the years that honor among nobles is usually inversely proportionate to their rank. As a result, we prefer to rely on more concrete methods for motivations—such as self-preservation. You already know we don't want you dead, but if you have ever been riding full tilt and had a horse buckle under you, you understand that death is always a possibility, and broken bones are almost a certainty."

"There's also the danger of missing the horse completely," Hadrian added. "I'm a good shot, but even the best archers have bad days. So to answer your question—yes, you can control your own horse."

⁂

They traveled at a moderate but steady pace for the remainder of the day. Royce guided them through fields, hedgerows, and forested trails. They stayed off the roads and away from the villages until at last there were no more of either. Even the farms disappeared as the land lost its tame face and they entered the wild highlands of Melengar. The ground rose, and forests grew thicker, with fewer passable routes. Ravines led to bogs at their bottoms, and hills sloped up into cliffs. This rough country, the western third of Melengar, lacked farmable land and remained unsettled. The area was home to wolves, elk, deer, bears, outlaws, and anyone seeking solitude, such as the monks of the Winds Abbey. Civilized men shunned it, and superstitious villagers feared its dark forests and rising mountains. Myths abounded about water nymphs luring knights to watery graves, wolf men devouring the lost, and ancient evil spirits that appeared as floating lights in the dense forest enticing children to their dark caves under the earth. Regardless of the legions of potential supernatural dangers, enough natural obstacles made the route one to avoid.

Hadrian never questioned his partner's choice of path or direction. He knew why Royce stayed clear of the Westfield road, which provided a clear and easy path along the riverbank to the fishing village of Roe. Despite its isolation at the mouth of the Galewyr, Roe had grown from a sleepy little dock into a thriving seaport. While it held the promise of food, lodging, and imagined safety, it would likely be watched. The other easy option was to travel north up the Stonemill road—the route Royce pretended to take by leaving enough tracks to hopefully mislead anyone who followed into thinking they were headed for Drondil Fields. Each path held obvious benefits, which anyone looking for them would understand as well. As a result, they plodded and hacked their way through the wilds, following whatever animal trails they could find.

After a particularly arduous fight through a dense segment

of forest, they came out unexpectedly on a ridge that afforded a magnificent view of the setting sun, which bathed the valley of Windermere and was reflected by the lake. Lake Windermere was one of the deepest in all of Avryn. Because it was too deep to support plant life, it was nearly crystal clear. The water shimmered in the folds and crevices of the three surrounding hills that shaped it in the form of a stretched, jagged triangle. The hills rose above the tree line, showing bald, barren peaks of scrub and stone. Hadrian could just make out a stone building on the top of the southernmost hill. Aside from Roe, the Winds Abbey was the only sign of civilization for miles.

The party aimed toward the building and descended into the valley, but night caught up with them before they were halfway there. Fortunately, a distant light from the abbey provided them a beacon. The weariness of being up for two stress-filled days combined with hard travel and no food was taking its toll on Hadrian, and he assumed the same was true of Royce, though his partner showed it less. The prince looked the worst. Alric rode just ahead of Hadrian. His head would droop lower and lower with each stride of his horse until he would nearly fall from his saddle. He would catch himself, straighten, and then the process would begin again.

Despite the warm day, night brought with it a bitter chill, and in the soft light of the rising moon, the breath of men and horses began to fog the crisp night air. Above, the stars shone like diamond dust scattered across the heavens. In the distance, the call of owls and the shrill static of crickets filled the valley. Had the party not been so exhausted and hungry, they might have described the trip that night as beautiful. Instead, they merely gritted their teeth and focused on the path ahead.

They began climbing the south hill as Royce led them with

uncanny skill along a switchback trail that only his keen eyes could see. The thin, worn clothes of the steward's son were a miserable defense against the cold, and soon the prince was shivering. To make matters worse, as they climbed higher, the temperature dropped and the wind grew. Soon trees began to shrink to stunted shrubs and the earth changed to lichen- and moss-covered stone. At last, they reached the steps of the Winds Abbey.

Clouds had moved in, and the moon was no longer visible. In the darkness, they could see very little except the steps and the light they had followed. They dismounted and approached the gate. A stone arch set within a peaked nave lay open on a porch of rock hewn from the hill itself. There was no longer the sound of crickets, nor of hooting owls; only the unremitting wind broke the silence.

"Hello?" Hadrian called. After a time, Hadrian called again. He was about to try a third time when he saw a light move within. Like a dim firefly weaving behind unseen trees, it vanished behind pillars and walls, reappearing closer each time. As it drew near, Hadrian saw that the strange will-o'-the-wisp was a small man in a worn frock holding a lantern.

"Who is it?" he asked in a soft, timid voice.

"Wayfarers," Royce answered. "Cold, tired, and hoping for a place to rest."

"How many are you?" The man poked his head out and swung the lantern about. He paused to study each face. "Just the three?"

"Yes," Hadrian replied. "We've been traveling all day with no food. We were hoping to take advantage of the famous hospitality of the legendary Monks of Maribor. Do you have room?"

The monk hesitated and then said, "I—I suppose." He stepped back to allow them entrance. "Come in, you can—"

"We have horses," Hadrian interrupted.

"Really? How exciting," the monk replied, sounding impressed. "Oh, I would like to see them, but it's very late and—"

"No, I just meant, is there somewhere we can stable them for the night? A barn or perhaps a shed?"

"Oh, I see." The monk paused, tapping his lip thoughtfully. "Ah, well, we had a lovely stable, mostly for cows, sheep, and goats, but that's not going to work tonight. We also had some animal pens where we kept pigs, but that really won't do either."

"I suppose we could just tie them up outside somewhere if that's all right," Hadrian said. "I think I remember a little tree or two."

The monk nodded, appearing relieved to have the issue resolved. After they stacked the saddles on the porch, the little man led them through an opening into what appeared to be a large courtyard.

With only the bleak glow of the monk's lantern, Hadrian could not see far beyond the stone walkway and was too tired for a tour even if the monk had been inclined to show off his home. The abbey had a heavy smell of smoke that conjured visions of warm crackling hearths where beds might be.

"We didn't mean to wake you," Hadrian said softly.

"Oh, not me," the monk said. "I actually don't sleep much. I was busy with a book, right in the middle of a sentence when I heard you. Most unnerving. It's a rare thing to hear someone in the middle of the day around here, much less a dark night."

Columns of freestanding stone rose beneath a cloudy sky, and various black silhouetted statues dotted the space. The smoky smell was stronger, but the only thing that appeared to be burning was the lantern in the monk's hand. They reached a small set of stone steps and he led the way down into what appeared to be a rough-hewn stone cellar.

"You can stay here," the monk told them.

The three stared at the tiny hovel, which Hadrian thought looked less inviting than the cells below Essendon Castle. Inside, it was very cramped, filled with piles of neatly stacked wood, tied bundles of twigs and heather, two wooden barrels, a chamber pot, a little table, and a single cot. No one said a word for a moment.

"It's not much, I know," the monk said regretfully, "but at the moment, it's all I can offer you."

"We'll make do, then, thank you," Hadrian assured him. He was so tired he did not care as long as he could lie down and be out of the wind. "Can we perhaps get a few blankets? As you can see, we really don't have any supplies with us."

"Blankets?" The monk looked concerned. "Well, there is one here." He pointed at the cot, where a single thin blanket lay neatly folded. "I truly am sorry I can't offer you any more. You can keep the lantern if you like. I know my way around without it." The monk left them without another word, perhaps fearful they would ask for something else.

"He didn't even ask us our names," the prince said.

"And wasn't that a pleasant surprise," Royce pointed out as he moved around the room with the lantern. Hadrian watched him take a thorough inventory of what little was there: a dozen or so bottles of wine hidden in the back, a small sack of potatoes under some straw, and a length of rope.

"This is intolerable," Alric said in disgust. "Surely an abbey of this size has better accommodations than this pit."

Hadrian found an old pair of burlap shoes that he cleared out before he lay down on the cellar floor. "I actually have to agree with the royal one there. I heard great things about the hospitality of this abbey. We do appear to be getting the dregs."

"Question is, why?" Royce said. "Who else is here? It would need to be several groups or a tremendously large party to turn us out to this hovel. Only nobility travel with such large retinues. They might be looking for us. They might be associated with those archers."

"I doubt it. If we were in Roe, I think we'd have more reason for concern," Hadrian said as he stretched and then yawned. "Besides, anyone who is here has turned in for the night and is probably not expecting any late arrivals."

"Still, I'm going to get up early and look around. We might need to make a hasty departure."

"Not before breakfast," Hadrian said, sitting on the floor and kicking off his boots. "We need to eat and I know abbeys are renowned for their food. If nothing else, you can steal some."

"Fine, but His Highness should not move about. He needs to keep a low profile."

Standing in the middle of the cellar with a sickened look on his face, Alric said, "I can't believe I'm being subjected to this."

"Consider it a vacation," Hadrian suggested. "For at least one day you get to pretend you are nobody, a common peasant, the son of a blacksmith perhaps."

"No," Royce said, preparing his own sleeping space but keeping his boots on. "They might expect him to know things like how to use a hammer. And look at his hands. Anyone could tell he was lying."

"Most people have jobs that require the use of their hands, Royce," Hadrian pointed out. He spread his cloak over himself and turned on his side. "What could a common peasant do that monks wouldn't know the first thing about and wouldn't cause calluses?"

"He could be a thief or a whore."

They both looked at the prince, who cringed at his prospects. "I'm taking the cot," Alric said.

Chapter 4

Windermere

The morning arrived cold and wet. A solid gray sky cast a steady curtain of rain on the abbey. The deluge streamed down the stone steps and pooled in the low pocket of the entryway. When the growing puddle reached Hadrian's feet, he knew it was time to get up. He turned over on his back and wiped his eyes. He had not slept well. He felt stiff and groggy, and the cold morning air chilled him to the bone. He sat up, dragged a large hand down the length of his face, and looked around. The tiny room appeared even more dismal in the drab morning light than it had the night before. He moved back away from the puddle and looked for his boots. Alric had the benefit of the cot, yet he did not appear to have fared much better. Despite having a blanket wrapped tightly around him, he lay shivering. Royce was nowhere to be seen.

Alric opened one eye and squinted at Hadrian as he pulled his big boots on.

"Good morning, *Your Highness*," Hadrian said in a mocking tone. "Have a pleasant sleep?"

"That was the worst night I have ever endured," Alric snarled through clenched teeth. "I have never felt such misery as this damp, freezing hole. Every muscle aches; my head is throbbing, and I can't stop my teeth from chattering. I'm going home today. Kill me if you must, but nothing short of my death will stop me."

"So that would be a no?" Hadrian got to his feet, rubbed his arms briskly, and looked out at the rain.

"Why don't you do something constructive and build a fire before we die of the cold?" the prince grumbled, pulling the thin blanket over his head and peering out as if it were a hood.

"I don't think we should build a fire in this cellar. Why don't we just run over to the refectory? That way we can warm up and get food at the same time. I'm sure they have a nice roaring fire. These monks get up early, probably been laboring for hours making fresh bread, gathering eggs, and churning butter just for the likes of us. I know Royce wants you to stay hidden, but I don't think he expected winter would arrive so soon, or so wet. I think if you keep your hood raised, we should be fine."

The prince sat up with an eager look. "Even a room with a door would be better than this."

"That may be," they heard Royce say from somewhere outside, "but you won't find it here."

The thief appeared a moment later, his hood up and his cloak slick with rain. Once he ducked in out of the downpour, he snapped it like a dog shaking his fur. This sent a spray of water at Hadrian and Alric. They flinched and with a grimace the prince opened his mouth to speak but he stopped short. Royce was not alone. Behind him followed the monk from the night before. He was soaked. His wool frock sagged with the weight of the water, and his hair laid plastered flat on his head. His skin was pale, his purple lips quivered, and his fingers were wrinkled as if he had been swimming too long.

"I found him sleeping outside," Royce said as he quickly grabbed an armful of the stacked wood. "Myron, take off that robe. We need to get you dry."

"Myron?" Hadrian said with an inquisitive look. "Myron

Lanaklin?" Hadrian thought the monk nodded in reply, but he was shivering so hard it was difficult to tell.

"You know each other?" Alric asked.

"No, but we are familiar with his family," Royce said. "Give him the blanket."

Alric looked shocked and held tightly to his covering.

"Give it to him," Royce insisted. "It's *his* blanket. This fool gave us his home to stay in last night while he huddled in a wind-lashed corner of the cloister and froze."

"I don't understand," Alric said, reluctantly pulling the blanket off his shoulders. "Why would you sleep outside in the rain when—"

"The abbey burned down," Royce told them. "Anything that wasn't stone is gone. We weren't walking through a courtyard last night—that was the abbey. The ceiling is missing. The outer buildings are nothing but piles of ash. The whole place is a gutted ruin."

The monk slipped out of his robe, and Alric handed the blanket to him. Myron hurriedly pulled it around his shoulders and, sitting down, drew his knees up to his chest, wrapping them in the folds as well.

"What about the other monks?" Hadrian asked. "Where are they?"

"I—I bu-buried them. In the garden mostly," Myron said through chattering teeth. "The gr-ground is softer there. I don't th-think they will mind. We all lo-loved the garden."

"When did this happen?"

"Night before last," Myron replied.

Shocked by the news, Hadrian did not want to press the monk further and a silence fell over the room. Royce built a fire near the entrance using various pieces of wood and some oil from the lantern. As it grew, the stone walls reflected the heat, and soon the room began to warm.

No one said anything for a long time. Royce prodded the fire with a stick, churning the glowing coals so that they sparked and spit. They each sat watching the flames, listening to the fire pop and crackle while outside the wind howled and the rain lashed the hilltop. Without looking at the monk, Royce said in a somber voice, "You were all locked in the church when it was burned, weren't you, Myron?"

The monk did not reply. His gaze remained focused on the fire.

"I saw the blackened chain and lock in the ash. It was still closed."

Myron, his arms hugging his knees, began to rock slowly.

"What happened?" Alric asked.

Still Myron said nothing. Several minutes passed. At last, the monk looked away from the fire. He did not look at them, but instead, he stared at some distant point outside in the rain. "They came and accused us of treason," he said with a soft voice. "There were maybe twenty of them, knights with helms covering their faces. They rounded us up and pushed us into the church. They closed the big doors behind us. Then the fire started.

"Smoke filled the church so quickly. I could hear my brothers coughing, struggling to breathe. The abbot led us in prayer until he collapsed. It burned very quickly. I never knew it contained so much dry wood. It always seemed to be so strong. The coughing got quieter and less frequent. Eventually, I couldn't see anymore. My eyes filled with tears, and then I passed out. I woke up to rain. The men and their horses were gone and so was everything else. I was under a marble lectern in the lowest nave, and all my brothers were around me. I looked for other survivors but there were none."

"Who did this?" Alric demanded.

"I don't know their names, or who sent them, but they were dressed in tunics with a scepter and crown," Myron said.

"Imperialists," Alric concluded. "But why would they attack an abbey?"

Myron did not reply. He merely stared out the window at the rain. A long time passed; finally Hadrian asked in a comforting voice, "Myron, you said they charged you with treason. What did they accuse you of doing?"

The monk said nothing. He just sat huddled in his blanket and stared. Alric finally broke the silence. "I don't understand. I gave no orders to have this abbey destroyed, and I can't believe my father did either. Why would Imperialists carry out such an act, especially without my knowledge?"

Royce cast a harsh and anxious look at the prince.

"What?" Alric asked.

"I thought we discussed the importance of keeping a low profile."

"Oh, please." The prince waved a hand at the thief. "I don't think it will get me killed if this monk knows I'm the king. Look at him. I've seen drowned rats more formidable."

"King?" Myron muttered.

Alric ignored him. "Besides, who is he going to tell? I'm heading back to Medford this morning anyway. Not only do I have a traitorous sister to deal with, but apparently there are things going on in my kingdom that I know nothing about. I need to address this."

"It might not have been one of your nobles," Royce said. "I wonder…Myron, did it have anything to do with Degan Gaunt?"

Myron shifted nervously in his seat as an anxious look came over his face. "I need to string a clothesline to dry my robe," he said while getting up.

"Degan Gaunt?" Alric inquired. "That deranged revolutionary? Why do you bring him up?"

"He's one of the leaders of the Nationalist movement, and he's rumored to be around this area," Hadrian confirmed.

"The Nationalist movement—ha! A grandiose name for that rabble." Alric sneered. "They're more like the peasant party. Those radicals want the commoners to have a say in how they're ruled."

"Perhaps Degan Gaunt was using the abbey for more than just a romantic rendezvous," Royce speculated. "Maybe he was meeting with Nationalist sympathizers as well. Perhaps your father did know, or it could have had something to do with his death."

"I'm going to gather some water to make us some breakfast. I'm sure you are all hungry," Myron said as he finished hanging his robe and began collecting various pots to set out in the rain.

Alric took no notice of the monk as he focused on Royce. "My father never would have ordered such a heinous attack! He'd be more upset at the Imperialists invading the abbey than the Nationalist revolutionaries using it for meetings. Those revolutionaries' dreams are just that, but the Imperialists are organized. They have the church behind them. My family has always been steadfast Royalists, believers in the god-given right for a king to rule through his nobles and in the independent sovereignty of each kingdom. Our greatest fear isn't from some rabble thinking they can organize and overthrow the rule of law. Our concern is that one day the Imperialists will find the Heir of Novron and demand all the kingdoms of the four nations of Apeladorn pledge fealty to a new empire."

"Yes, you prefer things exactly the way they are," Royce observed. "But being the king, that doesn't seem terribly surprising."

"You are no doubt a staunch Nationalist, in favor of lopping the heads off all the nobles, and the redistribution of their lands, to peasants, and letting them all have a say in how they are ruled," Alric told Royce. "That would solve all the problems of the world, wouldn't it? And that would certainly be in *your* favor."

"Actually," Royce said, "I don't have any political leanings. They get in the way of my job. Noble or commoner, people all lie, cheat, and pay me to do their dirty work. Regardless of who rules, the sun still shines, the seasons still change, and people still conspire. If you must place labels on attitudes, I prefer to think of myself as an individualist."

"And that's why the Nationalists will never organize enough to be a real threat."

"Delgos seems fairly well run and it's a republic—ruled by the people."

"They're nothing but a bunch of shopkeepers down there."

"They might be a bit more than that."

"It doesn't matter. What does is—why do Imperialists care so much about a few revolutionaries having meetings in Melengar?"

"Maybe Ethelred thought his marquis was plotting to help them—how did you put it?—lop off all the nobles' heads."

"Lanaklin? Are you serious? Victor Lanaklin isn't a Nationalist. Nationalists are commoners trying to steal power from the nobles. Lanaklin is an Imperialist, like all those Warric nobles. They're religious fanatics who want a single government under the control of the Heir of Novron. They think he will miraculously unite everyone and usher in some mythical age of paradise. It's as much wishful thinking as the Nationalists' dreams."

"Maybe this whole thing was just a romantic affair," Hadrian suggested.

Alric sighed and shook his head in resignation. He stood up and held his hands out to the fire. "So how long before breakfast is ready, Myron? I'm starving."

"I'm afraid I don't have much to offer you," Myron said. He set up a small elevated grate over the fire. "I have a few potatoes in a bag in the corner."

"That's all you have, isn't it?" Royce asked.

"I'm very sorry," Myron replied, looking sincerely pained.

"No, I mean those potatoes are all the food *you* have. If we eat them, you'll be left with nothing."

"Oh, well." He shrugged off the comment. "I'll manage somehow. Don't worry about me," he said optimistically.

Hadrian retrieved the bag, looked in it, and then handed it to the monk. "There are only eight potatoes in here. How long were you planning to stay?"

Myron did not answer for a while, until at last he said to no one in particular, "I'm not going anywhere. I have to stay. I have to fix it."

"Fix what, the abbey? That's an awfully big job for one man."

He shook his head. "The library, the books. That's what I was working on last night when you arrived."

"The library is gone, Myron," Royce reminded him. "The books were all burned. They're ash now."

"I know. I know," he said, brushing his wet hair back from his eyes. "That's why I have to replace them."

"How are you going to do that?" Alric asked with a smirk. "Rewrite all the books from memory?"

Myron nodded. "I was working on page fifty-three of *The History of Apeladorn* by Antun Bulard when you came." Myron went over to a makeshift desk and brought out a small box. Inside were about twenty pages of parchment and several curled sheets of thin bark. "I ran out of parchment. Not much survived the fire but the bark works all right."

Royce, Hadrian, and Alric shuffled through them. Myron wrote with small meticulous lettering, which extended to the edge of the page in every direction. No space was wasted.

The text was complete, including page numbers not placed at the end of the parchments but where the pages would have ended in the original document.

Staring at the magnificently rendered text, Hadrian asked, “How could you remember all of this?”

Myron shrugged. “I remember all the books I read.”

“And did you read all the books in the library here?”

Myron nodded. “I had a lot of time to myself.”

“How many were there?”

“Three hundred eighty-two books, five hundred twenty-four scrolls, and one thousand two hundred thirteen individual parchments.”

“And you remember every one?”

Myron nodded once more.

They all sat back, staring at the monk in awe.

“I was the *librarian*,” Myron said as if that would explain it all.

“Myron,” Royce suddenly said, “in all those books did you ever read anything about a place called Gutaria Prison or a prisoner called Esra…haddon?”

Myron shook his head.

“I suppose it’s unlikely anyone would write anything down concerning a secret prison,” Royce said, looking disappointed.

“But it was mentioned a few times in a scroll and once in a parchment. On the parchment, however, the name Esrahaddon was altered to *prisoner* and Gutaria was listed as *The Imperial Prison*.”

“Maribor’s beard!” Hadrian exclaimed, looking at the monk in awe. “You really did memorize the whole library, didn’t you?”

“Why ‘imperial prison’?” Royce asked. “Arista said it was ecclesiastical.”

Myron shrugged. “Maybe because in imperial times the

Church of Nyphron and the empire were linked. *Nyphron* is the ancient term for *emperor*, derived from the name of the first emperor, Novron. So, the Church of Nyphron is the *worshipers of the emperor* and anything associated with the empire could also be considered part of the church."

"That's why members of the Nyphron Church are so intent on finding the heir," Royce added. "He would be their god, so to speak, and not merely a ruler."

"There were several very interesting books on the Heir of the Empire," Myron said excitedly. "And speculation as to what happened to him—"

"What about the prison?" Royce asked.

"Well, that's a subject which isn't mentioned much at all. The only direct reference was in a very rare scroll called *The Accumulated Letters of Dioylion.* The original copy came here one night about twenty years ago. I was only fifteen at the time, but I was already the library assistant when a priest, wounded and near death, brought it. It was raining then, much as it is now. They took him to the healing rooms and told me to watch after his things. I took his satchel, which was soaked, and inside I found all sorts of scrolls. I was afraid the water might damage them, so I opened them up to dry. While they lay open, I couldn't resist reading them. I usually can't resist reading anything.

"Although he didn't look much better two days later, the priest left and took his scrolls. No one could convince him to stay. He seemed frightened. The scrolls themselves were several correspondences made by Archbishop Venlin, the head of the Nyphron Church at the time of the breaking of the empire. One of them was a post-imperial edict for the construction of the prison, which is why I thought the document was so important historically. It revealed the church exercised governmental control immediately following the disappearance of the emperor. I found it quite fascinating. It was also curious that the building of a prison had such high priority, considering the turmoil of that period. I now realize it was a very rare scroll, but of course, I didn't know that back then."

"Wait a minute," Alric interrupted. "So this prison was built—what—nine hundred years ago and exists in my kingdom and I don't know anything about it?"

"Well, based on the date of the scroll, it would have been started...nine hundred and ninety-six years, two hundred and fifty-four days ago. The prison was a massive undertaking. One letter in particular spoke of recruiting skilled artisans from around the world to design and build it. The greatest minds and the most advanced engineering went into its creation. They carved the prison out of solid rock from the face of the mountains just north of the lake. They sealed it not only with metal, stone, and wood but also with ancient and powerful enchantments. In the end, when it was finished, it was believed to be the most secure prison in the world."

"They must have had some really nasty criminals back then to go to so much trouble," Hadrian said.

"No," Myron replied matter-of-factly, "just one."

"One?" Alric asked. "An entire prison designed to hold just one man?"

"His name was Esrahaddon."

Hadrian, Royce, and Alric shared looks of surprise.

"What in the world did he do?" Hadrian asked.

"According to everything I read, he was responsible for the destruction of the empire. The prison was specifically designed to hold him."

They looked incredulously at the monk.

"And exactly how is he responsible for wiping out the most powerful empire the world has ever known?" Alric asked.

"Esrahaddon was once a trusted advisor to the emperor,

but he betrayed him, killing the entire imperial family, except, of course, for the one son who managed to miraculously escape. There are even stories that he destroyed the capital city of Percepliquis. The empire fell into chaos and civil war after the emperor's death. Esrahaddon was captured, tried, and imprisoned."

"Why not just execute him?" Alric asked, generating icy glares from the thieves.

"Is execution your answer to every problem?" Royce sneered.

"Sometimes it's the best solution," Alric replied.

Myron retrieved the pots from outside and combined the water into one. He added the potatoes and placed the pot over the fire to cook.

"Then Arista has sent us to bring her brother to see a prisoner who is over a thousand years old. Does anyone else see a problem with that?" Hadrian asked.

"See!" Alric exclaimed. "Arista is lying. She probably picked up the name Esrahaddon in her studies at Sheridan University and didn't realize when he lived. There is no way Esrahaddon could still be alive."

"He might be," Myron said casually, stirring the potatoes in the pot over the fire.

"How's that?" Alric queried.

"Because he's a wizard."

"When you say he was a wizard," Hadrian asked, "do you mean that he was a learned man of wisdom or that he could do card tricks and sleight of hand or maybe he was able to brew a potion to help you sleep? Royce and I know a man like that, and he is a bit of all three, but he can't hold off death."

"According to the accounts I have read," Myron explained, "wizards were different back then. They called magic 'the Art.' Most of the knowledge of the empire was lost when it fell. For instance, the ancient skills of Teshlor combat, which made warriors invincible, or the construction techniques that could create vast domes, or the ability to forge swords that could cut stone. Like these, the art of true magic was lost to the world with the passing of the true wizards. Reports say in the days of Novron, the Cenzars—that's what they called wizards—were incredibly powerful. There are stories of them causing earthquakes, raising storms, even blacking out the sun. The greatest of these ancient wizards formed into a group called the Great Cenzar Council. Members were part of the inner circle of government."

"Really," Alric said thoughtfully.

"Did you ever read anything about exactly where the prison was located?" Royce asked.

"No, but there was a bit about it in Mantuar's *Thesis on Architectural Symbolism in the Novronian Empire*. That's the parchment I mentioned where the name Esrahaddon was changed. Stuffed on a back shelf for years, I found it one day while clearing an old portion of the library. It was a mess, but it mentioned the date of construction, and a bit about the people commissioned to build it. If I hadn't first read *The Accumulated Letters of Dioylion*, I never would have made the connection between the two, because, as I said, it never mentioned the name of the prison or the prisoner."

"I don't understand how this prison could exist in Melengar without my knowing about it," Alric said, shaking his head. "And how does Arista know about it? And why does she want me to go there?"

"I thought you determined she was sending you there to kill or imprison you," Hadrian reminded him.

"That certainly makes more sense to me than a thousand-year-old wizard," Royce said.

"Maybe," Alric muttered, "but..." The prince, his eyes searching the ground before him for answers, tapped a finger on his lips. "Consider this: if she really wanted me dead, why choose such an obscure place? She could have sent you to this monastery and had a whole army waiting, and no one would hear a scream. It's unnecessarily complicated to drag me to a hidden place no one has heard of. Why would she mention this Esrahaddon or Gutaria at all?"

"Now you think she's telling the truth?" Royce asked. "Do you think there really is a thousand-year-old man waiting to talk to you?"

"I wouldn't go that far, but—well, consider the possibilities if he does exist. Imagine what I could learn from a man like that, an advisor to the last emperor."

Hadrian chuckled at the comment. "You're actually starting to sound like a king now."

"It might merely be the warmth of the fire or the smell of boiling potatoes, but I'm starting to think it might be a good idea to see where this leads. And look, the storm is breaking. The rain will be stopping soon, I think. What if Arista isn't trying to kill me? What if there really is something there I need to discover, something that has to do with the murder of our father?"

"Your father was killed?" Myron asked. "I'm so sorry."

Alric took no notice of the monk. "Regardless, I don't like this ancient prison existing in my kingdom without my knowledge. I wonder if my father knew about it, or his father. Perhaps none of the Essendons were aware of it. A thousand years would predate the founding of Melengar by several centuries. The prison was built when this land still lay contested during the Great Civil War. If it's possible for a man to live for a thousand years, if this Esrahaddon was an advisor to the last emperor, I think I should like to speak to him. Any noble in Apeladorn would give his left eye for a chance to speak to a true imperial advisor. Like the monk said, so much knowledge was lost when the empire fell, so much forgotten over time. What might he know? What advantage would a man like that be to a young king?"

"Even if he's just a ghost?" Royce asked. "It's unlikely there is a thousand-year-old man in a prison north of this lake."

"If the ghost can speak, what's the difference?"

"The difference is I liked this idea a lot better when you *didn't* want to go," Royce said. "I thought Esrahaddon was some old baron your father exiled who had put a contract out on you, or maybe the mother of an illegitimate half brother who was imprisoned to keep her quiet. But this? This is ridiculous!"

"Let's not forget you promised my sister." Alric smiled. "Let's eat. I'm sure those potatoes are done by now. I could eat them all."

Once more Alric drew a reproachful look from Royce.

"Don't worry about the potatoes," Myron told him. "There are more in the garden, I'm sure. These ones I found while digging in the—" He stopped himself.

"I'm not worried, monk, because you are coming with us," Alric told him.

"Wha—what?"

"You obviously are a very knowledgeable fellow. I'm sure you'll come in handy, in any number of situations that may lie before us. So you'll serve at the pleasure of your king."

Myron stared back. He blinked two times in rapid succession, and his face suddenly went pale. "I'm sorry, but I—I can't do that," he replied meekly.

"Maybe it would be best if you came with us," Hadrian told him. "You can't stay here. Winter is coming and you'll die."

"But you don't understand," Myron protested with increasing

anxiety in his voice, and shook his head adamantly. "I—I can't leave."

"I know. I know." Alric raised his hand to quell the protest. "You have all these books to write. That's a fine and noble task. I'm all for it. More people need to read. My father was a big supporter of the university at Sheridan. He even sent Arista there. Can you imagine that? A girl at the university? In any case, I agree with his views on education. Look around you, man! You have no parchment and likely little ink. If you do write these tomes, where will you store them? In here? There is no protection from the elements; they will be destroyed and blown to the wind. After we visit this prison, I'll take you back to Medford and set you up to work on your project. I'll see to it you have a proper scriptorium, perhaps with a few assistants to aid you in whatever it is you need."

"That is very kind but I can't. I'm sorry. You don't really understand—"

"I understand perfectly. You're obviously Marquis Lanaklin's third son, the one he sent away to avoid the unpleasant dividing of his lands. You're rather unique—a learned monk, with an eidetic mind, and a noble as well. If your father doesn't want you, I certainly could use you."

"No," Myron protested, "it's not that."

"What is it, then?" Hadrian asked. "You're sitting here, cold and wet in a stone and dirt hole, wrapped in only a blanket, looking forward to a grand feast consisting of a couple of boiled potatoes, and your king is offering to set you up like a landed baron and you're protesting?"

"I don't mean to be ungrateful, but I—well, I've never left the abbey before."

"What do you mean?" Hadrian asked.

"I've never left. I came here when I was four years old. I've never left—ever."

"Surely you've traveled to Roe, the fishing village?" Royce asked. Myron shook his head. "Never to Medford? What about the surrounding area? You've at least gone to the lake, to fish or just for a walk?"

Myron shook his head again. "I've never been off the grounds. Not even to the bottom of the hill. I'm not quite sure I can leave. Just the thought makes me nauseous." Myron checked the dryness of his robe. Hadrian could see his hand was shaking even though he had stopped shivering some time ago.

"So that's why you were so fascinated by the horses," Hadrian said mostly to himself. "But you have seen horses before, right?"

"I have seen them from the windows of the abbey when on rare occasions we would receive visitors who had them. I've never actually touched one. I've always wondered what it would be like to sit on one. In all the books, they talk about horses, jousts, battles, and races. Horses are very popular. One king—King Bethamy—he actually had his horse buried with him. There are many things I have read about that I've never seen—women, for one. They are also very popular in books and poems."

Hadrian's eyes widened. "You've never seen a woman before?"

Myron shook his head. "Well, some books did have drawings which depicted them, but—"

Hadrian hooked a thumb at Alric. "And here I thought the prince lived a sheltered life."

"But you've at least seen your sister," Royce said. "She's been here."

Myron did not say anything. He looked away and set about removing the pot from the fire and placing the potatoes on plates.

"You mean she came here to meet with Gaunt and never even tried to see you?" Hadrian asked.

Myron shrugged. "My father came to see me once about a year ago. The abbot had to tell me who he was."

"So you weren't a part of the meetings here at all?" Royce observed. "You weren't hosting them? Making arrangements for them?"

"*No!*" Myron screamed at them, and he kicked one of the empty pots across the room. *"I—don't—know—anything—about—letters—and—my—sister!"* He backed up against the cellar wall as tears welled up in his eyes, and he panted for breath. No one said a word as they watched him standing there, clutching his blanket and staring at the ground.

"I'm—I'm sorry. I shouldn't have yelled at you. Forgive me," Myron said, wiping his eyes. "No, I've never met my sister, and I saw my father only that once. He swore me to silence. I don't know why. Nationalists—Royalists—Imperialists—I don't know about any of it." There was a distance in the monk's voice, a hollow painful sound.

"Myron," Royce began, "you didn't survive because you were under a stone lectern, did you?"

The tears welled up once again and the monk's lips quivered. He shook his head. "At first, they made us watch while they beat the abbot bloody," Myron said, his voice choked and hitched in his throat. "They wanted to know about Alenda and some letters. He finally told them my sister was sending messages disguised in the form of love letters, but she wasn't meeting anyone. That was just a fabrication. The letters were arranged by my father and being picked up by a messenger from Medford. After they found out about my father's visit, that's when they started questioning me." Myron swallowed and took a ragged breath. "But they never hurt me. They didn't even touch me. They asked if my father was siding with the Royalists and plotting with Melengar against Warric and the church. They wanted to know who else was involved. I didn't say a word. I didn't know anything. I swear I didn't. But I could have said something. I could have lied. I could have said, 'Yes, my father is a Royalist and my sister is a traitor!' But I didn't. I never opened my mouth. Do you know why?"

Myron looked at them with tears running down his cheeks. "I didn't tell them because my father made me swear to be *silent*." He paused a moment then said, "I watched *in silence* as they sealed the church. I watched *in silence* as they set it on fire. And *in silence*, I listened to my brothers' screams. It was my fault. I let my brothers die because of an oath I made to a man who was a stranger to me." Myron began to cry uncontrollably. He slid down the wall into a crumpled ball on the dirt, his arms covering his face.

Hadrian finished serving the potatoes but Myron refused to eat. Hadrian stored two spuds away in the hopes that Myron might want them later.

By the time the measly meal ended, the monk's robe was dry, and he dressed. Hadrian approached him and placed his hands on Myron's shoulders. "As much as I hate to say it, the prince is right. You have to come with us. If we leave you here, you'll likely die."

"But I—" He looked frightened. "This is my home. I'm comfortable here. My brothers are here."

"They're all dead," Alric said bluntly.

Hadrian scowled at the prince and then turned to Myron. "Listen, it's time to move on with your life. There's a lot more out there besides books. I would think you'd want to see some of it. Besides, your *king*"—he said the last word sarcastically—"needs you."

Myron sighed heavily, swallowed hard, and nodded in agreement.

⁂

The rain lightened, and by midday, it stopped completely. After they packed Myron's parchments and whatever supplies they could gather from the abbey's remains, they were ready to leave. Royce, Hadrian, and Alric waited at the entrance of the abbey, but Myron did not join them. Eventually Hadrian went looking and found the monk in the ruined garden. Ringed by soot-stained stone columns, it would have formed the central courtyard among all the buildings. There were signs of flowerbeds and shrubs lining the pathway of interlocking paving stones now covered in ash. At the center of the cloister, a large stone sundial sat on a pedestal. Hadrian imagined that before the fire, this sheltered cloister had been quite beautiful.

"I'm afraid," Myron told Hadrian as he approached. Staring at the burnt lawn, the monk was sitting on a blackened stone bench, his elbows on his knees, his chin on his palms. "This must seem strange to you. But everything here is so familiar. I could tell you how many blocks of stone make up this walkway or the scriptorium. I can tell you how many windowpanes were in the abbey, the exact day of the year, and time of day, the sun peaks directly over the church. How Brother Ginlin used to eat with two forks because he vowed never to touch a knife. How Brother Heslon was always the first one up and always fell asleep during vespers."

Myron pointed across from them at a blackened stump of a tree. "Brother Renian and I buried a squirrel there when we were ten years old. A tree sprouted the following week. It grew white blossoms in spring, and not even the abbot could tell what species it was. Everyone in the abbey called it the Squirrel Tree. We all thought it was a miracle and that perhaps the squirrel was a servant of Maribor who was thanking us for taking such good care of his friend."

Myron paused a moment and used the long sleeves of his robe to wipe his face as he stared at the stump. He pulled his gaze away and looked once more at Hadrian. "I could tell you how in winter the snow could get up to the second-story windows, and it was like we were all squirrels living in this cozy burrow, all safe and warm. I could tell you how each one of us was the very best at what we did. Ginlin made wine so light it evaporated on your tongue, leaving only the taste of wonder. Fenitilian made the warmest, softest shoes. You could walk out in the snow and never know you left the abbey. To say Heslon could cook is an insult. He would make steaming plates of scrambled eggs mixed with cheeses, peppers, onions, and bacon, all in a light spicy cream sauce. He'd follow this with rounds of sweet bread—each topped with a honey-cinnamon drizzle—smoked pork rounds, salifan sausage, flaky powdered pastries, freshly churned sweet butter, and a ceramic pot of dark mint tea. And that was just for breakfast."

Myron smiled, his eyes closed, with a dreamy look on his face.

"What did Renian do?" Hadrian asked. "The fellow you buried the squirrel with? What was his specialty?"

Myron opened his eyes but was slow to answer. He looked back at the stump of the tree across from them and he said softly, "Renian died when he was twelve. He caught a fever. We buried him right there, next to the Squirrel Tree. It was his favorite place in the world." He paused, taking a breath that was not quite even. A frown pulled at his mouth, tightening his lips. "There hasn't been a day that has gone by since then that I haven't said good morning to him. I usually sit here and tell him how his tree is doing. How many new buds there were, or when the first leaf turned or fell. For the last few days I've had to lie, because I couldn't bring myself to tell him it was gone."

Tears fell from Myron's eyes, and his lips quivered as he looked at the stump. "All morning I've been trying to tell him goodbye. I've been trying..." He faltered and paused to wipe his eyes. "I've been trying to explain why I have to leave him now, but you see, Renian is only twelve, and I don't think he really understands." Myron put his face in his hands and wept.

Hadrian squeezed Myron's shoulder. "We'll wait for you at the gate. Take all the time you need."

When Hadrian emerged from the entrance, Alric barked at him, "What in the world is taking so bloody long? If he's going to be this much trouble, we might as well leave him."

"We aren't leaving him, and we'll wait as long as it takes," Hadrian told them. Alric and Royce exchanged glances but neither said a word.

Myron joined them only a few minutes later with a small bag containing all his belongings. Although he was obviously upset, his mood lightened at the sight of the horses. "Oh my!" he exclaimed. Hadrian took Myron by the hand like a young child and led him over to his speckled white mare. The horse, its massive body moving back and forth as the animal shifted its weight from one leg to another, looked down at Myron with large dark eyes.

"Do they bite?"

"Not usually," Hadrian replied. "Here, you can pat him on the neck."

"It's so... *big*," Myron said with a look of terror on his face. He moved his hand to his mouth as if he might be sick.

"Please, just get on the horse, Myron." Alric's tone showed his irritation.

"Don't mind him," Hadrian said. "You can ride behind me. I'll get on first and pull you up after, okay?"

Myron nodded but the look on his face indicated he was

anything but okay. Hadrian mounted and then extended his arm. With closed eyes, Myron reached out, and Hadrian pulled him up. The monk held on tightly and buried his face in the large man's back.

"Remember to breathe, Myron," Hadrian told him as he turned the horse and began to walk back down the switchback trail.

The morning started cold but it eventually warmed some. Still, it was not as pleasant as it had been the day before. They entered the shelter of the valley and headed toward the lake. Everything was still wet from the rain, and the tall fields of autumn-browned grass soaked their feet and legs as they brushed past. The wind came from the north now and blew into their faces. Overhead, a chevron of geese honked against the gray sky. Winter was on its way. Myron soon overcame his fear and picked his head up to look about.

"Dear Maribor, I had no idea grass grew this high. And the trees are so tall! You know, I had seen pictures of trees this size but always thought the artists were just bad at proportion."

The monk began to twist left and right to see all around him. Hadrian chuckled. "Myron, you squirm like a puppy."

Lake Windermere appeared like gray metal pooling at the base of the barren hills. Although it was one of the largest lakes in Avryn, the fingers of the round cliffs hid much of it from view. Its vast open face reflected the desolate sky and appeared cold and empty. Except for a few birds, little moved on the stony clefts.

They reached the western bank. Thousands of fist-sized rocks, rubbed smooth and flat by the lake, made a loose cobblestone plain where they could walk and listen to the quiet lapping of the water. From time to time, rain would briefly fall. They would watch it come across the surface of the lake, the crisp horizon blurring as the raindrops broke the stillness, and then it would stop while the clouds above swirled undecidedly.

Royce, as usual, led the small party. He approached the north side of the lake and found what appeared to be the faint remains of a very old and unused road leading toward the mountains beyond.

Myron's wriggling was finally subsiding. He sat behind Hadrian but did not move for quite some time. "Myron, are you okay back there?" Hadrian asked.

"Hmm? Oh, yes, I'm sorry. I was watching the way the horses walk. I've been observing them for the last few miles. They are fascinating animals. Their back feet appear to step in exactly the same place their front feet left an instant before. Although, I suppose they aren't feet at all, are they? Hooves! That's right! These are hooves! *Enylina* in Old Speech."

"Old Speech?"

"The ancient imperial language. Few people outside the clergy know it these days. It's something of a dead language. Even in the days of the empire it was only used in church services, but that has gone out of style and no one writes in it anymore."

Hadrian felt Myron rest his head against his back, and for the rest of the ride watched to make sure that Myron did not doze off and fall.

They turned away from the lakeside and started into a broad ravine that became rocky as they climbed. The more they progressed, the more apparent it was to Alric that they were traveling on what had once been a road. The path was too smooth to be wholly natural, and yet over time, rocks had fallen from the heights and cracks had formed where weeds forced themselves out of the crevices. Centuries had taken their toll, but there remained a faint trace of something ancient and forgotten.

Despite the cold, the intermittent rain, and the strange circumstance of his being there, Alric was not nearly as miserable as he let on. There was an odd tranquility to the trip that day. Not often had the prince traveled so simply in such inclement weather and he found it captivating by its sheer strangeness. The vast silence, the muted light, the haunting clip-clop of the horses' hooves, everything suggested adventure in a fashion he had never experienced before. His most daring escapades had always been organized and catered by servants. He had never been on his own like this, never truly in danger.

When he had found himself bound in the boat, he had been furious. No one had ever treated him with such disregard. Striking a member of the royal family was punishable by death, and because it was, most avoided even touching him. To be trussed up like an animal was humiliating beyond his comprehension. It had never occurred to him that he could come to harm. He had fully expected to be rescued at any moment. That prospect had dimmed dramatically as they had traveled into the deep forests on their way to Windermere.

He had been serious when he had said it was the worst night of his life, but in the morning when the rain let up, and after the meal, he found what he could describe only as a second wind. The prospect of seeking out this mysterious prison and its reputed inmate smacked of real adventure. Perhaps more than anything, it kept his mind occupied. He was busy trying to stay alive and determine the identity of a killer, which kept him from dwelling on the death of his father.

On occasion while riding, when no one spoke for a time and silence took hold, his mind would touch on his father's death. He would be back in the royal bedchamber seeing his father's pale face and that tiny tear of dried blood near the corner of his lips. Alric expected to feel something. He expected to cry but that never happened. He felt nothing and wondered what that meant.

Back at the castle, everyone would be wearing black and the halls would be filled with the sounds of weeping—just like when his mother had died. No music, no laughter, and it had seemed like more than a month without the sun shining. He was relieved, almost happy, when the period of mourning ended. Part of him felt guilty for that, and yet it was as if a terrible weight had been lifted. That was how it would be if he were at the castle—solemn faces, weeping, and the priests passing a candle for him to walk around the casket with while they chanted. He had done that as a child and hated it. Alric was glad he was not there, trapped and drowning in that well of sorrow that he could not tap. He would deal with it all the next day, but for today he was grateful to be on a distant road with no one of importance for company.

Royce drew his horse to a stop. They were alone, since the others had a tendency to lag behind, as their horse carried two.

"Why are we stopping?" Alric asked.

"It's leveling off, so we're probably close. Have you forgotten that this might be a trap?"

"No," the prince said. "I'm quite aware of that fact."

"Good, then in that case, farewell, Your Majesty," Royce told him.

Alric was stunned. "You're not coming?"

"Your sister only asked us to bring you here. If you want to get yourself killed, that's your affair. Our obligation is complete."

Instantly Alric felt foolish for his earlier misguided satisfaction in being alone with strangers. He could not afford to lose his only guides or he would never find his way back. After only a moment's thought, he said, "Then I suppose this is a perfect time to tell you I'm officially bestowing the title of *royal protectors* on you and Hadrian, now that I'm certain you aren't trying to kill me. You'll be responsible for defending the life of your king."

"Really? How thoughtful of you, Your Highness." Royce grinned. "I suppose this is a good time to tell you I don't serve kings—unless they pay me."

"No?" Alric smiled wryly. "All right then, consider it this way. If I live to return to Essendon Castle, I'll happily rescind your execution orders and forgive your unlawful entry of my castle. However, if I die out here or am taken captive and locked away in this prison, you'll never be able to return to Medford. My uncle has already labeled you murderers of the highest order. I'm sure there are already men searching. Uncle Percy might seem like a courtly old gentleman, but believe me, I've seen his ugly side and he can be quite scary. He's the best swordsman in Melengar. Did you know that? So if sovereign loyalty isn't good enough for you, you might consider the practical benefits of keeping me alive."

"The ability to convince others that your life is worth more than theirs must be a prerequisite for being king."

"Not a prerequisite but it certainly helps," Alric replied with a grin.

"It will still cost you," Royce said, and the prince's grin faded. "Let's say one hundred gold tenents."

"One hundred?" Alric protested.

"Do you think your life is worth less? Besides, it's what DeWitt promised, so that seems fair. But there's one other thing. If we're going to be your protectors, you'll have to do as I say. I can't safeguard you if you don't and since we aren't just risking your silly little life, but my future as well, I'll have to insist."

Alric huffed. He did not like the way they treated him. They should feel honored to do his bidding. Besides, he was granting them absolution of serious crimes, and instead of showing gratitude, the man demanded payment. This type of behavior was just what he expected from thieves. Still, he needed them. "Like all good rulers, it's understood there are times when we must listen to skilled advisors. Just remember who I am and who I'll be when we get back to Medford."

As Hadrian and Myron caught up, Royce said, "Hadrian, we've just been promoted to royal protectors."

"Does it pay more?"

"Actually, it does. It also weighs less. Give the prince back his sword."

Hadrian handed the huge sword of Amrath to Alric, who slipped the broad leather baldric over one shoulder and strapped on the weapon. The sword was too big for him and he felt a bit foolish, but at least he thought it looked better now that he was dressed and mounted.

"The captain of the guard took this off my father and handed it to me—was it only two nights past? It was Tolin Essendon's sword, handed down from king to prince for seven hundred years. We are one of the oldest unbroken families in Avryn."

Royce dismounted and handed the reins of his horse to Hadrian. "I'm going to scout up ahead and make sure there are no surprises waiting." He left with surprising swiftness in a hunched run. He entered the shadows of the ravine and vanished.

"How does he do that?" Alric asked.

"Creepy, isn't it?" Hadrian said.

"How did he do what?" Myron stared at a cattail he had plucked just before they left the lakeside. "These things are marvelous, by the way."

They waited for several minutes, and at the sound of a bird's song, Hadrian ordered them forward. The road curved left and then right until they could once again see the lake, which was now far below and looked like a large bright puddle. The road began to narrow and at last stopped. To either side, hills rose at a gradual slope, but directly in front of them the path ended at a straight, sheer cliff extending upward several hundred feet.

"Are we in the wrong place?" Hadrian asked.

"It's supposed to be a *hidden* prison," Alric reminded them.

"I just assumed," Hadrian said, "being up here in the middle of nowhere was what was meant by *hidden*. I mean, if you didn't know the prison was here, would you come to such a place?"

"If this was made by the best minds of what was left of the empire," Alric said, "it's likely to be hard to find and harder to enter."

"Legends hold it was mostly constructed by dwarves," Myron explained.

"Lovely," Royce said. "It's going to be another Drumindor."

"We had issues getting into a dwarf-constructed fortress in Tur Del Fur a few years back," Hadrian explained. "It wasn't pretty. We might as well get comfortable; this could take a while."

Royce searched the cliff. The stone directly before the path was exposed, as if recently sheared off, and while moss and small plants grew among the many cracks elsewhere, none were found anywhere near the cliff face.

"There's a door here; I know it," the thief said, running his hands lightly across the stone. "Damn dwarves. I can't find a hinge, crack, or seam."

"Myron," Alric asked, "did you read anything about how to open the door to the prison? I've heard tales about dwarves having a fondness for riddles, and sometimes they make keys out of sounds, words that when spoken unlock doors."

Myron shook his head as he climbed down off the horse.

"Words that unlock doors?" Royce looked at the prince skeptically. "Are these fairy tales you're listening to?"

"An invisible door sounds like a fairy tale to me," Alric replied. "So it seems appropriate."

"It's not invisible. You can see the cliff, can't you? It's merely well hidden. Dwarves can cut stone with such precision you can't see a gap."

"You do have to admit, Royce," Hadrian said, "what dwarves can do with stone is amazing."

Royce glared over his shoulder at him. "Don't talk to me."

Hadrian smiled. "Royce doesn't much care for the wee folk."

"Open in the name of Novron!" Alric suddenly shouted with a commanding tone, his voice echoing between the stony slopes.

Royce spun around and fixed the prince with a withering stare. "Don't do that again!"

"Well, *you* weren't making any progress. I just thought perhaps since this was, or is, a church prison, maybe a religious command would unlock it. Myron, is there some standard religious saying to open a door? You should know about this. Is there such a thing?"

"I'm not a priest of Nyphron. The Winds Abbey was a monastery of Maribor."

"Oh, that's right," Alric said, looking disappointed.

"I mean, I know *about* the Church of Nyphron," Myron

clarified, "but since I'm not a member, I'm not privy to any secret codes or chants or such."

"Really?" Hadrian said. "I thought you monks were just sort of like the poorer, younger brother of the Nyphron Church."

Myron smiled. "If anything, we'd be the older but still the poorer brother. Worshiping Emperor Novron is a relatively recent event that began a few decades after the emperor's death."

"So you monks worship Maribor while the Nyphrons worship Novron?"

"Close," the monk said, "the Nyphron Church also worships Maribor but they just put more emphasis on Novron. The main difference comes down to what you are looking for. We monks believe in a personal devotion to Maribor—seeking his will in quiet places. It's through ancient rituals, and in this silence, that he speaks to us in our hearts. We're striving to know Maribor better.

"The Church of Nyphron, on the other hand, focuses on trying to understand Maribor's will. They believe the birth of Novron demonstrates Maribor's desire to take a direct hand in controlling the fate of mankind. As such, they are very involved in politics. You're familiar with the story of Novron, aren't you?"

Hadrian pursed his lips. "Um...he was the first emperor and defeated the elves in some war a long time ago. I'm not sure why that makes him a god."

"He's not, actually."

"Then why do so many people worship him?"

"Novron is believed to be the son of Maribor, sent to aid us in our darkest hour. There are six actual gods. Erebus is the father of all of the gods and he made the world of Elan. He brought forth three sons and a daughter. The eldest son,

Ferrol, is a master of magic and created the elves. His second son is Drome, the master craftsman who created the dwarves. The youngest is Maribor and he, of course, created man. It was Erebus's daughter, Muriel, who created the animals, birds, and the fish in the sea."

"That's five."

"Yes, there is also Uberlin, the son of Erebus and Muriel."

"The god of darkness," Alric put in.

"Yeah, I've heard of him, but wait—are you saying the father had a child with his own daughter?"

"It was a terrible mistake," Myron explained. "Erebus forced himself on Muriel while in a drunken rage. Their union resulted in the birth of Uberlin."

"That must have been awkward at family gatherings—raping your own daughter and all," Hadrian said.

"Quite. In fact, Erebus's original sons, Ferrol, Drome, and Maribor, slew him because of the incident. When Uberlin tried to defend his father, all three turned on him and imprisoned their nephew, or would that be *brother*? I guess it's really both, isn't it? Well, anyway, they locked Uberlin in the depths of Elan. Even though he was born through a terrible violation, Muriel was heartbroken to lose her only son and refused to speak to her brothers again."

"So now we're back to five gods."

"Not exactly. Many people believe that a god is immortal and cannot die. There are some cults that believe Erebus still lives and wanders Elan as a man searching for forgiveness for his crime."

The day was growing dark and the wind picked up, heralding another possible storm. The horses started to become spooked, so Hadrian went to check on them. Alric got up and walked around, rubbing his legs and muttering about being saddle sore.

"Myron?" Hadrian called over. "Would you like to help me unsaddle them? I don't think we'll be leaving soon."

"Of course," the monk said eagerly. "Now, how do I do that?"

Together, Hadrian and Myron relieved the animals of their saddles and packs and stowed the gear under a small rock ledge. Myron summoned the courage every so often to stroke their necks. Once everything was put away, Hadrian suggested Myron gather some grass for the animals while he went to check on Royce.

His partner sat on the path, staring at the cliff. Occasionally, the thief would get up, examine a portion of the wall, and sit back down, grumbling.

"Well? How's it going?"

"I hate dwarves," Royce replied.

"Most people do."

"Yes, but I have a reason. The bastards are the only ones that can make boxes I can't open."

"You'll open it. It won't be pretty, and it won't be soon, but you'll open it. What I don't understand is why would Arista send us here knowing that we couldn't get in?"

Royce sat on his haunches, his cloak draped out around him. His eyes remained focused but he was frustrated. "I can't even see anything. If I could even find just a crack, then maybe . . . but how can I break a lock when I can't even find the door?"

Hadrian gave him a reassuring pat on the shoulder before returning to Myron, who had finished feeding the horses and had joined Alric, sitting over by the cliff's wall.

"How's it coming?" Alric asked with a bit of annoyance in his voice.

"Nothing yet, just leave him be. Royce will figure it out. It just takes some time." Hadrian turned his attention back to

Myron. "I was thinking about what you were saying before. If Uberlin is considered a god, why did you say Novron is not? After all, they're both children of gods, right?"

"Well, no, technically he's a demigod, part god, part human. You see, Maribor sent Novron to—well, let me jump back a bit. Okay, so Ferrol was the oldest and when he created the elves, they spread, albeit slowly, across all of Elan. When Drome came along, he granted his children control of the underground world. This left no place for Maribor's children. So mankind was forced to struggle in the most wretched corners left to us."

"So the elves got all the good places, and we got stuck with the dregs? That doesn't sound very fair," Hadrian said.

"Well, our ancestors weren't happy about that either. Not to mention humans reproduce much more quickly than elves, who have a much longer life span. This made conditions rather crowded and it only got worse when the dwarves were driven to the surface."

"Driven? By who?"

"You remember what I said about the gods locking Uberlin in the underworld? Well, he created his own race, just like Drome, Maribor, and Ferrol."

"Ah...the goblins. I can see how they would make things less *homey* down there."

"Exactly. Between mankind's growing numbers and the emergence of the dwarves, our ancestors were being crushed. So they begged Maribor for help. He heard their pleas and tricked his brother Drome into forging the great sword Rhelacan. Then he convinced his other brother Ferrol to enchant the weapon. All he needed was a warrior to wield it, so he came to Elan in disguise and slept with a mortal woman. Their union produced Novron the Great. He united all the tribes of mankind and led them in a war against the elves.

Armed with the Rhelacan, Novron was victorious and so began mankind's dominance, led by Novron, who had united all of humanity."

"Okay, that makes sense, but when did we start worshiping Novron as a god?"

"That occurred after his death. The Church of Nyphron was established to pay homage to Novron as the savior of mankind. The newly formed church became the official religion of the empire, but farther away from the imperial capital of Percepliquis, people remembered the old ways and continued to worship Maribor as they always had."

"And that would be you, the Monks of Maribor, I mean?"

Myron nodded.

During their discussion, storm clouds continued to form, filling the sky and darkening the ravine. What light remained was an odd hue, adding a sense of the surreal to the landscape. Soon the wind began gusting through the pass, blowing dirt into the air. In the distance echoed the low rumble of thunder.

"Any luck with the door, Royce?" Hadrian called over. He sat resting with his back against the cliff, his legs outstretched, and he tapped the tips of his boots together. "Because it looks like we're in for another cold, wet night, only this time we won't have any shelter."

Royce muttered something indiscernible.

Down below, framed by the walls of the ravine, the surface of the lake shone like a mirror facing the sky. Every now and then it would flash brilliantly as lightning flickered in the distance.

Royce grumbled again.

"What's that?" Hadrian asked.

"I was just thinking about what you said earlier. Why *would* Arista send us here if she knew we couldn't get in? She must have thought we could; maybe to her it was obvious."

"Maybe it's magic," Alric said, pulling his cloak tighter.

"Enough with the enchanted words," Royce told him. "Locks are mechanical. Believe me. I know a thing or two on the subject. Dwarves are very clever and very skilled, but they don't make doors that unlock because of a sound."

"I just brought it up because Arista could do some, so maybe getting in was easy for her."

"Do some what?" Hadrian asked.

"Magic."

"Your sister is a witch?" Myron asked, disturbed.

Alric laughed. "You could certainly say that, yes, but it has little to do with her magical prowess. She went to Sheridan University for a few years and learned magical theory. It never amounted to much, but she was able to do a few things. For instance, she magically locks the door to her room, and I think she made the countess Amril sick over some dispute about a boy. Poor Amril was covered in boils for a week."

Royce looked over at Alric. "What do you mean, magically locks her door?"

"There's never been a lock on it, but no one can open it but her."

"Did you ever see your sister unlock her door?"

Alric shook his head. "I wish I had."

"Myron," Royce said, "did you ever read anything about unusual locks or keys? Maybe something associated with dwarves?"

"There's the tale of *Iberius and the Giant*, where Iberius uses a key forged by dwarves to open the giant's treasure box, but it wasn't magical—just big. There's also the Collar of Liem, from the *Myth of the Forgotten*, which refused to unlock until the wearer was dead—I guess that doesn't help much, does it? Hmm...let me think...perhaps it has something to do with gemlocks."

"Gemlocks?"

"They're not magical either but they were invented by dwarves. They're gems that interact with other stones to create subtle vibrations. Gemlocks are generally used when several people need to open the same locked container. All they need is a matching gem. For particularly valuable containers, the lock might require a specific cut, which modifies the resonance. Truly gifted gemsmiths could make a lock that actually changed with the seasons, allowing different gems to unlock it at different times of the year. This is what gave rise to the idea of birthstones, because certain stones have more strength at certain times. I've—"

"That's it," Royce interrupted.

"What's it?" Alric asked. Royce reached into his breast pocket and pulled out a dark blue ring. Alric jumped to his feet. "That's my father's ring. Give it to me!"

"Fine," Royce said, tossing it toward the prince. "Your sister told us to return it to you when we got to the prison."

"She did?" Alric looked surprised. He slipped the ring on his finger, and like his sword, it did not quite fit and spun around from the weight of the gem. "I thought she took it. It has the royal seal. She could have used it to muster the nobles, to make laws, or to announce herself as steward. With it, she could have taken control of everything."

"Maybe she *was* telling the truth," Hadrian suggested.

"Let's not make snap judgments," Royce cautioned. "First, let's see if this works. Your sister said you would need the ring to get into the prison. I thought she meant to identify you as the king, but I think she meant it a bit more literally. If I'm correct, touching the stone with the ring will cause giant doors to open."

They all gathered at the cliff face close to Alric in anticipation of the dramatic event.

"Go ahead, Alric—do it."

He turned the ring so the gem was on top, made a fist, and attempted to touch it to the cliff. As he did, his hand disappeared into the rock. Alric recoiled, wheeling backward with a cry.

"What happened?" Royce asked. "Did it hurt?"

"No, it just felt sort of cold but I can't touch it."

"Try it again," Hadrian said.

Alric did not look at all happy with the suggestion but nodded just the same. This time he pressed farther, and the whole party watched as his hand disappeared into the wall up to his wrist before he withdrew it.

"Fascinating," Royce muttered, feeling the solid stone of the cliff. "I didn't expect that."

"Does that mean he has to go in alone?" Hadrian asked.

"I'm not sure I want to enter solid stone by myself," Alric said with fear in his voice.

"Well, you may have no choice," Royce responded, "assuming you still want to talk to the wizard. But let's not give up yet. Give me the ring a moment."

Despite his earlier desire for the ring, Alric now showed no concern at handing it over. Royce slipped it on, and when he pressed his hand to the cliff face, it passed into the mountainside just as easily as Alric's had. Royce pulled his hand back; then he took the ring off, and holding it in his left hand, he reached out with his right. Once more, his hand passed through the stone.

"So you don't have to be the prince, and you don't have to be wearing it. You only need to be touching it. Myron, didn't you say something about the gem creating a vibration?"

Myron nodded. "They create a specific resonance with certain stone types."

"Try holding hands," Hadrian suggested.

Alric and Royce did so, and this time, both could penetrate the stone.

"That's it," Royce declared. "One last test. Everyone join hands. Let's make sure it works with four." They all joined hands and each was able to pierce the surface of the cliff. "Everyone, make sure you remove your hands before breaking the chain."

"Okay, we need to make some decisions before we go any further. I've seen some unusual things before but nothing like this. I don't have a clue what will happen to us if we go in there. Well, Hadrian, what do you think?"

Hadrian rubbed his chin. "It's a risk, to be sure. Considering some of the choices I've made recently, I'll leave this one up to you. If you think we should go, then that's good enough by me."

"I have to admit," Royce responded, "my curiosity is piqued, so if you still want to go through with this, Alric, we'll go with you."

"If I had to go in alone, I would decline," Alric said. "But I'm also curious."

"Myron?" Royce asked.

"What about the horses? Will they be all right?"

"I'm sure they will be fine."

"But what if we don't come back? They'll starve, won't they?"

Royce sighed. "It's us or them. You'll have to choose."

Myron hesitated. Lightning and thunder tore through the sky, and it began to rain. "Can't we just untie them, so in case we don't—"

"I don't intend to make plans based on our expected deaths. We'll need the horses when we come out. They're staying—are you?"

The wind sprayed rain into the monk's face as he stole one

last look at the horses. "I'll go," he said finally. "I just hope they'll be all right."

"Okay," Royce told them, "this is how we'll do it. I'll go first, wearing the ring. Alric comes in behind me, then Myron, and Hadrian will take up the rear. When we get inside, we break the chain in reverse order: Hadrian first, then Myron, and Alric last. Enter in the same place I do, and don't pass me. I don't want anyone setting off any traps. Any questions?"

All but Myron shook their heads. "Wait a second," he said as he trotted off toward where they had stored their gear. He gathered the lantern and tinder kit he had brought from the abbey and paused a moment to pet the horses' wet noses one more time. "I'm ready now," he said when he returned to the party.

"All right, here goes, everyone hang on and follow me," Royce said as they rejoined their chain and moved forward. One by one, they passed through the rock cliff. Hadrian was last. When the barrier reached his shoulder, he took a deep breath as if he were swimming, and with that, Hadrian dipped his head inside the stone.

CHAPTER 5

ESRAHADDON

They entered into total darkness. The air was dry, still, and stale. The only sound came from the rainwater dripping from their clothes. Hadrian took a few blind steps forward to make sure he was completely through the barrier before releasing Myron's hand. "See anything, Royce?" he asked in a whisper so quiet it could scarcely be heard.

"No, not a thing. Everyone stay still until Myron gets the lantern lit."

Hadrian could hear Myron fiddling in the dark. He tilted his head, searching in vain for anything to focus on. There was nothing. He could have had his eyes closed. Myron scraped the tiny metal lever on his tinder pad, and a burst of sparks flashed on the monk's lap. In the flare, Hadrian saw faces glaring from the darkness. They appeared briefly and vanished with the dying brilliance.

No one moved or spoke as Myron scraped the pad again. This time the tinder caught fire, and the monk lit the wick of the lantern. The light revealed a narrow hallway, only five feet wide, and a ceiling that was so high it was lost in darkness. Lining both walls were carvings of faces, as if people standing on the other side of a gray curtain were pressing forward to peer at them. Seemingly caught in a moment of anguish frozen forever in stone, their terrible ghastly visages stared at the party with gaping mouths and wild eyes.

"Pass up the light," Royce ordered softly.

As the lantern moved from Myron to Royce, its light shone on more faces. To Hadrian, it seemed as if they screamed at the intruders, but the corridor remained still and silent. Some of the figures had eyes wide with fear, while others' eyes were shut tight, perhaps to avoid seeing something too frightening to look at.

"Someone certainly had a morbid taste in decorating," Royce said, taking the lantern.

"I'm just thankful they're only carvings. Imagine if we could hear them," Alric said.

"What makes you think they're carvings?" Hadrian asked, reaching out to gingerly touch the nose of a woman with glaring eyes. He half expected warm skin and was grateful when his fingers met cold stone. "Maybe they let go of their gemstones too soon."

Royce held the lantern up high. "The passage keeps going."

"More faces?" Alric asked.

"More faces," the thief confirmed.

"At least we're out of the rain," Hadrian said, trying to sound cheerful. "We could still be back..." When he turned around, he was shocked. The corridor extended behind them seemingly without end. "Where's the wall we just came through?" He took a step and reached out. "It's not an illusion. The hallway keeps going." Turning back, Hadrian saw Royce pressing on the sides of the corridor. Unlike with the wall outside, his hand did not penetrate the surface.

"Well, this is going to make matters difficult," the thief muttered.

"There must be another way out, right?" Alric asked, his voice a bit shaky.

The thief looked back, then forward, and sighed. "We might as well travel in the direction we entered. Here, Alric, take your ring back, although I'm not sure what good it will do you in here."

Royce led them down the corridor. He checked and tested anything that appeared suspicious. The passage went on for what seemed like eternity. Despite the hallway's appearing perfectly straight and level, Hadrian began to wonder if the dwarves had built in an imperceptible curve that made it loop back onto itself to form a circle. He also worried about the amount of oil left in Myron's lantern. It would not be long before they were cast back into utter darkness.

The lack of variation in their surroundings made it impossible to judge exactly how long they had been walking. After a while, something luminescent appeared in the distance. A tiny light bobbed and weaved. As the light drew closer, the echo of sharp, deliberate footsteps accompanied it. At last, Hadrian could discern the figure carrying a lamp. He was tall and trim and wore a long-hooded hauberk. Over this was a scarlet and gold tabard that shimmered in the lamplight. The tabard was marked with a regal coat of arms depicting a celestial crown and a jeweled scepter above a shield divided into quarters and supported on either side by combatant lions. At his side he wore a polished sword with decorative detailing, and on his head, a pointed silver helm exquisitely etched with gold ivy trim. Below the helm were a pair of dark eyes and an even darker look.

"Why are you here?" His tone was reproachful and threatening.

There was a pause before Royce replied. "We are here to see the prisoner."

"*That* is not allowed," he responded firmly.

"Then Esrahaddon is still alive?" asked Alric.

"*Do not speak that name!*" thundered the sentry. He cast a tense look over his shoulder into the darkness. "Not here, not *ever* here. You should not have come."

"That may be but we are here and we need to see Esra—the prisoner," Royce replied.

"That will not be possible."

"Make it possible," Alric ordered. His voice was loud and commanding. He stepped out from behind the others. "I'm King Alric of Melengar, lord of this land wherein you stand. You will not tell me what *is* and what *is not* possible within the boundaries of my own kingdom."

The sentry took a step back and eyed Alric critically. "You lack a crown, *King*."

Alric drew his sword. Despite its size, he handled it smoothly and extended the point at the sentry. "What I lack in a crown, I more than make up for in a sword."

"A sword will not avail you. None who dwell here fear death any longer." Hadrian could not tell whether it was the weight of the sentry's words or the weight of the sword but Alric lowered his blade. "Do you have proof of your rank?"

Alric extended a clenched hand. "This is the seal of Melengar, symbol of the House of Essendon and emblem of this realm."

The sentry stared at the ring and nodded. "If you are the reigning sovereign of the realm, you do have the right to enter. But know this: there is magic at work here. You will do well to follow me closely." He turned and led them back the way he had come.

"Do you recognize the emblem on the guard?" Hadrian whispered to Myron as they followed him.

"Yes, that's the coat of arms of the Novronian Empire, worn by the Percepliquis Imperial City Guard. It's very old."

Their guide led them out of the corridor filled with faces,

and Hadrian was grateful to be free of it. The hallway opened into a massive cavern with a vaulted ceiling carved from natural stone and supported by pillars of the same. Torches lining the walls revealed a magnificent expanse. It appeared large enough to hold all of Medford. They traversed it by crossing narrow bridges that spanned chasms and traveling through open arches that rose like great trees whose branches supported the mountain above.

There was no visible sign of wood, fabric, or leather. Everything—chairs, benches, desks, tables, shelves, and doors—was made of stone. Huge fountains hewn from rock gurgled with water from unseen springs. The walls and floors lacked the adornment of tapestries and carpets. Instead, carved into virtually every inch of the stone were intricate markings—strange symbols of elaborate twisted designs. Some of them were chiseled with a rough hand, while others were smoothly sculpted. At times, from the corner of his eye, Hadrian thought he saw the carved markings change as he passed them. Looking closely, he discovered it was not an illusion. The shifts were subtle, like the movement of cobwebs in the wake of their passing.

They moved deeper, and their escort did not pause or waver. He walked at a brisk pace, which at times caused Myron, who had the shortest legs, to trot in order to keep up. Their footfalls bounced off the hard walls throughout the stone chamber. The only other sounds Hadrian heard were voices, distant whispers of hidden conversations, but they were too faint for him to make out the words. Whether the sounds were from inhabitants around an unseen corner, or the result of some trick of the stone, was impossible to tell.

Farther in, sentinels began to appear, standing guard along their path. Most were dressed identically to their guide, but others, found deeper in the prison, wore black armor with a simple white emblem of a broken crown. Sinister-looking helms hid their faces as they stood at perfect attention. None of them moved or said a word.

Hadrian asked Myron about the emblem these men wore.

"The crest is used by the ancient order of the Seret Knights," the monk explained quietly. "They were first formed eight hundred years ago by Lord Darius Seret, who had been charged by Patriarch Linnev with the task of finding the lost Heir of Novron. The broken crown is symbolic of the shattered empire, which they seek to restore."

Finally they reached what Hadrian assumed was their final destination. They entered an oval chamber with an incredibly tall door dominating the far wall. Carved of stone, it stood wreathed in a glittering array of fine spiderweb-like designs, which appeared organic in nature. Like the veins of a leaf or the delicate, curling tendrils of sprawling roots, the doorframe spread out until its artistry was lost in the shadows. On either side of the door stood dramatic obelisks covered with runes cut deep in beveled stone. Between these and the door, blue flames burned in braziers mounted on high pedestals.

A man sat on a raised chair behind a six-foot-tall stone desk that was exquisitely sculpted with intricate patterns of swirling lines. On two sides of the worktable, barrel-thick candles twice the height of a man burned. So many melted wax tears streaked down their sides that Hadrian thought they might once have been as tall as the great door.

"Visitors," their guide announced to the clerk, who, until then, had been busy writing in a massive book with a black feathered quill. The man looked up from his work. His gray beard hung all the way to the floor. Deeply lined with wrinkles, his face looked like the bark of an ancient tree.

"What are your names?" the clerk asked.

"I'm Alric Brendon Essendon, son of Amrath Essendon,

King of Melengar, Lord of the Realm, and I demand an audience with the prisoner."

"The others?" The clerk motioned toward the rest.

"They are my servants, the royal protectors and my chaplain."

The clerk rose from his seat and leaned forward to examine each party member in more detail. He looked into the eyes of each for a moment before he resumed his seat. He dipped his feather quill and turned to a new page. After a few moments of writing, he asked, "Why do you wish to see the prisoner?" With his quill poised, he waited for a reply.

"My business is not your concern," Alric answered in a kingly voice.

"That may be; however, this prisoner *is* my concern, and if you have dealings with him, it *is my business*. I must know your purpose, or I will not grant you entry, king or not."

Alric stared at the clerk for some time before relenting. "I wish to ask him questions concerning the death of my father."

The clerk considered this a moment, then scratched his quill on the page of the great book. When he finished, he looked up. "Very well. You may enter the cell but you must obey our rules. They are for your own safety. The man to whom you wish to speak is no ordinary man. He is a thing, an ancient evil, a demon that we have successfully trapped here. Above all else, we are dedicated to keeping him confined. As you might imagine, he very much desires to escape. He is cunning and perpetually tests us. Constantly he is looking for a weakness, a break in a line, or a crack in the stone.

"First, proceed directly down the path to his confinement; do not tarry. Second, stay in the gallery; do not attempt to descend to his cage. Third—and this is the most important—do nothing he asks. No matter how insignificant it may sound. Do not be fooled by him. He is intelligent and cunning. Ask him your questions; then leave. Do not deviate from these rules. Do you understand?" Alric nodded. "Then may Novron have mercy on you."

Just then, the great doors split along the central seam and slowly started to open. The loud grinding of stone on stone echoed until at last the doors stood wide. Beyond them lay a long stone bridge that spanned an abyss. The bridge was three feet wide and as smooth as glass, and it appeared no thicker than a sheet of parchment. At the far end of the span rose a column of black rock. An island-like tower, its only visible connection to the world was the delicate bridge.

"You may leave your lantern. You will have no need for it," the clerk stated. Royce nodded but kept the lantern nevertheless.

As they stepped through the doorway, Hadrian heard a sound like singing, a faint mournful song as if a thousand voices joined in a somber dirge. The sad, oppressive music brought to mind the worst memories of his life and filled him with a misery so great it sapped his resolve. His feet felt weighted, his soul chilled. Moving forward became an effort.

Once the party crossed the threshold, the great doors began to close, shutting with a thundering boom. The chamber was well lit, although the source of the light was not apparent. It was impossible to judge the height or the depth of the chasm. Both stretched into seeming emptiness.

"Are other prisons like *this*?" Myron asked, his voice quavering as they began to inch their way across the bridge.

"I would venture to guess this is unique," Alric replied.

"Trust me, I know prisons," Royce told them. "This *is* unique."

The party fell into silence during the crossing. Hadrian was in the rear, concentrating on the placement of his feet. Partway across he paused and glanced up briefly to check on the others. Myron was holding his arms out at his sides like a tightrope walker. Alric, half crouching, reached out with his hands as if he might resort to crawling at any minute. Royce, however, strode casually forward with his head tilted up, and he frequently turned from side to side to study their surroundings.

Despite its appearance, the bridge was solid. They successfully crossed it to a small arched opening into the black tower. Once off the bridge, Royce turned to face Alric. "You were fairly free about revealing your identity back there, Your Majesty," he said, reproaching the monarch. "I don't recall discussing a plan where you walk in and blurt out, 'Hey, I'm the new king, come kill me.' "

"You don't actually think there are assassins in here, do you? I know I thought this was a trap, but look at this place! Arista never could have arranged this. Or do you honestly think others will be able to slip in the same cliff door we entered through?"

"What I think is that there is no reason to take unnecessary chances."

"Unnecessary chances? Are you serious? You don't consider crossing a slick, narrow bridge over a gorge, which is who knows how deep, a risk? Assassins are the least of our worries."

"Are you always this much trouble to those guarding you?"

Alric's only response was a look of disdain.

The archway led to a narrow tunneled corridor, which eventually opened into a large round room. Arranged like an amphitheater, the gallery contained descending stairs and stone benches set in rings, each lower than the one before it, which focused all attention on the recessed center of the room. At the bottom of the steps was a balcony, and twenty feet below it lay a circular stage. Once they descended the stairs,

Hadrian could see the stage was bare except for a single chair and the man who sat upon it.

An intense beam of white light illuminated the seated figure from high above. He did not appear terribly old, with only the start of gray entering his otherwise dark shoulder-length hair. Dark, brooding eyes gazed out from beneath a prominent forehead. No facial hair marred his high cheekbones, which surprised Hadrian, because the few wizards and magicians he knew about all wore long beards as a mark of their profession. He wore a magnificent robe, the color of which Hadrian could not quite determine. The garment shimmered somewhere between dark blue and smoky gray, but where it was folded or creased, it looked to be emerald green or at times even turquoise. The man sat with the robe gathered around him, his hands, lost in its folds, placed on his lap. He sat still as a statue, giving no indication he was aware of their presence.

"What now?" Alric whispered.

"You talk to him," Royce replied.

The prince looked around thoughtfully. "That man down there can't really be a thousand years old, can he?"

"I don't know. In here, anything seems possible," Hadrian said.

Myron looked around the room and up toward the unseen ceiling, a pained expression on his face. "That singing—it reminds me of the abbey, of the fire, as if I can hear them again—screaming." Hadrian gently put a hand on Myron's shoulder.

"Ignore it," Royce told the monk, and then turned to glare at Alric. "You have to talk to him. We can't leave until you do. Now go ahead and ask him what you came here to find out."

"What do I say? I mean, if he is, you know, really a wizard of the Old Empire, if he actually served the last emperor, how do I approach him?"

"Try asking what he's been up to," Hadrian suggested. That was met by a smirk from Alric. "No, seriously, look down there. It's just him and a chair. He has no books, no cards, nothing. I nearly went crazy with boredom cooped up in The Rose and Thorn last winter during a heavy snowfall. How do you suppose he's spent *a thousand years* just sitting in that chair?"

"And how do you not go insane, listening to that sound all that time?" Myron added.

"Okay, I've got something." Alric turned to address the wizard. "Excuse me, sir." The man in the chair slowly raised his head and blinked in response to the bright light from above. He looked weary, his eyes tired. "Sorry to disturb you. I'm Alric Ess—"

"I know well who art thee," Esrahaddon interrupted. His tone was relaxed and calm, his voice gentle and soothing. "Where be thy sinlister?"

"My what?"

"Thy *sinlister*, Arista?"

"Oh, my *sister*."

"*Sis-ter*," the wizard repeated carefully, and sighed, shaking his head.

"She's not here."

"Why doth not she come?"

Alric looked first to Royce and then to Hadrian.

"She asked us to come in her place," Royce responded.

Looking at the thief, the wizard asked, "And who art thee?"

"Me? I'm nobody," Royce replied.

Esrahaddon narrowed his eyes at the thief and raised one eyebrow. "Perhaps, perhaps not."

"My sister instructed me to come here and speak with you," Alric said, drawing the wizard's attention back to him. "Do you know why?"

“ ’Tis I who bade her send thee.”

“Neat trick since you’re locked in here,” Hadrian observed.

“*Neat?*” Esrahaddon questioned. “Dost thou intend ’twas a clean thing? For I see no filth upon the matter.” The four men responded with looks of confusion. “ ’Tis not a point upon which to dwell. Arista hath in habit graced me with her presence fair for a year and more, though difficult be it to determine the passage of the sun within this darkened hole. A student of the Art she fancies herself, but schools for wizards thy world abides not. A desert of want drove her to seek my counsel. She bade me teach those skills now long forgotten. Within these walls am I locked, as time skips across fingertips untethered, with naught but the sound of mine own voice to pose comfort. So did I acquiesce for pity’s sake. Tidings of the new world thy princess did provide. In return, I imparted gifts upon her—gifts of knowledge.”

“Knowledge?” Alric asked, concerned. “What kind of knowledge?”

“Trifles. Be not long ago thy father suffered ill? A henth bylin did I instruct her to create.” They all looked at him, puzzled. Esrahaddon’s gaze left them. He appeared to search for something. “By another name did she fix it. ’Twas . . .” His face strained with concentration until at last he scowled and shook his head.

“A healing potion?” Myron asked.

The wizard eyed the monk carefully. “Indeed!”

“You taught her to make a potion to give to my father?”

“Frightening, yes? To have such a devil as I administering potions to thy king. Yet no poison did I render nor death impart. Likeminded was she and did challenge me thus, so each did we drink from the same cup to prove it free of mischief. No horns did we grow nor deaths impart, but thy liege fared well upon the taking.”

"That doesn't explain why Arista sent me here."

"Death upon thy house hast come?"

"How do you know that? Yes, my father was murdered," Alric said.

The wizard sighed and nodded. "I forewarned a curse so dreadful hung above thy family's fate, but ear thy sister hast not. Still, I beckoned her to send thee forth should death imperil or accident belay the ruling House of Essendon."

Esrahaddon looked deliberately at Hadrian, Royce, and then Myron. "Innocents accused thy fellows be? For I counseled her thus—trustworthy only are those assigned blame for deeds most foul."

"So, do you know who killed my father?"

"A name I have not nor clairvoyant am I. Yet clear is the bow from which the arrow flew. Thy father died by the hand of man in league with the adversary that holds me fast."

"The Nyphron Church," Myron muttered softly, yet still the wizard heard and his eyes narrowed once more at the monk.

"Why would the Church of Nyphron wish to kill my father?"

"For deaf and blind be the passions of men once scent is sniffed. Watchful are they and listen well these walls, for while act benign and intent charitable my jailors believed my hand did point the way and thy father the Heir of Novron be."

"Wait a minute," Alric interrupted, "the church doesn't want to murder the heir. Their whole existence revolves around restoring him to the throne and creating the New Imperial Era."

"A thousand years renders not truth from lie. Death called for and death sought for the blood of god. 'Tis reason true that sealed away am I."

"And why is that?"

"Alone, muzzled and buried deep, chained to a stone-lined grave I am kept. For witness to this counterfeit of the truth I stand, the only lamp in a ceaseless night. The church, that bastion of faith, the wicked serpent whose fangs did wretch the life from the emperor and his family—all save one. Should heir be found, evidence shall I hold and such proof against slander wield. For 'tis I who fought to save our lord."

"The way we heard the story, *you* were the one who killed the imperial family and are responsible for the destruction of the entire empire," Hadrian said.

"From whence did such tale arise? From the adder tongue of mitered serpents? Dost thou truly believe such power resides in one man?"

"What makes you think they killed the emperor?" Alric inquired.

"'Tis not a question nor guess. 'Tis no supposition I extol but memory—as clear as yesterday. I *know.* 'Twas there and 'twas I who delivered the emperor's only son from death at pious hands."

"So you are telling us that you lived at the time of the emperor. Do you expect us to believe that you are over nine hundred years old?" Royce asked.

"Thou speak of doubt, but none have I. A question posed and a question answered."

"That's *just* an answer like this is *just* a prison," Royce countered.

"I still don't understand what all this has to do with my father. Why would the church kill him?"

"Kept alive by powers of enchantment am I, for I alone the heir can find. These serpents watch and hope to see me slip and cast into their hands the fruit of Novron. An interest upon him did I show. By kindness did I suggest deference toward thy father, and in haste to rid burdened souls of traceable guilt did the church slay thy king. Mores the blood to stain red hands. Never did I expect—but wonder nonetheless at their vicious thirst, so to Arista did I warn of perils and portents dark."

"And that's why you wanted me brought here? To explain this to me? To make me understand?"

"Nay! I did send summons but for a path of another course."

"And what is that?"

The wizard looked up at them, his expression revealing a hint of amusement. "Escape."

No one said anything. Myron took the moment to sit down on the stone bench behind him and whispered to Hadrian, "You were right. Life outside the abbey *is* much more exciting than books."

"You want us to help you to escape?" Royce asked incredulously. He held out his hands and looked around the black stone fortress. "From *here*?"

" 'Tis necessary."

" 'Tis also impossible. I have gotten out of a number of difficult situations in my time but nothing like this."

"And thou art aware of little. Measures thou see art but trifles. Walls, guards, and the abyss stand least among the gauntlet. Lo what works of magic ensnare me! Magical locks claim all the doors here as smoke and dream they vanish with passage. The bridge into the bargain, for it hath withered hence. Look and ye will find it so—'tis gone."

Royce raised an eyebrow skeptically. "Alric, I need your ring." The prince handed it to the thief, who climbed the steps and disappeared into the tunnel. He returned a few minutes later and gave the ring back to Alric. A slight nod of his head confirmed what Hadrian already suspected.

Hadrian turned his attention back to the wizard and

Esrahaddon continued. "More to the misery and serious still art the runes that line these prison walls. Magic defends this offending stone, which neither force of blow nor whit of wizardry shall let slip the portal of this hateful cage. 'Tis what thou hear as twisted euphony, this mournful wailing that plagues the ear. Within this spellbound grasp of symbols no new conjuration may manifest. Moreover, what more to trip hope and plague mind but that time itself lies captive in this hateful grip, suspended thus immobile. 'Tis why the years but wave in passing as they flee, never touching this cave nor inhabitants therein. In joining me, thou hast not aged one wink nor shall thou hunger nor thirst—lest no more than when thou entered. Shocking O this feat, this masterwork of mountainous achievement, built for one soul."

"Huh?" Alric asked.

"He says that no magic can be performed in here and… and…time does not pass," Myron explained.

"I don't believe that," Alric challenged.

"Put hand to thy breast and search for the meter of thy heart."

Myron inched his fingers across his chest and let out a tiny squeak.

"And with all these obstacles you expect us to help you escape?" Hadrian said.

The wizard replied with an impish grin.

"Although I'm dying to ask how," Royce said, "I'm even more compelled to ask why. If they went through this much effort to seal you in here, it seems to me they might have had a good reason. You've told us what we came to hear. We're done. So why would we be foolish enough to try and help you escape?"

"Little choice exists for the choosing."

"We have a great many choices," Alric countered bravely. "I'm the king and rule here. It's you who is powerless."

"Oh, 'tis not I that bars thy path, O prince. Thou understand rightly, helpless am I—a prisoner of weakness bound. 'Tis our jailors with whom thou need set thy argument. While every note in our words be measured and writ, I pray thee call out for release and greet the silence sure to follow. Shout, and hear the echo run unanswered. Trapped with me by walls or death they seek to claim thee."

"But if they are listening, they know I'm not the heir," Alric said, but the courage in his voice had melted away.

"Call out, and see which truth prevails."

Alric's concern showed on his face as he looked first to Hadrian and then to Royce. "He may be right," the thief said quietly.

Concern turned to panic and the prince began to shout commands for their release. There was no response, no sound of the great door opening or of approaching protectors to escort them to the exit. Everyone except the wizard looked worried. Alric wrung his hands, and Myron stood and held on to the rail of the balcony as if letting go would allow the world to spin away from him.

"It was a trap after all," Alric said. He turned to Royce. "My apologies for doubting your sound paranoia."

"Even I didn't expect this. Perhaps there's another way out." Royce took a seat on one of the observation benches and assumed the same contemplative look he had worn when he was trying to determine how to get inside the prison.

Everyone remained silent for some time. Finally, Hadrian approached Royce and whispered, "Okay, buddy, this is where you tell me you have this wonderfully unexpected plan to get us out of here."

"Well, I do have one, but it seems almost as frightening as the alternative."

"What's that?"

"We do what the wizard says."

They looked down at the man casually seated in the chair. His robe looked a slightly different shade of blue now. Hadrian waved the others over and explained Royce's plan.

"Could this be a trick?" Alric asked quietly. "The clerk did warn us not to do anything he said."

"You mean the nice clerk who took away our bridge and refuses to let us out?" Royce replied. "I'm not seeing an alternative, but if any of you have another idea, I'm willing to hear it."

"I'd just like to feel my heart again," Myron said, holding his palm to his chest and looking sick. "This is very disturbing. I almost feel like I'm actually dead."

"Your Majesty?"

Alric looked up at the thief with a scowl. "I just want to say for the record that as far as royal protectors go, you're not very good."

"It's my first day," Royce replied dryly.

"And already I'm trapped in a timeless prison. I shudder to think what might have happened if you had a whole week."

"Listen, I don't see we have a choice here," Royce told the group. "We either do what the wizard says and hope he can get us out, or we accept an eternity of sitting here listening to this dreadful singing."

The mournful wail of the music was so wretched that Hadrian knew listening to it would eventually drivc him mad. He tried to ignore it, but as it did for Myron, it brought him unpleasant memories of places and people. Hadrian saw the disappointment on his father's face when he had left to join the military. He saw the tiger covered in blood, gasping for breath as it slowly died, and he heard the sound of hundreds chanting the name: "*Galenti!*" He had reached his conclusion. Anything was better than staying there.

Royce stood and returned to the balcony, below which the wizard waited calmly. "I assume if we help you escape, you'll see to it we get out as well?"

"Indeed."

"And there is no way to determine if you are telling the truth right now?"

The wizard smiled. "Alas, nay."

Royce sighed heavily. "What do we have to do?"

"Precious little. Thy prince, this wayward and recent king, need but recite a bit of poetry."

"Poetry?" Alric pushed past Hadrian to join Royce at the balcony. "What poetry?"

The wizard stood up and kicked his chair to one side to reveal four stanzas of text crudely scratched into the floor.

"'Tis amazing what beauty time may grant," the wizard said with obvious pride. "Speak, and it wilt be so."

Hadrian silently read the lines brightly illuminated by the beam of the overhead light.

AS LORD OF THIS REALM AND KEEPER OF KEYS,
A DECREE WAS MADE AND COUNCILMAN SEIZED.

UNJUSTLY, I SAY, AND THE TIME 'TIS NIGH
TO OPEN THE GATE AND LET HIS SOUL FLY.

BY VIRTUE OF GIFT GRANTED TO ME,
BY RIGHTFUL BIRTH, THE SOVEREIGN I BE.

HEREBY I PROCLAIM THIS ROYAL DECREE,
ESRAHADDON THE WIZARD, THIS MOMENT IS FREE.

"How is that possible?" Alric asked. "You said spells don't work here."

"Indeed, and thou art no spell-caster. Thou art but granting freedom as the law allows the rightful ruler of this land—laws of control laid down before the birth of Melengar, laws built on assumptions false concerning the longevity of power and who might, in due course of time, wield it—at this moment, in this place, 'tis thee. Thou art the rightful and undisputed ruler of this land, and as such, the locks art thine to open. For here latch and bolt be forged with words of enchantment—words that in time hath changed their meaning.

"This gaol raised upon ground once claimed by imperial might, in absence of emperor slain did bend knee alone to the Nyphron Church Patriarch. Now within these walls never a grain of sand did drop to mark the passage of time but without thunder of war did rumble. Armies marched and lands divided, the empire lost to warlords' whim. Then through bloody strife did these hills birth Melengar, realm sovereign under lordly king. What privilege once reserved alone only for a mitered head hast now fallen to thee. To thee, good King of Melengar, who has the power to right wrong so long omit. Nine centuries of dust hast buried wit, dear king, for these jailers hath forgotten how to read their own runes!"

In the distance, Hadrian heard the grinding of stone on stone. Outside the cell, the great door was opening. "Speak those words, my lord, and thou will end nine hundred years of wrongful imprisonment."

"How does this help?" Alric asked. "This place is filled with guards. How does this get us out?"

The wizard smiled a great grin. "Thy words will cast aside the barrier enchantment and allow me the freedom to use the Art once more."

"You'll cast a spell. You'll disappear!"

Footsteps thundered on the bridge, which had apparently reappeared. Hadrian ran up the gallery stairs to look down the tunnel. "We have guards coming! And they don't look happy."

"If you're going to do this, you'd better make it fast," Royce told Alric.

"They've swords drawn," Hadrian shouted. "Never a good sign."

Alric glared down at the wizard. "I want your word you won't leave us here."

"Gladly given, my lord." The wizard inclined his head respectfully.

"This better work," Alric muttered, and began reading aloud the words on the floor below.

Royce raced to join Hadrian as he positioned himself at the mouth of the tunnel. Hadrian planned to use its confined space to limit the advantage of the guard's numbers and planted his feet while Royce took up position slightly behind him. In unison, they drew their weapons, preparing for the impending onslaught. At least twenty men stormed the gallery. Hadrian could see their eyes and recognized what burned there. He had fought numerous battles and he knew the many faces of combat. He had seen fear, recklessness, hatred, even madness. What came at him now was rage—blind, intense rage. Hadrian studied the lead man, estimating his footfalls to determine which leg his weight would land on when he came within striking range. He did the same with the man behind him. Calculating his attack, he raised his swords, but the prison guards stopped. Hadrian waited with his swords still poised, yet the guards did not advance.

"Let us away," he heard Esrahaddon say from behind. Hadrian whirled around and discovered the wizard was no longer on the stage below. Instead, he moved casually past Hadrian, navigating around the stationary guards. "Come, come," Esrahaddon called.

Without a word, the group hurried after the wizard. He led them through the tunnel and across the newly extended bridge. The prison was oddly silent, and it was then that Hadrian realized the music had stopped. The only remaining sound was their footfalls against the hard stone floor.

"Be at ease for perils past but tarry not and follow well," Esrahaddon told them reassuringly.

They did as instructed, and no one said a word. To pass the clerk, who stood peering through the great door, they needed to come within inches of his anxiety-riddled face. As Hadrian attempted to slip by without bumping him, he saw the man's eye move. Hadrian stiffened. "Can they see or hear us?"

"Nay. A ghostly breath is all thee be, a chill and swirl of air to their percept."

The wizard led them without hesitation, making turns, crossing bridges, and climbing stairs with total confidence.

"Maybe we're dead?" Myron whispered, glaring at each frozen guard he passed. "Maybe we're *all* dead now. Maybe we're ghosts."

Hadrian thought Myron might be on to something. Everything was so oddly still, so empty. The fluid movement of the wizard and his billowing robe, which now emitted a soft silvery light far brighter than any lantern or torch, only heightened the surreal atmosphere.

"I don't understand. How is this possible?" Alric asked, stepping around a pair of black-suited guards who watched the third bridge. He waved his hand before the face of one of them, who did not respond. "Is this your doing?"

" 'Tis the *ithinal*."

"Huh?"

"A magic box. Power to alter time eludes the grasp of man, for too vast be the scope and too great the field. Yet enclose the space, confine the effect, and tame the wild world within.

Upon these walls, my colleagues of old wove enchantments complex. Designed to affect magic and time, I had but to ever so slightly adjust a fiber or two within the weave to throw us out of phase."

"So, the guards can't see us, but that doesn't explain why they are just standing there," Hadrian said. "We disappeared, and you're free. Why are they not searching? Shouldn't they be locking doors to trap us?"

"Within these walls, locked art the sands of time for all but us."

"You turned it inside out!" Myron exclaimed.

Esrahaddon looked with an appraising eye over his shoulder at the monk. " 'Tis thrice thou hast impressed me. What did thou say thy name was?"

"He didn't," Royce answered for him.

"Thou dost not trust people easily, my black-hooded friend? 'Tis quite wise. Careful should be the dealings with the wise and wizards." Esrahaddon winked at the thief.

"What does he mean by 'turning it inside out'?" Alric asked. "So, time has stopped for them while we are free?"

"Indeed. Though time still moves, 'tis very slowly paced. Unaware will they remain sealed in an instant lost."

"I'm starting to see now why they were afraid of you," Alric said.

"Nine hundred years did I spend imprisoned for saving the son of a man we all swore our lives to serve and protect. Exceedingly kind is the reward I bestow, for there art worse moments in which for all eternity to be trapped."

They reached the great stair that led to the main entrance corridor and began the long, exhausting climb up the stone steps. "How did you stay sane?" Hadrian asked. "Or did time slip by in an instant like it is for them?"

"Slip it did but not so fast when measured in centuries.

Each day a battle did I fight. Patience is a skill learned as a practitioner of the Art. Yet times there were that...well, who can say what it means to be sane?"

When they approached the hall of faces, Esrahaddon looked down its length and paused. Hadrian noticed the wizard stiffen. "What is it?" he asked.

"Those faces, frozen thus, art the workers who built this gaol. Came I to this place during the final walling. Tented city did wreathed the lake. Hundreds of artisans with families came to the call to do their part for their fallen emperor. Such was the character of His Imperial Majesty. They all mourned his passing, and few in the vast and varied empire would not gladly give their lives for him. Labeled the betrayer, I beheld hatred in their eyes. Proud were they to be the builders of my tomb."

The wizard's gaze moved from face to face. "I recognize some—the stonecutters, sculptors, cooks, and wives. The church, for fear of secrets slipped from lips innocent, sealed them so. All before thee, ensnared by a lie. How many dead? How much lost to hide one secret, which even a millennium hast not erased?"

"There's no door down there," Alric warned the wizard.

Esrahaddon looked up at Alric as if awoken from a dream. "Be not a fool. Thou didst enter through it," he said, and promptly led them down the corridor at a brisk walk. "Thou wert merely out of phase with it."

Here, in the darkest segment of the prison, Esrahaddon's robe grew brighter still, and he looked like a giant firefly. In time, they came to a solid stone wall, and without hesitation or pause, Esrahaddon walked through it. The rest quickly followed.

The bright sunlight of a lovely, clear autumn morning nearly blinded them the moment they passed through the barrier. Blue sky and the cool fresh air were a welcome change.

Hadrian took a deep breath and reveled in the scent of grass and fallen leaves, a smell he had not even noticed prior to entering the prison. "That's strange. It should be nighttime and raining, I would think. We couldn't have been in there more than a few hours. Could we?"

Esrahaddon shrugged and threw his head back to face the sun. He stood and took long deep breaths of air, sighing contentedly with each exhale. "Unexpected be the wages of altering time. 'What morrow be it?' 'tis better to ask. This day, the next, or one after. 'Tis possible tens or hundreds did fly past." The wizard appeared amused at the shock on their faces. "Worry not, 'tis likely only hours hast thee skipped."

"That's rather unnerving," Alric said. "Losing time like that."

"Verily, for nine hundred years have I lost. Everyone I knew is dead, the empire gone, and who knows in what state the world is left. Should what thy sister reports prove true, much hath changed in the world."

"By the way," Royce mentioned, "no one uses the words *'tis* or *hath* anymore and certainly not *thou*, *thy*, or *verily*."

The wizard considered this a moment, then nodded. "In my day, classes oft did speak different in forms of speech. Assumed I did that ye were of a lower station or, in the case of the king, poorly educated."

Alric glared. "It's you who sound strange, not us."

"Indeed. Then I shall need to speak as all of—*you*—do. Even though—it is—crude and backward."

Hadrian, Royce, and Myron began the task of saddling the horses, which remained standing where they had left them. Myron smiled, obviously happy to be with the animals once again. He petted them while eagerly asking how to tie a cinch strap.

"We don't have an extra horse and Hadrian is already

riding double," Alric explained. He glanced at Royce, who showed no indication of volunteering. "Esrahaddon will have to ride with me, I suppose."

"Unnecessary will that be, for my own way I shall go."

"Oh no you're not. You're coming back with me. I have a great deal to speak with you about. You were an advisor to the emperor and are obviously very gifted and knowledgeable. I have great need for someone such as you. You'll be my royal counselor."

"Nay, 'twill..." He sighed, then continued. "No, *it will* come as a shock to—*you*—but I did not escape to help with *your* little problems. Matters more pressing I must attend to, and too long from them have I been."

The prince appeared taken aback. "What matters could you possibly have after nine hundred years? After all, it's not as if you have to get home to tend to your livestock. If it's a matter of compensation, you'll be well paid and live in as much luxury as I can afford. And if you are thinking you can make more elsewhere, only Ethelred of Warric is likely to offer as much, and trust me, you don't want to work for the likes of him. He's a dogmatic Imperialist and a loyal church supporter."

"I do not seek compensation."

"No? Look at you. You have nothing—no food, no place to sleep. I think you should consider your situation a bit more before refusing me. Besides, gratitude alone should compel you to help me."

"Gratitude? Has the meaning of this word changed as well? In my day, this meant to show appreciation for a favor."

"And it still does. I saved you. I released you from that place."

Esrahaddon raised an eyebrow. "Didst thou help me escape as favor to me? I think not. Thou—*you* freed me to save *yourself*. I owe *you* nothing, and if I did, I repaid *you* when I brought *you* out."

"But the whole reason I came here was to gain your assistance. I'm inheriting a throne handed down by blood! Thieves abducted and dragged me across the kingdom in my first few days as king. I still don't know who killed my father or how to find them. I'm in great need of help. You must know hundreds of things the greatest minds of today have never known—"

"Thousands at least but I am still not going with *you*. *You* have a kingdom to secure. My path lies elsewhere."

Alric's face grew red with frustration. "I insist you return with me and become my advisor. I can't just let you wander off. Who knows what kind of trouble you could cause? You're dangerous."

"Yes indeed, dear prince," the wizard said, and his tone grew serious. "So allow me to grant thee a bit of free counsel—use not the word *insist* with regards to me. Thou hast but only a small spill to contend with; do not tempt a deluge."

Alric stiffened.

"How long before the church starts hunting you?" Royce asked casually.

"What dost..." The wizard sighed. "What do *you* mean?"

"You locked things up nicely in the prison so no one will know you escaped. Of course, if we were to return and start bragging about how we broke you out, that might start inquiries," Hadrian said.

The wizard leveled his gaze at him. "Is it a threat you make?"

"Why would I do that? As you already know, I have nothing to do with this. Not to mention it would be pretty stupid of me to threaten a wizard. The thing is, though, the king here, he is not as bright as I am. He very well might get drunk and tell stories at the first tavern he arrives at, as nobles often do." Esrahaddon glanced at Alric, whose red face now turned pale. "Fact is, we came all this way to find out who killed Alric's father, and we really don't know much more than we did before we set out."

Esrahaddon chuckled softly. "Very well. Prithee, impart how 'tis—*it is*—*your* father died."

"He was stabbed with a knife," Alric explained.

"What kind of knife?"

"A common rondel military dagger." Alric held his hands about a foot apart. "About this long. It had a flat blade and a round pommel."

Esrahaddon nodded. "Where was he stabbed?"

"In his private chapel."

"Where physically?"

"Oh, in the back, upper left side, I think."

"Were there any windows or other doors in the chapel?"

"None."

"Who found the body?"

"These two." Alric pointed at Royce and Hadrian.

The wizard smiled and shook his head. "Nay, beside them, who announced the death of the king? Who raised the alarm?"

"That would be Captain Wylin, my master-at-arms. He was on the scene very quickly and apprehended them."

Hadrian thought about the night King Amrath had been killed. "No, that's not right. There was a dwarf there. He must have come around the corner of the hallway just as we left the room. He probably saw the king's body lying on the floor of the chapel and shouted. Right after he yelled, the soldiers came and surprisingly fast, I might add."

"That was just Magnus," Alric said. "He's been doing stonework about the castle for months."

"Didst thee—*you*—see this dwarf approach from the corridor?" the wizard asked.

"No," Hadrian replied, and Royce confirmed that with a shake of his head.

"And when *you* entered the chapel from the doorway, was the body of the king visible?"

Hadrian and Royce shook their heads.

"That solves it, then," the wizard said as if everything was perfectly clear. The party stared back at him in confusion. Esrahaddon sighed. "The dwarf killed Amrath."

"That's not possible," Alric said, challenging him. "My father was a big man, and the dagger thrust was downward. A dwarf couldn't possibly have stabbed him in the upper back."

"Your father was in his chapel, as any pious king, kneeling with head bowed. The dwarf killed him as he prayed."

"But the door was locked when we entered," Hadrian said. "And there was no one in the room besides the king."

"No one you could *see*. Did the chapel have an altar with a cabinet?"

"Yes, it did."

"They did a millennium ago as well. Religion changes slowly. The cabinet was likely too small for a man but could easily accommodate a dwarf. After he killed the king, he locked the door and waited for you two to find the body." Esrahaddon paused. "That cannot be right *you—two—to*?" He rolled his eyes and shook his head. "If this hast been done to language, I fear to know the fate of all else.

"With door locked, a night guard or cleaning steward would not find the body prematurely. Only a skilled thief would be able to enter, which I assume at least one of you is." He looked directly at Royce as he said the last part. "After you left, the dwarf crept out, opened the door, and sounded the alarm."

"So, the dwarf is an agent of the church?"

"No." The wizard sighed with a look of frustration. "Not a dwarf alive who would carry a common dagger. The traditions of dwarves change even slower than religion. Given the dagger he was by the one who hired him. Find that person and you will find the true killer."

Stunned, everyone looked at the wizard. "That's incredible," Alric said.

"Nay, not so difficult to determine." The wizard inclined his head toward the cliff. "Escape *was hard*. Speaking as you do *is hard*. Determining the murderer of King Amrath was... was... soft?"

"Soft?" Hadrian asked. "You mean easy."

"How be it that easy forms the opposite of hard? Sense this makes not."

Hadrian shrugged. "And yet, it is."

Esrahaddon looked frustrated. "Alas. Now, this is as much assistance as I shall lend in this matter. Therefore, I will be on my way. As I have said, I have affairs to attend. My help was sufficient to prevent any loose tongues?"

"You have my hand on it," Alric said, reaching out.

The wizard looked down at Alric's open palm and smiled. "Thy word is enough." He turned away and without so much as a parting gesture began walking down the slope.

"You're going to walk? You know, it's a long way to anywhere from here," Hadrian yelled after him.

"I am looking forward to the trip," the wizard replied without glancing back. Following the ancient road, he rounded the corner and slipped out of sight.

The remaining party members mounted their horses. Myron seemed more comfortable with the animals now and climbed confidently into his seat behind Hadrian. He even neglected to hold on until they began down the ravine back in the direction from which they had come. Hadrian expected they would pass Esrahaddon on the way down, but they reached the bottom of the ravine without seeing him.

"Not your run-of-the-mill fellow, is he?" Hadrian asked. He was continuing to look around for any signs of the wizard.

"The way he was able to get out of that place makes me wonder exactly what we did here today by letting him out," Royce said.

"No wonder the emperor was so successful." Alric frowned and knotted the ends of his reins. "Although I can tell it didn't come without aggravation. You know, I don't extend my hand often, but when I do, I expect it to be accepted. I found his reaction quite insulting."

"I'm not sure he was being rude by not shaking your hand. I think it's just because he couldn't," Myron told them. "Shake your hand, that is."

"Why not?"

"In *The Accumulated Letters of Dioylion*, they told a bit about Esrahaddon's incarceration. The church had both of his hands cut off in order to limit his ability to cast spells."

"Oh," Alric said.

"Why do I get the impression this Dioylion fellow didn't die a natural death?" Hadrian asked.

"He's probably one of those faces in the hallway." Royce spurred his horse down the slope.

Chapter 6

Revelations by Moonlight

"I heard you were looking for me, Uncle?" Princess Arista swept into his office. She was followed by her bodyguard, Hilfred, who dutifully waited by the door. Still dressing in clothing mourning her father's death, she wore an elegant black gown with a silver bodice. Standing straight and tall with her head held high, she maintained her regal air.

The Archduke Percy Braga rose as she entered. "Yes, I have some questions for you." He resumed his seat behind the desk. Her uncle was dressed in black as well. His doublet, cape, and cap were dark velvet, causing his gold chain of office to stand out more than usual. His eyes looked weary from lack of sleep, and a thickening growth of stubble shadowed his face.

"Do you, now?" she said, glaring at him. "Since when does the lord chancellor summon the acting queen to answer *his* questions?"

Percy raised his eyes to meet hers. "There is no proof your brother is dead, Arista. You are not queen yet."

"No proof?" She walked over to Braga's chart table, where maps of the kingdom lay scattered everywhere. They were littered with flags marking where patrols, garrisons, and companies were deployed. She picked up the soiled robe she saw there; it bore the Essendon falcon crest. Poking her fingers through the holes cut in the back, she threw it on his desk. "What do you call this?"

"A robe," the archduke responded curtly.

"This is my brother's, and these holes look as though a dagger or arrow would fit through them nicely. Those two men who murdered my father killed Alric as well. They dumped his body in the river. My brother is dead, Braga! The only reason I have not already ordered my coronation is that I'm observing the appropriate mourning period. That time will soon be over, so you should mind how you speak to me, Uncle, lest I forget we are family."

"Until I have his body, Arista, I must consider your brother alive. As such, he is still the rightful ruler, and I'll continue to do everything in my power to find him regardless of your interference. I owe that much to your father, who entrusted me with this position."

"In case you haven't noticed, my father is dead. You should pay more attention to the living, or you won't be the Lord Chancellor of Melengar for long."

Braga started to say something and then stopped to take a calming breath. "Will you answer my questions or not?"

"Go ahead and ask. I'll decide after I hear them." She casually walked back to the chart table and sat on it. She crossed her long legs at the ankles and absently studied her fingernails.

"Captain Wylin reports that he has completed his interviews with the dungeon staff." Braga got up and moved from behind his desk to face Arista. In his hand, he held a parchment, which he glanced at for reference. "He indicates you visited the prisoners after your brother and I left them. He says you brought two monks with you who were later found gagged and hanging in place of the prisoners. Is that true?"

"Yes," she replied without embellishment. The archduke

continued to stare at her, the silence growing between them. "I'm a superstitious woman by nature, and I wanted to be certain they had last rites so their ghosts didn't remain after their execution."

"There is a report you ordered the prisoners unchained?" Braga took another step closer to her.

"The monks told me the prisoners needed to kneel. I saw no danger in it. They were in a cell with an army of guards just outside."

"They also reported you entered with the monks and had the door closed behind you." The archduke took another step. He was now uncomfortably close, studying her manners and expression.

"Did they also mention I left before the monks did? Or that I wasn't there when the brutes grabbed them?" Arista pushed off the desk, causing her uncle to step back. She casually slipped past him and walked to the window, which looked down at the castle courtyard. A man was chopping and stacking wood for the coming winter. "I'll admit it wasn't the smartest thing I've ever done, but I never thought they would escape. They were just two men!" She continued to stare out the window absently. Her gaze drifted from the woodcutter to the trees, which had lost all their leaves. "Now, is that all you wanted to know? Do I have the chancellor's permission to return to my duties as queen of this realm?"

"Of course, my dear." Braga's tone turned warmer. The princess left the window and moved toward the exit. "Oh, but there is one last thing."

Arista paused at the doorway and glanced over her shoulder. "What is it?"

"Wylin also reports the dagger used to kill your father is missing from the storeroom. Do you have any idea where it might be?"

She turned to face him. "Are you now accusing me of stealing?"

"I'm simply asking, Arista," the archduke huffed in irritation. "You don't need to be so obstinate with me. I'm merely trying to do my job."

"Your job? I think you are doing much more than your job. No, I don't know anything about the dagger, and stop pestering me with accusations thinly veiled as inquiries. Do it again and we shall soon see who rules here!"

Arista stormed out of Braga's office, leaving Hilfred to jog a step to keep up with her. She promptly crossed the keep to the residences. Asking Hilfred to stand guard, she rushed up the steps of her personal tower. She entered her room, slammed the door shut, and locked it with a tap from the gemstone in her necklace.

Breathing heavily, she paused a moment, with her back pressed against the door. She tried to steady herself. She felt as if the room were swaying like a young tree in a breeze. She had been feeling that way often lately. The world seemed to be constantly swirling around her. Yet this was her sanctuary, her refuge. Here was the one place she felt safe, where she kept her secrets, where she could practice her magic, and where she dreamed her dreams.

Although she was a princess, her room was very modest. She had seen the bedrooms of the daughters of earls, and even one baroness had a finer abode. By comparison, hers was quite small and austere. It was, however, by her own choice. She could have her pick of the larger, more ornately decorated bedrooms in the royal wing, but she chose the tower for its isolation and the three windows, which afforded a view of all the lands around the castle. Thick burgundy drapes extended from ceiling to floor, hiding the bare stone. She had hoped they might keep the chill out as well but unfortunately they did not. Winter nights were often brutally cold despite her efforts to keep the little fireplace roaring. Still the soft presence of the drapes made it seem warmer just the same. Four giant pillows rested on a tiny canopy bed. There was no room for a larger one. Next to the bed was a small table with a pitcher inside a washbasin. Beside it stood a wardrobe, which had been passed down to her from her mother along with her hope chest. The solidly made trunk with a formidable lock sat at the foot of her bed. The only other pieces of furniture in the room were her dressing table, a mirror, and a small chair.

She crossed the room and sat at her dressing table. The mirror, which stood beside it, was of lavish design. The looking glass was clearer than most and was framed on either side by two elegant swans swimming away from one another. This too had once belonged to her mother. She fondly remembered nights sitting before it, watching its reflection as her mother brushed her hair. On the table, she kept her collection of hairbrushes. She had many, one from each of the kingdoms her father had visited on matters of state, including a pearl-handled brush from Wesbaden and an ebony one with fine fish-bone teeth from the exotic port city of Tur Del Fur. Looking at them now brought back memories of days when her father would return home with a hand hidden behind his back and a twinkle in his eye. Now the swan mirror and the brushes were all that remained of her parents.

With a sudden sweep of her hand, she threw the brushes across the room. *Why had it come to this?* She cried softly; it did not matter. She had work yet to do. There were things she had started that must now be finished. Braga was getting more suspicious each day—time was running out.

She unlocked and opened her hope chest. From inside, she removed the bundle of purple cloth she had hidden there. How ironic, she thought, for her to have used that cloth. Her father had wrapped the last hairbrush he had given her in it. She laid the bundle on her bed and carefully unfolded it to reveal the rondel dagger. The blade was still stained with her father's blood.

"Only one more job left for you to do," she told the knife.

⁂

The Silver Pitcher Inn was a simple cottage located on the outskirts of the province of Galilin. Fieldstone and mortar composed the lower half, while whitewashed oak beams supported a roof of thick field thatch, gone gray with time. Windows divided into diamond panes of poor-quality glass underscored by heldaberry bushes lined the sides. Several horses stood tied to the posts out front, with still more visible in the small stable to the side.

"Seems like a busy place for so far out," Royce observed.

Traveling east, they had ridden all day. Just as before, the trip through the wilds proved exhausting. As the evening light had faded, they had reached the farmland of Galilin. They passed through tilled fields and meadows until at last they stumbled onto a country lane. Because none of them knew for certain where they were, they decided to follow the road to a landmark. To their pleasant surprise, the Silver Pitcher Inn was the first building they found.

"Well, Majesty," Hadrian said, "you should be able to find your way back to the castle from here, if that's still your destination."

"It's about time I got back," Alric told him, "but not before I eat. Does this place have decent food?"

"Does it matter?" Hadrian chuckled. "I'd be happy for a bit of three-day-ripe field mouse at this point. Come on, we can have a last meal together, which, since you have no money on you, I'll be paying for. I hope you'll let me deduct it from my taxes."

"No need. We'll tack it on to the job as an additional expense," Royce interjected. He looked at Alric and added, "You haven't forgotten you still owe us one hundred tenents, have you?"

"You'll get paid. I'll have my uncle set the money aside. You can pick it up at the castle."

"I hope you don't mind if we wait a few days, just to make sure."

"Of course not." The prince nodded.

"And if we send a representative to pick up the money for us?" Royce asked. Alric stared at him. "One who has no idea how to find us in case he is captured?"

"Oh please, aren't you being just a tad bit too cautious now?"

"No such thing," Royce replied.

"Look!" Myron shouted suddenly, pointing at the stable.

All three of them jumped fearfully at the sudden outburst.

"There's a *brown* horse!" the monk said in amazement. "I didn't know they came in brown!"

"By Mar, monk!" Alric shook his head in disbelief, a gesture Royce and Hadrian mirrored.

"Well, I didn't," Myron replied sheepishly. His excitement, however, was still evident when he added, "What other colors do they come in? Is there a green horse? A blue one? I would so love to see a blue one."

Royce went inside and returned a few minutes later. "Everything looks all right. A bit crowded, but I don't see anything too out of the ordinary. Alric, be sure to keep your hood up and either spin your ring so the insignia is on the inside of your hand, or better yet, remove it altogether until you get home."

Just inside the inn was a small stone foyer, where several

cloaks and coats hung on a forest of wall pegs. A handful of walking sticks of various shapes and sizes rested on a rack to one side. Above, a shelf held an assortment of tattered hats and gloves.

Myron stood just inside the door, gaping at his surroundings. "I read about inns," he said. "In *Pilgrims' Tales*, a group of wayward travelers spend a night at an inn, where they decided to tell stories of their journeys. They made a wager for the best one. It's one of my favorites, although the abbot didn't much care for my reading it. It was a bit bawdy. There were several accounts about women in those pages and not in a wholesome fashion either." He scanned the crowd excitedly. "Are there women here?"

"No," Hadrian replied sadly.

"Oh. I was hoping to see one. Do they keep them locked up as treasures?"

Hadrian and the others just laughed.

Myron looked at them, mystified, then shrugged. "Even so, this is wonderful. There's so much to see! What's that smell? It's not food, is it?"

"Pipe smoke," Hadrian explained. "It probably was not a popular activity at the abbey."

A half dozen tables filled the small room. A slightly askew stone fireplace with silver tankards dangling from mantel hooks dominated one wall. Next to it stood the bar, which was built from rough and unfinished tree logs complete with bark. Some fifteen patrons lined the room, a handful of whom watched the group enter with passing interest. Most were rough stock, woodsmen, laborers, and traveling tinkers. The pipe smoke came from a few gruff men seated near the log bar, and a cloud of it hovered at eye level throughout the room, producing an earthy smell that mingled with that of the burning wood of the fireplace and the sweet scent of baking bread.

Royce led them to an open round table near the window, where they could see the horses outside.

"I'll order us something," Hadrian volunteered.

"This is a beautiful place," Myron declared, his eyes darting about the room. "There is so much going on, so many conversations. Speaking at meals wasn't allowed at the abbey, so it was always deathly silent. Of course, we got around that rule by using sign language. It used to drive the abbot crazy, because we were supposed to be focusing on Maribor, but there are times when you simply have to ask someone to pass the salt."

No sooner had Hadrian reached the bar than he felt someone press up behind him menacingly.

"You should be more careful, my friend," a man whispered softly.

Hadrian turned slowly and chuckled when he saw who it was. "I don't have to, Albert. I have a shadow who watches my back." Hadrian gestured toward Royce, who had slipped up behind the viscount.

Albert, who wore a dirty, tattered cloak with the hood pulled up, turned to face a scowling Royce. "I was just making a joke."

"What are you doing here?" Royce whispered.

"Hiding—" Albert started, but he fell quiet when the bartender came over with a pitcher of foaming beer and four mugs.

"Have you eaten?" Hadrian asked.

"No." Albert looked longingly at the pitcher.

"Could I get another mug and another plate of supper?" Hadrian asked the hefty man behind the bar.

"Sure thing," the bartender responded as he added another mug. "I'll bring the food over when it's ready."

They returned to the table with the viscount trailing them. Albert looked curiously at Myron and Alric for a moment.

"This is Albert Winslow, an acquaintance of ours," Hadrian explained as Albert pulled a chair over to their table. "These are—"

"Clients," Royce cut in quickly, "so no business talk, Albert."

"We've been out of town... traveling, the last few days," Hadrian said. "Anything been going on in Medford?"

"A lot," Albert said quietly as Hadrian poured the ale. "King Amrath is dead."

"Really?" Hadrian feigned surprise.

"The Rose and Thorn has been shut down. Soldiers tore through the Lower Quarter. A bunch of folks were rounded up and sent to prison. There's a small army surrounding Essendon Castle and the entrances to the city. I got out just in time."

"An army around the castle? What for?" Alric asked.

Royce motioned for him to calm down. "What about Gwen?"

"She's okay—I think," Albert replied, looking curiously at Alric. "At least she was when I left. They questioned her and roughed up a few of her girls but nothing more than that. She's been worried about you. I think she expected you to return from... traveling... days ago."

"Who are 'they'?" Royce asked, his voice several degrees colder.

"Well, a lot of them were royal guards, but they had a whole bunch of new friends as well. Remember those strangers in town we talked about a few days ago? They were marching with some of the royal guards, so they must be working for the crown prince, I would think." Again, Albert glanced at Alric. "They were combing the entire city and asking questions about a pair of thieves operating out of the Lower Quarter. That's when I made myself scarce. I left town and headed west. It was the same all over. Patrols are everywhere. They have been ripping apart inns and taverns, hauling people into the streets. I've stayed one step ahead of them so far. Last thing I heard, a curfew was ordered after nightfall in Medford."

"So, you just kept heading west?" Hadrian asked.

"Until I got here. This is the first place I came to that hadn't been ransacked."

"Which would explain the large turnout," Hadrian mentioned. "Mice leave a sinking ship."

"Yeah, a lot of people decided Medford wasn't so friendly anymore," Albert explained. "I figured I would stick around here for a few days and then start back and test the waters as I go."

"Has there been any word concerning the prince or princess?" Alric asked.

"Nothing in particular," the viscount responded. He took a drink, his eyes lingering on the prince.

The rear door to the inn opened and a slim figure entered. He was filthy, dressed in torn rags and a hat that looked more like a sack. He clutched a small purse tightly to his chest and paused for only a moment, his eyes darting around the room nervously. He walked quickly to the rear of the bar, where the innkeeper filled a sack of food in exchange for the purse.

"What do we have here?" asked a burly fellow from one of the tables as he got to his feet. "Take off the hat, elf. Show us them ears."

The ragged pauper clung to his bag tightly and looked toward the door. When he did, another man from the bar moved to block his path.

"I said take it off!" the burly man ordered.

"Leave him alone, Drake," the innkeeper told him. "He just came in for a bit of food. He ain't gonna eat it here."

"I can't believe you sell to *them*, Hall. Haven't you heard they're killing people up in Dunmore? Filthy things." Drake reached out to pull the hat off but the figure aptly dodged his reach. "See how they are? Fast little things when they want to be, but lazy bastards if you try to put 'em to work. They ain't nothing but trouble. You let 'em in here, and one day they'll end up stabbing you in the back and stealing you blind."

"He ain't stealing anything," Hall said. "He comes in here once a week to buy food and stuff for his family. This one has a mate and a kid. Poor things are barely alive. They're living in the forest. It's been a month since the town guard in Medford drove them out."

"Yeah?" Drake said. "If he lives in the forest, where's he getting the money to pay for the food? You stealing it, ain't you, boy? You robbing decent people? Breaking into farms? That's why the sheriffs drive 'em out of the cities, 'cause they're all thieves and drunks. The Medford guard don't want 'em on their streets, and I don't want 'em on ours!"

A man standing behind the vagabond snatched his hat off, revealing thick matted black hair and pointed ears.

"Filthy little elf," Drake said. "Where'd you get the money?"

"I said leave him be, Drake," Hall persisted.

"I think he stole it," Drake said, and pulled a dagger from his belt.

The unarmed elf stood fearfully still, his eyes darting back and forth between the men who menaced him and the door to the inn.

"Drake?" Hall said in a lower, more serious tone. "You leave him be, or I swear you'll never be served here again."

Drake looked up to see Hall, who was considerably larger than he, holding a butcher knife.

"You wanna go find him in the woods later, that's your business. But I won't have no fighting in my place." Drake put the dagger away. "Go on, get out," Hall told the elf, who carefully moved past the men and slipped back out the door.

"Was that really an elf?" Myron asked, astonished.

"They're half-breeds," Hadrian replied. "Most people don't believe pure-blood elves exist anymore."

"I actually pity them," Albert said. "They were slaves back in the days of the empire. Did you know that?"

"Well, actually, I—" Myron started, but he stopped short when he saw the slight shake of Royce's head and the look on his face.

"Why pity them?" Alric asked. "They were no worse off than the serfs and villeins we have today. And now they are free, which is more than the villeins can say."

"Villeins are bound to the land, true, but they aren't slaves," Albert said, correcting him. "They can't be bought and sold; their families aren't torn apart, and they aren't bred like livestock and kept in pens or butchered for entertainment. I heard they used to do that to the elves, and sure, they're free now, but they aren't allowed to be part of society. They can't find work, and you just saw what they have to go through just to get food."

Royce's expression had grown colder than usual, and Hadrian knew it was time to change the subject. "You wouldn't know it to look at him," he said, "but Albert here is a nobleman. He's a viscount."

"Viscount Winslow?" Alric said. "Of what holding?"

"Sad to say, none," Albert replied before taking a large drink of ale. "Granddad, Harlan Winslow, lost the family plot when he fell out of favor with the King of Warric. Although, truth be told, I don't think it was ever anything to boast about. From what I heard, it was a rocky patch of dirt on the Bernum River. King Ethelred of Warric gobbled it up a few years ago.

"Ah, the stories my father told me of Grandfather's trials

and tribulations trying to live with the shame of being a landless noble. My dad inherited a little money from him, but he squandered it trying to keep up the pretense he was still a wealthy nobleman. I myself have no problem swallowing my pride if it will fill my stomach." Albert squinted at Alric. "You look familiar. Have we met before?"

"If we did, I'm certain it was in passing," Alric replied.

The meal arrived and chewing replaced conversation. The food was nothing special: a portion of slightly overcooked ham, boiled potatoes, cabbage, onions, and a loaf of old bread. Yet after nearly two days of eating only a few potatoes, Hadrian considered it a feast. As the light outside faded, the inn boy began lighting the candles on each table, and they took the opportunity to order another pitcher.

While sitting there relaxing, Hadrian noticed Royce repeatedly looking out the window. After the third glance, Hadrian leaned over to see what was so compelling. With the darkness outside, the window was like a mirror. All he could see was his own face.

"When was The Rose and Thorn raided?" Royce asked.

Albert shrugged. "Two or three days ago, I guess."

"I meant, what time of day?"

"Oh, evening. At sunset, I believe, or just after. I suppose they wanted to catch the dinner crowd." Albert paused and sat up suddenly as his expression of contentment faded into one of concern. "Oh—ah...I hate to eat and run, but if it's all right with you boys, I'm going to make myself scarce again." He got up and exited quickly through the rear door. Royce glanced outside again and appeared agitated.

"What is it?" Alric asked.

"We have company. Everyone stay calm until we see which way the wind is blowing."

The door to the Silver Pitcher burst open, and eight men

dressed in byrnie with tabards bearing the Melengar falcon poured into the room. They flipped over a few tables near the door, scattering drinks and food everywhere. Soldiers brandishing swords glowered at the patrons. No one in the inn moved.

"In the name of the king, this inn and all its occupants are to be searched. Those resisting or attempting to flee will be executed!"

The soldiers broke into groups. One began pulling men from their tables and shoved them against the wall, forming a line. Others charged up the steps to the loft, while a third set descended into the tavern's cellar.

"I do an honest business here!" Hall protested as they pushed him up against the wall with the rest.

"Keep your mouth shut or I'll have this place torched," a man entering said. He did not wear armor, nor the emblem of Melengar. Instead, he was dressed in fine practical clothing of layered shades of gray.

"It was a pleasure having your company, gentlemen," Alric told those at the table, "but it seems my escort is here."

"Be careful," Hadrian told him as the prince stood up.

Alric moved toward the center of the room, pulled back his hood, and stood straight with his chin held high. "What is it you are looking for, good men of Melengar?" he asked in a loud clear voice that caught the attention of everyone in the room.

The man in gray spun around, and when he saw Alric's face, he showed a surprised smile. "Well! We are looking for you, Your Highness," he said with a gracious bow. "We were told you were kidnapped, possibly dead."

"As you can see, I'm neither. Now release these good people."

There was a brief hesitancy on the part of the soldiers, but the man in gray nodded, and the men stood at attention. The man in gray moved promptly to Alric. He looked the prince up and down with a quizzical expression. "Your choice of dress is a bit unorthodox, is it not, Your Majesty?"

"My choice of dress is none of your concern, sir..."

"It's Baron, Your Highness, Baron Trumbul. Your Majesty is needed back at Essendon Castle. Archduke Percy Braga ordered us to find you and escort you there. He has been worried about your welfare, considering all the recent events."

"As it happens, I was heading that way. You can, therefore, please the archduke and me by providing escort."

"Wonderful, my lord. Do you travel alone?" Trumbul looked at the others still seated at the table.

"No," Alric replied, "this monk is with me, and he will be returning to Medford as well. Myron, say goodbye to those nice people and join us." Myron stood up and with a smile waved at Royce and Hadrian.

"Is that all? Just the one?" The baron glanced at the remaining two of the party.

"Yes, just the one."

"Are you certain? It was rumored you might have been captured by two men."

"My dear baron," Alric replied sternly, "I think I would remember such a thing as that. And the next time you take it upon yourself to question your king, it may be your last. It's lucky for you that I find myself in a good mood, having just eaten and being too tired to take serious offense. Now give the innkeeper a gold tenent to pay for my meal and your disruption."

No one moved for a moment, and then the baron said, "Of course, Your Majesty. Forgive my impudence." He nodded to a soldier, who pulled a coin from his purse and flipped it toward Hall. "Now, Your Highness, shall we be going?"

"Yes," Alric replied. "I hope you have a carriage for me. I have had my fill of riding, and I'm hoping to sleep the rest of the way back."

"I'm sorry, Your Majesty, we do not. We can commandeer one just as soon as we reach a village, and hopefully some better clothes for you as well."

"That will have to do, I suppose."

Alric, Myron, Trumbul, and the troops left the inn. There was a brief discussion only partially heard through the open door as they arranged mounts. Soon the sound of hooves retreated into the night.

"That was Prince Alric Essendon?" Hall asked, coming over to their table and trying to see out their window. Neither Royce nor Hadrian replied.

After Hall returned to the bar, Hadrian asked, "Do you think we should follow them?"

"Oh, don't start that. We did our good deed for this month—two, in fact, if you count DeWitt. I'm content to just sit here and relax."

Hadrian nodded and drained his mug of ale. They sat there in silence while he stared out the window, drumming his fingers restlessly on the table.

"What?"

"Did you happen to notice the weapons that patrol was wearing?"

"Why?" Royce asked, irritated.

"Well, they were wearing Tiliner rapiers instead of the standard falchion swords carried by the Medford Royal Guard. The rapiers had steel rather than iron tangs but unmarked pommels. Either the Royal Armory has upgraded their standards or those men are hired mercenaries, most likely from eastern Warric. Not exactly the kind of men you'd hire to augment a search party for a lost Royalist king. And if I'm not mistaken, Trumbul is the name of the fellow Gwen pointed out as being suspicious in The Rose and Thorn the night before the murder."

"See," Royce said, irritated, "this is the problem with these good deeds of yours; they never end."

~

The moon was rising as Arista placed the dagger on her windowsill. While it would still be some time before the moonbeams would reach it, all the other preparations were ready. She had spent all day working on the spell. In the morning, she had gathered herbs from the kitchen and garden. To find a mandrake root of just the right size had required nearly two hours. The hardest step, however, had been slipping down to the mortuary to clip a lock of hair from her father's head. By evening, she had been grinding the mixture with her mortar and pestle while she muttered the incantations needed to bind the elements. She had sprinkled the resulting finely ground powder on the stained blade and had recited the last words of the spell. All that was required now was the moonlight.

She jumped when a knock on her door startled her. "Your Highness? Arista?" the archduke called to her.

"What is it, Uncle?"

"Can I have a word with you, my dear?"

"Yes, just a minute." Arista drew the curtain shut, hiding the blade on the sill. She placed her mortar and pestle in her trunk and locked it. Dusting off her hands, she checked her hair in the mirror. She went to the door, and with a tap of her necklace, she opened it.

The archduke entered, still dressed in his black doublet, his thumbs hooked casually in his sword belt. His heavy chain of office shimmered in the firelight from Arista's hearth. He looked around her bedroom with a critical expression. "Your father never did approve of you living up here. He always wanted you down with the rest of the family. I actually think it hurt him a bit that you chose to separate yourself like this, but you have always been a solitary person, haven't you?"

"Does this visit have a point?" she asked with irritation as she took a seat on her bed.

"You seem very curt with me lately, my dear. Have I done something to offend you? You are my niece, and you did just lose your father and possibly your brother. Is it so impossible to believe I'm concerned for your welfare? That I'm worried about your state of mind? People have been known to do… unexpected things in moments of grief—or anger."

"My state of mind is fine."

"Is it?" he asked, raising an eyebrow. "You have spent most of the last few days in seclusion up here, which cannot be healthy for a young woman who has just lost her father. I would think you would want to be with your family."

"I no longer have a family," she said firmly.

"*I* am your family, Arista. I'm your uncle, but you don't want to see that, do you? You want to see me as your enemy. Perhaps that's how you deal with your grief. You spend all your time in this tower, and when you do step out of this stronghold of yours, it's only to attack me for my attempts to find your brother. I don't understand why. I have also asked myself why I've not seen you cry at the loss of your father. You two were quite close, weren't you?"

Braga moved to the dresser with the swan mirror and paused as he stepped on something. He picked up a silver-handled brush lying on the floor. "This brush is from your father. I was with him when he bought this one. He refused to have a servant select it. He personally went to the shops in Dagastan to find just the right one. I honestly think it was the highlight of the trip for him. You should take more care with things of such importance." He replaced it on the table with the other brushes.

He returned his attention to the princess. "Arista, I know you were afraid he was going to force you to marry some old, unpleasant king. I suspect the thought of being imprisoned within the invisible walls of marriage terrified you. But despite what you might have thought, he *did* love you. Why do you not cry for him?"

"I can assure you, Uncle, I'm perfectly fine. I'm just trying to keep busy."

Braga continued to move around her small room, studying it in detail. "Well, that's another thing," he said to her. "You're very busy, but you are not trying to find your father's killer? I would be, if I were you."

"Isn't that *your* job?"

"It is. I have been working continuously without sleep for days, I assure you. Much of my focus, however, as you should know, has been on finding your brother in the hopes of saving his life. I hope you can understand my priorities. You, on the other hand, seem to do little despite being the *acting queen*, as you call yourself."

"Did you come here to accuse me of being lazy?" Arista asked.

"Have you been lazy? I doubt it. I suspect you've been hard at work these last few days, perhaps weeks."

"Are you suggesting I killed my father? I ask only because *that* would be a very dangerous thing to suggest."

"I'm not suggesting anything, Your Highness. I'm merely trying to determine why you have shown so little sadness at the passing of your father and so little concern for the welfare of your brother. Tell me, dear niece, what were you doing in the oak grove this afternoon, returning with a covered basket? I also heard you were puttering around the kitchen pantry."

"You've had me followed?"

"For your own good, I assure you," he said with a warm, reassuring tone, patting her on the shoulder. "As I said, I'm concerned. I have heard stories of some who took their own lives after a loss such as yours. That's why I watch you. However, in your case, it was unnecessary, wasn't it? Taking your own life is not at all what you have been up to."

"What makes you say that?" Arista replied.

"Picking roots and pilfering herbs from the kitchen sounds more like you were working on a recipe of some kind. You know, I never approved of your father sending you to Sheridan University, much less allowing you to study under that foolish magician Arcadius. People might think you a witch. Common folk are easily frightened by what they don't understand, and the thought of their princess as a witch could be a spark that leads to a disaster. I told your father not to allow you to go to the university, but he let you leave anyway."

The archduke walked around the bed, absently smoothing her coverlets.

"Well, I'm glad my father didn't listen to you."

"Are you? I suppose so. Of course, it really didn't matter. It wasn't such a terrible thing. After all, Arcadius is harmless, isn't he? What could he teach you? Card tricks? How to remove warts? At least, that was all I thought he could teach you. But as of late, I have become . . . concerned. Perhaps he did teach you something of value. Perhaps he taught you a name . . . *Esrahaddon*?"

Arista looked up sharply and then tried to mask her surprise.

"Yes, I thought so. You wanted to know more, didn't you? You wanted to learn real magic, only Arcadius doesn't know much himself. He did, however, know someone who did. He told you about Esrahaddon, an ancient wizard of the old order who knows how to unlock the secrets of the universe and control the primordial powers of the elements. I can only imagine your delight in discovering such a wizard was imprisoned right here in your own kingdom. As princess, you have the authority to see the prisoner, but you never asked for your father's permission, did you? You were afraid he might say no. You should have asked him, Arista. If you had, he would have told you that no one is allowed in *that* prison. The church explained it all to Amrath the day of his coronation. He learned how dangerous Esrahaddon is and what he can do with innocent people like you. That monster taught you real magic, didn't he, Arista? He taught you black magic, am I right?" The archduke narrowed his eyes, his voice losing even the pretense of warmth.

Arista did not reply. She sat in silence.

"What did he teach you? I wonder. Certainly not party tricks or sleight of hand. He probably didn't show you how to call down lightning or how to split the earth, but I'm sure he taught you simple things—simple yet useful things—didn't he?"

"I have no idea what you're talking about," she said as she started to stand. Her voice betrayed a hint of fear. She wanted to put distance between the two of them. Crossing to the dressing table, she picked up a brush and began running it through her hair.

"No? Tell me, my dear, what happened to the dagger that killed your father and still bears his blood?"

"I told you I don't know anything about that." She watched him in the mirror.

"Yes, you did say that, didn't you? But somehow I find that hard to believe. You are the only person who might have a purpose for that blade—a dark purpose. A very evil purpose."

Arista whirled on him, but before she could speak, Braga

went on. "You betrayed your father. You betrayed your brother. Now you would betray me as well and with the same dagger! Did you really think me such a fool?"

Arista looked toward the window and could see, even through the heavy curtain, the moonlight had finally reached it. Braga followed her glance and a puzzled expression washed over his face. "Why does only one window have its curtains drawn?"

He turned, grabbed the drape, and threw it back, revealing the dagger bathed in moonlight. He staggered at the sight of it, and Arista knew the spell had worked its magic.

❧

They had not gone far, only a handful of miles. The traveling was slow and the lack of sleep combined with his full stomach made Alric so drowsy he feared he might fall from the saddle. Myron did not look much better, riding along behind a guard, his head drooping. They traveled down a lonely dirt lane past a few farms and over footbridges. To the left lay a harvested cornfield, where empty brown stalks were left to wither. To the right stood a dark woodland of oak and hemlock, their leaves long since scattered to the wind; their naked branches reached out over the road.

It was another cold night, and Alric swore to himself he would never take another night ride as long as he lived. He was dreaming of curling up in his own bed with a roaring fire and perhaps a warmed glass of mulled wine when the baron ordered an unexpected halt.

Trumbul and five soldiers rode up beside Alric. Two of the men dismounted and took hold of the bridles of the prince's and Myron's horses. Four additional men rode ahead, beyond

Alric's sight, while three others turned and rode back the way they had come.

"Why have we stopped?" Alric asked, yawning. "Why have the men split up?"

"It's a treacherous road, Your Majesty," Trumbul explained. "We need to take precautions. Vanguards and rear guards are necessary when escorting one such as you, during times such as these. Any number of dangers might exist out here on dark nights. Highwaymen, goblins, wolves—there's no way to know what you might come across. There's even the legend of a headless ghost that haunts this road, did you know that?"

"No I didn't," the prince said. He did not care for the casual tone the baron was suddenly taking with him.

"Oh yes, they say it's the ghost of a king who died at this very spot. Of course, he wasn't really a king, just a crown prince who might have worn the crown one day. You see, as the tale goes, the prince was returning home one night in the company of his brave soldiers when one of them took it upon himself to chop the poor bastard's head off and put it in a sack." Trumbul paused as he pulled a burlap bag off his horse and held it up to the prince. "Just like this one here."

"What are you playing at, Trumbul?" Alric inquired.

"I'm not playing at all, Your Royal High-and-Mightiness. I just realized I don't need to return you to the castle to be paid; I only need to return part of you. Your head will do fine. It saves the horse the effort of carrying you the entire way, and I have always had a fondness for horses. So whatever I can do to help them, I try to do."

Alric spurred his mount, but the man with the reins held it firmly, and the horse only pivoted sharply. Trumbul took advantage of the animal's sudden lurch and pulled the prince to the ground. Alric attempted to draw his sword, but

Trumbul kicked him in the stomach. With the wind knocked out of him, Alric doubled over in the dirt, laboring to breathe.

Trumbul then turned his attention to Myron, who sat in his saddle with a look of shock as the baron approached him.

"You look familiar," Trumbul said as he pulled Myron roughly off the horse. He held the monk's head toward the moonlight. "Oh yes, I remember. You were the not-so-helpful monk at the abbey we burned. You probably don't remember me, do you? I was wearing a helm with a visor that night. We all were. Our employer insisted that we hide our faces." He stared at the monk, who had tears welling in his eyes. "I don't know if I should kill you or not. I was originally told to spare your life so you could deliver a message to your father, but you don't seem to be heading that way. Besides, keeping you alive was related to that job, and unfortunately for you, we have already been paid for its completion. So it seems what I do is completely at my discretion."

Without warning, Myron kicked the baron in the knee with such force that it broke the baron's grip on the monk, who leapt over a fallen log and bolted into the darkness of the trees, snapping twigs and branches as he ran into the night. Screaming in pain, the baron collapsed to the ground. "Get him!" he yelled, and two soldiers chased after Myron.

A commotion erupted in the trees. Alric heard Myron's cry for help, followed by the sound of a sword drawn from a scabbard. Another scream ended as quickly as it began, cut abruptly short. The silence returned. Still holding his leg, Trumbul cursed the monk. "That will teach the little wretch!"

"You all right, Trumbul?" asked the guard holding Alric's horse.

"I'm fine, just give me a second. Damn, that little monk kicked hard."

"He won't be kicking anyone anymore," another soldier added.

The baron slowly climbed to his feet and tested his leg. He walked over to where Alric lay and drew his sword. "Grab him by the arms and hold him tight. Make sure he doesn't cause me any trouble, boys."

The guard Myron had been riding behind dismounted and took Alric's left arm while another secured his right. "Just make sure you don't hit us by accident," he said.

Trumbul grinned in the moonlight. "I never do anything by accident. If I hit you, you've done something to deserve it."

"If you kill me, my uncle will hunt you down no matter where you try to hide!"

Trumbul chuckled at the young prince. "Your uncle is the one who will pay us for your head. He wants you dead."

"What? You lie!"

"Believe what you will." The baron laughed. "Turn him over so I get a clear stroke at the back of his neck. I want a pretty trophy. I hate it when I end up having to hack and hack."

Alric struggled but the two soldiers were stronger than he was. They twisted the prince's arms behind his back, forced him to his knees, and shoved his head to the ground.

There was the sound of snapping twigs from the thick brush by the side of the road. "It took you two a long time to kill that little monk," Trumbul said. "But you got back just in time for the night's finale."

The two soldiers holding Alric twisted his arms harder to keep him from moving. The prince struggled with all his strength, screaming into the dirt. "No! Stop! You can't! Stop!" His efforts were useless. The soldiers each had a firm grip, and years of wielding swords and shields in battle had turned their arms to steel. The prince was no match for them.

Alric waited for the blow. Instead of hearing Trumbul's blade whistling through the night air, he heard an odd gurgle, then a thud. The guards loosened their hold on him. One let go entirely, and Alric heard his rapid footfalls as he sprinted away. The other hauled the prince up, holding him tightly from behind. The baron lay dead on the ground. Two men stood on either side of the body. In the darkness, Alric saw only silhouettes, but they did not match the men who had chased Myron into the trees. The one nearest the baron held a knife, which seemed to glow with an eerie radiance in the moonlight. Next to him stood a taller, broader man, who held a sword in each hand.

Again the sound of twigs snapping came from the woods nearby.

"Everyone, over here!" shouted the soldier who still shielded himself with Alric.

The two guards holding the horses dropped the reins and drew their swords. Their faces, however, betrayed their fear.

Myron climbed out of the woods and stood in the moonlight, his rapid breath forming little clouds in the cold night air.

Alric heard Royce's voice: "Your friends aren't coming. They're already dead."

The two guards wielding swords looked at each other, then raced down the road in the direction of the Silver Pitcher Inn. The last remaining soldier, holding Alric, looked around wildly. As Royce and Hadrian took a stride toward him, he cursed abruptly, let go of the prince, and bolted.

Alric could not stop shaking as he wiped the tears and dirt from his face. Hadrian and Royce helped him to his feet. He stood on wobbly legs and looked at those around him.

"They were going to kill me," he said. "They were going to *kill me*!" he screamed.

He abruptly pushed Royce and Hadrian away and, drawing his father's sword, drove it deep into the torso of the dead

Trumbul. He staggered and stood there gasping, staring at the dead body before him, his father's sword swaying back and forth, the tip buried in the baron's back.

Soon men approached from both directions of the road. Many were from the Silver Pitcher Inn and carried crude weapons. Some of them were wet with blood but none appeared injured. Two of them led the horses that Royce, Hadrian, and Alric had been using since the Wicend Ford. There was also a thin figure in tattered rags wearing a shapeless hat. He bore only a heavy stick.

"Not a single one got past us," Hall declared as he approached the small group. "One tried to duck us, but the half-breed found him. I can see now why you asked him to come. Bastard can see better than an owl in the dark."

"As promised, you can keep the horses and everything on them," Hadrian said. "But make sure you bury these bodies tonight or you might find trouble in the morning."

"Is that really the prince?" one of the men asked, staring at Alric.

"Actually," Hadrian said, "I think you are looking at the new King of Melengar."

There was a quiet murmur of interest, and a few went through the bother of bowing, although Alric did not notice. He had retrieved his sword and was now searching Trumbul's body.

The men gathered in the road to look over the captured animals, weapons, and gear. Hall took charge and began to divvy up the loot as best he could.

"Give the elf one of the horses," Royce told him.

"What?" the innkeeper asked, stunned. "You want us to give *him* a horse? Are you sure? I mean, most of these men don't have a good horse."

Drake quickly cut in. "Listen, we all fought equally tonight.

He can have a share like everyone, but that miserable filth ain't walking off with no horse."

"Don't kill him, Royce," Hadrian said hurriedly.

The prince looked up to see Drake backing up as Royce took a step toward him. The thief's face was eerily calm but his eyes smoldered.

"What does the king say?" Drake asked quickly. "I mean—he is the king and all, right? Technically, them is his horses, right? His soldiers was a ridin' 'em. We should ask him to decide—okay?"

There was a pause while Alric stood up and faced the crowd. The prince felt sick. His legs were weak, his arms hurt, and he was bleeding from scrapes on his forehead, chin, and cheek. He was covered in dirt. He had come within seconds of death and the fear from it was still with him. He noticed Hadrian move away to where Myron was. The monk was crying off to his right, and Alric knew he was a hair away from joining him, but he was the king. He clenched his teeth and looked at them. A score of dirty, blood-splattered faces looked back. He stood there unable to think clearly. His mind was still on Trumbul. He was still furious and humiliated. Alric glanced at Royce and Hadrian and then looked back at the crowd.

"Do whatever these two men tell you to do," he said slowly, clearly, coldly. "They are my royal protectors. Any man who willfully disobeys them will be executed." There was silence in the wake of his voice. In the stillness, Alric pulled himself onto his horse. "Let's go."

Hadrian and Royce exchanged looks of surprise and then mounted. The monk was quiet now and walked in a daze. Hadrian pulled Myron up behind him.

As they started down the road, Royce stopped his horse near Hall and Drake and quietly told them both, "See to it the half-breed gets a horse and keeps it, or when I return, I'll hold everyone in this hamlet accountable—and for once, it will be legal."

The four rode along in silence for some time. Finally, Alric hissed, "It was my own uncle." Despite his efforts, his eyes began to water.

"I've been thinking about that," Hadrian mentioned. "The archduke stands next in line for the throne after you and Arista. But being family, I figured he'd be just as big a target as you, only he's not a blood uncle, is he? His last name is Braga, not Essendon."

"He married my mother's sister."

"Is she alive?"

"No, she died years ago, in a fire." Alric slammed his fist on the saddle's pommel. "He taught me the blade! He showed me how to ride. He's my uncle and he is trying to kill me!"

Nothing was said for a while, and then Hadrian finally asked, "Where are we going?"

Alric shook his head as if coming out of a dream. "What? Oh, to Drondil Fields, Count Pickering's castle. He is—was—one of my father's most trusted nobles and our closest friends. He's also the most powerful leader in the kingdom. I'll raise an army from there and march on Medford within the week. And Maribor help the man, or uncle, who tries to stop me!"

⁂

"Is this what you wanted to see?" the archduke asked Arista, picking up the dagger. He held it out so she could read the name Percy Braga clearly spelled out on the blade in her father's blood. "It looks like you have indeed learned a thing or two from Esrahaddon. This, however, proves nothing. I certainly didn't stab your father with it. I wasn't even near the chapel when he was killed."

"But you ordered it. You might not have driven the dagger into his body, but you were the one responsible." Arista wiped the tears from her eyes. "He trusted you. We all trusted you. You were part of our family!"

"There are some things more important than family, my dear—secrets, terrible secrets which must remain hidden at all costs. As hard as it may be for you to believe, I do care for you, your brother, and your—"

"Don't you dare say it!" she shouted at him. "You murdered my father."

"It was necessary. If you only knew the truth, you'd understand what is truly at stake. There are reasons why your father had to die and Alric as well."

"And me?"

"Yes, I'm afraid so. But these matters must be handled delicately. One murder is not unusual, and Alric's disappearance has actually been a great help. If things had occurred the way they were planned, it would have looked much more suspicious. I suspect your brother will meet death in some quiet remote area far from here. I had originally planned for you to die accidently in an unfortunate accident, but you have provided me with a better approach. It'll be easy to convince others you hired those two thieves to kill your father and your brother. You see, I already planted the seeds that something was amiss. The night your father was killed, I had Captain Wylin and a squad of men at the ready. I'll simply explain that having failed the double murder, you sought to correct matters by freeing the killers. We have several witnesses who can attest to the arrangements you made that evening. I'll announce your trial at once and call all the nobles to court. They'll hear of your treachery, your betrayals, and your foul acts. They'll learn how education and witchcraft turned you into a power-craving murderess."

"You won't dare! If you put me before the nobles, I'll tell them the truth."

"That will be difficult, since you'll be gagged. After all"—he looked at his name glistening on the blade—"you're a witch and we can't allow you to cast spells on us. I would have your tongue cut out now except that it might look suspicious, since I haven't yet called for the trial."

Braga looked around the bedroom once more and nodded. "I was wrong. I do approve of your choice of quarters after all. I had other plans for this tower once, but now I think it will be the perfect place for you to await the trial in isolation. With the amount of time you've spent here by yourself, practicing your crafts, no one will notice a difference."

He walked out, taking the dagger with him. As he left, she saw a bearded dwarf with a hammer in hand standing outside the door. When it closed, she heard pounding and knew she had been locked in.

Chapter 7

Drondil Fields

The four rode on through most of the night. They finally stopped when Myron toppled from the horse after falling asleep behind Hadrian. Leaving the horses saddled, they slept only briefly in a thicket. Soon they were back on the road, traveling through an orchard of trees. Each plucked an apple or two and ate the sweet fruit as they rode. There was little to see until the sun rose. Then a few workers began to appear. An older man drove an oxcart filled with milk and cheese. Farther down the lane, a young girl carried a basket of eggs. Myron watched her intently as they passed by, and she looked up at him, smiling self-consciously.

"Don't stare, Myron," Hadrian told him. "They will think you're up to something."

"They are even prettier than horses," the monk remarked, glancing back repeatedly over his shoulder as the girl fell behind them.

Hadrian laughed. "Yes, they are, but I wouldn't tell *them* that."

Ahead, a hill rose, and on top of it stood a castle. The structure was nothing like Essendon Castle—it looked more like a fortress than a house of nobility.

"Drondil Fields," Alric said. The prince had barely said anything since his ordeal the night before. He did not complain about the long ride or the cold night air. Instead, he rode in silence with his eyes fixed on the path that lay ahead.

"Odd name for a castle," Hadrian mentioned.

"Brodic Essendon built it during the wars following the fall of the Steward's Reign," Myron said. "His son, Tolin the Great, finished the work, defeated Lothomad the Bald, and proclaimed himself the first king of Melengar. They fought the battle on fields that belonged to a farmer named Drondil and later this whole area became known as Drondil Fields, or so the story goes."

"Who was Lothomad?" Hadrian asked.

"He was the King of Trent. After Glenmorgan III was executed, Lothomad seized his chance and sent his armies south. Ghent and Melengar would both be part of Trent today if it wasn't for Tolin Essendon."

"That's why they called him the Great, I assume."

"Exactly."

"Nice design. The five-pointed star shape makes it impossible to find a blind wall to scale."

"It's the strongest fortress in Melengar," Alric said.

"What brought the Essendons to Medford, then?" Royce asked.

"After the wars," Myron explained, "Tolin felt it was depressing living in such a gloomy fortress. He built Essendon Castle in Medford and entrusted Galilin to his most loyal general, Seadric Pickilerinon."

"Seadric's son was the one who shortened his name to Pickering," Alric added.

Hadrian noticed a distant look on Alric's face, a melancholy smile on his lips.

"My family has always been close to the Pickerings. There's

no direct blood relation, but Mauvin, Fanen, and Denek have always been like my brothers. We almost always spend Wintertide and Summersrule with them."

"I'll bet the other nobles aren't too happy about that," Royce said. "Particularly those who actually *are* blood relatives."

Alric nodded. "Nothing has ever come of their jealousies, though. No one would dare challenge a Pickering. They have a legendary family tradition with swords. Rumor has it that Seadric learned the ancient art of Tek'chin from the last living member of the Knights of the Order of the Fauld."

"Who?" Hadrian asked.

"The way I heard it—the way Mauvin told me—was that they were a post-imperial brotherhood who tried to preserve at least part of the ancient skills of the Teshlor Knights."

"And who were they?"

"Teshlors?" Alric glanced over at him, stunned. "The Teshlors are the greatest warriors who ever lived. They once guarded the emperor himself. But I guess like everything else, their techniques were lost with the fall of the empire. Still, what Seadric learned from the Order of the Fauld, and I guess it was just a tiny fraction of what the Teshlors knew, made him a legend. That knowledge has been faithfully passed from father to son for generations, and that secret gives the Pickerings an uncanny advantage in combat."

"We are well acquainted with that little bit of trivia," Hadrian muttered. "But like I was saying, it's a nice design for a fortress, except for those trees." He gestured toward the orchard. "That grove would provide good cover for an attacking army."

"This hill never used to look like it does now," Alric explained. "It used to be cut clear. The Pickerings planted this orchard only a couple of generations ago. Same with those rosebushes and rhododendrons. Drondil Fields hasn't seen warfare in five hundred years. I suppose the counts didn't see the harm in some fruit, shade, and flowers. The great fortress of Seadric Pickilerinon is now little more than a country estate."

They came up to the entrance and Alric led them in without pausing.

"Here now, hold on there!" an overweight gate warden ordered. He was holding a pastry in one hand and a pint of milk in the other. His weapon lay at his side. "Where do you think you're all going, riding up here as if this were your fall retreat?"

Alric pulled back his hood, and the warden dropped both his pastry and milk. "I—I'm sorry, Your Highness." He stumbled, snapping to attention. "I had no idea you were coming today. No one said anything to me." He wiped his hands and brushed the crumbs from his uniform. "Is the rest of the royal family coming as well?" Alric ignored him, continuing through the gate and across the plank bridge into the castle. The others followed him without a word as the astonished warden stared after them.

Like the outside of the castle, the interior courtyard showed little resemblance to its fortress heritage. The courtyard was an attractive garden of neatly trimmed bushes and the occasional small, carefully pruned tree. Colorful banners of greens and gold hung to either side of the keep's portico, rippling in the morning breeze. The grass looked carefully tended, although it was mostly yellow now with winter dormancy. Carts and wagons, most filled with empty bushel baskets possibly used to harvest the fruit, lay beneath a green awning. A couple of apples still lay in the bottom of one of them. A stable of horses stood near a barn where cows called for their morning milking. A shaggy black and white dog gnawed a bone at the base of the fieldstone well, and a family of white ducks followed each other in a perfect line as they wandered freely, quacking merrily as they went. Castle workers scurried about their morning chores, fetching water, splitting wood, tending animals, and quite often nearly stepping on the wandering ducks.

Near a blacksmith shed, where a beefy man hammered a glowing rail of metal, two young men sparred with swords in the open yard. Each of them wore a helm and carried a small heater shield. A third sat with his back to the keep steps. He was using a slate and a bit of chalk to score the match. "Shield higher, Fanen!" the taller figure shouted.

"What about my legs?"

"I won't be going after your legs. I don't want to lower my sword and give you the advantage, but you need to keep the shield high to deflect a downstroke. That's where you're vulnerable. If I hit you hard enough and you aren't ready, I can drive you to your knees. Then what good will your legs be?"

"I'd listen to him, Fanen," Alric yelled toward the boy. "Mauvin's an ass, but he knows his parries."

"Alric!" The taller boy threw off his helm and ran to embrace the prince as he dismounted. At the sound of Alric's name, several of the servants in the courtyard looked up in surprise.

Mauvin was close to Alric in age but was taller and a good deal broader in the shoulders. He sported a head of wild dark hair and a set of dazzling white teeth, which shone as he grinned at his friend.

"What are you doing here, and by Mar, what are you dressed up as? You look frightful. Did you ride all night? And your face—did you fall?"

"I have some bad news. I need to speak to your father immediately."

"I'm not sure he's awake yet, and he is awfully cranky if you wake him early."

"This can't wait."

Mauvin stared at the prince and his grin faded. "This is no casual visit, then?"

"No, I only wish it was."

Mauvin turned toward his youngest brother and said, "Denek, go wake Father."

The boy with the slate shook his head. "I'm not going to be the one."

Mauvin started toward his brother. "Do it now!" he shouted, scaring the young boy into running for the keep.

"What is it? What's happened?" Fanen asked, dropping his own helm and shield on the grass and walking over to embrace Alric as well.

"Has any word reached you from Medford in the last several days?"

"Not that I know of," Mauvin replied, his face showing more concern now.

"No riders? No dispatches for the count?" Alric asked again.

"No, Alric, what is it?"

"My father is dead. He was murdered in the castle by a traitor."

"What!" Mauvin gasped, taking a step back. It was a reaction rather than a question.

"That's not possible!" Fanen exclaimed. "King Amrath dead? When did this happen?"

"To be honest, I'm not sure how long it has been. The days following his murder have been confusing, and I've lost track of the time. If word has yet to reach here, I suspect it hasn't been more than a few days."

All the workers stopped what they were doing and stood

around listening intently. The constant ringing of the blacksmith's hammer ceased and the only sounds in the courtyard were the distant mooing of a cow and the quacking of the ducks.

"What's this all about?" Count Pickering asked as he stepped out of the castle, holding up an arm to shield his squinting eyes from the morning's bright sun. "The boy came in panting for air and said there was an emergency out here."

The count, a slim, middle-aged man with a long, hooked nose and a well-trimmed prematurely gray beard, was dressed in a gold and purple robe pulled over his nightshirt. His wife, Belinda, came up behind him, pulling on her robe and peering out into the courtyard nervously. Hadrian took advantage of Pickering's sun-blindness to chance a long look. She was just as lovely as rumor held. The countess was several years younger than her husband, with a slender, stunning figure and long golden hair, which spilled across her shoulders in a way she would never normally show in public. Hadrian now understood why the count guarded her jealously.

"Oh my," Myron said to Hadrian as he twisted to get a better view. "I don't even think of horses when I look at her."

Hadrian dismounted and helped Myron off the horse. "I share your feelings, my friend, but trust me, that's one woman you *really* don't want to stare at."

"Alric?" the count said. "What in the world are you doing here at this hour?"

"Father, King Amrath has been murdered," Mauvin answered in a shaky voice.

Shock filled Pickering's face. He slowly lowered his arm and stared directly at the prince. "Is this true?"

Alric nodded solemnly. "Several days ago. A traitor stabbed him in the back while he was at prayer."

"Traitor? Who?"

"My uncle, the archduke and lord chancellor—Percy Braga."

~

Royce, Hadrian, and Myron followed their noses to the kitchen after Alric had left for a private meeting with Count Pickering. There they met Ella, a white-haired cook who was all too happy to provide them with a hearty breakfast in order to have first chance at any gossip. The food at Drondil Fields was far superior to the meal they had eaten at the Silver Pitcher Inn. Ella brought wave upon wave of eggs, soft powdered pastries, fresh sweet butter, steaks, bacon, biscuits, peppered potatoes, and gravy along with a jug of apple cider and an apple pie baked with maple syrup for dessert.

They ate their fill in the relative quiet of the kitchen. Hadrian repeated little more than what Alric had already revealed in the courtyard; however, he did mention that Myron had lived his life in seclusion at the monastery. Ella seemed fascinated by this and questioned the monk mercilessly on the subject. "So, you never saw a woman before today, love?" Ella asked Myron, who was finishing the last of his pie. He was eating heartily and there was a ring of apples and crust around his mouth.

"You're the first one I've ever spoken to," Myron replied as if he were boasting a great achievement.

"Really?" Ella said with a smile and feigned bashfulness. "I'm so honored. I haven't been a man's first in years." She laughed but Myron only looked at her, puzzled.

"You've a lovely home," Myron told her. "It looks very… sturdy."

She laughed again. "It's not mine, ducky, I just work here. It belongs to the nobles, like all the nice places do. Us normal folk, we lives in sheds and shacks and fights over what they throw away. We're sorta like dogs that way, aren't we? Course, I ain't complaining. The Pickerings aren't a bad lot. Not as snooty as some of the other nobles, who think the sun rises and falls because it pleases them. The count won't even have a chambermaid. He doesn't let no one help him dress neither. I've even seen him fetch water for himself more than once. He's downright daft, that one. His boys take after him too. You can see it in the way they saddle their own horses. That Fanen, why, just the other day I seen him swinging a smith's hammer. He was having Vern show him how to mend a blade. Now I asks you, how many nobles you see trying to learn the blacksmith trade? Can I get anyone another cup of cider?"

They all shook their heads and took turns yawning.

"Lenare, now she takes after her mother. They're a pair, they are. Both are pretty as a rose and smell just as sweet, but they do has their thorns. The temper those two have is frightful. The daughter is worse than the mother. She used to train with her brothers and was beating the stuffing out of Fanen until she discovered she was a lady and they don't do such things."

Myron's eyes closed and his head drooped, and suddenly the chair toppled as the monk fell over. He woke with a start and struggled to his knees. "Oh, I'm terribly sorry, I didn't mean to—"

Ella was so busy laughing she couldn't answer and simply waved her hand at him. "You've had a long night, dear," she finally managed to say. "Let me set you up in the back before that chair bucks you off again."

Myron hung his head and said quietly, "I have the same problem with horses."

❧

Alric told his story to the Pickerings over breakfast. As soon as he finished, the count shooed his sons out and called for his staff to begin arranging for a full-scale mobilization of Galilin. While Pickering dispatched orders, Alric left the great hall and began wandering through the corridors of the castle. This was the first time he had been alone since his father's death. He felt as though he was caught up in the current of a river, whisked along by the events unfolding around him. Now it was time to take control of his destiny.

Alric saw few people in the corridors. Aside from the occasional suit of armor or painting on the wall, there was little to distract his thoughts. Drondil Fields, though smaller than Essendon, felt larger due to its horizontal layout, which sprawled across the better part of the hilltop. Where Essendon Castle had several towers and lofty chambers that rose many stories high, Drondil Fields was only four stories at its tallest point. Because it was a fortress, fireproofing was essential, so the roof was made of stone rather than wood, requiring thick walls to support its weight. Because the windows were small and deep, they let in little light, which made the interior cave-like.

He remembered running through these corridors as a child, chasing Mauvin and Fanen. They had held mock battles, which the Pickerings had always won. He had always trumped them by bringing up that he would be king someday. At the age of twelve, it had been wonderful to be able to taunt a friend who had bested him with "Sure, but I'll be king. You'll have to bow to me and do as I say." The thought that in order for him to become king his father would have to die had never really occurred to him. He had no idea what being the king really meant.

I am king now.

Being king had always been something he had imagined to be far, far in the future. His father had been a strong man, and Alric had looked forward to many years as prince of the realm. Only a few months ago, at the Summersrule Festival, he and

Mauvin had made plans to go on a yearlong trip to the four corners of Apeladorn. They had wanted to visit Delgos, Calis, and Trent and even planned to seek the location of the fabled ruined city of Percepliquis. To discover and explore the ancient capital of the Old Novronian Empire had been a childhood dream of theirs. They wanted to find fortune and adventure in the lost city. Mauvin hoped to discover the rest of the lost arts of the Teshlor Knights, and Alric was going to find the ancient crown of Novron. While they had mentioned the trip to their fathers, neither one had brought up Percepliquis. It hardly mattered, given that no one knew where the lost city was, but it was considered heresy even to search for the ancient capital of the Old Empire. Still, walking the fabled halls of Percepliquis was probably the boyhood dream of every youth in Apeladorn. For Alric, though, his adolescence was over.

I am king now.

Dreams of endless days of reckless adventures, exploring the frontier while drinking bad ale, sleeping beneath the open sky, and loving nameless women, blew away like smoke in the wind. In their place came visions of stone rooms filled with old men with angry faces. He had only occasionally watched his father hold court, listening while the clergy and the nobles demanded fewer taxes and more land. One earl had even demanded the execution of a duke and the custody of his lands for the loss of one of his prized cows. Alric's father sat, in what Alric felt must have been dull misery, as the court secretary read the many petitions and grievances on which the king was required to rule. As a child, Alric had thought being king meant doing whatever he wished. But over the years, he saw what it really meant—compromise and appeasement. A king could not rule without the support of his nobles and the nobles were never happy. They always wanted something and expected the king to deliver.

I am king now.

To Alric, being king felt like a prison sentence. He would spend the rest of his life in service to his people, his nobles, and his family, just as his father had done. He wondered if Amrath had felt the same way when his own father had died. It was something he had never considered before. Amrath as a man and the dreams he might have sacrificed were foreign concepts to the young prince. He wondered if his father had been happy. When Alric remembered him, the images that came to mind were his bushy beard and bright smiling eyes. His father had smiled a great deal. Alric wondered if it was due to his enjoyment of being king or because being with his son gave him a much-needed break from the affairs of state. Alric felt a sudden longing to see his father once more. He wished he had taken time to sit and talk with him, man to man, to ask for his father's council and guidance in preparation for this day. He felt completely alone and uncertain about whether he could live up to the tasks that lay before him. More than anything, he just wished he could disappear.

❧

The shrill ring of clashing metal awakened Hadrian. After Ella's breakfast, he had wandered into the courtyard. The weather was turning distinctly colder but he found a place to nap on a soft patch of lawn that caught the full face of the sun. He thought he had closed his eyes for only a moment, but when he opened them again, it was well past noon. Across the yard the Pickering boys were back at sparring.

"Come at me again, Fanen," Mauvin ordered, his voice muffled by his helm.

"Why? You're just going to whack me again!"

"You have to learn."

"I don't see why," Fanen protested. "It's not like I'm planning a life in the soldiery or the tournaments. I'm the second son. I'll end up at some monastery stacking books."

"Second sons don't go to abbeys; third sons do." Mauvin lifted his visor to grin at Denek. "Second sons are the spares. You've got to be trained and ready in case I die from some rare disease. If I don't, you'll get to roam the lands, fending for yourself. That means a life as a mercenary or on the tournament circuit. Or if you are lucky, you'll land a post as a sheriff, a marshal, or master-at-arms for some earl or duke. These days, it's almost as good as a landed title, really. Still, you won't get those jobs, or last long as a merc or swordsman, unless you know how to fight. Now come at me again and this time pivot, step, and lunge."

Hadrian walked over to where the boys were fighting and sat on the grass near Denek to watch. Denek, who was only twelve years old, glanced at him curiously. "Who are you?"

"My name is Hadrian," he replied as he extended his hand. The boy shook it, squeezing harder than was necessary. "You're Denek, right? The Pickerings' third son? Perhaps you should speak with my friend Myron, seeing as how I hear you are monastery-bound."

"Am not!" he shouted. "Going to the monastery, I mean. I can fight as well as Fanen."

"I wouldn't be surprised," Hadrian said. "Fanen is flat-footed, and his balance is off. He's not going to improve much either, because Mauvin is teaching him, and Mauvin is favoring his right and rocks back on his left too much."

Denek grinned at Hadrian and then turned to his brothers. "Hadrian says you both fight like girls!"

"What's that?" Mauvin said, whacking aside Fanen's loose attack once more.

"Oh, ah, nothing," Hadrian said, trying to recant, and

glared at Denek, who just kept grinning. “Thanks a lot,” he told the boy.

“So, you think you can beat me in a duel?” Mauvin asked.

“No, it’s not that. I was just explaining I didn’t think Denek here would have to go to the monastery.”

“Because we fight like girls,” Fanen added.

“No, no, nothing like that.”

“Give him your sword,” Mauvin told Fanen.

Fanen threw his sword at Hadrian. It dove point down in the sod not more than a foot before his feet. The hilt swayed back and forth like a rocking horse.

“You’re one of the thieves Alric told us about, aren’t you?” Mauvin swiped his sword deftly through the air in a skillful manner that he had not used in his mock battles with his brother. “Despite this great adventure you all have been on, I don’t recall Alric mentioning your great prowess with a blade.”

“Well, he probably just forgot,” Hadrian joked.

“Are you aware of the legend of the Pickerings?”

“Your family is known to be skillful with swords.”

“So you *have* heard? My father is the second-best swordsman in Avryn.”

“He’s the best,” Denek snapped. “He would have beaten the archduke if he had his sword, but he had to use a substitute, which was too heavy and awkward.”

“Denek, how many times do I have to tell you, when speaking of one’s reputation, it does not boost your position to make excuses when you lose a contest. The archduke won the match. You need to face that fact,” Mauvin admonished. Turning his attention back to Hadrian, he said, “Speaking of contests, why don’t you pick up that blade, and I’ll demonstrate the Tek’chin for you.”

Hadrian picked up the sword and stepped into the dirt ring

where the boys had been fighting. He made a feint, followed by a stab, which Mauvin easily deflected.

"Try again," Mauvin said.

Hadrian tried a slightly more sophisticated move. This time he swung right and then pivoted left and cut upward toward Mauvin's thigh. Mauvin moved with keen precision. He anticipated the feint and knocked the blade away once more.

"You fight like a street thug," Mauvin commented.

"Because that's what he is," Royce assured them as he approached from the direction of the keep, "a big, dumb street thug. I once saw an old woman batter him senseless with a butter churn." He shifted his attention to Hadrian. "*Now* what have you gotten yourself into? Looks like this kid will hand you a beating."

Mauvin stiffened and glared at Royce. "I would remind you that I'm a count's son, and as such, you will refer to me as *lord*, or at least *master*, but not *kid*."

"Better watch out, Royce, or he'll be after you next," Hadrian said, moving around the circle, looking for an opening. He tried another attack but that, too, was blocked.

Mauvin moved in now with a rapid step. He caught Hadrian's sword hilt-to-hilt, placed a leg behind him, and threw Hadrian to the ground.

"You're too good for me," Hadrian conceded as Mauvin held out a hand to help him to his feet.

"Try him again," Royce shouted.

Hadrian gave him an irritated look and then noticed a young woman entering the courtyard. It was Lenare. She wore a long gown of soft gold, which nearly matched her hair. She was as lovely as her mother and walked over to join the group.

"Who is this?" she asked, motioning at Hadrian.

"Hadrian Blackwater," he said with a bow.

"Well, Mr. Blackwater, it appears my brother has beaten you."

"It would appear so," Hadrian acknowledged, still dusting himself off.

"It's nothing to be ashamed of. My brother is a very accomplished swordsman—too accomplished, in fact. He has a nasty tendency to chase away any would-be suitors."

"They are not worthy of you, Lenare," Mauvin said.

"Try him again," Royce repeated. There was a perceptible note of mischief in his voice.

"Shall we?" Mauvin asked politely with a bow.

"Oh, please do," Lenare bade him, clapping her hands in delight. "Don't be afraid. He won't kill you. Father doesn't like them to actually hurt anyone."

With an evil smirk directed toward Royce, Hadrian turned to face Mauvin. This time he made no attempt to defend himself. He stood perfectly still, holding his blade low. His gaze was cool and he stared directly into Mauvin's eyes.

"Put up a guard, you fool," Mauvin told him. "At least *try* to defend yourself."

Hadrian raised his sword slowly, more in response to Mauvin's request than as a move to defend. Mauvin stepped in with a quick flick of his blade designed to set Hadrian off his footing. He then pivoted around behind the larger man and sought to trip him up once more. Hadrian, however, also pivoted and, swinging a leg, caught Mauvin behind the knees, dropping him to the dirt.

Mauvin looked curiously at Hadrian as he helped him to his feet. "Our street thug has some surprises, I see," Mauvin muttered with a smile.

This time, Mauvin struck at Hadrian in a fast set of sweeping attacks, most of which never caught anything but air as

Hadrian avoided the strokes. Mauvin moved in a flurry, his blade traveling faster than the eye could follow. The steel rang now as Hadrian caught the strokes with his blade, parrying them aside.

"Mauvin, be careful!" Lenare shouted.

The battle rapidly escalated from friendly sparring to serious combat. The strokes moved faster, harder, and closer. The shrill ring of the blades began to echo off the courtyard walls. The grunts and curses became grimmer. The match went on for some time, the two fighting toe to toe. Suddenly Mauvin executed a brilliant maneuver. Feinting left, he swung right, following through the stroke and spinning fully around, exposing his back to Hadrian. Seeing his opponent vulnerable, Hadrian made the obvious riposte, but Mauvin miraculously caught his blade instinctively without seeing it. Pivoting again, Mauvin brought his own sword to Hadrian's undefended side. Before he could finish the blow, however, Hadrian closed the distance between them and Mauvin's swing ran behind the larger man's back. Hadrian trapped the boy's sword arm under his own and raised his sword to the boy's throat. There was a gasp from Mauvin's siblings. Royce simply chuckled with sinister relish. Releasing his grip, Hadrian set Mauvin free.

"How did you do that?" Mauvin asked. "I performed a flawless Vi'shin Flurry against you. It's one of the most advanced maneuvers of the Tek'chin. No one has ever countered it before."

Hadrian shrugged. "First time for everything." He threw the sword back toward Fanen. It pierced the earth between the boy's feet. Unlike the previous time, it dove in edge first, so the hilt did not swing.

With his eyes on Hadrian and an expression of awe on his

face, Denek turned to Royce and said, "That must have been an awfully wicked old lady and a big butter churn."

ര

"Alric?"

The prince had wandered into one of the castle storerooms and was sitting on the thick sill of a barrel-vaulted window, looking out at the western hills. The sound of his friend's voice roused him from deep thoughts, and it was not until then that he realized he was crying.

"Sorry," Mauvin said, "but Father's been looking for you. The local nobles have started to arrive, and I think he wants you to talk to them."

"It's okay," Alric said, wiping his cheeks and glancing longingly once more out the window at the setting sun. "I've been here longer than I thought. I guess I lost track of the time."

"It's easy to do in here." Mauvin walked around the room and took a bottle of wine out of a crate. "Remember the night we snuck down here and drank three of these?"

Alric nodded. "I was really sick."

"So was I, and yet we still managed to make the stag hunt the next day."

"We couldn't let anyone know we were drinking."

"I thought I was going to die, and when we got back, it turned out Arista, Lenare, and Fanen had already turned us in the night before."

"I remember."

Mauvin studied his friend carefully. "You'll make a good king, Alric. And I'm sure your father would be proud."

Alric did not say anything for a moment. He picked up a bottle from the crate and felt its weight in his hand. "I'd better get back. I have responsibilities now. I can't hide down here drinking wine like the old days."

"I suppose we could if you really wanted to." Mauvin grinned devilishly.

Alric smiled and threw his arms around him. "You're a good friend. I'm sorry we'll never get to Percepliquis now."

"It's all right; besides, you never know. We might get there someday."

As they left the storeroom, Alric dusted off his hands dirt that he had picked up from Mauvin's back during their embrace. "Is Fanen getting so good now that he was able to put you in the dirt?"

"No, it was the thief you brought with you, the big one. Where did you find him? His skill at sword fighting is unlike anything I've ever seen. It's actually rather remarkable."

"Really? Coming from a Pickering, that's high praise indeed."

"I'm afraid the Pickering legend won't last long at this rate: Father loses to Percy Braga, and now I get thrown in the dirt by a common ruffian. How long will it be before we are being challenged for our land and title by the other nobles without fear?"

"If your father had his sword that day..." Alric paused. "Why didn't your father have his sword?"

"Misplaced it," Mauvin said. "He was certain it was in his room, but the next morning, it was gone. A steward found it later the same day laying somewhere strange."

"Well, sword or no, I can tell you, Mauvin, I think your father is still the best swordsman in the kingdom."

༄

Royce, Hadrian, and Myron continued to enjoy the hospitality of the Pickerings with a hearty lunch as well as supper served to them in the warm comfort of Ella's kitchen. They spent most of the day napping, recovering lost sleep from the previous days. By nightfall, they were beginning to feel like themselves again.

Hadrian had a newfound shadow as Denek followed him wherever he went. After supper, Denek asked Hadrian, Royce, and Myron to come watch the marshaling of the troops from one of his favorite spots. The boy led them to the parapet above the main gate. From there, they could see both the grounds outside the castle and inside the courtyard without being underfoot.

Around early evening people began to arrive. Small groups of knights, barons, squires, soldiers, and village officials trickled in and formed camps outside the castle. Tall poles bearing the banners of various noble houses stood in the courtyard, signaling their presence in accordance with their sworn duty. By moonrise, eight standards and about three hundred men gathered in camps around bonfires. Their tents littered the hillside and extended throughout the orchards.

Vern, along with five other blacksmiths from various villages, worked late, sharing his forge and anvil. They were hammering out last-minute requests. The rest of the courtyard was equally active, with every lamp lit and each shop busy. Leatherworkers adjusted saddle stirrups and helms. Fletchers fashioned bundles of arrows, which they stacked like cordwood against the stable wall. Woodcutters created large rectangular archer shields. Even the butchers and bakers worked hard, preparing sack meals from smoked meats, breads, onions, and turnips.

"The green one with the hammer on it is Lord Jerl's banner," Denek told them. The weather had turned sharply cold again, and his breath created a frosty fog. "I spent a summer at their estate two years ago. It's right on the edge of the

Longwood Forest, and they love to hunt. They must have two dozen of the realm's best hounds. It's where I learned to shoot a bow. I bet you know how to shoot a bow real well, don't you, Hadrian?"

"I've been known to hit the forest from the field on occasion."

"I bet you could outshoot any of Jerl's sons. He's got six, and they all think they are the best marksmen in the province. My father never taught us archery. He said it didn't make sense because we would never be fighting in ranks. He taught us to concentrate on the sword. Although I don't know what good it will do me if I'm sent to a monastery. I'll be stuck doing nothing but reading all day."

"Actually, there is a great deal more than that to do in an abbey," Myron explained, pulling the blanket around his shoulders tighter. "In spring, most of your time will be spent gardening, and in autumn, there is the harvest, preserving, and brewing. Even in winter, there is the mending and cleaning. Of course the bulk of your time is spent in prayer, either communal in the chapel or silently in the cloister. Then there is—"

"I think I'd rather be a foot soldier," Denek sighed with a grimace. "Or maybe I could join you two and become a thief! It must be a wonderfully exciting life running all over the world, accomplishing dangerous missions for king and country."

"You'd think that, wouldn't you?" Hadrian muttered softly.

Below them, a single rider quickly approached the front gate.

"Isn't that the banner of Essendon?" Royce asked, pointing to the falcon flag the rider carried.

"Yeah," Denek said, surprised. "It's the king's standard. He's a messenger from Medford."

They looked at each other, puzzled, as the messenger entered the castle and did not reemerge. They went on talking with Myron, who was trying in vain to convince Denek life in the monastery was not bad at all, when Fanen came running up the parapet.

"There you are!" he shouted at them. "Father has half the castle turned out looking for you."

"Us?" Hadrian asked.

"Yes." Fanen nodded. "He wants to see the two thieves in his chambers right away."

"You didn't steal the silver or anything, did you, Royce?" Hadrian asked.

"I would bet it has more to do with your flirting with Lenare this afternoon and threatening Mauvin just to show off," Royce retorted.

"That was your fault," Hadrian said, jabbing his finger at him.

"It's nothing like that," Fanen said, interrupting them. "The princess Arista is going to be executed for treason tomorrow morning!"

Once, long ago, the great hall of Drondil Fields had been the site of the first court of Melengar. It was there that King Tolin had drafted and signed the Drondil Charter, officially bringing the kingdom into existence. Now, old and faded, the parchment was mounted on one wall in a place of honor. Around it, massive burgundy drapes hung, tied back by gold cords with silken tassels. Today the hall served as the council chambers of Count Pickering; Royce and Hadrian hesitantly entered the hall.

At a long table in the center of the room sat a dozen men

dressed in the finery of nobles. Hadrian recognized most of the men and could make some good guesses at the identities of those he did not know. There were earls, barons, sheriffs, and marshals; the leadership of eastern Melengar sat assembled before them. At the head of the table was Alric, and at his right was Count Pickering. Standing behind the count was Mauvin, and as Hadrian and Royce entered, Fanen took up position next to his brother. Alric was dressed in fine clothes, no doubt borrowed from one of the Pickerings. Less than a day had passed since Hadrian had last seen the prince, but Alric looked much older than he remembered.

"Have you told them why they were summoned?" Count Pickering asked his son.

"I told them the princess was to be executed," Fanen replied. "Nothing more."

"I've been summoned by Archduke Percy Braga," Count Pickering explained, holding up the dispatch, "to report to Essendon Castle as witness for the immediate trial of Princess Arista on the grounds of witchcraft, high treason, and murder. He has accused her of killing not only Amrath but also Alric." He dropped the dispatch on the table and slammed his hand down on it in disgust. "The blackguard means to have the kingdom for his own!"

"It's worse than I feared." Alric summarized for the thieves: "My uncle planned to kill me and my father and then blame both murders on Arista. He will execute her and take the kingdom for himself. No one will be the wiser. He'll fool everyone into thinking he is the great defender of the realm. I'm sure his plan will work. Even I was suspecting her only a few days ago."

"It's true. It has long been rumored that Arista has dabbled in the arcane arts," Pickering confirmed. "Braga will have no trouble finding her guilty. People are afraid of what they don't understand. The thought of a woman with magical powers is terrifying to old men in comfortable positions. Even without the fear of witchery, most nobles are uncomfortable with the thought of a woman monarch. The verdict will be assured. Her sentence will be handed down quickly."

"But if the prince was to arrive," Baron Enild said, "and show he's alive, then—"

"That's exactly what Braga wants," Sir Ecton declared. "He can't find Alric. He's searched for days and couldn't locate him. He wants to draw him out before Alric has a chance to gather an army against him. He's counting on the prince's youth and lack of experience. He wants to manipulate the prince to react with emotion instead of reason. If he can't find Alric, he will lure the prince to him."

"Less than half our forces have mustered so far," Pickering grumbled despairingly. He walked to the great map of Melengar, which hung opposite the ancient charter, and slapped the western half of the map. "Our most powerful knights are the farthest from here, and because they have the most men to rally, it will take them longer to report. I don't expect them for another eight hours, maybe as long as sixteen.

"Even if we resign ourselves to employing only Galilin's forces, the earliest we could be ready to attack wouldn't be until tomorrow evening. By then Arista will be dead. I could march with what troops I have, leaving orders for the others to follow, but doing so would risk the whole army by dividing our forces. We cannot jeopardize the realm for the sake of one woman, even though she is the princess."

"Judging from the mercenaries we encountered at the inn," Alric told them, "I suspect the archduke anticipates an assault and has strengthened his forces with purchased arms loyal only to him."

"He will likely have scouts and ambushes prepared," Ecton

said. "At first sight of our march, he will tell the other nobles assembled for the trial that we are working for Arista and that they need to defend Essendon against us. There is simply no way for us to march until we have more forces."

"Waiting," Alric said sadly, "will surely see Arista burned at the stake. Now, more than ever, I feel guilty for not trusting her. She saved my life. Now hers is in jeopardy, and there is little I can do about it." He looked at Hadrian and Royce. "I can't simply sit idly by and let her die. But to act prematurely would be folly."

The prince stood and walked over to the thieves. "I have inquired about you two since we arrived. You've been holding out on me. I thought you were common thieves. So imagine my surprise when I discovered you two are famous." He glanced around at the other nobles in the room. "Rumor has it you two are unusually gifted agents known for taking difficult, sometimes nearly impossible, assignments of sabotage, theft, espionage, and even, on rare occasions, assassinations. Don't bother denying it. Many in this room have already confided in me that they have used your services in the past."

Hadrian looked at Royce and then around at the faces of the men before them. He nodded uncomfortably. Not only were some of the men past clients, some had been targets as well.

"They tell me you are independents and are not aligned with any established guilds. It's no small feat to operate with such autonomy. I have learned more in a few hours from them than I did after days riding with you. What I do know, however—what I discovered for myself—is that you saved my life twice, once to honor a promise to my sister and once for no reason I can discern. Last night, you challenged the might of the Lord Chancellor of Melengar and came to my aid against a superior force of trained killers. No one asked you to, no one would have faulted you for letting me die. You could expect no reward for saving me, and yet you did it. Why?"

Hadrian looked at Royce, who stood silent. "Well," he began as he glanced at the floor, "I guess—we'd just grown kind of fond of you, I suppose."

Alric smiled and addressed the room. "The life of the Prince of Melengar—the would-be king—was saved, not by his army, not by his loyal bodyguards, nor by a grand fortress—but by two treacherous, impudent thieves who didn't have the good sense to ride away."

The prince stepped forward and placed a hand on each of their shoulders. "I'm already deeply in your debt and have no right to ask, but I must beg you now to display the same poor judgment once again. Please save my sister and you can name whatever price you wish."

"Another last-minute, good-deed job," Royce grumbled as he stuffed supplies into his saddlebag.

"True," Hadrian said, slinging his sword belt over his shoulder, "but this is at least a *paying* job."

"You should have told him the real reason we saved him from Trumbul—because we wouldn't see the hundred tenents otherwise."

"That was *your* reason. Besides, how often do we get to do royal contracts? If word gets around, we'll be able to command top salaries."

"If word gets around, we'll be hanged."

"Okay, good point. But remember, she did save our skins. If Arista hadn't helped us out of the dungeon, we'd be ornaments for the Medford Autumn Festival right now."

Royce paused and sighed. "I didn't say we weren't doing it,

did I? Did I say that? No I didn't. I told the little prince we'd do it. Just don't expect me to be happy about it."

"I just want to make you feel better about your decision," Hadrian said. Royce glared at him. "Okay, okay, I'll see about the horses now." He grabbed his gear and headed for the courtyard, where a light snow was starting to fall.

Pickering had provided the thieves with two of his swiftest stallions and any supplies they thought they might need. Ella had a late-night snack and a sizable travel meal prepared for them. They took heavy woolen cloaks to brace against the cold and dark scarves that they wrapped around the lower half of their faces to keep the chill of the wind off their cheeks.

"I hope we will meet again soon," Myron told them as they prepared their mounts. "You two are the most fascinating people I have ever met, although I suppose that isn't saying a lot, is it?"

"It's the thought that counts," Hadrian told him, and gave the monk a bear hug, which caught the little man by surprise. As they climbed into their saddles, Myron bowed his head and muttered a soft prayer.

"There," Hadrian told Royce, "we've got Maribor on our side. Now you can relax."

"Actually," Myron said sheepishly, "I was praying for the horses. But I *will* pray for you as well," he added hastily.

Alric and the Pickerings came out to the courtyard to see them off. Even Lenare joined them, wrapped in a white fur cape. The fluffy muffler was wrapped so high on her shoulders that it hid the lower portion of her face. Only her eyes could be seen.

"If you can't get her out," Pickering said, "try to stall the execution until our forces can arrive. Once they do, however, you'd better have her secured. I'm certain Braga will kill her out of desperation. Oh, and one more thing: don't try to fight

Braga. He's the best swordsman in Melengar. Leave him for me." The count slapped the elegant rapier he wore at his side. "This time I'll have my own sword, and the archduke will feel its sting."

"I'll be leading the attack on Essendon," Alric informed them. "It's my duty as ruler. So if you do reach my sister and if I should fall before the end of this, let her know I'm sorry for not trusting her. Let her know..." He faltered for a moment. "Let her know I loved her and I think she will make a fine queen."

"You'll tell her yourself, Your Majesty," Hadrian assured him.

Alric nodded and then added, "And I'm sorry about what I said to you before. You two are the best royal protectors I could ever hope for. Now go. Save my sister or I'll have you both thrown back in my dungeon!"

They bowed respectfully in their saddles, then turned their horses and urged them into a gallop. They rode out the gate into the cold black of night.

Chapter 8

Trials

The morning of Arista Essendon's trial arrived along with the first snow. Despite not having slept, Percy Braga did not feel the least bit tired. Having set the wheels in motion the previous morning by sending the trial announcements, he had a hundred details demanding his personal attention. He was just rechecking his witness list when there was a knock at the door to his office and a servant entered.

"I'm sorry to disturb you, sir," the man said with a bow. "Bishop Saldur is here. He told me you wanted to see him?"

"Of course, of course, send him in," the archduke replied.

The elderly cleric entered, wearing his dress robes of black and red. Braga crossed the room and kissed his ring as he bowed. "Thank you for seeing me so early, Your Grace. Are you hungry? May I arrange for some breakfast?"

"No, thank you, I've already eaten. At my age, one tends to wake early whether one wants to or not. What exactly did you want to see me about?"

"I just wanted to make sure you didn't have any questions about your testimony today. We could go over it now if you do. I've scheduled some time."

"Ah, I see," the bishop replied, nodding slowly. "I don't

think that will be necessary. I have a clear understanding of what is required."

"Wonderful, then I think everything is in order."

"Excellent," the bishop said, and glanced toward the decanter. "Is that brandy I see?"

"Yes, would you like some?"

"Normally I wouldn't indulge so early, but this is a special occasion."

"Absolutely, Your Grace."

The bishop took a seat near the fire as Braga poured two glasses of brandy and handed one to him. "To the new Melengar regime," the archduke proposed. The crystal rang clear, like a bell, as their glasses touched. Then each took a deep drink.

"There's just something about a bit of brandy on a snowy day," Saldur remarked with a tone of satisfaction in his voice. The cleric had white hair and gentle-looking eyes. Sitting in the glow of the fire, casually cupping the glass in his wrinkled hand, he appeared the quintessential kindhearted grandfather. Braga knew better. He could not have risen to his present position without being ruthless. As bishop, Saldur was one of the chief officers of the Nyphron Church and the ranking clergy in the kingdom of Melengar. He worked and resided in the great Mares Cathedral, an edifice just as imposing as, and certainly more beloved than, Essendon Castle. As far as influence was concerned, Braga estimated that of the nineteen bishops who comprised the leadership of the faithful, Saldur must be in the top three.

"How long before the trial?" Saldur asked.

"We'll begin in about an hour or so."

"I must say, you've handled this very well, Percy." Saldur smiled at him. "The church is quite pleased. Our investment in you was substantial, but it would appear we made a wise choice. When dealing with timetables as long as we are, it's difficult to be sure we've put the right people in place. Each of these annexations needs to be handled delicately. We don't want anyone suspecting us of stacking the deck the way we are. When the time comes, it has to appear as if all the monarchies voluntarily accept the formation of the New Empire. I must admit, I had some doubts about you."

Braga raised an eyebrow. "I'm surprised to hear you say that."

"Well, you didn't look as though you had the makings of a king when we arranged your marriage to Amrath's sister. You were a scrawny, pretentious, little—"

"That was nearly twenty years ago," Braga protested.

"True enough. However, at the time, all I noticed about you was your skill with a sword and your staunch Imperialist view. I was afraid that being so young, you might—well, who knew if you'd stay loyal? But you proved me wrong. You've grown into an able administrator, and your ability to adapt in the face of unexpected events, like this sudden timetable shift Arista caused, proves your capability to manage problems effectively."

"Well, I'll admit it hasn't gone exactly as I planned. Alric's escape was unexpected. I clearly underestimated the princess, but at least she was good enough to provide me a convenient means to implicate her."

"So, exactly what are you planning to do about Arista's little brother? Do you know where he is?"

"Yes, he is at Drondil Fields. I have several reports of the mustering of Galilin. Troops are converging at Pickering's castle."

"And you're not concerned about that?"

"Let's just say I wish I could have caught the little brat before he reached Pickering. But I'll be turning my attentions to him as soon as I conclude with his sister. I hope to take care of him before he can bolster too much support. He's been quite elusive. He slipped through my fingers at the Wicend Ford. Not only did he escape but he also took horses from my men. I thought he would be easy to find, and I had scores of troops watching every road, valley, and village, but for several days he just vanished."

"And that's when he got through to Pickering?"

"Oh, no," Braga said. "I actually managed to catch him. A patrol picked him up at the Silver Pitcher Inn."

"Then I don't understand. Why isn't he here?"

"Because my patrol never came back. An advance rider brought the news Alric was captured, but the rest of them disappeared. I investigated and heard some amazing rumors. According to my reports, two men traveling with the prince organized the locals and staged an ambush on the men bringing Alric in."

"Do you know who these two men were who came to Alric's aid?"

"I have no names, but the prince called them his royal protectors. I'm certain, however, they're the same two thieves I set up to take the blame for Amrath's death. Somehow, the prince has managed to retain their services. He must have offered them riches, perhaps even land and title. The boy is more clever than I thought. But no matter, I have made adequate arrangements for him and his friends. I've been bolstering the ranks of the Melengar army for the last several weeks with mercenaries loyal to my money. Amrath never knew. One of the perks of being the lord chancellor is not having to get the royal seal on all orders."

There was another knock at the door, and the servant once again entered. "The Earl of Chadwick is here to see you, my lord."

"Archibald Ballentyne? What is he doing here? Get rid of him."

"No, wait," the bishop said, intervening. "I asked the earl to come. Please send him in." The servant bowed and left, closing the door behind him.

"I wish you had discussed this with me," Braga said. "Forgive me, Your Grace, but I have too much going on today to entertain a visit from a neighboring noble."

"Yes, yes. I know you are quite busy, but the church has its own matters to attend to. As you well know, you're not the only kingdom we administer to. The Earl of Chadwick possesses a certain interest to us. He is young, ambitious, and easily impressed by success. It will do him good to see firsthand just what kinds of things are possible with the right *friends*. Besides, having an ally on your southern border has benefits for you as well."

"Are you suggesting I try and sway him away from King Ethelred?"

"Ethelred is a good Imperialist, I admit, but there can be only one emperor. There's no reason it couldn't be you, assuming you continue to prove yourself worthy. Ballentyne has many assets that could help in that endeavor."

"I'm not even king yet and you're talking emperor?"

"The church hasn't lasted for three thousand years by not thinking ahead. Ah, here he is. Come in, come in, Archibald." Archibald Ballentyne entered, brushing the snow from his cloak and stomping his feet. "Toss your cloak aside and come to the fire. Warm up, lad. The carriage ride must have been a cold one."

Archibald crossed the room and kissed the ring of the still seated bishop. "Good morning, Your Grace," he said, then turned and bowed graciously to the archduke. "My lord."

He swept off his cloak and shook it out carefully. Perplexed, he looked around. "Your servant left before taking my cloak."

"Just throw it anywhere," Braga instructed.

The earl looked at him, aghast. "This is imported damask with gold thread embroideries." Just then, the servant reentered with a large comfortable chair. "Ah, there you are. Here, take this, and for Maribor's sake, don't hang it from a peg." He passed his cloak to the servant, who bowed and left.

"Brandy?" Braga asked.

"Oh, good lord, yes," Archibald replied. Braga handed him a glass, the bottom of which was filled with a smoky amber liquid.

"I appreciate your coming, Archibald," the bishop said. "I'm afraid we won't have much time to talk just now; there is quite a bit of turmoil in Melengar today. But as I was telling Braga, I thought it might be beneficial for the three of us to have a quick chat."

"I'm always at your service, of course, Your Grace. I appreciate any opportunity to meet with you and the new King of Melengar," Archibald said nonchalantly. Saldur and Braga exchanged looks. "Oh, come now, it can hardly be a secret. You are the archduke and lord chancellor. With King Amrath and the prince dead, if you execute Arista, you'll wear the crown. It's really rather nicely done. I commend you. Murder in broad daylight, right before the nobles—they'll cheer you on as you steal their crown."

Braga stiffened. "Are you accusing me of—"

"Of course not," the earl said, stopping him. "I accuse no one. What care do I have for the affairs of Melengar? My liege is Ethelred of Warric. What happens in your kingdom is none of my affair. I was merely offering my *sincere* congratulations"—he raised his glass and nodded at the bishop—"to both of you."

"Do you have a name for this game, Ballentyne?" Braga asked tentatively as both he and Saldur watched the young earl closely.

Archibald smiled again. "My dear gentlemen, I'm playing no game. I'm being truthful when I say I'm simply in awe. All the more because of my own recent failure. You see, I tried a gamble myself, to increase my station, only it was less than successful."

Braga became quite amused with this primly dressed earl. He understood what the bishop saw in him and he was curious now. "I'm very sorry to hear you suffered difficulties. Exactly what were you attempting?"

"Well, I acquired some letters and tried to blackmail the Marquis of Glouston into marrying his daughter to me so I could obtain his Rilan Valley. I had the messages locked in my safe in my private tower and was prepared to present them to Victor in person. Everything was perfect but—*poof*." Archibald made an exploding gesture with his fingers. "The letters vanished. Like a magic trick."

"What happened to them?" Saldur asked.

"They were stolen. Thieves sawed a hole in the roof of my tower and, in just a matter of minutes, slipped in and snatched them from underneath my very nose."

"Impressive," Saldur said.

"Depressing is what it was. They made me look like a fool."

"Did you catch the thieves?" Braga asked.

Archibald shook his head. "Sadly, no, but I finally figured out who they are. It took me days to reason it out. I did not tell anyone I possessed those letters. So the only ones who could have taken them are the same thieves which I hired in the first place. Cunning devils. They call themselves Riyria. I'm not sure why they stole them; perhaps they planned to charge me twice, but I won't give them the satisfaction, of course. I'll hire someone else to intercept the next set from the Winds Abbey."

"So, the letters you had were correspondences between the Marquis of Glouston and King Amrath?" Saldur asked.

Archibald looked at the bishop, surprised. "Interesting

guess, Your Grace. No, they were love letters between his daughter and her Nationalist lover, Gaunt. I planned to have Alenda marry me instead to spare Victor the embarrassment of his daughter being involved with a commoner."

Saldur chuckled.

"Have I said something funny?"

"You had more in your hands than you knew," Saldur informed him. "Those weren't love letters, and they weren't to Degan Gaunt."

"With all due respect, Your Grace, I had the letters in my possession. They were addressed to him."

"I'm sure they were, but that was merely a precaution against someone like you discovering them. It was quite clever, actually. It makes a fine diversion should someone intercept the letters. Degan Gaunt as a lover, I suspect, is meant to represent Lanaklin's desire for revolution against Ethelred. If the marquis stated his opinions openly, he would risk execution. Those letters were actually coded messages from Victor Lanaklin sent by Alenda to a messenger of King Amrath. The Marquis of Glouston is a traitor to his kingdom and the Imperialist cause. Had you realized, you could have had all of Glouston and Victor's head as a wedding gift."

"How do you know?"

"Archduke Braga learned of the meetings when the late king asked him to pay the messenger directly and without record. He of course told me."

Archibald stood silent and then swallowed the rest of his brandy in one mouthful. "But wait, why tell you?"

"Because as a good Imperialist, Percy here knows the importance of keeping the church informed of such things."

Archibald looked at Braga, puzzled. "But you're a Royalist, aren't you? I mean, how could the Lord Chancellor of Melengar be an Imperialist?"

"How indeed?" Saldur asked with a smile.

"By marrying into the royal family," Braga pointed out.

"The church has been surreptitiously placing Imperialists in key positions near the throne of nearly every Royalist kingdom in Avryn and even a few in the nations of Trent and Calis," Saldur explained. "Through unusual accidents, these men have managed to find themselves rulers of most of those realms. The church feels that when the heir is finally found, it will help make a smoother transition if all the various kingdoms are already prepared to pledge their allegiance."

"Incredible."

"Indeed. I must warn you, however, that you won't be able to obtain additional letters. There will be no more meetings at the Winds Abbey. Regrettably, I was forced to ask the archduke to teach the monks a lesson for hosting such meetings. The abbey was burned along with the monks."

"*You* killed your fellow shepherds of Maribor's flock?" Archibald asked Saldur.

"When Maribor sent Novron to us, it was as a warrior to destroy our enemies. Our god is not squeamish at the sight of spilled blood, and it's often necessary to prune weak branches to keep the tree strong. Killing the monks was a necessity, but I did spare one, the son of Lanaklin, so he could return home and let his father know the deaths were on his hands. We can't have Royalists organizing against us, can we?" Saldur smiled at him. The elderly cleric took another sip of his drink, the moment passed, and once more Braga observed the persona of the saintly grandfather.

"So, you were after Glouston, Archibald?" Braga said, refilling the earl's glass. "Perhaps I misjudged you. Tell me, my dear earl, were you more upset you lost the land or Alenda?"

Archibald waved his hand in the air as if he were shooing a fly. "She was merely an added benefit. It's the land I wanted."

"I see." Braga glanced at Saldur, who smiled and nodded. "You may still get it." Braga resumed speaking to the earl. "With me on the throne of Melengar, I'll want a strong Imperialist ally guarding my southern border with Warric."

"King Ethelred would call that treason."

"And what would you call it?"

Archibald smiled and drummed his fingernails on the beautiful cut crystal of the royal brandy glass, making it ring with a pleasant song. "Opportunity."

Braga sat back down and stretched out his feet to the fire. "If I help you obtain the marchland from Lanaklin, and you throw your allegiance to me, Melengar will replace Warric as the strongest kingdom in Avryn. Similarly, *Greater* Chadwick will be its most powerful province."

"That's assuming Ethelred doesn't declare war," Archibald warned. "Kings often frown upon losing a quarter of their realm, and Ethelred is not the type to take such an action without retaliation. He enjoys fighting. What's more, he's good at it. He has the best army in Avryn now."

"True," Braga said. "But he has no able general to command it. He doesn't have anyone near the talent of your Sir Breckton. That man is gifted when it comes to leading men. If you broke with Warric, could you count on his loyalty to you?"

"Breckton's loyalty to me is unwavering. His father, Lord Belstrad, is a chivalrous knight of archaic dimensions. He beat those values into his sons. Neither Breckton nor his brother—what's his name, the younger Belstrad boy, who went to sea—*Wesley*, would dishonor themselves by opposing a man they have sworn their allegiance to. I do admit, however, their honor can be an inconvenience. I remember once a servant dropped my new fustian hat in the mud, and when I commanded Breckton to cut off the clumsy oaf's hand in punishment, he refused. Breckton went on for twenty minutes explaining the code of chivalry to me. Oh yes, my lord, he is indeed loyal to House Ballentyne, but I would rather have a less loyal man who simply obeys without question. It's entirely possible that should I break with Warric, Breckton might refuse to fight at all, but I'm certain he would not oppose me. Personally, I would be more concerned with Ethelred himself. He is a fine commander in his own right."

"True," Braga acknowledged, "but so am I. I would welcome him engaging me personally. I already have a standing veteran army and a number of mercenaries at the ready. I'll be able to muster superior numbers should that prove necessary. The result will be that he would lose all of Warric, and that could provide me the keys to the rest of Avryn and, perhaps, all of Apeladorn."

This time Archibald chuckled. "My, but I do appreciate your ability to *think big*. I can see there would be many advantages to my joining with you. Do you really have your sights on the title of emperor?"

"Why not? If I'm poised to conquer, the Patriarch will be eager to throw his allegiance to me, just as the church did with Glenmorgan. If I promise certain rights to the church, he may even declare me the heir. Then no one will stand against me. In any case, this is for another day. We are getting ahead of ourselves." Braga turned his attention toward the bishop. "I want to thank you, Your Grace, for arranging this meeting. It was very educational. But now it's nearly midmorning, and I think it's time to get Arista's trial under way. I would, however, like to invite you to stay, Archibald. As it turns out, I think I may be able to offer you a gift to show you my commitment to you as a newfound friend of Melengar."

"I'm flattered, my lord. I'd welcome the opportunity to spend time with you, and I'm sure whatever gift you may have will be a generous one."

"You mentioned the thieves who spoiled your move against Victor Lanaklin called themselves Riyria?"

"Yes, I did. Why do you ask?"

"Well, it appears we share a common interest in these two rogues. They have also been a rather painful thorn in my own side. As you already discovered, they pay no respect to people who hire them, and are willing to turn against their employers. I, too, hired them for a task and now find them working against me. I have reason to believe they may be coming here today, and I have set plans in motion to capture them. If they do indeed make an appearance, I'll try them along with Arista. It's quite possible all three will be burning at the stake by early evening."

"You are, indeed, most generous, my lord," Archibald replied with a nod of his head and a smile on his lips.

"I thought you might enjoy that. You mentioned when you arrived that Alric is dead, and that's indeed the notion I've been circulating. Unfortunately, it's not so—that is, not yet. Arista actually arranged for those thieves to smuggle Alric out of this castle on the night of Amrath's death. I believe he has hired them and they will attempt to save her. Evidence indicates they used the sewers to exit the castle, so I've taken extra precautions there. The grate in the kitchen has been sealed, and Wylin, the captain of the castle guard, waits with his best men hidden to close the river grate behind them. I even failed to post guards near there, to make it more enticing. With luck, the fool of a prince might actually play the boyish hero and come with them. If he does—checkmate!"

Archibald nodded with obvious pleasure. "You really are very impressive."

Braga raised his glass in tribute. "To me."

"To you." Archibald drank to Braga's health.

There was a loud pounding on the door. "Come!" Braga called, irritated.

"Lord Chancellor!" One of Braga's hired soldiers burst into the room. His cheeks and nose were red, his armor dripping wet. On his head and shoulders a small bit of snow remained.

"Yes? What is it?"

"The wall guard reports footprints in the snow leading to the river near the sewers, my lord."

"Excellent," Braga replied, draining his glass. "Take eight men and support Captain Wylin from the river. I don't want them escaping. Remember, if the prince is with them, kill him on sight. Don't let Wylin stop you. Either way, I want the thieves alive. Lock them in the dungeons and gag them as before. I'll use them as further incriminating evidence against Arista and burn the whole lot together." The soldier bowed and left.

"Now, gentlemen, as I was saying, let's join the magistrate and the other nobles. I'm anxious to get this trial under way." They all stood, and walking three abreast, they exited the large double doors as one.

ර

The morning sun, magnified by the snow, entered the river grate as a stark white light. The wintry radiance splintered along the glistening ceiling, revealing ancient stone caked in mildew and moss. The frozen sweat of the sewer walls reflected the light, bouncing it back and forth until at last it scattered into the all-consuming darkness. In the gloom, the soldiers waited, crouching and cold. Their feet were ankle-deep in filthy cold water, which streamed between their legs, running from the castle drains to the river. For the better part of four hours, they lingered in silence, but now they could hear the sound of footsteps approaching. The sloshing of the dirty water echoed off the sewer walls, and the distant movement of shadows played upon the stone.

With a motion of his hand, Wylin ordered his troop to hold their position and maintain their silence. He wanted to be certain the rear guard was in place and his prey was in sight before he made his move. There were many avenues in the sewers where two men could run and hide in the dark. He did not want to be chasing the rats through a maze of tunnels. Not only was it unpleasant down there, but Wylin knew the archduke wanted the thieves for the morning festivities and would not be pleased with a long delay.

Soon they came into view. Two men—one tall and broad, the other shorter and slimmer—dressed in warm winter cloaks with hoods pulled high, rounded the corner slowly, pausing from time to time to look about.

"Remind me to compliment His Majesty on the quality of his sewers," one of them mentioned in a mocking tone.

"At least the slime is warmer than the river," the other replied.

"Yeah, too bad this is happening on the coldest day of the year. Why couldn't it be the middle of summer?"

"That would be warmer for sure, but could you imagine the smell?"

"Speaking of smell, do you think we're getting close to the kitchen yet?"

"You're the one leading; I can't see a thing in here."

Wylin waved his arm. *"Move in, now! Take them!"*

The castle guard rushed from their positions in an adjoining tunnel and charged the two men. From behind, more soldiers raced forward, blocking any retreat. The troops encircled the two, swords drawn and shields at the ready.

"Careful," Wylin said, "the archduke says they are full of surprises."

"I'll show you surprises," one of the soldiers from the rear said, and, stepping forward, struck the tall one with the pommel of his sword, dropping him to the ground. Another used his shield and the second man fell unconscious.

Wylin sighed and glared at his ranks, then shrugged. "I was planning on letting them walk but this works too. Chain 'em, gag 'em, and drag 'em to the dungeons. And for Maribor's sake, get their heads up before they drown. Braga wants them alive." The soldiers nodded and went to work.

ɞ

"This hearing of the High Court of Melengar has been assembled in good order to review allegations made against the princess Arista Essendon by the Lord Chancellor, the Archduke of Melengar, Percy Braga." The strong voice of the chief magistrate boomed across the chamber. "Princess Arista stands duly accused of treason against the crown, the murder of her father and brother, and the practicing of witchcraft."

The largest room in the castle, the Court of Melengar had a cathedral ceiling, stained-glass windows, and walls rimmed in emblems and shields of the noble houses of the kingdom. Bench seats and balconies were overflowing with spectators. The nobles and the city's affluent merchants pressed in to see the royal trial of the princess. Outside, many common people had been gathering since dawn and waited in the snow as runners reported the proceedings. A wall of armor-clad soldiers held them at bay.

The court itself was a boxed set of bleachers composed of

tiered armchairs, where the ranking nobles of the kingdom sat. Several of the seats were vacant but enough had arrived to serve Braga's purpose. Still frosty with the morning chill, most of the court wore fur wraps as they waited for the fire in the great hearth to warm the room. At the front stood the empty throne, its vacancy looming like an ominous specter before the court. Its presence was a stark reminder of the gravity and scope of the trial. The verdict could decide who would sit there next and control the reins of the kingdom.

"This judicial court, comprised of men of good standing and sound wisdom, will now hear the allegations and the evidence. May Maribor grant them wisdom."

The chief magistrate took his seat and a heavyset man with a short beard wreathing his small mouth stood up. He was dressed in expensive-looking robes that flowed behind him as he paced before the jury, eyeing each man carefully.

"Lords of the Court," the lawyer said, addressing the bleachers with a dramatic sweep of his arm. "Your noble personages have by now learned that our good king Amrath was murdered seven days past in this very castle. You may also be aware Prince Alric is missing, presumed abducted and murdered. But how could such things as these happen within a king's own castle walls? A king *might* be murdered. A prince *might* be abducted. But both in the same night and one after the other? How is this possible?"

The crowd quieted as they struggled to hear.

"How is it possible that two killers slipped inside the castle unnoticed, stabbed the king to death, and, despite being caught and locked in the dungeon, were able to escape? This in itself is incredible, because the cell in which they were locked was heavily guarded by skilled soldiers. Not only were they imprisoned, they were also chained by their wrists and ankles to the wall. But what is beyond amazing, what is beyond belief, is that after managing their miraculous escape, the two did not flee! No, indeed! Informed while in captivity that they would be drawn and quartered at dawn—a most painful and gruesome death, to be certain—for their most heinous crime, these two killers remained in a castle filled with hundreds of soldiers ready to thrust them back into their cell. Rather than flee for their lives, instead they sought out the prince, the most heavily guarded and high-profile personage in the castle, and kidnapped him! I ask you again, how is this possible? Were the castle guards asleep? Were they so totally incompetent as to let the killers of the king walk out? Or could it be that the assassins had help?

"Could a guard have done this? A foreign spy? Even a trusted baron or earl? No! None of them would have the authority to enter the dungeon to *see* the killers of the king, much less free them. Nay, gracious lords, no person in the castle that night had the authority to enter those jails so easily, save one—Princess Arista! Being the daughter of the victim, who could deny her the right to spit in the faces of the men who murdered her father so brutally? Only she wasn't there to defile the killers; she came to help them finish the job she started!"

The crowd murmured.

"This is an outrage!" an elderly man protested from the bleachers. "To accuse the poor girl of her father's death... You should be ashamed! Where is she? Why is she not present to dispute these claims?"

"Lord Valin," the lawyer addressed him, "we are honored to have you with us today. This court will call the princess forth shortly. She is not here for the presenting of facts, as it is a tedious and unpleasant matter, and this court does not want the princess to endure it. Likewise, those called to testify can speak freely, without the presence of their future queen, should she be found innocent. And there are still other, more unpleasant reasons, upon which I will elaborate in due time."

This did not appear to change Lord Valin's mood, but he made no further protest and sat back down.

"The court of Melengar calls Reuben Hilfred to testify."

The lawyer paused as the big soldier, still dressed in ring mail and the tabard of the falcon, stood before the court. His stance was proud and straight, but his expression was anything but pleased.

"Hilfred," the lawyer addressed him, "what is your position here at Essendon Castle?"

"I am personal bodyguard to Princess Arista," he told the court in a loud clear voice.

"Tell us, Reuben, what is your rank?"

"I am sergeant-at-arms."

"That's a fairly high rank, isn't it?"

"It is a respected position."

"How did you attain this rank?"

"I was singled out for some reason."

"For some reason? For some reason?" the lawyer repeated, laughing gaily. "Is it not true you were recommended for promotion by Captain Wylin for your years of consistent and unwavering loyalty to the crown? Moreover, is it not true that the *king himself* appointed you to be his daughter's personal bodyguard after you risked your life and saved Arista from the fire that killed the queen mother? Were you not also presented with a commendation for bravery by the king? Are not all these things true?"

"Yes, sir."

"I sense in you a reluctance to be here, Reuben. Am I correct?"

"Yes, sir."

"It is because you are loyal to your princess, and you do

not wish to be a part of anything which might harm her. That is an admirable quality. Still, you are also an honorable man, and as such, you must speak truthfully in your testimony before this court. So tell us, Reuben, what happened the night the king was murdered?"

Hilfred shifted his weight uncomfortably from one foot to the other and then took a breath and spoke. "It was late, and the princess was asleep in her bed. I was on post at the tower stairs when the king was found. Captain Wylin ordered me to check on Princess Arista. Before I reached her door, she came out, startled by the noise."

"How was she dressed?" the lawyer asked.

"In a gown, I am not sure which."

"But she was dressed? Was she not? Not in a robe or nightclothes?"

"Yes, she was dressed."

"You have spent years guarding Arista. Have you ever known her to sleep in her gowns?"

"No."

"Never?"

"Never."

"But I assume you have no doubt stood outside her door when she went to dress for meals or to change after traveling. Does she have servants to help her dress?"

"Yes."

"How many?"

"Three."

"And how long is the fastest you recall her dressing?"

"I am not certain."

"Make a guess; the court will not hold you to the exact time."

"Perhaps twenty minutes."

"Twenty minutes with three servants. That is actually quite

fast, considering all the ties and toggles that require lacing for most ladies' clothing. Now how long would you say it was between the discovery of the king's body and the time the princess came out of her room?"

Hilfred hesitated.

"How long?" the lawyer persisted.

"Perhaps ten minutes."

"Ten minutes, you say? And when she came out of her room, how many servants were with her?"

"None that I saw."

"Amazing! The princess woke up unexpectedly in the dark and managed to dress herself fully in a lavish gown in ten minutes without the help of a single servant!"

The lawyer paced the floor, his head down in thought, a finger tapping his lips. He paused with his back to Hilfred. Then, as if a sudden thought occurred to him, he spun abruptly.

"Tell us, how did she take the news of the king's death?"

"She was shocked."

"Did she weep?"

"I am sure she did."

"But did you *see* her?"

"No."

"Then what happened?"

"She went to Prince Alric's chambers to find him and was surprised he was not there. She then—"

"Please stop there just a minute. She went to *Alric's* chambers? She learns her father is murdered and her first inclination is to go to her brother's room? Did you not find it odd she did not immediately rush to her father's side? After all, no one had suggested any harm had come to Alric, had they?"

"No."

"What happened next?"

"She went to view her father's body, and Alric arrived."

"After the prince sentenced the prisoners to death, what did the princess do?"

"I do not understand what you mean," Hilfred replied.

"Is it true she went to visit them?" the lawyer questioned.

"Yes, she did."

"And were you with her?"

"I was asked to wait outside the cell."

"Why?"

"I do not know."

"Has she often asked you to wait outside when she is speaking with people?"

"Sometimes."

"Often?"

"Not often."

"Then what happened?"

"She called for monks to give last rites to the murderers."

"She called for monks?" the lawyer repeated with a clear note of skepticism in his voice. "Her father is murdered and she is concerned about the *murderers'* souls? Why did she call for two monks? Was one not sufficient to do the job for both? For that matter, why not call the castle priest?"

"I do not know."

"And did she also order the murderers unchained?"

"Yes, to be able to kneel."

"And when the monks entered the cell, did you go with them?"

"No, again she asked me to remain outside."

"So the monks could enter but not her trusted bodyguard? Not even when the known killers of her father were unchained and free? Then what?"

"She came out of the cell. She wanted me to stay behind and escort the monks to the kitchens after they were done giving last rites."

"Why?"

"She did not say."

"Did you ask?"

"No, sir. As a man-at-arms, it is not my place to question the orders from a member of the royal family."

"I see, but were you pleased with these orders?"

"No."

"Why?"

"I was fearful more assassins might be in the castle, and I did not wish the princess to be out of my sight."

"In point of fact, wasn't Captain Wylin in the process of searching the castle for additional threats, and didn't he make everyone aware he felt the castle was unsafe?"

"He did."

"Did the princess explain to you where she was going so you could find her after performing your duty to the monks?"

"No."

"I see. And how do you know the two you escorted to the kitchens were the monks? Did you see their faces?"

"Their hoods were up."

"Did they have their hoods up when they entered the cell?"

Hilfred thought a moment and then shook his head. "I do not think so."

"So, on a night when her father is killed, she orders her personal bodyguard to leave her unprotected and to escort two monks down to the empty kitchens—two monks who decided suddenly to pull their hoods up inside the castle, hiding their faces? And what about the murderers' possessions? Where were they?"

"They were in the custody of the cell warden."

"And what did she say to the warden concerning them?"

"She told him she was going to have the monks take them for the poor."

"And did they take them?"

"Yes."

The lawyer softened his address. "Reuben, you do not strike me as a fool. Fools don't rise to the rank and position you have achieved. When you heard the killers escaped, and the monks were found chained in their place, did it cross your mind that maybe the princess had arranged it?"

"I assumed the killers attacked the monks after the princess left the cell."

"You did not answer my question," the lawyer said. "I asked if it crossed your mind."

Reuben said nothing.

"Did it?"

"Perhaps, but only briefly."

"Let us turn our attention to more recent events. Were you present during the conversation between Arista and her uncle in his study?"

"Yes, but I was asked to wait outside."

"To wait just outside the door, correct?"

"Yes."

"Therefore, could you hear what transpired inside?"

"Yes."

"Is it true the princess entered the archduke's office, where he was diligently working at locating the prince, and informed him that Prince Alric was clearly dead and that no search was needed? That he would make a better use of his time"—he paused here and turned to face the nobles—"*to begin preparations for her coronation as our queen*!"

There was a decidedly unpleasant murmur from the crowd, and a few of the court whispered and nodded to one another.

"I do not remember her using those words."

"Did she, or did she not, indicate the archduke should stop looking for Alric?"

"Yes."

"And did she threaten the archduke, insinuating she would soon hold her coronation, and once she was queen, he might find he was no longer the lord chancellor?"

"I believe she did say something to that effect, but she was angry—"

"That will be all, Sergeant-at-arms. That is all I asked. You can step down." Hilfred began to leave the witness box when the lawyer spoke again. "Oh, I am sorry—just one last thing. Have you ever seen or heard the princess cry over the loss of her father or brother?"

"She is a very private woman."

"Yes or no?"

Hilfred hesitated. "No, I have not."

"I am prepared to call the cell warden to corroborate the testimony of Hilfred if the court feels his account of the events is not truthful," the lawyer told the magistrates.

They conferred in whispers, and then the chief magistrate replied, "That will not be necessary. The word of the sergeant-at-arms is recognized as honorable and we will not question it here. You may proceed."

"I am sure you are as perplexed as I was," the lawyer said, addressing the bleachers in a sympathetic voice. "Many of you know her. How could this sweet girl attack her own father and brother? Was it just to gain a throne? It is not like her, is it? I ask you to bear with me. The reason should become quite clear in a moment. The court calls Bishop Saldur to testify."

Eyes from the gallery swept the room, looking for the cleric, as the old man slowly stood up from his seat and approached the witness box.

"Your Grace, you have been in this castle on many occasions. You know the royal family extremely well. Can you shed some light on Her Highness's motivations?"

"Gentlemen," Bishop Saldur spoke to the court and judges in his familiar warm and humble tone, "I have watched over the royal family for years and this recent tragedy is heartbreaking and dreadful. The accusation the archduke brings against the princess is painful to my ears, for I feel almost like a grandfather to the poor girl. However, I cannot hide the truth, which is...she *is* dangerous."

This brought a round of whispers between the spectators.

"I can assure each of you she is no longer the sweet innocent child whom I used to hold in my arms. I have seen her, spoken to her, watched her in her grief—or rather, the lack of grief—for her father and brother. I can tell you truly, her lust for knowledge and power has caused her to fall into the arms of evil." The bishop paused, dropping his head into his hands and shaking it. He looked up with a remorse-filled face and said, "It's the result of what happens when a woman is educated and, in Arista's case, introduced to the wicked powers of black magic."

A collective gasp issued from the crowd.

"Against my advice, King Amrath allowed her to attend the university, where she studied sorcery. She opened herself up to the forces of darkness, and it created in her a craving for power. Education planted an evil seed in her, and it flowered into the horrible deaths of her father and her brother. She is no longer a princess of the realm but a *witch*. This is evident by the fact she hasn't wept for her father. You see, as a learned bishop of the church, I know—witches cannot cry."

The crowd gasped again. Braga heard a man say, "I knew it!" from somewhere in the gallery.

The lawyer called Countess Amril to the court, and she testified that two years earlier, Arista had hexed her when she had told the squire Davens that the princess fancied him. Amril went on to describe how she had suffered horribly of sickness and boils for days as a result.

Next the lawyer called the monks, who, like Countess Amril, were eager to relate how they had been ill-used by the princess. They told how she had insisted the thieves be unchained, despite their assurance it was not necessary, and explained they had been attacked the moment she had left the room.

The crowd's reaction grew louder, and even Lord Valin looked troubled.

Percy Braga observed the audience with satisfaction from his seat at the rear of the magistrates. The faces of the gentry were filling with anger. He had successfully coaxed the spark into a flame, and the flame would soon be a blaze.

In the crowd, he spotted Wylin moving in the wings toward him.

"We have them, my lord," Wylin reported in a whisper. "They are gagged and locked in the dungeon. A little banged up by two of my overzealous men but alive."

"Excellent, and has there been any movement on the roads? Has there been any indication nobles loyal to the traitor Arista may attack?"

"I don't know, sir. I came directly from the sewers."

"Very well, get to the gate and sound the horn if you see anything. I'm concerned there may be an assault from Pickering of Drondil Fields. Oh, and if you see that wretched little dwarf, tell him it's time to bring the princess down."

"Of course, Your Lordship." Wylin pulled a small parchment rolled into a tube from his tabard. "I was passed this on my way in. It just arrived via messenger addressed to you." Braga took the missive from Wylin and the master-at-arms left with a bow.

Braga grinned at the ease of it all. He wondered if the princess in her distant tower prison could sense her coming death. Her own beloved citizens would soon be begging—nay, demanding—her execution. He had yet to present the storeroom administrator who would attest to the stolen dagger that had later been found in Arista's possession. And then, of course, there were now the thieves. He would hold them until the last and drag them out to the floor gagged and chained. The mere sight of them was likely to start a riot. He would have Wylin explain how he apprehended them trying to save the princess. The magistrates would have no choice but to rule against Arista and grant him the throne.

He would still have to deal with the possibility of Alric's attacking, but that could not be helped now. He was certain he would defeat Alric. Several of the more disgruntled eastern lords had already agreed to join him the moment he was crowned king. Once the trial was complete, and Arista dead, he planned to hold the coronation. By the next day, he would marshal the kingdom. Alric would cease to be a prince and become a fugitive.

"The court calls storage clerk Kline Druess," the lawyer was saying, "who was in charge of keeping the knife used to kill the king."

More damning evidence, Braga thought as he unrolled the scroll that Wylin had presented him. It had no seal, no emblem of nobility, only a simple string tie. He read the message, which was as simple as its package.

You missed us in the sewers.
We now have the princess.
Your time is growing short.

The archduke crumpled the note in his fist and glared around at the numerous faces in the crowd, wondering if whoever had written it was watching him. His heart began beating faster, and he stood up slowly, trying not to draw attention to himself.

The lawyer caught sight of his movement and gave him a

curious look. Braga dismissed his concern with a slight wave of his hand. He left the court, forcing himself to walk slowly and calmly. The moment he passed through the chamber doors and out of sight of the crowd, he trotted through the castle halls, his cape whipping behind him. In his fist, he held on to the note, crushing it.

It isn't possible, he thought. *It can't be!* Hearing footfalls approaching rapidly from behind, he stopped and spun, drawing his sword.

"Is there a problem, Braga?" Archibald Ballentyne inquired. He held his hands up defensively before the point of the archduke's blade. Braga silently threw the crumpled note at him and resumed his march toward the dungeon.

"It's those thieves, those damned thieves," the Earl of Chadwick called out as he ran after Braga. "They're demons! Magicians! Evil mages! They are like smoke, appearing and disappearing at will."

Archibald caught up with Braga and they descended the stairs to the detention block, where the door guard dodged aside just in time to avoid the archduke. After trying the door and finding it locked, Braga hammered on it. The warden promptly left his desk and brought his keys for the red-faced archduke.

"My lord, I—"

"Open the cell to the prisoners Wylin's men just brought in. Do it now!"

"Yes, my lord." Fumbling with his great ring of keys, the warden moved quickly to the cell hall. Two castle guards stood watch to either side of a door and promptly stepped aside at his approach.

"Have you two been here since the prisoners were brought in?" Braga asked the guards.

"Aye, my lord," the guard on the left replied. "Captain

Wylin ordered us to stand guard and to allow absolutely no admittance to anyone except him or you."

"Very good," he said. Then, to the warden, he added, "Open it."

The warden unlocked the door and entered the cell. Inside, Braga saw two men chained to the wall, stripped to their waists with gags in their mouths. They were not the same men he had seen the night of the king's murder.

"Remove the gags," Braga ordered the warden. "Who are you? What are you doing here?"

"M-m-my name's Bendent, Your Lordship. I'm just a street sweeper from Kirby's End—honest. We weren't doing nothing wrong!"

"What were you two doing in the sewers under this castle?"

"Hunting rats, sir," the other one said.

"*Rats?*"

"Yes, sir, honest, we was. We was told there was a big event here in the castle this morning and the castle kitchen was complaining about rats climbing up from the sewers. 'Cause of the cold, you see, sir. We was told we'd get paid a silver tenent for every rat we done killed and brought out—only..."

"Only what?"

"Only we never seen no rats, Your Lordship."

"Before we found any, we were knocked out by soldiers and brought here."

"See? What did I tell you?" Archibald told Braga. "They took her already. They stole her right from under your nose just like they took my letters!"

"They couldn't have. There's no way to get up to Arista's tower. It's too high, and it can't be climbed."

"I'm telling you, Braga, these men are skilled. They scaled my Gray Tower well enough, and it's one of the tallest there is."

"Trust me, Archibald. Arista's tower can't be climbed."

"But they did it," Ballentyne insisted. "I didn't think it was possible when they did it to me either, not until I opened the safe and my prize was gone. Now your prize is gone, and what will you do with that crowd out there when you have no princess to burn?"

"It's just not possible," Braga repeated, pushing Ballentyne out of his way. "You two," he said to the guards, still standing outside the cell as he walked out, "come with me and bring one of those gags. It's time the princess came down for her court appearance."

Braga led them through the castle and up six flights of stairs to the residence level. The hallway here was empty. All the servants were gathered with the others, listening to the proceedings of the trial.

They passed the royal chapel and continued up the hallway to the next door. Braga threw it open and shouted, "Magnus!" Inside, a dwarf with a braided brown beard and a broad flat nose lay on a bed. He was dressed in a blue leather vest, large black boots, and a bright orange puffed-sleeve shirt that made his arms appear huge.

"Is it time?" the dwarf asked. Hopping off the bed, he yawned and rubbed his eyes.

"Is there any chance someone could have gotten up in her tower and stolen Arista out of there?" Braga asked urgently.

"None whatsoever," the dwarf said with a tone of total confidence. Braga looked back and forth between Ballentyne and the dwarf, scowling.

"I have to know for certain. Besides, she needs to come down for the burning, and I must get back to the trial. You'll have to fetch her. Take these guards with you. One of them has a gag. Make sure they use it before bringing her down." To the guards the archduke added, "The princess has been corrupted by dark magic; she's a witch and can play tricks with your mind, so don't let her talk to you. Get her and bring her to the court." The guards nodded and the dwarf led them down the hallway in the direction of the tower.

"Archibald, go get Wylin, the captain of the guards. He's stationed at the castle gate. Tell him to come to the royal residence wing and provide assistance guarding the princess. I can't take any chances. Do you understand me?"

"I'll do as you say, Percy, but I'm sure she is already gone," Archibald insisted. "These bastards are incredible. They're like ghosts, and they have no fear at all. They work right under your nose, steal you blind, and then have the audacity to send you a note *telling* you what they have done!"

Braga paused in thought. "Yes, why *did* they do that?" he asked himself. "If they took her, why let me know? And if they didn't, they must have suspected I would immediately check to..." He glanced over his shoulder in the direction the dwarf had gone then turned back to Archibald. "Get Wylin up here, *now*!"

Braga ran up the hallway, following the dwarf and the two guards. They were just entering the north corridor, which led directly to the tower, when he caught up to them.

"Stop where you are!"

The dwarf turned around with a puzzled expression on his face. The guards responded differently. The larger of the two pivoted, drawing his sword, and moved to block the archduke's passage.

~

"Time to move, Royce," Hadrian said, casting off his helm. The standard-issue sword of the castle guard felt heavy and awkward in his grip.

Royce removed his helm as well as he moved past the dwarf, running quickly down the hall.

"Stop him, you fool!" Braga ordered the dwarf, but he was too slow to react. The thief was already far down the hall and the small dwarf ran after him. Braga drew his own sword and turned his attention to Hadrian.

"Do you know who I am? I know we met in the dungeon recently when you were hanging in chains, but are you aware of my reputation? I'm Archduke Percy Braga, Lord Chancellor of Melengar and, more importantly, the winner of the title of Grand Circuit Tournament Swords Master for the last five years in a row. Do you have any titles? Any ribbons won? Any awards bestowed? Are there trophies shelved for your handling of a sword? I have bested the best in Avryn, even the famous Pickering and his magic rapier."

"The way I heard it, he didn't have his sword the day you two dueled."

Braga laughed. "That sword story is just that—a legend. He uses it as an excuse to account for his losses or when he is afraid of an opponent. His sword is just a common rapier with a fancy hilt."

Braga moved in and swiped at Hadrian in a savagely fast attack that drove him backward. He struck again and Hadrian had to leap backward to avoid being slashed across the chest.

"You're fast. That's good. It'll make this more interesting. You see, Mr. Thief, I'm sure you have the situation all wrong. You may be under the impression that you are holding me at bay while your friend races to rescue the damsel in distress. How noble for a commoner like yourself. You must entertain dreams of being a knight to be so idealistic." Braga lunged, dipped, and slashed. Hadrian fell back again, and once more,

Braga smiled and laughed at him. "The truth is, you are not holding me at all. I'm holding you."

The archduke feinted left and then short-stroked toward Hadrian's body. He dodged the attack, but it put him off balance and off guard. Although Braga's stroke missed, it allowed him the opportunity to punch the hilt of his sword hard into Hadrian's face, throwing him back against the corridor wall. His lip began to bleed. Immediately, Braga lashed out again, but Hadrian had moved, and the archduke's sword sparked across the stone wall.

"That looked like it hurt."

"I've had worse," Hadrian said. He was panting slightly, his voice less confident.

"I must admit, you two have been quite impressive. Your reputation is certainly well earned. It was very clever of you to slip into the sewers behind those rat catchers and use them as decoys. It was also intelligent of you to send that note causing me to direct you right to the princess but your genius ended there. You see, I can kill you whenever I want, but I want you alive. I need at least one person to execute. The mob will insist on that. In a few moments, Wylin and a dozen guards will come up here, and you'll be taken to the stake. Meanwhile, your friend, whom you are sure is rescuing Arista, will be the instrument of her death and his as well. You could run and warn him, but—oh, that's right—you are keeping me at bay, aren't you?"

Braga grinned and attacked again.

~

Royce reached a door at the end of the hall and was not surprised to find it locked. He pulled his tools from his belt. The lock was traditional, and he had no trouble picking it. The door swung open, but immediately Royce knew something was wrong. He felt, more than heard, a click as the door pulled back. His instincts told him something was not right. He looked up the spiral stairs that disappeared around the circle of the tower. Nothing looked amiss, but years of experience told him otherwise.

He tentatively put a foot on the first step and nothing happened. He moved to the second, and the third, inching his way up. Listening for any telltale sounds, he searched for wires, levers, and loose tiles. Everything appeared safe. Behind him down the hallway, he could hear the faint sounds of swordplay as Hadrian entertained the archduke. He needed to hurry.

He moved up five more steps. There were small windows, no more than three feet tall and only a foot wide, just enough to allow light to pass through but nothing else. The winter sun revealed the staircase in a washed-out brilliance. Weight, rather than mortar, held the smooth stone walls together. The steps were likewise made of solid blocks of stone also fitted with amazing artisanship so that a sheet of parchment could not slip between the cracks.

Royce moved up to the ninth step, and as he shifted his weight to the higher stone block, the tower shook. In reaction, he instinctively started to step back, and then it happened. The previous eight steps collapsed. They broke and fell out of sight into an abyss below him. Royce shifted his weight forward again just in time to avoid falling to his death and took another off-balance step upward. The moment he did, the previous step broke away and fell. The tower rumbled again.

"Your first mistake was picking the lock," Magnus told him.

Royce could hear the dwarf's voice from the doorway below. When he turned, he could see the dwarf standing just outside the door in the castle's corridor. He stood there, spinning a door key tied to a string around his index finger, winding and unwinding it. He absently stroked the hair of his beard.

"If you open the door without using the key, it engages the trap," Magnus explained with a grin.

The dwarf began to pace slowly before the open door like a professor addressing a class. "You can't jump the hole you made to get back here. It's already too far. And, in case you are wondering, the bottom is a long way down. You started climbing this tower on the sixth floor of the castle, and the base of the tower extends to the bedrock below the foundation. I also added plenty of jagged rocks at the bottom, just for fun."

"You made this?" Royce asked.

"Of course—well, not the tower. It was here already. I spent the last half year hollowing it out like a stone-eating termite." He grinned. "There's very little material left in it. All those solid-looking blocks of rock you see are parchment-thin. I left just the right amount of structure in place. The inside looks like a spiderweb made of stone rather than thread. Tiny strands of rock in a latticework of a classic crystalline matrix—strong enough to hold the tower up but extremely fragile if the right thread is broken."

"And I take it each time I take a step up, the previous one will fall?"

The dwarf's grin widened. "Beautiful, isn't it? You can't go down, but if you go up, you'll get into an even worse situation. The steps work as a horizontal support for the vertical planes. Without the steps to steady the structure, it will twist on itself and fall. Before you reach the top, the entire tower will collapse once enough supports fall away. Don't let my talk about hollow walls put you too much at ease. It's still stone, and the full weight of this tower remains immense. It will very easily crush you, and the lady at the top, should the fall and the sharp rocks at the bottom not manage to do the job. You've already weakened the structure to where it might fall on its own now. I can hear it with the blowing of the wind—the tiny little cracks and pops. All stone makes sounds as it grows, shrinks, twists, or erodes—it's a language I understand very well. It tells me stories of the past and of the future, and right now, this tower is singing."

"I hate dwarves," Royce muttered.

Chapter 9

Rescuers

The water pitcher and basin hit the floor and shattered. The crash jolted Arista, who sat on her bed, disoriented and confused. The room was shaking. All summer the tower had felt strange but nothing like this. She held her breath—waiting. Nothing happened. The tower stopped moving.

Tentatively, she slipped off the bed, crept gingerly toward the windows, and looked out. She saw nothing to explain the tremor. Outside, the world was blanketed white by a fresh layer of snow that was still falling and she wondered if it was snow sliding from the tower's eves that made the room shake. It did not seem likely nor did that matter.

How much time do I have left?

She looked down. The crowd still circled the front gate of the castle. There must have been more than a hundred people there, all pressing for news of her trial. Around the perimeter of the castle, three times the usual number of guards patrolled in full armor. Her uncle was not taking any chances. Perhaps he thought the people of the city might rise up against him rather than see their princess burned? She knew better. No one cared if she lived or died. While she knew all the lords, earls, and barons by name and had sat down with them for dozens of meals, she knew they were not her friends. She did not have any friends. Braga was right; she spent too much time in her tower. No one really knew her. She lived a solitary life, but this was the first time she ever really felt alone.

She had spent all night trying to determine exactly what words she would use when brought before the court. In the end, she concluded there was little she could do or say. She could accuse Braga of the murder of her father, but she had no proof. He was the one with all the evidence on his side. After all, she had released the two thieves and was responsible for Alric's disappearance.

What was I thinking?

She had handed her brother over to two unknown thugs. Alric had personally explained his intent to torture them and she had left him to their mercy. Arista felt sick whenever she imagined them laughing at her expense as they drowned poor Alric in the river. Now they were likely halfway to Calis or Delgos, taking turns wearing the royal signet ring of Melengar. When the scouts had returned with Alric's robe, she had been certain he was dead, and yet there was no body.

Is it possible Alric still lives?

No, she reasoned, it was far more likely Braga kept Alric's corpse hidden. Revealing it before her trial would allow her to make a bid for the throne. Once the trial was over, once she was found guilty and burned, he would miraculously reveal its discovery. It was very possible Braga had Alric's body locked away in one of the rooms below her or somewhere in the vault.

It was all her fault. If she had not interfered, perhaps Alric might have taken charge and discovered Braga's treachery. Perhaps he could have saved both of them. Perhaps she was nothing more than a foolish girl after all. At least her death would put an end to the questions and the guilt consuming her. She closed her eyes and once more felt the unsteadiness of the world around her.

ꟻ

The Galilin host was now a full five hundred strong as it marched through the wintry landscape. Sixty knights dressed in full armor carried lances adorned with long forked banners. They flicked like serpents' tongues in the numbing wind. When they were back at Drondil Fields, Myron had overheard Alric arguing with the other nobles, about marching too soon. Apparently, they were still missing the strength of several lords, and leaving when they did was a risk. Pickering had finally agreed to Alric's demands and convinced the others once Barons Himbolt and Rendon arrived, bringing another score of knights. To Myron, the force was impressive at any size.

At the head of the line rode Prince Alric, Myron, Count Pickering, and his two eldest sons, as well as the land-titled nobles. Following them were the knights, who rode together in rows four abreast. An entourage of squires, pages, and footmen traveled behind them. Farther back were the ranks of the common men-at-arms: strong, stocky brutes dressed in chain and steel with pointed helms, plate metal shin guards, and metal shank boots. Each was equipped with a kite shield, a short broad-blade sword, and a long spear. Next in line were the archers, in leather jerkins and woolen cloaks that hid their quivers. They marched holding their unstrung bows as though they were mere walking sticks. At the rear came the artisans, smiths, surgeons, and cooks, pulling wagons that hauled the army's supplies.

Myron felt foolish. After hours on the road, he was still having trouble keeping his horse from veering to the left into Fanen's gelding. He was starting to get the hang of the stirrups, but he still had much to learn. The front toe guard, which prevented his feet from resting on the soles, frustrated him. The Pickering boys took him under their wing and explained how only the ball of the foot was to rest on the stirrup brace. This provided better control and prevented a foot from catching in the event of a fall. They also told him how tight stirrups helped to hold his knees to the horse's sides. All Pickering's horses were leg trained and could be controlled by the feet, thighs, and knees. They were taught this way so that knights could fight with one hand on a lance or sword and the other on a shield. Myron was working on this technique now, squeezing his thighs, trying to persuade the horse to steer right, but it was no use. The more he used his left knee, the more his right knee also squeezed to compensate. The result was confusion on the part of the animal, and it wandered over and brushed against Fanen's mount once again.

"You need to be more firm," Fanen told him. "Show her who's in charge."

"She already knows—*she* is," Myron replied pathetically. "I think I should just stick with the reins. It's not like I'll be wielding a sword and shield in the coming battle."

"You never know," Fanen said. "Monks of old used to fight a lot, and Alric said you helped save his life by fighting against those mercenaries who attacked him in the forest."

Myron frowned and dropped his gaze. "I didn't fight anyone."

"But I thought—"

Myron shook his head. "I should have, I suppose. They were the ones who burned the abbey. They were the ones who killed... but..." He paused. "I would have died if Hadrian and Royce hadn't saved me. The king just assumed that I fought and I never bothered to tell the truth. I really have to stop doing that."

"Doing what?"

"Lying."

"That's not lying. You just didn't correct him."

"It amounts to the same thing. The abbot once told me that lying was a betrayal to one's self. It's evidence of self-loathing. When you are so ashamed of your actions, thoughts, or intentions, you lie rather than accepting yourself for who you really are—or, in this case, pretend something happened when it didn't. The idea of how others see you becomes more important than the reality of you. It's like when a man would rather die than be thought of as a coward. His life is not as important to him as his reputation. In the end, who is braver? The man who dies rather than be thought of as a coward or the man who lives willing to face who he really is?"

"I'm sorry, you lost me there," Fanen said with a quizzical look.

"It doesn't matter. But the prince asked me along as a chronicler of events, not as a warrior. I think he wants me to record what happens today in a book."

"Well, if you do, please leave out the way Denek threw a fit at not being allowed to come. It will reflect badly on our family."

Everything they passed was new to Myron. He had seen snow, of course, but only in the courtyard and cloister at the abbey. He never had seen how it settled on a forest or glittered on the edges of rivers and streams. They were traveling through populated country now, passing village after village; each one larger than the one before. Myron could only stare in fascination at the many different types of buildings, animals, and people he saw along the way. Each time they came into a town, the villagers came out to stare at them. They scurried out of their homes, aroused by the ominous *thrump*, *thrump*, *thrump* of the soldiers marching. Some summoned the courage to ask where they were going, but the men said nothing, under strict orders to maintain silence.

Children ran to the edge of the road, where parents quickly pulled them back. Myron had never seen a child before—at least, not since he had been one. It was not uncommon for a boy to be sent to the abbey at ten or twelve, but rarely, if ever, was one sent before the age of eight. The smallest of the children fascinated Myron, and he watched them in amazement. They were like short drunk people, loud and usually dirty, but all were surprisingly cute and looked at him in much the same way that he looked at them. They would wave, and Myron could not help waving back, although he assumed it was not very soldierly to do so.

The war host moved surprisingly fast. The foot soldiers, responding in unison to orders, alternated between periods of double-time marching and a more relaxed stride, which was only slightly slower. Each of them wore a grim face, without a smile among them.

For hours, they marched. No one interfered; there were no advance formations lying in ambush, no challenges along the road. To Myron, the trip felt more like an exciting parade than the preparation for an ominous battle. Finally, he saw his first glimpse of Melengar in the distance. Fanen pointed out the great bell tower of Mares Cathedral and the tall spires of Essendon Castle, where no standard flew.

A vanguard rode up and reported a strong force entrenched around the city. The nobles ordered their regiments to form ranks. Flags relayed messages, archers strung their bows, and the army transformed themselves into blocks of men. In long lines of three across, they moved as one. The archers were summoned forward and moved ahead just behind the foot soldiers.

Ordered to the rear, Myron and Fanen rode with the cooks to watch and listen. From his new vantage point, Myron noticed part of the army had broken away from the main line and was moving to the right side of the city. When the ranks of men reached the rise, which left them visible to the castle walls, a great horn sounded in the distance.

One of their own answered the castle horn, and the Galilin archers released a barrage of arrows upon the defenders. The shafts flew and appeared to hang briefly in the air like a dark cloud. As they fell, Myron could hear the distant cries of men. He watched with anticipation as the mounted knights broke into three groups. One stayed on the road, while the other two took up flanking positions on either side. The main line increased their pace to a brisk walk.

When they heard the horn, Mason Grumon and Dixon Taft led their mob up Wayward Street, effectively emptying the Lower Quarter. It was the sign Royce and Hadrian had told them to wait for—the signal to attack.

Ever since the two thieves had woken them in the middle of the night, they had spent their time organizing the resistance in the Lower Quarter of Medford. They spread news of Amrath's assassination by the archduke, of the innocence of the princess, and of the return of the prince. Those not moved by loyalty or justice were enticed by the chance to strike back at their betters. It was not difficult to convince the poor and the destitute to take up arms against the soldiery who policed them. In addition, there were those hoping for a possibility to do a little looting, or perhaps receive some reward from the crown if they prevailed.

They armed themselves with pitchforks, axes, and clubs.

Makeshift armor was constructed by strapping whatever thin metal they could find under their clothing. In most cases, this meant commandeering a baking sheet from their wives. They had the numbers, but they looked like a pathetic lot. Gwen had roused the Artisan Quarter, which provided not only strong workers but a few swords, bows, and bits of armor. With the city guards ordered to the perimeter and most of the Gentry Quarter at the trial, there was no one to stop them from openly organizing.

With Dixon at his side, Mason marched at the head of the commoner procession, his smithing hammer in one hand and a rough-hewn shield he had beaten together that morning in the other. Years of frustration and resentment steamed to the surface as the smith strode forward. Anger born from the life he had been denied overwhelmed him. When he could not pay the taxes on his late father's shop, the city sheriff and his guards had come. When he refused to leave, they had beaten him unconscious and thrown him into the gutter of Wayward Street. Mason blamed the guards for most of his life's misfortunes. The beating had weakened his shoulders, and for years afterward, wielding his hammer was so painful he could work only a few hours each day. This, and his gambling habit, kept him in poverty. Of course, he never really considered the gambling to be the real problem; it was the guards who were responsible. It did not matter to him that the soldiers and the sheriff who had beaten him were no longer with the guard. That day was his chance to fight back, to repay in kind for the pain he had endured.

Neither he nor Dixon was a warrior or even athletic, but they were large men with broad chests and thick necks, and the crowd followed behind them as if the citizens of the Lower Quarter were plowing the city with a pair of yoked oxen. They turned onto Wayward Street and marched unchallenged into the Gentry Quarter. Compared to the Lower Quarter, it was like another world. The streets were paved with decorative tile work and lined with metal horse hitches. Along the avenue, enclosed streetlamps and covered sewers accentuated the care taken for the comfort of the privileged few. Marking the center of the Gentry Quarter was a large spacious square. The great Essendon Fountain, with its statue of Tolin on a rearing horse above the pluming water, was its main landmark. Across from it, Mares Cathedral rose. In its towers high above, bells chimed loudly. They passed the fine three-story stone-and-brick houses, with their iron fences and decorative gates. That the stables here looked better than the house Mason lived in was not lost on him. The trip through the square only added fuel to the fire that was sweeping across the city.

When they reached Main Street, they saw the enemy.

ණ

The sound of the horn brought Arista to the window once more. What she saw amazed her. In the distance, at the edge of her sight, she could see banners rising above the naked trees. Count Pickering was coming, and he was not alone. There was a score of flags, representing most of the western provinces. Pickering was marching on Medford with an army.

Is it on my account?

She pondered the question and concluded the answer was no. Of all the nobles, she knew the Pickerings the best, but she doubted the count marched for her. The more likely explanation was that news of Alric's death had reached him, and he was challenging Braga for the crown. Arista doubted Pickering had given any thought to her. He merely saw his opportunity and he was reaching for it. The fact that she might still live was only a technicality. No one wanted a woman as their ruler. If Pickering won, he would force her abdication of the throne in favor of himself or perhaps Mauvin. She would be sent away, or locked up, but she would never be truly free. At least if Pickering won, Braga would never sit on the throne—but she did not like Pickering's chances. She was no tactician and certainly not a general but even she could see that the forces marching up the road lacked the numbers for a castle siege. Braga had his forces well entrenched. Looking at the courtyard below, she realized the attack was distracting everyone.

Perhaps this time it will be different.

She rushed to her door and with a tap of her necklace unlocked it. She grabbed the latch and pushed. As usual, the door refused to budge. "Damn that dwarf," she said aloud to herself. She pushed violently against the door, throwing her entire weight, such that it was, against it. The door did not give way.

There was another rumble, and her room shook once more. Dust fell from the rafters. *What is going on?* She staggered as the tower swayed like a ship at sea. She did not know what else to do. Terrified and bewildered, she returned to the illusionary safety of her bed. She sat there, hugging her knees, hardly breathing, her eyes darting at the slightest sound. The end was coming. One way or another, she was certain the end was coming soon.

⁂

The prince was new to combat and unsure what to expect. He had hoped that merely assembling a massive force would cause the city's defenders to surrender. The reality was altogether different. When they reached Medford, they found trenches built outside the walls filled with spearmen. His archers had launched three flights of arrows but still the defenders remained steadfast. Using shields, they fended off much of the barrage and sustained little noticeable damage.

Who are they? Alric wondered. *Are my own soldiers standing between me and my home? What lies has Braga spread among the guards? Or are they all hired men? Did my gold pay for those lines of pointed steel?*

Alric sat on one of Pickering's horses draped with a caparison hastily adorned with rough sewn images of the Melengar falcon. The animal was as restless as its rider, shuffling its hooves and snorting great clouds of frosty fog. Alric held the reins with his right hand, his left holding his woolen cloak tight about his neck. His eyes rose above the heads of the spearmen to look on the city of his birth. The walls and towers of Medford appeared faint and dreamlike through the falling snow. The vision slowly faded into white as an eerie silence muffled the world.

"Your Majesty," Count Pickering spoke, breaking the stillness.

"Another flight?" Alric proposed.

"Arrows will not conquer your city."

Alric nodded solemnly. "The knights, then—send them in."

"Marshal!" the count shouted. "Order the knights to break that line!"

Gallant men in shining armor spurred their steeds and charged forward with banners dancing overhead. A whirlwind of snow launched into the sky at their passing and obscured them from view. They vanished from sight but Alric listened to the thunder of their hooves.

The clash was dreadful. Alric felt it as much as heard it. Metal shrieked and men cried out, and until that moment, Alric had never known it was possible for horses to scream.

When the cloud of snow settled, the prince could at last see the bloody spectacle. Spears braced in the dirt pierced the breasts of man and mount. Horses collapsed, throwing the knights to the ground where they lay, like turtles struggling to right themselves. Spearmen drew forth short swords and thrust downward, punching their sharp points into eye slits and the armor gaps at the armpit or groin.

"This is not going as well as I hoped," Alric complained.

"Battle rarely ever does, Your Majesty," Count Pickering assured him. "But this is a large part of what being king means. Your knights are dying. Are you going to leave them to their fate?"

"Should I send in the foot soldiers?"

"If I were you, I certainly would. You need to break a hole in that wall, and you'd better do so before your men decide you're incompetent and vanish into the forests around them."

"Marshal!" Alric shouted. "Marshal Garret, order the foot soldiers to engage immediately!"

"Yes, Sire!"

A horn sounded and the men roared forward into battle. Alric watched as steel cut through flesh. The footmen fared better than the knights, but the defensive position of the city soldiers took a toll. Alric could hardly bear to watch. Never before had he seen such a sight—there was so much blood. The white snow was gone, stained pink and in some desperate places turned to a dark red. Littering the grounds were body parts—arms severed, heads split open, and legs chopped off. The wall of men blended in a whirling mass of flesh, dirt, blood, and an endless cacophony of screams.

"I can't believe this is happening," Alric said, sounding and feeling sick. "This is my city. These are my people. My men!" He turned to Count Pickering. "I'm killing my own men!" He was shaking now, his face red, and tears filled his eyes.

Hearing the shrieks and cries, he squeezed the pommel of his saddle until his hands hurt. He felt helpless.

I am king now.

He did not feel like a king. He felt like he had on the road near the Silver Pitcher when those men had held him facedown in the dirt. The tears were now streaming down his cheeks.

"Alric! Stop it!" Pickering snapped at him. "You mustn't let the men see you crying!"

Fury flared in Alric, and he spun on the count. "No? *No?* Look at them! They are dying for me. They are dying on *my* order! I say they do have a right to see their king! They *all* have a right to see their king!"

Alric wiped the tears from his cheeks and gathered his reins. "I'm tired of this. I'm tired of having my face put in the dirt! I won't stand it. I'm tired of being helpless. That's my city, built by my ancestors! If my people choose to fight, then by Maribor, I want them to know it's me they fight!"

The prince put on his helm, drew his father's large sword, and spurred his horse forward, not at the trench but at the castle gate itself.

"Alric, no!" Pickering shouted after him.

Mason rushed forward and drove his hammer through the helmet of the first guard he saw. Grinning with delight at his good fortune, he gathered the man's sword and looked up.

The mob had reached the main gate of the city. The great four-towered barbican of gray stone rose above them like a monstrous beast. It swarmed with soldiers shocked at the sight of the city rising against them. Surprise and the accompanying panic bought the mob time to clear the streets and reach the gatehouse. Mason heard Dixon shout, "For Prince Alric!" but the prince was the last thing on the smith's mind.

Mason picked out his next target—a tall guard absorbed in a swinging match with a street sweeper from Artisan Row. Mason stabbed the guard in the armpit and listened to him scream as he twisted the blade. The street sweeper grinned at the smith and Mason grinned back.

He had killed only two men but already Mason was slick with blood. His tunic felt heavy as it stuck to the skin of his chest and he could not tell if sweat or tears of blood dripped down his face. The grin he had shown to the sweeper remained glued to his lips by the thrill and elation.

This is freedom! This is living!

His heart thundered and his head swam as if he were drunk. Mason swung his sword again, this time at a man already down on one knee. His swing was so strong the blade cut halfway through his victim's neck. He kicked the dead man aside and cried aloud in his victory. He spoke no words; words were valueless at such a moment. He shouted the fury that pounded in his heart. He was a man again, a man of strength, a man to be feared!

A horn sounded and Mason looked up once more. A captain of the castle guard was on the ramparts shouting orders, rallying his troops. They responded to the call and fell back into ranks, struggling to defend the gate even as the mob closed in.

Mason stepped through the muddy, blood-soaked ground, now slick beneath his feet. He looked about and picked a new target. A castle guard with his back to the smith was in the process of retreating to the sound of his captain's voice. The smith aimed at the guard's neck, attempting to cleave off his head. His inexperience with a sword caused him to aim too high and the blade glanced off the man's helmet, ringing it loudly. He raised the sword for another blow when the man unexpectedly turned around.

Mason felt a sharp, burning pain in his stomach. In an instant, all the strength and fury drained from him. He let go his sword. He saw, rather than felt, himself drop to his knees. He looked down at the source of the pain and watched the soldier withdraw a sword from his stomach. Mason could not believe what he was seeing.

How could all that steel come out of me?

The smith felt a warm wetness on his hands as he instinctively pressed them to the wound. He tried as best he could to contain his organs as the blood flowed through a gash at least a foot wide. He no longer felt his legs, and lay helpless when, to his horror, he saw the soldier swing again—this time at his head.

❧

Alric charged the castle barbican. Immediately, Count Pickering, Mauvin, and Marshal Garret led the reserve knights in behind him. Arrows rained down from the parapets above the great gates. One deflected off Alric's visor, and another struck deep into the horn of his saddle. One hit Sir Sinclair's horse in the flank, causing it to rear unexpectedly, but the knight remained mounted. Countless more struck the ground harmlessly. The enraged prince rode directly to the gate and, standing up in his stirrups, shouted, "I am Prince Alric Brendon Essendon! Open this gate in the name of your king!"

Alric was not certain anyone had heard him as he stood there, his sword raised high over his head. Furthermore, if they had heard him, there was no reason to believe another arrow would not whistle down and end his life. Behind the prince, the remaining knights fanned out around him as the marshal attempted to build a wall around his monarch.

Another arrow did not fly but neither did the gate open.

"Alric," Count Pickering shouted, "you must fall back!"

"I am Prince Alric Essendon! Open the gate *now*!" he demanded again, and this time, he removed his helm and threw it aside, backing his horse into full view of the ramparts.

Alric and the others waited. Count Pickering and Mauvin stared at the prince in terror and tried to persuade him to come away from the gate. Nothing happened for several tense moments as the prince and his bodyguards sat outside waiting, staring up at the parapets. From inside they heard the sounds of fighting.

A shout came from atop the walls of the city. "The prince! Open the gate! Let him in! It's the prince!" More shouts, a scream, and then suddenly the massive gate split open, and the great doors pulled back. Inside was a mass of confusion as uniformed guards fought a horde of citizens dressed up like tinkers, wearing makeshift armor or stolen helms.

Alric did not pause. He spurred his mount and drove into the crowd. Mauvin, Count Pickering, Sir Ecton, and Marshal Garret struggled to form a personal defense for their king, but there was little need. At the sight of him, the defenders laid down their weapons. Word that the prince was alive spread, and those who saw him charging toward the castle, brandishing his father's sword, roared with cheers.

~

Royce heard the horn wail as he stood trapped on the steps of the tower. "Sounds like a fight outside," Magnus mentioned. "I wonder who will win." The dwarf scratched his beard. "For that matter, I wonder who is fighting."

"You don't take much interest in your employer's business, do you?" Royce said, studying the walls. When he tried to tap a spike into a seam, the stone broke like an eggshell. The dwarf was telling the truth about that.

"Only if it's necessary for the job. By the way, I wouldn't do that again. You were lucky you didn't hit a binding thread."

Royce cursed under his breath. "If you want to be helpful, why not just tell me how to get up and back?"

"Who said I was trying to be helpful?" The dwarf grinned at him wickedly. "I just spent half a year on this project. I don't want you to topple the whole thing in the first few minutes. I want to savor the moment."

"Are all dwarves this morbid?"

"Think of it as having built a sandcastle and wanting the pleasure of seeing it fall to a wave. I'm on the edge of my toes waiting to see exactly how and when it will finally collapse. Will it be a misstep, a loss of balance, or something amazing and unexpected?"

Royce drew his dagger and held it by the blade for the dwarf to see. "Are you aware I could put this through your throat where you stand?"

It was a false threat, as he would not dare throw away such a vital tool at this moment. Still, he expected a reaction of fear, or at least a mocking laugh. Instead, the dwarf did neither. He glared at the dagger, his eyes wide.

"Where did you get that blade?"

Royce rolled his eyes in disbelief. "I'm a little busy here. If you don't mind." He resumed his study of the steps. He observed the way they curved up and around the central trunk of the tower, how the steps above formed the ceiling to the ones below. He looked up ahead and then behind him.

"The step I am on doesn't collapse if I'm on it," Royce said to himself, but loud enough for the dwarf to hear. "It only falls if I step on the next one."

"Yes, quite ingenious, isn't it? As you might imagine, I'm quite proud of my work. I originally designed it to be an instrument of Arista's death. Braga hired me to set it up to look like an accident. A decrepit old tower in the royal residence collapses, and the poor princess is crushed in the process. Unfortunately, after Alric escaped, he changed his mind and decided to have her executed instead. I thought I would never get to see the fruits of all my hard work, but then you came along. How nice of you."

"All traps have weaknesses," Royce said. He looked ahead at the steps and smiled suddenly. Crouching, he leapt forward not one but two steps. The step in the middle slipped from its position and fell, but the step he had started from remained. "With no following step," Royce observed, "that step is now secure from breaking, isn't it?"

"Very clever," the dwarf replied, clearly disappointed.

Royce continued to leap two steps at a time until he moved around the circle out of sight of the dwarf. As he did, Magnus shouted, "It'll do you no good. The gap at the bottom is much too far for you to jump. You are still trapped!"

Arista was crouched on her bed when she heard someone outside her door. It was probably that dreadful little dwarf or Braga himself coming to take her to the trial. She could hear a scraping and an occasional thud. She remembered too late that she had not resealed the door with her gemlock. As she moved toward the door, it swung open. To her surprise, it was neither Braga nor the dwarf. Instead, there in the doorway was one of the thieves from the dungeon.

"Princess," was all Royce said, entering with a respectful though brief nod in her direction. He quickly moved past her and seemed to be looking for something; his eyes roamed over the walls and ceiling of her bedroom.

"You? What are *you* doing here? Is Alric alive?"

"Alric's fine," Royce said as he moved about the room. He

looked out the windows and examined the material of the drapes. "Well, that's not going to work."

"Why are you here? How did you get here? Did you see Esrahaddon? What did he say to Alric?"

"I'm a bit busy just now, Your Highness."

"Busy? Doing what?"

"Saving you but I'll admit I'm not doing very well at the moment." Without asking permission, Royce opened her wardrobe and began sifting through her clothes. Then he rifled through her dresser drawers.

"What do you want with my *clothes*?"

"I'm trying to figure a way out of here. I suspect this tower is going to collapse in a few minutes, and if we don't get out soon, we'll die."

"I see," she said simply. "Why can't we just go down the stairs?" She got up and crept to the doorway. "Sweet Maribor!" she cried as she saw every other step missing.

"We can leap those but the last six or seven steps at the bottom are totally gone. It's too far to jump to the corridor. I was hoping maybe we could jump out the window to the moat, but that looks like instant death."

"Oh," was all she could utter. A scream was growing in her and she covered her mouth with her hand, holding it back. "You're right. You're not doing very well."

Royce looked under her bed and then stood up. "Wait a minute, you're a sorceress, aren't you? Esrahaddon taught you magic. Can you get us down? Levitate us, or turn us into birds or something?"

Arista smiled awkwardly. "I was never able to learn much from Esrahaddon and certainly not self-levitation."

"Can you levitate a board or stone we could jump to?"

Arista shook her head.

"And the bird thing?"

"Even if I could, which I can't, we'd stay birds, because I couldn't turn us back after changing, now could I?"

"So magic is out," Royce said, and began pulling the feather-stuffed mattress off Arista's bed, revealing the rope net beneath it. "Okay, then help me untie your bed."

"The rope isn't long enough to reach the bottom of the tower," Arista told him.

"It doesn't have to be," he replied, pulling the rope through the holes in the bed frame.

The tower shuddered, and dust cascaded from the rafters. Arista held her breath for a moment, her heart pounding in anticipation of a sudden plummet, but the tower steadied itself once more.

"Clearly we are running out of time." Royce coiled the length of rope over his shoulder and headed toward the door.

Arista paused only a moment to look back at the dressing table and the brushes her father had given her, and then moved to what remained of the stairs.

"You're going to have to jump down. The steps that are still there should be very sturdy and it should be easier than jumping up. Just be sure you don't over jump, but if you do, I'll try to catch you." With that, he sprang down two steps so gracefully that she felt embarrassed for her own lack of confidence.

Arista stood on the landing and rocked back and forth, focusing on the first step. She leapt and landed on it a little too far forward. Waving her arms madly, she teetered on the edge, struggling desperately against falling. Royce held out his hands, ready to catch her, but she regained her balance. Shaking slightly, she took a deep breath.

"Don't over jump!" he reminded her.

No kidding, she thought. *As if I haven't already learned that lesson.*

The second jump was easier, and the third better still. Soon she developed a rhythm and moved down the steps at a brisk pace following Royce, who almost danced his way down. They were nearly to the bottom when Royce stopped.

"Keep going," he told her. "Stop when you reach the last step and wait there."

She nodded as he pulled the rope from around his shoulder and began tying it to the step he stood on. Arista continued to jump her way down, reminding herself not to be overconfident. When she saw the open expanse at the bottom, her remaining confidence fled. The gaping hole, which fell away into darkness, was enough to shake her back into terror.

"Well, well, princess!" the dwarf called to her. He stood in the open doorway of the corridor, grinning, showing a mouthful of yellowed teeth. "I really didn't expect to see you again. Where's the thief? Did he fall to his death?"

"You disgusting little beast!" she cried at him.

The tower shifted once more. Its shuddering caused Arista to stagger a bit on the step and her heart to pound in fear. Clouds of dust and bits of rock rained down, clattering off the walls and steps. Arista cowered, covering her head with her arms, until the shaking stopped and the debris settled.

"This old tower, she's almost ready to fall," the dwarf told her with a manic glee in his voice. "Such a pity to be so close to safety and yet still so very far. If only you were a frog, you might leap it. As it is, you still don't have a way out."

A coil of rope fell from the heights above. Suspended by a stair, the rope dangled midway between the princess and the dwarf. Along the slender line, Royce descended like a spider. When he reached a point level with Arista, he stopped and began to swing.

"Now *that* is impressive!" the dwarf exclaimed, and nodded, showing his approval.

Royce swung onto the step next to Arista and tied the rope around his own waist. "All we have to do is swing across. Just hang on to me."

The princess gladly threw her arms around the thief's shoulders and squeezed tight, as much out of fear as for safety.

"You might have actually made it," the dwarf said. "For that you have my respect, but you must understand I have a reputation to uphold. I can't have someone walking around boasting they escaped one of my traps." Then, without warning, he abruptly closed the door, sealing them in.

Hadrian heard the wail of a horn as he faced Braga in the corridor of the royal residence. "I think it will be quite some time until Wylin and the castle guards arrive," he said, taunting the archduke. "I suspect the master-at-arms has more on his mind than responding to the demands of an earl from Warric to report to the royal residence when his castle is being stormed."

"More's the pity for you, as I no longer have the luxury of keeping you alive," Braga said as he lunged once more.

He swiped at Hadrian with lightning-fast cuts. Hadrian danced away from Braga, retreating farther and farther down the hall. The archduke showed perfect form, his weight centered on his back foot while only the toe of his front foot touched the ground, his back straight, his sword arm outstretched, and his other arm raised in a graceful bent L. Even the fingers of his free hand were elegantly posed as if they were holding up an invisible wineglass. His long black hair, peppered with lines of gray, cascaded down to his shoulders, and not a trace of perspiration was on his brow.

Hadrian in contrast acted clumsy and unsure. The Melengar sword was far inferior to any of his own blades. The tip wavered as he tried to hold it steady with both hands. He inched backward, working to keep a distance between them.

The archduke lunged again. Hadrian parried and then dove past Braga, barely avoiding a return slice, which nicked a wall sconce. He took the opportunity to run down the hallway and slip into the chapel. "Are we playing hide-and-seek now?" Braga said, goading him.

Braga entered and crossed swiftly to the altar, where Hadrian stood. When the archduke swung at him, Hadrian stepped back, ducked a swiping stroke, and then leapt clear of a slash. Braga's attacks glanced off the statue of Novron and Maribor, taking part of the god's first three fingers off. Hadrian now stood before the wooden lectern, keeping his eyes on the archduke while he awaited the next attack.

"It's so poetic of you to choose to die in the same room as the king," Braga said. He swung right, and Hadrian glanced the stroke aside. Braga pivoted on his back foot and swung his sword overhead in a powerful downward stroke. Expecting this attack, counting on it, Hadrian dove and slid across the polished marble floor on his stomach in the direction of the chapel door.

Hadrian got to his feet and turned in time to see Braga's stroke had sliced into the vertical grain of the lectern. His swing had been so forceful that the blade was now wedged in the wood and the archduke struggled to free it. Taking advantage of his distraction, Hadrian ran to the door, slipped out, and closed it behind him. Driving his sword into the jamb, he wedged it shut.

"That should hold you for a while," Hadrian said to himself, pausing to catch his breath.

~

"That little worm!" Arista spat through clenched teeth at the closed door.

The tower shuddered again, and this time larger pieces fell. One block of stone plummeted down, taking out a step only a few feet from them. Both shattered on impact and fell into the abyss of the tower's foundation. With the loss of those blocks, the tower came free and began to twist and topple.

"Hang on!" Royce shouted as he pushed off the step. The two flew across the gap to the door. He grabbed hold of the large iron door ring, and they each found footholds on the ledge of the doorjamb.

"He locked it," Royce informed her. He looped one arm through the door ring and removed his lock-picking tools from his belt. With his free hand, he worked the lock. A deep, resonating thunder shook the castle, and suddenly the rope tied to Royce went slack. The thief dropped his tools and pulled out his dagger. He cut the rope around his waist just as the stone slab attached to it passed them heading down. The rest of the tower was collapsing now.

Royce drove his dagger deep into the wooden door for another handhold as the tower fell around them. Walls hollowed out by the dwarf splintered into shards, which burst and flew in all directions. Rocks and stone pummeled them as Royce and Arista cowered under the scant protection of the narrow stone arch of the doorframe.

A fist-size stone struck Arista's back. She lost her tenuous foothold and screamed as she fell. In an instant, Royce grabbed her. Grasping blindly, he caught the back of her dress and a substantial amount of hair. "I can't hold you!" he shouted.

He felt her sliding down his body, the back of her dress

tearing. Royce gave up his own toehold, hanging by his arm hooked through the door ring, so that he could wrap his legs around her. The princess's fingers clawed his body frantically, and when they finally found his belt, she latched on.

Royce was temporarily blinded by a cloud of dust and powdered stone. When it settled, he found they were dangling in the brilliant sunlight on what was now an exterior wall of the castle's keep. The debris of the tower fell into the moat, making a pile of broken rocks seventy feet below. The crowd of trial watchers screamed and gasped, pointing up at them. "It's the princess!" a voice shouted.

"Can you reach the ledge?" Royce asked.

"No! If I try, I'll fall. I can't—"

Royce felt her slipping again and tried to tighten his leg hold on her, but he knew it would not be enough.

"Oh no! My fingers—I'm slipping!"

Royce's arm, crooked in the ring, was wrenching his shoulder badly. His other hand, which gripped Arista's dress and hair, was slowly losing hold. She was sliding down once again; soon he would lose her altogether. Royce felt a tug on his arm. The door opened, and a strong hand reached out and grabbed Arista.

"I've got you," Hadrian told her as he hauled the princess up. Then he pulled the door open wide, dragging Royce into the hallway with it.

They lay on the floor exhausted and covered in bits of rock. Royce got to his feet and dusted off his clothes. "I thought I felt it unlock," he said, getting up and retrieving his dagger from the face of the door.

Hadrian stood in the threshold, looking out at the clearing blue sky. "Well, Royce, I love what you've done with the place."

"Where's the dwarf?" Royce asked, looking around.

"I didn't see him."

"And Braga? You didn't kill him, did you?"

"No. I locked him in the chapel but it won't hold. Which reminds me, could I borrow your sword? You're not going to use it, anyway."

Royce handed him the falchion sword that had been part of his castle guard disguise. Hadrian took the weapon, slipped it from its sheath, and weighed it in his hand. "I tell you, these swords are terrible. They are heavy and have all the balance of a drunken three-legged dog trying to take a piss." He then looked at Arista and added, "Oh, excuse me, Your Highness. How are you doing, Princess?"

Arista got to her feet. "Much better now."

"For the record, we're even, right?" Royce asked her. "You saved us from prison and a horrible death, and now we've saved you."

"Fine," she agreed, wiping the dust from her torn dress. "But I would like to point out my rescue of you was far less death defying." She ran a hand through her disheveled hair. "That really hurt, you know."

"Falling would have hurt more."

A loud bang echoed from down the hall.

"Gotta go," Hadrian told them. "His Lordship is loose."

"Be careful," Arista shouted after him. "He's a renowned swordsman!"

"I'm really tired of hearing that," Hadrian grumbled as he started back up the hall. He had not gone far when Braga rounded the corner, coming toward them.

"So, you got her out!" Braga bellowed. "I'll just have to kill her myself, then."

"You'll have to get by me first, I'm afraid," Hadrian told him.

"That won't be a problem."

The archduke charged Hadrian, swinging at him in a fury.

Braga hammered stroke after stroke on him in a rage. Hadrian fought to deflect the fierce blows, which fell so fast they whistled in the air. The look on Braga's reddening face was one of hatred as he continued to pummel Hadrian.

"Braga!" Alric shouted from the far end of the hall.

The archduke spun, panting for air.

Hadrian saw the prince standing at the far end of the corridor. He was dressed in plate armor and a white tabard marred by a spattering of blood. Alric's hand rested on the hilt of his sheathed sword, and at his side were the Pickerings and Sir Ecton. Each wore a grim and dangerous look.

"Put down your weapon," the prince ordered in a powerful voice. "It's over. This is my kingdom!"

"You filthy little creature!" Braga cursed at the prince. He turned his attention away from Hadrian and began walking toward Alric. Hadrian did not follow. Instead, he joined Royce and Arista to watch.

"Did you think I was after your precious little kingdom?" Braga bellowed. "Is that what you think? I was trying to save the *world*, you fools! Can't you see it? Look at him!" The archduke pointed at the prince. "Look at the little maggot prince!" He turned and pointed back at Arista. "And her, too! Just like their father; they aren't human!" Braga, his face still red from the fight, continued down the corridor toward Alric. "You would have filth rule you all, but not me. Not while there is breath in this body!"

Braga charged forward, raising his sword as he moved. When he came within reach of Alric, he brought it down toward the prince. Before Alric could react, the attack was deflected. An elegant rapier caught Braga's blade mid-stroke.

Count Pickering held Braga's sword in the air, and Sir Ecton pulled the prince out of harm's way.

"You have your sword, I see. So there will be no excuse for you this time, dear count," Braga said.

"There will be no need for one. You are a traitor to the crown, and in memory of my friend Amrath, I'll end this."

Blades flashed. Pickering was as much a master of fencing as Braga, and the two moved elegantly, their swords appearing as extensions of their bodies. Reaching for their weapons, Mauvin and Fanen started forward, but Ecton stopped them. "This is your father's fight."

Pickering and Braga fought to kill. Sword strokes swept faster than the eye could follow, their deadly blades whistling a song to each other, crashing in chorus. The incredibly lustrous blade of Pickering's rapier caught the faint light in the corridor and glowed as it streaked through the air. It flashed and sparked when steel met steel.

Braga lunged, nicked Pickering's side, and, sweeping back, cut him shallowly across the chest. Pickering barely blocked a second stab with a quick parry, which allowed him an overhead stroke. Braga raised his sword to block, but Pickering ignored the defense. He swung down with force and speed, streaking light from his sword.

Hadrian instinctually cringed. The high, overpowered stroke would leave Pickering vulnerable, open to a fatal riposte by Braga. Then the metal of the swords clashed. A brilliant spark flared as, incredibly, Pickering's blade sheared Braga's sword in two. The count's stroke continued unabated into the archduke's throat. The lord chancellor collapsed to the floor, his head rolling a foot away.

Mauvin and Fanen rushed to their father's side, beaming with obvious pride and relief. Alric ran down the hall to where his sister stood between the two thieves. "Arista!" he shouted as he threw his arms around her. “Thank Maribor you’re all right!”

“You aren’t angry with me?” she asked, pulling away from him with surprise in her voice.

Alric shook his head. “I owe you my life,” he said, hugging her again. “And as for you two—” he began, looking at Royce and Hadrian.

“Alric,” Arista interrupted, “it was not their fault. They didn’t kill Father, and they didn’t want to kidnap you. It was my doing. I was the one who forced them. They didn’t do anything.”

“Oh, you are quite wrong there, my dear sister. They did a *great* deal.” Alric smiled and placed a hand on Hadrian’s shoulder. “Thank you.”

“You’re not going to charge us for the tower, I hope,” Hadrian said. “But if you are, it was Royce’s fault and should come out of his share.”

Alric chuckled.

“My fault?” Royce growled. “Find that little bearded menace and take your payment out of *his* stubby little hide.”

“I don’t understand,” Arista replied, looking confused. “You wanted them executed.”

“You must be mistaken, dear sister. These two fine men are the royal protectors of Essendon, and it appears they have done a finc job today.”

“Your Lordship.” Marshal Garret appeared in the hall and approached the count, glancing only briefly at the dead body of Braga. “The castle has been secured and the mercenaries are slain or have fled. It would appear the castle guard is still loyal to the House of Essendon. The nobles are anxious to hear about the state of affairs and are waiting in the court.”

“Good,” the count replied. “Tell them His Majesty will

address them soon. Oh, and send someone to clean this mess up, will you?" The marshal bowed and left.

Alric and his sister walked hand in hand down the corridor toward the others. Hadrian and Royce followed behind them. "Even now it's hard for me to believe him capable of such treachery," Alric said, looking down at Braga's body. A large puddle of blood stretched across the floor of the hallway and Arista lifted the hem of her dress as she passed.

"What was all that ranting about us not being human?" Arista asked.

"He was clearly insane," Bishop Saldur said, approaching with Archibald Ballentyne in tow. Although Hadrian had never met the bishop in person, he knew who he was. Saldur greeted the prince and princess with a warm smile and fatherly expression. "It's so good to see you, Alric," he said, placing his hands on the boy's shoulders. "And my dear Arista, no one is more pleased than I about your innocence. I must beg your forgiveness, my dear, as I was misled by your uncle. He planted seeds of doubts in my mind. I should have followed my heart and realized you could not possibly have done the things he accused you of." He gently kissed her on one cheek and then the other.

The bishop looked down at the blood-soaked body at their feet. "I fear the guilt of killing the king was too much for the poor man, and in the end, he lost his mind completely. Perhaps he was certain you were dead, Alric, and seeing you in the hallway, he took you for a ghost or a demon back from the grave to haunt him."

"Perhaps," Alric said skeptically. "Well, at least it's over now."

"What about the dwarf?" Arista asked.

"Dwarf?" Alric replied. "How do you know about the dwarf?"

"He was the one who set the trap in the tower. He nearly killed me and Royce. Does anyone know where he has gotten to? He was just here."

"He's responsible for far more than that. Mauvin, run and tell the marshal to organize a search immediately," Alric instructed.

"Right away." Mauvin nodded and ran off.

"I, too, am pleased you are all right, Your Highness," Archibald told the prince. "I was told you were dead."

"And were you here to pay your respects to my memory?"

"I was here by invitation."

"Who invited you?" Alric asked, and looked at the slain corpse of Braga. "Him? What dealings do an Imperialist earl from Warric and a traitorous archduke have in Melengar?"

"It was a cordial visit, I assure you."

Alric glared at the earl. "Get out of my kingdom before I have you seized as a conspirator."

"You wouldn't dare," Archibald returned. "I'm a vassal of King Ethelred. Seize me or even treat me roughly and you risk war—a struggle Melengar can ill afford, particularly now, with an inexperienced boy at the helm."

Alric drew his sword, and Archibald took two steps back. "Escort the earl out before I forget Melengar has a treaty of peace with Warric."

"Times are changing, Your Highness," Archibald called to the prince as guards led him away. "The New Empire is coming, and there is no place for an archaic monarchy in the new order."

"Is there no way I can throw him in the dungeon, even for a few days?" Alric asked Pickering. "Can I try him as a spy perhaps?"

Before Pickering could reply, the bishop Saldur spoke. "The earl is quite right, Your Highness. Any hostile act made against Ballentyne would be considered by King Ethelred to be an act of war against Chadwick. Just consider how you would respond if Count Pickering here were hanged in Aquesta. You wouldn't stand for it any more than he would. Besides, the earl is all bluster. He is young and merely trying to sound important. Forgive him his youth. Have you not made errors in judgment as well?"

"Perhaps," Alric muttered. "Still, I can't help but suspect that snake is up to no good. I just wish there was some way I could teach him a lesson."

"Your Highness?" Hadrian said, stopping him. "If you don't mind, Royce and I have friends in the city we'd like to check on."

"Oh, yes, of course, go right ahead," Alric responded. "But there is the matter of payment. You've done me a great service," he said, looking fondly at his sister. "I intend to honor my word. You can name your price."

"If it's all right, we'll get back to you on that," Royce said.

"I understand." The prince revealed a hint of concern. "But I do hope you'll be reasonable in your request and not bankrupt the kingdom."

"You should address the court," Pickering told Alric.

Alric nodded and he, Arista, and Mauvin disappeared down the stairs. Pickering lingered behind with the two thieves.

"I think there's a chance that boy will actually make a decent king," he mentioned once the prince was too far away to hear. "I had my doubts in the past, but he seems to have changed. He is more serious, more confident."

"So, the sword is magic after all." Hadrian motioned toward the rapier.

"Hmm?" Pickering looked down at the sword he wore at his side and grinned. "Oh, well, let's just say it gives me an edge in a battle. That reminds me, why were you letting Braga beat you?"

"What do you mean?"

"I saw you fighting when we first came up. Your stance was defensive, your strokes all parries and blocks. You never once attacked."

"I was frightened," Hadrian lied. "Braga has won so many awards and tournament competitions, and I haven't won any."

Pickering looked puzzled. "But not being noble born, you aren't allowed to enter a tournament."

Hadrian pursed his lips and nodded. "Now that you mention it, I suppose you're right. You'd best see to your wounds, Your Lordship. You're bleeding on your nice tunic."

Pickering glanced down and looked surprised to see the slice Braga had given him across the chest. "Oh, yes, well, it doesn't matter. The tunic is ruined from the cut anyway, and the bleeding seems to have stopped."

Mauvin returned and trotted over to them. He stood next to his father, his arm around his waist. "I have soldiers looking for the dwarf but so far no luck." Despite the bad news, Mauvin was smiling broadly.

"What are you grinning at?" his father asked.

"I knew you could best him. I did doubt it for a time, but deep down I knew."

The count nodded and a thoughtful expression came over his face. He looked at Hadrian. "After so many years of doubt, it was fortuitous I had the opportunity and good fortune to defeat Braga, particularly with my sons watching."

Hadrian nodded and smiled. "That's true."

There was a pause as Pickering studied his face and then he placed a hand on Hadrian's shoulder. "To be quite honest, I for one am very pleased you're not noble, Mr. Hadrian Blackwater, quite pleased indeed."

"Are you coming, Your Lordship?" Sir Ecton called, and the count and his sons headed off.

"You didn't really hold back on Braga so Pickering could kill him, did you?" Royce asked after the two were left alone in the hallway.

"Of course not. I held off because it's death for a commoner to kill a noble."

"That's what I thought." Royce sounded relieved. "For a minute, I wondered if you'd gone from jumping on the good-deed wagon to leading the whole wagon train."

"Sure the gentry appear all nice and friendly, but if I'd killed him, even though they wanted him dead anyway, you can be sure they wouldn't be patting me on the back, saying, 'Good job.' No, it's best to avoid killing nobles."

"At least not where there are witnesses," Royce said with a grin.

As they headed out of the castle, they heard Alric's voice echoing: "...was a traitor to the crown and responsible for the murder of my father. He attempted to murder me and to execute my sister. Yet, due to the wisdom of the princess and the heroism of others, I am standing here before you."

This was followed by a roar of applause and cheers.

Chapter 10

Coronation Day

Seventy-eight people had died, and over two hundred bore wounds from what became known as the Battle of Medford. The timely attack by the citizenry at the gate had precipitated the prince's entrance into the city, and arguably had saved his life. Once news of Alric's return spread through the city, all resistance ended. This restored peace but not order. For several hours after the battle, roving gangs took the opportunity to loot shops and storehouses, mostly along the riverfront. A shoemaker died defending his cobbler shop, and a weaver was badly beaten. In addition to the general thieving, the sheriff, his two deputies, and a moneylender were murdered. Many believed there were those who took advantage of the chaos to settle old scores. The killers were never identified, and no one bothered to look for the looters. In the end, no one was even arrested; it was enough that the violence was over.

Most of the snow that had fallen the day of the battle had melted over the next few days, leaving only dirty patches hiding in the shadows. Still, for the most part, the weather remained decidedly cold. Autumn was officially finished, and winter had arrived. In the freezing winds, a silent crowd stood outside the royal crypt for hours as they removed Amrath's body for the official state funeral. Many others were buried the same day. The funerals provided a cleansing of the entire city's grief, followed by a weeklong period of mourning.

Among the dead was Wylin, the captain of the guard of Essendon Castle. He had fallen while directing the defenses at the castle gate. It was never determined if Wylin had been a traitor or had merely been deceived by the archduke's lies. Alric gave him the benefit of the doubt and granted him burial with full honors. Although Mason Grumon died, Dixon Taft, manager of The Rose and Thorn, survived the battle with only the loss of his right arm just above the elbow. He might have died, along with many others, except for the efforts of Gwen DeLancy and her girls. Prostitutes, it turned out, made excellent nurses. The maimed and wounded who lacked family to care for them filled Medford House for weeks. When word of this reached the castle, food, supplies, and linens were sent.

News spread throughout Melengar of Alric's heroic charge on the fortified gates. How he had survived the hail of arrows, only to bravely fling off his helm and dare them a second time—it made for great barroom stories. Few had thought much of the son of Amrath prior to the battle, but now he became a hero in the eyes of many. A somewhat lesser-known tale gained popularity a few days later as it, too, circulated through the city's taverns. This outlandish yarn described how two criminals, falsely accused of the king's murder, had escaped a torturous death by abducting the prince. The story grew with each telling, and soon these same thieves were said to have gone on a rollicking trip through the countryside with the prince, returning just in time to save the princess from the tower seconds before it collapsed. Some even claimed to have helped the thieves save the prince from a roadside execution, while others insisted they personally saw the princess and one of the criminals dangling from the side of the castle after the collapse of the tower.

Despite extensive searches, the dwarf whose hand had actually killed the king escaped. Alric posted a reward notice offering one hundred gold tenents on every crossroad sign and on the door of every tavern and church in the realm. Patrols rode the length of every road, searching barns, storehouses, mills, and even under the spans of bridges, yet he was not found.

Following the week of mourning, work began on repairing the castle. Crews cleared away the debris, and architects estimated at least a year to rebuild the lost tower. Though the falcon flag flew above the castle, the city saw little of Prince Alric. He remained sequestered within the halls of power, buried under hundreds of obligations. Count Pickering, acting as a counselor, remained in the castle along with his sons. He assisted the young prince in his efforts to assume his father's role.

One month to the day after the burial of King Amrath, the prince's coronation took place. By that time, the snows had returned and the city was white once more. Everyone came to the ceremony, yet only a fraction could fit inside the expansive Mares Cathedral, where the coronation took place. The majority caught a brief glimpse of their new monarch when he rode in an open carriage back to the castle or as he stood on the open balcony while trumpets blared.

It was a full day of celebration with minstrels and street performers hired to entertain the citizenry. The castle even provided free ale and rows upon rows of tables filled with all manner of food. In the evening, which came sooner with the shortening of the days, people crammed into the local taverns and inns, which were full of out-of-town visitors. The locals retold the stories of the Battle of Medford and the now famous legend of *Prince Alric and the Thieves.* These stories were still popular and showed no sign of going out of fashion. The day was long and eventually even the lights in the public houses winked out..

One of the few buildings still burning a candle was in the Artisan Quarter. It had originally been a haberdashery, but the previous owner, Lester Furl, had died in the battle the month before. Some said the plumed hat he had worn that day had caught the attention of an axe. Since then, the wooden sign of the ornate cavalier hat had still hung above the door, but no hats were for sale in the window. Even late into the night, the light was always on; however, no one was ever seen entering or exiting the shop. A small man in a simple robe greeted those nosy enough to knock. Behind him, visitors saw a room filled with the dried, hairless skins of animals. Most soaked in tubs or were stretched out on frames. There were pumice stones, needles and thread, and folded sheets of vellum piled neatly along the walls. The room also contained three desks with upright tops over which large sheets of parchment lay with carefully written text. Bottles of ink rested on shelves and in open drawers. The man was always polite, and when asked what he sold in his shop, he would reply, "Nothing." He simply wrote books. Because few people could read, most inquiries ended there.

The fact was there were very few books in the shop.

Myron Lanaklin sat alone in the store. He had written half a page of *Grigoles Treatise on Imperial Common Law* and then just stopped. The room was cold and silent. He stood up, walked to the shop window, and looked out at the dark, snowy street. In a city with more people than he had seen before in his lifetime, he felt utterly alone. A month had passed, but he had finished only half of his first book. He found himself spending most of his time just sitting. In the silence, he imagined he could hear the sound of his brothers speaking the evening vespers.

He avoided sleep because of the nightmares. They had started the third night he slept in the shop and were terrible. Visions of flames and sounds of pleading coming from his own mouth as the voices of his family died in the inferno. Every night they died again, and every day he awoke on the cold floor of the tiny room in a world more silent and isolated than the abbey had ever been. He missed his home and the mornings he spent with Renian.

Alric made good on his promise. The new King of Melengar provided him the shop rent-free and all the materials needed for making his books. Never was there a mention of cost. Myron should have been happy, but he felt more lost each day. Although he had more food than ever before, and no abbot to restrict his diet, he ate little. His appetite dwindled along with his desire to write.

When he had first arrived at the shop, he had felt obligated to replace the books, but as the days slipped by, he sat alone and confused. How could he *replace* the books? They were not missing. No shelf lay bare; no library stood wanting. What would he do if he ever completed the project? What would he do with the books? What would become of them? What would become of him? They had no home, and neither did he.

Myron sat down on the wooden floor in the corner, pulling his legs to his chest, and rested his head against the wall. "Why did I have to be the one who lived?" he muttered to the empty room. "Why did I have to be left behind? Why is it I'm cursed with an indelible memory, so that I can recall every face, every scream, every cry?"

As usual, Myron wept. There was no one to see, so he let the tears run unchecked down his cheeks. He cried there on the floor in the flickering candlelight and soon fell asleep.

The knock on the door startled him and he stood up. He could not have been asleep long; the candle still burned. Myron moved to the door and, opening it a crack, peered out. On the stoop outside, two men in heavy winter cloaks stood waiting.

"Myron? Are you going to let us in or leave us to freeze?"

"Hadrian? Royce!" Myron exclaimed as he threw open the door. He embraced Hadrian immediately and then turned to Royce and paused, deciding a handshake would suit him better.

"So it's been a while," Hadrian said, kicking the snow off his boots. "How many books have you finished?"

Myron looked sheepish. "I've had a little trouble adjusting but I'll get them done. Isn't this place wonderful?" he said, trying to sound sincere. "It was very generous of His Majesty to provide all this for me. I've enough vellum to last years, and ink? Well, don't get me started. As Finiless wrote, 'More could not be gotten though the world be emptied to the breath of time.' "

"So you like it here?" Hadrian asked.

"Oh, I love it, yes. I really couldn't ask for anything more." The two thieves exchanged looks, the meaning of which Myron could not discern. "Can I get either of you something—tea, perhaps? The king is very good to me. I even have honey to sweeten it."

"Tea would be nice," Royce said.

Myron moved to the counter to fetch a pot. "So what are you two doing out so late?" he asked, then laughed at himself. "Oh, never mind, I guess this isn't late for *you*. I suppose you work nights."

"Something like that," Hadrian said. "We just got back from a trip to Chadwick. We are heading back to The Rose and Thorn but wanted to stop by here on the way and deliver the news."

"News? What kind of news?"

"Well, I thought it might be good news, but now I'm not so sure."

"Why's that?" the monk asked, pouring water into the pot.

"Well, it would mean leaving here."

"It would?" Myron turned suddenly, spilling the water.

"Well, yes, but I suppose if you're really attached to this place, we could—"

"To go where?" Myron asked anxiously, setting down the pitcher, forgetting the tea.

"Well," Hadrian began, "Alric offered us whatever we wanted as payment for saving his sister, but seeing as how Arista saved our life first, it didn't seem right asking for money, or land, or anything personal like that. We got to thinking just how much was lost when the Winds Abbey was destroyed. Not just the books, mind you, but the safe haven for those lost in the wilderness. So we asked the king to rebuild the abbey just like it was."

"Are—are you serious?" Myron stammered. "And did he say yes?"

"To be honest, he sounded relieved," Royce said. "I think he felt as if there was a dagger dangling over his head for a month. I suppose he was afraid we'd ask for something ridiculous like his firstborn or the crown jewels."

"We might have, if we hadn't already stolen them." Hadrian chuckled, and Myron was not sure if he was joking or not.

"But if you really like this place..." Hadrian said, whirling his finger in the air. "I suppose we—"

"No! No—I mean, I think you are right. The abbey should be rebuilt for the sake of the kingdom."

"Glad you feel that way, because we need you to help the builders design it. I'm assuming you could draw a few floor plans and maybe some sketches?"

"Certainly, down to the finest detail."

Hadrian chuckled. "I bet you can. I can see you're going to drive the royal architect to drink."

"Who will be the abbot? Has Alric contacted the Dibben Monastery already?"

"He sent out a messenger this morning as one of his first acts as king. You're going to have a few guest monks trickling in over the winter, and this spring all of you'll have a great deal of work to do."

Myron was grinning widely.

"About that tea?" Royce inquired.

"Oh yes, sorry." He returned to pouring water into the pot. Stopping once more, he turned back to the thieves, and his grin faded.

"I would so much love to return to my home and see it rise again. But…" Myron paused.

"What is it?"

"Won't the Imperialists simply come back? If they hear the abbey is there again—I don't think I could…"

"Relax, Myron," Hadrian said. "That's not going to happen."

"But how can you be sure?"

"Trust me, the Imperialists won't advocate another foray into Melengar," Royce assured the monk. The smile on the thief's face made Myron think of a cat, and he was happy not to be a mouse.

ꕥ

In the hours before dawn, the Lower Quarter was quiet. Dampened by the snow, the only sound came from the muffled hoof falls of mounts as they moved slowly up the alley to The Rose and Thorn.

"Do you need any of the money?" Royce asked Hadrian.

"I have enough. Deposit the rest with Gwen. What does that come to now?"

"Well, we're in pretty good shape. We have our share of the fifteen gold tenents for returning Alenda's letters, and the twenty from Ballentyne for stealing them in the first place, plus DeWitt's one hundred, and Alric's one hundred. You know, one day we're going to have to find DeWitt—and *thank him* for that job." Royce grinned.

"Do you think it was fair asking for the money along with the abbey?" Hadrian asked. "I have to admit the guy was starting to grow on me, and I hate to think we took advantage of him."

"The hundred was for going into Gutaria with him," Royce reminded him. "The abbey was for saving his sister. We didn't ask for *anything* Alric didn't agree to in advance. And he did say anything, so we could easily have asked for land and noble rank."

"Why didn't we?"

"Oh? So you would like to be the count Blackwater, would you?"

"It might have been nice," Hadrian said, sitting up straighter in his saddle. "And you could be the infamous marquis Melborn."

"Why infamous?"

"Would you prefer notorious? Nefarious, perhaps?"

"What's wrong with *beloved*?"

Neither could hold a straight face at the thought.

"Come to think of it, we failed to bill the good king for saving him from Trumbul. Do you think—"

"It's too late, Royce," Hadrian told him.

Royce sighed, disappointed. "So, I think he wasn't too put out, all things considered. Besides, we *are* thieves, remember?

Anyway, the bottom line is, we won't be starving this winter."

"Yes, we've been good little squirrels, haven't we?" Hadrian said.

"Maybe this spring we can start that fishing enterprise you wanted."

"I thought you wanted the winery."

Royce shrugged.

"Well, you keep thinking. I'm going to go wake up Emerald and let her know I'm back. It's too cold to sleep alone tonight."

Royce passed the tavern and dismounted at Medford House. For some time, he stood, just staring at the top window, while his feet grew colder and colder in the snow.

"You *are* going to come up, aren't you?" Gwen asked from the doorway. She was still dressed and as pretty as ever. "Isn't it awfully cold out there?"

Royce smiled at her. "You waited up."

"You said you'd be coming back tonight."

Royce pulled his saddlebag off his horse and carried it up the steps. "I have another deposit to make."

"Is that why you were standing in the snow for so long? You were trying to decide whether or not to trust me with your money?"

Her words stung him. "No!"

"Then why were you standing there so long?"

Royce hesitated. "Would you prefer me if I were a fisherman, or perhaps a winemaker?"

"No," she said. "I prefer you as you are."

Royce took her hand. "Wouldn't you be better off with a nice farmer or rich merchant? Someone you can raise children with, someone you can grow old with, someone who will stay at home and not leave you alone and wondering."

She kissed him.

"What was that for?"

"I'm a prostitute, Royce. There aren't many men who consider themselves unworthy of me. I love you as you are and always will no matter what path you choose. If I did have the power to change anything, it would be to convince you of that."

He put his arms around her, and she pulled him close. "I missed you," she whispered.

❧

Archibald Ballentyne woke with a start.

He had fallen asleep in the Gray Tower of Ballentyne Castle. The fire had burned out, and the room was growing cold. It was also dark, but the dim glow of the faint orange embers in the hearth gave a little light. There was an odd and unpleasant odor in the air, and he felt the weight of something large and round on his lap. He could not make it out in the darkness. It seemed like a melon wrapped in linen. He stood up and set the object in his chair. He moved aside the brass screen and, taking two logs from the stack nearby, placed them on top of the hot coals. He prodded the embers with a poker, blew on them, and coaxed the fire back to life. As he did, the room filled with light once more.

He set the poker back to its stand, replaced the screen, and dusted his hands off. As he turned around, he looked at the chair he had been sleeping in and immediately pinwheeled backward in horror.

There on his seat was the head of the former archduke of Melengar. The cloth, which was covering it, had partially fallen away, revealing a large portion of what had once been Braga's face. The eyes were rolled back, leaving white and milky orbs in their sockets. The yellowed skin, stretched and leathery, was shriveled. A host of some kind of worms moved in the gaping mouth, slithering in a heaving mass, which made it almost appear as if Braga's tongue was trying to speak.

Archibald's stomach twisted in knots. Too frightened to scream, he looked around the room for intruders. As he did, he saw writing on the wall. Painted in what appeared to be blood, in letters a foot tall, were the words:

NEVER INTERFERE WITH MELENGAR AGAIN
BY ORDER OF THE KING
...AND US

BOOK II

Avempartha

CHAPTER 1

COLNORA

As the man stepped out of the shadows, Wyatt Deminthal knew this would be the worst, and possibly the last, day of his life. Dressed in raw wool and rough leather, the man was vaguely familiar, a face seen briefly by candlelight over two years earlier, a face Wyatt had hoped he would never see again. The man carried three swords, each one battered and dull, the grips sweat-stained and frayed. Taller than Wyatt by nearly a foot, with broader shoulders and powerful hands, he stood with his weight distributed across the balls of his feet. He locked his eyes on Wyatt the way cats stare at mice.

"Baron Delano DeWitt of Dagastan?" It was not a question but an accusation.

Wyatt felt his heart shudder. Even after he recognized the face, a part of him—the optimist that had somehow managed to survive after all these dreadful years—still hoped the man was only after his money. But with the sound of those words, that hope died.

"Sorry, you must be mistaken," he replied to the man blocking his path, trying his best to sound friendly, carefree—guiltless. He even tried to mask his Calian accent to further the charade.

"No, I'm not," the man insisted as he crossed the width of the alley, moving closer, eating up the comforting space between them. His hands remained in full view, which was more worrisome than if they had rested on the pommels of his swords. Even though Wyatt wore a fine cutlass, the man had no fear of him.

"Well, as it happens, my name is Wyatt Deminthal. I think, therefore, that you must be mistaken."

Wyatt was pleased he had managed to say all this without stammering. With great effort, he concentrated on relaxing his body, letting his shoulders droop, resting his weight on one heel. He even forced a pleasant smile and glanced around casually as an innocent man might.

They faced each other in the narrow, cluttered alley only a few yards from where Wyatt rented a loft. It was dark. A lantern hung a few feet behind him, mounted on the side of the feed store. He could see its flickering glow, the light glistening in puddles the rain had left on the cobblestone. Behind him, he could still hear the music of the Gray Mouse Tavern, muffled and tinny. Voices echoed in the distance, laughter, shouts, arguments; the clatter of a dropped pot followed the cry of an unseen cat. Somewhere a carriage rolled along, its wooden wheels clacking on wet stone. It was late. The only people on the streets were drunken men, whores, and those with business best done in the dark.

The man took another step closer. Wyatt did not like the look in his eyes. They held a hard edge, a serious sense of resolve, but it was the hint of regret he detected that jarred Wyatt the most.

"You're the one who hired me and my friend to steal a sword from Essendon Castle."

"I'm sorry. I really have no idea what you are talking about. I don't even know where this *Essendon* place is. You must have me confused with some other fellow. It's probably the hat." Wyatt took off his wide-brimmed cavalier and showed it to the man. "See, it's a common hat in that anyone can buy one, but uncommon at the same time, as few people wear them these days. You most likely saw someone in a similar hat and just assumed it was me. An understandable mistake. No hard feelings, I can assure you."

Wyatt placed his hat back on, tilting it slightly down in front and cocking it a bit to one side. In addition to the hat, he wore an expensive black and red silk doublet and a short flashy cape; however, the lack of any velvet trimming, combined with his worn boots, betrayed his station. Thc single gold ring piercing his left ear revealed even more; it was his one concession, a memento to the life he had left behind.

"When we got to the chapel, the king was on the floor. Dead."

"I can see this is not a happy story," Wyatt said, tugging on the fingers of his fine red gloves—a habit he had when nervous.

"Guards were waiting. They dragged us to the dungeons. We were nearly executed."

"I'm sorry you were ill used, but as I said, I'm not DeWitt. I've never heard of him. I'll be certain to mention you should our paths ever cross. Who shall I say is looking?"

"Riyria."

Behind Wyatt, the feed store light winked out and a voice whispered in his ear, "It's elvish for *two*."

His heartbeat doubled, and before he could turn, he felt the sharp edge of a blade at his throat. He froze, barely allowing himself to breathe.

"You set us up to die." The voice behind him took over. "You brokered the deal. You put us in that chapel so we would take the blame. I'm here to repay your kindness. If you have any last words, say them now, and say them quietly."

Wyatt was a good cardplayer. He knew bluffs and the man behind him was not bluffing. He was not there to scare, pressure, or manipulate him. He was not looking for information; he knew everything he wanted to know. It was in his voice, his tone, his words, the pace of his breath in Wyatt's ear—he was there to kill him.

"What's going on, Wyatt?" a small voice called.

Down the alley, a door opened and light spilled forth, outlining a young girl, whose shadow ran across the cobblestones and up the far wall. She was thin with shoulder-length hair and wore a nightgown that reached to her ankles, exposing bare feet.

"Nothing, Allie—get back inside!" Wyatt shouted, his accent fully exposed.

"Who are those men you're talking to?" Allie took a step toward them. Her foot disturbed a puddle, which rippled. "They look angry."

"I won't allow witnesses," the voice behind Wyatt hissed.

"Leave her alone," Wyatt begged. "She wasn't involved. I swear. It was just me."

"Involved in what?" Allie asked. "What's going on?" She took another step.

"Stay where you are, Allie! Don't come any closer. Please, Allie, do as I say." The girl stopped. "I did a bad thing once, Allie. You have to understand. I did it for us, for you, Elden, and me. Remember when I took that job a few winters back? When I went up north for a couple of days? I—I did the bad thing then. I pretended to be someone I wasn't and I almost got some people killed. That's how I got the money for the winter. Don't hate me, Allie. I love you, honey. Please just get back inside."

"No!" she protested. "I can see the knife. They're going to hurt you."

"If you don't, they'll kill us both!" Wyatt shouted harshly, too harshly. He had not wanted to do it, but he had to make her understand.

Allie was crying now. She stood in the alley, in the shaft of lamplight, shaking.

"Go inside, honey," Wyatt told her, gathering himself and trying to calm his voice. "It will be all right. Don't cry. Elden will watch over you. Let him know what happened. It will be all right."

She continued to sob.

"Please, honey, you have to go inside now," Wyatt pleaded. "It's all you can do. It's what I need you to do. Please."

"I—love—you, Da—ddy!"

"I know, honey. I know. I love you too, and I'm *so sorry*."

Allie slowly stepped back into the doorway, the sliver of light diminishing until the door snapped shut, leaving the alley once more in darkness. Only the faint blue light from the cloud-shrouded moon filtered into the narrow corridor where the three men stood.

"How old is she?" the voice behind him asked.

"Leave her out of this. Just make it quick—can you give me that much?" Wyatt braced himself for what was to come. Seeing the child had broken him. He shook violently, his gloved hands in fists, his chest so tight it was difficult to swallow and hard to breathe. He felt the metal edge against his throat and waited for it to move, waited for it to drag.

"Did you know it was a trap when you came to hire us?" the man with three swords asked.

"What? *No!*"

"Would you still have done it if you knew?"

"I don't know—I guess—yes. We needed the money."

"So, you're not a baron?"

"No."

"What, then?"

"I was a ship's captain."

"Was? What happened?"

"Are you going to kill me anytime soon? Why all the questions?"

"Each question you answer is another breath you take," the voice from behind him spoke. It was the voice of death, emotionless, and empty. Hearing it made Wyatt's stomach lurch as if he were looking over the edge of a high cliff. Not seeing his face, knowing that he held the blade that would kill him, made it feel like an execution. He thought of Allie, hoped she would be all right, then realized—she would see him. The thought struck with surprising clarity. She would rush out after it was over and find him on the street. She would wade through his blood.

"What happened?" the executioner asked again, his voice instantly erasing all other thoughts.

"I sold my ship."

"Why?"

"It doesn't matter."

"Gambling debts?"

"No."

"Why, then?"

"What difference does it make? You're going to kill me anyway. Just do it!"

He had steadied himself. He was ready. He clenched his teeth, shut his eyes. Still, the killer delayed.

"It makes a difference," the executioner whispered in his ear, "because Allie is not your daughter."

The blade came away from Wyatt's neck.

Slowly, hesitantly, Wyatt turned to face the man holding the dagger. He had never seen him before. He was smaller than his partner, dressed in a black cloak with a hood that shaded his features, revealing only hints of a face—the tip of a sharp nose, highlight of a cheek, end of a chin.

"How do you know that?"

"She saw us in the dark. She saw my knife at your throat as we stood deep in shadow across the length of twenty yards."

Wyatt said nothing. He did not dare move or speak. He did not know what to think. Somehow, something had changed. The certainty of death rolled back a step, but its shadow lingered. He had no idea what was happening and was terrified of making a misstep.

"You sold your ship to buy her, didn't you?" the hooded man guessed. "But from whom, and why?"

Wyatt stared at the face beneath the hood—a bleak landscape, a desert dry of compassion. Death was there, a mere breath away; an utterance remained all that separated eternity from salvation.

The bigger man, the one with three swords, reached out and placed a hand on his shoulder. "A lot is riding on your answer. But you already knew that, didn't you? Right now you're trying to decide what to say, and of course, you're trying to guess what we want to hear. Don't. Go with the truth. At least that way, if you're wrong, your death won't have been because of a lie."

Wyatt nodded. He closed his eyes again, took a deep breath, and said, "I bought her from a man named Ambrose."

"Ambrose Moor?" the executioner asked.

"Yes."

Wyatt waited but nothing happened. He opened his eyes. The dagger was gone and the three-sword man was smiling at him. "I don't know how much that little girl cost, but it was the best money you ever spent."

"You aren't going to kill me?"

"Not today. You still owe us one hundred tenents, for the balance on that job," the man in the hood told him coldly.

"I—I don't have it."

"Get it."

Light burst into the alley as the door to Wyatt's loft flew open with a bang and Elden charged out. He held his mammoth two-headed axe high above his head as he strode toward them with a determined look.

The man with three swords rapidly drew two of them.

"Elden, *no*!" Wyatt shouted. "They're not going to kill me! Just stop."

Elden paused, his axe held aloft, his eyes looking back and forth between them.

"They're letting me go," Wyatt assured him, then turned to the two men. "You are, aren't you?"

The hooded man nodded. "Pay off that debt."

As the men walked away, Elden moved to Wyatt's side and Allie ran out to hug him. The three returned to the loft and slipped inside the doorway. Elden took one last look around, then closed the door behind them.

❧

"Did you see the size of that guy?" Hadrian asked Royce, still glancing over his shoulder as if the giant might try to sneak up on them. "I've never seen anyone that big. He had to be a good seven feet tall, and that neck, those shoulders, and that axe! It would take two of me just to lift it. Maybe he isn't human; maybe he's a giant, or a troll. Some people swear they exist. I've met a few who say they have seen them personally."

Royce looked at his friend and scowled.

"Okay, so it's mostly drunks in bars who say that, but that doesn't mean it's not possible. Ask Myron, he'll back me up."

The two headed north toward the Langdon Bridge. It was quiet here. In the respectable hill district of Colnora, people were more inclined to sleep at night than to carouse in taverns. This was the home of merchant titans, affluent businessmen who owned houses grander than many of the palatial mansions of upper nobility.

Colnora had started out as a meager rest stop at the intersection of the Wesbaden and Aquesta trade routes. Originally, a farmer named Hollenbeck and his wife had watered caravans there and granted room in their barn to the traders in return for news and goods. Hollenbeck had an eye for quality and always picked the best of the lot.

Soon his farm became an inn and Hollenbeck added a store and a warehouse to sell what he acquired to passing travelers. The merchants deprived of first pick bought plots next to his farm and opened their own shops, taverns, and roadhouses. The farm became a village, then a city, but still, the caravans gave preference to Hollenbeck. Legend held that the reason was their fondness for his wife, a wonderful woman who, in addition to being uncommonly beautiful, sang and played the mandolin. It was said she baked the finest cobblers of peach, blueberry, and apple. Centuries later, when no one could accurately place the location of the original Hollenbeck farm, and few remembered there had ever been such a farmer, they continued to remember his wife—Colnora.

Over the years the city flourished, until it became the largest urban center in Avryn. Shoppers found the latest style in clothes, the most exquisite jewelry, and the widest variety of exotic spices from hundreds of shops and marketplaces. In addition, the city was home to some of the best artisans and boasted the finest, most popular inns and taverns in the country. Entertainers had long congregated there, prompting Cosmos DeLur, the city's wealthiest resident and patron of the arts, to construct the DeLur Theatre.

Crossing the district, Royce and Hadrian halted abruptly

in front of the theatre's large white painted board. It depicted the silhouette of two men scaling the outside of a castle tower and read:

THE CROWN CONSPIRACY
HOW A YOUNG PRINCE AND TWO THIEVES SAVED A KINGDOM
EVENING SHOWS DAILY

Royce raised an eyebrow while Hadrian slipped the tip of his tongue along his front teeth. They glanced at each other, but neither said a word before continuing on their way.

Leaving the hill district, they continued along Bridge Street as the land sloped downward toward the river. They passed rows of warehouses—mammoth buildings emblazoned with company brands like royal crests. Some were simply initials, usually the new businesses that had no sense of themselves. Others bore trademarks, like the boar's head of the Bocant Company, an empire whose genesis had been pork, or the diamond symbol of DeLur Enterprises.

"You realize he'll never be able to pay us the hundred?" Hadrian asked.

"I just didn't want him to think he was getting off easy."

"You didn't want him to think Royce Melborn went soft at the sight of a little girl's tears."

"She wasn't just *any* girl, and besides, he saved her from Ambrose Moor. For that alone he earned one life."

"That's something that has always puzzled me. How is it Ambrose is still alive?"

"I've been sidetracked, I suppose," Royce said in his *let's not talk about it* tone, and Hadrian dropped the subject.

Of the city's three main bridges, the Langdon was the most ornate. Made from cut stone, it was lined every few feet by large lampposts fashioned in the shapes of swans, which, when lit, gave the bridge a festive look. Now, however, with the lights out, the stone was wet and appeared oily and dangerous.

"Well, at least we didn't spend the last month looking for DeWitt for nothing," Hadrian said sarcastically as they crossed the bridge. "I would have thought—"

Royce stopped walking and abruptly raised his hand. Both men looked around and, without a word, drew their weapons as they moved back to back. Nothing seemed amiss. The only sound was the roar of the tumultuous waters that rushed and churned below them.

"Impressive, Duster," a man said, addressing Royce, as he stepped out from behind one of the bridge lampposts. His skin was pale, and his body so slender and bony that he swam in his loose britches and shirt. He looked like a corpse someone forgot to bury.

Behind them, Hadrian noted three more men crawling onto the span. They all had similar appearances, thin and muscular, each in dark-colored clothes. They circled like wolves.

"What tipped you off we were here?" the thin man asked.

"I'm guessing it was your breath, but body odor really can't be ruled out," Hadrian replied with a grin while noting their positions, their movements, and the direction of their eyes.

"Mind yer mouth, bub," the tallest of the four threatened.

"To what do we owe this visit, Price?" Royce asked.

"Funny, I was about to ask you the same," the thin man replied. "This is our city, after all, not yours—not anymore."

"Black Diamond?" Hadrian asked.

Royce nodded.

"And you would be Hadrian Blackwater," Price noted. "I always thought you'd be bigger."

"And you're a Black Diamond. I always thought there were more of you."

Price smiled, held his gaze long enough to suggest a threat, and returned his attention to Royce. "So what are you doing here, Duster?"

"Just passing through."

"Really? No business?"

"Nothing that would interest you."

"Well now, you see, that's where you're wrong." Price stepped away from the swan lamppost and began slowly circling them as he talked. The wind blowing down the river whipped his loose shirt like a flag at mast. "The Black Diamond is interested in everything that happens in Colnora, most particularly when it involves you, Duster."

Hadrian leaned over and asked, "Why does he keep calling you *Duster*?"

"That was my guild name," Royce replied.

"*He* was a Black Diamond?" asked the youngest-looking of the four. He had round, chubby cheeks blown red and blotchy and a narrow mouth wreathed by a thin mustache and goatee.

"Oh yes, that's right, Etcher, you've never heard of Duster before, have you? Etcher is new to the guild, only been with us, what—six months? Well, you see, not only was Duster a Diamond, he was an officer, bucket man, and one of the most notorious members in the guild's history."

"Bucket man?" Hadrian asked.

"Assassin," Royce explained.

"He's a legend, this one is," Price went on, pacing around the stone bridge, carefully avoiding the puddles. "Wonder boy of his day, he rose through the ranks so fast it unnerved people."

"Funny," Royce said, "I only remember one."

"Well, when the First Officer of the guild is nervous, so is everyone else. You see, back then the Jewel had a man named Hoyte running the show. He was an ass to most of us—a good thief and administrator, but an ass just the same. Duster here had a lot of support from the lower ranks and Hoyte was concerned Duster might replace him. He began ordering Duster on the most dangerous jobs—jobs that went suspiciously bad. Still, Duster always escaped unscathed, making him even more a hero. Rumors began circulating we might have a traitor in the guild. Rather than being concerned, Hoyte saw this as an opportunity."

Price paused in his orator's trek around the bridge and stopped in front of Royce. "You see, at that time there were three bucket men in the guild and all of them good friends. Jade, the guild's only female assassin, was a beauty who—"

"Is this going somewhere, Price?" Royce snapped.

"Just giving Etcher a little background, Duster. You wouldn't begrudge me the chance to educate my boys, would you?" Price smiled and returned to his casual pacing, slipping his thumbs into the loose waistline of his pants. "Where was I? Oh yes, Jade. It happened right over there." He pointed back across the bridge. "That empty warehouse with the clover symbol on its side. That's where Hoyte set them up, pitting one against the other. Then, like now, bucket men wore masks to prevent being marked." Price paused and looked at Royce with feigned sympathy. "You had no idea who she was until it was over, did you, Duster? Or did you know and kill her anyway?"

Royce said nothing but glared at Price with a dangerous look.

"The last of the three bucket men was Cutter, who was understandably upset to learn Duster murdered Jade, since Cutter and Jade were lovers. The fact that his friend was responsible made it personal, and Hoyte was happy to let Cutter settle the score.

"But Cutter didn't want Duster dead. He wanted him to

suffer and insisted on something more elaborate, more painful. The man is a strategic mastermind—our best heist planner—and arranged for Duster to be apprehended by the city guard. Cutter traded a few favors and, with some money, bought a trial that resulted in Duster going to Manzant Prison. The hole no one ever comes back from. Escape was thought to be impossible—only somehow Duster managed it. You know, we still don't know how you got out." He paused, giving Royce a chance to reply.

Again, Royce remained silent.

Price shrugged. "When Duster escaped, he returned to Colnora. First, the magistrate who presided over his trial was found dead in his bed. Then the false witnesses—all three on the same night—and finally the lawyer. Soon, one by one, members of the Black Diamond started disappearing. They turned up in the strangest places: the river, the city square, even the steeple of the church.

"After losing more than a dozen members, the Jewel made a deal. He gave Hoyte to Duster, who forced him to confess publicly. Then Duster killed Hoyte and left his body in the Hill Square Fountain—it was pure artistry. It stopped the war, but the wounds were too deep to forgive. Duster left, only to reemerge years later working out of Crimson Hand territory up north. But you're not a member, are you?"

"I don't have much use for guilds anymore," Royce replied coldly.

"And who's that?" Etcher asked, pointing at Hadrian. "Duster's servant? He's carrying enough weapons for the both of them."

Price smiled at Etcher. "That's Hadrian Blackwater, and I wouldn't point at him—you're likely to lose that arm."

Etcher looked at Hadrian skeptically. "What? He's some kind of master swordsman? Is that it?"

Price chuckled. "Sword, spear, arrow, rock, whatever is at hand." He turned to Hadrian. "The Diamond doesn't know as much about you, but there are a lot of rumors. One says you were a gladiator. Another reports you were a general in a Calian army—successful, too, if the stories can be trusted. There's even one tale circulating that you were the enslaved courtier of an exotic eastern queen."

Some of the other Diamonds, including Etcher, chuckled.

"As much fun as this trip down memory lane has been, Price, do you have a reason for stopping us?"

"You mean beyond entertainment? Beyond harassment? Beyond reminding you that this is a Black Diamond–controlled city? Beyond informing you that unguilded thieves like yourselves are not allowed to practice here, and that you personally are not welcome?"

"Yeah, that's what I meant."

"Actually, there is one more thing. There's a girl looking for you two."

Royce and Hadrian glanced at each other curiously.

"She's been going around asking about two thieves named Hadrian and Royce. Now, as entertaining as it has been to hear your names publicly advertised, it's embarrassing for the Black Diamond to have anyone asking for thieves in Colnora that are not members of our guild. People are apt to get the wrong impression about this city."

"Who is she?" Royce asked.

"No idea."

"Where is she?"

"Sleeping under the Tradesmen's Arch on Capital Boulevard, so I think we can rule out her being a noble debutant or a rich merchant's daughter. Since she is traveling alone, I think you can also rule out the possibility that she is here to kill you or have you arrested. If I had to guess, I should think she is looking to hire you. I must say, if she is typical of the kind of patrons you two attract, I would consider a more traditional line of work. Perhaps there's a pig farm you might be able to get a job at—at least you would be keeping the same level of company."

Price's tone and expression dropped to a serious level. "Find her and get her, and yourselves, out of our city by tomorrow night. You might want to hurry. Cleaned up, she could be pretty and might fetch a fair price or at least provide several minutes of pleasure for someone. I suspect the only reason she hasn't been touched so far is that she's been dropping your names everywhere. Around here, Royce Melborn is still something of a bogeyman."

Price turned to leave and his mocking tone returned. "It's actually a shame you can't stay around; the theatre is showing a play about a couple of thieves lured into being accused of murdering the King of Medford. It's loosely based on the real murder of Amrath several years ago." Price shook his head. "Completely unrealistic. Can you imagine a seasoned thief being lured into a castle to steal a sword to save a man from a duel? Authors!"

Price continued to shake his head as he and the other thieves left Hadrian and Royce on the bridge and headed down the streets on the far bank.

"Well, that was pleasant, don't you think?" Hadrian said as they retraced their steps, heading back up the hill toward Capital Boulevard. "Nice bunch of guys. I feel a little disappointed they only sent four."

"Trust me, they were plenty dangerous. Price is the Diamond's First Officer, and the other two quiet ones were bucket men. There were also six more, three on each side of the bridge, hiding under the ambush lip, just in case. They weren't taking any chances with us. Does that make you feel better?"

"Much, thanks." Hadrian rolled his eyes. "Duster, huh?"

"Don't call me that," Royce said, his tone serious. "Don't ever call me that."

"Call you what?" Hadrian asked innocently.

Royce sighed, then smiled at him. "Walk faster; apparently, we have a client waiting."

⁂

She awoke to a rough hand on her thigh.

"Whatcha got in the purse, honey?"

Disoriented and confused, the girl wiped her eyes. She was in the gutter beneath the Tradesmen's Arch. Her hair was a filthy tangle of leaves and twigs, her dress a tattered rag. She clutched a tiny purse to her chest, the drawstring tied around her neck. To most passing by, she might appear as a bundle of trash discarded on the side of the road, or a pile of cloth and twigs absently left behind by the street sweepers. Still, there were those who were interested even in piles of trash.

The first thing she saw when her eyes could focus was the dark, haggard face and gaping mouth of a man crouching over her. She squealed and tried to crawl away. A hand grabbed her by the hair. Strong arms forced her down, pinning her wrists to her sides.

She felt his hot breath on her face and it smelled of liquor and smoke. He tore the tiny purse from her fingers and pulled it from around her neck.

"No!" She wrenched a hand free and reached out for it. "I need that."

"So do I." The man cackled, slapping her hand aside. Feeling the weight of coins in the bag, he smiled and stuffed the small pouch in his breast pocket.

"No!" she protested.

He sat on her, pinning her to the ground, and ran his fingers down her face, along her lips, stopping at her neck. Slowly they circled her throat and he gave a little squeeze. She gasped, struggling to breathe. He pressed his lips hard against hers, so hard she could tell he was missing teeth. The rough stubble of his whiskers scratched her chin and cheeks.

"Shush," he whispered. "We're only getting started. You need ta save your strength." He lifted off, pushing himself up to his knees, and reached for the buttons of his britches.

She struggled, clawing at him, kicking. He pinned her arms under his knees and her feet found only air. She screamed. The man replied by slapping her hard across the face. The shock left her stunned, staring blindly while he returned to work on his buttons. The pain did not hit her yet, not fully. It was there welling up, fire hot on her cheek. Through watering eyes, she saw him on top of her as if viewing the scene from a distance. Individual sounds were lost, replaced by a dull hum. She saw his cracked, peeling lips moving, his throat muscles shifting, long gangly cords, but never heard the words. She freed one arm, but it was captured and stuffed back down out of sight once more.

Behind him, she could see two figures approaching. Somewhere inside her, a thread of hope came alive, and she managed a weak whisper: "Help me."

The foremost man drew a massive sword and, holding it by the blade, swung the pommel. Her attacker fell sprawling across the gutter.

The man with the sword knelt down beside her. He was merely an outline against the charcoal sky, a phantom in the dark.

"May I be of assistance, milady?" She heard his voice—a nice voice. His hand found hers and he pulled her to her feet.

"Who are you?"

"My name is Hadrian Blackwater."

She stared at him. "Really?" she managed, refusing to let go of his hands. Before she realized it, she began to cry.

"What'd you do to her?" the other man asked, coming up behind them.

"I—I don't know."

"Are you squeezing her hand too hard? Let her go."

"I'm not holding her. She's holding me."

"I'm sorry. I'm sorry." Her voice quavered. "I just never thought I would ever find you."

"Oh, okay. Well, you did." He smiled at her. "And this fellow here is Royce Melborn."

She gasped and threw her arms around the smaller man's neck, hugging him tight and crying even harder. Royce stood awkward and stiff while Hadrian peeled her off.

"So I get the impression you're glad to see us; that's good," Hadrian told her. "Now, who are you?"

"I'm Thrace Wood of Dahlgren Village." She was smiling. She could not help herself. "I have been looking for you for a very long time."

She staggered.

"Are you all right?"

"I'm a little dizzy."

"When was the last time you had anything to eat?"

Thrace stood thinking, her eyes shifting back and forth as she tried to remember.

"Never mind." Hadrian turned to Royce. "This was once your city. Any ideas where we can get help for a young woman in the middle of the night?"

"It's a shame we aren't in Medford. Gwen would be great for this sort of thing."

"Well, isn't there a brothel here? After all, we're in the trade capital of the world. Don't tell me they don't sell *that*."

"Yeah, there's a nice one on South Street."

"Okay, Thrace is it? Come with us, we'll see if we can get you cleaned up and perhaps a bit of food in you."

"Wait." She knelt down beside the unconscious man and pulled her purse from his pocket.

"Is he dead?" she asked.

"Doubt it. Didn't hit him that hard."

Rising, she felt light-headed and darkness crept in from the edges of her vision. She hovered a moment like a drunk, began to sway, and finally collapsed. She woke only briefly and felt arms gently lifting her. Through a dull buzzing she heard the sound of a chuckle.

"What's so funny?" she heard one of them say.

"This is the first time, I suspect, anyone has ever visited a whorehouse and brought his own woman."

Chapter 2

Thrace

"Shines up purty as a new copper piece, that one does," Clarisse noted as the three looked through the doorway at Thrace, waiting in the parlor. Clarisse was a large rotund woman with rosy cheeks and short pudgy fingers that had a habit of playing with the pleats of her skirt. She and the other women of the Bawdy Bottom Brothel had done wonders with the girl. Thrace was clothed in a new dress. It was cheap and simple—a brown linen kirtle over a white smock with a starched brown bodice—but still decidedly more fetching than the rag she had worn. She hardly resembled the ragamuffin they had met the night before. In addition to giving her a bed to sleep in, the women had scrubbed, combed, and fed her. Her lips and eyes were even painted and the results were stunning. She was a young beauty with startling blue eyes and golden hair.

"Poor girl was in awful shape when you dropped her off. Where'd you find her?" Clarisse asked.

"Under the Tradesmen's Arch," Hadrian replied.

"Poor thing." The large woman shook her head sadly. "You know, if she needs a place, I'm sure we could put her on the roster. She'd get a bed to sleep in, three meals a day, and with her looks she could do well for herself."

"Something tells me she's not a prostitute," Hadrian told her.

"None of us are, honey. Not until you find yourself sleeping under the Tradesmen's Arch, that is. You shoulda seen her at breakfast. She ate like a starved dog. Course she wouldn't touch a thing till we convinced her that the food was free, given by the chamber 'a commerce to visitors of the city as a welcome. Maggie came up with that one. She's a hoot, she is. That reminds me, the bill for the room, dress, food, and general cleanup comes to sixty-five silver. We threw in the makeup for free, 'cause Delia just wanted to see how she'd look, on account she says she's never worn it 'afore."

Royce handed her a gold tenent.

"Well, well, you two really need to drop by more often, and next time without the girl, eh?" She winked. "Seriously, though, what's the story with this one?"

"That's just it; we don't know," Hadrian replied.

"But I think it's time we found out," Royce added.

Not nearly as nice as Medford House back home, the Bawdy Bottom Brothel was decorated with gaudy red drapes, rickety furniture, pink lampshades, and dozens of pillows. Everything had tassels and fringe, from the threadbare carpets to the cloth edging adorning the top of the walls. It was old, weathered, and worn but at least it was clean.

The parlor was a small oval room just off the main hall with two bay windows that looked out on the street. It contained two love seats, a few tables crowded with ceramic figures, and a small fireplace. Seated on one of the love seats, Thrace waited, her eyes darting about as if she were a rabbit in an open field. The moment the two men entered, she leapt from her seat, knelt, and bowed her head.

"Hey! Watch it, that's a new dress," Hadrian said with a smile.

"Oh!" She scrambled to her feet, blushing, then curtsied and bowed her head once more.

"What's she doing?" Royce whispered to Hadrian.

"Not sure," he whispered back.

"I'm trying to show the proper reverence, Your Lordships," she whispered to both of them while keeping her head down. "I'm sorry if I'm not very good at it."

Royce rolled his eyes and Hadrian began to laugh.

"Why are you whispering?" Hadrian asked her.

"Because you two were."

Hadrian chuckled again. "Sorry, Thrace—ah, your name is Thrace, right?"

"Yes, my lord, Thrace Annabell Wood of Dahlgren Village." She awkwardly curtsied again.

"Okay, well—Thrace." Hadrian struggled to continue with a straight face. "Royce and I are not lords, so there is no need to bow or curtsy."

The girl looked up.

"You saved my life," she told them in such a solemn tone Hadrian stopped laughing. "I don't remember a lot of last night, but I remember that much. And for that you deserve my gratitude."

"I would settle for an explanation," Royce said, moving to the windows. He began closing the drapes. "Straighten up, for Maribor's sake, before a sweeper sees you, thinks we're noble, and marks us. We're already on thin ice here as it is. Let's not add to it."

She stood up straight, and Hadrian could not help staring. Her long yellow hair, now free of twigs and leaves, shimmered in waves over her shoulders. She was a vision of youthful beauty and Hadrian guessed she could not be more than seventeen.

"Now, why have you been looking for us?" Royce asked, closing the last curtain.

"To hire you to save my father," she said, untying the purse from around her neck and holding it up with a smile. "Here. I have twenty-five silver tenents. Solid silver stamped with the Dunmore crown."

Royce and Hadrian exchanged looks.

"Isn't it enough?" she asked, her lips starting to tremble.

"How long did it take you to save up this money?" Hadrian asked.

"All my life. I saved every copper I was ever given, or earned. It was my dowry."

"Your dowry?"

She lowered her head, looking at her feet. "My father is a poor farmer. He would never—I decided to save for myself. It's not enough, is it? I didn't realize. I'm from a very small village. I thought it was a lot of money; everyone said so, but..." She looked around at the battered love seat and faded curtains. "We don't have palaces like this."

"Well, we really don't—" Royce began in his usual insensitive tone.

"What Royce is about to say," Hadrian interrupted, "is we really don't know yet. It depends on what you want us to do."

Thrace looked up, her eyes hopeful.

Royce just glared at him.

"Well, it does, doesn't it?" Hadrian shrugged. "Now, Thrace, you say you want us to save your father. Has he been kidnapped or something?"

"Oh no, nothing like that. As far as I know he's fine. Although I have been away a long time looking for you. So I'm not sure."

"I don't understand. What do you need us for?"

"I need you to open a lock for me."

"A lock? To what?"

"A tower."

"You want us to break into a tower?"

"No. I mean—well, yes, but it isn't like—it's not illegal.

The tower isn't occupied; it has been deserted for years. At least I think so."

"So you just want us to open a door to an empty tower?"

"Yes!" she said, nodding vigorously so that her hair bounced.

"Doesn't sound too hard." Hadrian looked at Royce.

"Where is this tower?" Royce asked.

"Near my village on the west bank of the Nidwalden River. Dahlgren is very small and has only been there a short time. It's in the new province of Westbank, in Dunmore."

"I've heard about that place. It's supposedly being attacked by elven raiders."

"Oh, it's not the elves. The elves have never caused us any trouble."

"I knew it," Royce said to no one in particular.

"Leastways, I don't think so," Thrace went on. "We think it's a beast of some kind. No one has ever seen it. Deacon Tomas says it's a demon, a minion of Uberlin."

"And your father?" Hadrian asked. "How does he fit into this?"

"He's going to try and kill the beast, only..." She faltered and looked at her feet once more.

"Only you think it will kill him instead?"

"It has killed fifteen people and over eighty head of livestock."

A freckle-faced woman with wild red hair entered the parlor dragging a short potbellied man who looked like he had shaved for the occasion, his face nicked raw. The woman was laughing, walking backward as she hauled him along with both hands. The man stopped short when he saw them. His hands slipped through hers and she fell to the wooden floor with a hollow thud. The man looked from the woman to them and back, frozen in place. The woman glanced over her shoulder and laughed.

"Oops," was all she could manage. "Didn't know it was taken. Give us a hand up, Rubis."

The man helped her to her feet. She paused to give Thrace a long appraising look, then winked at them. "We do good work, don't we?"

"That was Maggie," Thrace told them after the woman hauled her man back out again.

Hadrian moved to the sofa and gestured for Thrace to sit. She sat gingerly and straight, not allowing her back to touch the rear of the sofa, and carefully smoothed out her skirt.

Royce remained on his feet. "Does Westbank have a lord? Why isn't he doing something about this?"

"We had a fine margrave," she said. "A brave man with three good knights."

"Had?"

"He and his knights rode out to fight the beast one evening. Later, all that was found was bits and pieces of armor."

"Why don't you just leave?" Royce asked.

Thrace's head drooped and her shoulders slouched a bit. "Two nights before I left to come here, the beast killed everyone in my family except for me and my father. We weren't home. My father had worked late in the fields and I went to look for him. I—I accidentally left the door open. Light attracts it. It went right for our house. My brother, Thad, his wife, and their son were all killed.

"Thad—he was the joy of my father's life. He was the reason we moved to Dahlgren in the first place—so he could become the town's first cooper." Tears welled in her eyes. "Now they're all gone and my father has nothing left but his grief and the beast that brought it. He'll see it dead, or die himself before the month is out. If I had only closed the door... If I had just checked the latch..."

Her hands covered her face and her slender body quivered. Royce gave Hadrian a stern look, shaking his head very slightly and mouthing the word *no*.

Hadrian scowled and placed his hand on her shoulder and brushed the hair away from her eyes. "You're going to ruin all your pretty makeup," he said.

"I'm sorry. I really don't want to be such a bother. These aren't your problems. It is just that my father is all I have left and I can't bear the thought of losing him too. I can't reason with him. I asked him to leave, but he won't listen."

"I can see your problem, but why us?" Royce asked coldly. "And how does a farmer's daughter from the frontier know our names and how to find us in Colnora?"

"A crippled man told me. He sent me here. He said you could open the tower."

"A cripple?"

"Yes. Mr. Haddon told me the beast can't—"

"Mr. Haddon?" Royce interrupted.

"Uh-huh."

"This Mr. Haddon...he wouldn't be missing his hands, would he?"

"Yes, that's him."

Royce and Hadrian exchanged glances.

"What exactly did he say?"

"He said the beast can't be harmed by weapons made by man, but inside Avempartha there is a sword that can kill it."

"So, a man with no hands told you to find us in Colnora and hire us to get a sword for your father from a tower called *Avempartha*?" Royce asked.

The girl nodded.

Hadrian looked at his partner. "Don't tell me...it's a dwarven tower?"

"No..." Royce replied, "it's elvish." He turned away with a thoughtful expression.

Hadrian returned his attention to the girl. He felt awful. It was bad enough that her village was so far away, but now they faced an elven tower. Even if she offered them a hundred gold tenents, he would not be able to convince Royce to take the job. She was so desperate, so in need of help. His stomach knotted as he considered the words he would say next.

"Well," Hadrian began reluctantly, "the Nidwalden River is several days' travel over rough ground. We'd need supplies, for what—a six-, seven-day trip? That's two weeks there and back. We'd need food and grain for the horses. Then you'd have to add in time at the tower. That's time we could be doing other jobs, so that right there is money lost. Then there is the danger involved. Risk of any kind can bump our price and a mass-murdering phantom-demon-beast that can't be harmed by weapons has got to be classified as a risk."

Hadrian looked into her eyes and shook his head. "I hate to say it, and I'm very sorry, but we can't take—"

"Your money," Royce abruptly interjected as he spun around. "It's too much. To take the full twenty-five silver for this job... Ten really seems like more than enough."

Hadrian raised an eyebrow and stared at his partner but said nothing.

"Ten silver each?" she asked.

"Ah—no," Hadrian replied, keeping his eyes on Royce. "That would be together. Right? Five each?"

Royce shrugged. "Since I'll be doing the actual lock picking, I think I should get six, but we can work that out between us. It's not something she needs to be concerned about."

"Really?" Thrace asked, looking as if she might explode with happiness.

"Sure," Royce replied. "After all... we're not thieves."

❧

"Want to explain why we are taking this job?" Hadrian asked, shielding his eyes as they stepped outside. The sky was a perfect blue, the morning sun already working to dry the lingering puddles from the night before. All around them people rushed to market. Carts loaded with spring vegetables and tarp-covered barrels sat trapped behind three wagons mounded high with hay. Out of the crowd in front of them, a fat man charged forward with a flapping chicken gripped tightly under each arm. He danced around the puddles, dodging people and carts and offering a muttered "Excuse me," as he pressed by.

"She's paying us ten silver for a job that has already cost us a gold tenent," Hadrian continued after successfully skirting the chicken man. "It will cost us several more before we're done."

"We're not doing it for the money," Royce informed him as he cut a path through the crowd.

"Obviously, but why are we doing it? I mean, sure, she's cute as a button and all, but unless you're planning on selling her, I don't see the angle here."

Royce looked over his shoulder, displaying an evil grin. "I never even considered selling her. That could defray the costs considerably."

"Forget I brought it up. Just tell me why we're doing this."

Royce led them out of the crowd toward Ognoton's Curio Shop, whose window exhibited hookahs, porcelain animal figurines, and jewelry boxes with brass latches. They ducked around the side into the narrow bricked space between it and a confectioner shop that was offering free samples of hard candy.

"Don't tell me you haven't wondered what Esrahaddon has

been doing," Royce whispered. "That wizard was imprisoned for nine hundred years, then disappears the day we break him out and we don't hear a word about him until now? The church must know, and yet the Imperialists haven't launched search parties or posted notices. I would think that if the most dangerous man alive was on the loose, there might be a bit more of a commotion.

"Two years later he turns up in a tiny village and invites us to come visit. On top of that, he picks the elven frontier and Avempartha as the meeting place. Don't you want to find out what he wants?"

"What is this Avempartha?"

"All I know is that it's old. Real old. Some kind of ancient elven citadel. Which also begs the question, wouldn't you like to get a peek inside? If Esrahaddon thinks there's value in opening it, I'm guessing he's right."

"So we're going after ancient elven treasure?"

"I have no idea, but I'm sure there is something valuable in there. But for that we need supplies and we need to get out of town before Price lets loose the hounds."

"Well, as long as you promise not to sell the girl."

"I won't—if she behaves herself."

&

Hadrian felt Thrace leaning again, this time gazing at a two-story country home of stucco and stone with a yellow thatch roof and orange clay chimney. It was surrounded by a waist-high wall overgrown with lilacs and ivy.

"It's so beautiful," she whispered.

It was early afternoon and they were only a few miles out of Colnora, traveling east along the Alburn road. The country lane twisted through the tangle of tiny villages that comprised the hill region surrounding the city, little hamlets where poor farmers worked their fields alongside the summer cottages of the idle rich, who for three months a year pretended to be country squires. Royce rode beside them or trotted forward as congestion demanded. His hood was up despite the pleasant weather. Thrace rode behind Hadrian on his bay mare, her legs dangled off one side, bobbing to the rhythm of the horse's stride.

"It's a different world here," she said. "A paradise, really. Everyone is wealthy. Everyone a king."

"Colnora does all right, but I wouldn't go that far."

"Then how do you explain all the grand houses? The horse carts have metal rims on their wheels. The vegetable stands overflow with bushels of onions and green peas. In Dahlgren all we have are footpaths and they are an awful mess after a rain, but here you have such wide roads and they even have names on posts. And back there a farmer was wearing gloves—gloves on his hands—while working. In Dahlgren, even the church deacon doesn't own fancy gloves, and he certainly wouldn't work in them if he did. You all are so rich."

"Some of them are."

"Like you two."

Hadrian laughed.

"But you have nice clothes and beautiful horses."

"She's not much of a horse really."

"No one in Dahlgren but the lord and his knights own horses, and yours are so pretty. I especially like her eyes—such long lashes. What's her name?"

"I call her Millie, after a woman I once knew who had the same habit of not listening to me."

"Millie is a pretty name. I like it. What about Royce's horse?"

Hadrian frowned and looked over at him. "I don't know. Royce, did you ever name her?"

"What for?"

Hadrian glanced back at Thrace, who returned an appalled look.

"How about..." She paused, shifting and twisting as she scanned the roadside. "Lilac, or Daisy? Oh wait, no, how about Chrysanthemum?"

"*Chrysanthemum?*" Hadrian repeated. As funny as it might be to have Royce riding a Chrysanthemum, or even a Lilac or Daisy, he had to point out that flower names just did not fit Royce's short, dirty gray mare. "How about Shorty or Sooty?"

"No!" Thrace scolded him. "It will make the poor animal feel awful."

Hadrian chuckled. Royce ignored the conversation. He clicked his tongue, kicked the sides of his horse, and trotted forward to avoid an approaching wagon, but remained there even after the road was clear.

"How about Lady?" Thrace asked.

"It seems a bit haughty, don't you think? She's not exactly a prancing show horse."

"Then it will make her feel better. Give her confidence."

They were coming upon a stream where honeysuckle and raspberry bushes crowned the heads of smooth granite banks with brilliant springtime green. A gristmill stood at the edge, its great wheel creaking and dripping. A pair of small square windows, like dark eyes, created a face in the stone exterior beneath the steeply peaked wooden roof. A low wall separated the mill from the road and on it rested a white and gray cat. Its green eyes opened lazily and blinked at them. When they drew closer, the cat decided they had come close enough and leapt from the wall, darting across the road into the thickets.

Royce's horse reared and whinnied, dancing across the dirt. As the horse shuffled backward, Royce cursed and tightened the reins, pulling her head down and forcing her to turn completely around.

"Ridiculous!" Royce complained once the horse was under control. "A thousand-pound animal terrified by a five-pound cat; you'd think she was a mouse."

"Mouse! That's perfect," Thrace shouted, causing Millie's ears to twist back.

"I like it," Hadrian agreed.

"Oh, good lord," Royce muttered, shaking his head as he trotted forward again.

As they rode farther east, the country estates became farms, rosebushes became hedges, and fences that divided fields gave way to mere tree lines. Still Thrace pointed out curiosities, like the unimagined luxury of covered bridges and the ornately decorated carriages that still occasionally thundered by.

The road climbed higher and soon they lost the shade as the land opened up into vast fallow fields of goldenrod, milkweed, and wild salifan. Flies dogged them in the heat and the drone of cicadas whined. Thrace at last grew quiet and laid her head against Hadrian's back. He became concerned she might fall asleep and topple off, but occasionally she would stir to look about or swat at a fly.

Higher and higher they climbed until they reached the top of Amber Heights. The prominent highland stood out as a bald spot of short grass and bare rock. Part of a long ridge that ran along the eastern edge of Warric, it served as the border between the kingdom of Warric and the kingdom of Alburn. Alburn was the third most powerful and prosperous kingdom in Avryn, after Warric and Melengar. Most of its lands were deeply forested and its coast was often subjected to attacks by the Ba Ran Ghazel, who made lightning assaults, abducting the unfortunate and burning what they could not carry. Its ruler, King Armand, had only recently gained the throne, after the unexpected death of the old king. While King Reinhold had been a Royalist, Hadrian had the impression the new king was an Imperialist sympathizer, if not an open supporter, which was unfortunate for Melengar, whose list of allies seemed to grow shorter each day.

Amber Heights was a curiosity even to the local residents due to the standing stones, the massive blue-gray rocks carved into uniquely fluid shapes. They appeared almost organic in their rounded curves, like a series of writhing serpents burrowing in and out of the hilltop. Hadrian did not have the slightest idea what purpose the stones might have originally served. He doubted anyone did. Remnants of campfires were scattered around the stones, etched with messages of true love or the occasional slogan: "Maribor Is God!" "Nationalists Are Barmy," "The Heir Is Dead," and even "Gray Mouse Tavern—it's all downhill from here." Reaching the crest, they could all see the city of Colnora spread out behind them, while to the northeast lay the endless miles of dense and untamed woodland where the kingdoms of Alburn and Dunmore blurred together. To Hadrian the forest appeared as an ocean of unbroken green—miles and miles of rugged wilderness, on the other side of which lay a tiny village called Dahlgren.

Because the wind on the hilltop was cool and strong enough to drive off the flies, it made a perfect place to break for a midday meal. They ate salted pork, hard dark bread, onions, and pickles. It was the kind of meal Hadrian would loathe to eat in a town, but it seemed somehow wonderful on the road, where his appetite was greater and options were fewer. He watched Thrace sitting on the grass, nibbling on a pickle, being careful not to stain her new dress. She gazed off with a faraway look, inhaling the air in deep appreciative breaths.

"What are you thinking?" he asked.

She smiled at him a bit self-consciously and he thought he noticed a sadness about her. "I was just thinking how wonderful it is here. How nice it would be to live on one of those farms we passed. We wouldn't need anything grand, not even a house—my father can build a house all by himself and he can turn any soil. There's nothing he can't do once he sets his mind to it, and once he sets his mind, there's no changing it."

"Sounds like a great guy."

"Oh, he is. He's very strong, very determined."

"I'm surprised he would allow you to set off alone across the country like you did."

Thrace smiled.

"You didn't walk all the way, did you?"

"Oh no, I got a ride with a peddler and his wife who stopped in Dahlgren. They refused to spend a second night and let me ride in the back of their wagon."

"Have you done much traveling before?"

"No. I was born in Glamrendor, the capital of Dunmore. My family worked a tenant farm for His Lordship there. We moved to Dahlgren when I was about nine, so I've never been out of Dunmore until now. I can't even say I remember all that much of Glamrendor. I do recall it was dirty, though. All the buildings were made of wood, and the roads very muddy—at least that's how I remember it."

"Still that way," Royce mentioned.

"I can't believe you had the courage to just go off like that," Hadrian said, shaking his head. "It must have been a shock leaving Dahlgren and a few days later finding yourself in the largest city in the world."

"Oh, it was," she replied, using her pinky finger to draw away a number of hairs that had blown into her mouth. "I felt foolish when I realized just how hard it was going to be to find you. I expected it would be like back home, where I would be able to walk up to anyone and they would know who you were. There are a lot more people in Colnora than I expected. To be honest, there's a lot more of everything. I looked and looked and I thought I would never find you."

"I expect your father will be worried."

"No he won't," she said.

"But if—"

"What are these things?" she asked, pointing at the standing stones with her pickle. "These blue stones. They're so odd."

"No one knows," Royce replied.

"Were they made by elves?" she asked.

Royce cocked his head and stared at her. "How did you know that?"

"They look a bit like the tower near my village—the one I need you to open. Same kind of stone—at least, I think so. The tower looks bluish too, but it might be because of the distance—ever notice how things get blue in the distance? I suppose if we could actually get near it, we might find it was just a common gray, you know?"

"Why can't you get near it?" Hadrian asked.

"Because it's in the middle of the river."

"Can't you swim?"

"You would have to be a real strong swimmer. The tower is built on a rock that hangs over a waterfall. Beautiful falls—really high, you know? Lots of water going over. On sunny days, you can see rainbows in the mist. Of course, it's very dangerous. At least five people have died—only two are for sure, the other three are just guesses, because—" She paused when she saw the looks on their faces. "Is something wrong?"

"You might have said something earlier," Royce replied.

"About the waterfall? Oh, I thought you knew. I mean, you

acted like you knew the tower when I mentioned it before. I'm sorry."

They ate in silence for a few moments. Thrace finished her lunch and walked around looking at the stones, her dress billowing behind her. "I don't understand," she finally said, raising her voice over the wind. "If the Nidwalden is the border, why are there elven stones here?"

"This used to be elven land," Royce explained. "All of it. Before there was a Colnora, or a Warric, it was part of the Erivan Empire. Most don't like to acknowledge that; they prefer to think that men always ruled here. It bothers them. Funny thing is many of the names we use are elvish. Ervanon, Rhenydd, Glamrendor, Galewyr, and Nidwalden are all elven. The very name of this country, Avryn, means *green fields*."

"Try and tell that to someone in a bar sometime and see how fast you get cracked in the head," Hadrian mentioned, drawing looks from both of them.

While they finished eating, Thrace stood among the great stones, staring west, her hair and dress whipping about. Her sight rose to the horizon, out beyond Colnora, beyond the blue hills to the thin line of the sea. She looked so small and delicate he half expected the wind to carry her away like some golden leaf, and then he noticed the look in her eyes. She was little more than a child and yet her eyes were older—the glow of innocence and the sparkle of wonder were absent. There was a weight to her face, a determination in her gaze. Whatever childhood she had known had long since abandoned her.

They finished their food, packed up, and set off again. Descending the far side of the heights, they continued to follow the road for the remainder of the day, but as sunset neared, the road narrowed to little more than a simple trail. Farmhouses still appeared from time to time, but they were less frequent. The forest grew thicker and the road darker.

As sunlight faded, Thrace grew very quiet. There was nothing to see or point out anymore but Hadrian guessed it was more than that. Mouse skipped a stone into a windblown pile of the past year's leaves and Thrace jumped, grabbing his waist. She dug her nails in deep enough to make him wince.

"Shouldn't we find shelter?" she asked.

"Not much chance of that out here," Hadrian told her. "From this point on we'll be leaving civilization behind. Besides, it's a lovely evening. The ground is dry and it looks like it will be warm."

"We're sleeping outside?"

Hadrian turned around to see her face. Her mouth was open slightly, her forehead creased, her eyes wide and looking up at the sky. "We're still a long way from Dahlgren," he assured her. She nodded but held on to him tighter.

They stopped at a clearing near a little creek that flowed over a series of rocks, making a friendly rushing sound. Hadrian helped Thrace down and pulled the saddles and gear off the horses.

"Where's Royce?" Thrace asked in a whispered panic. She stood with her arms folded across her chest, looking around anxiously.

"It's okay," Hadrian told her as he pulled the bridle off Millie's head. "He always does a bit of scouting whenever we stop for the night. He'll circle the area making sure we're alone. Royce hates surprises."

Thrace nodded but remained huddled, as if standing on a stone amidst a raging river.

"We'll be sleeping right over there. You might want to clear it some. A single stone can ruin a night's sleep. I ought to know; it seems whenever I sleep outside, I always end up with a stone under the small of my back."

She walked into the clearing and gingerly bent over, tossing aside branches and rocks, nervously glancing skyward and jumping at the slightest sound. By the time Hadrian had the horses settled, Royce had returned. He carried an armload of small branches and a few shattered logs, which he used to build a fire.

Thrace stared at him, horrified. "It's so bright," she whispered.

Hadrian squeezed her hand and smiled. "You know, I bet you're a wonderful cook, aren't you? I could make us dinner, but it would be miserable. All I know how to do is boil potatoes. How about you give it a try? What do you say? There are pots and pans in that sack over there and you'll find food in the one next to it."

Thrace nodded silently and, with one last glance upward, shuffled over to the packs. "What kind of meal would you like?"

"Something edible would be a pleasant surprise," Royce said, adding more wood.

Hadrian threw a stick at him. The thief caught it and placed it on the fire.

She dug into the packs, going so far as to stick her head inside, and emerged moments later with an armload of items. She borrowed Hadrian's knife and began cutting vegetables on the bottom of a turned-up pan.

It grew dark quickly, the fire becoming the only source of light in the clearing. The flickering yellow radiance illuminated the canopy of leaves around them, creating the feel of a woodland cave. Hadrian picked out a grassy area upwind from the smoke and laid out sheets of canvas coated in pitch. It blocked the wetness that would otherwise soak in. The treated fabric was something they had come up with after years on the road. But they did not have time to make one for Thrace. He sighed, threw Thrace's blankets on his canvas, and went in search of pine boughs for his own bed.

When dinner was ready, Royce called for Hadrian. He returned to the fire, where Thrace was dishing out a thick broth of carrots, potatoes, onions, and salted pork. Royce was sitting with a bowl on his lap and a smile on his face.

"You don't have to be that happy," Hadrian told him.

"Look, Hadrian—food."

They ate mostly in silence. Royce made a few comments about things they should pick up when they passed through Alburn, such as another length of rope and a new spoon to replace the cracked one. Hadrian mostly watched Thrace, who refused to sit near the fire; she ate alone on a rock in the shadows near the horses. When they finished, she stole away to the river to wash the pot and wooden bowls.

"Are you all right?" Hadrian asked, finding her along the stony bank.

Thrace was crouched on a large moss-capped rock, her gown tucked tight around her ankles, as she washed the pot and bowls by scooping up what sand she could find and scrubbing them with her fingers.

"I'm fine, thank you. I'm just not used to being out at night."

Hadrian settled down beside her and began cleaning his bowl.

"I can do that," she said.

"So can I. Besides, you're thc customer, so you should get your money's worth."

She smirked at him. "I'm not a fool, you know. Ten silver won't even cover the feed for the horses, will it?"

"Well, what you have to understand is Mouse and Millie are very spoiled. They only eat the best grain." He winked. She could not help smiling back.

Thrace finished the pot and the other bowls and they walked back to camp.

"How much farther is it?" she asked, replacing the pot and bowls in the sack.

"I'm not sure. I've never been to Dahlgren, but we made good time today, so maybe only another four days."

"I hope my father is all right. Mr. Haddon said he would try to convince him to wait until I returned before hunting the beast. I hope he did. As I said, my father is a very stubborn man and I can't imagine anyone changing his mind."

"Well, if anyone can, I suspect that Mr. Haddon could," Royce remarked, prodding the coals of the fire with a long stick. "How did you meet him?"

Thrace found the bed Hadrian had laid out for her near the fire and sat down on her blanket. "It was right after my family's funeral. It was very beautiful. The whole village turned out. Maria and Jessie Caswell hung wreaths of wild salifan on the markers. Mae Drundel and Rose and Verna McDern sang the 'Fields of Lilies,' and Deacon Tomas said a few prayers. Lena and Russell Bothwick held a reception at their house. Lena and my mother were very close."

"I don't remember you mentioning your mother; was she—"

"My mother died two years ago."

"I'm sorry. Sickness?"

Thrace shook her head.

No one spoke for a while, then Hadrian said, "You were telling us how you met Mr. Haddon—"

"Oh yeah, well, I don't know how many funerals you've been to, but it starts to feel...smothering. All the weeping and old stories. I snuck out. I was just wandering, really. I ended up at the village well and there he was...a stranger. We don't get many of those, but that wasn't all. He had on this robe that shimmered and kinda seemed to change colors from time to time, but the big thing was he had no hands. The poor man was trying to get himself a drink of water, struggling with the bucket and rope.

"I asked his name and then, oh, I don't know, I did something stupid like starting to cry and he asked me what was wrong. The thing was, at that moment, I wasn't crying because my brother and his wife just died. I was crying because I was terrified my father would be next. I don't know why I told him. Maybe because he was a stranger. It was easy to talk to him. It all just spilled out. I felt stupid afterward, but he was very patient. That's when he told me about the weapon in the tower and about you two."

"How did he know where we were?"

Thrace shrugged. "Don't you live there?"

"No...we were visiting an old friend. Did he talk oddly? Did he use *thee* and *thou* a lot?"

"No, but he spoke a bit more educated than most. He said his name was Mr. Esra Haddon. Is he a friend of yours?"

"We only met him briefly," Hadrian explained. "Like you, we helped him with a little problem he was having."

"The question is, why is he keeping tabs on us?" Royce asked. "And how, since I don't recall dropping our names and he couldn't have known we would be going to Colnora."

"All he told me is that you were needed to open the tower and if I left right away, I could find you there. Then he arranged for me to ride with the peddler. He's been very helpful."

"Rather amazing, isn't it, for a man who can't even get himself a cup of water," Royce muttered.

CHAPTER 3

THE AMBASSADOR

Arista stood at the tower window, looking down at the world below. She could see the roofs of shops and houses. They appeared as squares and triangles of gray, brown, and red pierced by chimneys left dormant on the warm spring day. The rain had washed through, leaving the world below fresh and vibrant. She watched the people walking along the streets, gathering in squares, moving in and out of doorways. Occasionally a shout reached her ears, soft and faint. Most of the noise came from directly below in the courtyard, where a train of seven coaches had just arrived and servants were loading trunks.

"No. No. No. Not the red dress!" Bernice shouted at Melissa. "Novron, protect us. Look at that neckline. Her Highness has a reputation to protect. Put that in storage, or better yet—burn it. Why, you might as well salt her, put a garnish behind her ear, and hand her over to a pack of starving wolves. No, not the dark one either; it's nearly black—it's spring, for Maribor's sake. Where's your head? The sky blue gown, yes, that one can stay. Honestly, it's a good thing I'm here."

Bernice was an old plump woman with a doughlike face

that sagged at the cheeks and doubled at the chin. The color of her hair was unknown, as she always wrapped it in a barbette veil that looped her head from crown to neck. To this she added a tall cloth filet that made it seem like the top of her head was flat. She stood in the center of Arista's bedroom, flailing her arms and shouting amidst the chaotic maelstrom that she had created.

Piles of clothes lay everywhere except in Arista's wardrobes. Those stood empty, waiting with doors wide, as Bernice sorted each gown, boxing the winter dresses for storage. In addition to Melissa, Bernice had drafted two other girls from downstairs to assist in the packing. Bernice had filled one chest but still her bedroom remained carpeted in gowns, and Arista already had a headache from all the shouting.

Bernice had been one of her mother's handmaids. Queen Ann had kept several. Drundiline, a beautiful woman, had been her secretary and close friend. Harriet ran the residence, organizing the cleaning staff, seamstresses, and laundry. Nora, whose lazy eye always made it impossible to tell who she was actually looking at, handled the children. Arista remembered how she would tell her fairy tales at bedtime about greedy dwarves who kidnapped spoiled princesses, but a dashing prince always saved them in the end. In all, Arista could remember no fewer than eight maids, but she could not remember Bernice.

She had come to Essendon Castle nearly two years earlier, only a month after Arista's father, King Amrath, had been murdered. Bishop Saldur explained that she had served the queen and was the only maid to survive the fire that had killed her mother so many years earlier. He mentioned Bernice had been away for years, suffering from melancholy and sickness, but after Amrath's death, she insisted on returning to care for her beloved queen's daughter.

"Oh, Your Highness," Bernice said, holding two separate

pairs of Arista's shoes, "I do wish you would come away from that window. The weather may look pleasant, but drafts are not something to toy with. Trust me, I know all about it—intimately. Pray you never have to go through what I did—the aches, the pains, the coughing. Not that I'm complaining, of course; I'm still here, aren't I? I'm blessed with the gift of seeing you grow into a lady, and Maribor willing, I will see you as a bride. What a fine bride you'll make! I hope King Alric picks a husband for you soon. Who knows how long I have left, and we don't want people gossiping about you any more than they already are."

"People are gossiping?" Arista turned and sat on the open windowsill.

Watching her on the edge, Bernice panicked and froze in place, her mouth opening and closing with silent protests, both hands waving the shoes at her. "Your Highness," she managed to gasp, "you'll fall!"

"I'm fine."

"No. No, you're not." Bernice shook her head frantically. "Please. I beg of you."

She dropped the shoes, planted her feet, and reached out her hand as if standing on the edge of a precipice. "Please."

Arista rolled her eyes, stood up, and walked away from the window. She crossed the room to her bed, which lay beneath several layers of clothes.

"No, wait!" Bernice shouted again. She shook her hands at the wrists as if trying to dry them. "Melissa, clear Her Highness a place to sit."

Arista sighed and ran a hand through her hair while she waited for Melissa to gather the dresses.

"Careful now, don't wrinkle them," Bernice cautioned.

"I'm sorry, Your Highness," Melissa told her as she gathered an armful. She was a small redhead with dark green eyes who had served Arista for the past five years. The princess got the distinct impression the maid's apology did not refer to the mess on the bed. Arista fought to keep from laughing and a smile emerged. It only made matters worse when she saw Melissa grinning as well.

"The good news is the bishop delivered a list of potential suitors to His Majesty this morning," Bernice said, and Arista no longer had any trouble quelling laughter, the smile disappeared as well. "I'm hoping it will be that nice prince Rudolf, King Armand's son." Bernice was raising her eyebrows and grinning mischievously like some deranged pixie. "He's very handsome—many say dashing—and Alburn is a very nice kingdom—at least so I have heard."

"I've been there and I've met him. He's an arrogant ass."

"Oh, that tongue of yours!" Bernice clasped her hands to the sides of her face and gazed upward, mouthing a silent prayer. "You must learn to control yourself. If anyone else had heard you—thankfully, we're the only two here."

Arista glanced at Melissa and the other two girls busy sorting through her things. Melissa caught her look and shrugged.

"All right, so you aren't certain about Prince Rudolf, that's fine. How about King Ethelred of Warric? You can't do better than him. The poor widower is the most powerful monarch in Avryn. You would live in Aquesta and be queen of the Wintertide festivals."

"The man has to be in his fifties. Not to mention he's an Imperialist. I'd slit my throat first."

Bernice staggered backward and threw one hand to her own neck while the other reached for the wall.

Melissa snickered and tried to cover it with a pretend cough.

"I think you're done here, Melissa," Bernice said. "Take the chamber pot when you go."

"But the sorting isn't—" Melissa protested.

Bernice gave her a reproachful look.

Melissa sighed. "Your Highness," she said, and curtsied to Arista, then picked up the chamber pot and left.

"She didn't mean anything by it," Arista told Bernice.

"It doesn't matter. Respect must be maintained at all times. I know I'm only an old crazy woman who doesn't matter to anyone, but I can tell you this: if I were here—if I had been well enough to help raise you after your mother died, people wouldn't be calling you a witch today."

Arista's eyes widened.

"Forgive me, Your Highness, but that's the truth of it. With your mother gone, and me away, I fear you were brought up poorly. Thank Maribor I came back when I did, or who knows what would become of you? But no worries, my dear, we have you on the right track now. You'll see, everything will work out once we find you a suitable husband. All that nonsense from your past will soon be forgotten."

~

Her dignity, as well as the length of her gown, prevented Arista from running down the stairs. Hilfred trotted behind her, struggling to keep up with the sudden burst of speed. She had caught her bodyguard by surprise. She had surprised herself. Arista had had every intention of walking calmly up to her brother and politely asking if he had gone mad. The plan had worked fine up until she passed the chapel; then she started moving faster and faster.

The good news is the bishop delivered a list of potential suitors to His Majesty this morning.

She could still see the grin on Bernice's face and hear the perverse glee in her words, as if she were a spectator at the foot of a gallows waiting for the hangman to kick the bucket.

I'm hoping it will be that nice prince Rudolf, King Armand's son.

It was hard to breathe. Her hair broke loose from the ribbon and flew behind her. As Arista rounded the turn near the ballroom, her left foot slipped out from under her and she nearly fell. Her shoe came off and spun across the polished floor. She left it, pressing on, hobbling forward like a wagon with a broken wheel. She reached the west gallery. It was a long, straight hallway lined with suits of armor, and here she picked up speed. Jacobs, the royal clerk, spotted her from his perch outside the reception hall and jumped to his feet.

"Your Highness!" he exclaimed with a bow.

"Is he in there?" she barked.

The little clerk with the round face and red nose nodded. "But His Majesty is in a state meeting. He's requested that he not be disturbed."

"The man is already disturbed. I'm just here to beat some sense into his feeble little brain."

The clerk cringed. He looked like a squirrel in a rainstorm. If he had had a tail, it would have been over his head. Behind her she heard Hilfred's familiar footsteps approach.

She turned toward the door and took a step.

"You can't go in," Jacobs told her, panicking. "They are having a state meeting," he repeated.

The soldiers who stood to either side of the door stepped forward to block her.

"Out of my way!" she yelled.

"Forgive us, Your Highness, but we have orders from the king not to allow anyone entrance."

"I'm his sister," she protested.

"I am sorry, Your Highness; His Majesty—he specifically mentioned you."

"He—what?" She stood stunned for a moment, then spun

on the clerk, caught wiping his nose with a handkerchief. "Who's in there with him? Who's in this *state meeting*?"

"What's going on?" Julian Tempest, the lord chamberlain, asked as he rushed out of his office. His long black robe with gold hash marks on the sleeve trailed behind him like the train of a bride. Julian was an ancient man who had been Lord Chamberlain of Essendon Castle since before she was born, perhaps even before her father was born. Normally he wore a powdered wig that hung down past his shoulders like the floppy ears of an old dog, but she had caught him by surprise and all he had on was his skullcap, a few tufts of white hair sticking out like seed silk from a milkweed pod.

"I want to see my brother," Arista demanded.

"But—but, Your Highness, he's in a state meeting; surely it can wait."

"Who is he meeting with?"

"I believe Bishop Saldur, Chancellor Pickering, Lord Valin, and, oh, I'm not sure who else." Julian glanced at Jacobs for support.

"And what is this meeting about?"

"Why, actually, I think it has to do with"—he hesitated—"your future."

"My future? They are determining my life in there and I can't go in?" She was livid now. "Is Prince Rudolf in there? Lanis Ethelred, perhaps?"

"Ah...I don't know—I don't think so." Again he glanced at the clerk, who wanted no part of this. "Your Highness, please calm down. I suspect they can hear you."

"Good!" she shouted. "They should hear me. I want them to hear me. If they think I am going to just stand here and wait for the verdict, to see what they will decide my fate to be, I—"

"Arista!"

She turned to see the doors to the throne room open. Her

brother, Alric, stood trapped behind the guards, who quickly stood aside. He was wearing the white fur mantle Julian insisted he drape over his shoulders at all state functions and the heavy gold crown, which he pushed to the back of his head. "What is your problem? You sound like a raving lunatic."

"I'll tell you what my problem is. I'm not going to let you do this to me. You are not going to send me off to Alburn or Warric like some—some—state commodity."

"I'm not sending you to Warric or Alburn. We've already decided you are going to Dunmore."

"Dunmore?" The word hit her like a blow. "You're joking. Tell me you're joking."

"I was going to tell you tonight. Although, I thought you'd take it better. I figured you'd like it."

"Like it? Like it! Oh yeah, I love the idea of being used as a political pawn. What are they giving you in return? Is that what you were doing in there, auctioning me off?" She rose on her toes, trying to get a look over her brother's shoulders to see who he was hiding in the throne room. "Did you have them bidding on me like a prized cow?"

"Prized cow? What are you talking about?" Alric glanced behind him self-consciously and closed the doors. He waved at Julian and Jacobs, shooing them away. In a softer voice he said, "It will give you some respect. You'll have genuine authority. You won't be just *the princess* anymore and you'll have something to do. Weren't you the one that said you wanted to get out of your tower and contribute to the well-being of the kingdom?"

"And—and this is what you thought of?" She was ready to scream. "Don't do this to me, Alric, I beg of you. I know I've been an embarrassment. I know what they say about me. You think I don't hear them whispering *witch* under their breath? You think I don't know what was said at the trial?"

"Arista, those people were coerced. You know that." He glanced briefly at Hilfred, who stood beside her, holding the lost shoe.

"I'm just saying I know about it. I'm sure they complain to you all the time." She gestured toward the closed door behind him. She did not know whom she meant by *they* and hoped he did not ask. "But I can't help what people think. If you want, I'll come to more events. I'll attend the state dinners. I'll take up needlepoint. I'll make a damn tapestry. Something cute and inoffensive. How about a stag hunt? I don't know how to make a tapestry, but I bet Bernice does—she knows all that crap."

"*You're* going to make a tapestry?"

"If that's what it takes. I'll be better—I will. I haven't even put the lock on my door in the new tower. I haven't done a thing since you were crowned, I swear. Please don't sentence me to a life of servitude. I don't mind being just a princess—I don't."

He looked at her, confused.

"I mean it. I really do, Alric. Please, don't do this."

He sighed, looking at her sadly. "Arista, what else can I do with you? I don't want you living like a hermit in that tower for the rest of your life. I honestly think this is for the best. It will be good for you. You might not see it now but—don't look at me like that! I am king and you'll do as I tell you. I need you to do this for me. The kingdom needs you to do this."

She could not believe what she was hearing. Arista felt tears working their way forward. She locked her jaw, squeezing her teeth together, breathing faster to stave them off. She felt feverish and a little light-headed. "And I suppose I am to be shipped off immediately. Is that why the carriages are outside?"

"Yes," he said firmly. "I was hoping you would be on your way in the morning."

"Tomorrow?" Arista felt her legs weaken, the air empty from her lungs.

"Oh, for Maribor's sake, Arista—it's not like I'm ordering you to marry some old coot."

"Oh—well! I am so pleased you are looking out for me," she said. "Who is it, then? One of King Roswort's nephews? Dearest Maribor, Alric! Why Dunmore? Rudolf would have been misery enough, but at least I could understand an alliance with Alburn. But Dunmore? That's just cruel. Do you hate me that much? Am I that horrible that you must marry me to some no-account duke in a backwater kingdom? Even Father wouldn't have done that to me—why—why are you laughing? Stop laughing, you insensitive little hobgoblin!"

"I'm not marrying you off, Arista," Alric managed to get out.

She narrowed her eyes at him. "You're not?"

"God, no! Is that what you thought? I wouldn't do that. I'm familiar with the kind of people you know. I'd find myself floating down the Galewyr again."

"What, then? Julian said you were deciding my fate in there."

"I have—I've officially appointed you Ambassador of Melengar."

She stood silent, staring at him for a long moment. Without turning her head, she shifted her eyes and grabbed her shoe from Hilfred. Leaning on his shoulder, she slipped it back on.

"But Bernice said Sauly brought a list of eligible suitors," she said tentatively, cautiously.

"Oh yes, he did," Alric said, and chuckled. "We all had a good laugh at that."

"We?"

"Mauvin and Fanen are here." He hooked his thumb at the door. "They're going with you. Fanen plans to enter the contest the church is organizing up in Ervanon. You see, it was supposed to be this big surprise, but you ruined everything as usual."

"I'm sorry," she said, her voice quavering unexpectedly. She threw her arms around her brother and hugged him tight. "Thank you."

⁂

The front wheels of the carriage bounced in a hole, followed abruptly by the rear ones. Arista nearly struck her head on the roof and lost her concentration, which was frustrating, because she was certain she was on the verge of recalling the name of Dunmore's Secretary of the Treasury. It started with a Bon, a Bonny, or a Bobo—no, it could not be Bobo, could it? It was something like that. All these names, all these titles, the third baron of Brodinia, the Earl of Nith—or was it the third baron of Nith and the Earl of Brodinia? Arista looked at the palm of her hand, wondering if she could write them there. If caught, it would be an embarrassment not just for herself, but for Alric, and all of Melengar as well. From now on, everything she did, every mistake, every stumble would not just hurt her, it would reflect poorly on her kingdom. She had to be perfect. The problem was she did not know how to be perfect. She wished her brother had given her more time to prepare.

Dunmore was a new kingdom, only seventy years old, an overgrown fief reclaimed from the wilderness by ambitious nobles with only passing pedigrees. It had none of the traditions or refinement found in the rest of Avryn, but it did have a plethora of mind-numbing titled offices. She was convinced King Roswort created them the way a self-conscious man might overdecorate a modest house. He certainly had more ministers than Alric, with titles twice as long and uniquely vague, such as the Assistant Secretary of the Second Royal Avenue Inspection Quorum. *What does that even mean?* And then there was the simply unfathomable, since Dunmore was landlocked, Grandmaster of the Fleet! Nevertheless, Julian had provided her with a list and she was doing her best to memorize it, along with a tally sheet of their imports, exports, trade agreements, military treaties, and even the name of the king's dog. She laid her head back on the velvet upholstery and sighed.

"Something wrong, my dear?" Bishop Saldur inquired from his seat directly across from her, where he sat pressing his fingers together. He stared at her with unwavering eyes that took in more than her face. She would have considered his looks rude if he had been anyone else. Saldur—or Sauly, as she always called him—had taught her the art of blowing dandelions that had gone to seed when she was five. He had shown her how to play checkers and pretended not to notice when she climbed trees or rode her pony at a gallop. For commencement on her sixteenth birthday, Sauly had personally instructed her on the Tenets of the Faith of Nyphron. He was like a grandfather. He always stared at her. She had given up wondering why.

"There's too much to learn. I can't keep it all straight. The bouncing doesn't help either. It's just that"—she flipped through the parchments on her lap, shaking her head—"I want to do a good job, but I don't think I will."

The old man smiled at her, his eyebrows rising in sympathy. "You'll do fine. Besides, it's only Dunmore." He gave her a wink. "I think you'll find His Majesty King Roswort an unpleasant sort of man to deal with. Dunmore has been slow to gain the virtues that the rest of civilization has learned to enjoy. Just be patient and respectful. Remember that you'll be standing in *his* court, not Melengar, and there you are subject to his authority. Your best ally in any discussion is silence. Learn to develop that skill. Learn to listen instead of speaking and you'll weather many storms. Also, avoid promising anything. Give the impression you are promising, but never actually say the words. That way Alric always has room to maneuver. It is a bad practice to tie the hands of your monarch."

"Would you like something to drink, my lady?" Bernice asked, sitting beside Arista on the cushioned bench, guarding a basket of travel treats. She sat straight, her knees together, hands clutching the basket, thumbs rubbing it gently. Bernice beamed at her, fanning deep lines from the corners of her eyes. Her round pudgy cheeks were forced too high by a smile too broad—a condescending smile, the sort displayed to a child who had scraped her knee. At times Arista wondered if the old woman was trying to *be* her mother.

"What have you got in there, dear?" Saldur asked. "Anything with a bite to it?"

"I brought a pint of brandy," she said, and then hastily added, "in case it got cold."

"Come to think of it, I feel a bit chilled," Saldur said, rubbing his hands up and down his arms, pretending to shiver.

Arista raised an eyebrow. "This carriage is like an oven," she said while pulling on the high dress collar that ran to her chin. Alric had emphasized that she needed to wear properly modest attire, as if she had made a habit of strolling about the castle in bosom-baring scarlet tavern dresses. Bernice took this edict as carte blanche to imprison Arista in antiquated costumes of heavy material. The sole exception was the dress for her meeting with the King of Dunmore. Arista wanted all the help she could get to make a good impression and decided to wear the formal reception gown that had once belonged to her mother. It was simply the most stunning dress Arista had ever seen. When her mother had worn it, every head had turned. She had looked so impressive, so magnificent—every bit the queen.

"Old bones, my dear," Saldur told her. "Come, Bernice, why don't you and I share a little cup?" This brought a self-conscious smile to the old lady's face.

Arista pulled the velvet curtain aside and looked out the window. Her carriage was in the middle of a caravan consisting of wagons and soldiers on horseback. Mauvin and Fanen were somewhere out there, but all she could see was what the window framed. They were in the kingdom of Ghent, although Ghent had no king. The Nyphron Church administered the region directly and had for several hundred years. There were few trees in this rocky land and the hills remained a dull brown, as if spring were tardy—off playing in other realms and neglecting its chores here. High above the plain a hawk circled in wide loops.

"Oh dear!" Bernice exclaimed as the carriage bounced again. *Oh dear!* was as close as Bernice ever came to cursing. Arista glanced over to see that the jostling was making the process of pouring the brandy a challenge. Sauly with the bottle, Bernice with the cup, their arms shifting up and down, struggling to meet in the middle like in some test-of-skill at a May Fair—a game that was designed to look simple but ultimately embarrassed the players. At last, Sauly managed to tip the bottle and they both cheered.

"Not a drop lost," he said, pleased with himself. "Here's to our new ambassador. May she do us proud." He raised the cup, took a large mouthful, and sat back with a sigh. "Have you been to Ervanon before, my dear?"

Arista shook her head.

"I think you'll find it spiritually uplifting. Honestly, I am surprised your father never brought you here. It is a pilgrimage every member of the Church of Nyphron needs to make once in their life."

Arista nodded, failing to mention her late father had not been terribly devout. He had been required to play his part in the religious services of the kingdom, but often skipped them if the fish were biting, or if the huntsmen reported spotting a stag in the river valley. Of course, there had been times when even he had sought solace. She had long wondered about his death. Why had he been in the chapel the night that miserable dwarf had stabbed him? More importantly, how had her uncle Percy known he would be there and used this knowledge to plot his death? It puzzled her until she realized he had not been there praying to Novron or Maribor—he had been talking to *her*. It had been the anniversary of the fire. The date Arista's mother had died. He had probably visited the chapel every year and it bothered Arista that her uncle knew more about her father's habits than she did. It also disturbed her that she had never thought to join him.

"You'll have the privilege of meeting with His Holiness the Archbishop of Ghent."

She sat up, surprised. "Alric never mentioned anything about that. I thought we were merely passing through Ervanon on our way to Dunmore."

"It is not a formal engagement, but he is eager to see the new Ambassador of Melengar."

"Will I be seeing the Patriarch as well?" she asked, concerned. Not being prepared for Dunmore was one thing, but meeting the Patriarch with no preparation would be devastating.

"No." Saldur smiled like a man amused by a child's struggle to take her first steps. "Until the Heir of Novron is found, the Patriarch is the closest thing we have to the voice of god. He lives his life in seclusion, speaking only on rare occasions. He is a very great man, a very holy man. Besides, we can't keep you too long. You don't want to be late for your appointment with King Roswort in Glamrendor."

"I suppose I'll miss the contest, then."

"I don't see how," the bishop said after taking another sip, which left his lips glistening.

"If I push on to Dunmore, I won't be in Ervanon to see—"

"Oh, the contest won't be held in Ervanon," Saldur explained. "Those broadsides you've no doubt seen only indicated that contestants are to *gather* there."

"Then where will it be?"

"Ah, well now, that's something of a secret. Given the gravity of this event, it is important to keep things under control, but I can tell you this: Dunmore will be on the way. You'll stop there long enough to have your audience with the king and then you'll be able to continue on to the contest with the rest of them. Alric will most assuredly want to have his ambassador on hand for this momentous occasion."

"Oh, wonderful, I would like that—Fanen Pickering is competing. But does that mean you won't be coming?"

"That will be up to the archbishop to decide."

"I hope you can. I'm sure Fanen would appreciate as many people as possible cheering him on."

"Oh, it's not a competition. I know all those heralds are promoting it that way, which is unfortunate, because the Patriarch did not intend it so."

Arista stared at him, confused. "I thought it was a tournament. I saw an announcement declaring the church was hosting a grand event, a test of courage and skill, the winner to receive some magnificent reward."

"Yes, and all of that's true but misleading. Skill will not be needed so much as courage and... Well, you'll find out."

He tipped the cup and frowned, then looked hopefully at Bernice.

Arista stared at the cleric a moment longer, wondering what all that meant, but it was clear Sauly would not be adding anything further on the topic. She turned back to the window, peering out once more. Hilfred trotted beside the carriage on his white stallion. Unlike Bernice, her bodyguard was unobtrusive and silent. He was always there, distant, watchful, respectful of her privacy, or as much as a man who was required to follow her everywhere could be. He was always in sight of her but never looking—the perfect shadow. It had always been that way, but since the trial, he had been different. It was a subtle change but she sensed he had withdrawn from her. Perhaps he felt guilty for his testimony, or maybe, like so many others, he believed some of the accusations brought against her. It was possible Hilfred thought he was serving a witch. Maybe he even regretted saving her life from the fire that night. She threw the curtain shut and sighed.

∽

It was dark by the time the caravan arrived in Ervanon. Bernice had fallen asleep, her head hanging limp over the basket, which threatened to fall. Saldur had nodded off as well, his head drooping lower and lower, popping up abruptly only to droop again. Through her window, Arista felt the cool, dewy night air splash across her face as she craned her neck to look ahead. The sky was awash in stars, giving it a light dusty appearance, and Arista could see the dark outline of the city rising on the great hill. The lower buildings were nothing more than shadows, but from within them rose a singular finger. The Crown Tower was unmistakable. The alabaster battlements that ringed the top appeared like a white crown floating high in the air. The ancient remnant of the Steward's

Empire was distinctive as the tallest structure ever made by man. Even at a distance it was awe-inspiring.

Surrounding the city were campfires, flickering lights scattered across the flats like a swarm of resting fireflies. As they approached, she heard voices, shouts, laughter, arguments rising up from the many camps along the roadside. They were the contestants, and there must be hundreds of them. Arista saw only glimpses as the carriage rolled past. Faces were illuminated by the glow of firelight. Silhouetted figures carried plates; men and boys sat on the ground laughing, tipping cups to their mouths. Tents filled the spaces in between and lines of tethered horses and wagons lay in the shadows.

The wheels and hooves of her carriage began a loud click-clack as they rolled onto cobblestone. They entered through a gate and all she could see were torches illuminating the occasional wall, or a light in a nearby window. Arista was disappointed. She had learned about the city's history at Sheridan University and looked forward to seeing the ancient seat that had once ruled the world. In the power vacuum left after the fall of the ancient Novronian Empire, civil wars broke out and the people divided along their old Apelanese ethnic lines, forming the four nations of Apeladorn: Trent, Avryn, Calis, and Delgos. Within each of these, various warlords struggled for supremacy, battling their neighbors for land and power. After more than three hundred years of warfare, only one ruler ever managed to make a serious attempt at unifying the four nations into one empire again. Glenmorgan of Ghent ended the era of civil wars and, through brilliant and brutal conquests, unified Trent, Avryn, Calis, and Delgos under one banner once more. The Church of Nyphron threw its support behind him but reminded the people that Glenmorgan was not the Heir of Novron by naming him the Defender of the Faith and Steward to the Heir. They solidified the union by establishing the church's base in Ervanon and built their great cathedral alongside Glenmorgan Castle.

The Steward's Reign did not last. According to Arista's professor, Glenmorgan's son was ill suited to the task he inherited, and the Steward's Empire ended only seventy years after it began, collapsing with the betrayal of Glenmorgan III by his nobles. It was not long before Calis and Trent broke away and Delgos declared itself a republic.

Ervanon was mostly ruined in the warfare that followed, but in the aftermath, the Patriarch moved into the last remaining piece of Glenmorgan's great palace—the Crown Tower. From then on, the tower and the city became synonymous with the church and recognized as the holiest place in the world behind the ancient—but lost—Novronian capital of Percepliquis itself.

The carriage stopped with a jerk that rocked the inhabitants, waking Saldur and causing the old maid to gasp when her basket spilled to the floor.

"We've arrived," Saldur said with a groggy voice as he wiped his eyes, yawned, and stretched.

The coachman locked the brake, climbed down, and opened the door. A rush of cool damp air flooded inside and chilled Arista. She stepped out, stiff and weak, her head hazy. It felt strange to be standing still. They were at the very base of the massive Crown Tower. She looked up and doing so made her dizzy. Even at that dark hour, the top stood out brightly against the night sky. The tower rested on a domed crest known as Glenmorgan's Rise, which was the highest point for miles. Even though she didn't climb a step, it appeared as if she stood at the top of the world as she looked beyond the ancient wall and down to the sprawling valley below.

She yawned and shivered and instantly Bernice was there, throwing a cloak over her shoulders and buttoning it. Sauly took longer getting out of the carriage. He slowly extended each thin leg, stretching them out and testing his weight.

"Your Grace." A boy appeared. "I hope you had a pleasant journey. The archbishop asked me to tell you he is waiting in his private chambers for the princess."

Arista was stunned. "Now?" She turned to the bishop. "You don't expect me to meet him with a day's coating of road dust and sweat on me. I look a fright, smell like a pig, and I'm exhausted."

"You look lovely as always, my lady," Bernice cooed while stroking the princess's hair. It was a habit that Arista particularly disliked. "I'm sure the archbishop, being a spiritual man, will be looking at your soul, not your physical person."

Arista gave Bernice a quizzical look, then rolled her eyes.

Servants dressed in clerical frocks appeared around them, hauling luggage, breaking down the harnesses, and watering the horses.

"This way, Your Grace," the boy said, and led them into the tower.

They entered a large rotunda with a polished marble floor and columns that divided the center from a walkway that encircled the wall. As if from a great distance, she could hear soft singing. Dozens of voices, perhaps a choir, were rehearsing. Flickering light from unseen lamps bounced off polished surfaces. Their footsteps echoed loudly.

"Couldn't I see him in the morning?"

"No," Saldur said, "this is a very important matter."

Arista furrowed her brow and pondered this. She had taken for granted that visiting the archbishop was just a formality, but now she was not so sure. As part of Percy Braga's plot to usurp the kingdom of Melengar, he had placed her on trial for her father's death. Barred from attending the proceedings, she later heard rumors of testimony others had given, including her beloved Sauly. If the stories were true, Sauly had denounced her not only for killing her father, but also for witchery. She had never spoken to the bishop about the allegations, nor had she demanded an explanation from Hilfred. Percy Braga was to blame for all of it. He had tricked everyone. Hilfred and Sauly had only done what they had thought best for the sake of the kingdom. Still, she could not help wondering if perhaps she had been the one fooled.

According to the church, witchery and magic of any kind were an abomination to the faith. *If Sauly thought I was guilty, might he take steps against me?* She considered it incredible that the bishop, who had been like a family member to her, who always seemed so kind and benevolent, could do such a thing. On the other hand, Braga had been her actual uncle, and after nearly twenty years of loyal service, he had murdered her father and tried to kill her and Alric as well. His desire for power knew no loyalties.

She was increasingly aware of Hilfred's presence coming up the stairs behind her. Normally giving her a comfortable feeling of security, it now seemed threatening. *Why is it he never looks at me?* Perhaps she was wrong. Perhaps it was not guilt or dislike; perhaps it was a matter of distancing himself. She heard farmers who raised cows for milking often named them Bessie or Gertrude, but those same farmers never named the beef cows, those destined for slaughter.

Arista's mind began to race. Were they leading her to a locked cell in yet another tower? Would they execute her, the way the church had executed Glenmorgan III? Would they burn her at a stake and later justify it as a purifying act for the crime of heresy? What would Alric do when he found out? Would he declare war on the church? If he did, all the other kingdoms would turn against him. He would have no choice but to accept the edict of the church.

They reached a door and the bishop asked Bernice to go and prepare the princess's room for her arrival. He asked Hilfred to wait outside while he led Arista in and closed the door behind her.

It was a surprisingly small room, a tiny study with a cluttered desk and only a few chairs. Wall sconces revealed old thick books, parchments, seals, maps, and clerical vestments for various occasions.

Two men waited inside. Seated behind the desk was the archbishop, an old man with white hair and wrinkled skin. He sat wrapped in a dark purple cassock with an embroidered shoulder cape and a golden stole that hung around his neck like an untied scarf. He had a long and pallid face, made longer by his unkempt beard, which, when he was seated as he was, reached to the floor. Similarly, his eyebrows were whimsically bushy. On a high wooden seat he sat bent in a hunched posture, giving the impression he was leaning forward with interest.

Searching through the clutter was another, much younger, thin little man, with long fingers and darting eyes. He, too, was pale, as if he had not seen the sun in years. His long black hair pulled back in a tight tail gave him the stark and intense look of a man consumed by his work.

"Your Holiness Archbishop Galien," Saldur said after they had entered, "may I introduce the princess Arista Essendon of Melengar."

"So pleased you could come," the old cleric told her. His mouth, which had lost many of its teeth, frequently sucked in his thin lips. His voice was windy, with a distinctive rasp. "Please, take a seat. I assume you had a rough day bouncing around in the back of a carriage. Dreadful things, really. They tear up the roads and shake you to a frazzle. I hate getting in one. It feels like a coffin and at my age you are wary of getting into boxes of any kind.

But I suppose I must endure it for the sake of the future, a future I won't even see." He unexpectedly winked at her. "Can I offer you a drink? Wine, perhaps? Carlton, make yourself useful, you little vagabond, and get Her Highness a glass of Montemorcey."

The little man said nothing but moved rapidly to a chest in the corner. He pulled a dark bottle from the contents and drew out the cork.

"Sit down, Arista," Saldur whispered in her ear.

The princess selected a red velvet chair in front of the desk and, brushing out her dress, sat down stiffly. She was not at ease but made an effort to control her growing fear.

Carlton presented her with a glass of red wine on an engraved silver platter. She considered that it might be drugged or even poisoned, but dismissed this notion as ridiculous. *Why poison or drug me? I already made the fatal error of blindly blundering into your web.* If Hilfred had defected to their side, she had only Bernice to protect her against the entire armed forces of Ghent. She was already at their mercy.

Arista took the glass, nodded at Carlton, and sipped.

"The wine is imported through the Vandon Spice Company in Delgos," the archbishop told her. "I have no idea where Montemorcey is, but they do make incredible wine. Don't you think?"

"I must apologize," Arista blurted out nervously. "I was unaware I was coming directly here. I assumed I would have a chance to freshen up after the long trip. I am generally more presentable. Perhaps I should retire and meet you tomorrow?"

"You look fine. You can't help it. Lovely young princesses are blessed that way. Bishop Saldur did the right thing bringing you here immediately, even more than he knows."

"Has something happened?" Saldur asked.

"Word has come down"—he looked up and pointed at the ceiling—"literally, that Luis Guy will be traveling with us."

"The sentinel?"

Galien nodded.

"That might be good, don't you think? He'll bring a contingent of seret, won't he? And that will help maintain order."

"I am certain that's the Patriarch's mind as well. I, however, know how the sentinel works. He won't listen to me and his methods are heavy handed. But that's not what we are here to discuss."

He paused a moment, took a breath, and returned his attention to Arista. "Tell me, my child, what do you know of Esrahaddon?"

Arista's heart skipped a beat but she said nothing.

Bishop Saldur placed his hand on hers and smiled. "My dear, we already know that you visited him in Gutaria Prison for months and that he taught you what he could of his vile black magic. We also know that Alric freed him. Yet none of that matters now. What we need to know is where he is and if he has contacted you since his release. You are the only person he knows who might trust him and therefore the only one he might reach out to. So tell us, child, have you had any communication with him?"

"Is this why you brought me here? To help you locate an alleged criminal?"

"He *is* a criminal, Arista," Galien said. "Despite what he told you, he is—"

"How do you know what he told me? Did you eavesdrop on every word the man said?"

"We did," he replied passively.

The blunt answer surprised her.

"My dear girl, that old wizard told you a story. Much of it is actually true; only he left out a great deal."

She glanced at Sauly, whose fatherly expression looked grim as he nodded his agreement.

"Your uncle Braga wasn't responsible for the murder of your father," the archbishop told her. "It was Esrahaddon."

"That's absurd," Arista scoffed. "He was in prison at the time and couldn't even send messages."

"Ah—but he could, and he did—through you. Why do you think he taught you to make the healing potion for your father?"

"Besides curing him of sickness, you mean?"

"Esrahaddon didn't care about Amrath. He didn't even care about you. The reality is he needed your father dead. Your mistake was going to him. Trusting him. Did you think he would be your friend? Your sage old tutor, like Arcadius? Esrahaddon is no tame beast, no honorable gentleman. He is a demon and he is dangerous. He used you to escape. From the moment you visited him, he calculated your use as a tool. To escape he needed the ruling monarch to come and release him. Your father knew who and what he was, so he would never do it. But Alric, because of his ignorance, would. So he needed your father dead. All Esrahaddon had to do was make the church believe your father was the heir. He knew it would cause us to act against him."

"But why would the church want the heir dead? I don't understand."

"We'll get to that in due time. But suffice it to say his interest in you and your father got our attention. It was the healing potion Esrahaddon had you create that sealed your father's fate. It tainted his blood to appear as if he was a descendent of the imperial bloodline. When Braga learned this, he followed what he thought was the church's wishes and put plans in motion to remove Amrath and his children."

"Are you saying that Braga was working for the church when he had my father murdered?"

"Not directly—or officially. But Braga was devout in his beliefs. He acted rashly, not waiting for the church *bureaucracy*, as he used to call it. Both the bishop and I speak for the whole church when we tell you we are truly sorry for the tragedy that occurred. Still, you must understand we did not orchestrate it. It was the design of Esrahaddon that set the wheels of your father's fate in motion. He used the church just as he used you."

Arista glared at the archbishop and then at Sauly. "You knew about this?"

The bishop nodded.

"How could you allow Braga to kill my father? He was your friend."

"I tried to stop it," Sauly told her. "You must believe me when I tell you this. The moment the test was done, and your father implicated, I called for an emergency council of the church, but Braga couldn't be stopped. He refused to listen to me and said I was wasting valuable time."

Fears of her own murder fled and anger filled the vacuum. She stood up, fists clenched, her eyes filled with hate.

"Arista, I know you are upset, and have every right to be, but let me explain further." The archbishop waited for her to sit down again. "What I am about to tell you is the most highly guarded secret of the Church of Nyphron. This information is strictly reserved for top-ranking members of the clergy. I am trusting you with this information because we need your help and I know you'll not extend it unless you understand why." He took the glass of wine, sipped it, then leaned forward and spoke to Arista in a quiet tone. "In the last few years of the empire, the church uncovered a dark and twisted scheme whose goal was no less than to enslave all of humanity. The conspiracy led directly to the emperor. Only the church could save mankind. We killed the emperor and tried to eliminate his bloodline, but the emperor's son was aided by Esrahaddon. His heritage contains the power to raise the demons of the past and once more bring humanity to the brink. For this reason, the church has sought to find the heir and destroy the lineage whose existence is a knife at the throat of all of us. After so long, the heir might not even be aware of his power, or even who he is. But Esrahaddon knows. If that wizard finds the heir, he can use him as a weapon against us. No one will be safe."

The archbishop looked at her carefully. "Esrahaddon was once part of the high council. He was one of the key members in the effort to save the empire from the conspirators, but at the last moment, he betrayed the church. Instead of a peaceful transition, he callously caused a civil war that destroyed the empire. The church cut off his hands and locked him away for nearly a millennium. What do you think he'll do if he has the chance to exact revenge? Whatever humanity he might have possessed died in Gutaria Prison. What remains is a powerful demon bent on our destruction—revenge for revenge's sake; he is mad with it. He is like a wildfire that will consume all if not stopped. As a princess of a kingdom, you must understand—sacrifices must be made to ensure the future of the realm. We deeply regret the error that occurred in respect to your father but hope you'll come to understand why it happened, accept our apologies, and help us prevent the end of all that we know.

"Esrahaddon is an incredibly intelligent madman bent on destroying everyone. The heir is his weapon. If he finds him before we do, if we cannot prevent him from reawakening the horror we managed to put to sleep centuries ago, then all this—this city, your kingdom of Melengar, all of Apeladorn will be lost. We need your help, Arista. We need you to help us find Esrahaddon."

The door opened abruptly and a priest entered.

"Your Grace," he said, out of breath, "the sentinel is calling the curia to order."

Galien nodded and looked back at Arista. "What say you, my dear? Can you help us?"

The princess looked at her hands. Too much was whirling in her head: Esrahaddon, Braga, Sauly, mysterious conspiracies, healing potions. The one image that remained steadfast was the memory of her father lying on his bed, his face pale, blood soaking the covers. It had taken so long to put the pain behind her, and now...had Esrahaddon killed him? Had they? "I don't know," she muttered.

"Can you at least tell us if he has contacted you since his escape?"

"I haven't seen or heard from Esrahaddon since before my father's death."

"You understand, of course," the archbishop told her, "that be this as it may, you are the most likely person he would trust and we would like you to consider working with us to find him. As Ambassador of Melengar you could travel between kingdoms and nations and never be suspected. I also understand that right now you may not be ready to make such a commitment, so I won't ask; but please consider it. The church has let you down grievously; I only request that you give us a chance to redeem ourselves in your eyes."

Arista drained the rest of her wine and slowly nodded.

"Do you think she is telling the truth?" the archbishop asked him. There was a faint look of hope on his face, clouded by an overall expression of misery. "There was a great deal of resistance in her."

Saldur was still looking at the door Arista had exited. "*Anger* would be a more accurate word, but yes, I think she was telling the truth."

He did not know what Galien had expected. Had he thought Arista would embrace him with open arms after they admitted to killing her father? The whole idea was absurd, desperate measures from a man sinking in quicksand.

"It was worth it," the archbishop said without any conviction.

Saldur played with a loose thread on his sleeve, wishing he had taken the remainder of Bernice's bottle with him. He had never cared much for wine. More than anything, the tragedy of Braga's death was the loss of a great source of excellent brandy. The archduke had really known his liquor.

Galien stared at him. "You're quiet," the archbishop said. "You think I was wrong, of course. You said so, didn't you? You were very vocal about it at our last meeting. You were watching her every move. You have that—that—" The old man waved his hand toward the door as if this would make his fumbling clearer. "That old handmaid monitoring her every breath. Isn't that right? And if Esrahaddon had contacted her, we would have known and they would be none the wiser, but now..." The archbishop threw up his hands, feigning disgust in a sarcastic imitation of Saldur.

Saldur continued to fiddle with the thread, wrapping it around the end of his forefinger, winding it tighter and tighter.

"You're too arrogant for your own good," Galien accused him defensively. "The man is an imperial wizard. What he is capable of is beyond your comprehension. For all we know, he may have been visiting her in the form of a butterfly in the garden or a moth that entered her bedroom window each night. We had to be sure."

"A butterfly?" Saldur said, genuinely amazed.

"He's a wizard. Damn you. That's what they do."

"I highly doubt—"

"The point is we didn't know for sure."

"And we still don't. All I can say is I don't think she was lying, but Arista is a clever girl. Maribor knows she has proven that already."

Galien lifted his empty wineglass. "Carlton!"

The servant looked up. "I'm sorry, Your Grace, but I can't say I know her well enough to offer much of an opinion."

"Good god, man. I'm not asking you about her; I want more wine, you fool."

"Ah," Carlton said, and headed for the bottle, then pulled the cork out with a dull, hollow pop.

"The problem is that the Patriarch blames me for Esrahaddon's disappearance," Galien continued.

For the first time since Arista's departure, Saldur leaned forward with interest. "He's told you this?"

"That's just it; he's told me nothing. He only speaks to the sentinels now. Luis Guy and that other one—Thranic. Guy is unpleasant, but Thranic..." He trailed off, shaking his head and frowning.

"I've never met a sentinel."

"Consider yourself lucky. Although your luck, I think, is running out on that score. Guy spent all morning upstairs in a long meeting with the Patriarch." He played with the empty glass, running his finger around the rim. "He's in the council hall right now, giving his address to the curia."

"Shouldn't we be there?"

"Yes," he said miserably, but he made no effort to move.

"Your Grace?" Saldur asked.

"Yes, yes." He waved at him. "Carlton, get me my cane."

~

Saldur and the archbishop entered to the sound of a man's booming voice. The grand council chamber was a three-story circular room encompassing the entire width of the tower. It was lined in thin ornate columns set in groups of two that represented the relationship between Novron, the Defender of Faith, and Maribor, the god of man. Between each set was a tall thin window, which provided the room with a complete panoramic view of the surrounding countryside. Seated in circular rows, radiating out from the center, gathered the curia, the college of chief clerics of the Nyphron Church. The other eighteen bishops were present to hear the words of the Patriarch as spoken by Luis Guy.

Sentinel Luis Guy, a tall thin man with long black hair and disquieting eyes, stood in the center of the room. He was sharp; that was Saldur's first impression of the man, clean, ordered, focused, both in manner and looks. His hair was very black yet his skin was light, providing a striking contrast. His mustache was narrow, his beard short and severe, trimmed to a fine point. He dressed in the traditional red cassock, black cape, and black hood, with the symbol of the broken crown neatly embroidered on his chest. Not a hair or a pleat was out of place. He stood straight, his eyes not scanning the crowd but glaring at them.

"...the Patriarch feels that Rufus has the strength to persuade the Trent nobles and the church will deliver the rest. Remember, this isn't about picking the best horse. The Patriarch must choose the one that can win the race and Rufus is the most likely candidate. He's a hero to the south and a native of the north. He has no visible ties to the church. Crowning him emperor will immediately stifle a large segment of the population that might otherwise oppose us. While Rufus may not cause Trent and Calis to submit to the New Empire, it should prevent them from uniting against us. In their hesitation we shall find the time to consolidate the whole of Avryn under one emperor. After which time, we shall systematically, one-by-one, force Trent, then Calis to join or face invasion. Given the vastly superior wealth and power of Avryn, it is more than likely they will submit without a fight—all the more so with Rufus as emperor."

"You speak as if the unification is already complete," Bishop Tildale of Dunmore said. "But Avryn has eight kingdoms and only Dunmore, Ghent, and Warric are Imperialist. What about the Royalists? They aren't going to accept this without a fight. It's not like the time of Glenmorgan, when all he faced were a handful of warlords—these are kings with lands and titles that they've held for generations. The kingdoms of Alburn and Melengar are old and proud realms. Even King Urith of Rhenydd, as poor as he is, will not simply take a knee to Rufus merely because we say so. And what about Maranon? Their fields supply most of Avryn with the food we eat. If King Vincent resists, he could starve us into submission. And Galeannon? King Fredrick has often threatened to cede to Calis, where he could be the strong leader of a weak pack rather than a weak leader of a strong one. If we insist on his giving up what little independence he has, we could lose him."

"I can assure you King Fredrick will bow before the imperial throne when the time comes," the bishop of Galeannon announced.

"And you needn't worry about Maranon's wheat fields," the bishop of Maranon said.

"As you can see, the Royalist problem has been eliminated," Guy assured them. "It has taken nearly a generation, but the church has managed to successfully insert loyal Imperialists in key positions in each kingdom, with the minor exception of Melengar, where our plans did not proceed as expected. This failure will easily be mitigated by its singularity. Once Rufus is declared emperor, all the other kingdoms will pledge allegiance and Melengar will be alone. They will capitulate or face a war with the rest of Avryn. So yes, with just a few minor issues, the unification of Avryn has indeed already been accomplished. We just have not made this fact public."

This caused a murmur throughout the chamber.

"I knew we were progressing successfully on this project," Saldur told the archbishop, "but I had no idea we were so far along."

"Braga's appointment as king of Melengar was to be the final step," Galien replied with a disappointed tone. Of all the kingdoms the church had prepared for the coming New Empire, only Saldur's had failed.

"And the Nationalists?" the Prelate of Ratibor asked. "They have been growing in number. You can't simply ignore them."

"The Nationalists will be an issue," Guy admitted. "For years now the seret have been watching Gaunt and his followers. They are being funded by the DeLur family and several other powerful merchant cartels in the Republic of Delgos. Delgos has enjoyed its freedom for too long to be convinced of the advantages of a central authority. They already fear the very idea of a unified empire. So yes, we know they will fight. They will need to be defeated on the battlefield, which is another reason why the Patriarch has selected Rufus. He's a ruthless warlord. He'll crush the Nationalists as his first act as emperor. Delgos will fall soon after."

"Do we have the troops to take Delgos?" Prelate Krindel, the resident historian, asked. "Tur Del Fur is defended by a dwarven fortress. It held out against a two-year siege by the Dacca."

"I have been working on that very problem and I think I'll have a—unique—solution."

"And what might that be?" Galien asked suspiciously.

Luis Guy looked up. "Ah, Archbishop, so good of you to join us. I sent word we were beginning nearly an hour ago."

"Do you plan to spank me for being tardy, Guy? Or are you simply trying to avoid my question?"

"You are not ready to hear the answer to that question," the sentinel replied, which brought a reproachful look from the archbishop. "You would not believe me if I told you and certainly would not approve. But when the time comes, and it is necessary, then rest assured the fortress of Drumindor will fall, and Delgos along with it."

The archbishop frowned at the slight, but before he could comment, Saldur spoke up. "What about the common people? Will they embrace a new emperor?" he asked.

"I have traveled the length and breadth of the four nations, promoting the contest. Heralds have announced it from Dagastan in the south to Lanksteer in the north; all of Apeladorn is aware of the event. In the marketplaces, taverns, and castle courts, anticipation is high. Once we announce the true intent of the contest, the people will be beside themselves. Gentlemen, these are exciting times. It is no longer a question of if, but when the New Empire will rise. The groundwork is laid. All we need to do is bestow the crown."

"And King Ethelred of Warric?" Galien asked. "Is he on board?"

Guy shrugged. "He isn't pleased with giving up his throne to become a viceroy, but few of the monarchs are, even those we placed in power. It is amazing how quickly rulers become accustomed to being called Your Majesty. Yet he has been assured that for being the first to take off his crown, he will be first in line in the new order. It is very likely he will assume the role of regent, administering the empire on behalf of Lord Rufus as the new emperor is away handling any uprisings. I also suggested that he might remain as chief council. He appeared satisfied with that."

"I still don't like handing over power to Rufus and Ethelred," Saldur said.

"We won't be," Galien assured him. "The church will be in control. They are the faces, but we are the mind. The church will have a permanent appointee in the palace of the New Empire who will be charged with overseeing the construction of the new order." He looked to Guy. "Did the Patriarch mention this to you?"

"He did."

"And did he say if he would accept this responsibility himself?"

"Due to his advanced age, the Patriarch will not be taking on this burden but will instead select someone from this council who will be empowered to act autonomously on behalf of the entire church. That person will be appointed co-regent alongside Ethelred at least for the duration of the reconstruction phase."

"Such a man would be immensely powerful," the archbishop said. Saldur could tell from his tone—perhaps everyone could—that he knew it would not be him. "Would that person be you?"

Guy shook his head. "My task, as my father before me, and his before that, is to find the Heir of Novron. The Patriarch has asked me to assist in these matters concerning the immediate establishment of the empire, which I am happy to do, but I'll not be deterred from my life's goal."

"Who will it be, then?"

"His Holiness has not yet decided. I suspect he will wait to see how events with the contest play out." There was a pause as they waited for Guy to speak again. "This is a historic moment. All that we have worked for, all that has been carefully nurtured for centuries, is about to bear fruit. We now stand at the threshold of a new dawn for mankind. What began nearly a millennium ago will conclude with this generation. May Novron bless our hands."

"He's impressive," Saldur told Galien.

"You think so?" the archbishop replied. "Good, because you're coming with us."

"To the contest?"

He nodded. "I need someone to counterbalance Guy. Perhaps you can be just as big a pain to him as you've been to me."

☙

Arista hesitated outside the door, holding a single candle. Inside, she could hear Bernice shuffling about, turning down the bed, pouring water into the basin, laying out Arista's bed clothes in that ghastly nursemaid way of hers. As tired as she was, Arista had no desire to open that door. She had too much to think about and could not bear Bernice just now.

How many days?

She tried counting them in her head, ticking them off, tracking her memories of those muddled times between the death of her father and the death of her uncle; so much had happened so quickly. She still remembered the pale white look of her father's face as he lay on the bed, a single tear of blood on his cheek, and the dark stain spreading across the mattress beneath him.

Arista glanced awkwardly at Hilfred, who stood behind her. "I'm not ready to go to bed yet."

"As you wish, my lady," he said quietly, as if understanding her need not to alert the nurse-beast within.

Arista began walking aimlessly. She traveled down the hallway. This simple act gave her a sense of control, of heading toward something instead of being swept along. Hilfred followed three paces behind, his sword clapping against his thigh, a sound she had heard for years, like the swing of a pendulum ticking off the seconds of her life.

How many days?

Sauly had known Uncle Percy would kill her father. He knew before it happened! How long in advance did he know? Was it hours? Days? Weeks? He said he had tried to stop him. That was a lie—it had to be. Why not expose him? Why not just tell her father? But maybe Sauly had. Maybe her father refused to listen. Was it possible Esrahaddon really had used her?

The dimly lit hall curved as it circled around the tower. The lack of decoration surprised Arista. Of course, the Crown Tower was only a small part of the old palace, a mere corner staircase. The stones were old hewn blocks set in place centuries earlier. They all looked the same—dingy, soot-covered, and yellow, like old teeth. She passed several doors, then came to a staircase and began climbing. It felt good to exert her legs after being idle so long.

How many days?

She remembered her uncle searching for Alric, watching her, having her followed. If Saldur had known about Percy, why had he not intervened? Why had he allowed her to be locked in the tower and put through that dreadful trial? Would Sauly have allowed them to execute her? If he had just spoken up, if he had backed her, she could have called for Braga's imprisonment. The Battle of Medford could have been avoided and all those people would still be alive.

How many days before Braga's death did Saldur know... and do nothing?

It was a question without an answer. A question that echoed in her head, a question she was not certain she wanted answered.

And what was all this about the destruction of humanity? She knew they thought she was naïve. *Do they think I am ignorant as well?* No one person had the power to enslave an entire race. Not to mention the very idea that this threat emanated from the emperor was absurd. The man had already been the ruler of the world!

The stairs ended in a dark circular room. No sconces, torches, nor lanterns burned. Her little candle was the only source of illumination. Followed by Hilfred, Arista exited the stairs. They had entered the alabaster crown near the tower's pinnacle. An immediate sense of unease washed over her. She felt like a trespasser on forbidden grounds. There was nothing to give her that impression except perhaps the darkness. Still, it felt like exploring an attic as a child—the silence, the shadowy suggestion of hidden treasures lost to time.

Like everyone, she had grown up hearing the tales of Glenmorgan's treasures and how they lay hidden at the top of the Crown Tower. She even knew the story about how they had been stolen yet returned the following night. There were many stories about the tower, tales of famous people imprisoned at its top. Heretics like Edmund Hall, who had supposedly discovered the entrance to the holy city Percepliquis and paid by spending the remainder of his life sealed away—isolated where he could tell no one of its secrets.

It was here. It was all here.

She walked the circle of the room. The sounds of her footsteps echoed sharply off the stone, perhaps because of the low ceiling, or maybe it was just her imagination. She held up her candle and found a door at the far side. It was an odd door. Tall and broad, not made of wood as the others in the tower, nor was it made of steel or iron. This door was made of stone, one single solid block that looked like granite and appeared out of place beside the walls of polished alabaster.

She looked at it, perplexed. There was no latch, knob, or hinges. Nothing to open it with. She considered knocking.

What good will it do to knock on granite except to bloody my knuckles? Placing her hand on the door, she pushed, but nothing happened. Arista glanced at Hilfred, who stood silently watching her.

"I just wanted to see the view from the top," she told him, imagining what he might be thinking.

She heard something just then, a shuffle, a step from above. Tilting her head, she lifted the candle. Cobwebs lined the underside of the ceiling, which was made of wood. Clearly someone or something was up there.

Edmund Hall's ghost!

The idea flashed through her mind and she shook her head at her foolishness. Perhaps she should go and cower in bed and have Auntie Bernice read her a nice bedtime story. Still, she had to wonder. What lay behind that very solid-looking door?

"Hello?" a voice echoed, and she jumped. From below Arista saw the glow of another light rising, the sound of steps climbing. "Is someone up here?"

She had an instant desire to hide and she might have tried if there had been anything to hide behind and Hilfred had not been with her.

"Who's there?" A head appeared, coming around the curve of the steps from below. It was a man—a priest of some sort by the look of him. He wore a black robe with a purple ribbon that hung down from either side of his neck. His hair was thin, and from that angle, Arista could see the beginning of a bald spot on the back of his head, a tanned island in a sea of graying hair. He held a lantern above his head and squinted at her, looking puzzled.

"Who are you?" he asked in a neutral tone. It was neither threatening nor welcoming, merely curious.

She smiled self-consciously. "My name is Arista, Arista from Melengar."

"Arista from Melengar?" he said thoughtfully. "Might I ask what you are doing here, Arista from Melengar?"

"Honestly? I was—ah—hoping to get to the top of the tower to see the view. It's my first time here."

The priest smiled and began to chuckle. "You are sightseeing, then?"

"Yes, I suppose so."

"And the gentleman with you—is he also sightseeing?"

"He is my bodyguard."

"Bodyguard?" The man paused in his approach. "Do all young women from Melengar have such protection when they travel abroad?"

"I am the Princess of Melengar, daughter of the late king Amrath and sister of King Alric."

"Aha!" the priest said, entering the room and walking the curve toward them. "I thought so. You were part of the caravan that arrived this evening, the lady who came in with the Bishop of Medford. I saw the royal carriage, but didn't know what royalty it contained."

"And you are?" she asked.

"Oh yes, I'm very sorry, I am Monsignor Merton of Ghent, born and raised right down below us in a small village called Iberton, a stone's throw from Ervanon. Wonderful fishing in Iberton. My father was a fisherman, by the way. We fished year-round, nets in the summer and hooks in the winter. Teach a man to fish and he'll never go hungry, I always say. I suppose in a way that's how I came to be here, if you get my meaning."

Arista smiled politely and glanced back at the stone door.

"I'm sorry but that door doesn't go to the outside, and I'm afraid you can't get to the top." He tilted his head toward the ceiling and lowered his voice. "That's where *he* lives."

"He?"

"His Holiness, Patriarch Nilnev. The top floor of this tower is his sanctuary. I come up here sometimes to just sit and listen. When it is quiet, when the wind is still, you can sometimes hear him moving about. I once thought I heard him speak, but that might have just been hopeful ears. It is as if Novron himself is up there right now, looking down, watching out for us. Still, if you like, I do know where you can get a good view. Come with me."

The monsignor turned and descended back down the stairs. Arista looked one last time at the door, then followed.

"When does he come out?" Arista asked. "The Patriarch, I mean."

"He doesn't. At least not that I have ever seen. He lives his life in isolation—better to be one with the Lord."

"If he never comes out, how do you know he's really up there?"

"Hmm?" Merton glanced back at her and chuckled. "Oh, well, he does speak with people. He holds private meetings with certain individuals, who bring his words to the rest of us."

"And who are these people? The archbishop?"

"Sometimes, though lately his decrees have come down to us by way of the sentinels." He paused in their downward trek and turned to look at her. "You know about them, I assume?"

"Yes," she told him.

"Being a princess, I thought you might."

"We actually haven't had one visit Melengar for several years."

"That's understandable. There are only a few left and they have a very wide area to cover."

"Why so few?"

"His Holiness hasn't appointed any new ones, not since he ordained Luis Guy. I believe he was the last."

This was the first good news Arista had heard all day. The sentinels were notorious watchdogs of the church. Originally charged with the task of finding the lost heir, they commanded the famous order of the Seret Knights. These knights enforced the church's will—policing layman and clergy alike for any signs of heresy. When the seret investigated, it was certain someone would be found guilty, and usually anyone who protested would find themselves charged as well.

Monsignor Merton led her to a door two floors down and knocked.

"What is it?" an irritated voice asked.

"We've come to see your view," Merton replied.

"I don't have time for you today, Merton. Go bother someone else and leave me be."

"It's not for me. The princess Arista of Medford is here, and she wants to see a view from the tower."

"Oh no, really," Arista told him, shaking her head. "It's not that important. I just—"

The door popped open and behind it stood a fat man without a single hair on his head. He was dressed all in red, with a gold braided cord around his large waist. He was wiping his greasy hands on a towel and peering at Arista intently.

"By Mar! It is a princess."

"Janison!" Merton snapped. "Please, that's no way for a prelate of the church to speak."

The fat man scowled at Merton. "Do you see how he treats me? He thinks I am Uberlin himself because I like to eat and enjoy an occasional drink."

"It is not I that judges you, but our lord Novron. May we enter?"

"Yes, yes, of course, come in."

The room was a mess of clothes, parchments, and paintings that lay on the floor or leaned on baskets and chests. A desk stood at one end and a large flat, tilted table was at the other. On it were stacks of maps, ink bottles, and dozens of quills. Nothing appeared to be in its place or even to have one.

"Oh—" Arista nearly said *dear* but stopped short, realizing she had almost imitated Bernice.

"Yes, it is quite the sight, isn't it? Prelate Janison is less than tidy."

"I am neat in my maps and that's all that matters."

"Not to Novron."

"You see? And, of course, I can't retaliate. How can anyone hope to compete with His Holiness Monsignor Merton, who heals the sick and speaks to god?"

Arista, who was following Merton across the wretched room toward a curtain-lined wall, paused as a memory from her childhood surfaced. Looking at Merton, she recalled it. "You're the savior of Fallon Mire?"

"Aha! Of course he didn't tell you. It would be too prideful to admit he is the chosen one of our lord."

"Oh stop that." It was Merton's turn to scowl.

"Was it you?" she asked.

Merton nodded, sending Janison a harsh stare.

"I heard all about it. It was some years ago. I was probably only five or six when the plague came to Fallon Mire. Everyone was afraid because it was working its way up from the south and Fallon Mire was not very far from Medford. I remember my father spoke of moving the court to Drondil Fields, only we never did. We didn't have to because the plague never moved north of there."

"Because *he* stopped it," Janison said.

"I did not!" Merton snapped. "Novron did."

"But he sent you there, didn't he? Didn't he?"

Merton sighed. "I only did what the lord asked of me."

Janison looked at Arista. "You see? How can I hope to compete with a man whom god himself has chosen to hold daily conversations with?"

"You actually heard the voice of Novron telling you to go save the people of Fallen Mire?"

"He directed my footsteps."

"But you talk to him too," Janison pressed, looking at Arista. "He won't admit that, of course. Saying so would be heresy and Luis Guy is just downstairs. He doesn't care about your miracle." Janison sat down on a stool and chuckled. "No, the good monsignor here won't admit that he holds little conversations with the lord, but he does. I've heard him. Late at night, in the halls, when he thinks everyone else is asleep." Janison raised his voice an octave as if imitating a young girl. *"Oh Lord, why is it you keep me awake with this headache when I have work in the morning? What's that? Oh, I see, how wise of you."*

"That's enough, Janison," Merton said, his voice serious.

"Yes, I'm certain it is, Monsignor. Now take your view and leave me to my meal."

Janison picked up a chicken leg and resumed eating while Merton threw open the drapes to reveal a magnificent window. It was huge, nearly the width of the room, divided only by three stone pillars. The view was breathtaking. The large moon revealed the night as if it were a lamp one could reach out and touch, hanging among a scattering of brilliant stars.

Arista placed a hand on the windowsill and peered down. She could see the twisting silver line of a river far below, shimmering in the moonlight. At the base of the tower, campfires circled the city, tiny flickering pinpricks like stars themselves. Looking straight down, she felt dizzy and her heartbeat quickened. Wondering how close she was to the top of the tower, she looked up and counted three more levels of windows above her, to the alabaster crown of white.

"Thank you," she told Merton, and nodded toward Janison.

"Rest assured, Your Highness. He is up there."

She nodded but was not certain if he was referring to god or the Patriarch.

Chapter 4
Dahlgren

For five days, Royce, Hadrian, and Thrace made their way north through the nameless sea of trees that made up the eastern edge of Avryn, a region disputed by both Alburn and Dunmore. Each laid claim to the vast, dense forest between them, but until the establishment of Dahlgren, neither appeared in any hurry to settle the land. The great forest, referred to merely as either the East or the Wastes, remained uncut, untouched, unblemished. The road they traveled, once a broad lane as it had plowed north out of Alburn, quickly became two tracks divided by a line of grass, and finally squeezed down to a single dirt trail that threatened to vanish entirely. No fences, farms, nor wayside inns broke the woodland walls, nor did travelers cross their path. Here in the northeast, maps were vague, with few markings, and went entirely blank past the Nidwalden River.

At times, the beauty of the forest was breathtaking, even spiritual. Monolithic elms towered overhead, weaving a lofty tunnel of green. It reminded Hadrian of the few times he had poked his head into Mares Cathedral in Medford. The long-trunked trees arched over the trail like the buttresses of the great church, forming a natural nave. Delicate shafts of muted light pierced the canopy at angles as if entering through a gallery of windows far above. Along the ground, fans of finely fingered ferns grew up from the past year's brown leaves, creating a soft swaying carpet. A choir of birds sang in the unseen heights, and from the bed of brittle leaves came the rustle of squirrels and chipmunks like the coughs, whispers, and shifts of a congregation. It was beautiful yet disturbing, like swimming out too far, delving into unknown, unseen, and untamed places.

Over the last days, travel became increasingly difficult. The recent spring storms had dropped several trees across the trail, which blocked the route as formidably as any castle gate. They dismounted and struggled through the thick brush as Royce searched for a way around. Hours passed yet they failed to rejoin the road. Scratched and sweaty, they led their horses across several small rivers and on one occasion faced a sharp drop. Looking down from the rocky cliff, Hadrian offered Royce a skeptical look. Usually Hadrian didn't question Royce's sense of direction or his choice of path. Royce had an unerring ability to find his way in the wilderness, a talent proven on many occasions. Hadrian tilted his head up. He could not see the sun or sky; there was no point of reference—everything was limbs and leaves. Royce had never let him down, but they had never been in a place like this before.

"We're all right," Royce told them, a touch of irritation in his voice.

They worked their way down, Royce and Thrace leading the horses on foot while Hadrian cleared a path. When they reached the bottom, they found a small stream, but no trail. Again, Hadrian glanced at Royce, but this time the thief made no comment as they pressed on along the least dense route.

"There," Thrace said, pointing ahead to a clearing revealed by a patch of sun that managed to sneak through the canopy.

A few more steps revealed a small road. Royce looked at it for a moment, then merely shrugged, climbed back on his horse, and kicked Mouse forward.

They emerged from the forest as if escaping from a deep cave, into the first open patch of direct sun they had seen in days. In the glade, beside a rough wooden wellhead, stood a child among a herd of eight grazing pigs. The child, no more than five years old, held a long, thin stick, and an expression of wonder was on the little round face, covered in sweat-trapped dirt. Hadrian had no idea if it was a boy or a girl, as the child displayed no definite indication of either, wearing only a simple smock of flax linen, dirty and frayed with holes and rips so plentiful they appeared by design.

"Pearl!" Thrace called out as she scrambled off Millie so quickly the horse sidestepped. "I'm back." She walked over and tousled the child's matted hair.

The little girl—Hadrian now guessed—gave Thrace little notice and continued to stare at them, eyes wide.

Thrace threw out her arms and spun around. "This is Dahlgren. This is home."

Hadrian dismounted and looked around, puzzled. They stood on a small patch of close-grazed grass beside a well constructed of ill-fitted planks with a wooden bucket, wet and dripping, resting on a rail. Two other rutted trails intersected with the one they followed, forming a triangle with the well at its center. On all sides, the forest surrounded them. Massive trees of dramatic size still blocked the sky, except for the hole above the clearing, through which Hadrian could see the pale blue of the late-afternoon sky.

Hadrian scooped a handful of water from the bucket to wash the sweat from his face and Millie nearly shoved him aside as she pushed her nose into the bucket, drinking deeply.

"What's with the bell?" Royce asked, climbing down off Mouse and gesturing toward the shadows.

Hadrian looked over, surprised to see a massive bronze bell hanging from a rocker arm, which in turn hung from the lower branch of a nearby oak. Hadrian guessed that if it had been on the ground, Royce could have stood inside it. A rope dangled, with knots tied at several points along its length.

"That's different," he said, walking toward it. "How does it sound?"

"Don't ring it!" Thrace exclaimed. Hadrian pivoted his eyebrows up. "We only ring it for emergencies."

He looked back at the bell, noting the relief images of Maribor and Novron, along with lines of religious script circling its waist. "Seems sort of extravagant for . . . well . . ." He looked around at the empty clearing.

"It was Deacon Tomas's idea. He kept saying, 'A village isn't a village without a church, and a church isn't a church without a bell.' Everyone pitched in a little. The old margrave matched what we had and ordered it for us. The bell was finished long before we had time to build the church. Mr. McDern took his oxen and fetched it all the way from Ervanon. When he got back, we had no place to put it and he needed his wagon. It was my father's idea to hang it here and use it as an alarm until the church went up. That was a week before the attacks started. At the time no one had any idea how much use we'd get out of it." She stared at the huge bell for a moment and then added, "I hate the sound of that bell."

A gusty breeze rustled the leaves and threw a lock of hair in her face. She brushed it back and turned away from the oak and the bell. "Over there"—she pointed across the rutted path—"is where most of us live." Hadrian spotted structures hidden in shadow within a shallow dip, behind a blind of goldenrod and milkweed. They were small wooden-framed buildings plastered with wattle and daub—a mixture of mud, straw, and manure. The roofs were thatch, the windows no more than holes in the walls. Most lacked doors, making do with curtains across the entrances, which fluttered with the wind, revealing dirt floors. Beside one, he spotted a vegetable garden that managed to catch a sliver of sun.

"That's Mae and Went Drundel's place there in front," Thrace said. "Well, I guess it's just Mae's now. Went and the boys...they...were taken not long ago. To the left, the one with the garden is the Bothwicks'. I used to babysit Tad and the twins, but Tad's old enough now to watch the twins himself. They are like family really. Lena and my mother were very close. Behind them, you can just see the McDerns' roof. Mr. McDern is the village smith and the owner of the only pair of oxen. He shares them with everyone, which makes him popular come spring. To the right, the place with the swing is the Caswells'. Maria and Jessie are my best friends. My father hung that swing for us not long after we moved here. I spent some of the best days of my life on that swing."

"Where's your place?" Hadrian asked.

"My father built our house a ways down the hill." She gestured toward a small trail that ran to the east. "It was the best house—best farm, really—in the village. Everyone said so. There's almost nothing left now."

Pearl was still staring at them, watching every move.

"Hello," Hadrian said to her with a smile, bending down on his haunches, "my name is Hadrian, and this is my friend Royce." Pearl glared and took a step back, brandishing the stick before her. "You don't talk much, do you?"

"Her parents were both killed two months ago while planting," Thrace told them, looking at the girl with sympathetic eyes. "It was daylight, and like everyone else, they thought they were safe, but it was a stormy day. The clouds had darkened the sky." Thrace paused, then added, "A lot of people have died here."

"Where is everyone else?" Royce asked.

"They'll all be in the fields now, bringing in the first cutting of hay, but they'll be coming back soon; it's getting late. Pearl minds the pigs for the entire village, don't you, Pearl?" The girl nodded fiercely, holding her stick with both hands and keeping a wary eye on Hadrian.

"What's up there?" Royce asked. He had moved down off the green and was looking up the trail as it ran north.

Hadrian followed, leaving Millie with the bucket, her tail swishing vigilantly against a handful of determined flies. Moving past a stand of spruce, Hadrian could see a hill cleared of trees rising just a few hundred yards away. On its crest rested a stockade-style wall of hewn logs and, in the center, a large wooden house.

"That's the margrave's castle. The deacon Tomas has taken on the responsibility of steward until the king appoints a new lord. He's very nice and I don't think he'd mind you using the stables, considering there aren't any other horses in the village. For now just tie them to the well, I guess, and we can go see my father.

"Pearl, watch their stuff, and keep the pigs away. If Tad, Hal, or Arvid comes back before I do, have them take the horses up to the castle and ask the deacon if they can stable them there, okay?"

The little girl nodded.

"Does she talk?" Hadrian asked.

"Yes, just not very often anymore. C'mon, I'll take you to—to what used to be my home. Dad's probably there. It's not far and a pretty pleasant walk." She began leading them east along a footpath that ran downhill behind the houses. As they circled around, Hadrian got a better look at the village. He could see more houses, all of them tiny things, most likely single rooms with lofts. There were other, smaller structures, a few crated feed bins built on stilts to keep clear of rodents and what looked to be a community outhouse; it too lacked a solid door.

"I'll ask the Bothwicks to take you in while you're here. I'm staying with them myself; they—" Thrace stopped. Her hands flew to her face as she sucked in a sudden breath and her lips started to quiver.

Beside the path, not far from the house with the swing, two wooden markers stood freshly driven into the earth. Carved into them were the names Maria and Jessie Caswell.

☙

The Wood farm appeared down the footpath. Several acres lay cleared of trees, most at the bottom of a hill where lush wheat grew in perfectly straight rows. A low stone wall built from carefully stacked rocks ran the perimeter. It was a beautiful field of rich dark earth, well turned, well planted, and well drained.

The homestead itself stood on the rise overlooking the field. The house was a ruined shell, its roof gone, thatch scattered across the yard, blown by the wind. Only a few timbers remained—splintered poles jutting up like broken bones punching through skin. The lower half of the building and the chimney were both made of irregularly shaped fieldstone and remained mostly intact. Some stones lay in piles where they had slipped from their stacks, but the majority appeared eerily untouched.

Little things caught Hadrian's attention. Mounted beneath one window hung a flowerbox with a scallop edge and the image of a deer carved into it. The front door, made of solid oak, did not reveal a single peg or visible joint. The stones that created the walls, in alternated colors of gray, rose, and tan, were each chipped to a fine flat profile. The curved walkway was bordered with bushes trimmed to resemble a hedge.

Theron Wood sat amidst the ruins of his home. The big farmer, with dark leathery skin, had a short mangle of forgotten gray hair that crowned a face cut by wind and sun. He looked like a part of the earth itself, a gnarled trunk of a great tree with a face like a weathered cliff. Holding a grass cutter between his legs, he rested on the remaining wall of his home, slowly dragging a sharpening stone along the length of the huge curved scythe blade. Back and forth the stone scraped while the man stared down at the green field below, an expression on his face Hadrian could describe only as one of contempt.

"Daddy! I'm back." Thrace ran to the old farmer, hugging him around his neck. "I missed you."

Theron endured the squeeze and glared at them. "Are these the ones, then?"

"Yes. This is Hadrian and Royce. They've come all the way from Colnora to help. They can get the weapon Esra told us about."

"I have a weapon," the farmer growled, and resumed sharpening his blade. The sound was cold and grating.

"This?" Thrace asked. "Your grass cutter? The margrave had a sword, a shield, and armor and he—"

"Not this, I have another weapon, much bigger, much sharper."

Puzzled, she looked around. The old man offered no insight.

"I don't need what lies in that tower to kill the beast."

"But you promised me."

"And I am a man of my word," he replied, and drew the stone along the edge of the blade once more. "The waiting only made my weapon sharper." He dipped the stone into a bucket of water that sat beside him. He raised it back to the blade but paused and said, "Every day I wake up, I see Thad's broken bed and Hickory's cradle. I see the shattered barrel that Thad made, the fields I planted for him—growing despite me. Best season in a decade. I woulda reaped more than enough to pay for the contract and tools. I woulda had extra. I coulda built him a shop. I might even have afforded a sign and real glass windows. He coulda had a planed wooden door with hinges and studs. His shop woulda been better than any house in the village. Better than the manor. People would walk by and stare, wondering what great man owned such a business. How great an artisan was this town's cooper that he could manage such a fine store?

"Those bastards back in Glamrendor who wouldn't let Thad hang a shingle, they would never have seen the like. It woulda had a shake roof and scalloped eaves, a hard oak counter, and iron hooks to hold lanterns for when he needed to work late at night to complete all his orders. His barrels would be stacked in a storage shed beside the shop. A beautiful barn-size one, and I would paint it bright red so no one could miss it. I woulda got him a wagon too, even if I had to build it myself. That way he could send orders all over Avryn—back to Glamrendor too. I woulda driven them there myself just to see the shock and anger on their faces.

" 'Morning!' I'd say, grinning like a lipless crocodile. Here's another fine delivery of barrels from Thaddeus Wood, the best cooper in Avryn. They'd cringe and curse. Yep, that boy o' mine, he's no farmer, no sir. Starting with him, the Woods were gonna be artisans and shopkeepers.

"This village, it'd have grown. People woulda moved in

and started businesses of their own, only Thad's woulda always been the first, the biggest, and the best. I'd have seen to that. Soon this here woulda been a city, a fine city, and the Woods the most successful family—a merchant family giv'n money to the arts and riding around in fine carriages. This here house woulda been a true mansion, 'cause Thad woulda insisted, but I wouldn't care 'bout that, no sir. I'd have been content just watching Hickory grow up, seeing him learn to read and write—appointed magistrate, maybe. My grandson in the black robes! Yes sir, Magistrate Wood is going to court in a fine carriage and me standing there watching him.

"I see it. Every morning I get up; I sit; I look down Stony Hill and I see all of it. It's right there, right in that field growing in front of me. I haven't hoed. I haven't tilled, but look at it. The best crop I ever grew getting taller every day."

"Daddy, please come back with us to the Bothwicks'. It's getting late."

"This is my home!" the old man shouted, but not at her. His eyes were still on the field. He scraped the blade again. Thrace sighed.

There was a long silence.

"You and your friends go. I swore not to seek it, but there is always a chance it might come to me."

"But, Daddy—"

"I said take them and go. I don't need you here."

Thrace glanced at Hadrian. There were tears in her eyes. Her lips trembled. She stood for a moment, wavering, then abruptly broke and ran back up the path toward town. Theron ignored her. The old farmer tilted the blade of his grass cutter to the other side and resumed sharpening. Hadrian watched him for a moment, the sounds of the stone on metal drowning out Thrace's fading sobs. He never looked up, not at Hadrian, not to glance down the trail. The man was indeed a rock.

Hadrian found Thrace only a few dozen yards up the trail. She was on her knees, crying. Her small body jerked, her hair rocking with the movement. He placed his hand gently on her shoulder. "Your father is right. That weapon of his is very sharp."

Royce caught up with them, carrying a fractured piece of wood. He looked down at Thrace with an uncomfortable expression.

"What's up?" Hadrian asked before Royce said anything callous.

"What do you think of this?" Royce replied, holding out the scrap, which might have been part of the house framing. The beam was wide and thick, good strong oak taken from the trunk of a well-aged tree. The piece bore four deeply cut gouges.

"Claw marks?" Hadrian took the wood and placed his hand against the board with his fingers splayed out. "Giant claw marks."

Royce nodded. "Whatever it is, it's huge. So how come no one has seen it?"

"It gets very dark here," Thrace told them, wiping her cheeks as she stood. A curious expression crossed her face and she walked to where a yellow-flowered forsythia grew at the base of a maple tree. Taking a hesitant step, Thrace bent down and drew back what Hadrian thought was a wad of cloth and old grass. As she carefully cleaned away the leaves and sticks, he saw it was a crude doll with thread for hair and X's sewn for eyes.

"Yours?" Hadrian ventured.

She shook her head but did not speak. After a moment, Thrace replied, "I made this for Hickory, Thad's son. It was his Wintertide gift, his favorite. He carried it everywhere." Plucking the last bits of grass from the doll, she rubbed it.

"There's blood on it." Her voice quavered. Clutching the doll to her chest, she said softly, "He forgets—they were my family too."

ॐ

Royce guessed it was still early evening when they returned to the village common, but already the light was fading, the invisible sun quickly consumed by the great trees. The little girl and her herd of pigs were gone, and so were their horses and gear. In their place, they found a host of people rushing about with an urgency that left him uneasy.

Men crossed the clearing carrying hoes, axes, and piles of split wood over their shoulders. Most were barefoot, dressed in sweat-stained tunics. Women came behind, carrying bundles of twigs, reeds, thick marsh grasses, and stalks of flax. They too traveled barefoot, with their hair pulled up, hidden under simple cloth wraps. Royce could see why Thrace had made such a big deal out of the dress they had bought her, as all the village women wore simple homemade smocks of the same natural off-white color, lacking any adornment.

They looked hot and tired, focused on reaching the shelter of their homes and dumping their burdens. As the three approached the village, one boy looked up and stopped. He had a long-handled hoe across his shoulders, his arms threaded around it.

"Who's that?" he said.

This got the attention of those nearby. An older woman glared, still clutching her bag of twigs. A bare-chested man with thick, powerful arms lowered his pack of wood, holding tight to his axe. The topless man glanced at Thrace, who was still wiping her red eyes, and advanced on them, shifting the axe to his right hand.

"Vince, we got visitors!" he shouted.

A shorter, older man with a poorly kept beard turned his head and dropped his bundle as well. He looked at the boy who had first spotted them. "Tad, go fetch your pa." The boy hesitated. "Go now, son!"

The boy ran off toward the houses.

"Thrace, honey," the old woman said, "are you all right?"

The bearded man glared at them. "What they do to you, girl?"

As the men advanced, Royce and Hadrian moved together, each one looking expectantly at Thrace. Royce's hand slipped into the folds of his cloak.

"Oh no!" Thrace burst out. "They didn't do anything."

"Doesn't look like nothing. Disappear for weeks and you pop up crying, dressed like—"

Thrace shook her head. "I'm fine. It's just my father."

The men stopped. They kept a wary eye on the strangers but shot looks of sympathy at Thrace.

"Theron's a fine man," Vince told her, "a strong man. He'll come around, you'll see. He just needs some time."

She nodded, but it was forced.

"Now, who might you two be?"

"This is Hadrian and Royce," Thrace finally got around to saying, "from Colnora in Warric. I asked them here to help. This is Mr. Griffin, the village founder."

"Came out here with an axe, a knife, and not much else. The rest of these poor souls were foolish enough to follow, on account I told them life was better, and they was stupid enough to believe me." He extended his hand. "Just call me Vince."

"I'm Dillon McDern," the big bare-chested man said. "I'm the smith round here. Figure you fellas might want to know that. You got horses, right? My boys say they took two up to the manor a bit ago."

"This is Mae," Vince said, presenting the old woman. She nodded solemnly. Now that it was clear that Thrace was all right, the old woman slouched, and the look in her eyes became dull and distant as she turned away with her bundle of twigs.

"Don't mind her. She's—well, Mae's had it hard lately." He glanced at Dillon, who nodded.

The boy sent running returned with another man. Older than McDern, younger than Griffin, thinner than both, he dragged his feet as he walked, squinting despite the dim light. In his hands he held a small pig, which struggled to escape.

"Why'd you bring your pig, Russell?" Griffin asked.

"Boy said you needed me—said it was an emergency."

Griffin glanced at Dillon, who looked back and shrugged. "You find emergencies often call for pigs, do you?"

Russell scowled. "I just got hold of her. She gets riled up with Pearl all day, hard as can be to catch her. No way I'm letting her go with night coming on. What is it? What's the emergency?"

"Turns out there ain't one. False alarm," Griffin said.

Russell shook his head. "By Mar, Vince, scare a body to death. Next you'll be swinging from the bell rope just to see folks faint."

"Twarn't on purpose." He dipped his head at Royce and Hadrian. "We thought these fellas were up to something."

Russell looked at them. "Visitors, eh? Where'd you two come from?"

"Colnora," Thrace answered. "I invited them. Esra said they could help my father. I was hoping you'd let them stay with us."

Russell looked at her and sighed heavily, a frown pulling hard at the corners of his mouth.

"Oh, well—ah, that's okay, I guess," Thrace said, stumbling, looking embarrassed. "I can ask Deacon Tomas if he'll—"

"Of course they can stay with us, Thrace. You know better than to even ask." Tucking the pig under one arm, he placed his hand to the side of her face and rubbed her cheek. "It's just that, well, Lena and me—we was sure you were gone for good. Figured you'd found a new home, maybe."

"I'd never leave my father."

"No. No, I s'pose you wouldn't. You and your pa—you're alike that way. Rocks, the both of you, and Maribor help the plow that finds either of you in its path."

The pig made an attempt to escape, twisting, kicking its legs, and squealing. Russell caught it just in time. "Need to get back. The wife will be after me. C'mon, Thrace, and bring your friends." He led them toward the clump of tiny houses. "By Mar, girl, where'd you get that dress?"

Royce remained where he was as the rest started to go. Hadrian gave him a curious look but continued ahead with the others. Royce remained on the trail, unmoving, watching the villagers racing the light: fetching water, hanging out clothes, gathering animals. Pearl wandered past the well, her herd of pigs reduced to only two. Mae Drundel came out of her house, her kerchief pulled free, her gray hair hanging. Unlike the rest, she walked slowly. She crossed to the side of her home, where Royce noticed three markers like those of the Caswells'. She stood for a moment, knelt down for a time, then walked slowly back inside. She was the last villager to disappear indoors.

That left only Royce and the man at the well.

He was no farmer.

Royce had spotted him the moment they had returned, his long slender frame leaning silently against the side of the wellhead, resting in shadow where he nearly faded into the background. The man's hair hung loose to his shoulders, dark with a few threads of gray. He had high cheekbones and deep brooding eyes. His long enveloping robe shimmered with the last rays of sunlight. He sat motionless. This was a man comfortable with waiting and well versed in patience.

He did not look old, but Royce knew better. He had not changed much in the two years since Royce, Hadrian, a young prince Alric, and a monk named Myron had aided his escape from Gutaria Prison. The color of his robe was different, yet still not quite discernible. This time Royce guessed it shimmered somewhere between a turquoise and a dark green. As always, the sleeves hung down, hiding the absence of his hands. He also bore a beard, but that, of course, was new.

They watched each other, staring across the green. Royce walked forward, crossing the distance between them in silence. Two ghosts meeting at a crossroad.

"It's been a while—Esra is it? Or should I call you Mr. Haddon?"

The man tilted his head, lifting his eyes. "I am delighted to see you as well, Royce."

"How do you know my name?"

"I'm a wizard, or did you miss that from our last meeting?"

Royce paused and smiled. "You know, you're right; I might have. Perhaps you should write it down for me lest I forget again."

Esrahaddon raised an eyebrow. "That's a bit harsh."

"How do you know who I am?"

"Well, I did see *The Crown Conspiracy* while in Colnora. I found the sets pathetic and the orchestration horrible, but the story was good. I particularly loved the daring escape from the tower, and the little monk was hilarious—by far my favorite character. I was also pleased there was no wizard in the tale. I wonder who I should thank for that oversight—certainly not you."

"They also didn't use our real names. So again, how do you know it?"

"How would you find out your name, if you were me?"

"I'd ask people that would know. So who did you ask?"

"Would *you* tell me?"

Royce frowned. "Do you ever answer a question with an answer?"

"Sorry, it's a habit. I was a teacher most of my free life."

"Your speech has changed," Royce observed.

"Thank you for noticing. I worked very hard. I sat in many taverns over the last two years and listened. I have a talent for languages; I speak several. I don't know all the colloquial terms yet, but the general grammar wasn't hard to adjust to. It is the same language, after all; the dialect you speak is merely…less sophisticated than what I was used to. It's like talking with a crude accent."

"So you found out who we were by asking around and watching bad plays and you picked up the language by listening to drunks. Now tell me, why are you here, and why do you want us here?"

Esrahaddon stood up and slowly walked around the well. He looked at the ground where the last light of the sun spilled through the leaves of a poplar tree.

"I could tell you that I am hiding here and that would sound plausible. I could also say that I heard about the plight of this village and came here to help, because that's what wizards do. Of course, we both know you won't believe those answers. So let's save time. Why don't *you* tell me why I am here? Then you can try and judge by my reaction if you are correct or not, since that's what you're planning to do anyway."

"Were all wizards as irritating as you are?"

"Much worse, I'm afraid. I was one of the youngest and nicest."

A young man—Royce thought his name was Tad—trotted

over with a bucket. "It's getting late," he said with a harried look, filling his bucket with water. A few yards away Royce spotted a woman struggling to pull a stubborn goat into a house as a small boy pushed the animal from behind.

"Tad!" a man shouted, and the boy at the well turned abruptly.

"Coming!"

He smiled and nodded at each of them, grabbed his bucket of water, and ran back the way he came, spilling half the contents in the process.

They were alone again.

"I think you're here because you need something from Avempartha," Royce told the wizard. "And I don't think it is a sword of demon-slaying either. You're using this poor girl and her tormented father to lure me and Hadrian here to turn a knob you obviously can't manage."

Esrahaddon sighed. "That's disappointing. I thought you were smarter than that, and these constant references to my disability are dull. I am not *using* anyone."

"So you are saying there really is a weapon in that tower?"

"That is exactly what I am saying."

Royce studied him for a moment and scowled.

"Can't tell if I am lying or not, can you?" Esrahaddon smiled smugly.

"I don't think you're lying, but I don't think you're telling the truth either."

The wizard's eyebrows rose. "Now that's better. There might be hope for you yet."

"Maybe there is a weapon in that tower. Maybe it can help kill this... whatever it is they have here, but maybe you also conjured the beast in the first place as an excuse to drag us here."

"Logical," Esrahaddon said, nodding. "Morbidly manipulative, but I can see the reasoning. Only, if you recall, the attacks on this village started while I was still imprisoned."

Royce scowled again. "So why are you here?"

Esrahaddon smiled. "Something you need to understand, my boy, is that wizards are not fonts of information. You should at least know this much—the farmer Theron and his daughter would be dead today if I hadn't arrived and sent her to fetch you."

"All right. Your purpose here is none of my business. I can accept that. But why am *I* here? You can tell me that much, can't you? Why go to the bother of finding out our names and locating us—which was really impressive, by the way—when you could have gotten any thief to pick your lock and open the tower for you?"

"Because not just anyone will do. You are the only one I know who can open Avempartha."

"Are you saying I am the only thief you know?"

"It helps if you actually listen to what I say. You are the only one I know who can open Avempartha."

Royce glared at him.

"There is a monster here that kills indiscriminately," Esrahaddon told him with great and unexpected seriousness. "No weapon made by man can harm it. It comes at night and people die. Nothing will stop it except the sword that lies in that tower. You need to find a way inside and get that sword."

Royce continued to stare.

"You are right. That is not the whole truth, but it is the truth nonetheless and all that I am willing to explain...for now. To learn more you need to get inside."

"Stealing swords," Royce muttered mostly to himself. "Okay, let's take a look at this tower. The sooner I see it, the sooner I can start cursing."

"No," the wizard replied. He looked back at the ground, where the sun had already faded. He glanced up at the darkening sky. "Night is coming and we need to get indoors. In the morning we will go, but tonight we hide with the rest."

Royce considered the wizard for a moment. "You know, when I first met you, there was all this talk about you being this scary wizard that could call lightning and raise mountains and now you can't even fight a little monster, or open an old tower. I thought you were more powerful than this."

"I was," Esrahaddon said, and for the first time the wizard held up his arms, letting his sleeves fall back, revealing the stumps where his hands should have been. "Magic is a little like playing the fiddle. It's damn hard to do without hands."

❧

Dinner that evening was a vegetable pottage, a weak stew consisting of leeks, celery, onions, and potatoes in a thin broth. Hadrian took only a small portion that was far from filling, but he found it surprisingly tasty, filled with a mixture of unusual flavors that left a burning sensation in his mouth.

Lena and Russell Bothwick made good on their promise to put them up for the night, a kindness made all the more generous when they discovered how cramped the little house was. The Bothwicks had three children, four pigs, two sheep, and a goat they called Mammy, all of whom clustered in the single open room. Mosquitoes joined them as well, taking over the night shift from the flies. It was hard to breathe in the house filled with smoke, the scent of animals, and the steam from the stew pot. Royce and Hadrian staked out a bit of earth as near the open doorway as possible and sat on the floor.

"I didn't know the first thing about farming," Russell Bothwick was saying. Like most men in the village, he was dressed in a frayed and flimsy shirt that hung to his knees, belted around the waist with a length of twine. There were large dark circles under his eyes, another trait consistent with the other inhabitants of Dahlgren. "I was a candle maker back in

Drismoor. I worked as a journeyman in a trade shop on Hithil Street. It was Theron who kept us alive our first year here. We woulda starved or froze to death if not for Theron and Addie Wood. They took us under their wing and helped build this house. It was Theron that taught me how to plow a field."

"Addie was my midwife when I had the twins," Lena said while ladling out bowls, which Thrace handed to the children. The twin girls and Tad, exiled to the loft, looked down from their beds of straw, chins on hands, eyes watchful. "And Thrace here was our babysitter."

"There was never a question about taking her in," Russell said. "I only wish Theron would come too, but that man is stubborn."

"I just can't get over how beautiful that dress is," Lena Bothwick said again, looking at Thrace and shaking her head. Russell grumbled something, but since he had a mouthful of stew, no one understood him.

Lena scowled. "Well, it is."

She stopped talking about it but continued to stare. Lena was a gaunt woman with light brown hair cut straight and short, giving her a boyish look. Her nose came to a point so sharp it looked like it could cut parchment. She had a rash of freckles and no eyebrows to speak of. The children all took after her, each sporting the same cropped hairstyle, son and daughters alike, while Russell had no hair at all.

Thrace entertained them with stories of her adventure to the big city, of the sights and number of people she found there. She explained that Hadrian and Royce had taken her to a lavish hotel. This brought worried looks from Lena but she relaxed as more details were revealed. Thrace raved about her bath in a hot-water tub with perfumed soap and about how she had spent the night in a huge feather bed under a solid beamed roof. She never mentioned the Tradesmen's Arch, or what happened underneath it.

Lena was mesmerized to the point of nearly letting the remainder of the stew boil over. Russell continued to grunt and grumble his way through the meal. Esrahaddon sat with his back to the side wall between Lena's spinning wheel and the butter churn. His robe was now a dark gray. He was so quiet he could have been just a shadow. During dinner, Thrace spoon-fed the wizard.

How must that feel? Hadrian thought while watching them. *What is it like to have held so much power and now be unable to even hold a spoon?*

After dinner, while helping Lena clean up, Thrace was placing the washed bowls on a shelf and called out, "I remember this plate." A smile appeared on her face as she spotted the only ceramic dish in the house. The pale white oval with delicate blue traceries lay carefully tucked in a back corner of the cupboard with all the other treasured family heirlooms. "I remember when I was little, Jessie Caswell and I—" She stopped and the house quieted. Even the children stopped fussing.

Lena stopped cleaning the dishes and put her arms around Thrace, pulling her close. Hadrian noticed lines on the woman's face he had not seen previously. The two stood before the bucket of dirty water and silently cried together. "You shouldn't have come back," Lena whispered. "You should have stayed in that hotel with those people."

"I can't leave him." Hadrian heard Thrace's small voice muffled by Lena's shoulder. "He's all I have left."

Thrace pulled back and Lena struggled to offer her a smile.

It was dark outside now. From his vantage point at the doorway, Hadrian could not see much of anything—a tiny patch of moonlight scattered here and there. Fireflies blinked, leaving trails of light. The rest was lost in the vast black of the forest.

Russell pulled over a stool to sit across from Royce and Hadrian. Lighting a long clay pipe with a thin sliver of wood, he commented, “So, you two are here to help Theron kill the monster?”

“We’ll do what we can,” Hadrian replied.

Russell puffed hard on his pipe to ensure it lit, and then crushed the burning tip of the wooden sliver into the dirt floor. “Theron is over fifty years old. He knows the sharp end of a pitchfork from the handle, but I don’t ’spect he’s ever held a sword. Now you two look to me like the kind of fellas that have seen a fight up close, and Hadrian here not only has a sword—he’s got three. A man carries three swords, he, like as not, knows how to use ’em. Seems to me a couple fellas like you could do more than just help an old man get himself killed.”

“Russell!” Lena reprimanded him. “They’re our guests. Why don’t you scald them with hot water while you’re at it?”

“I just don’t want to see that damn fool kill himself. If the margrave and his knights didn’t stand a chance, how well will Theron do out there? An old man with that scythe of his. What’s he trying to prove? How brave he is?”

“He’s not trying to prove anything,” Esrahaddon said suddenly, and his voice silenced the room like a plate dropping. “He’s trying to kill himself.”

“What?” Russell asked.

“He’s right,” Hadrian said, “I’ve seen it before. Soldiers—career soldiers—brave men just reach a point where it’s all too much. It can be anything that sets them off—one too many deaths, a friend dying, or even something as trivial as a change in the weather. I knew a man once who led charges in dozens of battles. It wasn’t until a dog he befriended was butchered for food that he gave up. Of course, a fighter like that can't surrender, can't just quit. He needs to go out swinging. So they rush in unguarded, picking a battle they can't win."

"Then I needn't have wasted your time," Thrace said. "If my father doesn't want to live, whatever is in the tower can't save him."

Hadrian regretted speaking and added, "Every day your father is alive, there is the chance he can find hope again."

"Your father will be fine, Thrace," Lena told her. "That man is tough as granite. You'll see."

"Mom," one of the kids from the loft called.

Lena ignored the child. "You shouldn't listen to these people talking about your father that way. They don't know him."

"Mom."

"Honestly, telling a poor girl something like that right after she's lost her family."

"Mom!"

"What on earth is it, Tad?" Lena nearly screamed at the child.

"The sheep. Look at the sheep."

Everyone noticed it then. Crowded into the corner of the room, the sheep had been quiet through the meal. A content woolly pile that Hadrian had forgotten was there. Now they pushed each other, struggling against the wooden board Russell had put up. The little bell around Mammy's neck rang as the goat shifted uneasily. One of the pigs bolted for the door and Thrace and Lena tackled it just in time.

"Kids. Get down here!" Lena shouted in a whisper.

The three children descended the ladder with precision movements, veterans of many drills. Their mother gathered them near her in the center of the house. Russell got off his stool and doused the fire with the wash water.

Darkness enveloped them. No one spoke. Outside, the

crickets stopped chirping. The frogs fell silent an instant later. The animals continued to shift and stomp. Another pig bolted. Hadrian heard its little feet skitter across the dirt floor in the direction of the door. Beside him he felt Royce move; then there was silence.

"Here, someone take this," Royce whispered. Tad crawled toward the sound and took the pig from him.

They waited.

The sound began faint and hollow. A puffing, thought Hadrian, like bellows stoking a furnace. It grew nearer, louder, less airy—deep and powerful. The sound rose overhead and Hadrian instinctively looked up, but found only the darkness of the ceiling. His hands moved to the pommels of his swords.

Thrump. Thrump. Thrump.

They sat huddled in the darkness, listening, as the sound withdrew, then grew louder once more. A pause—total silence. Inside the house, even the noise of breathing vanished.

Crack!

Hadrian jumped at the loud burst that sounded as if a tree across the common exploded. Snapping, tearing, splintering, a war of violent noise erupted. A scream. A woman's voice. The shriek cut across the common, hysterical and frantic.

"Oh dear Maribor! That's Mae," Lena cried.

Hadrian leapt to his feet. Royce was already up.

"Don't bother," Esrahaddon told them. "She's dead, and there's nothing you can do. The monster cannot be harmed by your weapons. It—"

The two were out the door.

Royce was quicker and raced across the common toward the little house of Mae Drundel. Hadrian could not see a thing and found himself blindly chasing Royce's footfalls.

The cries stopped—a harsh, abrupt end.

Royce halted and Hadrian nearly plowed through him.

"What is it?"

"Roof is ripped away. There's blood all over the walls. She's gone. It's gone."

"It? Did you see something?"

"Through a patch in the canopy—just for a second, but it was enough."

Chapter 5

The Citadel

Royce and Esrahaddon left at first light, following a small trail out of the village. Ever since they had arrived in Dahlgren, Royce had noticed a distant sound, a dull, constant noise. As they approached the river, the sound grew into a roar. The Nidwalden was massive—an expanse of tumultuous green water flowing swiftly, racing by and bursting against rocks. Royce stood for a moment just staring. He spotted a branch out in the middle, a black and gray fist of leaves bobbing helplessly against the current. It sped along, riding through gaps in the boulders, ripping over rocks, until it vanished into a cloud of white. In the center, he saw something tall rising up, most of it lost in the mist and tree branches that extended over the water.

"We need to go farther downriver," Esrahaddon explained as he led Royce to a narrower trail that hugged the bank. River grass grew along the edge, glistening with dew, and songbirds sang shrill melodies in the soft morning breeze. Even with the thundering river, and the vivid memory of a roofless home and bloodstained walls, the place felt tranquil.

"There she is," Esrahaddon said reverently as they reached a rocky clearing that afforded them an unobstructed view of the river. It was wide and the water rushed by with a furious strength, then disappeared over the edge of a sudden fall.

They stood very near the ridge of the cataract and could see the white mist rising from the abrupt drop like a fog. Out in the middle of the river, at the edge of the falls, a massive shelf of bedrock jutted out like the prow of a mighty ship that ran aground just before toppling over the precipice. On this fearsome pedestal rose the citadel of Avempartha. Formed entirely of stone, the tower burst skyward from the rock shelf. A bouquet of tall, slender shards stretched upward like splinters of crystal or slivers of ice, its base lost in the billowing white clouds of mist and foam. At first sight it looked to be a natural stone formation, but a more careful study revealed windows, walkways, and stairs carefully integrated into the architecture.

"How am I supposed to get out there?" Royce asked, yelling over the roar, his cloak whipping and snapping like a snake.

"That would be problem number one," Esrahaddon shouted back, offering nothing more.

Is this some kind of test, or does he really not know?

Royce followed the river over the bare rocks to the drop. Here the land plummeted more than two thousand feet to the valley below. What stood before him was a vision of unsurpassed beauty. The falls were magnificent. The sheer power of the titanic surge was hypnotizing. The massive torrent of blue-green water spilled and sparkled into the billowing white bejeweled mist, the voice of the river thundering in his ears, rattling his chest. Beyond it, to the south, was an equally breathtaking vision. Royce could see for miles and marked the remaining passage of the river as it wound like a long shiny snake through the lush green landscape to the Goblin Sea.

Esrahaddon moved to a more sheltered escarpment farther inland and behind a brace of upward-thrust granite that blocked him from the gusting wind and spray. Royce climbed toward him when he noticed a depressed line in the trees running away from the river. A course of trees stood shorter than those around them, creating a trench in the otherwise uniform canopy. He made his way down to the forest floor and found that what he thought might be a gully was instead a section of younger growth. More importantly, the line was perfectly straight. Old vines and thornbushes masked unnatural mounds. He dug away some of the undergrowth and swept layers of dirt and dead leaves back until he touched flat stone.

"Looks like there might have been a road here," he shouted up to the wizard.

"There was. A great bridge once reached out across the river to Avempartha."

"What happened to it?"

"The river," the wizard told him. "The Nidwalden does not abide the efforts of man for long. Most of it likely washed away, leaving the remains to fall."

Royce followed the buried road to the river's edge, where he stood looking at the tower across the violent expanse. A vast gray volume rushed by him, its speed concealed by its size. The dark gray became a swirling translucent green as it reached the edge. The moment it fell, the water burst into white foam, billions of flying droplets, and all he could hear was the thundering roar.

"Impossible," he muttered.

He returned to where the wizard stood and sat down on the sun-warmed rock, looking at the distant tower that rose up in the haze where rainbows played.

"Do you want me to open that thing?" the thief asked with all seriousness. "Or is this some kind of game?"

"It's no game," Esrahaddon replied as he sat leaning against a rock, folding his arms, and closed his eyes.

It irritated Royce how comfortable he looked. "Then you'd better start saying more than you have so far."

"What do you want to know?"

"Everything—everything you know about it."

"Well, let's see, I was here once a very long time ago. It looked different then, of course. For one thing Novron's bridge was still up and you could walk right out to the tower."

"So the bridge was the only way to reach it?"

"Oh no, I don't think so. At least, it wouldn't make any sense if that were the case. You see, the elves built Avempartha before mankind walked on the face of Elan. No one—well, no human—knows why or what for. Its location here on the falls, facing south toward what we call the Goblin Sea, suggests perhaps the elves might have employed it as a defense against the Children of Uberlin—I believe you call them by the dwarven name, the Ba Ran Ghazel—*goblins of the sea*. But that seems unlikely, as the tower predates them as well. There might have even been a city here at one time. So little is left of their achievements in Apeladorn, but the elves had a fabulous culture rich in beauty, music, and the Art."

"When you say *the Art*, you mean magic?"

The wizard opened a single eye and frowned at him. "Yes, and don't give me that look, as if magic is dirty or vile. I have seen that too many times since I escaped."

"Well, magic isn't something people consider a good thing."

Esrahaddon sighed and shook his head with a stern look. "It is demoralizing to see what has happened to the world during my years of incarceration. I stayed alive and sane because I knew that one day I would be able to do my part to protect humanity, but now I discover it's almost no longer worth the effort. When I was young, the world was an incredible place. Cities were magnificent. Your Colnora wouldn't even rank as a slum in the smallest city of my time. We had indoor plumbing—spigots would pump water right into people's homes. There were extensive, well-maintained sewer systems that kept the streets from smelling like cesspools. Buildings were eight and nine stories tall, and some reached as high as twelve. We had hospitals where the sick were treated and actually got better. We had libraries, museums, temples, and schools of every kind.

"Mankind has squandered its inheritance from Novron. It's like having gone to sleep a rich man and waking up a pauper." He paused. "Then there's what you so feebly call magic. The Art separated us from the animals. It was the greatest achievement of our civilization. Not only has it been forgotten, it is now reviled. In my day, those who could weave the Art, and summon the natural powers of the world to their bidding, were considered agents of the gods—sacrosanct. Today they burn you if you accidentally guess tomorrow's weather.

"It was very different then. People were happy. There were no poor families living on the streets. No destitute hopeless peasants struggling to find a meal, or forced to live in hovels with three children, four pigs, two sheep, and a goat, where the flies in the afternoon are thicker than the family's evening stew."

Esrahaddon looked around sadly. "As a wizard, my life was devoted to the study of truth and the application of it in the service of the emperor. Never had I managed to find more truth or serve him more profoundly than when I came here. And yet, in many ways I regret it. Oh, if only I had stayed home. I would be long dead, having lived a happy, wonderful life."

Royce smiled at him. "Wizards aren't a font, I thought."

Esrahaddon scowled.

"Now, what about the tower?"

The wizard looked back at the elegant spires rising above

the mist. “Avempartha was the site of the last battle of the Great Elven Wars. Novron drove the elves back to the Nidwalden, but they held on by fortifying their position in the tower. Novron was not about to be stopped by a little water, and ordered the building of the bridge. It took eight years and cost the lives of hundreds, most of whom went over the falls, but in the end, the bridge was completed. It took Novron another five years after that to take the citadel. The act was as much symbolic as it was strategic and it forced the elves to accept that nothing would stop Novron from wiping them off the face of Elan. A very curious thing happened then, something that’s still unclear. Novron is said to have obtained the Horn of Gylindora and with it forced the unconditional surrender of the elves. He ordered them to destroy their war agents and machines and to retreat across the river—never to cross it again.”

“So there was no bridge until Novron built one? Not on either side?”

“No, that was the problem. There was no way to reach the tower.”

“How did the elves get there?”

“Exactly.” The wizard nodded.

“So you don’t know?”

“I’m old, but not that old. Novron is farther in the past for me than my day is to you.”

“So there is an answer to this puzzle. It’s just not obvious.”

“Do you think Novron would have spent eight years building a bridge if it was?”

“And what makes you think I can find the answer?”

“Call it a bunch.”

Royce looked at him curiously. “You mean *hunch*?”

The wizard looked irritated. “Still a few holes in my vocabulary, I suppose.”

Royce stared out at the tower in the middle of the river and considered why jobs involving stealing swords were never simple.

~

The service they held for Mae Drundel was somber and respectful, although to Hadrian it felt rehearsed. There were no awkward moments, no stumbling over words or miscues. Everyone was well versed in his or her role. Indeed, the remaining residents of Dahlgren were about as professional about funerals as mourners could be without being paid.

Deacon Tomas said the only customized portion of the service, when he mentioned her devotion to her late family and her church. Mae was the last of them to pass. Her sons had died of sickness before their sixth year and her husband had been killed by the beast less than five months earlier. In his eulogy, Tomas publicly shared what nearly everyone was thinking—that even though Mae's death was terrible, perhaps for her it was not so bad. Some even reported that she had left an inviting candle in her window for the past two nights.

As usual, there was nobody to bury, so they merely drove a whitewashed stake into the ground with her name burned into it. It stood next to the stakes marked DAVIE, FIRTH, and WENT DRUNDEL.

Everyone turned out for the service except Royce and Esrahaddon. Even Theron Wood made a showing to pay his respects. The old farmer looked even more haggard and miserable than he had the day before and Hadrian suspected he had been awake all night.

After the service ended, the village shared their midday dinner. The men placed a row of tables, end to end, across the village common, and each family brought a dish. Smoked fish, black pudding (a sausage made from pig's blood, milk, animal fat, onions, and oatmeal), and mutton were the most popular.

Hadrian stood back, leaning against a cedar tree, watching the others form lines.

"Help yourself," Lena told him.

"There doesn't look like there is a lot here. I have provisions in my bag," he assured her.

"Nonsense—we'll have none of that—everyone eats at a wake. Mae would want it that way, and what else is a funeral for if not to pay respects to the dead?"

She glared at him until he nodded and began looking about the tables for a plate.

"So those are your horses I have up in the castle stables?" a voice said, and he turned to see a plump man in a cleric frock. He was the first person who did not look in desperate need of a meal. His cheeks were rosy and large, and when he smiled, his eyes squinted nearly shut. He did not look terribly old, but his hair was pure white, including his short beard.

"If you are Deacon Tomas, then yes," Hadrian replied.

"I am indeed, and think nothing of it. I get rather lonely up on the hill at night all by myself with all those empty rooms. You hear every sound at night, you know. The wind slapping a shutter, the creak of rafters—it can be quite unnerving. Now at least I can blame the noises I hear on your horses. Being way down in the stables, I doubt I could hear them, but I can pretend, can't I?" The deacon chuckled to himself. "But honestly, it can be miserable up there. I'm used to being with people, and the isolation of the manor house is such a burden," he said while heaping his plate full of mutton.

"It must be awful for you. But I'll bet there is good food. Those nobles really know how to fill a storehouse, don't they?"

"Well, yes, of course," the deacon replied. "As a matter of fact, the margrave had put by a remarkable amount of smoked meats, not to mention ale and wine, but I only take what I need, of course."

"Of course," Hadrian agreed. "Just looking at you, I can tell that you're not the kind of man to take advantage of a situation. Did you supply the ale for the funeral?"

"Oh no," the deacon replied, aghast. "I wouldn't dare pillage the manor house like that. Like you just said, I am not the kind of man to take advantage of a situation and it's not my stores to give, now is it?"

"I see."

"Oh my, look at the cheese," said the deacon, scooping up a wedge and shoving it in his mouth. "Have to admit one thing," he spoke with his mouth full, "Dahlgren can really throw a funeral."

When they reached the end of the tables, Hadrian looked for a place to sit. The few benches were filled with folks eating off their laps.

"Up, you kids!" the deacon shouted at Tad and Pearl. "You don't need to be taking up a bench. Go sit on the grass." They frowned but got up. "You there, Hadrian is it? Come sit here and tell me what brings a man who owns a horse and three swords to Dahlgren. I trust you aren't noble or you'd have knocked on my door last night."

"No, I'm not a noble, but that brings up a question. How did you inherit the manor house?"

"Hmm? Inherit? Oh, I didn't inherit anything. It is merely my station as a public servant to help in a crisis like this. When the margrave and his men died, I knew I had to administer to this troubled flock and watch after the king's interests. So I endure the hardships and do what I can."

"Like what?"

"What's that?" the deacon asked, tearing into a piece of mutton, which left his lips and cheeks shiny with grease.

"What have you done to help?"

"Oh—well, let's see...I keep the house clean, the yard maintained, and the garden watered. You really have to keep after those weeds, you know, or the whole garden would be swallowed up and not a single vegetable would survive. And oh—the toll it takes on my back. I've never had what you would call a good back as it is."

"I meant about the attacks. What steps have you taken to safeguard the village?"

"Well now," the deacon said, chuckling, "I'm a cleric, not a knight. I don't even know how to hold a sword properly and I don't have an army of knights at my disposal, do I? So aside from diligent prayer, I'm not in a position where I can really *do* anything about that."

"Have you considered letting the villagers stay in the manor at night? Whatever this creature is, it doesn't have much trouble with thatched roofs, but the manor has what looks to be a sturdy roof and some thick walls."

The deacon shook his head, still smiling at Hadrian as an adult might look at a child who just asked why there must be poor people in the world. "No, no, that wouldn't do at all. I am quite certain the next lord of the house would not appreciate having a whole village taking over his home."

"But you are aware that the responsibility of a lord is to protect his subjects? That is why his subjects pay him a tax. If the lord isn't willing to protect them, why should they honor him with money, crops, or even respect?"

"You might not have noticed," the deacon replied, "but we are between lords at the moment."

"So then, you don't intend to continue taxing these people for the time they are without protection?"

"Well, I didn't mean that—"

"So you do intend to uphold the responsibility of a steward?"

"Well, I—"

"Now, I can understand your hesitation to overstep your authority and open the manor house to the village, so I am certain you'll want to take the other option."

"Other option?" The cleric was holding another slice of mutton to his mouth but sat too distracted to bite.

"Yes, as steward and acting lord, it falls on you to protect this village in his stead, and since inviting them into the house at night is out of the question, then I presume you'll be taking to the field to fight the beast."

"Fight it?" He dropped the mutton on his lap. "I don't think—"

Before he could say any more, Hadrian went on. "The good news is that I can help you there. I have an extra sword if you are missing one, and since you have been so kind as to let me board my horse at the stable, I think the least I can do is lend her to you for the fight. Now, I have heard that some people have determined where the lair of the beast is, so it really seems a simple matter of—"

"I—I don't recall saying that lodging the people in the manor at night was out of the question," the deacon said loudly to interrupt Hadrian. Several heads turned. He lowered his voice and added, "I was merely stating that it was something I had to consider carefully. You see, the mantle of leadership is a heavy one indeed, and I need to weigh the consequences of every act I make, as they can break as well as mend. No, no, you can't rush into these things."

"That is very understandable and very wise, I might add," Hadrian agreed, keeping his voice loud enough for others to hear him. "But the margrave was killed well over two weeks ago, so I am certain you have come to a decision by now?"

The deacon caught the interested looks of several of the villagers. Those who had finished their meals wandered over.

One was Dillon McDern, who was taller than the rest and stood watching them.

"I—ah."

"Everyone!" Hadrian shouted. "Gather round, the deacon wants to talk with us about the defense of the village."

The crowd of mourners, plates in hand, turned and gathered in a circle around the well. All eyes turned to Deacon Tomas, who suddenly looked like a defenseless rabbit caught in a trap.

"I—um—" the deacon started, then slumped his shoulders and said in a loud voice, "In light of the recent attacks on houses, everyone is invited to spend nights in the protection of the castle."

The crowd murmured to each other and then Russell Bothwick called out, "Will there be enough room for everyone?"

The deacon looked as if he was about to reconsider when Hadrian stood up. "I'm sure there's plenty of room in the house for all the women and children and most of the married men. Those single men, thirteen or older, can spend the night in the stables, smokehouse, and other outbuildings. Each of them has stronger walls and roofs than any of the village homes."

The inhabitants of the village began to cluster now in earnest.

"And our livestock? Do we abandon them to the beast?" another farmer asked. Hadrian did not recognize him. "Without the livestock we'll have no meat, no wool, or field animals for work."

"I've got Amble and Ramble to think of," McDern said. "Dahlgren would be in a sorry state if'n I let sumpin' happen to those oxen."

Hadrian jumped to the rim of the well, where he stood above them with one arm on the windlass. "There's plenty of room inside the stockade walls for all the animals where they will be safer than they have been in your homes. Remember there is safety in numbers. If you sit alone in the dark, it is easy for anything to kill you, but the creature will not be so bold as to enter a fenced castle with the entire village watching. We can also build bonfires outside the walls for light."

This brought gasps. "But light draws the creature!"

"Well, from what I can see, it doesn't have difficulty finding you in the dark."

The villagers looked from Hadrian to Deacon Tomas and back again.

"How do you know?" someone asked from the crowd. "How do you know any of this? You're not from here. How do you know anything?"

"It's a demon from Uberlin!" someone Hadrian did not recognize shouted.

"You can't stop it!" a woman on the right yelled. "Grouping together could just make killing us that much easier."

"It doesn't want to kill you all at once and it isn't a demon," Hadrian assured the villagers.

"How do you know?"

"It kills only one or two, why? If it can tear apart Theron Wood's house, or rip the roof off Mae Drundel's home in seconds, it could easily destroy this whole village in one night, but it doesn't. It doesn't because it isn't trying to kill you all. It's killing for food. The beast isn't a demon; it's a predator." The villagers considered this, and while they paused, Hadrian continued, "What I have heard about this creature is that no one has ever seen it and no victim has survived. Well, that doesn't surprise me at all. How do you expect to survive when you sit alone in the dark just waiting to be eaten? No one has ever seen it because it doesn't want to be seen. Like any predator, it conceals itself until it springs, and like a predator, it hunts the weakest prey; it looks for the stray, the young, the old, or the sick. All of you have been dividing yourselves up into tidy little meals. You've made yourselves too convenient to resist. If we group together, it might prefer to hunt a deer or a wolf that night instead of us."

"What if you're wrong? What if no one has seen it because it is a demon and can't be seen? It could be an invisible spirit that feeds on terror. Isn't that right, Deacon?"

"Ah—well—" the deacon began.

"It could be, but it isn't," Hadrian assured them.

"How do you know?"

"Because my partner saw it last night."

This caught the group by surprise and several conversations broke out at once. Hadrian spotted Pearl sitting on the grass staring at him. Several asked questions at once and Hadrian waved at them to quiet down.

"What did it look like?" a woman with a sunburned face and a white kerchief over her head asked.

"Since I didn't see it, I would prefer Royce tell you himself. He'll be back before dark."

"How could he have seen anything in the dark?" one of the older farmers asked skeptically. "I looked outside when I heard the scream and it was as black as the bottom of that well yer standing on. There's no way he could have seen anything."

"He saw the pig!" Tad Bothwick shouted.

"What's that, boy?" Dillon McDern asked.

"The pig, in our house last night," Tad said excitedly. "It was all dark and the pig ran, but he saw it and caught him."

"That's right," Russell Bothwick recalled. "We had just put the fire out and I couldn't see my hand in front of my face, but this fellow caught a running pig. Maybe he did see something."

"The point is," Hadrian went on, "we'll all stand a better chance of survival if we stick together. Now, the deacon has graciously invited all of us to join him behind the protection of walls and a solid roof. I think we should listen to his wisdom and start making plans to resettle and gather wood before the evening arrives. We still have plenty of time to build up strong bonfires."

They were looking at Hadrian now and nodding. There were still those who looked unconvinced, but even the skeptics appeared hopeful. Small groups were forming, talking, planning.

Hadrian sat back down and ate. He was not a fan of blood pudding and stayed with the smoked fish, which was wonderful.

"I'll bring the oxen over," he heard McDern say. "Brent, you go bring yer wagon and fetch yer axe too."

"We'll need shovels and Went's saw," Vince Griffin said. "He always kept it sharp."

"I'll send Tad to fetch it," Russell announced.

"Is it true?" Hadrian looked up from his plate to see Pearl standing before him. Her face was just as dirty as it had been the day before. "Did yer friend—did he really catch a pig in the dark?"

"If you don't believe me, you can ask him tonight."

Looking over the little girl's head, he spotted Thrace. She was sitting alone on the ground down the trail past the Caswells' graves. He noticed her hands wiping her cheeks. He set his empty plate on the table, smiled at Pearl, and walked over. Thrace did not look up, so he crouched down beside her. "What is it?"

"Nothing." She shook her head, hiding her face with her hair.

Hadrian glanced around the trail and then back up at the villagers. The women were putting away the uneaten food as the men gathered tools, all of them chattering quickly.

"Where's your father? I saw him earlier."

"He went back home," she said, sniffling.

"What did he say to you?"

"I told you, it's all right." She stood up, brushed off her dress, and wiped her eyes. "I should help with the cleaning. Excuse me."

ॐ

Hadrian entered the clearing and once more faced the remains of the Woods' farmhouse. The roofing poles listed to one side; the framing was splintered; the thatch was scattered. *This is what shattered dreams look like.* The farm seemed cursed, haunted by ghosts, only one of the ghosts was not at home. There was no sign of the old farmer, and the scythe rested, abandoned, up against the ruined wall. Hadrian took the opportunity to peer inside at the shattered furniture, broken cupboards, torn clothes, and bloodstains. A single chair stood in the center of the debris, beside a wooden cradle.

Theron Wood came up from the river a few moments later, carrying a shoulder yoke with two buckets full of water hanging from the ends. He did not hesitate when he spotted Hadrian standing before the ruins of his house. He walked right by. He set the buckets down and began pouring the water into three large jugs.

"You back again?" he asked without looking up. "She told me she paid you silver to come here. Is that what you do? Take advantage of simple girls? Steal their hard-earned money, then eat their village's food? If you came here to see if you can squeeze more coins out of me, you're gonna be disappointed."

"I didn't come here for money."

"No? Then why did you?" he asked, tipping the second bucket. "If you really are here to get that club or sword or whatever that crazy cripple thinks is in the tower, shouldn't you be trying to swim the river right now?"

"My partner is working on that as we speak."

"Uh-huh, he's the swimmer, is he? And what are you, the guy that squeezes the money out of poor miserable farmers? I've seen your kind before, highwaymen and cheats—you scare people into paying you just to live. Well, that's not gonna work this time, my friend."

"I told you I didn't come here for money."

Theron dropped the bucket at his feet and turned. "So why did you come here?"

"You left the wake early and I was concerned you might not have heard the news that everyone in the village is going to spend the night inside the castle walls."

"Thanks for the notice." He turned back and corked the jugs. When he finished, he looked up, annoyed. "Why are you still here?"

"What exactly do you know about combat?" Hadrian asked.

The farmer glared at him. "What business is it of yours?"

"As you pointed out, your daughter paid my partner and me good money to help you kill this monster. He's working on providing you with a proper weapon. I am here to ensure you know how to use it when it gets here."

Theron Wood ran his tongue along his teeth. "You're fixin' to educate me, are you?"

"Something like that."

"I don't need any training." He picked up his buckets and yoke and began walking away.

"You don't know the first thing about combat. Have you ever even held a sword?"

Theron whirled on him. "No, but I plowed five acres in one

day. I bucked half a cord of wood before noon. I survived being caught eight miles from shelter in a blizzard and I lost my whole damn family in a single night! Have *you* done any of that?"

"Not your *whole* family," Hadrian reminded him.

"The ones that mattered."

Hadrian drew his sword and advanced on Theron. The old farmer watched his approach with indifference.

"This is a bastard sword," Hadrian told him, and dropped it at the farmer's feet and walked half a dozen steps away. "I think it suits you rather well. Pick it up and swing at me."

"I have more important things to do than play games with you," Theron said.

"Just like you had more important things to do than take care of your family that night?"

"Watch yer mouth, boy."

"Like you were watching that poor defenseless grandson of yours? What was it really, Theron? Why were you really working so late that night? And don't give me this bull about benefitting your son. You were trying to get some extra money this year for something *you* wanted. Something you felt you needed so badly you let your family die."

The farmer picked up the sword, puffing his cheeks and rocking his shoulders back, his breath hissing through his teeth. "I didn't let them die. It wasn't me!"

"What did you trade them for, Theron? Some fool's dream? You didn't give a damn about your son; it was all about you. You wanted to be the grandfather of a magistrate. You wanted to be the big man, didn't you? And you'd do anything to make that dream come true. You worked late. You weren't there. You were out in the field when it came, because of your dream, your desires. Is that why you let your son die? You never cared about them at all. Did you? All you care about is yourself."

The farmer charged Hadrian with the sword in both hands and swung at him. Hadrian stepped aside and the wild swing missed, but the momentum carried the farmer around and he fell to the dirt.

"You let them die, Theron. You weren't there like a man is supposed to be. A man is supposed to protect his family, but what were you doing? You were out in the fields working on what *you* wanted. What *you* had to have."

Theron got up and charged again. Once more Hadrian stepped aside. This time Theron managed to remain standing and delivered more wild swings. Hadrian drew his short sword and deflected the blows. The old farmer was in a rage now and struck out maniacally, swinging the sword like an axe with single, hacking strokes that stole his balance. Soon Hadrian did not need to parry anymore and merely sidestepped out of the way. Theron's face grew redder with each miss. Tears filled his eyes. At last, the old man collapsed to the dirt, frustrated and exhausted.

"It wasn't me that killed them," he yelled. "It was *her*! She left the light on. She left the door open."

"No, Theron." Hadrian took the sword from the farmer's limp hands. "Thrace didn't kill your family and neither did you—the beast did." He slipped his sword back in its sheath. "You can't blame her for leaving a door open. She didn't know what was coming. None of you did. Had you known, you would have been there. Had your family known, they would have put out the light. The sooner you stop blaming innocent people and start trying to fix the problem, the better off everyone will be.

"Theron, that weapon of yours may be mighty sharp, but what good is a sharp weapon when you can't hit anything or, worse, hit the wrong target? You don't win battles with hate. Anger and hate can make you brave, make you strong, but they also make you stupid. You end up tripping over your own two feet." Hadrian stared down at the old man. "I think that's enough for today's lesson."

ര

Royce and Esrahaddon returned less than an hour before sunset and found a parade of animals driving up the road. It looked like every animal in the village was on the move and most of the people were out along the edges with sticks and bells, pots and spoons, banging away, herding the animals up the hill toward the manor house. Sheep and cows followed each other fine enough, but the pigs were a problem, and Royce spotted Pearl with her stick, masterfully bringing up the rear.

Rose McDern, the smithy's wife, was the first to spot them and suddenly Royce heard "He's back!" excitedly repeated among the villagers.

"What's going on?" Royce asked Pearl, purposely avoiding the adults.

"Movin' the critters to the castle. We all stay'n there tonight, they says."

"Do you know where Hadrian is? You remember, the man I arrived with? Thrace was riding with him?"

"The castle," Pearl told him, and narrowed her eyes at the thief. "You really catch a pig in the dark?"

Royce looked at her, puzzled. Just then, a pig darted up the road and the girl was off after it, waving her long switch in the air.

The castle of the Lord of Westbank was a typical motte-and-bailey fortress, with the great manor house built on a steep man-made hill, surrounded by a wall of sharp-tipped wooden logs that enclosed the outbuildings. A heavy gate barred the entrance. A halfhearted attempt at a moat ringed it but amounted to nothing more than a shallow ditch. Cut trees left about forty yards of sharpened stumps in all directions.

A group of men worked at the tree line, cutting pines. Royce was still a bit vague on names but he recognized Vince Griffin and Russell Bothwick working a dual-handled saw. Tad Bothwick and a few other boys raced around, trimming branches with axes and hatches. Three girls tied the branches into bundles and stacked them on a wagon. Dillon McDern and his sons used his oxen to haul the logs up the hill to the castle, where more men labored to cut and split the wood.

Royce found Hadrian splitting logs near the stockade gate. He was naked to the waist except for the small silver medallion that dangled from his neck as he bent forward to place another wedge. He had a solid sweat worked up along with a sizable pile of wood.

"Been meddling, have you?" Royce asked, looking around at the hive of activity.

"You must admit they didn't have much in the way of a defense plan," Hadrian said, pausing to wipe the sweat from his forehead.

Royce smiled at him. "You just can't help yourself, can you?"

"And you? Did you find the doorknob?"

Hadrian picked up a jug and downed several swallows, drinking so quickly some of the water dripped down his chin. He poured some in his palm and rinsed his face, running his fingers through his hair.

"I didn't even get close enough to see a door."

"Well, look on the bright side"—Hadrian smiled—"at least you weren't captured and condemned to death this time."

"That's the bright side?"

"What can I say? I'm a glass-half-full kinda guy."

"There he is," Russell Bothwick shouted, pointing. "That's Royce over there."

"What's going on?" Royce asked as throngs of people suddenly moved toward him from the field and the castle interior.

"I mentioned that you saw the thing and now they want to know what it looks like," Hadrian explained. "What did you think? They were coming to lynch you?"

He shrugged. "What can I say? I'm a glass-half-empty kinda guy."

"Half empty?" Hadrian chuckled. "Was there ever any drink in that glass?"

Royce was still scowling at Hadrian when the villagers crowded around them. The women wore kerchiefs over their hair, dark and damp where they crossed their foreheads. Their sleeves were rolled up, their faces smudged with dirt. Most of the men, like Hadrian, were topless, wood shavings and pine needles sticking to their skin.

"Did you see it?" Dillon asked. "Did you really get a look at it?"

"Yes," Royce replied, and several people murmured.

"What did it look like?" Deacon Tomas asked. The priest stood out from the crowd, looking fresh, clean, and rested.

"Did it have wings?" Russell asked.

"Did it have claws?" Tad asked.

"How big was it?" Vince Griffin asked.

"Let the man answer!" Dillon thundered, and the rest quieted.

"It does have wings and claws. I saw it only briefly because it was flying above the trees. I caught sight of it through a small opening in the leaves, but what I saw was long, like a snake, or lizard, with wings and two legs that—that were still clutching Mae Drundel."

"A lizard with wings?" Dillon repeated.

"A dragon," a woman declared. "That's what it is. It's a dragon!"

"That's right," Russell said. "That's what a winged lizard is."

"There's supposed to be a weak spot in their armor near the armpit, or whatever a dragon has for an armpit," a woman with a particularly dirty nose explained. "I heard an archer once killed a dragon in mid-flight by hitting him there."

"I heard you weaken a dragon by stealing its treasure hoard," a bald-headed man told them all. "There was a tale where this prince was trapped in the lair of a dragon and he threw all the treasure into the sea and it weakened the beast so much the prince was able to kill him by stabbing him in the eye."

"I heard that dragons were immortal and couldn't be killed," Rose McDern said.

"It's not a dragon," Esrahaddon said with a tone of disgust. He stepped out from the crowd and they turned to face him.

"Why do you say that?" Vince Griffin asked.

"Because it isn't," he replied confidently. "If it was a dragon whose wrath you had incurred, this village would have been wiped from the face of Elan months ago. Dragons are very intelligent beings, far more than you or even I, and more powerful than we can begin to comprehend. No, Mrs. Brockton, no archer ever killed a dragon by shooting him in a soft spot with an arrow. And no, Mr. Goodman, stealing a dragon's treasure doesn't weaken it. In fact, dragons don't have treasures. What exactly would a dragon do with gold or gems? Do you think there is a dragon store somewhere? Dragons don't believe in possessions, unless you count memories, strength, and honor as possessions."

"But that's what he said he saw," Vince countered.

The wizard sighed. "He said he saw a snake or lizard with wings and two legs. That should have been your first clue." The wizard turned to Pearl, who had finished driving the last of the pigs into the courtyard of the castle and had run back out to join the crowd. “Tell me, Pearl, how many legs does a dragon have?”

“Four,” the child said without thinking.

“Exactly. This is not a dragon.”

“Then what is it?” Russell asked.

“A Gilarabrywn,” Esrahaddon replied casually.

“A—a what?”

“Gil...lar...ah...brin,” the wizard pronounced slowly, mouthing the syllables carefully. “Gilarabrywn, a magical creature.”

“What does that mean? Does it cast spells like a witch?”

“No, it means it’s unnatural. It wasn’t born; it was created—conjured, if you will.”

“That’s just crazy,” Russell said. “How gullible do you think we are? This thingamabob—whatever you called it—killed dozens of people. It ain’t no made-up thing.”

“No, wait,” Deacon Tomas said, intervening, waving to them from deep in the sea of villagers. They backed away to reveal the cleric standing with his hand still up in the air, his eyes thoughtful. “There *was* a beast known as the Gilarabrywn. I learned about it in seminary. In the Great Elven Wars they were tools of the Erivan Empire, beasts of war, terrible things that devastated the landscape and slaughtered thousands. There are accounts of them laying waste to cities and whole armies. No weapon could harm them.”

“You know your history well, Deacon,” Esrahaddon said. “The Gilarabrywn were devastating instruments of war—intelligent, powerful, silent killers from the sky.”

“How could such a thing still be alive after so long?” Russell asked.

“They aren’t natural. They can’t die a normal death, because they really aren’t alive as we understand living to be.”

“I think we’re going to need more wood,” Hadrian muttered.

As the sun set, the farmers provisioned the castle for the night. The children and women gathered beneath the great beams of the manor house while the men worked to the last light of day building the woodpiles. Hadrian had organized effective teams for cutting, dragging, and tying the stacks such that by nightfall they had six great piles surrounding the walls and one in the center of the yard itself. They doused the piles in oil and animal fat to make the lighting faster. It was going to be a long night and they did not want the fires to burn out, nor would it do to have them lit too late.

"Hadrian!" Thrace yelled as she ran frantically through the courtyard.

"Thrace," Hadrian said, working to the last minute on the courtyard woodpile. "It's dark. You should be in the house."

"My father's not here," she cried. "I've looked everywhere around the castle. No one saw him come in. He must still be at home. He's out there alone, and if he's the only one alone tonight—"

"Royce!" Hadrian shouted, but it was unnecessary, as Royce was already leading their saddled horses out of the stable.

"She found me first," the thief said, handing him Millie's reins.

"That damn fool," Hadrian said, grabbing his shirt and weapons and pulling himself up on the horse. "I told him about coming to the castle."

"So did I," she said, her face a mask of fear.

"Don't worry, Thrace. We'll bring him back safe."

They spurred the animals and rode out the gate at a gallop.

෴

Theron sat in the ruins of his house on a wooden chair. A small fire burned in a shallow pit just outside the doorway.

The sky was finally dark and he could see stars. He listened to the night music of the crickets and frogs. A distant owl began its hunt. The fire snapped and popped, and beneath it all, the distant roaring of the falls. Mosquitoes entered the undefended house. They swarmed, landed, and bit. The old man let them. He sat as he had every night, staring silently at memories.

His eyes settled on the cradle. Theron remembered building the little rocker for his first son. He and Addie had decided to name their firstborn Hickory—a good, strong, durable wood. Theron had hunted the forest for the perfect hickory tree and found it one day on a hill, bathed in sunlight as if the gods had marked it. Each night Theron had carefully crafted the cradle and finished the wood so it would last. All five of his children had slept in it. Hickory died there before his first birthday from a sickness for which there was no name. All his sons had died young, except for Thad, who had grown to be a fine man. He had married a sweet girl named Emma, and when she had given birth to Theron's grandson, they had named him Hickory. Theron remembered thinking that it seemed as if the world was finally trying to make up for the hardships in his life—that somehow the unwarranted punishment of his firstborn's premature death was healed through the life of his first grandson. But it was all gone now. All he had left was the blood-sprayed bed of five dead children.

Behind the cradle lay one of Addie's two dresses. It was a terrible, ugly thing, stained and torn, but to his watering eyes it looked beautiful. She had been a good wife. For more than thirty years she had followed him from one dismal town to the next as he had tried to find a place he could call his own. They had never had much, and many times, they had gone hungry, and on more than one occasion nearly froze to death. In all that time, he had never heard her complain. She had mended his clothes and his broken bones, made his meals, and looked after him when he was sick. She had always been too thin, giving the biggest portions of each meal to him and their children. Her clothes had been the worst in the family. She never found time to mend them. She had been a good wife and Theron could not remember ever having said he loved her. It had never seemed important before. The beast had taken her too, plucked her from the path between the village and the farm. Thad's Emma had filled the void, making it easy to move on. He had avoided thinking about her by staying focused on the goal, but now the goal was dead, and his house had caved in.

What must it have been like for them when the beast came? Were they alive when it took them? Did they suffer? The thoughts tormented the farmer as the sounds of the crickets died.

He stood up, his scythe in his hands, preparing to meet the darkness, when he heard the reason for the interruption of the night noises. Horses thundered up the trail and the two men Thrace had hired entered the light of the campfire in a rush.

❧

"Theron!" Hadrian shouted as he and Royce arrived in the yard of the Woods' farm. The sun was down, the light gone, and the old man had a welcome fire burning—only not for them. "Let's go. We've got to get back to the castle."

"You go back," the old man growled. "I didn't ask you to come here. This is my home and I'm staying."

"Your daughter needs you. Now get up on this horse. We don't have much time."

"I'm not going anywhere. She's fine. She's with the Bothwicks. They'll take good care of her. Now get off my land!"

Hadrian dismounted and marched up to the farmer, who stood his ground like a rooted tree.

"My god, you're a stubborn ass. Now either you're going to get on that horse or I'll put you on it."

"Then you'll have to put me on it," he said, setting his scythe down and folding his arms across his chest.

Hadrian looked over his shoulder at Royce, who sat silently on Mouse. "Why aren't you helping?"

"It's really not my area of expertise. Now, if you want him dead—that I can do."

Hadrian sighed. "Please get on the horse. You're going to get us all killed staying out here."

"Like I said, I never asked you to come."

"Damn," Hadrian cursed as he removed his weapons and hooked them on the saddle of his horse.

"Careful," Royce leaned over and told him. "He's old, but he looks tough."

Hadrian ran full tilt at the old farmer and tackled him to the ground. Theron was larger than Hadrian, with powerful arms and hands made strong by years of unending work, but Hadrian was fast and agile. The two grappled in a wrestling match that had them rolling in the dirt grunting as each tried to get the advantage.

"This is so stupid," Hadrian muttered, getting to his feet. "If you would just get on the horse..."

"You get on the horse. Get out of here and leave me alone!" Theron yelled at them as he struggled to catch his breath, standing bent over, hands resting on his knees.

"Maybe you can help me this time?" Hadrian said to Royce.

Royce rolled his eyes and dismounted. "I didn't expect you'd have so much trouble."

"It's not easy to subdue a person bigger than you and not hurt him in the process."

"Well, I think I found your problem, then. Why don't we try hurting him?"

When they turned back to face Theron, the farmer had a good-size stick in his hand and a determined look in his eyes.

Hadrian sighed, “I don’t think we have a choice.”

“Daddy!” Thrace shouted, running into the ring of firelight, her face streaked with tears. “Daddy,” she cried again, and reaching the old man, threw her arms around him.

“Thrace, what are you doing here?” Theron yelled. “It’s not safe.”

“I came to get you.”

“I’m staying here.” He pulled his daughter off and pushed her away. “Now you take your hired thugs and get back to the Bothwicks right now. You hear me?”

“No,” Thrace cried at him, her arms raised, still reaching. “I won’t leave you.”

“Thrace,” he bellowed, his huge frame towering over her, “I am your father and you’ll do as I say!”

“No!” she shouted back at him, the firelight shining on her wet cheeks. “I won’t leave you to die. You can whip me if you want, but you’ll have to come back to the castle to do it.”

“You stupid little fool,” he cursed. “You’re gonna get yourself killed. Don’t you know that?”

“I don’t care!” Her voice ran shrill, her hands crushed into fists, arms punched down at her sides. “What reason do I have to live if my own father—the only person I have left in the world—hates me so much he would rather die than look at me?”

Theron stood stunned.

“At first,” she began in a quavering voice, “I thought you wanted to make sure no one else was killed, and then I thought maybe it was—I don’t know—to put their souls to rest. Then I thought you wanted revenge. Maybe the hate was eating you up. Maybe you had to see it killed. But none of that’s true. You just want to die. You hate yourself—you hate me. There’s nothing in this world for you anymore, nothing you care about."

"I don't hate you," Theron said.

"You do. You do because it was my fault. I know what they meant to you—and I wake up every morning with that." She wiped the tears enough to see. "If it was me, it would have been just like it was with Mom—you would have driven a stick into Stony Hill with my name on it and the next day gone back to work. You would have driven the plow and thanked Maribor for his kindness in sparing your son. I should have been the one to die, but I can't change what happened and your death won't bring him back. Nothing will. Still, if all I can do now—if all that's left for me—is to die here with you, then that's what I'll do. I won't leave you, Daddy. I can't. I just can't." She fell to her knees, exhausted, and in a fragile voice said, "We'll all be together again, at least."

Then, as if in response to her words, the wood around them went silent once more. This time the crickets and frogs stopped so abruptly the silence seemed suddenly loud.

"No," Theron said, shaking his head. He looked up at the night sky. "*No!*"

The farmer grabbed his daughter and lifted her up. "We're going." He turned. "Help us."

Hadrian pulled Millie around. "Up, both of you." Millie stomped her hoovcs and started to pull and twist, nostrils flaring, ears twitching. Hadrian gripped her by the bit and held tight.

Theron mounted the horse and pulled Thrace up in front of him, then, with a swift kick, he sent Millie racing up the trail back toward the village. Royce leapt on the back of Mouse and, throwing out a hand, swung Hadrian up behind him even as he sent the horse galloping into the night.

The horses needed no urging as they ran full out with the sweat of fear dampening their coats. Their hooves thundered, pounding the earth like violent drumbeats. The path ahead was only slightly lighter than the rest of the wood and for Hadrian it was often a blur as the wind drew tears from his eyes.

"Above us!" Royce shouted. Overhead they heard a rush of movement in the leaves.

The horses made a jarring turn into the thick of the wood. Invisible branches, leaves, and pine boughs slapped them, whipped them, beat them. The animals raced in blind panic. They drove through the underbrush, glancing off tree trunks, bouncing by branches. Hadrian felt Royce duck and mimicked him.

Thrump. Thrump. Thrump.

He could hear a slow beating overhead, a dull, deep pumping. A blast of wind came from above, a massive downdraft of air. Along with it came the frightening sounds of cracking, snapping, splintering. The treetops shattered and exploded.

"Log!" Royce shouted as the horses jumped.

Hadrian kept his seat only by virtue of Royce's agile grab. In the darkness, he heard Thrace's scream, a grunt, and a sound like an axe handle hitting wood. The thief reined Mouse hard, wrestling with her, pulling the animal's head around as she reared and snorted. Hadrian could hear Millie galloping ahead.

"What's going on?" Hadrian asked.

"They fell," Royce growled.

"I can't see them." Hadrian leapt down.

"In the thickets, there to your right," Royce said, climbing off Mouse, who was in a panic, thrashing her head back and forth.

"Here," Theron said, his voice labored, "over here."

The farmer stood over his daughter. She lay unconscious, sprawled and twisted. Blood dripped from her nose and mouth.

"She hit a branch," Theron said; his voice was shaking, frightened. "I—I didn't see the log."

"Get her on my horse," Royce commanded. "Theron, take her and ride for the manor. We're close. You can see the light of the bonfires burning."

The farmer made no protest. He climbed on Mouse, who was still stomping and snorting. Hadrian picked up Thrace. A patch of moonlight showed a dark blemish on her face, a long wide mark. He lifted her. Her head fell back, limp; her arms and legs dangled free. She seemed dead. He handed her to Theron, who cradled his daughter to his chest and held her tight. Royce let loose the bit, and the horse thundered off, racing for the open field, leaving Royce and Hadrian behind.

"Think Millie's around?" Hadrian whispered.

"I think Millie is already an appetizer."

"I suppose the good news is that she bought Thrace and Theron safe passage."

They slowly moved to the edge of the wood. They were very close to where Dillon and his boys had been hauling logs earlier that day. They could see three of the six bonfires blazing away, illuminating the field.

"What about us?" Royce asked.

"Do you think the Gilarabrywn knows we're still in here?"

"Esrahaddon said it was intelligent, so I presume it can count."

"Then it will come back and find us. We have to reach the castle. The distance across the open is about—what? Two hundred feet?"

"About that," Royce confirmed.

"I guess we can hope it's still munching on Millie. Ready?"

"Run spread out so it can't get both of us. Go." The grass was slick with dew and filled with stumps and pits. Hadrian got only a dozen yards before falling on his face.

"Stay behind me," Royce told him.

"I thought we were spreading out?"

"That's before I remembered you're blind."

They ran again, dodging in and out, as Royce picked the path up the hillside. They were nearly halfway across when they heard the bellows again.

Thrump. Thrump. Thrump.

The sound rushed toward them. Looking up, Hadrian saw something dark pass across the face of the rising moon, a serpent with batlike wings gliding, arcing, circling like a hawk hunting mice in a field.

The bellows stopped.

"It's diving!" Royce shouted.

A massive burst of wind blew them to the ground. The bonfires were instantly snuffed out. A second later, a loud rumble shook the earth and a monolithic wall of green fire exploded in a great ring, surrounding the entire hill. Astounding flames, thirty feet high, flashed up like trees of light spewing intense heat.

No longer having any trouble seeing his way, Hadrian jumped to his feet and sped to the gate, Royce on his heels. Behind them the flames roared. Above them they heard a chilling scream.

Dillon, Vince, and Russell slammed the gate shut the instant they were inside. The bonfire in the courtyard, which had been unlit so far, startled everyone as it exploded into a brilliant blue-green flame, reaching like a pillar into the sky. Once more from the darkness above, the Gilarabrywn screamed at them.

The emerald inferno slowly burned down. The flames lost

their green color and diminished until only natural flames remained. The fires crackled and hissed, sending storms of sparks skyward. The men in the courtyard stared upward, but there were no further signs of the beast, only darkness and the distant sound of crickets.

Chapter 6

The Contest

I can assure you, Your Royal Majesty," Arista said in her most congenial voice, "there will be no change in foreign or domestic policy under King Alric's reign. He will continue to pursue the same agenda as our father—upholding the dignity and honor of the House of Essendon. Melengar will continue to remain your friendly neighbor to the west."

Arista stood before the King of Dunmore in her mother's best dress—the stunning silver silk gown. Forty buttons lined the sleeves. Dozens of feet of crushed velvet trimmed the embroidered bodice and full skirt. The rounded neckline clung to her shoulders. She stood erect, chin high, eyes forward, hands folded.

King Roswort, who sat on his throne wearing furs that looked to have come from wolves, drained his cup and belched. He was short and immensely fat. His round pudgy face sagged under its own weight, gathering at the bottom and forming three full chins. His eyes were half closed, his lips were wet, and she was certain she could see a bit of spittle dribbling down through the folds of his neck. His wife, Freda, sat beside him. She, too, was large, but thin by comparison. Whereas the king seeped liquid, she was dry as a desert—in both looks and manner.

The throne room was small with a wooden floor and beams that supported a lofty cathedral ceiling. Protruding from the walls were heads of stags and moose, each covered in enough dust to make its fur look gray. Near the door stood the famous nine-foot stuffed bear named Oswald, its claws up, mouth open, snarling. Dunmore legend held that Oswald killed five knights and an unknown number of peasants before King Ogden—King Roswort's grandfather—slew him with nothing more than a dagger. That had been seventy years earlier, when Glamrendor was just a frontier fort, and Dunmore little more than a forest with trails. Roswort himself could not claim such glory. He had abandoned the hunting traditions of his sires in favor of courtly life, and it showed.

The king held up his cup and shook it.

Arista waited and the king yawned. Somewhere behind her, loud heels crossed the throne room. There was a muttering, then the heels again, followed by the snapping of fingers. Finally, a figure approached the dais, thin and delicate—an elf. He was dressed in a rough woolen uniform of dull brown. Around his neck was a heavy iron collar that was riveted in place. He approached with a pitcher and filled the king's cup, then backed away. The king drank, tipping the cup too high, wine dribbling down, leaving a faint pink line and a droplet dangling from his stubbly whiskers. He belched again, this time more loudly, and sighed with contentment. The king looked back at Arista.

"But what about this matter of Braga's death?" Roswort asked. "Do you have evidence to show that he was involved in this so-called conspiracy?"

"He tried to kill me."

"Yes, so you say, but even if he did, he had good reason, it seems. Braga was a good and devout Nyphron and you are—after all—a witch."

Arista squeezed her hands together. It was not for the first time and her fingers were starting to ache. "Forgive me, Your Royal Majesty, but I fear you may be misinformed on that subject."

"Misinformed? I have—" He coughed, coughed again, then spat on the floor beside the throne. Freda glared rigidly at the elf until he stepped over and wiped it up with the bottom of his tunic.

"I have very good information gatherers," the king went on, "who tell me both Braga and Bishop Saldur brought you to trial to answer charges of witchcraft and the murder of your father. Immediately afterwards Braga was dead, decapitated, and accused of the very charges he leveled against you. Now you come before us as Ambassador of Melengar—a woman. I fear this is all too convenient for my tastes."

"Braga also accused me of killing His Royal Majesty King Alric, who appointed me to this office, or do you also deny his existence?"

The royal eyebrows rose. "You are young," he said coldly. "This is your first audience as ambassador. I'll ignore your affront—this time. Insult me again, and I'll have you expelled from my kingdom."

Arista bowed her head silently.

"It does not bode well with us that the throne of Melengar was taken by blood. Nor that House Essendon pays only lip service to the church. Also, your kingdom's tolerance for elves is disgusting. You let the vile beasts run free. Novron never meant for this to be. The church teaches us that the elf is a disease. They must be broken into service or vanquished altogether. They are like rats and Melengar is the woodpile next door. Yes, I have no doubt that Alric will continue his father's policies. Both were born with blinders. Changes are coming and I can already see that Melengar is too foolish to bend with the wind. All the better for Dunmore, I think."

Arista opened her mouth, but the king held up a finger.

"This interview is over. Go back to your brother and tell him we fulfilled the favor of seeing you and were not impressed."

The king and queen stood together and walked out through the rear archway, leaving Arista facing two empty wooden chairs. The elf, which stood nearby, watched her intently but said nothing. She half considered going on with the rest of her prepared speech. The level of futility would remain; empty thrones could not be any less responsive and most certainly would be more polite.

She sighed. Her shoulders drooped. *Could it have gone any worse?* She turned and walked out, listening to her beautiful dress rustling.

She stepped outside the castle gate and looked down at the city. Deep baked ruts scarred the uneven dirt roads, so rough and littered with rocks they appeared as dry riverbeds. Sun bleached the tight rows of similarly framed wooden buildings to a pale gray. Most of the residents wore drab colors, clothes made of undyed wool or linen. Dozens of people with weary faces sat on corners or wandered about aimlessly with hands out. They appeared invisible to those walking by. It was Arista's first visit to Glamrendor, the capital of Dunmore. She shook her head and muttered softly, "We have seen you too."

Despite the meager offerings, the city was bustling, but she suspected few of those rushing by were locals. It was easy to tell the difference. Those from out of town wore shoes. Wagons, carriages, coaches, and horses flowed through the center of the capital that morning, all heading east. The church had opened the contest to all comers, common and noble alike. It was their shot at glory, wealth, and fame.

Her own coach waited, flying the Melengar falcon, and Hilfred stood holding the door. Bernice sat inside with a tray of sweets on her lap and a smile on her lips. "How did it go, my dear? Were you impressive?"

"No, I wasn't impressive, but we are also not at war, so I should thank Maribor for that kindness." She sat opposite Bernice, making certain to pull the full length of her gown inside the door before Hilfred closed it.

"Have a gingerbread man?" Bernice asked, holding up the tray with a look of pity that included pushing out her lower lip. "He is bound to steal the pain away."

"Where is Sauly?" she asked, eyeing the man-shaped cookies.

"He said he had some things to speak to the archbishop about and would ride in His Grace's coach. He hoped you did not mind."

Arista did not mind and only wished Bernice had joined him. She was tired of the constant company and missed the solitude of her tower. She took a cookie and felt the carriage rock as Hilfred climbed up with the driver. The coach lurched and they were off, bouncing over the rutted road.

"These are stale," Arista said with a mouthful of gingerbread that was hard and sandy.

Bernice looked horrified. "I'm so sorry."

"Where did you get them?"

"A little bakery up—" She started to point out the window, but the movement of the carriage confused her. She looked around, then gave up and put her hand down again. "Oh, I don't know now, but it was a very nice shop and I thought you might need—you know—something to help you feel better after the meeting."

"*Need* them?"

Bernice nodded her head with a forced smile, and reaching out, she patted the princess's hand and said, "It's not your fault, dear. It really isn't fair of His Majesty to put you in this position."

"I should stay in Medford and receive suitors," Arista guessed.

"Exactly. This just isn't right."

"Neither is this cookie." She placed the gingerbread man back on the tray minus the leg she had bitten off. She then sat raking her tongue with her upper teeth like a cat with hair in its mouth.

"At least His Royal Majesty must have been impressed by how you looked," Bernice said, eyeing her with pride. "You're beautiful."

Arista gave her a sidelong glance. "The dress is beautiful."

"Of course it is, but—"

"Oh dear Maribor!" Arista cut her off as she glanced out the window. "How many are there now? It will be like traveling with an army."

As the carriage reached the end of town, she saw the masses. There could be as many as three hundred men standing behind the banners of the Nyphron Church. They all waited in a single line, but they could not have been more different—the muscular, scrawny, tall, and short. All ranks were represented: knights, soldiers, nobles, and peasants. Some wore armor, some silk, others linen or wool. They sat on chargers, draft horses, ponies, mules, or inside coaches, open-air carriages, wagons, and buckboards. They appeared a strange and unlikely assortment, but each bore the same smile of expectation and excitement, all eyes looking east.

Arista's first official session as ambassador was finished. As bad as it had been, it was over. With Sauly gone, she could shelve thoughts of church and state, guilt and blame. Stress that had smothered her for days evaporated and at last she was able to feel the growing excitement that bubbled all around her.

From everywhere people rushed to join the growing train.

Some arrived with nothing but a small linen bag tucked under one arm, while others led their own personal train of packhorses.

There were those who commanded multiple wagons loaded with tents, food, and clothes. One well-dressed merchant carried velvet upholstered chairs and a canopy bed on top of a wagon.

A loud banging hammered the roof of the coach, shocking both of them. Gingerbread men flew. "Oh dear!" Bernice gasped. A moment later Mauvin Pickering's head appeared in the window, looking down and inside from the back of his horse so that his dark hair hung wildly.

"So how did it go?" He grinned mischievously. "Do I need to prepare for war?"

Arista scowled.

"That good, huh?" Mauvin went on, heedless of the commotion he had caused. "We'll talk later. I have to find Fanen before he starts dueling someone. Hiya, Hilfred. This is going to be great. When was the last time we were all camping together? See ya."

Bernice was fanning herself with both hands, staring up at the roof of the coach, her mouth slack. Seeing her and the little army of gingerbread men scattered on the benches, in the curtains, on the floor, and in her lap, Arista could not help smiling.

"You were right, Bernice. The cookies did cheer me up."

"See him?" Fanen pointed to the man in the brown suede doublet. "That's Sir Enden, possibly the greatest living knight after Sir Breckton."

After another day's travel that left her drowsy, Arista was

at the Pickerings' camp, hiding from Bernice. The two boys shared an elegant single-peak tent of alternating gold and green stripes, which they had pitched at the eastern edge of the main camp. The three sat out front under the scallop-edged canopy held up by two tall wooden poles. On the left flew the gold falcon on the red field of the House of Essendon, on the right the gold sword on the green field of the House of Pickering. It was a modest camp compared to most of the nobles'. Some looked like small castles and took hours for a team of servants to erect. The Pickerings traveled lightly, carrying everything they needed on their stallions and two packhorses. They did not have tables or chairs and Arista sprawled in a modest gown on a sheet of canvas. If Bernice saw, the old woman would have a heart attack.

Arista did not mind. She thought it was wonderful to lie back and stretch out under the sky. It reminded her of Summersrule when they were kids. At night the adults would dance and the children would lie on the south hill at the Pickerings' home of Drondil Fields, counting the falling stars and fireflies. It had been all of them then—Mauvin, Fanen, Alric, even Lenare—back before the boys' sister became too much of a lady. She remembered the feel of the cool night breeze rushing over her, the sensation of grass on her bare feet, the vast spray of stars above, and the faint melody of the band as it played "Calide Portmorc," the Galilin folk song.

"And there, see the large man in the green tunic? That's Sir Gravin; he's a quester. He does most of his work for the Church of Nyphron. You know—recovering artifacts, slaying monsters, those kinds of things. He's known to be one of the greatest adventurers alive. He's from Vernes; that's all the way down near Delgos."

"I know where Vernes is, Fanen," Arista replied.

"That's right, you have to know all that stuff now, don't you?" Mauvin said. "Your High Exulted Ambassadorship." The elder Pickering offered an elaborate seated bow.

"Laugh now—just you wait," she told him. "You'll get yours—one day you'll be marquis. Then it won't be all fun and games. You'll have responsibilities, mister."

"I won't," Fanen said sadly.

If not for his being three years younger, Fanen could be Mauvin's twin. Both had the dashing Pickering features: sharp angled faces, dark thick hair, bright white teeth, and sweeping shoulders that tapered to narrow, athletic waists. Fanen was just leaner and a bit shorter, and unlike Mauvin, whose hair was always a frightful mess, Fanen kept his neatly combed.

"That's why you need to win this thing," Mauvin told his brother. "And, of course, you will, because you're a Pickering, and Pickerings never fail. Look at that guy over there. He doesn't stand a chance."

Arista did not bother sitting up. He had been doing this all night—pointing out people and explaining how he could tell by the way they walked or wore their swords that Fanen could best them. She had no doubt he was right; she was just tired of hearing it.

"What is the prize for this contest?" she asked.

"They haven't said yet," Fanen muttered.

"Gold, most likely," Mauvin replied, "in the form of some award, but that's not what makes it valuable. It's the prestige. Once Fanen takes this trophy, he will have a name; well, he already has the Pickering name, but he hasn't any titles yet. Once he does, opportunities will open up for him. Of course, it could be land. Then he'd be set."

"I hope so; I certainly don't want to end up at a monastery."

"Do you still write poetry, Fanen?" Arista asked.

"I haven't—in a while."

"It was good—what I remember, at least. You used to write all the time. What happened?"

"He learned the poetry of the sword. It will serve him far better than the pen," Mauvin answered for him.

"Who's that?" Fanen asked, pointing to the west.

"That's Rentinual," Mauvin replied, "the self-proclaimed genius. Get this. He's brought this thing, a huge contraption, with him."

"Why?"

"He says it's for the contest."

"What is it?"

Mauvin shrugged. "Don't know, but it's big. He keeps it covered under a tarp and wails like a girl whenever the wagon team bounces it through a rut."

"Say, isn't that Prince Rudolf?"

"Where?" Arista popped her head up, moving to her elbows.

Mauvin chuckled. "Just kidding. Alric told us about… your misunderstanding."

"Have you met Rudolf?" she asked.

"Actually, I have," Mauvin said. "The man has donkeys wondering why they got stuck with him as a namesake." It took a second, then Fanen and Arista broke into laughter, dragging Mauvin with them. "He's a royal git, that's certain, and I'd have been plenty upset if I thought I was facing a life kissing that ass. Honestly, Arista, I'm surprised you didn't turn Alric into a toad or something."

Arista stopped laughing. "What?"

"You know, put a hex on him. A week as a frog would—what's wrong?"

"Nothing," she said, lying back down and turning onto her stomach.

"Hey—look—I didn't mean anything."

"It's okay," she lied.

"It was just a joke."

"Your first joke was better."

"Arista, I know you're not a witch."

A long uncomfortable silence followed.

"I'm sorry," Mauvin offered.

"Took you long enough," she said.

"It could have been worse." Fanen spoke up. "Alric could have forced you to marry Mauvin."

"That's really sick," Arista said, rolling over and sitting up. Mauvin looked at her with hurt, surprised eyes. She shook her head. "I just meant it would be like marrying a brother. I've always thought of you all as family."

"Don't tell Denek," Mauvin replied. "He's had a crush on you for years."

"Seriously?"

"Oh, and don't tell him I told you either. Uh—better yet, just forget I said that."

"What about those two?" Fanen asked abruptly, pointing toward a massive red and black striped tent from which two men had just exited. One was huge, with a wild red mustache and beard. He wore a sleeveless scarlet tunic with a green draped sash and a metal cap with several dents in it. The other man was tall and thin, with long black hair and a short trimmed beard. He was dressed in a red cassock and black cape with the symbol of a broken crown on his chest.

"I don't think you want to mess with either of them," Mauvin finally said. "That's Lord Rufus of Trent, Warlord of Lingard, a clan leader and veteran of dozens of battles against the wild men of Estrendor, not to mention being the hero of the battle of Vilan Hills."

"That's Rufus?" Fanen muttered.

"I've heard he's got the temperament of a shrew and the arm of a bear."

"Who's the other guy, the one with the broken crown standard?" Fanen asked, pointing at the other man.

"That, my dear brother, is a sentinel, and let's just hope this is the closest either of us ever get to one."

While Arista was watching the two men, she saw a silhouette appear against the light of the distant campfire—very short, with a long beard and puffy sleeves.

"By the way, I want to start early tomorrow, Fanen," his brother said. "I want to get out ahead of the train. I'm tired of eating dust."

"Anyone know exactly where we are going?" Fanen asked. "It feels like we are traveling to the end of the world."

Arista nodded. "I heard Sauly talking about it with the archbishop. I think it is a little village called Dahlgren."

She looked back, trying to find the figure once more, but it was gone.

Chapter 7

Of Elves and Men

Thrace lay on the margrave's bed in the manor house, her head carefully wrapped in strips of cloth. Her hair was bunched and snarled, blond strands slipping out between the bandages. Purple and yellow bruises swelled around her eyes and nose. Her upper lip puffed up to twice its size and a line of dark dried blood ran its length. Thrace coughed and mumbled but never spoke, never opened her eyes.

And Theron never left her side.

Esrahaddon ordered Lena to boil feverfew leaves in a big pot of apple cider vinegar. She did as he instructed. Everyone did now. After the previous night, the residents of Dahlgren treated the cripple with newfound respect and looked at him with awe and a bit of fear. It was Tad Bothwick and Rosc McDern who had seen him raise the green fire that had chased away the beast. No one said the word *witch* or *wizard*. No one had to. Soon the steam from the pot filled the room with a pungent flowery odor.

"I'm so sorry," Theron whispered to his daughter.

The coughing and mumbling had stopped and she lay still as death. He held her limp hand to his cheek, unsure if she could hear him. He had been saying that for hours, begging her to wake up. "I didn't mean it. I was just so angry. I'm sorry. Don't leave. Please come back to me."

He could still hear the sound in the dark of his daughter's cry, cut horribly short by a muffled crack. If it had been a tree trunk or a thicker branch, Theron guessed, she would have died instantly. As it was, she still might die.

No one but Lena and Esrahaddon dared enter the room that Theron filled with his grief. They all expected the worst. Blood had covered the girl's face and her father's shirt by the time they arrived at the manor. Skin white, lips an odd bluish hue, Thrace had not moved nor opened her eyes. Esrahaddon had whispered to her and instructed them to take the girl to the manor and keep her warm. It was the kind of thing one did for the dying, making them as comfortable as possible. Deacon Tomas had prayed for her and remained on hand to bless her departing soul.

In the past year, the village of Dahlgren had seen many deaths. Not all were by the beast. There were the normal accidents and sicknesses, and in the winter, wolves hunted the area. There were also some unexplained disappearances. Often attributed to the beast, they could just as likely have been the result of getting lost in the forest or accidentally falling in the Nidwalden. In no more than a year, over half the village's population had perished or gone missing. Everyone knew someone who had died, and nearly every family had lost at least one member. The people of Dahlgren had grown accustomed to death. He was a nightly visitor, a guest at every breakfast table. They knew his face, the sound of his voice, the way he walked, his peculiar habits. He was always there. If it were not for the mess he left, they might neglect to notice him altogether. No one expected Thrace to survive.

The sun came up, casting a dull light into the room where Theron wept for his daughter. The last of his family was leaving him. Only now he realized how much she meant to him. Thoughts came, uninvited, to his mind. Time and time again, it had been she who had always come for him. He remembered the night the beast attacked his farm, when he was coming home late. Only she had braved the darkness to search for him. It was Thrace, a young girl, little more than a child, who had traveled alone halfway across Avryn and spent her life savings to bring him help. Then, the previous night, when his stubbornness had kept him at the farm, she had come to him in the darkness, running alone through the forest, ignoring the dangers. There had been only one thought in her mind—to save him. She had succeeded. She had deprived the beast of his flesh, but more than that, she had pulled him back into the world of the living. She had ripped the black veil away from his eyes and freed his heart from the weight of guilt, but the price had been her life.

Tears ran down his cheeks. They hung on his upper lip. He kissed his daughter's hand, leaving a wet spot, an offering, an apology.

How could I have been so blind?

The even, constant breaths his daughter took slowed with each inhale, less frequent, shorter than the one before. He listened to their descent, like the sound of footsteps receding, walking away, growing fainter, quieter.

He clutched her hand, kissing it repeatedly and rubbing it to his wet cheek. It felt like his heart was being ripped out through his chest.

At last, the regular pace of her breathing stopped.

Theron sobbed. "Oh, god."

"Daddy?" He jerked his head up. His daughter's eyes were open. She was looking at him. "Are you all right?" she whispered.

His mouth opened but he could not speak. His tears continued to flow, and like a barren bit of land seeing water for the first time in years, a smile of joy grew on his face.

৵

Swift clouds moved across a capricious sky as growing winds and the portents of a coming storm marked the new day. Royce sat on the rock ledge where the cliff met the river and the spray of the falls dampened the stone. His feet and legs were soaked from a morning spent trekking through the damp forest underbrush. His eyes stared out across the ridgeline of the falls at the promontory rock and the towering citadel that sat tantalizingly upon it. He thought that perhaps there might be a tunnel running under the river. He looked for an access in the trees but found nothing. He was getting nowhere.

After almost two days, he was no closer to his goal. The tower still lay out of reach. Unless he could learn to swim the current, walk on water, or fly, he had no chance of traversing the gulf that lay between.

"They're over there right now, you know," Esrahaddon said.

Royce had forgotten about the wizard. He had arrived some time earlier, mentioning only that Thrace had survived, was awake, and looked to make a full recovery. After that, he took a seat on a rock and spent the next hour or so staring across the river much as Royce had done all day.

"Who?"

"The elves. They're on their side of the river looking back at us. They can see us, I suspect, even at this range. They are surprising like that. Most humans consider them inferior—lazy, filthy, uneducated creatures—but the fact is they are superior to humans in nearly every way. I suppose that's why humans are so quick to denounce them; they are unwilling to concede that they may be second best.

"Elves are truly remarkable. Just look at that tower. It's fluid and seamless, as if growing right out of the rock. How elegant. How perfect. It fits into the landscape like a thing of nature, a natural wonder, only it isn't. They created it using skills and techniques that our best masons couldn't begin to understand. Just imagine how glorious their cities must be! What wonders those forests across the river must hold."

"So you have never crossed the river?" Royce asked.

"No man ever has, and no man is ever likely to. The moment a man touches that far shore, he will fall dead. The thread by which the fate of man hangs is a thin one indeed."

"How's that?"

Esrahaddon only smiled. "Did you know that no human army ever won a battle against the elves before the arrival of Novron? At that time, elves were our demons. The Great Library of Percepliquis had reams on it. Once we even thought they were gods. Their life span is so long that no one noticed them aging. Their death rites are so secret no human has ever seen an elven corpse.

"They were the firstborn, the Children of Ferrol, great and powerful. In combat, they were feared above all things. Sickness could be treated. Bears and wolves could be hunted and trapped. Storms and droughts prepared for. But nothing, nothing could stand before the elves. Their blades broke ours, their arrows pierced our armor, their shields were impenetrable, and, of course, they knew the Art. Imagine a sky darkened with a host of Gilarabrywn. And they are only one of their weapons. Even without all that, without the Art, their speed, eyesight, hearing, balance, and ancient skills are all beyond the abilities of man."

"If that's true, how come they're over there and we're sitting here?"

"It is all because of Novron. He showed us their weaknesses. He taught mankind how to fight, how to defend, and he taught us the art of magic. Without it we were naked and helpless against them."

"I still don't see how we won," Royce challenged. "Even with that knowledge, they still seem to have the advantage."

"True, and in an even fight we would have lost, but it wasn't even. You see, elves live for a very long time. I don't think any human actually knows how long, but they live for many centuries at least. There may be elves right now watching us that remember what Novron looked like. But no people can live that long and reproduce quickly. Elves have few children and a birth for them is quite significant. Birth and death in the elven world are rare and holy things.

"Imagine the devastation and misery it must have been for them during the wars. No matter how many battles they won against us, each time their numbers were fewer than before. While we humans recovered our losses in a generation, it would take a millennium for the elves. They were consumed—drowned, if you will—in a flooding sea of humanity." Esrahaddon paused, then added, "Only now Novron is gone. There will be no savior this time."

"This time?"

"What do you think keeps them over there? These are their lands. To us it seems eons ago, but to them it is just yesterday when they walked this side of the river. By now, their numbers have likely recovered."

"What keeps them on that side of the river, then?"

"What keeps anyone from what they want? Fear. Fear of annihilation, fear that we would destroy them utterly, but Novron is dead."

"You mentioned that," Royce pointed out.

"I told you before that mankind has squandered the legacy of Novron, and it has done so at its own peril. Novron brought magic to man, but Novron is gone, and the magic forgotten. We sit here like children, naked and unarmed. Mankind is inviting the wrath of a race so far beyond us they won't even hear our cries. The elves' ignorance of our weakness and this fragile agreement between the Erivan Empire and a dead emperor is all that remains of humanity's defense."

"It's a good thing they don't know, then."

"That's just it," the wizard told him. "They are learning."

"The Gilarabrywn?"

Esrahaddon nodded. "According to Novron's decree, the banks of the river Nidwalden are *ryin contita*."

"Off limits to everyone," Royce roughly translated, garnering a faint smile from the wizard. "I can read and write too."

"Ah, a truly educated man. So as I was saying, the banks of the river Nidwalden are *ryin contita*."

A look of realization washed over the thief's face. "Dahlgren is in violation of the treaty."

"Exactly. The decree also stipulates that elves are forbidden to take human lives, except should they cross the river. It says nothing about humans killed through benign actions. If I release a boulder, it could roll anywhere, but odds are it will roll downhill. If houses and people are downhill, it may destroy them, but it isn't me that's killing them; it is the boulder and the unfortunate fact they live downhill from it."

"And they are watching what we do, how we deal with it. They are sizing up our strengths and weaknesses. Much like you are doing with me."

Esrahaddon smiled. "Perhaps," he said. "There is no way to be certain if they are responsible for the beast's presence, but one thing is certain: they are watching. When they see we are helpless against one Gilarabrywn, if they feel the treaty is broken, or when it runs out, fear will no longer be a deterrent."

"Is that why you are really here?"

"No." The wizard shook his head. "It plays a part, but the war between the elves and man will come despite any action I can take. I am merely trying to lessen the blow and give humanity a fighting chance."

"You might begin by teaching some others to do what you did last night."

The wizard looked at the thief. "What do you mean?"

"Coy doesn't suit you," Royce told him.

"No, I suppose not."

"I thought you couldn't do your art without your hands?"

"It is very hard and takes a great deal of time and it isn't very accurate. Imagine trying to write your name with your toes. I began working on that spell before you arrived here, thinking it would come in handy at some point. As it was, the flame wall nearly consumed you two. It was supposed to be several yards farther away, and last for hours instead of minutes. With hands I could have..." He trailed off. "No sense going there, I suppose."

"Were you really that powerful before?"

Esrahaddon showed him a wicked smile. "Oh, my dear boy, you couldn't begin to imagine."

◆

Word of Thrace's recovery quickly spread through the village. She was still a little groggy, but remarkably sound. She could see clearly, all her teeth were in her head, and she had an appetite. By midmorning, she was sitting up, eating soup. That day there was a decidedly different look in the villagers' eyes. The unspoken thought in every mind was the same—the beast had attacked and no one had died.

Most had seen the winged beast outlined in the brilliant green flames that night. Alongside each of them that morning walked a strange companion, a long-lost friend who had returned unexpectedly—hope.

They got busy at dawn preparing more wood fires. They had a system down now and were able to build up the piles with just a few hours' work. Suspecting that the beast—obviously able to see well in the dark—might not be able to see through thick smoke, Vince Griffin suggested they use smudge pots. For centuries, farmers had used smudge pots to drive off insects that threatened to devour their crops, and Dahlgren was no different. Old pots were promptly gathered and filled as if a cloud of locusts was on its way. At the same time, Hadrian, Tad Bothwick, and Kline Goodman began surveying the outbuildings of the lower bailey for the best shelters.

Hadrian busied himself organizing small groups of men. One group started to expand the cellar they had found in the smokehouse, and another went to work digging a tunnel with the idea of trying to capture the beast. A huge serpent chasing a man might follow him into a tunnel, but if the tunnel gradually narrowed, they might be able to seal the exits before it realized its mistake. No weapon made by man might be able to slay it, but Hadrian guessed there were no restrictions on imprisoning the beast.

Deacon Tomas was far from delighted with all the digging, cutting, and burning inside the castle grounds, but already it was clear that the villagers had found a new leader in Hadrian. Tomas remained quietly indoors caring for Thrace.

"Hadrian?"

He was washing at the well in the village, where he could find some privacy, when he looked up to see Theron.

"Been doing some digging, I see," the farmer said. "Dillon mentioned you had them making a tunnel. Pretty smart thinking."

"The odds of it working are slim," Hadrian explained, dousing his face with handfuls of water. "But at least it's a shot."

"Listen," the farmer began with a pained look on his face, and then said nothing.

"Thrace is doing well?" Hadrian asked after a minute or so.

"She's great, as solid as her old man," he said proudly, thumping his own chest. "It'll take more than a tree to break her. That's the thing about us Woods. We might not look like it, but we're a strong lot. It might take us a while, but we come back, and when we do, we're stronger than ever. Thing is, we need something—you know—a reason. I didn't have one—at least, I didn't think I did. Thrace showed me different."

They stood facing each other in an awkward silence.

"Listen," Theron said again, and once more paused. "I'm not used to being beholden to anyone, you see. I've always paid my own way. I got what I have by work and lots of it. I don't ask anyone's help and I don't apologize for the way I am, see?"

Hadrian nodded.

"But—well, a lot of what you said yesterday was true. Only today, some things are different—you follow? Thrace and me, we're gonna be leaving this place just as soon as she's able. I'm figuring a couple of days' rest and she'll be okay to travel. We'll head south, maybe to Alburn or even Calis; I hear it stays warm longer there, better growing season. Anyway, that still leaves a few nights we'll be here. A few more nights we'll have to live under this shadow. I'm not gonna lose my little girl the way I lost the others. Now, I know an old farmer like me ain't much good to her swinging a scythe or a pitch-fork against that thing, but if it comes to that, it would be good if I knew how to fight proper. That way if it comes calling before we leave, at least there will be a chance. Now, I haven't got much, but I do have some silver set aside and I was wondering if your offer to teach me how to fight was still good."

"First, we need to get something straight," Hadrian told him sternly. "Your daughter already paid us in full to do whatever we could to help you, so you keep your silver for the trip south or I won't teach you a thing. Agreed?"

Theron hesitated, then nodded.

"Good. Well, I suppose we can begin right now if you're ready."

"Should we get your swords?" Theron asked.

"That would be a problem, considering I put my swords on Millie last night and no one has seen her since, but that shouldn't matter for now."

"Should I cut sticks, then?" the farmer asked.

"No."

"What, then?"

"How about sitting down and just listening? There's a lot to learn before you're ready to swing at anything."

Theron looked at Hadrian skeptically.

"You want me to teach you, right? If I said I wanted you to teach me to be a great farmer in a few hours, what would you say?"

Theron nodded in submission and sat down on the dirt not far from where Hadrian had first met Pearl. Hadrian slipped his shirt on, took a bucket, turned it over, and sat down in front of him.

"As with everything, fighting takes practice. Anything can look easy if you're watching someone who's mastered whatever it is they are doing, but what you don't see is the hours and years of effort that go into perfecting their craft. I am sure you can plow a field in a fraction of the time it would take me for this very reason. Sword fighting is no different. Practice will allow you to react without thought to events, and even to anticipate those events. It becomes a form of foresight, the ability to look into the future and know exactly what your opponent will do even before he does. Without practice, you'll need to think too much. When fighting a more skilled opponent, even a split second of hesitation can get you killed."

"My opponent is a giant snake with wings," Theron said.

"And it has killed more than a score of men. Most certainly a more skilled opponent, wouldn't you say? So practice is paramount. The question is, what do you need to practice?"

"Swinging a sword, I should think."

"True, but that's only a small part of it. If it were merely swinging a sword, everyone with two legs and at least one arm would be experts. No, there is much more to it. First, there is concentration, and that means more than just paying attention to the fight. It means not worrying about Thrace or thinking about your family, the past, or the future. It means focusing on what you are doing beyond all else. It might sound easy, but it isn't. Next comes breathing."

"Breathing?" Theron asked dubiously.

"Yeah, I know we breathe all the time, but sometimes we stop breathing or stop breathing correctly. Ever get startled and discover you were holding your breath? Ever find yourself panting when you're really nervous or frightened? Some people can actually pass out that way. Trust me, in a real fight, you'll be scared, and unless you train, you'll end up breathing shallow or not at all. Less air saps your body of strength and makes it hard to think clearly. You'll become tired and slow, something you can't afford in a battle."

"So how do you breathe correctly?" Theron asked, still with a hint of sarcasm.

"You have to breathe deep and slow even before you need

to, before your exertion demands it. At first, it will be a conscious thought and it will feel counterproductive, even distracting. But over time, it will become second nature. It is also good to keep in mind that you have the most strength for a blow on an exhale. It adds power and focus to a stroke. Sometimes actually yelling or shouting helps. I'll want you to do that during your training. I want to hear it when you swing. Later on, it won't be necessary, although sometimes it can help to startle your opponent." Hadrian paused briefly and Theron noted the faint hint of a smile tug at his lips.

"Next comes balance, and that means more than not falling down. Sadly, humans only have two feet. That's only two points to support us. Pick up one and you are vulnerable. This is why you want to keep your feet on the ground. That doesn't mean you don't move, but when you move, you slide your feet rather than pick them up. You need to keep your weight forward, your knees slightly bent, and your balance on the balls of your feet rather than in your heels. Drawing your feet together reduces your two points of balance to one, so keep your feet apart, about shoulder width.

"Timing is, of course, very important. I warn you now, you'll be terrible at it to begin with, as timing improves with experience. You saw from swinging at me yesterday how frustrating it can be to swing and miss. Timing is what allows you to hit, and not only to hit, but also to do damage. You'll learn to see patterns in movement. You'll know when to expect an opening, or a weakness. Frequently you can anticipate an attack by watching how your opponent moves—the placement of his feet, the look in his eyes, a telltale drop of his shoulder, the tightening of a muscle."

"But I'm not fighting a person," Theron interrupted. "And I don't even think it has a shoulder."

"Even animals give signs about what they will do. They

hunch up, twist and shift their weight, just like people. Such signals do not have to be obvious. Most skilled fighters will try to mask their intentions or, worse, purposely try to mislead you. They want to confuse your timing, throw you off balance, and make an opening for themselves. Of course, this is exactly what you want to do to them. If done well, your opponent sees the false move, but not the attack. The result—in your case—is a headless flying serpent.

"The last thing to learn is the hardest. It can't be taught. It can barely be explained. It is the idea that the fight—the battle—doesn't really exist so much in your hands or your feet, but in your head. The real struggle is in your own mind. You must know you are going to win before you start the fight. You have to see it, smell it, and believe it utterly. It is a form of confidence, but you must guard against overconfidence. You have to be flexible—able to adapt in an instant and never allow yourself to give up. Without this, nothing else is possible. Unless you believe you'll win, fear and hesitation will hold you down while your opponent kills you. Now, let's get a couple of stout sticks and we will see how well you listened."

~

That night they lit the bonfires once more and everyone stayed sheltered in either the manor house or the cellar of the smokehouse. Royce and Hadrian were the only two moving outside and even they remained in the shelter of the smokehouse doorway, watching the night by bonfire light.

"How's Thrace doing?" Royce asked, his eyes on the sky.

"Great considering the fact that she broke a tree branch with her head," Hadrian replied as he sat on a barrel, cleaning a mutton bone of the last of its meat. "I even heard she was walking around asking to help with dinner." He shook his head and smiled. "That girl, she's something, that's for sure. Hard to imagine it seeing her under that arch in Colnora, but she's tough. The real change is in the old man. Theron says they plan on leaving in a day or two, as soon as Thrace can travel."

"So we're out of a job?" Royce feigned disappointment.

"Why, were you getting close?" Hadrian asked, throwing the bone away and wiping his hands on his vest.

"Nope. I can't figure out how to reach it."

"Tunnel?"

"I thought of that, but I've been over every inch of the forest and the rocks and there's nothing; no cave, no sunken dell, nothing that could be confused with a tunnel. I'm completely stumped on this."

"What about Esra? Doesn't the wizard have any ideas?"

"Maybe, but he's being elusive. He's hiding something. He wants access to that tower but won't say why and avoids direct questions about it. Something happened to him here years ago. Something he doesn't want to talk about. But maybe I can get him to open up more tomorrow if I let him know the Woods no longer require our services and that there is no reason for me to try anymore."

"Don't you think he'll see through that?"

"See through what?" Royce asked. "Honestly, I'm giving it one more try tomorrow and if I can't find something, I say we head out with Theron and Thrace."

Hadrian was silent.

"What?" Royce asked.

"I just hate to run out on them like that. I mean, they're starting to turn it around now."

"You do this all the time. You get these lost causes under your skin—"

"I'd like to remind you, coming here was your idea. I was in the process of declining the job, remember?"

"Well, a lot can happen in a day; maybe I'll find a way in tomorrow."

Hadrian stepped to the doorway and peered out. "The forest is loud. Looks like our friend isn't coming to visit us tonight. Maybe Esrahaddon's flames singed its wings and it's dining on venison this evening."

"The fires won't keep it away forever," Royce said. "According to the wizard, the fires didn't hurt it; they just confused it—bright lights do that, apparently. Only the sword in the tower can actually harm it. It will be back."

"Then we'd best take advantage of its absence and get a good night's sleep."

Hadrian went down into the cellar, leaving Royce staring out at the night sky and the gathering clouds that crossed the stars. The wind was still up, whipping the trees and battering the fires. He could almost smell it: change was in the air and it was blowing their way.

Chapter 8

Myths and Legends

Royce stood on the bank of the river in the early morning light, trying to skip stones out toward the tower. None of them made more than a single jump before the turbulent water consumed them. His most recent idea for reaching the tower centered on building a small boat and launching himself upriver in the hopes of landing on the rocky parapet before the massive current washed him over the falls. Although there was no clear landing ground for such an attempt, it might be possible if he caught the current just right and landed against the rock. The force of the water would likely smash the boat or drive it under when it met the wall, but he might be able to scramble onto the precipice before going over. The problem was even if he managed to perform this harrowing feat, there was no way back.

He turned to see the wizard walking up the river trail. Perhaps to keep an eye on him but more likely to be on hand should he discover the entrance.

"Morning," the wizard said. "Any epiphanies today?"

"Just one. There is no way to reach that tower."

Esrahaddon looked disappointed.

"I have exhausted all the possibilities I can think of.

Besides, Theron and Thrace are going to be leaving Dahlgren. I no longer have a reason to bang my head against this tower."

"I see," Esrahaddon said, staring down at him. "What about the welfare of the village?"

"Hardly my problem. This village shouldn't even be here, remember? It's a violation of the treaty. It would be best if all these people left."

"If we allow it to be wiped out, it could be seen as a sign of weakness and invite the elves to invade."

"And allowing the village to survive is breaking the treaty, resulting in the same possibility. Fortunately for me, I am not wearing a crown. I am not the emperor, or a king, so it's not something I need to deal with."

"You're just going to leave?"

"Is there a reason for me to stay?"

The wizard raised an eyebrow and looked long at the thief. "What do you want?" he asked at length.

"Are you proposing to pay me now?"

"We both know I have no money, but still you want something from me. What is it?"

"The truth. What are you after? What happened here nine hundred years ago?"

The wizard studied Royce for a moment and looked down at his feet. After a few minutes, he nodded. He walked over to a beech log that lay across the granite rock, and sat down. He looked out toward the water and the spray as if searching for something in the mist, something that was not there.

"I was the youngest member of the Cenzars. We were the council of wizards that worked directly for the emperor. The greatest wizards the world had ever seen. There was also the Teshlors, comprised of the greatest of the emperor's knights. Tradition dictated that a mentor from each council was to serve as teacher and full-time protector to the emperor's son and heir. Because I was the youngest, it fell to me to be Nevrik's Cenzar instructor, while Jerish Grelad was picked from the Teshlors. Jerish and I didn't get along. Like most of the Teshlors, he held a distrust of wizards, and I thought little of him and his brutish, violent ways.

"Nevrik, however, brought us together. Like his father, the emperor Nareion, Nevrik was a breed apart, and it was an honor to teach him. Jerish and I spent nearly all our time with Nevrik. I taught him lore, books, and the Art, while Jerish instructed him in the schools of combat and warfare. Though I still felt the practice of physical combat was beneath the emperor and his son, it was very clear that Jerish was as devoted to Nevrik as I was. In that middle ground, we found a foothold where we could stand together. When the emperor decided to break tradition and travel here to Avempartha with his son, we went along."

"Break tradition?"

"It had been centuries since an emperor had spoken directly to the elves."

"After the war, there wasn't tribute paid or anything like that?"

"No, all contact was severed at the Nidwalden, so it was a very exciting time. No one really knew what to expect. I personally knew very little about Avempartha beyond the historical account of how it was the site of the last battle of the Great Elven Wars. The emperor met with several top officials of the Erivan Empire in the tower while Jerish and I attempted, without much luck, to continue Nevrik's studies. The sight of the waterfall and the elven architecture was too much to compete with for the attention of a twelve-year-old boy.

"It was around dusk, nearly night. Nevrik had been pointing things out to us all day, reveling in the fact that neither Jerish nor I could identify any of the elven things he found. For example, there were several sets of elven clothes made of a shimmering material that we couldn't name drying in the sun. This was, of course, the first time in centuries that humans had met with elves, placing us at a distinct disadvantage. Nevrik delighted in stumping his teachers, so when he asked about the *thing* he saw flying toward the tower, I thought he saw a bird, or a bat, but he said it was too large and that it looked like a serpent. He mentioned it had flown into one of the high windows of the tower. Nevrik was so adamant about it that we all went back inside. We had just started up the main staircase when we heard the screams.

"It sounded like a war was being fought above us. The personal bodyguards of the emperor—a detachment of Teshlors—were fighting off the Gilarabrywn, protecting the emperor as they fled down the stairs. I saw groups of elves throwing themselves at the creature, dying to protect our emperor."

"The elves were?"

Esrahaddon nodded. "I was amazed by the sight. The whole scene is still so vivid to me even after nearly a thousand years. Still, nothing the knights or the elves could do stopped the attacking beast, which seemed determined to kill the emperor. It was a terrible battle, with knights falling on the stairs and dying upon the wet steps, elves joining them. The emperor ordered us to get Nevrik to safety.

"Jerish grabbed the boy and dragged him out of the tower kicking and screaming, but I hesitated. I realized that once outside, the flying beast would be able to swoop down and kill at will. The Art could not defeat it. The creature was magic and without the key to unlock the spell, nothing I could do would alter that enchantment. A thought came to me, and as the emperor exited the door, I cast an enchantment of binding—not on the beast, but on the tower, trapping the Gilarabrywn inside. Those knights and elves still inside died, but the beast was trapped."

"Where did it come from? What caused the thing to attack?"

Esrahaddon shrugged. "The elves insisted they knew nothing of the attack, and that they had no idea where the Gilarabrywn came from, except that one Gilarabrywn had been left unaccounted for after the wars. They assumed it destroyed. They mentioned a militant society, a growing movement of elves within the Erivan Empire that sought to incite a war. It was speculated they were responsible. The elven lords apologized and assured us they would investigate the matter fully. The emperor, convinced that to retaliate or even make the incident public was unwise, chose to ignore the attack and returned home."

"So what's this about a weapon?"

"The Gilarabrywn is a conjured creature, a powerful magic endowed with a life of its own beyond the existence of its creator. The creature is not truly alive; it cannot reproduce, grow old, or appreciate existence, but it also cannot die. It can, however, be dispelled. No enchantment is perfect; every magic has a seam where the weave can be unraveled. In the case of the Gilarabrywn, the seam is its name. Whenever a Gilarabrywn is created, so is an object—a sword, etched with its name. It is used to control the beast and, if necessary, destroy it. According to the elves, at the end of the war they placed all the Gilarabrywn swords in the tower, per Novron's orders. At that time all the swords were accounted for and all but one was notched to show their associated beast was destroyed."

Royce got up to stretch his legs. "Okay, so the elven lords held one of their monsters back just in case, or this militant group hid one to cause trouble. The elven leaders tell you all the swords are in there. Maybe they are, or maybe they aren't, and they just want—"

"It's in there," Esrahaddon interrupted.

"You saw it?"

"We were given a tour when we first arrived. Near the top is a sort of memorial to the war. All the swords are on display."

"All right, so there is a sword," Royce said, "but that's not why you want in. You didn't come here to save Dahlgren. Why are you really here?"

"You didn't allow me to finish," Esrahaddon replied, sounding every bit like the wise teacher letting his student know to be patient. "The emperor believed he had prevented a war with the elves and returned home, but what waited for him was an execution. While we were away, the church, under the leadership of Patriarch Venlin, planned the emperor's assassination. The attack came on the steps of the palace during a celebration commemorating the anniversary of the empire's founding. Jerish and I escaped with Nevrik. I knew that many of the Cenzars and the Teshlors were involved in the church's plot and that they would find us, so Jerish and I came up with a plan—we hid Nevrik and I created two talismans. One I gave to Nevrik and the other to Jerish. These amulets would hide them from the clairvoyant search the Cenzars were certain to make, but allow me to find them. Then I sent them away."

"And you?" Royce asked.

"I stayed behind. I tried to save the emperor." He paused, looking far away. "I failed."

"So what happened to the heir?" Royce asked.

"How should I know? I was locked up in a prison for nine hundred years. Do you think he wrote me? Jerish was supposed to take him into hiding." The wizard allowed himself a grim smile. "We both thought it would only be for a month or so."

"So you don't even know if an heir exists anymore?"

"I'm pretty confident the church didn't kill him or they would have killed me shortly thereafter, but what became of Jerish and Nevrik I don't know. If anyone could have kept

Nevrik alive, it would have been Jerish. Despite his age, he was one of the best knights the emperor had. The fact that he trusted his son to his care was testament to that. Like all Teshlor knights, Jerish was a master of all the schools of combat; there wouldn't have been a man alive who could beat him in battle, and he would have died before surrendering Nevrik. They would both be dead now, of course—time would have seen to that. So would their great-great-grandchildren if they had any. I suspect Jerish would have known the need to perpetuate the line and would have settled down somewhere quiet and encouraged Nevrik to marry and have children."

"And wait for you?"

"What's that?"

"That was the plan, wasn't it? They run and hide and you stay behind and find them when it was safe?"

"Something like that."

"So you had a way to contact them. A way to locate the heir? Something to do with the amulets."

"Nine hundred years ago I would have said yes, but finding their descendants now is probably a fool's dream. Time can destroy so many things."

"But you are trying nevertheless."

"What else is there for an old crippled outlaw to do?"

"Care to tell me how you plan to find them?"

"I can't do that. I've already told you more than I should have. The heir has enemies and, as fond as I have grown of you, that kind of secret stays with me. I owe that much to Jerish and Nevrik."

"But something in that tower is part of it. That's why you want to get inside." Royce thought a moment. "You sealed that tower just before you went to prison, and since the Gilarabrywn was only recently released, you can be almost certain that the interior of that tower hasn't been touched in all that time. It's the only place that's still the same as the day you left it. There's something in there you saw that day, or something you left there—something you need to find the heir."

"It is a shame you aren't as good at deciphering a way to get into the tower."

"About that," Royce said. "You mentioned that the emperor met with the elves in the tower. They aren't allowed on this bank, right?"

"Correct."

"And there was no bridge on their side of the river, right?"

"Again correct."

"But you never saw how they entered the tower?"

"No."

Royce thought a moment, then asked, "Why were the stairs wet?"

Esrahaddon looked at him, puzzled. "What's that?"

"You said earlier that when the knights were fighting off the Gilarabrywn, they died on the wet steps. Was it blood?"

"No, water, I think. I remember how the stairs were wet when we were climbing up, because it made the stone so slippery I nearly fell. Some of the knights did fall; that's why I remember it."

"And you said the elves had clothes drying in the sun?"

Esrahaddon shook his head. "I see where you are going with this, but not even an elf can swim to the tower."

"That may be true, but then why were they wet? Was it a hot day? Could they have been swimming?"

Esrahaddon raised his eyebrows incredulously. "In that river? No, it was early spring and still cold."

"Then how'd they get wet?"

Royce heard a faint sound behind him. He started to turn but stopped himself.

"We're not alone," he whispered.

"When you lunge, step in with the leg on your weapon side; it will give you more reach and better balance," Hadrian told Theron.

The two were at the well again. They had gotten up early and Hadrian was putting Theron through some basic moves using two makeshift swords they had created out of rake handles. To his surprise, Theron was spryer than he looked, and despite his size, the old man moved well. Hadrian had gone over the basics of parries, ripostes, flèches, presses, and the lunge, and they were now working on a compound attack comprising a feint, a parry, and a riposte.

"Cuts and thrusts must follow one upon the other without pause. The emphasis is always on speed, aggression, and deception. And everything is kept as simple as possible," Hadrian explained.

"I'd listen to him. If anyone knows stick fighting, it's Hadrian."

Hadrian and Theron turned to see two equestrians riding into the village clearing, each leading a pack pony laden with poles and bundles. They were young men not much older than Thrace, but dressed like young princes, in handsome doublets and hose complete with box-pleated frill and lace edging.

"Mauvin! Fanen?" Hadrian said, astonished.

"Don't look so surprised." Mauvin gave his horse rein to graze on the common's grass.

"Well, that's a little hard at this point. What in Maribor's name are you two doing here?"

Just then a procession of musicians, heralds, knights, wagons, and carriages emerged from the dense forest. Long banners of red and gold streamed in the morning light as standard-bearers preceded the march, followed by the plumed imperial guards of the Nyphron Church.

Hadrian and Theron moved aside against the trees for safety as the grand parade of elegantly draped stallions and gold-etched white carriages rolled in. There were well-dressed clergy and chain-mailed soldiers, knights with their squires leading packhorses laden with fine sets of shining metal armor. There were nobility with standards from as far away as Calis and Trent, but also commoners, rough men with broad swords and scarred faces, monks in tattered robes, and woodsmen with long bows and green hoods. Such an assortment of diverse characters made Hadrian think of a circus he had once seen, although this column of men and horses was far too grim and serious to be a carnival. Bringing up the rear echelon was a group of six riders in black and red with the symbol of a broken crown on their chests. At their head rode a tall thin man with long black hair and a short trimmed beard.

"So they've finally decided to do something about this," Hadrian said. "I'm impressed the church would go to such an effort to save a little village so far out that even its own king doesn't care. But that still doesn't explain why you two are here."

"I'm hurt." Mauvin feigned a chest pain. "Granted, I'm only here to help Fanen, but I might try my hand as well. Although, if you're going to be competing, it looks as if we shouldn't have bothered with the trip."

Theron whispered to Hadrian, "Who are these people? And what is he talking about?"

"Ah—sorry, this is Mauvin and Fanen Pickering, sons of Count Pickering of Galilin in Melengar, who are apparently very lost. Mauvin, Fanen, this is Theron Wood; he's a farmer."

"And he's paying you for lessons? Smart idea, but how did you two get here ahead of the rest of us? I didn't see you at any of the camps. Oh, what am I thinking? You and Royce probably had no trouble discovering the location of the contest."

"Contest?"

"Royce was probably hiding under the archbishop's desk as he set up the rules. So will it be swords? If it's swords, Fanen has a real chance to win, but if it's a joust, well..." He glanced at his brother, who scowled. "He's really not that good. Do you know how the eliminations will work? I can't imagine they will pit noble against commoner, which means Fanen won't be competing with you, so—"

"You're not here to slay the Gilarabrywn? Are you saying these people are here for that stupid contest?"

"Gilarabrywn? What's a Gilarabrywn? Is that like Oswald the bear? Heard about him coming through Dunmore. Terrorized villages for years until the king killed him with just a dagger."

The entourage traveled past them without pause up toward the manor house. One of the coaches separated from the group just after it cleared the well. It stopped, and a young well-dressed woman exited and ran to them, holding the edge of her skirt up to avoid the dirt.

"Hadrian!" she cried with a bright smile.

Hadrian bowed, and Theron joined him.

"Is this your father, Hadrian?" she asked.

"No, Your Highness. May I present Theron Wood of Dahlgren Village. Theron, this is Her Royal Highness Princess Arista of Melengar."

Theron stared at Hadrian, shocked. "You really get around, don't you?"

Hadrian smiled awkwardly and shrugged.

"Hey, Arista," Fanen said. "Guess what. Hadrian says the contest is to kill a beast."

"I didn't say that."

"Which is just fine by me, because if Hadrian was going to be competing, I think I would have to withdraw. But now, a hunt is a much different story. You know luck is often a deciding factor in these things."

" 'These things'?" Arista laughed at him. "Attended several beast-slaying contests, have you, Fanen?"

"Bah!" Fanen scoffed. "You know what I mean. Sometimes you are just in the right place at the right time."

Mauvin shrugged. "Doesn't sound like much of a contest for noblemen, really. If it turns out to be true, I'll be disappointed. Slaughtering a poor animal is no good use for a Pickering's sword."

"Say, did you also hear what the prize will be?" Fanen asked. "The way they've been selling this contest in every square, church, and tavern across Avryn, it has to be big. Will it just be a gold trophy, or is it land? I'm hoping to get an estate out of this. Mauvin will inherit our father's title, but I have to fend for myself. What does this animal look like? Is it a bear? Is it big? Have you seen it?"

Hadrian and Theron exchanged stunned looks.

"What is it?" Fanen asked. "It's not dead already?"

"No," Hadrian said. "It's not dead already."

"Oh good."

"Your Highness!" A woman's voice came from the carriage still lingering up the trail. "We need to be going—the archbishop will be waiting."

"I'm sorry," she told them. "I have to go. It was good seeing you again." She waved and ran back to her waiting carriage.

"We should probably be going too," Mauvin said. "We want to get Fanen's name as near to the top of the list as we can."

"Wait," Hadrian told them. "Don't enter the contest."

"What?" they both said.

"We rode days to get here for this," Fanen complained.

"Take my advice. Turn around right now and head back home. Take Arista with you too and anyone else you can convince to go. If it is a competition to kill the Gilarabrywn, don't sign up. You don't want to fight this thing. I'm serious. You don't know what you're dealing with. If you try and fight this creature, it will kill you."

"But you think you can kill it?"

"I'm not fighting it. Royce and I were just here doing a job for Theron's daughter and we were about to leave."

"Royce is here too?" Fanen asked, looking around.

"Do your father a favor and leave now."

Mauvin frowned. "If you were anyone else, I would take your tone as insolent. I might even call you a coward and a liar, but I know you're neither." Mauvin sighed and rubbed his chin thoughtfully. "Still, we did ride an awfully long way to just turn around. You say you were preparing to leave? When will that be?"

Hadrian looked at Theron.

"Another two days, I think," the old farmer told Hadrian. "I don't want to go until I know Thrace will be okay."

"Then we will stay here for that long and see for ourselves what's what. If it turns out to be as you say, we will leave with you. Is that fair, Fanen?"

"I don't see why you can't go and I stay. After all, I'm the one going to enter the contest."

"No one is going to kill that thing, Fanen," Hadrian told him. "Listen, I have been here for 3 nights. I have seen it and I know what it can do. It's not a matter of skill or courage. Your sword won't harm it; no one's will. Fighting that creature is nothing more than suicide."

"I'm not deciding yet," Fanen declared. "We aren't even certain what the contest is. I won't sign up right away, but I'm not leaving either."

"Do me a favor, then," Hadrian told them. "At least stay indoors tonight."

ઙ

Something, or someone, was in the thickets.

Royce left Esrahaddon and moved away to the river's edge, careful not to look in the direction of the sound. He descended from the rocks to the depression near the river and slipped into the trees, circling back. Something was there and it was working hard to be quiet.

At first, Royce caught a glimpse of orange and blue through the leaves and almost thought it was nothing more than a bluebird, but then it shifted. It was far too large to be a bird. Royce drew closer and saw a light brown braided beard, a broad flat nose, a blue leather vest, large black boots, and a bright orange shirt with puffed sleeves.

"Magnus!" Royce greeted the dwarf loudly, causing him to stumble and fall out of the bramble. He slipped backward off the little grassy ledge and fell on his back on the bare rock not far from where Esrahaddon sat. With the wind knocked out of him, the dwarf lay gasping for breath.

Royce leapt down and placed his dagger to the dwarf's throat.

"A lot of people have been looking for you," Royce told him menacingly. "I have to admit, I rather wanted to see you again myself to thank you for all the help you gave me in Essendon Castle."

"Don't tell me this is the dwarf that killed King Amrath of Melengar," Esrahaddon said.

"His name is Magnus, or at least that's what Percy Braga called him. He's a master trap builder and stone carver, isn't that right?"

"It's my business!" the dwarf protested, still struggling for air. "I'm a craftsman. I take jobs the same as you. You can't fault a guy for working."

"I almost died due to your work," Royce told him. "And you killed the king. Alric will be very pleased when I tell him I finally eliminated you. And as I recall, there's a price on your head."

"Wait—hang on!" Magnus shouted. "It was nothing personal. Can you tell me you never killed anyone for money, Royce?"

Royce hesitated.

"Yes, I know who you are," the dwarf told him. "I wanted to find out who beat my trap. You used to work for the Black Diamond, and not as a delivery boy either. It was my job, I tell you. I don't care about politics, or Braga, or Essendon."

"I suspect he's telling the truth," Esrahaddon said. "I've never known a dwarf to care at all for the affairs of humans beyond the coin they can obtain."

"See, he knows what I am saying. You can let me go."

"I said you were telling the truth, not that he should let you live. In fact, now that I can see you have been eavesdropping on our conversations, I have to encourage the notion of ending your life. I can't be sure how much you heard."

"What?" the dwarf cried.

"After slitting his throat, you can just roll his little body off the ledge here." The wizard stepped up and looked over the cliff.

"No," Royce replied, "it will be better to toss him off the falls. He's not that heavy; his body will likely carry all the way to the Goblin Sea."

"Do you need his head?" Esrahaddon asked. "To take back to Alric?"

"It would be nice, but I'm not carrying a severed head for a week while traveling through those woods. It would draw every fly for miles and it would stink after a few hours. Trust me, I speak from experience."

The dwarf looked at both of them in horror.

"No! No!" he shouted in panic as Royce pressed his blade to his neck. "I can help you. I can show you how to get to the tower!"

Royce looked at the wizard, who appeared skeptical.

"For the love of Drome. I'm a dwarf. I know stone. I know rock. I know where the tunnel to the tower is."

Royce relaxed his dagger.

"Let me live and I'll show it to you." He turned his head toward Esrahaddon. "And as for what I heard, I care nothing about the affairs of wizards and men. I'll never say a word. If you know dwarves, well, then you know we're a lot like stone when we choose to be."

"So there *is* a tunnel," Royce said.

"Of course there is."

"Before I decide," Royce asked, "what are you doing here?"

"I was finishing another job, that's all."

"And what was this job?"

"Nothing sinister, I just made a sword for a guy."

"All the way out here? Who is this person?"

"Lord Rufus somebody. I was hired to come here to make it. I was told he would meet me. Honest, no traps, no killings."

"And how are you still alive? How did you get out of Melengar? How is it you haven't been caught?"

"My employer is very powerful."

"This Rufus guy?"

"No. I'm making the sword for him, but Rufus isn't my employer."

"So who is?"

Royce heard footfalls. Someone was running up the trail. Thinking it might be the dwarf's associates, he slipped behind

Magnus. He gripped his hair, pulled his head back, and prepared to slit his throat.

"Royce!" Tad Bothwick shouted up to them from down near the water.

"What is it, Tad?" he asked cautiously.

"Hadrian sent me. He says you should come back to the village right away, but that Esra should steer clear."

"Why?" the wizard asked.

"Hadrian said to tell you that the Church of Nyphron just arrived."

"The church?" Esrahaddon muttered. "Here?"

"Is there a Lord Rufus with them?" Royce asked.

"Could be. There's a whole lot of fancy folk around. Must be at least one lord in the bunch."

"Any idea why they're here, Tad?"

"Nope."

"You might want to make yourself scarce," Royce told the wizard. "Someone might have mentioned your name. I'll go see what's happening. In the meantime"—he looked down at the dwarf—"it would appear your employer has just arrived. Your death sentence has been suspended. This kindly old man is going to watch you this afternoon, and you're going to stay right here. Then later you're going to show us where this tunnel is, and if you're telling the truth about knowing, then you live. Anything short of that and you're going over the falls in two pieces. Agreed? Good." He looked back at the wizard. "Want me to tie him up or just hit him over the head with a rock?" Royce asked, panicking the dwarf again.

"Won't be necessary. Magnus here looks like the honorable type. Besides, I can still manage a few surprisingly unpleasant things. Do you know what it is like to have live ants trapped inside your head?"

The dwarf did not move or speak. Royce searched him. He

found a belt under his clothes with little hammers and some rock-shaping tools and a dagger. Royce looked at the dagger, surprised.

"I tried copying it," the dwarf told him nervously. "It's not very good; I was working from memory."

Royce compared it to his own dagger. The two were very similar in design, though the blades were clearly different. Royce's weapon was made of an almost translucent metal that shimmered in the light, while Magnus's dagger seemed dull and heavy by comparison. The thief threw the dagger over the cliff.

"That's a magnificent weapon you have," the dwarf told him, mesmerized by the blade that a moment before had been at his throat. "It's a Tur blade, isn't it?"

Royce ignored him and spoke to Esrahaddon. "Keep an eye on him. I'll be back later."

❧

Arista took her seat on the balcony above the entrance to the great hall of the manor house, along with the entourage of the archbishop, which included Sauly and Sentinel Luis Guy. It was a very small balcony, created of rough logs and thick ropes, where only a few could fit, but Bernice managed to squeeze her way in and remained standing just behind her. Bernice's hovering out of sight was as irritating as a mosquito in the dark.

Arista had no idea what was going on—few people appeared to.

When they had arrived, everything was in chaos. The lord of the manor was apparently dead and the place was filled with peasants. They were promptly chased out. Luis Guy and his seret established order and assigned quarters based on rank. She was given a cramped but private room on the second level. It was a ghastly place, lacking even a single window. A bear rug lay on the floor, the head of a moose looked down at her from above the bed, and a coatrack made from deer antlers hung from the wall. Bernice was busy unpacking her clothes from the trunk when Sauly stopped by, insisting Arista join him on the balcony. At first, she thought the contest might be starting, but it was common knowledge it would begin at nightfall.

A trumpeter stepped up to the rail and blared a fanfare on his horn. Below, in the courtyard, a crowd formed. Men rushed over, some holding drinks or half-eaten meals. One man trotted up still buttoning his pants. The growing audience created a mass of heads and shoulders bunched together, all staring up at them.

The archbishop slowly stood up. Dressed in full regalia of long embroidered robes, he spread his arms in a grand gesture and spoke, his raspy voice barely adequate to the task.

"It is time to announce the details of this event and reveal the profound happening that you, the devoted of Novron, are about to take part in, an event so monumental that its conclusion will see the world altered forever."

Several people in the back complained they could not hear, but the archbishop ignored them and went on. "I know some of you came believing this contest was to be a battle of swords or lances, like some Wintertide tournament. Instead, what you will see is nothing less than a miracle. Some of you will die, one will succeed, and the rest will bear witness to the world.

"A terrible evil haunts this place. Here on the Nidwalden River, at the edge of the world, there is a beast. Not a great bear like Oswald that terrorized Glamrendor. This creature is none other than the legendary Gilarabrywn, a horror not seen since the days of Novron himself. A monster so terrible that even in those days of heroes and gods, only Novron, or one of his blood, could slay it. It will be your task, your challenge, to slay the creature and save this poor village from the ancient curse."

A murmur broke out among those gathered, and the archbishop raised his hands to quiet them. "Silence. For I have not yet told you of the reward!"

He waited as the mob grew quiet, many pushing closer to hear.

"As I said, the Gilarabrywn is a beast that only Novron or one of his bloodline can slay, and as such, he that succeeds in vanquishing this terror can be none other than the heir to the imperial crown, the long-lost Heir of Novron!"

The reaction was surprisingly quiet. There were no cheers, no shouts of jubilation. The crowd as a whole appeared stunned. They remained staring, as if expecting more. The archbishop in turn looked around, equally bewildered by the hesitancy of the congregation.

"Did he just say the winner would be the heir?" Arista asked, looking at Sauly, who appeared as if he'd just smelled something unpleasant. He smiled at her and, standing up, whispered in the archbishop's ear. The older man took his seat and Bishop Saldur addressed the crowd.

"For centuries the church has struggled to find the true heir, to restore the bloodline of our holy lord Novron the Great." Sauly's voice was loud and warm and carried well on the pine-scented afternoon air. "We have searched, but all we had to guide us were old books and rumors. Speculation, really, hopes and dreams. There has never been a means of finding him, no absolute method to determine where the heir was, or who he may be. Many have falsely claimed to be his descendent, many unworthy men have striven to take that lofty crown, and the church has sat helpless.

"Still, we have faith he is out there. Novron would not allow his own blood to die. We know he lives. He may be oblivious to who he is. A thousand years have passed since his disappearance, and who of us can accurately trace our lineage back to the days of the Old Empire? Who knows if one of us might have an ancestor who went to his grave with a terrible secret? A terrible, wonderful secret.

"The Gilarabrywn is a miracle Novron has sent. It is a tool to show us his son. He has confided this to the Patriarch and told His Holiness that he should hold a contest and if he did, the heir would be among the contestants, the truth of his lineage, oblivious even to himself.

"So you see, you—any one of you—may be the Heir of Novron, possessor of divine blood—a god. Have any of you sensed a power within? A belief in your own worth beyond that of others? This is your chance to prove to all of Elan that you are no fool, no mere man. Place your name upon the roster, ride out at nightfall, slay the beast, and you will become our divine ruler. You will not be a mere king, but *emperor*, and all kings will bow to you. You will take the imperial throne in Aquesta. All loyal Imperialists and the full force of the church will support you as we usher in a new age of order that will bring peace and harmony to the land. All you need do is destroy one lonely beast.

"What say you?"

This time the crowd cheered. Saldur glanced briefly at the archbishop and stepped away from the balcony to take a seat.

ஃ

When Royce reached Dahlgren, the village was in turmoil. People were everywhere. Most of the villagers were heading toward the common well. There were plenty of new faces, all of them men, most carrying some sort of weapon. Royce found Hadrian mobbed by villagers at the well. None of them looked happy.

"Where do we go now?" Selen Brockton asked, in tears.

Hadrian once more stepped up on the well, standing over the crowd and looking like he wanted to break something. "I don't know, Mrs. Brockton. Home, I guess—for now, at least."

"But our home has a thatched roof."

"Try digging cellars and getting as low as possible."

"What's going on?" Royce asked.

"The Archbishop of Ghent has arrived and moved into the manor house. He and his clergy, as well as a few dozen nobles, have taken over the castle and driven everyone else out. Well, except for Russell, Dillon, and Kline, whom he ordered to fill in the shelter and the tunnel we were digging, saying they could repair the damages or hang for destruction of property. Good old Deacon Tomas, he stands there nodding and saying, 'I told them not to do it, but they wouldn't listen.' They kept most of the livestock too, saying it was in the castle, so it belonged to the manor. Now everyone blames me for losing their animals."

"What about the bonfires?" Royce asked. "We could still build one here in the commons."

"No good," Hadrian told him. "His Lordship declared it unlawful to cut trees in the area and confiscated the oxen with the rest of the animals."

"Did you tell him what will happen when the sun goes down?"

"I can't tell him anything." Hadrian threw up his hands, running his fingers through his hair as if he might start pulling it out. "I can't get past the twenty-odd soldiers he has at the castle gate. Which is a good thing too or I might kill the guy."

"Why is the church here at all?"

"That's the kicker," Hadrian told him. "You know that competition the church has been announcing? Turns out that contest is to slay the Gilarabrywn."

"What?"

"They intend to send contestants out to fight the thing at nightfall, and if they die, they'll send the next one. They've got a damn list nailed to the castle gate."

"It's all right, it's all right," Deacon Tomas shouted.

Everyone turned to see the cleric coming down the trail from the castle, approaching the crowd at the well. He walked with his hands raised as if in blessing. On his face he had a great smile, which turned his eyes into half-moons. "Everything is going to be fine," he told them in a loud confident voice. "The archbishop has come to help us. They are going to kill the beast and save us from this nightmare."

"What about our livestock?" Vince Griffin asked.

"They will need most of them to feed the troops, but what isn't used will be returned after the beast has been slain."

The crowd grumbled.

"Now, now, what price do you put on safety? What price do you put on the lives of your children? Are a pig and a cow worth the lives of your children? Your wife? Consider it a tithe and be thankful the church has come to Dahlgren to save us. No one else has. The King of Dunmore ignored us, but your church has responded by sending not just some knight or margrave, but the Archbishop of Ghent himself. Soon the beast will be dead and Dahlgren will be a place of happiness once more. If that means one year of no meat, and plowing without an ox, surely that's not too high a price to pay. Now, everyone, please, back to your homes. Stay out of their way and let them do their work."

"What about my daughter?" Theron growled, and pushed forward, looking like he might kill the deacon.

"It's all right, I've spoken with the archbishop and Bishop Saldur; they have agreed to let her stay. They have moved her to a smaller room, but—"

"They won't let me in to see her!" the old farmer snapped.

“I know, I know,” Tomas said in a soothing voice. “But I can. I just came down to explain things. I am heading right back, and I promise you, I’ll stay by her side and watch over her until she is well.”

Hadrian slipped out of the crowd that now shifted around the deacon. He turned to Royce with a bitter look. “Tell me you found a way into the tower.”

Royce shrugged. “Maybe. We’ll need to check it out tonight.”

“Tonight?” Hadrian asked. “Shouldn’t such things be done in the daylight? When we can both see and things with complicated names aren’t flying around?”

“Not if I’m right.”

“And if you’re wrong?”

“If I’m wrong, we’ll both certainly die—most likely by being eaten.”

“The thing is, I know you’re not kidding. Did I mention I lost my weapons?”

“With any luck we won’t need them. What we will need, however, is a good length of rope, sixty feet at least,” Royce told him. “Lanterns, wax, a tinderbox—”

“I’m not going to like this, am I?” Hadrian asked miserably.

“Not at all,” Royce replied.

Chapter 9

Trials by Moonlight

Back in bed," the man shouted. "Back in bed this instant!" Arista was wandering the hallway of the manor house, as much to get to know her surroundings as to evade Bernice, who was insisting she take a nap. Initially she thought the yelling was directed at her, and while she put up with Bernice and her pampering, she was certainly not about to allow anyone to address her in such a manner as this brassy fellow seemed to be doing. She was no longer in her native kingdom of Melengar, where she was princess of the realm, but she was still a princess and an ambassador and no one had the right to speak to her like that.

With a fury in her countenance, she marched forward and, turning a corner, spotted a middle-aged man and a young girl. The girl was dressed only in her nightgown, her face battered and bruised. He held her wrist, attempting to drag her into a bedroom.

"Unhand her!" Arista ordered. "Hilfred! Guards!"

The man and girl both looked at her, bewildered.

Hilfred raced around the corner and in an instant stood with sword drawn between his princess and the source of her anger.

"I said get your filthy hands off her this instant, or I'll have them removed at the wrists."

"But I—" the man began.

From the other direction, two imperial guards arrived. "Milady?" the guards greeted her.

Hilfred said nothing but merely pointed his sword at the man's throat.

"Take this wretch into custody," Arista ordered. "He's forcing himself on this girl."

"No, no, please," the girl protested. "It was my fault. I—"

"It is not your fault." Arista looked at her with pity. "And you needn't be afraid. I can see to it that he never bothers you, *or anyone*, again."

"Oh dear Maribor, protect me," the man prayed.

"Oh no, you don't understand," the girl said. "He wasn't hurting me. He was trying to help me."

"How's that?"

"I had an accident." She pointed to the bruises on her face. "Deacon Tomas was taking care of me, but I was feeling better today and wanted to get up and walk, but he thought it best if I stay in bed another day. He is really only trying to look out for me. Please don't hurt him. He's been so kind."

"You know this man?" Arista asked the guards.

"He was cleared for entrance by the archbishop as the deacon of this village, my lady, and he was indeed attending to this girl, who is known as Thrace." Tomas, with his eyes wide with fear and Hilfred's sword steady at his throat, nodded as best he could and attempted a friendly though strained smile.

"Well," Arista said, pursing her lips, "my mistake, then." She looked at the guards. "Go back about your business."

"Princess." The guards bowed briskly, turned, and walked back the way they had come.

Hilfred slowly sheathed his sword.

She looked back at the two. "My apologies, it's just that—that—well, never mind." She turned away, embarrassed.

"Oh no, Your Highness," Thrace said, attempting as best she could to curtsy. "Thank you so much for coming to my aid, even if I didn't actually need it. It is good to know that someone as great as you would bother to help a poor farmer's daughter." Thrace looked at her in awe. "I've never met a princess before. I've never even seen one."

"I hope I'm not too much of a disappointment, then." Thrace was about to speak again but Arista beat her to it. "What happened to you?" She gestured at her face.

Thrace reached up, running her fingers over her forehead. "Is it that bad?"

"It was the Gilarabrywn, Your Highness," Tomas explained. "Thrace and her father, Theron, were the only two to ever survive a Gilarabrywn attack. Now please, my dear girl, please get back in bed."

"But really, I am feeling much better."

"Let her walk with me a bit, Deacon," Arista said, softening her tone. "If she feels worse, I'll get her back to bed."

Tomas nodded and bowed.

Arista took Thrace by the arm and led her up the hallway, Hilfred walking a few steps behind. They could not travel far, only thirty yards or so; the manor house was not a real castle. It was built from great rough-cut beams—some with the bark still on—and she guessed there were only about eight bedrooms. In addition, there were a parlor, an office, and the great hall, with a high ceiling and mounted heads of deer and bears. It reminded Arista of a cruder, smaller version of King Roswort's residence. The floor was made of wide pine planks, and the outer walls were thick logs. Nailed along them were iron lanterns holding flickering candles that cast semicircles of quivering light, for even though it was midafternoon, the interior of the manor was dark as a cave.

"You're so kind," the girl told her. "The others treat me... as if I don't belong here."

"Well, I'm glad you are here," Arista replied. "Other than my handmaiden, Bernice, I think you are the only other woman here."

"It is just that everyone else was sent back home and I feel so out of place, like I'm doing something wrong. Deacon Tomas says I'm not. He says I'm hurt and I need time to recover and that he'll see to it no one bothers me. He's been very nice. I think he feels as helpless as everyone else around here. Maybe taking care of me is a battle he feels he can win."

"I misjudged the deacon," Arista told her, "and you. Are all farmers' daughters in Dahlgren so wise?"

"Wise?" Thrace looked embarrassed.

Arista smiled at her. "Where is your family?"

"My father is in the village. They won't let him in to see me, but the deacon is working on that. I don't think it matters, as we will be leaving Dahlgren as soon as I can travel, which is another reason I want to get my strength back. I want to get away from here. I want us to find a new place and start fresh. I'll find a man, get married, have a son, and call him Hickory."

"Quite the plan, but how are you feeling—really?"

"I still have headaches and to be honest I'm getting a little dizzy right now."

"Maybe we should head back to your bedroom, then," Arista said, and they turned around.

"But I am feeling so much better than I was. That's another reason why I got up. I haven't been able to thank Esra. I thought he might be in the halls here somewhere."

"Esra?" Arista asked. "Is he the village doctor?"

"Oh no, Dahlgren's never had a doctor. Esra is—well, he's a very smart man. If it hadn't been for him, both me and my father would be dead by now. He was the one who made the medicine that saved me."

"He sounds like a great person."

"Oh, he is. I try to pay him back by helping him eat. He's very proud, you understand, and he would never ask, so I offer and I can see he appreciates it."

"Is he too poor to afford food?"

"Oh no, he just doesn't have any hands."

❧

"Tur is a myth," Esrahaddon was saying to the dwarf as Royce and Hadrian arrived at the falls.

"Says you," Magnus replied.

The wizard and the dwarf sat on the rocky escarpment facing each other, arguing over the roar. The sun, having dropped behind the trees, left the two in shadow, but the crystalline spires atop Avempartha caught the last rays of dying red light.

Esrahaddon sighed. "I'll never understand what it is about religion that causes otherwise sensible people to believe in fairy tales. Even in the world of religion, Tur is a parable, not a reality. You're dealing with myths based on legends based on superstitions and taking it literally. That is very undwarf-like. Are you certain you don't have some human blood in your ancestry?"

"That's just insulting." Magnus glared at the wizard. "You deny it, but the proof is right before you. If you had dwarven eyes, you could see the truth in that blade." Magnus gestured at Royce.

"What's this all about?" Hadrian asked. "Hello, Magnus, murder anyone lately?"

The dwarf scowled.

"This dwarf insists that Royce's dagger was made by Kile," Esrahaddon explained.

"I didn't say that," the dwarf snapped. "I said it was a Tur blade. It could have been made by anyone from Tur."

"What's Tur?" Hadrian asked.

"A misguided cult of lunatics that worship a fictitious god. They named him Kile, of all things. You'd think they could have at least come up with a better name."

"I've never heard of Kile," Hadrian said. "Now, I'm not a religious scholar, but if I remember what a little monk once told me, the dwarven god is Drome, the elvish god is Ferrol, and the human god is Maribor. Their sister, the goddess of flora and fauna, is...Muriel, right? And her son, Uberlin, is the god of darkness. So how does this Kile fit in?"

"He's their father," Esrahaddon explained.

"Oh right, I forgot about him, but his name isn't Kile, it's... Erebus or something, isn't it? He raped his daughter and his sons killed him, but he's not really dead? It didn't make a lot of sense to me."

Esrahaddon chuckled. "Religion never does."

"So who is Kile?"

"Well, the Cult of Tur, or Kile, as it is also known, insists that a god is immortal and cannot die. This deranged group of people appeared during the imperial reign of Estermon II and began circulating this story that Erebus had been drunk, or whatever equivalent there is to a god, when he raped his daughter, and he was ashamed for what he did. The story goes that Erebus allowed his children—the gods—to believe they had killed him. Then he came to Muriel in secret and begged her forgiveness. She told her father that she wasn't ready to forgive him and would only do so after he did penance. She said he had to do good deeds throughout Elan, but as a commoner, not as a god or even a king. For each act of sacrifice and kindness that she approved of, she would grant him a feather from her marvelous robe, and when her robe was gone, she would forgive and welcome him home.

"The Kile legend says that ages ago a stranger came to a poor village called Tur. No one knows where it was, of course, and over the centuries its location has changed in response to various claims, but the most common legend places it in Delgos, because it was being regularly attacked by the Dacca and, of course, because of the similarity in names to the port city of Tur Del Fur. The story goes that this stranger called himself Kile and, entering into Tur and seeing the terrible plight of the desperate villagers, taught them the art of weapon making to help in their defense. The weapons he taught them to make were reputed to be the greatest in the world, capable of cleaving through solid iron as if it were soft wood. Their shields and armor were light and yet stronger than stone. Once he taught them the craft, they used it to defend their homes. After driving off the Dacca, legend says there was a thunderclap on a cloudless day, and from the heavens, a single white feather fell into Kile's hands. He wept at the gift and bid them all farewell, never to be seen again. At least not by the residents of Tur. Throughout the various reigns of different emperors, there always seemed to be at least one or two stories of Kile appearing here and there, doing good deeds and obtaining his feather. The legend stood out beyond all others because the poor village of Tur was now famous for its great weaponry."

"I've never heard of a town by that name."

"You aren't the only one," Esrahaddon said. "So the myth

experts added a page to their story, as so often happens with these ridiculous tales when they crash into the face of reality. Supposedly, the village was inundated with requests for arms. The Turists didn't feel it was right to make weapons for just anyone, so they only made a few, and only for those who had a just and good need. Powerful kings, however, decided to take the god-given craft secrets for themselves and prepared to battle for control of the village. On the day of the battle, however, the armies marched in to discover that the village of Tur—all its inhabitants and buildings—was gone. Not a trace was left of their existence except for a single white feather that came from no known bird."

"Convenient," Hadrian said.

"Exactly," the wizard replied. "One mystery covered by another, but never any real evidence. Still it doesn't stop people from believing."

"For your information," Magnus spoke up, "Tur Del Fur was once a dwarven city, and in my tongue, its name means Village of Tur, and there are legends among my people of it once having been the source of great craftsmen who knew the secrets of folding metal and making great swords.

"Any dwarf in Elan would give his beard for the secrets of Tur, or even the chance to study a Tur blade."

"And you think Alverstone is a Tur blade?" Hadrian asked.

"What did you call it?" Magnus asked, his beady eyes abruptly focusing on him.

"Alverstone, that's what Royce calls his dagger," Hadrian explained.

"Don't encourage him," Royce said, his eyes fixed on the tower.

"Where did he get this Alverstone?" the dwarf asked, lowering his voice.

"It was a gift from a friend," Hadrian said, "right?"

"Who? And where did the friend get it from?" the dwarf persisted.

"You are aware I can hear you?" Royce told them; then, seeing something, he pointed toward Avempartha. "There, look."

They all scrambled up to peer at the outline of the fading tower. The sun was down now and night was upon them. Like great mirrors, the river and the tower captured the starlight and the luminous moon. The mist from the falls appeared as an eerie white fog skirting the base. Near the top of the spires, a dark shape spread its wings and flew down along the course of the river. It wheeled and circled back over the falls, catching air currents and rising higher until, with a flap of its massive wings, the beast headed out over the trees above the forest, flying toward Dahlgren.

"That's its lair?" Hadrian asked incredulously. "It lives in the tower?"

"Convenient, isn't it," Royce remarked, "that the beast resides at the same place as the one weapon that can kill it."

"Convenient for whom?"

"I guess that remains to be seen," Esrahaddon said.

Royce turned to the dwarf. "All right, my little mason, shall we head to the tunnel? It's in the river, isn't it? Somewhere underwater?"

Magnus looked at him, surprised.

"I am only guessing, but from the look on your face, I must be right. It's the only place I haven't looked. Now, in return for your life, you'll show us exactly where."

❧

Arista stood with the Pickerings on the south stockade wall watching the sunset over the gate. The wall provided the best view of both the courtyard and the hillside beyond while keeping them above the turmoil. Below, knights busied themselves dressing in armor; archers strung their bows, horses decorated in caparisons shifted uneasily, and priests prayed to Novron for wisdom. The contest was about to commence. Beyond the wall the village of Dahlgren remained silent. Not a candle was visible. Nothing moved.

Another scuffle broke out near the gate where the list of combatants hung on the hitching post. Arista could see several men pushing and swinging, rising dust.

"Who is it this time?" Mauvin asked. The elder Pickering leaned back against the log wall. He was in a simple loose tunic and a pair of soft shoes that day. This was the Mauvin she most remembered, the carefree boy who had challenged her to stick duels back when she stood a foot taller and could overpower him, in the days when she had a mother and father and her greatest challenge was making Lenare jealous.

"I can't tell," Fanen replied, peering down. "I think one is Sir Erlic."

"Why are they fighting?" Arista asked.

"Everyone wants a higher place on the list," Mauvin replied.

"That doesn't make sense. It doesn't matter who goes first."

"It does if the person in front of you kills the beastie before you get a chance."

"But they can't. Only the heir can kill the beast."

"You really think that?" Mauvin asked, turning around, grasping the sharpened points of the logs, and peering down the outside of the wall. "No one else does."

"Who's first on the list?"

"Well, Tobis Rentinual was."

"Which one is he?" she asked.

"He's the one we told you about with the big mysterious wagon."

"There"—Fanen pointed down in the courtyard—"the foppish-looking one leaning against the smokehouse. He has a shrill voice and a superior attitude that makes you want to throttle him."

Mauvin nodded. "That's him. I peeked under his tarp; there's this huge contraption made of wood, ropes, and pulleys. He managed to find the list first and sign his name. No one had a problem with it when they thought the contest was a tournament. Everyone was just itching to have a go at him, but now, well, the thought of Tobis as emperor has become a communal fear."

"What do you mean *was*?"

"He got bumped," Fanen said.

"Bumped?"

"Luis Guy's idea," Mauvin explained. "The sentinel decreed that those farther down on the list could move up via combat. Those unsatisfied with their place could challenge anyone for their position to a fight. Once issued, the challenged party could trade positions on the list or enter into combat with the challenger. Sir Enden of Chadwick challenged Tobis, who gave up his position. Who could blame him? Only Sir Gravin had the courage to challenge Enden, but several others drew swords against one another for lesser spots. Most expected the duels would be by points, but Guy declared battles over only when the opponent yielded, so they have gone on for hours. Many have been injured. Sir Gravin yielded only after Enden pierced his shoulder. He's announced he's withdrawing and will be leaving tomorrow, and he's not the only one. Several have already left wrapped in bandages."

Arista looked at Fanen. "You aren't challenging?"

Mauvin chuckled. "It was kinda funny. The moment Guy made the announcement, everyone looked at us."

"But you didn't challenge?"

Fanen scowled and glared at Mauvin. "He won't let me. And my name is near the bottom."

"Hadrian Blackwater told us not to sign up," Mauvin explained.

"So?" Fanen stared at his brother.

"So the one man here who could take that top spot without breaking a sweat doesn't even have his name on the list. Either he knows something we don't, or he thinks he does. That's worth waiting out the first night at least. Besides, you heard Arista; it doesn't matter who goes first."

"You know who else isn't on the list?" Fanen asked. "Lord Rufus."

"Yeah, I saw that. Thought he'd be the one to challenge Enden—it would have been worth the trip just to see that duel. He's not even out in the yard with the rest."

"He's been with the archbishop a lot."

From their elevated position, Arista scanned the courtyard below. The light was gone from the yard, the walls and trees casting the interior in shade. Men went around lighting torches and mounting them. There were hundreds assembled within the grounds and more outside all gathered into small groups. They talked; some shouted. She could hear laughter and even a bit of singing—she could not tell the song, but by its rhythm, she guessed it was a bawdy tavern tune. There was a lot of toasting going on. Dark figures in the failing light, broad, powerful men slamming cups together with enough force to spill foam. Above it all, on a wooden platform raised in the center of the yard, stood Sentinel Luis Guy. He was high enough to catch the last rays of the sun and the last breaths of the evening wind. The light made his red cassock look like fire and the wind blowing his cape lent him an ominous quality.

She looked back at the brothers. Mauvin had his mouth open, struggling to clear something from a back tooth with his forefinger. Fanen had his head up, looking at the sky. She was glad they were with her. It was a little bit of home in the wilderness and she imagined the smell of apples.

Arista and Alric had spent summer months at Drondil Fields to escape the heat of the city. She remembered how they used to climb the trees in the orchard outside the country castle and have apple fights in early autumn. The rotten apples would burst on the branches and spray pulp, soaking them until they all smelled like cider. Each tree a sovereign castle, they would make alliances. Mauvin always teamed with Alric, shouting, "My king! My king!" Lenare paired with Fanen, wanting to protect her younger brother from the "brutes," as she called them. Arista always remained on her own, fighting both groups. Even when Lenare stopped climbing trees, it became the boys against the girl. She did not mind. She did not notice. She did not even think about it until now.

There was so much in her head. So much she needed to sort out. It had been hard to think bouncing around in the coach with Bernice staring at her. She desperately wanted to talk to someone, if only to hear her own words aloud. The idea that Sauly was a conspirator was growing in her mind despite her reluctance to accept it. If Sauly could betray her father, who could be trusted? Could Esrahaddon? Had he used her to escape? Was he responsible for her father's death? Now it seemed the old wizard was nearby, somewhere just outside the walls perhaps, spending the night in one of the village houses. She did not know what to do, or who to trust.

Mauvin found what he was looking for and flicked it from his finger over the wall.

She opened her mouth to speak, hesitating to find the

proper words to say. The whole trip there she had planned to discuss the issues raised at Ervanon with the Pickerings; well, Mauvin, at least. She closed her mouth and bit her lip, once more thinking back to the long-ago orchard and the smell of apples.

"There you are, Your Highness," Bernice said, rushing to her with a shawl for her shoulders. "You shouldn't be out so late; it's not proper."

"Honestly, Bernice, you should have had children when you had the chance. This preoccupation with pampering me has got to stop."

The older woman only smiled warmly. "I'm just looking after you, dear. You need looking after. This foul place is full of rough men. There is little but thin walls and the grace of the archbishop separating them from your virtue. A lady such as yourself is a strong temptation, and given the untamed surroundings of this wilderness, it could easily drive many a good man to acts of rashness." She glanced suspiciously at the brothers, who looked back sheepishly. "And there are more than a few here who I couldn't even describe as good men. In a great castle with a proper retinue, men can be kept at bay by holding them in awe of royalty, but here, my lady, in this barbaric, feral landscape, they will surely lose their heads."

"Oh, Bernice, please."

"Here we go," Fanen said excitedly.

As the last of the sun's light faded, the gates opened and Sir Enden and his retinue of two squires and three pages rode out, torches flaming. They trotted to the open plain, where the knight prepared to do battle.

A shout rose from the crowd just then and Arista looked up to see a dark shadow sweep across the moonlit sky. It drifted in like a hawk, a silhouette of wings and tail. The crowd murmured and gasped as it circled the castle briefly, moving hesitantly before having its attention caught by torches waved by Sir Enden's entourage on the hillside.

It folded its wings and dove, falling out of the sky like an arrow aimed at the knight of Chadwick. Torches moved frantically and Arista thought she saw Sir Enden level his lance and charge forward. There were screams, cries of anguish and terror, as one by one the torches in the field went out.

"Next!" shouted Luis Guy.

❧

The dwarf led them up the river path to where the moon revealed a large rock protruding out toward the water. To Hadrian it looked vaguely like the dull tip of a broad spear. Magnus thumped the dirt with his boot, then pointed toward the river. "We go in here. Swim straight down about twenty feet—there's an opening in the bank. The tunnel runs right under us, curves down, and then runs under the river to the tower."

"You can tell all that with your foot?" Royce asked.

Hadrian looked at Esrahaddon. "How are you at swimming?"

"I can't say I've had the opportunity since..." he said, lifting his arms. "But I can hold my breath a good long time. Drag me if necessary."

"Let me go first," Royce announced, his eyes on Magnus. He threw his coil of rope on the ground and tied one end around his waist. "Feed this out to me, but hang on to it. I don't know how swift the current is."

"There is no current here," Magnus told them. "There's an underwater shelf that juts out, creating an eddy. It's like a little pond down there."

"You'll forgive me if I don't take your word for it. Once I am down I'll give three tugs indicating that it's safe to follow. Tie off the end and follow the line down. If, on the other hand, I jump in and the rope runs out like you just caught a marlin, haul me back so I can personally kill him."

The dwarf sighed.

Royce slipped off his cloak, and with Hadrian holding the rope, he descended into the river as if he were rappelling off the side of a wall. He dropped and vanished under the dark water. Hadrian felt the rope slip out gradually from between his fingers. At his side, Magnus showed no signs of concern. The dwarf stood with his head cocked back, looking up at the sky. "What do you suppose it's doing tonight?" he asked.

"Eating knights would be my guess," Hadrian replied. "Let's just hope they keep the thing busy."

Deeper and deeper, the rope trolled out; then it stopped. Hadrian watched where the line entered the water; it made a little white trail as it cut the current.

Tug. Tug. Tug.

"That's it. He's in," Hadrian announced. "You next, little man."

Magnus glared at him. "I'm a dwarf."

"Get in the river."

Magnus walked to the edge. Holding his nose and pointing his toes, he jumped and disappeared with a plop.

"That leaves you and me," Hadrian said, tying the end of the rope to a birch tree that leaned a bit out toward the river. "You go first—I'll follow—see how well you do. If need be, I'll pull you through."

The wizard nodded, and for the first time since Hadrian had known him, he looked unsure of himself. Esrahaddon took three deep breaths, rapidly blowing each out; on the fourth inhale, he held it and jumped feetfirst. Hadrian leapt in right after.

The water was cold—not icy or breathtaking, but colder than expected. The immediate shock caught Hadrian off guard for an instant. He kicked out with his feet, pointed his head down, and began to swim along the rope. Magnus had been right about the current. The water was still as a pond. He opened his eyes. Above him, there was a faint blue-gray shimmer; below, it was black. Panic gripped Hadrian when he realized he could not see Esrahaddon. Almost in response, a faint light appeared directly below him. The wizard's robe gave off a blue-green glow as he swam, paddling with his feet and stroking with his arms. Despite the lack of hands, he made good headway.

The light from the robe revealed the riverbank and the rope running down. It disappeared inside a dark hole. He watched the wizard slip through, and with his lungs starting to burn, followed him. Once inside, he kicked upward, and almost together their heads emerged from a quiet pool in a small cave.

Royce had the other end of the rope tied to a rock. There was a lantern burning beside him. The single flame easily illuminated the room. The chamber was a natural cave with a tunnel leading out. Magnus stood off to the side, either studying the cavern walls or just keeping his distance from Royce.

When Esrahaddon surfaced, Royce hauled him out. "You might have had an easier time swimming if you'd taken off—" Royce stopped as he saw the wizard's robe. It was dry.

Hadrian climbed out of the pool, feeling the river water drizzle down his body. He could hear the drops echoing in the cave like a rainstorm, but Esrahaddon was exactly as he had been before entering the river. With the exception of his hair and beard, he was not even damp.

Hadrian and Royce exchanged glances but said nothing.

Royce picked up his lantern. "Coming, short stuff?"

The dwarf grumbled and, taking hold of his beard with both hands, twisted a bit of water out. "You realize, my friend, dwarves are an older and far more accomplished—"

"Less chatter, more walking," Royce interrupted, pointing at the tunnel. "You lead. And you're not my friend."

Traveling forward, they entered into a new world. The walls were smooth and seamless, as if cut by the flow of water. The glossy surface magnified the light from Royce's lantern, making the curved interior surprisingly bright.

"So where are we?" Hadrian asked.

"Under the bank, not far below where we were standing before entering the water," Magnus told him. "The tunnel here corkscrews down."

"Incredible," Hadrian said, looking about him in amazement at the sparkling walls. "It's as though we're on the inside of a diamond."

Just as the dwarf had predicted, the tunnel curved around and around, sloping down. Right about the time Hadrian lost all sense of direction, it stopped spinning and ran straight. It was not long before they could hear and feel the thunder of the falls. It vibrated through the stone. Here the ceiling and walls seeped water. A thousand years of neglect had allowed stalactites of crystal to form on the ceiling, and jagged mounds of mineral deposits on the floor.

"This is a bit disturbing," Hadrian remarked, noticing a buildup of water on the floor that was getting deeper as they moved forward.

"Bah!" Magnus muttered, but failed to add anything more.

They slogged through the water, dodging stone spikes. Examining the walls, Hadrian noticed designs carved into them. Etchings of geometric shapes and patterns lined the corridor. Some of the more delicate lines were faded, missing, perhaps lost to the erosion of a billion water droplets. No words were visible and there were no recognizable symbols. The etching appeared to be nothing more than decorative. Above, almost lost in the growing stone, were brackets for what might have once been banner poles, and on the side walls he spotted mountings for lamps. Hadrian tried to imagine how the tunnel looked before the time of Novron, when multicolored banners and rows of bright lamps might have illuminated the causeway. It was not long before the tunnel pitched upward again and they could all see a faint light.

The tunnel ended at a stairway going up. The steps curved and were wide enough for them to take two strides before climbing the next step. When they reached the top, the star-filled sky was above them once more, and before long, they stood aboveground on the outcropping of rock that made up the base of the citadel. A strong wind met them. The gale was damp, filled with a wet mist. They stood at the end of a short stone bridge spanning a narrow crevasse, beyond which stood the spires of the monolithic tower. It loomed above them so high it was impossible to see the top.

More stairs awaited them on the far side and they moved at a slow but even pace, staying single file, even though the stairs were wide enough for two, or even three, to walk abreast. They climbed five sets of steps, zigzagging in a half circle around the outside of the tower. As they started their sixth flight, Royce waited until they had moved to the lee of the citadel, then called a halt for them to catch their breath. Below, the roar of the falls boomed, but from their perch, protected from the wind, the night seemed still. There were no sounds, no crickets or owls, just the deep voice of the river and the howl of the wind.

"This is ridiculous," Royce shouted over the roar. "Where's the damn door? I don't like being so exposed."

"It's just up ahead, not too much farther," Esrahaddon replied.

"How long do we have?" Hadrian asked, looking at the wizard, who shrugged in reply.

"Does it return here directly after killing, or does it enjoy the night?" Royce inquired. "I should think having been locked up in this tower for nine hundred years, it would want to spend some time flying about."

"It isn't a person, or an animal. It's a conjuration, a mystic embodiment of power. It mimics life and understands threats to its existence, certainly, but I doubt it has any concept of pleasure or freedom. Like I said, it's not alive."

"Then why does it eat?" Royce asked.

"It doesn't."

"Then why is it killing a person or two a night?"

"I've wondered that myself. It should attempt to fulfill its last instructions, and that was clearly to kill the emperor. It is possible that not finding its target, and not able to travel far from this tower—conjurations are often limited to a specific distance from their creator or point of origin—it might be trying to lure him here. It could have deduced that the emperor would not tolerate the slaughter of his people and would come to aid the village."

"Regardless, we'd better be quick," Hadrian concluded.

The wind resumed as they circled around. It whistled in their ears and buffeted their steps. The damp clothes chilled them despite the hard work of the march. Above, the spires still rose far into the night sky, and they all felt a grim sense of drudgery when they reached yet another short bridge, which ended abruptly at a solid wall.

Hadrian watched Royce sigh in disappointment as he looked at the dead end.

"I thought you said there was a door." Royce addressed the wizard.

"There was, and is."

Hadrian did not see a door. There was what appeared to be a faint outline of a door's frame etched in the wall in front of them, but it was solid stone.

Royce grimaced. "Another invisible stone portal?"

"Don't waste your time," Magnus told him. "You'll never open it. Trust me, I'm a dwarf. I spent hours trying to get in and nothing. That stone is enchanted and impenetrable. Crossing the river to get here was nothing compared to opening that door."

Royce turned to the dwarf with a puzzled look in his eyes. "You've been here? You tried to enter the tower. Why?"

"I told you, I was doing a job for the church."

"You said you made Lord Rufus a sword."

"I did, but the archbishop didn't want just any sword made for him. He wanted a replica of a sword, an elvish sword. He gave me a bunch of old drawings, which I used to make it. They were pretty good, with dimensions and material listed, but it's not like being able to examine the real thing." The dwarf's stare lingered on Royce suggestively. "I was told others of the same type could be found inside this tower. I came out here and spent all day climbing around, but never found a way in. No doors or windows, just things like this."

"This sword you made," Esrahaddon said. "Did it have writing on the blade?"

"Yep," Magnus replied. "They were real insistent that the inscription on the replica was exactly like that in the books."

"That's it," Esrahaddon muttered. "The church isn't here because of me, and they aren't here to find the heir; they're here to *make* an heir."

"Make an heir? I don't get it," Hadrian said. "I thought you said they wanted the heir dead."

"They do, but they are going to make a puppet. This Rufus has been picked to replace the true heir. There is a legend that only the bloodline of Novron can kill a Gilarabrywn. They will use this creature's death as undisputed proof that their boy is the true heir. Not only will it provide them legitimate means to dictate laws to the kings, but it will also hinder my efforts to reinstate the real heir to power. Who will believe an old outlawed wizard when their boy slew a Gilarabrywn? They will let a few bumpkins try to fight only to die, in order to prove the invincibility of the beast. Then this Rufus will step up, and with his sword etched with the name, he'll slay it and become emperor. With Rufus as their figurehead, the church will return to power and reform the empire. Excellent move, I must say. I'll admit I hadn't expected it."

"A few moderate kings might have something to say about that," Hadrian replied.

"And they know that as much as you do. They have a plan to deal with it, I'm sure."

"So do we still need to get inside?" Hadrian asked.

"Oh yes," the wizard told them. "Now more than ever." He chuckled. "Just imagine if before their boy Rufus slays this beast, another contestant slays it first."

The dwarf snorted. "Bah! I told you, you aren't getting through that door. It's solid stone."

The wizard considered the archway once more. "Open it, Royce."

Royce looked skeptical. "Open what? That's a wall. There's

no latch, no lock, not even a seam. Anyone have a gem we can try?"

"This isn't a gemlock," the wizard explained.

"I agree and I would know," Magnus told them.

"Try opening it anyway," the wizard insisted, staring at Royce. "That's why I brought you here, remember?"

Royce looked at the wall before him and scowled. "How?"

"Use your instincts. You opened the door to my prison and it had no latch either."

"I was lucky."

"You might be lucky again. Try."

Royce shrugged. He stepped forward and placed his hands lightly on the stone, letting his fingertips drift across the surface, searching by feel for what his eyes might not be able to see.

"This is a waste of time," Magnus said. "This is clearly a very powerful lock and without the key there is no way to open it. I know these things. I've *made* these things. They are designed to prevent thieves like him from entering."

"Ah," Esrahaddon said to the dwarf, "but you underestimate Royce. He is no ordinary lock picker. I sensed it the moment I first saw him. I know he can open it." The wizard turned to Royce, who was quickly showing signs of exasperation. "Stop *trying* to open it and just open it. Don't think about it. Just do it."

"Do what?" he asked, irritated. "If I knew how, don't you think I would have opened it by now?"

"That's just it; don't think. Stop being a thief. Just open the door."

Royce glared at the wizard. "Fine," he said as he pushed his palm against the stone wall and pulled it back with a look of shock on his face.

Esrahaddon's expression was one of sheer delight. "I knew it," the wizard said.

"Knew what? What happened?" Hadrian asked.

"I just pushed." Royce laughed at the absurdity.

"And?"

"What do you mean, *and*?" Royce asked, pointing at the solid wall.

"And what happened? Why are you smiling?" Hadrian studied the wall for something he missed, a tiny crack, a little latch, a keyhole, but he saw nothing. It was the same as it had always been.

"It opened," Royce said.

Hadrian and the dwarf looked at Royce, puzzled. "What are you talking about?"

Royce looked back over his shoulder as if that would make everything clear. "Are you both blind? The door is standing wide open. You can see there's a corridor that—"

"They can't see it," the wizard interrupted.

Royce looked from the wizard to Hadrian. "You can't see that the door is standing open now? You can't see this huge, three-story double door?"

Hadrian shook his head. "It looks just like it always has."

Magnus nodded his agreement.

"They can't see it because they can't enter," the wizard explained. Hadrian watched Royce look up, following the wizard's glance, and Royce's eyes widened.

"What?" Hadrian asked.

"Elven magic. Designed to prevent enemies from passing through these walls. All they see, and all they will encounter, is solid stone. The portal is closed to them."

"You can see it?" Royce asked Esrahaddon.

"Oh yes, quite plainly."

"So why is it we can see it and they can't?"

"I already told you, it is magic to stop enemies from entering. As it happens, I was invited into this tower nine hundred years ago. It was abandoned immediately after my visit, so I am guessing there was no one to revoke that permission." He looked back at what Hadrian still saw as solid stone. "I don't think I could have opened it, though, even if I had hands. That's why I needed you."

"Me?" Royce said; then a sudden shocked realization filled his expression and he glared at the wizard before him. "So you knew?"

"I wouldn't be much of a wizard if I didn't, now would I?"

Royce looked self-consciously at his own feet, then slowly turned to look cautiously at Hadrian, who only smiled. "You knew too?"

Hadrian frowned. "Did you really think I could work with you all these years and not figure it out? It is a little obvious, you know."

"You never said anything."

"I figured you didn't want to talk about it. You guard your past jealously, pal, and you have many doors on which I don't knock. Honestly, there were times I wondered if you knew."

"Knew what? What's going on?" Magnus demanded.

"None of your business," Hadrian told the dwarf, "but it does leave us with a parting of the ways, doesn't it? We can't come in, and I can tell you I am not fond of sitting here on the doorstep waiting for the flying lizard to come home."

"You should go back," Esrahaddon told them. "Royce and I can go on from here alone."

"How long will this take?" Hadrian asked.

"Several hours, a day perhaps," the wizard replied.

"I had hoped to be gone before it returned," Royce said.

"Not possible. Besides, this shouldn't be a problem for you, of all people. I am certain you have stolen from occupied homes before."

"Not ones where the owner can swallow me in a single bite."

"So we'll have to be extra quiet now, won't we?"

Chapter 10

Lost Swords

I thought last night went well," Bishop Saldur stated, slicing himself a wedge of breakfast cheese. He sat at the banquet table in the great hall of the manor along with Archbishop Galien, Sentinel Luis Guy, and Lord Rufus. The lofty cathedral ceiling of bound logs did little to elevate the dark, oppressive atmosphere caused by the lack of natural light. The entire manor had few windows and made Saldur feel as if he were crouching in an animal's den, some woodchuck's burrow or beaver's lodge. The thought that this miserable hovel would see the birth of the New Empire was a disappointment, but he was a pragmatic man. The method was irrelevant. All that mattered was the final solution. Either it worked or it did not—this was the only measure of value. Aesthetics could be added later.

Right now they needed to establish the empire. Mankind had drifted too long without a rudder. A firm hand was what the world needed, a solid grip on the wheel with a keen set of eyes that could see into the future and direct the vessel into clear, tranquil waters. Saldur envisioned a world of peace through prosperity, and security through strength. The feudal system so prevalent across the four nations held them back, chaining the kingdoms to a poverty of weakness and divided interests. What they needed was a centralized government with an enlightened ruler and a talented, educated bureaucracy overseeing every aspect of life. It was impossible to imagine the many goals that could be accomplished with the entire strength of mankind under one yoke. They could revolutionize farming, its fruits distributed evenly at a price that even the poorest could afford, vanquishing hunger. Laws could be standardized, eliminating arbitrary punishment by vindictive tyrants. Knowledge from the corners of the land could be gathered into a single repository where great minds could learn and develop new ideas, new techniques. They could improve transportation with standardized roads and they could clear the stench of cities with standardized sewage systems. If all this had to begin here in this little wood hut on the edge of the world, it was a small price to pay. "How many died?" he asked.

The archbishop shrugged and Rufus did not bother looking up from his plate.

"Five contestants were killed by the beast last night." Luis Guy answered his question as he plucked a muffin off the table with the point of his dagger.

The Knight of Nyphron continued to impress Saldur. He was a sword manifested in the form of a man—sharp, pointed, cutting, and just as elegant in appearance. He always stood straight, shoulders back, chin up, eyes focused directly on his target, his face a hard chiseled mask of contention, daring, almost begging for a confrontation from anyone fool enough to challenge him. Even after days in the wilderness, not a thread lay out of place. He was a paragon of the church, the embodiment of the ideal.

"Only five?"

"After the fifth was ripped in two, few were eager to step forward, and while they hesitated, the beast flew off."

"Do you think five deaths are sufficient to prove the beast is invincible?" Galien asked, looking at all of them.

"No, but we may have no choice. After last night, I'm not certain any more will volunteer," Guy replied. "The previously witnessed enthusiasm for the hunt has waned."

"And will you be ready, Lord Rufus? If no one else steps forward?" the archbishop asked, turning to the rough warrior seated at the end of the table.

Lord Rufus looked up. He was taking full advantage of the meal, chewing on a mutton leg that slicked his unruly beard with grease. His eyes stared at them from beneath the heavy hedges of his bushy red eyebrows. He spit a bit of bone out. "That depends," he said. "This sword the dwarf made, can it cut the beastie's hide?"

"We had our scribes check the dwarf's work against the ancient records," Saldur replied. "They match perfectly with the markings recorded on previous weapons that were capable of killing beasts of this kind."

"If it can cut it, I'll kill it." Rufus grinned a greasy smile. "Just be ready to crown me emperor." He bit into the leg again and ripped a large hunk of dark meat off, filling his mouth.

Saldur could hardly believe the Patriarch had chosen this oaf to be the emperor. If Guy was a sword, Rufus was a mallet, a blunt instrument of dull labor. Being a native of Trent, he would ensure the loyalty of the unruly northern kingdoms that most likely could not be gained any other way. That would easily double their strength going in. There was also his popularity, which extended down through Avryn and Calis. This reduced the number of protests against him. The fact that he was a renowned warrior would certainly help him in his first obstacles of killing the Gilarabrywn and crushing any opposition offered by the Nationalists. The problem, as Saldur saw it, was that Rufus, a rough, unreasonable dolt, had not only the heart of a warrior, but the mind as well. His answer to every problem was beating it to death. It would be hard to control him, but it made little sense to worry about the headaches of administrating an empire before one even existed. They needed to create it first and worry about the quality of the emperor later. If Rufus became a problem, they could merely ensure that once he had a son, and once that son was safe in their custody, Rufus could meet an untimely end.

"Well then," Galien said. "It would seem everything is in hand."

"Is that all you called me here for?" Guy asked with a tone of irritation.

"No," Galien replied, "I received some unexpected news this morning and I thought you might like to hear of it, Luis, as I suspect it will interest you very much. Carlton, will you ask the deacon Tomas to come in?"

Galien's steward, Carlton, who was busy pouring watered-down wine, promptly left the table and opened the door to the hallway. "His Grace will see you now."

In walked a plump, pudgy man in a priest's frock. "Luis Guy, Lord Rufus, let me introduce Deacon Tomas of Dahlgren Village. Tomas, this is Lord Rufus, Sentinel Guy, and you already know Bishop Saldur, of course."

Tomas nodded with a nervous smile.

"What's this all about?" Guy asked as if Tomas was not there.

"Go ahead, Tomas, tell the sentinel what you told me."

The deacon shifted his feet and avoided eye contact with anyone in the room. When he spoke, his voice was so soft they strained to hear him. "I was just mentioning to His Grace how I had stepped up and handled things here in the absence of the margrave. It has been hard times in this village, hard indeed, but I tried my best to keep the great house in order. It wasn't my idea that they should invade the place, I tried to stop them, but I am only one man, you see. It was impossible—"

"Yes, yes, tell him about the cripple," the archbishop put in.

"Oh, certainly. Ah yes, Esra came to live here, I don't know, about a month ago, he—"

"Esra?" Guy said, and glanced abruptly at the archbishop and Saldur, who both smiled knowingly at him.

"Yes," Deacon Tomas replied. "That's his name. He never said too much, but the villagers are a good lot and they took turns feeding him, as the poor man was in dire straits missing both hands as he is."

"Esrahaddon!" Guy hissed. "Where is the snake?"

The sudden violent reaction of the sentinel shocked Tomas, who took a step back.

"Ah, well, I don't know, he comes and goes, although I remember he was around the village a lot more before the two strangers arrived."

"Strangers?" Guy asked.

"Friends of the Wood family, I think. At least, they arrived with Thrace and spend a lot of time with her and her father. Since they got here, Esra spends most of his days off with the quiet one—Royce, I think they call him."

"Royce Melborn and Hadrian Blackwater, the two thieves that broke the wizard out of Gutaria, and Esrahaddon are all here in this village?" Saldur and Galien nodded at Luis.

"Very curious, isn't it?" the archbishop commented. "Perhaps we focused on the wrong hound when we approached Arista. It looks as if the old wizard has put his trust in the two thieves instead. The real question is, why would they all be here? It can't be coincidence that he turns up in this little backwater village at the precise moment when the emperor is about to be crowned."

"He couldn't know our plans," Guy told him.

"He *is* a wizard; they are good at discovering things. Regardless, you might want to see if you can determine what he's up to."

"Remember to keep your distance," Saldur added. "We don't want to tree this fox until we know he's led us to his den."

ೞ

Hadrian folded the blanket twice in length, then rolled it tight, buckling the resulting cloth log with two leather straps. He had all the gear left to them on the ground in neat piles. They still had all their camping gear, food, and feed. Royce had his saddle, bridle, and bags, but Hadrian had lost his tack along with his weapons when Millie had disappeared. It would be impossible to ride double and haul the gear. They would have to load Mouse up with everything and walk the trip home.

"There you are."

Hadrian looked up to see Theron striding from the direction of the Bothwicks', heading for the well with an empty bucket in his hand.

"We didn't see you around last night. Was worried something happened to you."

"Looks like everyone had a lucky night," Hadrian said.

"Everyone in the village—yeah. But I don't think them fellas up at the castle did so well. We heard a lot of shouting and screaming and they ain't celebrating this morning. My guess is their plan to kill the beast didn't go as hoped." The farmer scanned the piles. "Packing, eh? So you're leaving too?"

"I don't see why not. There's nothing keeping us here anymore. How's Thrace?"

"Doing well, rubbing elbows with the nobility, she tells me. She's walking around just fine; the headaches are mostly gone. We'll be on our way tomorrow morning, I expect."

"Good to hear it," Hadrian said.

"Who's your friend?" Theron motioned to the dwarf seated a few feet away in the shade of a poplar tree.

"Oh yeah. Theron, meet Magnus. He's not so much a friend as an associate." He thought about that and added, "Actually, he's more like an enemy I'm keeping an eye on."

Theron nodded, but with a puzzled look, and the dwarf grumbled something neither caught.

"What about my lesson?" Theron asked.

"Are you kidding? I don't really see the point in a lesson if you're both leaving tomorrow."

"You have something else to do? Besides, the road is a dangerous place and it wouldn't hurt to know a few more tricks, or is this your way of saying you want money now?"

"No." Hadrian waved his hand at the farmer. "Grab the sticks."

By noon, the sun was hot and Hadrian had worked up a sweat sparring with Theron, who was showing real improvement. Magnus sat on an overturned well bucket, watching the two with interest. Hadrian explained proper form, how to obtain penetrating thrusts and grips, which was hard using only rake handles.

"If you hold the sword with both hands, you lose versatility and reach, but you gain tremendous power. A good fighter knows when to switch from two hands to one and vice versa. If you are defending against someone with longer reach, you'd better be using one hand, but if you need to drive your sword deep through heavy armor—assuming you aren't holding a shield in your off hand—grip the pommel with both palms and thrust. Remember to yell as you do, like I taught you before. Then drive home the blow using all your power. A solid breastplate won't stop a sword thrust. They aren't designed to. Armor prevents a swing or a slice, and can deflect the point of a thrust; that's why professional fighters wear smooth, unadorned armor. You always see these princes and dukes with all their fancy gilded breastplates and light thin metal heavily engraved—it's like walking around in a death trap. Of course, they don't really fight. They have knights do that for them. They just walk around and look pretty. So the idea is when you thrust, you aim for a crease, groove, or seam in the armor, something that will catch and hold the tip. The armpits are excellent targets, or up under the nose guard. Drive a four-foot sword up under a nose guard and you don't have to worry much about a counterattack."

"How can you teach that poor fellow anything without swords?"

They both turned to see Mauvin Pickering walking toward them in his simple blue tunic. Gone was the dapper lord of Galilin; instead, he looked much like the boy Hadrian had first seen at Drondil Fields. In his hands, he carried two swords, and slung over his back were two small round shields.

"I saw you from the walls and thought you might like to borrow these," he said, handing a sword and shield to Theron, who accepted them awkwardly. "They are my and Fanen's spares."

Theron eyed the young man suspiciously, then looked to Hadrian.

"Go ahead," Hadrian told him, wiping the sweat from his brow with his sleeve. "He's right. You should know the feel of the real thing."

When Theron appeared confused by how to hold the shield, Mauvin began instructing him, showing the farmer where his arm slipped through the leather straps.

"See, Hadrian? It helps to actually teach your pupil how to put on a real shield; unless, of course, you expect he'll be spending all of his time warring against maple trees. Where are your weapons, anyway?"

Hadrian looked sheepish. "I lost them."

"Don't you carry enough for five people?"

"I've had a bad week."

"And who might you be?" Mauvin asked, looking at the dwarf.

Hadrian started to answer, then stopped himself. Alric had likely told Mauvin all about the dwarf who had murdered his father. "Him? He's... nobody."

"Okay..." Mauvin laughed, raising his hand and waving. "Pleased to meet you, Mr. Nobody." He then went and sat on the edge of the well, where he folded his arms across his chest. "Go on. Show me what he's taught you."

Hadrian and Theron returned to fighting, but slower now, as the sharp swords made Theron nervous. He soon became frustrated and turned to Mauvin, scowling.

"You any good with these things?"

The young man raised an eyebrow in surprise. "My dear sir, weren't we already introduced? My name is Mauvin Pickering." He grinned.

Theron narrowed his eyes in confusion, glanced at Hadrian, who said nothing, then faced the boy once more. "I asked if you knew how to use a sword, son, not your name."

"But—I—oh, never mind. Yes, I have been trained in the use of a sword."

"Well, I spent all my life on farms, or in villages not much bigger than this one, and I've never had much chance to see fellas beating each other with blades. It might help if'n I was to see what I'm s'posed to be doing. You know, all proper like."

"You want a demonstration?"

Theron nodded. "I have no way of knowing if Hadrian here even knows what he's doing."

"All right," Mauvin said, flexing his fingers and shaking his hands as he walked forward. He had a bright smile on his face, as if Theron had just invited him to play his favorite game.

The two paired off. Magnus and Theron took seats in the dirt and watched as Mauvin and Hadrian first walked through the basic moves and then demonstrated each at actual combat speed. Hadrian would explain each maneuver and comment on the action afterward.

"See there? Mauvin thought I was going to slice inward toward his thigh and dropped his guard briefly. He did that because I told him to by suggesting with a dip of my shoulder that this was my intention, so before I even started my stroke, I knew what Mauvin was going to do, because I was the one dictating it. In essence I knew what he would do before he did and in a battle that's very handy."

"Enough of the lessons," Mauvin said, clearly irritated at being the illustration of a fencing mistake. "Let's show him a real demonstration."

"Looking for a rematch?" Hadrian asked.

"Curious if it was luck."

Hadrian smiled and muttered, "Pickerings."

He took off his shirt and, wiping his face and hands, threw it on the grass and raised his sword to ready position. Mauvin lunged and immediately the two began to fight. The swords sang as they cut the air so fast their movements blurred. Hadrian and Mauvin danced around on the balls of their feet, shuffling in the dirt so briskly that a small cloud rose to knee height.

"By Mar!" the old farmer exclaimed.

Then abruptly they stopped, both panting from the exertion.

Mauvin glared at Hadrian with a look that was both amazed and irritated. "You're playing with me."

"I thought that was the point. You don't really want me to kill you?"

"Well no, but—well, like he said—by Mar! I've never seen anyone fight like you do; you're amazing."

"I thought you both were pretty amazing," Theron remarked. "I've never seen anything like that."

"I have to agree," Magnus chimed in. The dwarf was on his feet, nodding his head.

Hadrian walked over to the well and poured half a bucket over himself, then shook the water from his hair.

"Seriously, Hadrian," Mauvin asked, "where did you learn it?"

"From a man named Danbury Blackwater."

"Blackwater? Isn't that your name?"

Hadrian nodded and a melancholy look stole over his face. "He was my father."

"Was?"

"He died."

"Was he a warrior? A general?"

"Blacksmith."

"Blacksmith?" Mauvin asked in disbelief.

"In a village not much bigger than this. You know, the guy who makes horseshoes, rakes, pots."

"Are you telling me a village blacksmith knew the secret disciplines of the Teshlors? I recognized the Tek'chin moves, the ones my father taught me. The rest I can only assume were from the other lost disciplines of the Teshlors."

Mauvin drew blank stares from everyone.

"The Teshlors?" He looked around—more stares. He rolled his eyes and sighed. "Heathens, I'm surrounded by ignorant heathens. The Teshlors were the greatest knights ever to have lived. They were the personal bodyguards of the emperor. It's said they were taught the Five Disciplines of Combat from Novron himself. Only one of which is the

Tek'chin, and the knowledge of the Tek'chin alone is what has made a legend out of the Pickering dynasty. Your father clearly knew the Tek'chin, and apparently other Teshlor disciplines that I thought had been lost for nearly a thousand years, and you're telling me he was a blacksmith? He was probably the greatest warrior of his time. And you don't know what your father did before you were born?"

"I assume the same thing he did afterward."

"Then how did he know how to fight?"

Hadrian considered this. "I just assumed he picked it up serving in the local army. Several of the men in the village served His Lordship as men-at-arms. I assumed he saw combat. He used to talk like he had."

"Did you ever ask him?"

The thunder of hooves interrupted them as three men on horseback entered the village from the direction of the margrave's castle. The riders were all in black and red with the symbol of a broken crown on their chests. At their head rode a tall thin man with long black hair and a short trimmed beard.

"Excellent swordsmanship," the lead man said. He rode right up to Hadrian and reined in his animal roughly. The black stallion was draped in a scarlet and black caparison complete with braided tassels, a scarlet headpiece with a foot-tall black plume spouting from his head. The horse snorted and stomped. "I was wondering why the son of Count Pickering wasn't partaking in the combat today, but I see now you found a worthier partner to spar against. Who would this delightful warrior be and why haven't I seen you at the castle?"

"I'm not here to compete for the crown," Hadrian said simply, slipping on his shirt.

"No? Pity, you certainly appear to be worthy of a chance. What's your name?"

"Hadrian."

"Ah, good to meet you, Sir Hadrian."

"Just Hadrian."

"I see. Do you live here, *just* Hadrian?"

"No."

The horseman seemed less than pleased with the curt answer and nudged his horse closer in a menacing manner. The animal puffed out a hot moist breath into Hadrian's face. "Then what are you doing here?"

"Just passing through," Hadrian replied in his usual amiable manner. He even managed a friendly little smile.

"Really? Just passing through Dahlgren? To where in the world, might I ask, is Dahlgren on the way?"

"Just about everywhere, depending on your perspective, don't you think? I mean, all roads lead somewhere, don't they?" He was tired of being on the defensive and took a verbal swing. "Is there a reason you're so interested?"

"I'm Sentinel Luis Guy and I'm in charge of managing the contest. I need to know if everyone participating is listed."

"I already told you I wasn't here for the contest."

"So you did," Guy said, and slowly looked around at the others, taking particular notice of Magnus. "You are just passing through, you said, but perhaps those traveling with you wish to be listed on the roll."

A feint, perhaps? Hadrian decided to parry anyway. "No one I'm with will want to be on that list."

"No one you're with?"

Hadrian gritted his teeth. It *was* a feint. Hadrian mentally scolded himself.

"So you're not alone?" the sentinel observed. "Where are the others?"

"I couldn't tell you."

"No?"

Hadrian shook his head—fewer words, smaller chance of mistakes.

"Really? You mean they could be washing over the falls right now and you couldn't care less?"

"I didn't say that," Hadrian replied, irritated.

"But you see no need to know where they are?"

"They're grown men."

The sentinel smiled. "And who are *these men*? Please tell me so that I might inquire of them later perhaps."

Hadrian's eyes narrowed as he realized too late his mistake. The man before him was clever—too clever.

"Did you forget their names too?" Luis Guy inquired, leaning forward in his saddle.

"No." Hadrian tried to hold him off while he struggled to think.

"Then what are they?"

"Well," he began, wishing he had his own swords rather than a borrowed one. "Like I said, I don't know where *both* of them are. Mauvin is here, of course, but I have no idea where Fanen has gotten to."

"Surely you are mistaken. The Pickerings traveled with me and the rest of the entourage," Guy pointed out.

"Yes, they *were*, but they are planning on returning home with me."

Guy's eyes narrowed. "So you are saying that you traveled all the way out here *alone*—passing through, as you put it—and just happened to join up with the Pickerings?"

Hadrian smiled at the sentinel. It was weak, clumsy, and the fencing equivalent of dropping his sword and tackling his opponent to the ground, but it was all he could do.

"Is this true, Pickering?"

"Absolutely," Mauvin replied without hesitation.

Guy looked back at Hadrian. "How convenient for you," he said, disappointed. "Well, then don't let me keep you from your practice. Good day, gentlemen."

They all watched as the three men rode off toward the river trail.

"That was creepy," Mauvin remarked, staring off in their direction. "It can never be good when any sentinel takes an interest in you, much less Luis Guy."

"What's his story?" Hadrian asked.

"I really only know rumors. He's a zealot for the church, but I know many even in the church who are scared of him. He's the kind of person that can make kings disappear. He's also rumored to be obsessed with finding the Heir of Novron."

"Aren't all seret?"

"According to church doctrine, sure. But he really is, which explains why he's here."

"And the two with him?"

"Seret, the Knights of Nyphron, they are the sentinel's personal shadow army. They're answerable to no king or nation, just to sentinels and the Patriarch."

Mauvin looked at Hadrian. "You might want to keep that sword. It looks like a bad time to be without your weapons."

ꟹ

Although he had put his lantern out long before the creature's return, Royce could see just fine. Light permeated the walls of Avempartha, seeping through the stone as if it were smoky glass. It was daylight outside, of that he was certain, as the color of light had changed from dim blue to soft white.

As the sun rose, the interior of the citadel became an illuminated world of wondrous color and beauty. Ceilings stretched in tall, airy arches, meeting hundreds of feet above the floor and giving the illusion of not being indoors at all but rather in a place where the horizon was merely lost in mist. The roar of the nearby cataracts, tamed by the walls of the tower, was a soft, muffled, undeniably soothing hum.

Thin gossamer banners hung from the lofty heights. Each shimmered with symbols Royce did not understand. They might have been standards of royalty, rules of law, directions to halls, or meaningless decorations. All Royce knew was that even in the wake of a thousand years, the detailed patterns still appeared fluid and vibrant. It was artistry beyond mortal hands, born of a culture unfathomable. Being the only elven structure Royce had ever entered, it was his only glimpse into that world and it felt oddly peaceful. Still and silent, it was beautiful. Although it looked nothing like anything Royce had ever seen, his reason fought against the growing sensation that somehow all this was familiar. Royce felt calm as he wandered the corridors. The very shapes and shadows touched chords in his mind he never realized were there. It all spoke to him in a language he could not understand. He caught only a word or a phrase in an avalanche of sensations that both mystified and captivated him as he wandered aimlessly, like a man blinded by a dazzling light.

He walked from room to room, up stairs and across balconies, following no conscious course, but merely moving, staring, and listening. Royce noticed with concern that every movement he made was recorded clearly in centuries of dust that blanketed the interior. Still, he was fascinated to discover that where he disturbed the dust, the floor revealed a glossy surface as clear as still water.

Passing through the various chambers, he felt as if he were in a museum, lost in a moment of frozen time. Plates were still out before empty chairs, some fallen on their sides—overturned in the confusion and alarm of nearly a millennium earlier. Books lay open to pages someone had been reading nine hundred years before, yet Royce knew that even to that person who had sat there so long ago, this place, this tower, had been ancient. Aside from its dramatic history, by its age alone Avempartha would be a monument—a sacred structure—to the elves, a link to an ancient era. This was not a citadel. He did not know how he knew, but he was certain this was something far more than a mere fortress.

Esrahaddon had left Royce almost immediately after entering the tower and pointing him in the direction he was now following. He had told Royce that he would find the sword he sought somewhere above the entrance, but that the wizard's path led elsewhere. It had been hours now since they had parted, and the light outside was already starting to dim. Royce still had not found the sword. Sights, sounds, and smells sidetracked him. It was too much to process at once, too much to classify, and soon he found himself lost.

He started to follow his trail in reverse when he discovered his footprints overlapped, leaving him a path that moved in circles. He was starting to become concerned when he heard a new sound. Unlike everything he had encountered so far, this noise was disturbing. It was the thick rhythmical resonance of heavy breathing.

Every path open to the thief was marred with his own tracks except one. This led to yet another stair, where the breathing was louder. How many floors up Royce had wandered, he was not certain, but he knew he had not come across any swords. Slowly, and as silently as he could, he began to creep upward.

He had not gone more than five steps when he spotted his first sword. It lay blanketed in dust on a step beside a bony form. What cloth there might have been was gone, but the armor remained. Farther up, he spotted another and yet another. There were two different types of bodies—humans in broad heavy breastplates and greaves, and elves in delicate blue armor. This was the last stand, the last defense to protect the emperor. Elves and men fallen one upon the other.

Royce reached down and slid his thumb along the flat of the blade at his feet. As the dust wiped clear, the amazing shine of the elven steel glimmered as if new, but no etching was on it. Royce looked up the stairs and reluctantly stepped over the bodies as he continued his climb.

The breathing grew louder and deeper, like wind blowing through an echoing cavern. A room lay ahead, and with the silence of a cat's shadow, Royce crept inside. The chamber was round with yet another staircase leading up. As he entered, he could feel and smell fresh air. Tall thin windows allowed unfettered shafts of light into the room, but Royce felt that somewhere above him a much larger window lay.

At last, Royce found a rack of elven swords mounted ceremoniously to the wall in ornate cases. Divided from the rest of the room by a delicate chain, the area appeared as a memorial, a remembrance set aside in honor. A plaque on a pedestal stood before the rack and on the walls were numerous lines of elven script carved into the stone. Royce knew only a few words and those before him had been written with such flair and embellishment that he was at a loss to recognize even a single word, although he was certain he recognized several letters.

On the rack were dozens of swords. They all appeared to be identical, and without having to touch them, Royce could see the etchings clearly cut into the blades and the notches hewn into the metal. One spot remained vacant.

With a silent sigh, he steadied himself and began to climb upward once more. With each step, the air grew fresher; currents banished dust to the cracks and corners. Along the stair, more openings and hallways appeared to either side, but Royce had a hunch and continued to climb, moving toward the sound of breathing.

At last, the steps ended and Royce looked up at open sky. Above him was a circular balcony with sculpted walls like petals on a flower. Statues that had once lined this open-air pavilion lay in broken heaps on the floor. At their center rested the malevolent sleeping figure of the Gilarabrywn, an enormous black-scaled lizard with wings of gray membrane and bone. It lay curled, its head on its tail, its body heaving with deep, long breaths. Muscular claws were armed with four twelve-inch-long black nails; encrusted with dried blood, they left deep groves in the surface of the floor where they scraped in the beast's sleep. Long sharp fangs protruded from beneath leathery lips, as did a row of frightening teeth that followed no visible scheme but seemed to mesh together like a wild fence of needles. Ears lay back upon its head, its eyes cloaked by broad lids, beneath which pupils darted about in a fretful slumber, of what dark visages Royce could not begin to imagine. The long tail, barbed at the end with a saber-like bone, twitched.

Royce caught himself staring and cursed at his own stupidity. It was a sight, to be certain, but this was no time to be distracted. Focus was all that separated him from certain death.

He had always hated places with animals. Hounds bellowed at the slightest sound or smell. He had managed to step past many a sleeping dog, but there had been a few that managed to sense him without warning. He mentally gripped himself and pulled his eyes away from the giant to study the rest of the room. It was a shambles, broken fixtures and rubble. On closer study, however, Royce noticed that the rubble held terrible treasures. He recognized torn bits of Mae Drundel's dress, matted with dark stains; and tangled within its folds was a bit of scalp and a long lock of gray hair. Other equally disturbing items lay around him. Arms, feet, fingers, hands, all cast aside like shrimp tails. He spotted Millie, Hadrian's bay mare, or rather one of her rear legs and her tail. Not too far away he was stunned to see Millie's saddle and Hadrian's swords. Luckily, they were within easy reach.

As he began to move around the pile, inching his way with the slow discipline of a mantis on the hunt, he saw something. The bodies and torn clothes lay atop the pile of bones and stone. But deep beneath, on the bottom stratum of built-up sediment, Royce caught the singular glint of mirrored steel. It was only a tiny patch, no larger than a small coin, which was what he initially took it for, but its brilliance was unmistakable. It possessed the same gleam as the swords on the stairs and in the rack below.

Barely breathing—each movement keyed to a painfully slow pace that might defy even a direct look—Royce stole closer to the beast and his vile treasure trove. He slipped his hand under the strands of Millie's tail and meticulously began to draw forth the blade.

It came loose with little effort or sound, but even before he had it free, Royce knew something was wrong. It was not heavy enough. Even given that elven blades might weigh dramatically less, it was ridiculously light. He soon realized why as he drew forth only part of a broken blade. Seeing the etching on the unnotched metal, Royce realized his hunch was correct. This Gilarabrywn was no animal, no dumb beast trained to kill. This conjured demon was self-aware enough to realize it had only one mortal fear in this world—a blade with its name on it. It took precautions. The monster had broken the blade, severing the name and rendering it useless. He could not see the other half of the sword, but it seemed obvious to him where it lay. The remainder of the sword rested in the one place from which Royce could not steal it—beneath the sleeping body of the Gilarabrywn itself.

Chapter 11

Gilarabrywn

It was nearing dusk when Royce, hauling three swords over his shoulder, found Hadrian and Magnus waiting at the well. The village was empty, its inhabitants holed up in their hovels, and the night was quiet except for the faint sounds of distant activity coming from the castle.

"It's about time," Hadrian said, jumping to his feet at Royce's approach.

"Here's your gear." Royce handed Hadrian his weapons. "Be careful next time where you stow it. I do have more important things to do than be your personal valet."

Hadrian happily took the swords and belts and began strapping them on. "I was starting to worry the church had grabbed you."

"Church?" Royce asked.

"Luis Guy was harassing me earlier."

"The sentinel?"

"Yeah. He was asking about my partners and rode off toward the river and I haven't seen him come back. I got the impression he might be fishing for Esra. Where is Esra, anyway? Did you leave him at the river?"

"He didn't stop back here?" Royce asked. They shook their

heads. "Doesn't mean anything; he'd be a fool to come back to the village. He's likely hiding in the trees."

"Assuming he didn't get swept away by the river," Hadrian said. "Why did you leave him?"

"He left me with a very *don't follow me* attitude, which under normal circumstances would ensure that I followed him, but I had other things on my mind. Before I knew it, the sun was going down. I thought he had already left."

"So did you find anything valuable inside? Gems? Gold?"

Royce suddenly felt stupid. "You know, it never even crossed my mind to look."

"What?"

"I completely forgot about it."

"So what did you do in there all day?"

Royce pulled the bare half blade from his belt. It gleamed even in the faint light. "All the other swords were in a neat display case, but I found this buried almost directly under the Gilarabrywn's foot."

"Its foot?" Hadrian said, stunned. "You saw it?"

Royce nodded with a grimace. "And trust me—it isn't a sight you want to see drunk or sober."

"You think *it* broke the blade?"

"Kinda makes you wonder, doesn't it?"

"So where's the other piece?"

"I'm guessing it's sleeping on it, but I wasn't about to try and roll it over to look."

"I'm surprised you didn't wait until it left."

"With our client leaving in the morning, what's the point? If it was an easy grab—if I could see it and didn't have to spend hours digging through... well, stuff—fine, but I'm not about to risk my neck for Esra's personal war with the church. Besides, remember the hounds in Blythin Castle?"

Hadrian nodded with a sick look on his face.

"If it can smell scents, I didn't want to be around when it wakes up. The way I see it, Thrace has her father, Esra has access to the tower, and Rufus will rid the village of the Gilarabrywn. I say our work here is done." Royce looked at the dwarf, then back at Hadrian. "Thanks for keeping an eye on him." He drew his dagger.

"Wha—wait!" The dwarf backpedaled as Royce advanced. "We had a deal!"

Royce grinned at him. "Do I really look trustworthy to you?"

"Royce, you can't," Hadrian said.

The thief looked at him and chuckled. "Are you kidding? Look at him. If I can't slit his throat in ten seconds, tops, I'll buy you a beer as soon as we get back to Alburn. Tell me when you're ready to count."

"No, I meant he's right. You made a bargain with him. You can't go back on it."

"Oh please. This little...dwarf...tried to kill me and damn near succeeded, and you want me to let him go because I said I would? Hey, he lived a whole day longer for helping us. That's plenty reward."

"Royce!"

"What?" The thief rolled his eyes. "You aren't serious? He killed Amrath."

"It was a job, and you aren't a member of the royal guard. He upheld his end just as agreed. And there's no benefit to killing him."

"Enjoyment," Royce said. "Enjoyment and satisfaction are benefits."

Hadrian continued to glare.

Royce shook his head and sighed. "All right, okay, he can live. It's stupid, but he can live. Happy?"

Royce looked up at the great motte of the castle, where already the torches of that night's contestants were assembling. "It's nearly dark; we need to get inside. Where's the best seat for this dinner theatre I hear they've been holding at the castle? And when I say *best*, I mean *safest*."

"We still have an open invitation to the Bothwicks'. Theron is there now and we've been—"

A screeching cry from the direction of the river cut through the night.

"What in the land of Novron's ghost is that?" Magnus asked.

"You think maybe lizard wings found out his rattle was stolen?" Hadrian asked apprehensively.

Royce looked back toward the trees and then at his friend. "I think we'd better find a better place to hide tonight than the Bothwicks'."

"Where?" Hadrian asked. "If it comes looking for that blade, it will rip every house apart until it finds it, and we already know the local architecture doesn't pose much of a challenge. It's gonna kill everyone in the village."

"We could run them all to the castle; there might still be time," Royce suggested.

"No good," Hadrian countered. "The guards won't let us in. The forest, maybe?"

"The trees only slow it down. It won't stop it any more than the houses."

"Damn it." Hadrian looked around desperately. "I should have built the pit out in the village."

"What about the well here?" the dwarf asked, peering into the wooden-rimmed hole.

Royce and Hadrian looked at each other.

"I feel so stupid right now," Royce said.

Hadrian ran to the bell, grabbed hold of the dangling rope,

and began to pull it. The bell, intended for the future church of Dahlgren, raised the alarm.

"Keep ringing it," Hadrian yelled at Magnus as he and Royce raced to the houses, sweeping their cloth drapes aside and banging on the frames.

"Get out. Everyone out," they yelled. "Your houses won't protect you tonight. Get in the well. Everyone in the well now!"

"What's going on?" Russell Bothwick asked, peering out into the darkness.

"No time to explain," Hadrian shouted back. "Get in the well if you want to live."

"But the church? They are supposed to save us," Selen Brockton said, huddling in a blanket in the arch of her doorway.

"Are you willing to bet your life? You're all gonna have to trust me. If I am wrong, you'll spend one miserable night, but if I am right and you don't listen, you'll all die."

"That's good enough for me," Theron said, storming out of the Bothwick house, buttoning his shirt, his massive figure and loud harsh voice commanding everyone's attention. "And it had better be good enough for the lot of you too. Hadrian has done more to save this village from death in the past few days than all of us—and all of them—combined. If he says sleep in the well tonight, then by the beard of Maribor that's what I'll do. I don't care if the beast was known to be dead. I'd still do it, and any of you who refuse, why, you deserve to be eaten."

The inhabitants of Dahlgren ran to the well.

Loops were tied into the rope for footholds, and while the well was wide enough to lower four or even five people at a time, because they did not trust the strength of the windlass, they lowered them in groups of only twos and threes, depending on weight.

Although people moved quickly and orderly, obeying

Hadrian's instructions without argument, the process was excruciatingly slow. Magnus volunteered to go in and drive pegs into the walls to form footholds. Young Hal, Arvid, and Pearl, being too small to go down first, raced around the village fetching more shafts of wood for the dwarf to drive into the sides. Tad Bothwick went down and worked with Magnus, feeding him the wooden spikes as the little dwarf built makeshift platforms.

"Whoa, mister." Tad's voice echoed out of the mouth of the well. "I ain't never seen no one use a hammer like that. It took six weeks to build up these walls, and I swear you look like you coulda done it in six hours."

Outside, Hadrian, Theron, Vince, and Dillon did the work of lowering villagers in. Hadrian lined them up, sending women and children down first into the darkness, where only a single candle that Tad held for Magnus revealed anything below.

"How long?" Hadrian asked as they waited to lower the next set down.

"It would have been here by now if it had flown the moment we heard it," Royce replied. "It must be searching the tower. That gives us some time, but I don't know how much."

"Get up in a tree and yell when you see it."

When everyone was in, Hadrian lowered Theron and Dillon, leaving only Hadrian, Vince, and Royce aboveground, where they waited for Magnus to finish the last set of wall pegs. Up in a poplar tree, Royce stood out on a thin branch, scanning the sky while listening to the dwarf hammering the last stakes into place.

"Here it comes!" he shouted, spotting a shadow darting across the stars.

Seconds later the Gilarabrywn screamed from somewhere above the dark canopy of leaves and the three cringed, but nothing happened. They stood still, staring into the darkness around them, listening. Another cry ripped through the night. The Gilarabrywn flew straight for the torches of the manor house.

Royce spotted it in the night sky flying over the hill where the next challenger for the crown prepared to meet the beast. It descended, then rose once more. It issued another screech; then the beast let loose a roar and fire exploded from its mouth. Instantly, everything grew brighter as fire engulfed the hillside.

"That's new," Hadrian declared nervously as he watched the ghastly sight. The crowd of challengers lost their lives with hardly the time to scream. "Magnus, hurry!"

"All set. Go! Climb down," the dwarf shouted back.

"Wait!" Tad cried. "Where's Pearl?"

"She's looking for wood," Vince said. "I'll get her."

Hadrian grabbed his arm. "It's too dangerous; get in the well. Royce will go."

"I will?" Royce asked, surprised.

"It's lousy being the only one to see in the dark sometimes, isn't it?"

Royce cursed and ran off, pausing in homes and sheds to call the little girl's name as loudly as he dared. It got easier to see his way as the light from the hill grew larger and brighter. The Gilarabrywn screamed repeatedly and Royce looked over his shoulder to see the castle walls engulfed in flames.

"Royce," Hadrian shouted, "it's coming!"

Royce gave up stealth. "Pearl!" he yelled aloud.

"Here!" she screamed, darting out from the trees.

He grabbed the little girl up in his arms and raced for the well.

"Run, damn it!" Hadrian shouted, holding the rope for them.

"Forget the rope. Get down and catch her."

While Royce was still sprinting across the yard, Hadrian slid down the coil.

Thrump. Thrump. Thrump.

Hugging Pearl close to his chest, Royce reached the well and jumped. The little girl screamed as they fell in together. An instant later, there came a loud unearthly scream and a terrible vibration as the world above the well erupted in a brilliant light accompanied by a thunderous roar.

~

Arista paced the length of the little room, painfully aware of Bernice's head turning side to side, following her every move. The old woman was smiling at her; she always smiled at her, and Arista was about ready to gouge her eyes out. She was used to her tower, where even Hilfred gave her space, but for more than a week, she had been subjected to constant company—Bernice, her ever-present shadow. She had to get out of the room, to get away. She was tired of being stared at, of being watched after like a child. She walked to the door.

"Where are you going, Highness?" Bernice was quick to ask.

"Out," she said.

"Out where?"

"Just out."

Bernice stood up. "Let me get our cloaks."

"I am going alone."

"Oh no, Your Highness," Bernice said, "that's not possible."

Arista glared at her. Bernice smiled back. "Imagine this, Bernice: you sit back down and I walk out. It is possible."

"But I can't do that. You are the princess and this is a dangerous place. You need to be chaperoned for your own safety. We'll need Hilfred to escort us, as well. Hilfred," she called.

The door popped open and the bodyguard stepped in, bowing to Arista. "Did you need something, Your Highness?"

"No—yes," Arista said, and pointed at Bernice, "keep her here. Sit on her, tie her up, hold her at sword point if you must, but I am leaving and I don't want her following me."

The old maid looked shocked and put both hands to her cheeks in surprise.

"You're going out, Your Highness?" Hilfred asked.

"Yes, yes, I am going out!" she exclaimed, throwing her arms up. "I may roam the halls of this cabin. I may go to watch the contest. Why, I might even leave the stockade altogether and wander into the forest. I could get lost and die of starvation, eaten by a bear, tumble into the Nidwalden and get swept over the falls—but I'll do so alone."

Hilfred stood at attention. His eyes stared back at hers. His mouth opened and then closed.

"Is there something you want to say?" she asked, her tone harsh.

Hilfred swallowed. "No, Your Highness."

"At least take your cloak," Bernice insisted, holding it up.

Arista sighed, snatched it from her hands, and walked out.

The moment she left, regret set in. Storming down the corridor, dragging the cloak, she paused. The look on Hilfred's face left her feeling miserable. She recalled having a crush on him as a girl. He was the son of a castle sergeant, and he used to stare at her from across the courtyard. Arista had thought he was cute. Then one morning she had awoken to fire and smoke. He saved her life. Hilfred had been just a boy, but he had run into the flaming castle to drag her out. He spent two months suffering from burns and coughing fits that caused him to spit up blood. For weeks he awoke screaming from nightmares. As a reward, King Amrath appointed Hilfred to the prestigious post of personal bodyguard to the princess.

But she had never thanked him, nor forgiven him for not saving her mother. Her anger was always between them. Arista wanted to apologize, but it was too late. Too many years had passed, too many cruelties, followed by too many silences like the one that had just hung between them.

"What's going on?" Arista heard Thrace's voice and walked toward it.

"What's wrong, Thrace?" The princess found the farmer's daughter and the deacon in the main hallway. The girl was dressed in her thin chemise nightgown. They both looked concerned.

"Your Highness!" the girl called to her. "Do you know what is happening? Why was the bell ringing?"

"The contest is starting soon, if that's what you mean. I was on my way to watch. Are you feeling better? Would you like to come?" Arista found herself asking. She was aware of the irony, but being with Thrace was not the same as being escorted by Bernice and Hilfred.

"No, you don't understand. Something must be wrong. It's dark. No one would ring the bell at night."

"I didn't hear a bell," Arista said, pulling the cloak over her shoulders.

"The village bell," Thrace replied. "I heard it. It has stopped now."

"It's probably just part of the combat announcement."

"No." Thrace shook her head, and the deacon mimicked her. "That bell is only rung in emergencies, dire emergencies. Something is terribly wrong."

"I'm sure it's nothing. You forget. There is practically an army outside just itching for their chance to fight. Anyway, we certainly can't find out standing here." Arista took Thrace's hand and led them out to the courtyard.

Because it was the second night, the event had moved into

full extravagance. Outside, the high grassy yard of the manor's hill was set up like a pavilion at a tournament joust. The raised mound of the manor's motte offered a perfect view of the field below. Colorful awnings hung stretched above rows of chairs with small tables holding steins of mead, ale, and bowls of berries and cheese. The archbishop and Bishop Saldur sat together near the center, while several other clergy and servants stood watching the distant action unfolding on the hillside beyond the castle walls.

"Oh, Arista, my dear," Saldur called to her, "come to see history being made, have you? Good. Have a seat. That's Lord Rufus out there on the field. It seems he tires of waiting for his crown, but the vile beast is late in showing this evening and I think it is making His Lordship a tad irritated. Do you see how he paces his stallion? So like an emperor to be impatient."

"Who is to come after Rufus?" Arista asked, remaining on her feet, looking down at the field below.

"After?" Saldur looked puzzled. "Oh, I'm not sure, actually. Well, I hardly think it matters. Rufus will likely win tonight."

"Why is that?" Arista asked. "It isn't a matter of skill really, is it? It is a matter of bloodline. Is Lord Rufus suspected of bearing some known ties to the imperial family?"

"Well, yes, as a matter of fact he has claimed such for years now."

"Really?" Arista questioned. "I have never heard of him ever making such a boast."

"Well, the church doesn't like to promote unproven theories or random claims, but Rufus is indeed a favorite here. Tonight will prove his words, of course."

"Excuse me, Your Grace?" Tomas said with a bow. He and Thrace stood directly behind Arista, both still appearing as nervous as mice. "Do you happen to know why the village bell was rung?"

"Hmm? What's that? The bell? Oh that, I have no idea. Perhaps some quaint method the villagers use to call people to dinner."

"But, Your Grace—" Tomas was cut off.

"There," Saldur shouted, pointing into the sky as the Gilarabrywn appeared and swooped into the torchlight.

"Oh, here we go!" the archbishop shouted excitedly, clapping his hands. "Everyone pay attention to what you see here tonight, for surely many people will ask how it came to be."

The beast descended to the field and Lord Rufus trotted forward on his horse, which he had had the foresight to blind with a cloth bag to prevent it from witnessing the pending horror. With his sword held aloft, he shouted and spurred his mount forward.

"In the name of Novron, I—the true heir—smite thee." Rufus rose in the stirrups and thrust at the beast, which seemed startled by the bold confidence of the knight.

Lord Rufus struck the chest of the creature, but the blow glanced away uselessly. He struck again and again, but it was like striking stone with a stick. Lord Rufus looked shocked and confused. Then the Gilarabrywn slew Rufus and his horse with one casual swipe of a claw.

"Oh dear lord!" the archbishop cried, rising to his feet in shock. A moment later the shock turned to horror as the beast cast out its wings and, rising, bathed the hillside in a torrent of fire. Those in the yard staggered backward, spilling drinks and knocking over chairs. One of the pavilion legs toppled and the awning fell askew as people began to rush about.

With the hillside alight, the beast turned toward the castle and, rising higher, let forth another blast that exploded the wooden stockade walls into sheets of flame. The fire spread from dry log to dry log until the flames swept fully around, ringing the castle. It did not take long for those buildings close to the walls, those roofed with thatch, to catch, and soon the bulk of the lower castle and even the walls surrounding the manor house were burning. With the light of fire surrounding them, it was impossible to see where the Gilarabrywn had gone. Blind as to the whereabouts of the flying nightmare, and feeling the intensity of the heat growing all around them, the servants, guards, and clerics alike scattered in terror.

"We need to get to the cellar!" Tomas shouted, but amidst the screams and the roar of the flames devouring the wood, few heard him. Tomas took hold of Thrace and began to pull her back toward the manor. With her free hand Thrace grabbed Arista's arm, and Tomas pulled both back up the slope.

In shock, Arista put up no resistance as they dragged her from the yard. She had never experienced anything like this. She saw a man on fire running down the slope screaming, thrashing about as flames spiraled up his body. A moment later, he collapsed, still burning. There were others, living pyres racing blindly about the yard in ghastly brilliance, one by one collapsing on the grass. By instinct, Arista looked for the protection of Hilfred, but somewhere in her soup-like mind, she remembered she had ordered him to remain on guard in her room. He would be looking for her now.

Thrace held her arm in a vise grip as the three moved in a human chain. To her left she saw a soldier attempt to breach the wall. He caught on fire and joined the throng of living torches, screaming as his clothes and skin burned away. Somewhere not far off where the fire had spread to the forest, a tree trunk exploded with a tremendous crack. It rattled the building.

"We have to get down in the cellar," Tomas insisted. "Quickly! Our only hope is to get underground. We need—"

Arista felt her hair blowing in a sudden wind.

Thrump. Thrump.

Deacon Tomas began praying aloud as out of the smoke-clouded night sky, the Gilarabrywn descended upon them.

Chapter 12

Smoke and Ash

Crawling out of the well into the gray morning light, Hadrian entered an alien world. Dahlgren was gone. Only patches of ash and some smoldering timber marked the missing homes, but even more startling was the absence of trees. The forest that had hugged the village was gone. In its place was a desolate plain, scorched black. Limbless, leafless poles stood at random, tall dark spikes pointing at the sky. Fed by smoldering piles, smoke hung in the air like a dull gray fog, hiding the sky behind a hazy cloud from which ash fell silently like dirty snow, blanketing the land.

Pearl came out of the well. Not surprisingly, she said nothing as she wandered about the scorched world, stooping to turn over a charred bit of wood, then staring up at the sky as if surprised to find it still there now that the world had been cast upside down.

"How did this happen?" Russell Bothwick asked no one in particular, and no one answered.

"Thrace!" Theron yelled as he emerged from the well, his eyes focusing on the smoking ruins atop the hill. Soon everyone was running up the slope.

Like the village, the castle was a burned-out hull; the walls were gone, as were the smaller buildings. The great manor house was a charred pile. Bodies lay scattered, blackened by fire, torn and twisted. The corpses still smoked.

"Thrace!" Theron cried in desperation as he dug furiously into the pile of rubble that had been the manor house. All of the village men, along with Royce, Hadrian, and even Magnus, dug in the debris, more out of sympathy than hope.

Magnus directed them to the southeast corner, muttering something about the earth speaking with a hollow voice. They cleared away walls and a fallen staircase and heard a faint sound below. They dug down, revealing the remains of the old kitchen and the cellar beneath.

As if from the grave itself, they pulled forth Deacon Tomas, who looked battered but otherwise unharmed. Just as the villagers had, Tomas wiped his eyes, squinting in the morning light at the devastation around him.

"Deacon!" Theron shook the cleric. "Where is Thrace?"

Tomas looked at the farmer and tears welled in his eyes. "I couldn't save her, Theron," he said in a choked voice. "I tried, I tried so hard. You have to believe me, you must."

"What happened, you old fool?"

"I tried. I tried. I was leading them to this cellar, but it caught us. I prayed. I prayed so hard, and I swear it listened! Then I heard it laugh. It actually *laughed*." Tomas's eyes filled with tears. "It ignored me and took them."

"Took them?" Theron asked frantically. "What do you mean?"

"It spoke to me," Tomas said. "It spoke with a voice like death, like pain. My legs wouldn't hold me up anymore and I fell before it."

"What did it say?" Royce asked.

The deacon paused to wipe his face, leaving dark streaks of soot on his cheeks. "It didn't make sense, perhaps in my fear I lost my mind."

"What do you *think* it said?" Royce pressed.

"It spoke in the ancient speech of the church. I thought it said something about a weapon, a sword, something about trading it for the women. Said it would return tomorrow night for it. Then it flew away with Thrace and the princess. It doesn't make any sense at all, I'm probably mad now."

"The princess?" Hadrian asked.

"Yes, the princess Arista of Melengar. She was with us. I was trying to save them both—I was trying to—but—and now..." Tomas broke down crying again.

Royce exchanged looks with Hadrian and the two quickly moved away from the others to talk. Theron promptly followed.

"You two know something," he said accusingly. "You got in, didn't you? You took it. Royce got the sword after all. That's what it wants."

Royce nodded.

"You have to give it back," the farmer said.

"I don't think giving it back will save your daughter," Royce told him. "This thing, this Gilarabrywn, is a lot more cunning than we knew. It will—"

"Thrace hired you to bring me that sword," Theron growled. "That was your job. Remember? You were supposed to steal it and give it to me, so hand it over."

"Theron, listen—"

"Give it to me now!" the old farmer shouted as he towered menacingly over the thief.

Royce sighed and drew out the broken blade.

Theron took it with a puzzled look, turning the metal over in his hands. "Where's the rest?"

"This is all I could find."

"Then it will have to do," the old man said firmly.

"Theron, I don't think you can trust this creature. I think

even if you hand this over, it will still kill your daughter, the princess, and you."

"It's a risk I am willing to take!" he shouted at them. "You two don't have to be here. You got the sword—you did your job. You're done. You can leave anytime you want. Go on, get out!"

"Theron," Hadrian began, "we are not your enemy. Do you think either of us wants Thrace to die?"

Theron started to speak, then closed his mouth, swallowed, and took a breath. "No," he sighed, "you're right. I know that. It's just..." He looked into Hadrian's eyes with an expression of horrible pain. "She's all I've got left, and I won't stand for anything that can get her killed. I'll trade myself to the bloody monster if it will let her live."

"I know that, Theron," Hadrian said.

"I just don't think it will honor the trade," Royce said.

"We found another over here!" Dillon McDern shouted as he hauled the foppish scholar Tobis Rentinual out of the remains of the smokehouse. The skinny courtier, covered from head to foot in dirt, collapsed on the grass, coughing and sputtering.

"The soil was soft in the cellar..." Tobis managed, then sputtered and coughed. "We—dug into it with our—with our hands."

"How many?" Dillon asked.

"Five," Tobis replied, "a woodsman, a castle guard, I think, Sir Erlic, and two others. The guard—" Tobis entered into a coughing fit for a minute, then sat up, doubled over, and spat on the grass.

"Arvid, fetch water from the well!" Dillon ordered his son.

"The guard was badly burned," Tobis continued. "Two young men dragged him to the smokehouse, saying it had a cellar. Everything around us was on fire except the smokehouse, so the woodsman, Sir Erlic, and I all ran there too. The dirt floor was loose, so we started burrowing. Then something hit the shed and the whole thing came down on us. A beam caught my leg. I think it's broken."

The villagers excavated the collapsed shed. They pulled off a wall and dug into the wreckage, peeling back the fragments. They reached the bottom, where they found the others buried alive.

They dragged them out into the light. Sir Erlic and the woodsman looked near dead as they coughed and spat. The burned guard was worse. He was unconscious, but still alive. The last two pulled from the smokehouse ruins were Mauvin and Fanen Pickering, who, like Tobis, were unable to speak for a time but, other than numerous cuts and bruises, were all right.

"Is Hilfred alive?" Fanen asked after having a chance to breathe fresh air and drink a cup of water.

"Who's Hilfred?" Lena Bothwick asked, holding the cup of water Verna had brought. Fanen pointed to the burned guard across from him and Lena nodded. "He's not awake, but he's alive."

Search parties spread out and combed the rest of the area, finding many more bodies, mostly those of would-be contestants. They also discovered the remains of Archbishop Galien. The old man appeared to have died not from fire, but from being trampled to death. His servant, Carlton, lay inside the manor, apparently not content to die by his master's side. Arista's handmaid, Bernice, was also found inside the manor, crushed when the house collapsed. They found no one else alive.

The villagers created stretchers to carry Tobis and Hilfred

out of the smoky ruins to the well, where the women tended their wounds. The old common green was a charred patch of black. The great bell, having fallen, lay on its side in the ash.

"What happened?" Hadrian asked, sitting down next to Mauvin. The two brothers huddled where Pearl had once grazed pigs. Both sat hunched, sipping from cups of water, their faces stained with soot.

"We were outside the walls when the attack came," he said, his voice soft, not much louder than a strained whisper. He hooked his thumb at his brother. "I told him we were going home, but Fanen, the genius that he is, decided he wanted his shot at the beast, his chance at glory."

Fanen drooped his head lower.

"He tried to sneak out, thought he'd give me the slip. I caught him outside the gate and a little way down the hill. I told him it was suicide; he insisted; we got into a fight. It ended when we saw the hill catch on fire. We ran back. Before we reached the front gate, a couple of carriages and a bunch of horses went by at full gallop. I spotted Saldur's face peeking out from one of the windows. They didn't even slow down.

"We went looking for Arista and found Hilfred on the ground just out front of the burning manor house. His hair was gone, skin coming off in sheets, but he was still breathing, so we grabbed him and just ran for the smokehouse. It was the last building still standing that wasn't burning. The dirt floor was soft and loose, like it had recently been dug up, so we just started burrowing with our hands like moles, you know. That Tobis guy, Erlic, and Danthen followed us in. We only managed to dig a few feet when the whole thing came down on us."

"Did you find Arista?" Fanen asked. "Is she..."

"We don't know," Hadrian replied. "The deacon says it took her and Theron's daughter. She might still be alive."

The women of the village tended the wounds of those found at the castle while the men began gathering what supplies, tools, and food stores they could find into a pile at the well. They were a motley bunch, haggard and dirty, like a band of shipwrecked travelers left on a desert island. Few of them spoke, and when they did, it was always in whispered tones. From time to time, villagers would weep softly, kick a scorched board, or merely wander off a ways only to drop to their knees and shake.

When, at last, the men were bandaged and the supplies stacked, Tomas, who had cleaned himself up, stood and said a few words over the dead, and they all observed a moment of silence. Then Vince Griffin stood up and addressed them.

"I was the first to settle here," he said with a sad voice. "My house stood right there, the closest to this here well. I remember when most of you were considered newcomers, strangers even. I had great hopes for this place. I donated eight bushels of barley every year to the village church, though all I seen come of it was this here bell. I stayed here through the hard frost five years ago and I stayed here when people started to go missing. Like the rest a' you, I thought I could live with it. People die tragically everywhere, be it from the pox, the plague, starvation, the cold, or a blade. Sure, Dahlgren seemed cursed, and maybe it is, but it was still the best place I'd ever lived. Maybe the best place I ever will live, mostly because of you all and the fact that the nobles hardly ever bothered us, but all that's over now. There's nothing here no more, not even the trees that was here before we came, and I don't fancy spending another night in the well." He wiped his eyes clear. "I'm leaving Dahlgren. I s'pose many a' you will be too, and I just wanted to say that when you all came here, I saw you as strangers, but as I am leaving, I feel I'm gonna be saying goodbye to family, a family that has gone through a lot together. I...I just wanted you all to know that."

They all nodded in agreement and exchanged muttered conversations with the people nearest them. It was decided by all that Dahlgren was dead and that they would leave. There was talk about trying to stay together, but it was only talk. They would travel as a group, including Sir Erlic and the woodsman Danthen, south at least as far as Alburn, where some would turn west, hoping to find relatives, while others would continue south, hoping to find a new start.

"So much for the church's help," Dillon McDern said to Hadrian. "They were here two nights and look."

Dillon and Russell Bothwick walked over to where Theron sat against a blackened stump.

" 'Spect you'll be staying to find Thrace?" Dillon asked.

Theron nodded. The big man had not bothered to wash and he was coated in dirt and soot. He had the broken blade on his lap and stared at it.

"You think it'll be back tonight, do ya?" Russell asked.

"I think so. It wants this. Maybe if I give it back, it will give Thrace to me."

The two men nodded.

"You want us to stay behind and give you a hand?" Russell asked.

"A hand with what?" the old farmer asked. "Nothing you can do, either of ya. Go on, you both have families of your own. Get out while you can. Enough good people have died here."

The two men nodded again.

"Good luck to you, Theron," Dillon said.

"We'll wait awhile in Alburn to see if you show up," Russell told him. "Good luck."

Russell and Tad fashioned a sled from charred saplings and loaded what little they had on it. Lena mashed up a salve, which she applied to Hilfred's burns, and left it and a pile of bandages with Tomas, who took it on himself to stay with the soldier. And so it was that with only a few things to pack up and carry with them, the bulk of the villagers were on their way westward by early afternoon. No one wanted to be anywhere near Dahlgren after sunset.

ණ

"What are we doing here?" Royce asked Hadrian as the two sat on a partially burned tree trunk. They were just up the old village path from the well, near where the Caswells' two little wooden grave markers used to be. Like everything else, they were gone, nothing left to mark their passing. Hadrian and Royce could see Deacon Tomas sitting with Hilfred, who still lay unconscious.

"This job has cost us two horses and over a week's worth of provisions, and for what?" Royce went on, and with a sigh broke off a bit of charred bark and absently tossed it. "We should head out with the rest of them. The girl is likely dead already. I mean, why would it keep her alive? The Gilarabrywn holds all the cards. It can kill us at will, but we can't harm it. It has hostages, while all we have is half a sword that it doesn't really need but apparently would just like to have. If we had both parts of the sword, Magnus could put them back together and we could at least bargain from a position of some strength. We could even have the dwarf make us all swords, and maybe even spears with the right name on it. Then we could have a go at the bastard, but right now, we have nothing. We are no threat to it at all. Theron thinks he's going to bargain, but he doesn't have anything to bargain with. The Gilarabrywn set this up only to save itself the tedium of hunting for that sword."

"We don't know that."

"Sure we do. It won't keep those girls alive. It probably had them for lunch already, and when night comes, old Theron will be standing out there like a fool with exactly what it wants. He'll die and that will be that. On the other hand, his stupidity will buy time for the rest of us to get away. Considering his whole family is gone and his daughter is most likely already dead, it's probably for the best."

"He won't be standing there alone," Hadrian said.

Royce turned with a sick look on his face. "Tell me you're joking."

Hadrian shook his head.

"Why?"

"Because you're right; because everything you just said will happen if we leave."

"And you think if we stay, it will be different?"

"We've never quit a job before, Royce."

"What are you talking about? What job?"

"She paid us to get the sword for her."

"I got the sword. Her old man's got it right now."

"Only part of it, and the job won't be finished until he has both parts in his hands. That's what we were hired to do."

"Hadrian." Royce ran a hand over his face and shook his head. "For the love of Maribor, she paid us *ten silver*!"

"You accepted it."

"I hate it when you get like this." Royce stood suddenly, picking up a charred piece of scrap. "Damn it." He threw it into a pile of smoking wood that had once been the Bothwicks' home. "You're just going to get us killed, you know that, right?"

"You don't have to stay. This is my decision."

"And what are you going to do? Fight it when it comes? Are you going to stand there in the dark swinging swords that can't hurt it?"

"I don't know."

"You're insane," Royce told him. "The rumors are all true; Hadrian Blackwater is a damn loon!"

Hadrian stood to face his friend. "I'm not going to abandon Theron, Thrace, and Arista. And what about Hilfred? Do you think he can travel? You try dragging him through the woods and he'll be dead before nightfall, or do you want to try stuffing him in the well all night and think he'll be just fine in the morning? And what about Tobis? How far do you think he'll get on a broken leg? Or don't you give a damn about them? Has your heart gotten so black you can just walk away and let them all die?"

"They will all die anyway," Royce snapped at him. "That's just my point. We can't stop it from killing them. All we can do is decide whether to die with them or not, and I really don't see the benefit in sympathy suicide."

"We can do something," Hadrian asserted. "We're the ones who stole the treasure from the Crown Tower and put it back the very next night. The same two that broke into the invincible Drumindor, we put a human head in the Earl of Chadwick's lap while he slept in his tower, and busted Esrahaddon out of Gutaria, the most secure prison ever built. I mean, we can do *something*!"

"Like what?"

"Well..." Hadrian thought. "We can dig a pit, lure it there, and trap it."

"We'd have better luck asking Tomas to pray for Maribor to strike the Gilarabrywn dead. We really don't have the time or the manpower for excavating a pit."

"You have a better idea?"

"I'm sure I could come up with something better than luring it into a pit we can't dig."

"Like what?"

Royce began walking around the still smoldering stick forest, angrily kicking anything in his path. "I don't know, you're the one who thinks we can do something, but I know one thing: we can't do squat unless we can get the other half of that sword. So the first thing I would do is steal it tonight while it's gone."

"It would kill Thrace and Arista for certain if you did that," Hadrian pointed out.

"But then you could kill it. At least there would be the closure of revenge."

Hadrian shook his head. "Not good enough."

Royce smirked. "I could always steal the sword while you and Theron fool it with the blade Rufus was using." Royce allowed himself a morbid chuckle. "There's at least about a single chance in a million that might work."

Hadrian's brow furrowed in thought, and he sat down slowly.

"Oh no, I was joking," Royce said, backpedaling. "If it could tell the blade was missing last night, it can tell the difference between the real thing and a copy."

"But even if it doesn't work," Hadrian said, "it might give me time to get the girls away from it. Then *we* could dive in a hole—a small hole that we do have time to dig."

"And hope it doesn't dig us out? I've seen its claws; it won't be hard."

Hadrian ignored him and went on with his train of thought. "Then you could bring the other half of the sword, have Magnus forge it, and then I can kill it. See, it was a good thing you didn't kill him after all."

"You realize how stupid this is, right? That thing decimated this whole village and the castle last night, and you are going to take it on with an old farmer, two women, and a broken sword?"

Hadrian said nothing.

Royce sighed and sat down beside his friend, shaking his head. He reached into his robe and pulled his dagger out. He held it out in its sheath.

"Here," he said, "take Alverstone."

"Why?" Hadrian looked at him, puzzled.

"Well, I'm not saying Magnus is right, but, well, I've never found *anything* that this dagger can't cut, and if Magnus is right, if the father of the gods did forge this, I would think it could come in handy even against an invincible beast."

"So you're leaving?"

"No." Royce scowled and looked in the direction of the tower of Avempartha. "Apparently I have a job to finish."

Hadrian smiled at his friend, took the dagger, and weighed it in his hand. "I'll give it back to you tomorrow, then."

"Right," Royce replied.

❧

"Did your partner leave?" Theron asked as Hadrian approached him, walking up the slope of the scorched hill that had once been the castle. The old farmer stood on the blackened hillside, holding the shattered sword and looking up at the sky.

"No—well, sort of. He's headed back inside Avempartha to steal the other half of the sword just in case the Gilarabrywn tries to double-cross us. There is even a chance it might leave Thrace and Arista in the tower while it comes here, and if it does, Royce can get them out."

Theron nodded thoughtfully.

"You two have been real good to me and my daughter. I still don't know why, and don't tell me it's the money." Theron sighed. "You know, I never gave her credit for much. I ignored her, pushed her away for so many years. She was only my daughter, not a son—an extra mouth to feed that would cost us money to marry off. How she ever found the two of you and got you to come all this way to help us is...well, I just don't think I'll ever understand that."

"Hadrian," Fanen called to him. "Come down here and see what we've got."

Hadrian followed Fanen down the hill to the north edge of the burn line, where he found Tobis, Mauvin, and Magnus working on a huge contraption.

"This is my catapult," Tobis declared, standing proudly next to a wagon on which a wooden machine sat. Tobis looked comical in his loud-colored court clothes, propped up on a crutch Magnus had fashioned for him, his broken leg strapped down between two stiff pieces of wood. "They dragged it out here when I was bumped from the roster. She's exquisite, isn't she? I named her Persephone after Novron's wife. Only fitting, I thought, since I studied ancient imperial history to devise it. Not easy to do either. I had to learn the ancient languages just to read the books."

"Did you just build this?"

"No, of course not, you silly man. I am a professor at Sheridan. That's in Ghent, by the way. You know, the same place as the seat of the Nyphron Church? Well, being brilliant, I bribed some church officials, who let slip the true nature of the competition. It would not be a ridiculous bashing match between sawdust-filled heads, but a challenge to defeat a legendary creature. This was a puzzle I could solve, one that I knew did not require muscle and a lack of teeth, but rather a staggering intellect such as mine."

Hadrian walked around the device. A massive center beam rose a good twelve feet, and the long thick arm was a foot or two longer than that. It had a sack bucket joined to a lower beam with torsion-producing cords. On either side of the wagon were two massive hand cranks connected to a series of gears.

"Well, I must say, I have seen catapults before and this doesn't look much like them."

"That's because I modified it for fighting the Gilarabrywn."

"Well, he tried," Magnus added. "It wouldn't have worked the way he had it set up, but it will now."

"In fact, we fired a few rocks already," Mauvin reported.

"I've had some experience with siege weapons before," Hadrian said. "And I know they can be useful against something big, like a field of soldiers, or something that doesn't move, like a wall, but they're useless against a solitary moving enemy. They just aren't that fast or accurate."

"Yes, well, that's why I devised this one to fire not only projectiles but nets as well," Tobis said proudly. "I'm very clever that way, you see. The nets are designed to launch like large balls that open in mid-flight and snare the beast as it is flying, dropping it to the ground, where it will lie helpless while I reload and take my time crushing it."

"And this works?" Hadrian asked, impressed.

"In theory," Tobis replied.

Hadrian shrugged. "What the heck, it couldn't hurt."

"Just need to get it in position," Mauvin said. "Care to help push?"

They all put their backs to the catapult, except, of course, for Tobis, who limped along spouting orders. They rolled it to the ditch that ringed the bottom of the motte and within range to fire on anything in the area near the old manor house.

"Might want to get something to hide it—rubble or burnt

wood, maybe, so that it looks like a pile of trash," Hadrian said. "Which shouldn't be hard to do. Magnus, I was wondering if you could do me a favor."

"What kind?" he asked as Hadrian led him back up the hill toward the ruins of the manor house. The grass was gone, and they walked on a surface of ash and roots that made Hadrian think of warm snow.

"Remember that sword you made for Lord Rufus? I found it, still with him and his horse on the hill. I want you to fix it."

"Fix it?" The dwarf looked offended. "It's not my fault the sword didn't work; I did a perfect replica. The records were likely at fault."

"That's fine, because I have the original, or part of it, at least. I need you to make an exact copy of what we have. Can you do it?"

"Of course I can, and I will, in return for your getting Royce to let me look at the Alverstone."

"Are you crazy? He wants you dead. I saved your neck from him once already. Doesn't that count?"

The dwarf stood firm, his arms crossed over the braids in his beard. "That's my price."

"I'll talk to him, but I can't guarantee it."

The dwarf pursed his lips, which made his beard and mustache bristle. "Very well. Where are these swords?"

Theron agreed to the plan as long as he got the piece back, and brought the broken blade to the manor's smithy, which now consisted of no more than the brick forge and the anvil. He would hold the blade during the exchange and hand it over immediately should the ruse be discovered.

"Hrumph!" The dwarf looked disgusted.

"What?" Hadrian asked.

"No wonder it didn't work. There are markings on both sides. There's this whole other inscription. See, this is the incantation, I bet." The dwarf showed Hadrian the blade, where a seemingly incomprehensible spiderweb of thin sweeping lines formed a long design. Then he flipped it over to reveal a significantly shorter design on the back. "And this side, I'm guessing, holds the name that Esrahaddon mentioned. It makes sense that all the incantations are the same; only the name is unique."

"Does that mean you can create a weapon that will work?"

"No, it's broken right along the middle of the name, but I can make an awfully good copy of this, at least."

The dwarf removed his tool belt, hidden beneath his clothes, and laid it on the anvil. He had a number of hammers of different sizes and shapes, and chisels all in separate loops. He unrolled a leather apron and tied it on. Then he took Rufus's sword and strapped it to the anvil.

"Carry those everywhere, do you?" Hadrian asked.

"You won't catch me leaving them on a horse's saddle," Magnus replied.

Hadrian and Theron began digging a pit on the side of the courtyard. They dug it on the site of the old smokehouse, making use of the already turned soil to ease their effort. Without a shovel, they used old boards that left their hands black. Within a couple of hours, they had a small hole big enough for the two of them to get down fully under the earth. It was not deep enough to avoid being dug up, but it might hide them from a blast of fire as long as it did not come straight down. If it did, they would be like a couple of clay pots fired in sand.

"Won't be long now," Hadrian told Theron as the two men sat covered in dirt and ash, looking up at the fading light. Magnus was using his smallest hammer, tapping away with a resounding *tink*, *tink*. He muttered something, then pulled a heavy cloth from a pouch on his belt and began rubbing the surface of the metal.

Hadrian looked out over the trees, feeling Alverstone inside his tunic. He wondered if Royce had made it to the tower. *Is he inside? Has he found Esrahaddon? Can the old wizard do anything to help them?* He thought of the princess and Thrace. *What has it done with them?* He bit his lip. Royce was probably right. *Why would it keep them alive?*

The sound of horses approached from the south. Theron and Hadrian exchanged surprised looks and stood up to see a troop of riders racing out of the trees. Eight horsemen crossed the desolate plain, knights in black armor with a standard of a broken crown flying before them. Leading them was Luis Guy in his red cassock.

"Look who is finally back." Hadrian looked over at Magnus. "You done yet?"

"Just polishing," the dwarf replied. He then noticed the riders for the first time. "This can't be good," he grumbled.

The riders trotted into the remains of the courtyard and pulled up at the sight of them. Guy surveyed the smoldering ruins of the old castle for a moment, then dismounted and walked toward the dwarf, pausing to pick up a burnt bit of timber, which he turned over twice in his hands before tossing it away. "It would seem Lord Rufus didn't do as well last night as we hoped. Did you forget to dot an *i*, Magnus?"

Magnus took a frightened step back. Theron stepped forward quickly, grabbed the original broken blade, and hid it under his shirt.

Guy noticed the act but ignored the farmer and faced the dwarf. "Care to explain yourself, Magnus, or shall I just kill you for lousy workmanship?"

"Wasn't my fault. There were markings on the other side that none of the pictures showed. I did what you asked; your research was to blame."

"And what are you up to now?"

"He's duplicating the blade so we can use it to trade with the Gilarabrywn," Hadrian explained.

"Trade?"

"Yes, the creature took the princess Arista and a village girl. It said if we return the blade we took from its lair, it will free the women."

"It *said*?"

"Yes," Hadrian confirmed. "It spoke to Deacon Tomas last night just before he watched it take the women."

Guy laughed coldly. "So the beast is talking now, is it? And abducting women too? How impressive. I suppose it also rides horses and I should expect it to be representing Dunmore at the next Wintertide joust in Aquesta."

"You can ask your own deacon if you don't believe me."

"Oh, I believe you," he said, walking up to face Hadrian. "At least the part about stealing a sword from the citadel. That is what you're referring to, isn't it? So, someone actually got into Avempartha and took the real sword? Clever, particularly when I know that only someone with elvish blood can enter that tower. You don't look very elf-like to me, Hadrian. And I know the Pickerings' heritage quite well. I also know Magnus here couldn't get in. That leaves only your partner in crime, Royce Melborn. He's rather small, isn't he? Slender, agile? Those qualities would certainly serve him well as a thief. He can see easily in the dark, hear better than any human, has uncanny balance, and is so light on his feet that he can move in almost total silence. Yes, it would be most unfair to all the other poor thieves out there using their normal, human abilities."

Guy looked around carefully. "Where is your partner?" he asked, but Hadrian remained silent. "That's one of the biggest problems we have; some of these crossbred elves can pass for human. They can be so hard to spot sometimes. They don't have the pointed ears, or the squinty eyes, because they take after their human parent, but the elven parent is always there. That's what makes them so dangerous. They look normal, but deep down they are inhumanly evil. You probably don't even see it. Do you? You are like those fools that try and tame a bear cub or a wolf, thinking that they will come to love you. You probably think that you can banish the wild beast that lurks inside. You can't, you know. The monster is always there, just looking for the chance to leap out at you."

The sentinel glanced at the anvil. "And I suppose one of you was planning on using the sword to kill the beast and claim the crown of emperor?"

"Actually, no," Hadrian replied. "Getting the women and running real fast was more the plan."

"And you expect me to believe that? Hadrian Blackwater, the consummate warrior who handles a blade like a Teshlor Knight of the Old Empire. You really expect me to believe that you're just passing through this remote village? That you just happen to be in possession of the only weapon that can kill the Gilarabrywn at the precise moment in time when the emperor will be chosen by the one who does so? No, of course not, you are just using what is arguably the most powerful sword in the world to make a trade with an insanely dangerous, but now talking, monster, for a peasant girl and the Princess of Melengar, whom you barely know."

"Well—when you put it that way, it does sound bad, but it's the truth."

"The church will be returning to continue the trials here," Luis Guy told them. "Until then, it is my job to make certain no one who is, shall we say, unworthy of the crown kills the Gilarabrywn. That most certainly includes a thieving elf-lover and his band of cutthroats." Guy walked over to Theron. "So I'll have that blade you're holding."

"Over my dead body," Theron growled.

"As you wish." Guy drew his sword and all seven seret dismounted and drew their blades as well.

"Now," Guy told Theron, "give me the blade or both of you will die."

"Don't you mean all four?" a voice behind Hadrian said, and he looked over to see Mauvin and Fanen coming up the slope, spreading out, each with his sword drawn. Mauvin held two, one of which he tossed to Theron, who caught it clumsily.

"Make that five," Magnus said, holding two of his larger hammers in his hands. The dwarf looked over at Hadrian and swallowed hard. "He's planning on killing me anyway, so why not?"

"There are still eight of us," Guy pointed out. "Not exactly an even fight."

"I was thinking the same thing," Mauvin said. "Sadly, there's no one else here we can ask to join your side."

Guy looked at Mauvin, then Hadrian, for a long moment as the men glared across the ash at each other. Then he nodded and lowered his blade. "Well, I can see I'll have to report your misconduct to the archbishop."

"Go ahead," Hadrian said. "His body is buried with the rest of them just down the hillside."

Guy gave him a cold look, then turned to walk away, but as he did, Hadrian noticed his shoulder dip unnaturally to his right and his foot pivot, toe out, as he stepped. It was a motion Hadrian had taught Theron to watch for, the announcement of an attack.

"Theron!" he shouted, but it was unnecessary. The farmer had already moved and raised his sword even before Guy spun. The sentinel thrust for his heart. Theron was there a second faster and knocked the blade away. Then, out of reflex, the farmer shifted his weight forward, took a step, and performed the combination move Hadrian had drilled into him: parry, pivot, and riposte. He thrust forward, extending, going for reach. The sentinel staggered. He twisted and narrowly avoided being run through the chest, taking the sword thrust in his shoulder. Guy cried out in agony.

Theron stood shocked at his own success.

"Pull it out!" Hadrian and Mauvin both yelled at him.

Theron withdrew the blade and Guy staggered back, gripping his bleeding shoulder.

"Kill them!" the sentinel shouted through clenched teeth.

The Seret Knights charged.

Four Knights of Nyphron attacked the Pickering brothers. One rushed Hadrian, another launched himself at Theron, and the last took Magnus. Hadrian knew Theron would not last long against a skilled seret. He drew both his short sword and the bastard and slew the first Knight of Nyphron the moment he came within range. Then he stepped in the path of the second. The knight realized too late he was walking into a vise of two attackers as both Hadrian and Theron cut him down.

Magnus held up his hammers as menacingly as he could, but the little dwarf was clearly no match for the knight, and he retreated behind his anvil. As the seret got nearer, he threw one hammer at him, which hit the seret in the chest. It rang off his breastplate, causing no real harm, but it staggered him slightly. Realizing that the dwarf was no threat, the seret turned to face Hadrian, who raced at him.

The seret swung down in an arc at Hadrian's head. Hadrian caught the blade with the short sword in his left hand, holding the knight's sword arm up as he drove his bastard sword into the man's unprotected armpit.

Mauvin and Fanen fought together against the four attackers. The elegant rapiers of the Pickerings flew—catching, blocking, slicing, slamming—every attack turned back, every thrust blocked, every swing answered. Yet the two brothers could only defend. They stood their ground against the onslaught of the armored knights, who struggled to find a weakness. Mauvin finally managed to find a moment to jump to the offense and slipped in a thrust. The tip of his blade stabbed into the throat of the seret, dropping him with a rapid jab, but no sooner had he done so than Fanen cried out.

Hadrian watched as a seret sliced Fanen across his sword arm, the blade continuing down to his hand. The younger Pickering's sword fell from his fingers. Defenseless, Fanen desperately stepped backward, retreating from his two opponents. He tripped on the wreckage and fell. They rushed him, going for the kill.

Hadrian was too many steps away.

Mauvin ignored his own defense to save his brother. He thrust out. In one move, he blocked both attacks on Fanen—but at a cost. Hadrian saw the seret standing before Mauvin thrust. The blade penetrated Mauvin's side. Instantly the elder Pickering buckled. He fell to his knees with his eyes still on his brother. He could only watch helplessly as the next blow came down. Two swords entered Fanen's body. Blood coated the blades.

Mauvin screamed, even as his own assailant began his killing blow, a cross slice aimed at Mauvin's neck. Mauvin, on his knees, ignored the stroke, much to the delight of the seret. What the knight did not see was Mauvin did not need to defend. Mauvin was done defending. He thrust his sword upward, slicing through the attacker's rib cage. He twisted the blade as he pulled it out, ripping apart the man's organs.

The two who had killed his brother turned on Mauvin. The elder Pickering raised his sword again but his side was slick with blood, his arm weak, eyes glassy. Tears streamed down his cheeks. He was no longer focusing. His stroke went wide. The closest knight knocked Mauvin's sword away and the two remaining seret stepped forward and raised their swords, but that was as far as they got. Hadrian had crossed the distance and Mauvin's would-be killers' heads came loose, their bodies dropping into the ash.

"Magnus, get Tomas up here fast," Hadrian shouted. "Tell him to bring the bandages."

"He's dead," Theron said as he bent over Fanen.

"I know he is!" Hadrian snapped. "And Mauvin will be too if we don't help him."

He ripped open Mauvin's tunic and pressed his hand to his side as the blood bubbled up between his fingers. Mauvin lay panting, sweating. His eyes rolled up in his head, revealing their whites.

"Damn you, Mauvin!" Hadrian shouted at him. "Get me a cloth. Theron, get me anything."

Theron grabbed one of the seret who had killed Fanen and tore off his sleeve.

"Get more!" Hadrian shouted. He wiped Mauvin's side, finding a small hole spewing bright red blood. At least it was not the dark blood, which usually meant death. He took the cloth and pressed it against the wound.

"Help me sit him up," Hadrian said as Theron returned with another strip of cloth. Mauvin was a limp rag now. His head slumped to one side.

Tomas came running up, his arms filled with long strips of cloth that Lena had given him. They lifted Mauvin, and Tomas tightly wrapped the bandages around his torso. The blood soaked through the cloth, but the rate of bleeding had slowed.

"Keep his head up," Hadrian ordered, and Tomas cradled him.

Hadrian looked over at where Fanen lay. He was on his back in the dirt, a dark pool of blood still growing around his body. Hadrian gripped his swords with blood-soaked hands and stood up.

"Where's Guy?" he shouted through clenched teeth.

"He's gone," Magnus answered. "During the fight, he grabbed a horse and ran."

Hadrian stared back down at Fanen and then at Mauvin. He took a breath and it shuddered in his chest.

Tomas bowed his head and said the Prayer of the Departed:

"Unto Maribor, I beseech thee
Into the hands of god, I send thee
Grant him peace, I beg thee
Give him rest, I ask thee
May the god of men watch over your journey."

When he was done, he looked up at the stars and in a soft voice said, "It's dark."

Chapter 13

Artistic Vision

Arista did not want to breathe. It caused her stomach to tighten and bile to rise in her throat. Above her stretched the star-filled sky, but below—the pile. The Gilarabrywn built its mound, like a nest, from collected trophies, gruesome souvenirs of attacks and kills. The top of a head with dark matted hair, a broken chair, a foot still in its shoe, a partially chewed torso, a blood-soaked dress, an arm, so pale it was blue, reaching up out of the heap as if waving.

The pile rested on what looked to be an open balcony on the side of a high stone tower, but there was no way off. Instead of a door leading inside, there was only an archway, an outline of a door. Such false hope teased Arista as she longed for it to be a real door.

She sat with her hands on her lap, not wanting to touch anything. There was something underneath her, long and thin like a tree branch. It was uncomfortable, but she did not dare move. She did not want to know what it really was. She tried not to look down. She forced herself to watch the stars and look out at the horizon. To the north, the princess could see the forest, divided by the silvery line of the river. To the south lay large expanses of water that faded into darkness. Something out of the corner of her eye would catch her attention and she would look down. She always regretted it.

Arista realized with a shiver that she had slept on the pile, but she had not fallen asleep. It had felt like drowning—terror so absolute that it had overwhelmed her. She could not recall the flight she must have taken, or most of the day, but she did remember seeing it. The beast had lain inches away, basking in the afternoon sun. She had stared at it for hours, not able to look at anything else—her own death sleeping before her had a way of demanding her complete attention. She sat, afraid to move or speak. She was expecting it to wake and kill her—to add her to the pile. Muscles tense, heart racing, she locked her eyes on the thick scaly skin that rippled with each breath, sliding over what looked like ribs. She felt as if she were treading water. She could feel the blood pounding in her head. She was exhausted from not moving. Then the drowning came over her once more and everything went mercifully black.

Now her eyes were open again, but the great beast was missing. She looked around. There was no sign of the monster.

"It's gone," Thrace told her. It was the first either of them had spoken since the attack. The girl was still dressed in her nightgown, the bruises forming a dark line across her face. She was on her hands and knees, moving through the pile, digging like a child in a sandbox.

"Where is it?" Arista asked.

"Flew away."

Somewhere nearby, somewhere below, she heard a roar. It was not the beast. The sound was constant, a rumbling hum.

"Where are we?" she asked.

"On top of Avempartha," Thrace answered without looking up from her macabre excavation. She dug down beneath a layer of broken stone and turned over an iron kettle, revealing a torn tapestry, which she began tugging.

"What is Avempartha?"

"It's a tower."

"Oh. What are you doing?"

"I thought there might be a weapon, something to fight with."

Arista blinked. "Did you say 'to fight with'?"

"Yes, maybe a dagger, or a piece of glass."

Arista would not have believed it possible if it had not happened to her, but at that moment, as she sat helplessly, trapped on a pile of dismembered bodies, waiting to be eaten, she laughed.

"A piece of glass? A piece of glass?" Arista howled, her voice becoming shrill. "You're going to use a dagger or a piece of glass to fight—*that thing*?"

Thrace nodded, shoving the antlered head of a buck aside.

Arista continued to stare openmouthed.

"What have we got to lose?" Thrace asked.

That was it. That summed up the situation perfectly. The one thing they had going for them was that it could not get worse. In all her days, even when Percy Braga had been building the pyre to burn her alive, even when the dwarf had closed the door on her and Royce as they dangled from a rope in a collapsing tower, it had not been worse than this. Few fates could compare to the inevitability of being eaten alive.

Arista fully shared Thrace's belief, but something in her did not want to accept it. She wanted to believe there was still a chance.

"You don't think it will keep its promise?" she asked.

"Promise?"

"What it told the deacon."

"You—you could understand it?" the girl asked, pausing for the first time to look at her.

Arista nodded. "It spoke the old imperial language."

"What did it say?"

"Something about trading us for a sword, but I might have gotten it wrong. I learned Old Speech as part of my religious studies at Sheridan and I was never very good at it, not to mention I was scared. I'm still scared."

Arista saw Thrace thinking and envied her.

"No," the girl said at last, "it won't let us live. It kills people. That's what it does. It killed my mother and brother, my sister-in-law, and my nephew. It killed my best friend, Jessie Caswell. It killed Daniel Hall. I never told anyone this before, but I thought I might marry him one day. I found him near the river trail one beautiful fall morning, mostly chewed, but his face was still fine. That's what bothered me the most. His face was perfect, not a scratch on it. He just looked like he was sleeping under the pines, only most of his body was gone. It will kill us."

Thrace shivered with the passing wind.

Arista slipped off her cloak. "Here," she said. "You need this more than I do."

Thrace looked at her with a puzzled smile.

"Just take it!" she snapped. Her emotions breached the surface, threatening to spill. "I want to do *something*, damn it!"

She held out the cloak with a wavering arm. Thrace crawled over and took it. She held it up, looking at it as if she were in the comfort of a dressing room. "It's very beautiful, so heavy."

Again Arista laughed, thinking how strange it was to fly from despair to laughter in a single breath. One of them was surely insane—maybe they both were. Arista wrapped it around the young girl as she clasped it on. "And here I was ready to kill Bernice—"

Arista thought of Hilfred and the maid left—no, ordered—to stay in the room. Had she killed them?

"Do you think anyone survived?"

The girl rolled aside a statue's head and what looked like a broken marble tabletop. "My father is alive," Thrace said simply, digging deeper.

Arista did not ask how she knew this, but believed her. At that moment, she would believe anything Thrace told her.

With a nice hole dug into the heart of the debris, Thrace had yet to find a weapon beyond a leg bone, which she set aside with grisly indifference, to use in case she found nothing better, Arista guessed. The princess watched the excavation with a mix of admiration and disbelief.

Thrace uncovered a beautiful mirror that was shattered, and struggled to free a jagged piece, when Arista saw a glint of gold and pointed, saying, "There's something under the mirror."

Thrace pushed the glass aside and, reaching down, grabbed hold and drew forth the hilt half of a broken sword. Elaborately decorated in silver and gold encrusted with fine sparkling gems, the pommel caught the starlight and sparkled.

Thrace took the sword by the grip and held it up. "It's light," she said.

"It's broken," Arista replied, "but I suppose it's better than a piece of glass."

Thrace stowed the hilt in the lining pocket of the cloak and went on digging. She came across the head of an axe and a fork, both of which she discarded. Then, pulling back a bit of cloth, she stopped suddenly.

Arista hated to look but once more felt compelled.

It was a woman's face—eyes closed, mouth open.

Thrace placed the cloth back over the hole she had made. She retreated to the far edge and sat down, squeezing her knees while resting her head. Arista could see her shaking and Thrace did not dig anymore after that. The two sat in silence.

Thrump. Thrump.

Arista heard the sound and her heart raced. Every muscle in her body tightened and she dared not look. A great gust of air struck from above as she closed her eyes. She heard it land and waited to die. Arista could hear it breathing and still she waited.

"*Soon*," she heard it say.

Arista opened her eyes.

The beast rested on the pile, panting from the effort of its flight. It shook its head, spraying the platform with loose saliva from its lips, which failed to hide the forest of jagged teeth. Its eyes were larger than Arista's hand, with tall narrow pupils on a marbled orange and brown lens that reflected her own image.

"*Soon?*" She didn't know where she found the courage to speak.

The massive eye blinked and the pupil dilated as it focused on her. It would kill her now, but at least it would be over.

"*Thou know'st my speech?*" The voice was large and so deep she felt it vibrating her chest.

She both nodded and said, "*Yes.*"

Across from her, the princess could see Thrace with her head up off her knees, staring.

The beast looked at Arista. "*Thou art regal.*"

"*I am a princess.*"

"*The best bait*," the Gilarabrywn said, but Arista was not sure she heard that right. It might also have said, "The greatest gift." The phrase was difficult to translate.

She asked, "*Wilt thou honor thy trade or kill us?*"

"*The bait stays alive until I catch the thief.*"

"*Thief?*"

"*The taker of the sword. It comes. I crossed the moon to deceive it that the way 'twas clear, and have returned flying low. The thief comes now.*"

"What's it saying?" Thrace asked.

"It said we are bait to catch a thief that stole a sword."

"Royce," Thrace said.

Arista stared at her. "What did you say?"

"I hired two men to steal a sword from this tower."

"You hired Royce Melborn and Hadrian Blackwater?" Arista asked, stunned.

"Yes."

"How did you—" She gave that thought up. "It knows Royce is coming," Arista told her. "It pretended to fly away, letting him see it leave."

The Gilarabrywn's ears perked up, suddenly tilting forward toward the false door. Abruptly, but quietly, it stood and, with a gentle flap of its wings, lifted off. Catching the thermals, the beast soared upward above the tower. Thrace and Arista heard movement somewhere below, footsteps on stone.

A figure appeared in a black cloak. It stepped forward, passing through the solid stone of the false door, like a man surfacing from below a still pond.

"It's a trap, Royce!" Arista and Thrace shouted together.

The figure did not move.

Arista heard the whispered sound of air rushing across leathery wings. Then a brilliant light abruptly burst forth from the figure. Without a sound or movement, it was as if a star appeared in place of the man, the light so bright it blinded everyone. Arista closed her eyes in pain and heard the Gilarabrywn screech overhead. She felt frantic puffs of air beat down on her as the beast flapped its wings, breaking its dive.

The light was short-lived. It faded abruptly though not entirely and soon they could all see the man in the shimmering robe before them.

"*YOU!*" The beast cursed at him, shaking the tower with its voice. It hovered above them, its great wings flapping.

"Escaped thy cage beast of Erivan, hunter of Nareion!" Esrahaddon shouted in Old Speech. *"I shall cage thee again!"*

The wizard raised his arms, but before he made another move, the Gilarabrywn screeched and fluttered back in horror. It beat its great wings and rose, but in that last second, it reached down with one talon, snatching Thrace off the tower. It dove over the side, vanishing from sight. Arista raced to the railing, looking down in horror. The beast and Thrace were gone.

"We can do nothing for her," the wizard said sadly.

She turned to see Esrahaddon and Royce Melborn beside her, both looking over the edge into the dark roar of the river below. "Her fate lies with Hadrian and her father now."

Arista's hands squeezed the railing stiffly. She felt the drowning sensation again. Royce grabbed her by the wrist. "Are you all right, Your Highness? It's a long way down, you know."

"Let's get her downstairs," Esrahaddon said. "The door, Royce. The door."

"Oh right," the thief replied. *"Grant entry to Arista Essendon, Princess of Melengar."*

The archway became a real door that stood open. They all entered a small room. Off the pile, safe behind walls, Arista felt the impact at last and she was forced to sit before she fell.

She buried her face in her hands and wailed, "Oh god, dear Maribor. Poor Thrace!"

"She may yet be all right," the wizard told her. "Hadrian and her father are waiting with the broken sword."

She rocked as she cried but she did not cry only for Thrace. The tears were the bursting of a dam that could resist the flood no longer. In her mind flashed images of Hilfred and that last unspoken word; of Bernice and the cruel way she had treated her; and of Fanen and Mauvin, all of them lost. So much sorrow could not be put into words; instead, the emotions exploded out of her as she shouted, "The sword, what sword? What is all of this about a sword? I don't understand!"

"You explain," Royce said. "I need to find the other half."

"It's not there," Arista told him.

"What?"

"You said the sword was broken?" Arista asked.

"In two parts. I stole the blade half yesterday; now I need to get the hilt half. I'm pretty certain it is in that pile up there."

"No it isn't," Arista said, shocked that her brain was still working enough to connect the dots. "Not anymore."

⁂

The wizard led the way down the long crystalline steps, pausing from time to time to peer down a corridor, or at a staircase. He would think for a moment, then shake his head and push on, or mutter, "Ah, yes!" and turn.

"Where are we?" she asked.

"Avempartha," the wizard replied.

"I got that much already. What *is* Avempartha? And don't say it's a tower."

"It is an elven construction, built several millennia ago. More recently it has been a trap that has held the Gilarabrywn, and more recently still, it has apparently been its nest. Does that help?"

"Not really."

Although perplexed, Arista did feel better. It surprised her how easy it was to forget. It felt wrong. She should be thinking about the ones lost. She should be grieving, but her mind fought against it. Like broken limbs that refused to support any more weight, her heart and mind were hungry for relief. She needed a rest, something else to think about, something that did not involve death and misery. The tower of Avempartha provided the remedy. It was astounding.

Esrahaddon led them up and down stairs, through great rooms, and across interior bridges that spanned between spire shafts. Not a torch or lantern burned, but she could see perfectly, the walls themselves giving off a soft blue light. Vaulted ceilings a hundred feet high spread out like the canopy of a forest, with intricately lined designs that suggested branches and leaves. Railings, appearing as curling tendrils of creeping vines, sculptured from solid stone in vivid detail, ran along walkways and down steps. Nothing was without adornment, every inch imbued with beauty and care. Arista walked with her mouth open, her eyes shifting from one wonder to the next—a giant statue of a magnificent swan taking flight, a bubbling fountain in the shape of a school of fish. She recalled the crude barbarity of King Roswort's castle and his disdain for the elves—beings he likened to rats in a woodpile. *Some woodpile.*

There was a music to this place. The muted humming of the falls created a low, comforting bass. The wind across the tips of the tower played as woodwinds in an orchestra—soft reassuring tones. The bubbling and trickling of fountains lent light, satisfying rhythms to the symphony. Into this harmony crashed the voice of Esrahaddon as he recounted his first visit to the tower centuries before and how he had trapped the beast inside.

"So since you trapped the Gilarabrywn nine hundred years ago," she said, "you plan to trap it here again?"

"No," Esrahaddon told her. "No hands, remember? I can't cast that powerful of a binding spell without fingers, girl; you should know that better than anyone."

"I heard you threaten to cage it again."

"The Gilarabrywn doesn't know Esra doesn't have hands, does it?" Royce put in.

"The beast remembered me," the wizard said, taking over. "It assumed I was just as powerful as before, which means aside from the sword, I am about the only thing the Gilarabrywn fears."

"You just wanted to scare it off?"

"That was the idea, yes."

"We were trying to get the sword and hoped we might also save the both of you in the process," Royce told her. "I obviously didn't expect it to grab Thrace, and there was absolutely no way I could have guessed she would have taken the sword with her. You're certain she took a sword hilt from the pile?"

"Yes, I was the one who spotted it, but I still don't understand. How does the sword help? The Gilarabrywn isn't an enchantment; it's a monster that the heir must kill and..."

"You've been listening to the church. The Gilarabrywn *is* a magical creation. The sword is the countermeasure."

"A sword is? That doesn't make sense. A sword is metal, a physical element."

Esrahaddon smiled, looking a bit surprised. "So you paid attention to my lessons. Excellent. You're right, the sword is worthless. It is the word written on the blade that has the power to dispel the conjuration. If it is plunged into the body of the beast, it will unlock the elements holding it in existence and break the enchantment."

"If only you had been the one to take it, we'd have a way to fight the thing."

"Well, you did save me, at least," Arista reminded them. "Thank you."

"Don't thank us too soon. It's still out there," Royce told her.

"Okay, so Thrace hired Royce—I don't know how that transpired, but okay—still I don't understand why *you're* here, Esra," she admitted.

"To find the heir."

"There isn't an heir," she told them. "All the contestants failed and the rest are dead, I'm sure. That monster destroyed everything."

"I'm not talking about that foolishness. I'm speaking about the real Heir of Novron."

The wizard came to a T-intersection and turned left, heading for a staircase that lead down again.

"Wait a minute." Royce stopped them. "We didn't come this way."

"No *we* didn't, but I did."

Royce looked around him. "No, no, this is all wrong. Here I was letting you lead and you clearly don't have a clue where the exit is."

"I'm not leading you to the exit."

"What?" Royce asked.

"We're not leaving," the wizard replied. "I am going to the Valentryne Layartren and the two of you are coming with me."

"You might want to explain why," Royce told him, his voice chilling several degrees. "Otherwise you are jumping to a pretty big conclusion."

"I'll explain on the way."

"Explain now," Royce told him. "I have other appointments to consider."

"You can't help Hadrian," the wizard said. "The Gilarabrywn is already at the village by now. Hadrian is either dead or safe. Nothing you can do will change that. You can't help him, but you can help me. I spent the better part of two days trying to access the Valentryne Layartren, but without your hands, Royce, I can't reach it, and it would take days, perhaps weeks, for me to operate alone, but with Arista here, we can do it all tonight. Maribor has seen fit to deliver both of you to me at the precise moment I need you most."

"Valentryne Layartren," Royce muttered, "that's elvish for *artistic vision*, isn't it?"

"You know some elvish, good for you, Royce," Esrahaddon said. "You should pursue your roots more."

"Your roots?" Arista said, confused.

They both ignored her.

"You can't help the people back at the village, but you can help me do what I came here to do. What I brought you here to help me with."

"You need us to help you find the true Heir of the Empire?"

"You're normally quicker than this, Royce. I'm disappointed."

"I thought you were keeping it a secret."

"I was, but circumstances have forced me to reconsider. Now quit being so stubborn and come with me. You might look back on this moment one day and reflect on how you changed the course of the world by simply walking down these steps."

Royce continued to hesitate.

"Think," Esrahaddon said. "What can you do for Hadrian?"

Royce didn't answer.

"If you run down the steps, race through the tunnel, swim out to the woods, and kill yourself running to the village, what will that accomplish? Even if you miraculously manage to reach the town before Hadrian is killed, how will that help? You will be standing there exhausted and dripping wet. You don't have the sword. You can't harm it. You can't scare it. I doubt you can even distract it, and if you do, it will only be for a moment. If you go, it will only be to your own death, and for no reason at all. Hadrian's fate does not lie in your hands. You know I'm right, or you wouldn't still be listening to me. Now stop being stubborn."

Royce sighed.

"Thank the gods," the wizard said. "Let's get moving."

"Wait a minute." Arista stopped them. "Don't I get a say in this too?"

The wizard looked back at her. "Do you know the way out?"

"No," she replied.

"Then no, you don't get a say," the wizard told her. "Now, please, we've wasted enough time. Follow me."

"I remember you being nicer," Arista shouted at the wizard.

"And I remember both of you being faster."

They were off again, heading deeper into the center of the tower. As they did, Esrahaddon spoke again. "Most people believe this tower was built by the elves as a defensive fortress for the wars against Novron. As both of you most likely have guessed, that's not true. This tower predates Novron by many millennia. Others think it was built as a fortress against the sea goblins, the infamous Ba Ran Ghazel, only that's also not true, since the tower predates their appearance as well. The common mistake here is that this is a fortress at all—that's the result of human thinking. The fact is, the elves lived for eons before man or goblin, and perhaps even before dwarves entered the world. In those days they had no need for fortresses. They didn't even have a word for war, as the Horn of Gylindora controlled all of their internal strife. No, this wasn't some defensive bulwark guarding the only crossing point on the Nidwalden River, although that certainly became its use many eons later. Originally, this tower was designed as a center for the Art."

"He means magic," Arista clarified.

"I know what he means."

"Elven masters would travel here from the world over to study and practice advanced Art. Still, this wasn't just a school. The building itself is an enormous tool, like a giant furnace for a blacksmith, only in this case, the building works as a focusing element. The falls function as a source of power and the tower's numerous spires are like the antennae on a grasshopper or the whiskers of a cat. They reach out into the world, sensing, feeling, drawing into this place the very essence of existence. It is like a giant lever and fulcrum, allowing a single artist to magnify their power almost beyond reason."

"Artistic vision..." Royce said. "It's a device that will allow you to use magic to find the heir?"

"Sadly, not even Avempartha has that much power. I can't find something I've never seen, or something I don't know exists. What I can do, however, is find something I do know, something that I am very well acquainted with, and something I created for the specific purpose of finding later.

"Nine hundred years ago when Jerish and I decided to split up in order to hide Nevrik, I made amulets for them. These amulets served two purposes: one was to protect them from the Art, thus preventing anyone from locating them by divination; the other was to provide me with a means to track them with a signature only I know how to recognize.

"Of course, Jerish and I assumed it would only take a few years to assemble a group of loyalists to restore the emperor, but as we all now know, that didn't happen. I can only hope that Jerish was smart enough to impress upon the descendants of the heir to keep the necklaces safe and to hand them down from one generation to the next. That might be asking too much, since—well, who could imagine that I would live so long?"

They crossed another narrow bridge, which spanned a disturbingly deep gap. Overhead were several colorful banners with iconic images embroidered on them with large single elven letters. Arista noticed Royce staring at them, his mouth working as if he was trying to read. On the far side of the bridge, they reached a doorstep where a tall ornately decorated archway was drawn into the stone, but no door was present.

"Royce, if you wouldn't mind?"

Royce stepped forward and, laying his hands on the polished stone, pressed.

"What's he doing?" Arista asked the wizard.

Esrahaddon turned and looked at Royce.

The thief stood before them uncomfortably for a moment, then said, "Avempartha has a magical protection that prevents anyone who doesn't have elvish blood from entering. Every lock in the place works the same way. Originally, we thought no one else but I could enter—oh, and Esra, because he had been invited years ago—but it turns out that if an elf invites you, that's all that is needed. Esra found the exact elvish wording for me to memorize for the invite. That's how I got you in."

"Speaking of which..." Esrahaddon motioned toward the stone arch.

"Sorry," Royce said, and added in a clear voice, "Melentanaria, en venau rendin Esrahaddon, en Arista Essendon adona Melengar," which Arista understood as *Grant entry to the wizard Esrahaddon and Arista Essendon, Princess of Melengar.*

"That's Old Speech," Arista said.

"Yes." Esrahaddon nodded. "There are many similarities between Elvish and Old Imperial."

"Whoa!" Looking back at the archway, Arista suddenly saw an open door. "But I still don't understand. How is it you can grant us—oh." The princess stopped with her mouth still open. "But you don't look at all—"

"I'm a *mir.*"

"A what?"

"A mix," Esrahaddon explained, "some elven, some human blood."

"But you never—"

"It's not the kind of thing you brag about," the thief said. "And I'd appreciate it if you kept this to yourself."

"Oh—of course."

"Come along. Arista still needs to play her part," Esrahaddon said, entering.

Inside, they found a large chamber carved perfectly round. It was like entering the inside of a giant ball. Unlike the rest of the tower, and despite its size, the room was unadorned. It was merely a vast smooth chamber with no seam, crack, nor crevice. The only feature was a zigzagging stone staircase that rose from the floor to a platform that extended out from the steps and stood at the exact center of the sphere.

"Do you remember the Plesieantic Incantations I taught you, Arista?" the wizard asked as they climbed the stairs, his voice echoing loudly, ricocheting repeatedly off the walls.

"Um...the ah..."

"Do you or don't you?"

"I'm thinking."

"Think faster; this is no time for slow wits."

"Yes, I remember. Lord, but you've gotten testy."

"I'll apologize later. Now, when we get up there, you are going to stand in the middle of the platform on the mark laid out on the floor as the apex. You will begin and maintain the Plesieantic Phrase. Start with the Gathering Incantation; when you do, you will likely feel a bit more of a jolt than you would normally, because this place will amplify your power to gather resources. Don't be alarmed, don't stop the incantation, and whatever you do, don't scream."

Arista looked fearfully back at Royce.

"Once you feel the power moving through your body, begin the Torsonic Chant. As you do, you will need to form the crystal-matrix with your fingers, making certain you fold inward, not outward."

"So with my thumbs pointing out and the rest of my fingers pointing at me, right?"

"Yes," Esrahaddon said, irritated. "This is all basic formations, Arista."

"I know it, I know it—it's just been a while. I've been busy being Melengar's ambassador, not sitting in my tower practicing conjurations."

"So you've been frivolously wasting your time?"

"No," she said, exasperated.

"Now, when you've completed the matrix," the wizard went on, "just hold it. Remember the concentration techniques I taught you and focus on keeping the matrix even and steady. At that point, I'll tap into your power field and conduct my search. When I do, this room is likely to do some extraordinary things. Images and visions will become visible at various places in the room and you might even hear sounds. Again don't be alarmed. They aren't really here; they will merely be echoes of my mind as I search for the amulets."

"Does that mean *all* of us will be able to see who the real heir is?" Royce asked as they reached the top.

Esrahaddon nodded. "I would like to have kept it to myself, but fate has seen fit to force me a different way. When I find the magical pulse of the amulets, I'll focus on the owners and they will likely appear as the largest image in the room, as I'll be concentrating to determine not only who wears them, but where they are as well."

The platform was only faintly dust-covered and they could easily see the massive converging geometric lines marked on the floor like rays of the sun, all gathering to a single point in the exact center of the dais.

"Them?" Arista asked as she took her position at the central point.

"There were two necklaces: one I gave to Nevrik, which

will be the heir's amulet, and the other to Jerish, which will be the bodyguard's. If they still exist, we should see both. I would ask that you not tell anyone what you are about to see, for if you do, you could put the heir's life in immense danger and possibly imperil the future of mankind as we know it."

"Wizards and their drama." Royce rolled his eyes. "A simple *please keep your mouth shut* would do."

Esrahaddon raised an eyebrow at the thief, then turned to Arista and said, "Begin."

Arista hesitated. Sauly had to be wrong. All that talk about the heir having the power to enslave mankind was just to frighten her into being their spy. His warnings that Esrahaddon was a demon must be more lies. He was secretive, certainly, but not evil. He had saved her life that night. What had Sauly done? How many days before Braga's death had Saldur known…and done nothing? Too many.

"Arista?" Esrahaddon pressed.

She nodded, raised her hands, and began the weave.

Chapter 14

As Darkness Falls

The night wind blew gently across the hilltop. Hadrian and Theron stood alone on the ruins of the manor above what had been a village. A place of countless hopes that lay buried in ash and wreckage.

Theron felt the breeze on his skin and remembered the ill wind he had felt the night his family died. The night Thrace ran to him. He could still see her as she raced down the slope of Stony Hill, running to the safety of his arms. He had thought that was the worst day of his life. He had cursed his daughter for coming to him. He had blamed her for the death of his family. He had put on her all the woe and despair that he had been too weak to carry. She was his little girl, the one who always walked beside him wherever he went, and when he shooed her away, as he always did, he would catch her following at a distance, watching him, mimicking his actions and his words. Thrace was the one who laughed at his faces, cried when he was hurt; the one who sat at his bedside when he lay with fever. He never had a good word for his daughter. Never a pat or praise that he could remember. Not once did he ever say he was proud of her. Most of the time he had not acknowledged her at all. But he would gladly give his own life merely to see his little girl run to him again, just once more.

Theron stood shoulder to shoulder with Hadrian. He held the broken blade hidden beneath his clothes, ready to draw it out in an instant to appease the beast if needed. Hadrian held the false blade the dwarf had fashioned, and he, too, kept it hidden, explaining that if the Gilarabrywn knew in advance where its prize was, it might not bother with the trade. Magnus and Tobis waited down the hill out of sight behind a hunting blind of assembled wreckage while Tomas worked at making Hilfred and Mauvin as comfortable as possible at the bottom of the hill.

The moon had risen and climbed above the trees and still the beast had not come. The torches Hadrian had lit in a circle around the hilltop were burning out. Only a few remained, but it did not seem to matter, as the moon was bright, and with the canopy of leaves gone, they could see well enough to read a book.

"Maybe it's not coming," Tomas said to them, climbing up the hill. "Maybe it wasn't supposed to be tonight or maybe I was just hearing things. I've never been very good with the Old Speech."

"How's Mauvin?" Hadrian asked.

"The bleeding stopped. He's sleeping peacefully now. I covered him in a blanket and created a pillow for him from a spare shirt. He and the soldier Hilfred should—"

There came a cry from the tower that turned their heads. To his amazement, Theron saw a brilliant explosion of white light flare at the pinnacle of the tower. It was there one moment and then faded as suddenly as it had appeared.

"What in the name of Maribor was that?" Theron asked.

Hadrian shook his head. "I don't know, but if I had to guess, I'd say Royce had something to do with it."

There was another cry from the Gilarabrywn, this one louder.

"Whatever it was," Hadrian told him, "I think it's headed our way."

Behind them, they could faintly hear Tomas praying.

"Put in a good word for Thrace, Tomas," Theron told him.

"I'm putting a word in for all of us," the cleric replied.

"Hadrian," Theron said, "if by chance I don't survive this and you do, keep an eye on my Thrace for me, will you? And if she dies too, see to it we are buried on my farm."

"And if I should die and you live," Hadrian said, "make sure this dagger I have in my belt gets back to Royce before the dwarf steals it."

"Is that all?" the farmer asked. "Where do you want us to bury you?"

"I don't want to be buried," he said. "If I die, I think I would like my body to be sent down the river, over the falls. Who knows, I might make it all the way to the sea."

"Good luck," Theron told him. The sounds of night fell silent, save only for the breath of the wind.

This time, with no forest in the way, Theron could see it coming, its wide dark wings stretched out like the shadow of a soaring bird, its thin body curling, its tail snapping as it flew. It did not dive as it approached. It did not breathe fire or land. Instead, it circled in silent flight, arcing in a wide ellipse.

As it circled, they could see it was not alone. Within its claws, it held a woman. At first, Theron could not tell who it was. She appeared to be wearing a richly tailored robe but she had Thrace's sandy-colored hair. As it circled the second time, he knew it was his daughter. A wave of relief and heightened anxiety gripped him. *What has become of the other?*

After several circles, the beast lowered like a kite and softly touched the ground. It landed directly in front of them, not more than fifty feet away, on the site of the now collapsed manor house.

Thrace was alive.

A massive claw of scale-covered muscle and bone tipped with four foot-long black nails surrounded her like a cage.

"Daddy!" she cried, in tears.

Seeing her, Theron made a lunge forward. Instantly the Gilarabrywn's claw tightened and she cried out. Hadrian grabbed Theron and pulled him back.

"Wait!" he shouted. "It'll kill her if you get too close."

The beast glared at them with huge reptilian eyes. Then the Gilarabrywn spoke.

Neither Theron nor Hadrian understood a word.

"Tomas," Hadrian shouted over his shoulder. "What's it saying?"

"I'm not very good at—" Tomas began.

"I don't care how well you did in grammar at seminary, just translate."

"I think it said it chose to take the females because it would create the greatest incentive for cooperation."

The creature spoke again and Tomas did not wait for Hadrian to tell him to translate.

"It says: 'Where is the blade that was stolen?' "

Hadrian looked back at Tomas. "Ask it 'Where is the other female?' "

Tomas spoke and the beast replied.

"It says the other escaped."

"Ask it 'How do I know you will let us all live if I tell you where the blade is hidden?' "

Tomas spoke and the beast replied again.

"It says it will offer you a gesture of good faith, since it knows it has the upper hand and understands your concern."

It opened its claw and Thrace ran to her father. Theron's heart leapt as his little girl raced across the hill to his waiting arms. He hugged her tight and wiped her tears.

"Theron," Hadrian said, "get her out of here. Both of you get back to the well if you can." Theron and his daughter did not argue and the Gilarabrywn's great eyes watched carefully as Theron and Thrace began to sprint down the hill. Then it spoke again.

" 'Now, where is the blade?' " Tomas translated.

⁂

Looking up at the towering beast and feeling the sweat dripping down his face, Hadrian drew the false blade out of his sleeve and held it up. The Gilarabrywn's eyes narrowed.

" 'Bring it to me.' " Tomas translated its words.

This was it. Hadrian felt the metal in his hands. "Please let this work," he whispered to himself, and tossed the blade. It landed in the ash before the beast. The Gilarabrywn looked down at it and Hadrian held his breath. The beast casually placed its foot upon the blade and gathered it into its long talons. Then it looked at Hadrian and spoke.

"The deal is complete," Tomas said. "But..."

"But?" Hadrian repeated nervously. "But what?"

Tomas's voice grew weak. "But it says, 'I cannot allow those who have seen even half my name to remain alive.' "

"Oh, you bastard," Hadrian cursed, pulling his great spadone sword from his back. "Run, Tomas!"

The Gilarabrywn rose, flapping its great wings, causing a storm of ash to swirl into a cloud. It snapped forward with its head like a snake. Hadrian dove aside and, spinning, drove his sword at the beast. Rather than feeling the blade tip penetrate, however, Hadrian felt his heart sink as the point of the spadone skipped off as if the Gilarabrywn were made of stone. The sudden shock broke his grip and the sword fell.

Not losing a beat, the Gilarabrywn swung its tail around in a sharp snap. The long bone blade on the tip hummed as it sliced the air two feet above the ground. Hadrian leapt over it and the tail glanced off the hillside, stabbing into a charred timber. A quick flick and the several-hundred-pound log flew into the night. Hadrian reached inside his tunic and drew Alverstone from its sheath. He crouched like a knife fighter in a ring, up on the balls of his feet, waiting for the next attack.

Once more, the Gilarabrywn's tail came at him. This time it stabbed like a scorpion. Hadrian dove aside, and the long point sunk into the earth.

He ran forward.

The Gilarabrywn snapped at Hadrian with its teeth. He was ready for that, expecting it, counting on it. He jumped aside at the last minute. It was so close one tooth sliced through his tunic and gashed his shoulder. It was worth it. He was inches from the beast's face. With all his strength, Hadrian stabbed Royce's tiny dagger into the monster's great eye.

The Gilarabrywn screeched an awful cry that deafened Hadrian. It reared back, stomping its feet. The tiny blade pierced and cut a slice. It shook its head, perhaps as much in disbelief as in pain, and glared at Hadrian with its one remaining eye. Then it spat out words so laced with venom that Tomas did not need to translate.

The beast spread its wings and drew itself up in the air. Hadrian knew what was coming next and cursed his own stupidity for having allowed the creature to move him so far from the pit. He could never make it there in time now.

The Gilarabrywn screeched and arched its back.

There was a loud *twack!* A wad of rope netting flew into the air like a ball. With small weights tied to the edges, which traveled faster than the center, the net flew open like a giant wind sock, enveloping the flapping beast even as it tried to take flight.

Its wings tangled in the net, the Gilarabrywn dropped to the hilltop, crashing down with a heavy thud, the impact throwing up bits of the manor house's stairway banister, which flew end over end before shattering in a cloud of ash.

"It worked!" Tobis shouted, as much in shock as in triumph, from the far side of the hill.

Hadrian saw his opportunity and, spinning around, charged the monster. As he did, he noticed Theron following him.

"I told you to take Thrace and run," Hadrian yelled.

"You looked like you needed help," Theron shouted back, "and I told Thrace to head for the well."

"What makes you think she will listen to you any more than you listen to me?"

Hadrian reached where the Gilarabrywn lay on its side thrashing about wildly, and dove at its head. He found its open eye and attacked, stabbing repeatedly. With a terrible scream, the beast raked back with its legs, ripping the net open, and rolled to its feet again.

Hadrian, so intent on blinding the beast, had stepped on the netting. When the monster rose, Hadrian's feet went out from under him. He fell flat on his back, the air knocked from his lungs.

Blind, the beast resorted to lashing out with its tail, sweeping it across the ground. Caught trying to stand up, Hadrian was struck by the blunt force of the tail.

ô

Hadrian rolled and tumbled like a rag doll, sliding across the ash until he stopped in a patch of dirt, where he lay unmoving.

Freeing itself fully of the net, the beast sniffed the air and began moving toward the one who had caused it pain.

"No!" Theron shouted, and charged. He ran for Hadrian, thinking he could drag him clear of the blind beast before it reached him, only the beast was too fast and reached Hadrian at the same time Theron did.

Theron picked up a rock and drew forth the broken blade he still carried. He aimed for the exposed creature's side and, using the rock as a hammer, drove the metal home like a nail.

This stopped the Gilarabrywn from killing Hadrian, but the beast did not cry out as it had when Hadrian had stabbed it. Instead, it turned and laughed. Theron struck the blade with the rock again, forcing the metal deep, but still the beast did not cry out. It spoke to him, but Theron could not understand the words. Then, having little trouble guessing where the farmer stood, the Gilarabrywn swiped at him with his claw.

Theron did not have the speed or agility that Hadrian had. Strong as he was for his age, his old body could not move clear of the blow in time, and the great nails of the beast stabbed into him like four swords.

"*Daddy!*" Thrace screamed, running to him. She scrambled up the slope, crying as she came.

From their blind, Tobis and the dwarf fired a rock at the Gilarabrywn and managed to hit its tail. The beast spun and charged furiously in their direction.

Falling to her hands and knees, Thrace crawled to Theron's side and found her father lying broken on the hill. His left arm lay twisted backward, his foot facing the wrong direction. His chest was soaked in dark blood and his breath hitched as his body convulsed.

"Thrace," he managed to say weakly.

"Daddy," she cried as she cradled him in her arms.

"Thrace," he said again, gripping her with his remaining hand and pulling her close. "I'm so—" His eyes closed tightly in pain. "I'm so—pr—proud of you."

"Oh god, Daddy. No. No. No!" she cried, shaking her head.

She held him, squeezing as hard as she could, trying by the force of her arms to keep him with her. She would not let him go. She could not; he was all there was. She sobbed and wailed, clutching his shirt, kissing his cheek and forehead, and as she held him, she felt her father pass away into the night.

Theron Wood died on the scorched ground in a pool of blood and dirt. As he did, the last tiny remnant of hope Thrace had held on to—the last foothold she had in the world—died with him.

There was a darkness of night, a darkness of senses, and a darkness of spirit. Thrace felt herself drowning in all three. Her father was dead. Her light, her hope, her last dream, they had all died with his last breath. Nothing remained upon the world that *it* had not taken from her.

It had killed her mother.

It had killed her brother, his wife, and her nephew.

It had killed Daniel Hall and Jessie Caswell.

It had burned her village.

It had killed her father.

Thrace raised her head and looked across the hill at *it*.

No one who had been attacked had ever lived. There were never any survivors.

She stood and began to walk forward slowly. She reached into the robe and pulled out the sword that had remained hidden there.

The beast found the catapult and shattered it. It turned and blindly began to search its way back down the hillside, sniffing. It did not notice the young girl.

The thick layer of ash that it had created quieted her steps.

"No, Thrace!" Tomas shouted at her. "Run away!"

The Gilarabrywn paused and sniffed at the sound of the shout, sensing danger but unable to determine its source. It tried to look in the direction of the voice.

"No, Thrace—don't!"

Thrace ignored the cleric. She had passed beyond hearing, beyond seeing, beyond thinking. She was no longer on the hill. She was no longer in Dahlgren, but rather in a tunnel, a narrow tunnel that led inescapably to only one destination...*it*.

It kills people. That's what it does.

The beast sniffed the air. She could tell it was trying to find her; it was searching for the smell of fear it created in its victims.

She had no fear. *It* had destroyed that too.

Now she was invisible.

Without hesitation, fear, question, or regret, Thrace quietly walked up to the towering monster. She gripped the elven sword in both hands and raised it above her head. Putting the full weight of her small body into it, she thrust the broken sword into the Gilarabrywn's body. She did not have to put so much effort into it; the blade slipped in easily.

The beast shrieked in mortal fear and confusion.

It turned, recoiling, but it was already too late. The sword penetrated all the way to the hilt. The essence that was the Gilarabrywn and the forces that bound it shattered. With the snapping of the bonds that held it fast, the world reclaimed the energy in a sudden violent outburst. The eruption of force threw Thrace and Tomas to the ground. The shock wave continued down the hill, radiating out in all directions, beyond the burnt desolation to the forest, launching flocks of birds into the night.

Dazed, Tomas staggered to his feet and approached the small slender figure of Thrace Wood at the center of a cleared depression, where the great Gilarabrywn had once been. He walked forward in awe and fell prostrate on his knees before the girl.

"Your Imperial Majesty," was all he said.

Chapter 15

The Heir of Novron

The sun rose brightly over the Nidwalden River. The clouds had moved off and by midmorning the sky was clear and the air cooler than it had been. A light wind skimmed across the surface of the river, raising ripples, while the sun cast a brilliant gold face upon the water. A fish jumped above the surface and fell back with a plop. Overhead, birds sang morning songs and cicadas droned.

Royce and Arista stood on the bank of the river, wringing water out of their clothes. Esrahaddon waited.

"Nice robe," the princess said.

The wizard only smiled.

Arista shivered as she looked out across the river. The trees on the far bank looked different than the ones on their side, a different species, perhaps. Arista thought they appeared prouder, straighter, with fewer lower branches and longer trunks. While the trees were impressive, there was no evidence of civilization.

"How do we know they are over there?" Arista asked.

"The elves?" Esrahaddon questioned.

"I mean, no one has seen an elf"—she glanced at Royce—"a pure-blood elf—in centuries, right?"

"They are there. Thousands of them by now, I should think. Tribes of the old names, with bloodlines that can be traced to the dawn of time. The Miralyith, masters of the Art; Asendwayr, the hunters; Nilyndd, the crafters; Eiliwin, the architects; Umalyn, the spiritualists; Gwydry, the shipwrights; and Instarya, the warriors. They are all still there, a congress of nations."

"Do they have cities? Like we do?"

"Perhaps, but probably not like ours. There is a legend of a sacred place called Estramnadon. It is the holiest place in elven culture . . . at least that we humans know of. Estramnadon is said to be over there, deep in the forests. Some think it is their capital city and seat of their monarch; others speculate it is the sacred grove where the first tree—the tree planted by Muriel herself—still grows and is cared for by the Children of Ferrol. No one knows for certain. No human is likely ever to know, as the elves do not suffer the trespasses of others."

"Really?" The princess looked at the thief with a playful smirk. "Perhaps if I knew that before, I might have guessed Royce's heritage sooner."

Royce ignored the comment and turned to the wizard. "Can I assume you'll not be returning to the village?"

Esrahaddon shook his head. "I need to leave before Luis Guy and his pack of hounds track me down. Besides, I have an heir to talk to and plans to make."

"Then this is goodbye. I need to get back."

"Remember to keep silent about what you saw in the tower—both of you."

"Funny, I expected the heir and his guardian to be unknown farm boys from someplace—well—like this, I suppose. Someone I never heard of."

"Life has a way of surprising you, doesn't it?" Esrahaddon said.

Royce nodded and started to head off.

"Royce," Esrahaddon said softly, stopping him, "we know that what happened last night wasn't pleasant. You should prepare yourself for what you're going to find."

"You think Hadrian's dead," Royce said flatly.

"I would expect so. If he is, at least know that his death may have been the sacrifice that saved our world from destruction. And while that may not comfort you, I think we both know that it would have pleased Hadrian."

Royce thought a moment, nodded, then entered the trees and disappeared.

"He's definitely elvish," Arista said, shaking her head and sitting down opposite Esrahaddon. "I don't know why I didn't see it before. You've grown a beard, I see."

"You just noticed?"

"I noticed before, been kinda busy until now."

"I can't really shave, can I? It wasn't a problem while I was in Gutaria, but now—does it look all right?"

"You have some gray coming in."

"I ought to. I am nine hundred years old."

She watched the wizard staring across the river.

"You really should practice your art. You did well in there."

She rolled her eyes. "I can't do it, not the way you taught me. I can do most of the things Arcadius demonstrated, but it's a bit impossible to learn hand magic from a man without hands."

"You boiled water, and you made the prison guard sneeze. Remember?"

"Yes, I'm a veritable sorceress, aren't I?" she said sarcastically.

He sighed. "What about the rain? Have you worked on that incantation any more?"

"No, and I'm not going to. I am the Ambassador of Melengar now. I've put all that behind me. Given time, they may even forget I was tried for witchcraft."

"I see," the wizard said, disappointed.

The princess shivered in the morning chill and tried to run her fingers through her hair but caught them in tangles. Stains and wrinkles dotted her dress. "I'm a mess, aren't I?"

The wizard said nothing. He appeared to be thinking.

"So," she began, "what will you do when you find the heir?"

Esrahaddon only stared at her.

"Is it a secret?"

"Why don't you ask me what you really want to know, Arista?"

She sat trying to look naïve and offered a slight smile. "I don't understand."

"You aren't sitting here shivering in a wet dress making small talk with me for nothing. You have an agenda."

"An agenda?" she asked, not at all convincingly, even for her own tastes. "I don't know what you mean."

"You want to know if what the church told you about your father's death is true or not. You think I used you as a pawn. You are wondering if I tricked you into being an unwitting accomplice to your own father's death."

The act was over. She stared, stunned at the wizard's bluntness, barely breathing. She did not speak but slowly nodded her head.

"I suspected they might come after you because they are having trouble following me."

"Did you?" she asked, finding her voice. "Did you orchestrate my father's death?"

Esrahaddon let the silence hang between them a moment, then at last replied.

"Yes, Arista. I did."

At first, the princess did not say a word. It did not seem possible that she had heard him correctly. Slowly her head began to shake back and forth in disbelief.

"How..." she started. "How could you do that?"

"Nothing I nor anyone else says can explain that to you—not now, at least. Perhaps someday you'll understand."

Tears welled up in her eyes. She brushed them away and glared at the wizard.

"Before you judge me completely, as I know you will, remember one thing. Right now, the Church of Nyphron is trying to persuade you that I am a demon, the very Apostle of Uberlin. You are likely thinking they are right. Before you damn me forever and run into the embrace of the Patriarch, ask yourself these questions. Who approved your entrance into Sheridan University? Who talked your disapproving father into letting you attend? How did you learn about me? How was it that you found your way to a hidden prison that only a handful of people knew existed? Why were you taught to use a gemstone lock, and isn't it interesting that the very gem you used on your door was the same as the signet ring that unlocked the prison entrance? And how was it that a young girl, princess or not, was allowed to enter Gutaria Prison and leave unmolested not once, not twice, but repeatedly for months without her activities ever being questioned or reported back to her father the king?"

"What are you saying?"

"Arista," the wizard said, "sharks don't eat seafood because they like it, but because chickens don't swim. We all do the best we can with the tools we have, but at some point you have to ask yourself where the tools came from."

She stared at him. "You knew they would kill my father.

You counted on it. You even knew they would eventually kill me and Alric, and yet you pretended to be my friend, my teacher." Her face hardened. "School's over." She turned her back on him and walked away.

⸙

When Royce reached the edge of the burnt forest, he spotted a series of colorful tents set up around the old village common. The tents displayed pennants of the Nyphron Church, and he could see several priests as well as imperial guards. Other figures moved slowly over the hill near the old castle grounds, but nowhere did he see anyone he knew.

He kept to the cover of the trees when he caught the sound of a snapping twig not too far off. Slipping around, he quickly spotted Magnus crouched in the underbrush.

The dwarf jumped in alarm and fell backward at his approach.

"Relax," Royce whispered, sitting down next to where the dwarf now lay, nervously watching the thief.

Glancing down the slope, Royce realized that the dwarf had found an excellent position to watch the camp. They were on a rise behind a series of burnt trees where some of the underbrush had survived. Below, they had a perfect view of each of the tent openings, the makeshift horse corral, and the latrine. Royce guessed there were about thirty of them.

"What are you still doing here?" Royce asked.

"I was breaking a sword for your partner. But I'm leaving now."

"What happened?"

"Huh? Oh, Theron and Fanen were killed."

Royce nodded, showing no outward sign of surprise or grief.

"Hadrian? Is he alive?"

The dwarf nodded and went on to explain the events that had transpired that evening.

"After it was dead, or dispelled, or whatever, Tomas and I checked on Hadrian. He was unconscious, but alive. We made him comfortable, covered him in a blanket, and put a lean-to over him, the Pickering kid, and that Melengarian soldier. Before dawn, Bishop Saldur and his crew returned, dragging two wagons with them. The way I figure it, either Guy reported what happened and he was coming back with help, or they heard it when the beastie died. They pulled in and, fast as rabbits, had these tents up and breakfast cooking. I spotted the sentinel in their ranks, so I hid up here. They moved Hadrian, Hilfred, and Mauvin into that white tent, and soon after, they put a guard on it."

"Is that all?"

"Well, they sent a detail out to bury the dead. Most they buried on the hill up there near the castle, including Fanen, but Tomas made some big stink and they took Theron down the road to that last farm near the river and they buried him there."

"Perhaps you forgot to mention how you found my dagger?"

"The Alverstone? I thought you had it."

"I do," Royce said.

Magnus reached for his boot and cursed.

"When you investigated my background, you must have stumbled across the fact that I survived my youth by picking pockets."

"I remember something about that," the dwarf growled.

Royce pulled Alverstone from its sheath as he glared at the dwarf.

"Look, I'm sorry about killing that damn king. It was just a job I was hired to do, okay? I wouldn't have taken the job if it hadn't required a uniquely challenging masonry effort. I'm not an assassin. I'm not even good enough to be considered a pathetic fighter. I'm an artisan. Truth be told, I specialize in weapons. That's my first love, but all dwarves can cut stone, so I was hired to do the tower work; then the job got changed, and after half a year's work, I was going to be stiffed if I didn't knife the old man. In hindsight, I can see I should have refused, but I didn't. I didn't know anything about him. Maybe he was a bad king; maybe he deserved to die; Braga certainly thought so and he was the king's brother-in-law. I try not to involve myself in human affairs, but I was caught up in this one. It's not something I wanted; it's not something I looked for; it just happened. And it's not like someone else wouldn't have done it if I hadn't."

"What makes you think I'm upset you killed Amrath? I'm not even mad that you trapped the tower. Closing the door on me was the mistake you made."

Magnus inched away.

"Killing you would be as easy as—no, easier than—slaughtering a fatted pig. The challenge would lie in causing the maximum amount of pain before inflicting the death."

Magnus's mouth opened, but no words came out.

"But you are a very lucky dwarf, because there's a man still alive in that tent who wouldn't like it—a man you covered in a blanket and put a lean-to over."

Down below he spotted Arista as she entered the camp. She talked to a guard, who pointed toward the white tent. She rushed to it.

Royce looked back at the dwarf and spoke clearly and evenly. "If you ever touch Alverstone again without my permission, I'll kill you."

Magnus looked at him bitterly; then his expression changed

and he raised an eyebrow. "Without your *permission*? So there's a chance you'll *let* me study it?"

Royce rolled his eyes. "I'm going to get Hadrian out of there. You are going to steal two of the archbishop's horses and walk them over to the white tent without being spotted."

"And then we can talk about the *permission* thing?"

Royce sighed, "Did I mention I hate dwarves?"

"But, Your Grace—" Deacon Tomas protested as he stood in the large striped tent before Bishop Saldur and Luis Guy. The pudgy cleric made a poor showing of himself in his frock caked with dirt and ash, his face smudged, his fingers black.

"Look at you, Tomas," Bishop Saldur said. "You're so exhausted you look as if you'll fall down any minute. You've had a long two days, and you've been under tremendous stress for months now. It is only natural that you might see things in the dark. No one is blaming you. And we don't think you are lying. We know that right now you believe you saw this village girl destroy the Gilarabrywn, but I think if you just take a nap and rest, when you get up, you'll find that you were mistaken about a great many things."

"I don't need a nap!" Tomas shouted.

"Calm down, Deacon," Saldur snapped, rising abruptly to his feet. "Remember whose presence you are standing in."

The deacon cowed and Saldur sighed. His face softened to his grandfatherly visage and he put an arm around the man's shoulders, patting him gently. "Go to a tent and rest."

Tomas hesitated, turned, and left Saldur and Luis Guy alone.

The bishop threw himself down in the little cushioned

chair beside a bowl of red berries some industrious servant had managed to gather for him. He popped two in his mouth and chewed. They were bitter and he grimaced. Despite the early hour, Saldur was desperate for a glass of brandy, but none had survived the flight from the castle. Only the grace of Maribor could account for the survival of the camping gear and provisions, all of which they had lazily left in the wagons when they had first arrived at the manor. In the turmoil of their exodus, they had given little thought to provisions.

That he lived at all was a miracle. He could not recall how he had crossed the courtyard, or how he had reached the gate. He must have run down the hill, but had no recollection of it. His memory was like a dream, vague and fading. He did remember ordering the coachman to whip the horses. The fool wanted to wait for the archbishop. The old man could barely walk, and the moment the flames hit, his servants deserted him. He had had as much chance of survival as Rufus.

With Archbishop Galien's death, the command of the church's interest in Dahlgren fell to Saldur and Guy. The two inherited a disaster of mythic proportions. They were alone in the wilderness, faced with crucial decisions. How they handled them would decide the fate of future generations. Who actually held authority remained vague. Saldur was a bishop, an appointed leader, while Guy was only a constabulary officer whose jurisdiction extended mostly to apostate members of the church. Still, the sentinel actually spoke with the Patriarch. Saldur liked Guy, but appreciation for his effectiveness would not prevent him from sacrificing the sentinel if necessary. Saldur was certain that if Guy still had had his knights about him, the sentinel would have taken command and he would have had no choice but to accept it, but the seret were dead and Guy himself wounded. With Galien also dead, a door had opened, and Saldur planned to be the first one through.

Saldur looked at Guy. "How could you let this happen?"

The sentinel, who sat with his arm in a sling and his shoulder wrapped in bandages, stiffened. "I lost seven good men, and barely escaped with my life. I wouldn't call that *allowing* it to happen."

"And how exactly did a bunch of farmers defeat the infamous seret?"

"They weren't farmers. Two were Pickerings and there was Hadrian Blackwater."

"The Pickerings I can understand, but Blackwater? He's nothing but a rogue."

"No, there's more to him—him and his partner."

"Royce and Hadrian are excellent thieves. They proved that in Melengar and again in Chadwick. Poor Archibald still has fits over them."

"No," Guy said, "I think they're more than that. Blackwater knows Teshlor combat, and his friend Royce Melborn is an elf."

Saldur blinked. "An elf? Are you sure?"

"He passes as human, but I'm certain of it."

"And this is the second time we've found them with Esrahaddon," Saldur muttered in concern. "Is this Hadrian still here?"

"He is in the infirmary tent."

"Put a guard on him at once."

"I've had him under guard since he was dragged to the tent. What we need to concern ourselves with is the girl. She's going to prove herself to be an embarrassment if we don't do something," Guy said, and slipped his sword partway out of its sheath. "She is in grief over the loss of her father. It wouldn't be surprising if she threw herself over the falls in a fit of despair."

"And Tomas?" Saldur asked, reaching for another handful of berries. "It is clear he won't be quiet. Will you kill him too? What excuse will you give for that? And what about all the others in this camp that heard him going on all morning about her being the heir? Do we kill everyone? If we did, who would carry our bags back to Ervanon?" he added with a smile.

"I don't see the humor in this," Guy snapped, letting his sword slide back down in its sheath.

"Perhaps that's because you are not looking at it the right way," Saldur told him. Guy was a well-trained and vicious guard dog, but the man lacked imagination. "What if we didn't kill her? What if we actually made her the empress?"

"A peasant girl? Empress?" Guy scoffed. "Are you mad?"

"Despite his political clout, I don't think any of us, including the Patriarch, were particularly happy with the choice of Rufus. He was a fool, to be sure, but he was also a stubborn, powerful fool. We all suspected that he might have had to be killed within a year, which would have thrown the infant empire into turmoil. How much better would it be to have an empress that would do whatever she was told right from the very start?"

"But how could we possibly sell her to the nobles?"

"We don't," Saldur said, and a smile appeared on his wrinkled face. "We sell her to the people instead."

"How's that?"

"Degan Gaunt's Nationalist movement proved that the people themselves have strength. Earls, barons, even kings are afraid of the power which that commoner can gather. A word from him could launch a peasant uprising. Lords would have to kill their own people, their own source of revenue, just to keep order. This presents them with the undesirable choice of accepting either poverty or death. The landholders will do almost anything to avoid such an event. What if we tapped that? The peasants already revere the church. They follow its teachings as divine truth. How much more inspiring would it be to offer them a leader plucked from their own stock? A ruler who is one of them and able to truly understand the plight of the poor, the unwashed, the destitute. Not only is she a peasant queen, but she is also the Heir of Novron, and all the wonderful expectations that go with that. Indeed, in our greatest hour of need, Maribor has once again delivered unto his people a divine leader to show us the way out of darkness.

"We could send bards across the land repeating the epic tale of the pure, chaste girl who slew the elven demon that even Lord Rufus was powerless against. We'll call it *Rufus's Bane*. Yes, I like it—so much better than the unpronounceable *Gilarabrywn*."

"But can she be made to play her part?" Guy asked.

"You saw her. She's nearly comatose. Not only does she have no place to go, no friends or relatives, no money or possessions, she is also emotionally shattered. She'd slit her own wrists, I suspect, if she gets a knife. Still, the best part is that once we establish her as empress, once we have the support of the people so fervently on our side, no noble landholder would dare challenge us. We can do what we planned to do with Rufus. Only instead of a messy murder that would certainly invite suspicion and accusations, with the girl, we can simply marry her. The new husband will rule as emperor and we can lock her in a dark room somewhere, pulling her out for Wintertide showings."

Guy smiled at that.

"Do you think the Patriarch will agree?" Saldur asked him. "Perhaps we should send a rider back today."

"No, this is too important. I'll go myself. I'll leave as soon as I can saddle a horse. In the meantime—"

"In the meantime, we will announce that we are considering the possibility that this girl is the heir, but will not accept her unconditionally until a full investigation is conducted. That should buy us a month. If the Patriarch agrees, then we can send out rabble-rousers to incite the people with rumors that the church is being forced by the nobles and the monarchs to not reveal the girl as the true heir. The people will be denouncing our enemies and demanding that she take the throne before we even announce her."

"She will make the perfect figurehead," Guy said.

Saldur looked up, picturing the future. "An innocent girl linked with a mythic legend. Her beautiful name will be everywhere and she will be loved." The bishop paused and thought. "What is her name, anyway?"

"I think Tomas called her... Thrace."

"Seriously?" Saldur grimaced. "Well, no matter, we'll change it. After all, she's ours now."

ర

Royce looked around. There was not a single sentry left outside. Several still moved about on the hilltop, but they were far enough away to ignore. Satisfied, he ducked through the flap of the white tent. Inside, he found Tobis, Hadrian, Mauvin, and Hilfred on cots. Hadrian was naked to his waist, his head and chest wrapped in white bandages, but he was awake and sitting up. Mauvin, though still pale, was alert, his bandages bright white. Hilfred lay wrapped like a mummy and Royce could not be sure if he was awake or sleeping. Arista stood bent over his cot, checking on him.

"I was wondering when you would get here," Hadrian said.

Arista turned. "Yes, I thought you would have arrived much sooner."

"Sorry, you know how it is when you're having fun. You lose all track of time, but I did locate your weapons, again. You know how upset you get when you don't have your swords. Can you ride?"

"If I can walk, why not?" He raised an arm and Royce offered his shoulder, helping him to stand.

"What about me?" Mauvin asked, holding his side and sitting up on his cot. "You're not going to leave me, are you?"

"You have to take him," Arista declared. "He killed two of Guy's men."

"Can you ride?" Royce asked.

"If I had a horse under me, I could at least hang on."

"What about Thrace?" Hadrian asked.

"I don't think you need worry about her," Royce told him. "I was just by the bishop's tent. Tomas is demanding that they declare her empress."

"Empress?" Hadrian said, stunned.

"She killed the Gilarabrywn right in front of the deacon. I guess it made an impression."

"But what if they don't? We can't leave her."

"Don't worry about Thrace," Arista said. "I'll see she's taken care of. Now you all need to get out of here."

"Theron wanted at least one of his children to be successful," Hadrian muttered, "but empress?"

"You need to hurry," Arista said, helping Royce pull Mauvin to his feet. She gave all three of them a kiss and a gentle hug and then pushed them out like a mother sending her children to school.

Outside the tent, Magnus arrived with three saddled horses. The dwarf looked around nervously and whispered, "I could have sworn I saw guards watching this tent earlier."

"You did," Royce replied. "Three horses—you read my mind."

"I figured I needed one for myself," the dwarf replied, pointing at the shortened stirrups. He looked at Mauvin with a scowl. "Now it looks like I'll need to get another."

"Forget it," Royce whispered. "Ride with Mauvin. Take it slow and make sure he stays in the saddle."

Royce helped Hadrian up onto a gray mare, then started to chuckle to himself.

"What is it?" Hadrian asked.

"Mouse."

"What's that?"

Royce pointed to the horse Hadrian sat on. "Of all the animals he had to choose from, the dwarf stole Mouse."

Royce led them away from the camp, walking the horses across the scorched land, where the ash muffled their movement. He kept a close eye on the distant sentries. No outcry, no shouts, no one appeared to notice, and soon they slipped into the leafy forest. Once there, he turned back toward the river in order to throw off anyone who might look for their tracks. Once he had them safe in a shallow glen near the Nidwalden, Royce ordered them to stay put while he went back.

He crept up to the edge of the burned area. The camp was as it had been before. Satisfied they had made a clean escape, he walked back toward the river. He found himself on the trail that led to the Woods' farm and the shell of the old building. Inexplicably, the fire had never reached this far and it remained untouched. There was one change, however; in the center of the yard, where they had first seen the old farmer sharpening his scythe, there was a mound of earth. A stack of stones borrowed from the walls of the farmhouse circled the oblong mound. At its head, driven into the ground, was a broad plank, and burned into it were the words:

THERON WOOD
FARMER

Royce could just make out the additional words scratched into the plank below that:

Father of the Empress

As Royce stood reading the words, he noticed it—a chill making the hair on his skin stand up. Someone was watching him. On the edge of his sight, a figure stood in the trees. Another stood to his left. He sensed more behind him. He turned his head, focused his eyes to see who they were—nothing. All he saw were trees. He glanced to his left and again nothing. He stood still, listening. Not a twig snapped, nor a leaf crinkled, but he could still feel it.

He moved away from the clearing into the brush and circled around. He moved as quietly as he could, but when he stopped, he was alone.

Royce stood, puzzled. He looked for tracks where he had seen the figures, but none existed, not even a bent blade of grass. At last, he gave up and returned to where he had left the others.

"All's well?" Hadrian asked, sitting atop Mouse with the sun on his bare shoulders and his chest wrapped in broad strips of white cloth.

"I suppose," he said, mounting up.

He led them southwest along the highlands near the falls, following a deer trail that cut through the deep forest. It was the same trail he had found in his hours searching for a tunnel to the tower. Hadrian and Mauvin appeared to be doing better than expected, though each of them winced in pain whenever his horse took a misstep.

Royce continued to look back over his shoulder but nothing was ever there.

By midafternoon they had cleared the trees and found the main road heading south to Alburn. Here they paused to check Mauvin's and Hadrian's bandages. Mauvin started to bleed again, but it was not bad and Magnus turned out to be almost as good a nurse as he was a sword smith, fashioning a new pad for his side. Royce searched through the saddlebags and found Hadrian a suitable shirt.

"We should be fine," Royce told them, going through their inventory. "With a little luck we should reach Medford in a week."

"In a hurry, are you?" Hadrian asked.

"You might say that."

"Thinking about Gwen?"

"I'm thinking it's time I told her a few things about myself."

Hadrian smiled and nodded.

"You think Thrace will be all right?"

"Tomas seems to be watching out for her pretty well."

"Do you think they'll really make her empress?"

"Not a chance." Royce shook his head and handed the shirt to him. "What do you plan on doing now?" Royce asked Magnus.

The dwarf shrugged. "You mean assuming you don't kill me?"

"I'm not going to kill you, but your old employer, the

church, might now that you've turned on them. They will be coming after you just the same as they'll be after Mauvin and Hadrian. And without the church's support, you won't last long on your own. Towns in Avryn aren't too friendly to your kind."

"Nowhere is."

"That's what I meant." Royce sighed. "I know of a very out-of-the-way place you might be able to hold up at. A place the church isn't likely to visit. They need a lot of stonework done and could use an experienced craftsman like you."

"How do they feel about dwarves?"

"I don't think you'll have a problem. They're the kind of people who tend to like everyone."

"I could do with getting back to stonecutting." Magnus nodded.

"Myron will drive him crazy with his quest to get the monastery exactly the way it was," Hadrian said. "They've gone through five builders so far."

"I know," Royce replied with a little grin.

Royce climbed back on top of Mouse as Magnus went ahead to check on Mauvin.

Hadrian shook out his shirt before slipping his arm in the sleeve. "Arista told me you two were with Esrahaddon in the tower last night. She said he needed help with something, but wouldn't tell me what it was."

"He was using the tower to look for the Heir of Novron," Royce replied.

"Did he find him?"

"I think so, but you know how Esra is. It's hard to be sure of anything when dealing with him." Hadrian nodded and winced as he pulled the shirt over his shoulders.

"Having troubles?"

"You try getting dressed with broken ribs sometime. It isn't so easy."

Royce continued to look at him.

"What is it? Am I that entertaining?" Hadrian asked.

"It's just that you've worn that silver medallion ever since I've known you, but you never told me where you got it."

"Hmm? This?" Hadrian said. "I've had this forever. My father left it to me."

Glossary of Terms and Names

Addie Wood: Mother of Thrace, wife of Theron

Albert Winslow, Viscount: Landless nobleman used by Riyria to arrange assignments from the gentry

Alburn: Kingdom of Avryn ruled by King Armand and Queen Adeline

Alenda Lanaklin, Lady: Daughter of Marquis Victor Lanaklin and sister of Brother Myron of the Winds Abbey

Allie: Daughter of Wyatt Deminthal

Alric Brendon Essendon, Prince: Member of ruling family of Melengar, son of Amrath, brother of Arista

Alverstone: \al-ver-stone\ Royce's dagger

Ambrose Moor: Administrator of the Manzant Prison and Salt Works

Amrath Essendon, King: \am-wrath\ Ruler of Melengar, father of Alric and Arista

Amril, Countess: \am-rill\ Noblewoman that Arista cursed with boils

Antun Bulard: Historian and author of *The History of Apeladorn*

Apeladorn: \ah-pell-ah-dorn\ Four nations of man, consisting of Trent, Avryn, Delgos, and Calis

Aquesta: \ah-quest-ah\ Capital city of the kingdom of Warric

Arcadius Vintarus Latimer: Professor of lore at Sheridan University

Archibald Ballentyne: Earl of Chadwick

Arista Essendon, Princess: Member of ruling family of Melengar, daughter of Amrath, sister of Alric

ARMAND, KING: Ruler of Alburn, married to Adeline

ART, THE: Magic, generally feared by nobles and commoners due to superstition

ARVID MCDERN: Son of Dillon McDern of Dahlgren

AVEMPARTHA: Ancient elven tower

AVRYN: \ave-rin\ Central and most powerful of the four nations of Apeladorn, located between Trent and Delgos

BALLENTYNE: \bal-in-tine\ Ruling family of the earldom of Chadwick

BA RAN GHAZEL: Goblins of the sea

BELINDA PICKERING: Extremely attractive wife of Count Pickering, mother of Lenare, Mauvin, Fanen, and Denek

BELSTRADS: \bell-straads\ Family of knights from Chadwick, including Sir Breckton and Wesley

BERNICE: Handmaid of Princess Arista

BERNUM RIVER: Waterway that bisects the city of Colnora

BETHAMY, KING: Ruler reputed to have had his horse buried with him

BLACK DIAMOND, THE: International thieves' guild centered in Colnora

BLACKWATER: Last name of Hadrian and his father, Danbury

BLYTHIN CASTLE: Castle in Alburn

BOCANT: Family who built a lucrative industry from pork, second most wealthy merchants in Colnora

BOTHWICKS: Family of peasant farmers of Dahlgren

BRECKTON BELSTRAD, SIR: Son of Lord Belstrad, knight of Chadwick, considered by many to be the best knight of Avryn

BRODRIC ESSENDON: Founder of the Essendon dynasty

BUCKET MEN: Term for assassin used by the Black Diamond thieves' guild

BYRNIE: Long (usually sleeveless) tunic of chain mail formerly worn as defensive armor

CALIAN: \cal-lay-in\ Pertaining to the nation of Calis

CALIANS: Residents of the nation of Calis, darker in skin tone, with almond-shaped eyes

CALIS: \cal-lay\ Southern- and easternmost of the four nations of Apeladorn, considered exotic, in constant conflict with the Ba Ran Ghazel

CASWELL: Family of peasant farmers from Dahlgren

CENZARS: \sen-zhars\ Wizards of the ancient Novronian Empire

CHAMBERLAIN: Someone who manages the household of a king or nobleman

COLNORA: \call-nor-ah\ Largest and wealthiest city of Avryn, merchant-based, grew from a rest stop at a central crossroads from various major trade routes

COSMOS DELUR: Colnora's richest resident

CRIMSON HAND: Thieves' guild operating out of Melengar

CROWN TOWER: Home of the Patriarch, center of the Nyphron Church

CUTTER: Assassin of the Black Diamond, best friend of Royce, boyfriend of Jade

DAGASTAN: Major and easternmost trade port of Calis

DAHLGREN: \dall-grin\ Remote village on the bank of the Nidwalden River

DANBURY BLACKWATER: Father of Hadrian

DANTHEN: Woodsman from Dahlgren

DAREF, LORD: Nobleman of Warric, associate of Albert Winslow

DARIUS SERET: Founder of the Seret Knights

DAVENS, SQUIRE: Boy who Arista had a youthful crush on

DEGAN GAUNT: Leader of the Nationalists

DELANO DEWITT, BARON: Nobleman who hires Hadrian to steal Count Pickering's sword

DELGOS: One of the four nations of Apeladorn. The only

republic in a world of monarchies, Delgos revolted against the Steward's Empire after Glenmorgan III was murdered and after surviving an attack by the Ba Ran Ghazel with no aid from the empire.

DELORKAN, DUKE: Calian nobleman

DELUR: Family of wealthy merchants

DENEK PICKERING: Youngest son of Count Pickering

DILLON MCDERN: Dahlgren's blacksmith

DIOYLION: \die-e-leon\ *The Accumulated Letters of Dioylion*, a very rare scroll

DIXON TAFT: Bartender and manager of The Rose and Thorn Tavern

DROME: God of the dwarves

DRONDIL FIELDS: Count Pickering's castle, once the fortress of Brodric Essendon, the original seat of power in Melengar

DRUMINDOR: Dwarven-built fortress located at the entrance to Terlando Bay in Tur Del Fur

DRUNDEL: Peasant family from Dahlgren consisting of Mae, Went, Davie, and Firth

DUSTER: Moniker used by Royce while a member of the Black Diamond

ECTON, SIR: Chief knight of Count Pickering and military general of Melengar

EDMUND HALL: Professor of geometry at Sheridan University, reputed to have found Percepliquis, declared a heretic by the Nyphron Church, imprisoned in the Crown Tower

ELAN: The world

ELDEN: Large man, friend of Wyatt Deminthal

ELLA: Cook at Drondil Fields

ELVEN: Pertaining to elves

ENDEN, SIR: Knight of Chadwick, considered the second best to Breckton

EREBUS: Father of the gods, also known as Kile
ERIVAN: \ear-ah-van\ Elven empire
ERLIC, SIR: Knight competing in Dahlgren contest
ERVANON: \err-vah-non\ City in northern Ghent, seat of the Nyphron Church, once the capital of the Steward's Empire as established by Glenmorgan I
ESRAHADDON: \ez-rah-hod-in\ Wizard, onetime member of the ancient order of the Cenzar, convicted of destroying the Novronian Empire and sentenced to imprisonment
ESSENDON: \ez-in-don\ Royal family of Melengar
ESSENDON CASTLE: Home of ruling monarchs of Melengar
ESTRAMNADON: \es-tram-nah-don\ Believed to be the capital or at least a very sacred place in the Erivan Empire
ESTRENDOR: \es-tren-door\ Northern wastes
ETCHER: Member of the Black Diamond thieves' guild
FALINA BROCKTON: Real name of Emerald, waitress at The Rose and Thorn Tavern
FANEN PICKERING: \fan-in\ Middle son of Count Pickering
FAULD, THE ORDER OF: \fall-ed\ Post-imperial order of knights dedicated to preserving the skill and discipline of the Teshlor Knights
FENITILIAN, BROTHER: Monk of Maribor, made warm shoes
FERROL: God of the elves
FINILESS: Noted author
FLETCHER: Maker of arrows
GALEANNON: \gale-e-an-on\ Kingdom of Avryn, ruled by Fredrick and Josephine
GALENTI: \ga-lehn'-tay\ Calian term
GALEWYR RIVER: \gale-wahar\ Marks the southern border of Melengar and the northern border of Warric and reaches the sea near the fishing village of Roe
GALIEN, ARCHBISHOP: \gal-e-in\ High-ranking member of the Nyphron Church

GALILIN: \gal-ah-lin\ Province of Melengar ruled by Count Pickering

GEMKEY: Gem that opens a gemlock

GEMLOCK: Dwarven invention that seals a container and can only be opened with a precious gem of the right type and cut

GENTRY SQUARE: Affluent district of Melengar

GHAZEL: \gehz-ell\ Ba Ran Ghazel, dwarven name for goblins, literally: Sea goblins

GHENT: Ecclesiastical holding of the Nyphron Church

GILARABRYWN: \gill-lar-ah-bren\ Elven beast of war

GINLIN, BROTHER: \gin-lin\ Monk of Maribor, winemaker, refuses to touch a knife

GLAMRENDOR: \glam-ren-door\ Capital of Dunmore

GLENMORGAN: 326 years after the fall of the Novronian Empire, this native of Ghent reunited the four nations of Apeladorn; founder of Sheridan University; creator of the great north-south road; builder of the Ervanon palace (of which only the Crown Tower remains)

GLENMORGAN II: Son of Glenmorgan. When his father died young, the new and inexperienced emperor relied on church officials to assist him in managing his empire. They in turn took the opportunity to manipulate the emperor into granting sweeping powers to the church and nobles loyal to the church. These leaders opposed defending Delgos against the invading Ba Ran Ghazel in Calis and the Dacca in Delgos, arguing the threat would increase dependency on the empire.

GLENMORGAN III: Grandson of Glenmorgan. Shortly after assuming the stewardship, he attempted to reassert control over the realm his grandfather had created by leading an army against the invading Ghazel that had reached southeastern Avryn. He defeated the Ghazel at the First

Battle of Vilan Hills and announced plans to ride to the aid of Tur Del Fur. Fearing his rise in power, in the sixth year of his reign, his nobles betrayed and imprisoned him in Blythin Castle. Jealous of his popularity and growing strength, and resentful of his policy of stripping the nobles and clergy of their power, the church charged him with heresy. He was found guilty and executed. This began the rapid collapse of what many called the Steward's Empire. The church later claimed the nobles had tricked them, and condemned many, most of whom reputedly ended their lives badly.

GLOUSTON: Province of northern Warric bordering on the Galewyr River, ruled by the marquis Lanaklin

GREAT SWORD: Long sword designed to be held with both hands

GRIGOLES: \gry-holes\ Author of *Grigoles Treatise on Imperial Common Law*

GUARDIAN OF THE HEIR: Teshlor Knight sworn to protect the Heir of Novron

GUTARIA: \goo-tar-ah\ Secret Nyphron prison designed to hold Esrahaddon

GWEN DELANCY: Calian prostitute and proprietor of Medford House and The Rose and Thorn Tavern

HADRIAN BLACKWATER: Mercenary, one-half of Riyria

HALBERD: Two-handed pole used as a weapon

HEIR OF NOVRON: Direct descendant of demigod Novron, destined to rule all of Avryn

HELDABERRY: Wild-growing fruit often used to make wine

HESLON, BROTHER: Monk of Maribor, great cook

HILFRED: Bodyguard of Princess Arista

HIMBOLT, BARON: Nobleman of Melengar

HOUSE, THE: Nickname used for Medford House

HOYTE: Onetime First Officer of the Black Diamond

IMPERIALISTS: Political party that desires to unite all the kingdoms of men under a single leader who is the direct descendant of the demigod Novron

JADE: Assassin in the Black Diamond, girlfriend of Cutter, friend of Royce

JERISH GRELAD: Teshlor Knight and first Guardian of the Heir

JERL, LORD: Neighbor of the Pickerings known for his prize-winning hunting dogs

JULIAN TEMPEST: Chamberlain of Melengar

KILE: Master sword smith, named used by Erebus when in the form of a man

KRINDEL: Prelate of the Nyphron Church and historian

KRIS DAGGER: Weapon with a wavy blade, sometimes used in magic rituals

LANAKLIN: Ruling family of Glouston

LANIS ETHELRED: \eth-el-red\ King of Warric, Imperialist

LANKSTEER: Capital city of the Lordium kingdom of Trent

LENA BOTHWICK: Wife of Russell, farmer in Dahlgren

LENARE PICKERING: Daughter of Count Pickering and Belinda, sister of Mauvin, Fanen, and Denek

LINGARD: Capital city of Relison, kingdom of Trent

LONGWOOD: Forest in Melengar

LOTHOMAD, KING: Lothomad the Bald, ruler of Lordium, Trent, expanded territory dramatically following the collapse of the Steward's Reign, pushing south through Ghent into Melengar, where Brodric Essendon defeated him in the Battle of Drondil Fields in 2545

LOWER QUARTER: Impoverished section of the city of Medford

LUIS GUY: Sentinel of the Nyphron Church

MAGNUS: Dwarf

MANDALIN: \man-dah-lynn\ Capital of Calis

MANZANT: \man-zahnt\ Infamous prison and salt mine located in Manzar, Maranon

MARANON: \mar-ah-non\ Kingdom in Avryn, ruled by Vincent and Regina

MARES CATHEDRAL: Center of the Nyphron Church in Melengar, run by Bishop Saldur

MARIBOR: \mar-eh-bore\ God of men

MASON GRUMON: \grum-on\ Blacksmith in Medford

MAURICE SALDUR, BISHOP: Head of Nyphron Church in Melengar, friend of the Essendon ruling family

MAUVIN PICKERING: \maw-vin\ Eldest of Count Pickering's sons

MCDERN: Peasant family living in Dahlgren

MEDFORD: Capital of Melengar

MEDFORD HOUSE: Brothel run by Gwen DeLancy and attached to The Rose and Thorn Tavern

MELENGAR: \mel-in-gar\ Kingdom in Avryn, ruled by the Essendon royal family

MELENGARIANS: Residents of Melengar

MELISSA: Head servant of Princess Arista, nickname Missy

MERCS: Mercenaries

MERLONS: Solid section between two crenels in a crenellated battlement

MERTON, MONSIGNOR: Eccentric priest from Ghent, known to talk aloud to Maribor

MILLIE: Hadrian's horse

MIR: Person with both elven and human blood

MONTEMORCEY: \mont-eh-more-ah-sea\ Excellent wine imported through the Vandom Spice Company

MOTTE: Man-made hill

MOUSE: Royce's horse

MURIEL: Goddess of nature, daughter of Erebus, mother of Uberlin

MYRON: Monk of Maribor, son of Victor, brother of Alenda

NAREION: \nare-e-on\ Last emperor of the Novronian Empire

NATIONALISTS: Political party led by Degan Gaunt that desires rule by the will of the people

NEVRIK: \nehv-rick\ Son of Nareion, the heir who went into hiding

NIDWALDEN RIVER: Marks the eastern border of Avryn and the start of the Erivan realm

NOVRON: Savior of mankind, son of the god Maribor, demigod who defeated the elven army in the Great Elven Wars, founder of the Novronian Empire, builder of Percepliquis

NOVRONIAN: \nov-ron-e-on\ Pertaining to Novron

NYPHRON CHURCH: The worshipers of Novron and Maribor, his father

NYPHRONS: \nef-rons\ Devout members of the church

PARTHALOREN FALLS: \path-ah-lore-e-on\ The great cataracts on the Nidwalden near Avempartha

PATRIARCH: Head of the Nyphron Church who lives in the Crown Tower of Ervanon

PAULDRON: A piece of armor covering the shoulder at the junction of the body piece and the arm piece

PERCEPLIQUIS: \per-sep-lah-kwiss\ The ancient capital of the Novronian Empire, named for the wife of Novron

PERCY BRAGA, ARCHDUKE: Lord Chancellor of Melengar, winner of the title of Grand Circuit Tournament Champion in Swords, the Silver Shield, and Golden Laurel; uncle to Alric and Arista, having married King Amrath's sister

PICKERING: Noble family of Melengar and rulers of Galilin. Count Pickering is known to be the best swordsman in Avryn and believed to use a magic sword.

PICKILERINON: Seadric, who shortened the family name to Pickering

PLESIEANTIC INCANTATION: \plass-e-an-tic\ A method used in the Art to draw power from nature

PRICE: First Officer of the Black Diamond thieves' guild

RATIBOR: Capital of the kingdom of Rhenydd

RENDON, BARON: Nobleman of Melengar

RENIAN, BROTHER: \rhen-e-ahn\ Childhood friend of Myron the monk

RHELACAN: \rell-ah-khan\ Great sword that Maribor tricked Drome into forging and Ferrol into enchanting, given to Novron to defeat the elves

RHENYDD: \ren-yaed\ Kingdom of Avryn, ruled by King Urith

RILAN VALLEY: Fertile land that separates Glouston and Chadwick

RIONILLION: \ri-on-ill-lon\ Name of the city that first stood on the site of Aquesta but was destroyed during the civil wars that occurred after the fall of the Novronian Empire

RIYRIA: \rye-ear-ah\ Elvish for *two*, a team or a bond

RONDEL: Common type of stiff-bladed dagger with a round handgrip

ROSE AND THORN, THE: Tavern in Medford run by Gwen DeLancy, used as a base by Riyria

ROSWORT, KING: Ruler of Dunmore

ROYCE MELBORN: Thief, one-half of Riyria

RUFUS, LORD: Ruthless northern warlord, respected by the south

RUSSELL BOTHWICK: Farmer in Dahlgren, husband of Lena

SALIFAN: \sal-eh-fan\ Fragrant wild plant used in incense

SAULY: Nickname of Maurice Saldur, used by those closest to him

SENON UPLAND: Highland plateau overlooking Chadwick

SENTINEL: Inquisitor generals of the Nyphron Church, charged with rooting out heresy and finding the lost Heir of Novron

SERET: \sir-ett\ Knights of Nyphron. The military arm of the church first formed by Lord Darius Seret, who was charged with finding the Heir of Novron.

SHERIDAN UNIVERSITY: Prestigious institution of learning, located in Ghent

SPADONE: Long two-handed sword with a tapering blade and an extended flange ahead of the hilt allowing for an extended variety of fighting maneuvers. Due to the length of the handgrip and the flange, which provides its own barbed hilt, the sword provides a number of additional hand placements, permitting the sword to be used similarly to a quarterstaff, as well as a powerful cleaving weapon. The spadone is the traditional weapon of a skilled knight.

SUMMERSRULE: Popular midsummer holiday celebrated with picnics, dances, feasts, and jousting tournaments

TABARD: A tunic worn over armor usually emblazoned with a coat of arms

TEK'CHIN: Single fighting discipline of the Teshlor Knights that was preserved by the Knights of the Fauld and handed down to the Pickerings

TENENT: Most common form of semi-standard international currency. Coins of gold, silver, and copper stamped with the likeness of the king of the realm where the coin was minted.

TERLANDO BAY: Harbor of Tur Del Fur

TESHLORS: Legendary knights of the Novronian Empire, greatest warriors ever to have lived

THERON WOOD: Father of Thrace Wood, farmer of Dahlgren

THRACE WOOD: Daughter of Theron and Addie

TILINER: Superior side sword used frequently by mercenaries in Avryn

TOBIS RENTINUAL: History professor at Sheridan University

TOLIN ESSENDON: Son of Brodric, who moved the capital to Medford and built Essendon Castle

TOMAS, DEACON: Priest of Dahlgren village

TORSONIC: Torque-producing, as in the cable used in crossbows

TRENT: Northern mountainous kingdoms

TRUMBUL, BARON: Mercenary

TUR: Small legendary village believed to have once been in Delgos, site of the first recorded visit of Kile, mythical source of great weapons

TUR DEL FUR: Coastal city in Delgos, on Terlando Bay, originally built by dwarves

UBERLIN: The god of the Dacca and the Ghazel, son of Erebus and his daughter, Muriel

URITH, KING: Ruler of Ratibor

VALIN, LORD: Elderly knight of Melengar known for his valor and courage but lacking strategic skills

VANDON: Port city of Delgos, home to the Vandom Spice Company, which began as a pirate haven until Delgos became a republic, when it became a legitimate business

VENLIN, PATRIARCH: Head of the Nyphron Church during the fall of the Novronian Empire

VERNES: Port city at the mouth of the Bernum River

VILLEIN: Person who is bound to the land and owned by the feudal lord

VINCE GRIFFIN: Dahlgren village founder

WARRIC: Kingdom of Avryn, ruled by Ethelred

WESBADEN: Major trade port city of Calis

WESTBANK: Newly formed province of Dunmore

WESTERLANDS: Unknown frontier to the west

WICEND: \why-send\ Farmer in Melengar who lends his name to the ford that crosses the Galewyr into Glouston

WINDS ABBEY: Monastery of the Monks of Maribor near Lake Windermere in western Melengar

WINTERTIDE: Chief holiday, held in midwinter, celebrated by feasts and jousts

WYATT DEMINTHAL: Onetime ship captain, father of Allie

WYLIN: \why-lynn\ Master-at-arms at Essendon Castle

extras

about the author

about the author

After finding a manual typewriter in the basement of a friend's house, **Michael J. Sullivan** inserted a blank piece of paper and typed *It was a dark and stormy night, and a shot rang out*. He was just eight. Still, the desire to fill the blank page and see where the keys would take him next wouldn't let go. As an adult, Michael spent ten years developing his craft by reading and studying authors such as Stephen King, Ayn Rand, and John Steinbeck, to name just a few. He wrote ten novels, and after finding no traction in publishing, he quit, vowing never to write creatively again.

Michael discovered forever is a very long time and ended his writing hiatus ten years later. The itch returned when he decided to write books for his then thirteen-year-old daughter, who was struggling in school because of dyslexia. Intrigued by the idea of a series with an overarching story line, yet told through individual, self-contained episodes, he created the Riyria Revelations. He wrote the series with no intention of publishing it. After presenting his book in manuscript form to his daughter, she declared that it had to be a "real book," in order for her to be able to read it.

So began his second adventure on the road to publication, which included drafting his wife to be his business manager, signing with a small independent press, and creating a publishing company. He sold more than sixty thousand books as a self-published author and leveraged this success to achieve mainstream publication through Orbit (the fantasy imprint of Hachette Book Group) as well as foreign translation rights including French, Spanish, Russian, German, Polish, and Czech.

Born in Detroit, Michigan, Michael presently lives in Fair-fax, Virginia, with his wife and three children. He continues to fill the blank pages with three projects under development: a modern fantasy, which explores the relationship between good and evil; a literary fiction piece, profiling a man's descent into madness; and a medieval fantasy, which will be prequel to his best-selling Riyria Revelations series.

Find out more about Michael J. Sullivan and other Orbit authors by registering for the free monthly newsletter at www.orbitbooks.net

interview

When did you know you wanted to be an author?

I was really young, no more than seven or eight, and a friend and I were playing hide-and-seek, and I found a typewriter in his basement. It was a huge black metal upright with small round keys. I completely forgot about the game and loaded a sheet of paper. I swear, the very first thing I wrote was: "It was a dark and stormy night, and a shot rang out." I thought I was a genius.

When my friend found me, he was clearly oblivious to the value of the discovery I had made. He wanted to go outside and do something fun. I thought about explaining to him that I couldn't imagine anything that could be more fun than what I was doing. I looked at the blank page and wondered what might come next: Was it a murder mystery? A horror story? I wanted to find out; I wanted to fill the page; I wanted to see where the little keys would take me.

We ended up going alley-picking until my mother called me for dinner. Alley-picking was the art of walking down the alley between the houses and seeing if there was anything cool being thrown away that we could take for ourselves. I had hoped that someone was throwing away a typewriter—no one was, and I went to bed that night thinking about that typewriter, thinking about that page and that first sentence.

What made you start writing? Were you a big reader? Did you ever add to that first sentence?

I'm a bit ashamed to admit that I hated reading in my youth. The first novel I tried was a book called *Big Red*, which was about a boy and his dog. I was on my way to my sister's farm and would have nothing to do for four hours. This was before DSs, DVDs, VCRs — before all the entertainment acronyms. It was also before Sirius, and I knew that twenty minutes after we left Detroit there would be nothing but static on the radio — hence the reason for the book. I finished it out of a sense of perseverance rather than enjoyment. When I was forty I wanted to be able to say, "Yes! I read a book once! It was excruciating, and took half a year, but by god, I did it!" Then whomever I was speaking to would look upon me with awe and know they were in the presence of a learned man. The reality was, the book was boring and put me to sleep.

Then I read Tolkien's *The Hobbit* and *The Lord of the Rings*. I loved them in a way I never dreamed it was possible to love a book. When I closed the last page of *The Return of the King*, I was miserable. My favorite pastime was over. As I mentioned before, this was before all those letters, before Xboxes and PS 2s and 3s, back when television had only three stations and cartoons were something shown only on Saturday morning. I went to the bookstore with my brother looking for another series like that one and was dismayed to come up empty.

There was nothing to read. I sat in my room, miserable. I made the mistake of telling my mother I was bored and she put me to work cleaning the front closet. I pulled out what looked like a plastic suitcase.

"What's this?" I asked.

"That? That's your sister's old typewriter. Been in there for years."

I never finished cleaning the closet.

•

Can you tell us about your background in writing? Where did you go to college? Do you have an MFA?
Usually this question comes from aspiring writers, and they always look disappointed when I tell them the answer: I never took a class in writing or English, beyond those required in high school. I never read a book on creative fiction. I never went to a seminar or a writers' conference. And I didn't attend my first writers' group until after I had published my first book. What I know about writing I taught myself.

My family didn't have the money to help me pay for college. My father, a crane operator at Great Lake Steel, died when I was nine, and after that my mother paid the bills with the money she made as a gift wrapper for Hudson's department store and my social security checks (that stopped coming when I turned eighteen). Still, I was pretty good at art and received a scholarship to the Center for Creative Studies in Detroit, but it ran out just after my first year. I did manage to land a job as an illustrator/keyliner, though. Then kids came along and my wife made more money, so I stayed home. I was twenty-three.

By this time we had moved to the remote northern corner of Vermont, literally over a thousand miles away from everyone we knew. I had lots of time on my hands, particularly when our daughter was taking naps and the idea of trying to write a publishable book rose to the top of my consciousness. I was teaching myself to write by reading books. I went to the local general store (yes, just like in Green Acres) and looked for the books with the golden seal indicating they were Nobel or Pulitzer Prize winners. These were not the books I would normally choose to read. At the time, I was into Stephen King, Isaac Asimov, and Frank Herbert, but I was trying to learn — so I figured I should learn from the best, right? I purposely forced myself to read widely, especially the stuff I did not like. They were the ones that always won the awards, the abysmally boring novels with paper-thin plots and elaborate prose.

I would pick a particular author, read several books by them, and then write a novel using what I had gleaned from reading their books. I didn't just write a short story—I wrote whole novels, then rinsed and repeated with the next author. I found something in each writer's style, or technique, that I could appreciate, and worked at teaching myself how to do what they did. In a way, I was like Silar from the television series *Heroes*, where I stole powers from other authors and added them to my toolbox. From Steinbeck I learned the transporting value of vivid setting descriptions. From Updike I found an appreciation for indirect prose that could more aptly describe something by not describing it. From Hemingway I discovered an economy for words. From King, his ability to get viscerally into the minds of his characters . . . and so on. In addition, I wrote in various genres: mystery, science fiction, horror, coming-of-age, literary fiction—anything and everything. I did this for ten years.

My writing improved with each novel. I finally wrote what I thought was something worthy of publishing and spent maybe a year and a half trying to get an agent before I finally gave up. Ten years and untold thousands of hours is a long time to work at something and achieve at least what I thought at the time to be nothing. Ten years, ten books, a ton of rejections, and not a single reader. It was time to give up this pipe dream.

So how did you "get back on the horse" as it were? What got you to start writing again?

It was years later; we had left Vermont and were living in North Carolina. The kids were old enough for day care and I went back into advertising. I had been a one-man band running an advertising department at a software company, and then I left that to create my own advertising agency, where I was the creative director. As to writing novels, I had vowed never to write another creative word.

Years passed, and my second daughter, Sarah, was struggling in school. She's dyslexic, which makes reading difficult. Not being good at something means it isn't any fun. So I got her books — good books — books I loved: *The Hobbit*, *Watership Down*, Chronicles of Narnia, Chronicles of Prydain, and that new book that I was hearing about — that thing about the kid who was a wizard or something . . . *Harry Potter*. It was sitting around on a table one afternoon. Beautiful, brand-new book — I'm a sucker for a pretty book. I cracked it and started reading and was transported. What I liked the most was how easy it was to read — it was just plain fun.

I started writing again, but this time for the sheer fun of it and with the hopes of making something for my daughter that would help her to like reading. I wasn't writing in anyone's style. I was done trying to make the great American novel. I just wanted to enjoy making something I would like to read. Still, the authors I had studied were there, lurking beneath the surface. When I wanted to paint a vivid setting, Steinbeck was whispering in my ear. When I hunted for a special turn of phrase, Updike lent me his hounds, King gave me a road map into the characters' heads, and when I wrote a run-on sentence, "Papa" scowled at me.

Why did you decide on a series instead of writing a single book and adding sequels after?

It may seem strange, but two of the biggest inspirations for the Riyria Revelations were the television shows *Babylon 5* and *Buffy the Vampire Slayer*. The thing about them that I found fascinating was the layered plots. *B5* in particular was amazing in that the entire five-year series was mapped out before the first episode was shot. I think this might be the first, and only, time that's ever happened. Yet it allowed for the unique opportunity for viewers to watch episodes and look for clues to the bigger questions that were hinted at from time to time and in small doses. In addition, Straczynski — the show's creator — layered his plots, something that was mimicked to a lesser degree in *Buffy*. This really impressed me, and I wondered if it could be done in a book series. So I actually mapped out the entire series before writing it. I was never making a series of books, but rather one long story in six episodes.

You use a lot of humor in your books; talk to us about that. During the late sixties and early seventies a lot of the movies were pretty depressing. Many of them were tough dramas like *Chinatown* or were dreary accounts of the aftermath of the Vietnam War, such as *Coming Home*. For me, it was a terrible time to be a moviegoer. Then I saw *Butch Cassidy and the Sundance Kid*. I really liked the mix of drama and humor. Sometimes at the most tense spots a bit of humor is the perfect ingredient, and to me, far more realistic.

I also mentioned *Buffy the Vampire Slayer* and that's another great example. Joss Whedon is a master of mixing drama and humor. I don't presume to put myself into his league, but the hours of enjoyment I had in watching something I wouldn't normally be attracted to was definitely an influence on me.

Royce and Hadrian are a great pair; where did the inspiration for them come from?
It's funny, because many people assume I'm a big fan of Fafhrd and the Gray Mouser, but I've never read any of those stories. Any similarities are purely coincidental. I already mentioned

Butch Cassidy and the Sundance Kid, and there was a television show called *I Spy* that I enjoyed while growing up, and I'm sure at a subconscious level there is a lot of that seeping into my characters, but their origins actually go way, way back—more than twenty years. It was when I was living in Vermont, and to help pass the cold, boring winters I started writing a chain story with two other friends. It basically started with two characters walking into a tavern and getting together a crack team to go on an adventure into an ancient dungeon. We would write a few pages and mail it on to the next to add to the tale. Yes, it was long ago . . . before there was e-mail.

My friends soon became bored, and not too happy that I would rewrite the parts they wrote, but I really loved the concept of two buddies, each with their own strengths, each very different, but having a relationship that really works for them. My daughter tells me it's classic bromance, but that's a term that came into vogue long after Royce and Hadrian came to life. I really like creating characters that I would like to hang out with. Being a writer means you get to create your own imaginary friends.

How did you decide on the writing style for the series?

The Riyria Revelations was born out of my trying something new. My last novel before this, even though it was written years previously, was a true literary fiction piece. Short on plot, long on character development, with sentences that were composed with great care and required a tremendous amount of contemplation and polishing. As I already mentioned, I loved the *fun* of *Harry Potter*. This wasn't Steinbeck; it was simple, and light, and just a good enjoyable read. Riyria just flowed from my head to the keyboard. I wrote the first book in a month, the second a month later. Its style was designed to be light. I had a huge story to tell, one of complex themes, numerous characters, and dozens of twists where things are not always what they seem. This idea would be unmanageable in a heavy-handed style. I'm already asking a great deal of the reader — to keep track of everything that happens over the course of six separate novels as if they were one long book. To make the trip as comfortable as possible for my readers I attempted a style I had never tried before — invisibility. The idea is to make the story pop off the page and make the writing disappear. Neither awkward prose nor eloquent phrases should distract the reader from immersion in the action and the world unfolding before them. I have needed on many occasions to rewrite passages that were too pretty, too sophisticated, for fear the reader would notice them and pause to reflect. I have other works that do this. For the Riyria Revelations I wanted to keep it simple. The result, I have discovered — much to my delight — is a book that reads like a movie in the reader's mind. As you can tell, a lot of my references have been from television and movies, and I think that also sets the tone and pace in these books. I'm not so much trying to create another Lord of the Rings so much as a good old-fashioned Errol Flynn movie or sixties Western.

This, then, is the "light-hand" approach that some have read about on my website. While I know that I am not the first to employ it, it remains something of a rarity in the fantasy realm. For me, this is a great disappointment, for while I enjoy a beautifully written novel — I love a great story.

Why did you choose to use such established fantasy tropes in your series?

For years now I have heard fans of the traditional "Tolkienesque" fantasy novels lament the repetitive themes and exhausted archetypes of the genre. They are tired of the same old hero-vanquishing-evil and want something new, something more real, more believable. Which to me sounds like someone saying they love chocolate, they just wished it wasn't so chocolaty and that it tasted more like vanilla. Many writers struggle to appease, whether that means turning an old theme on its head or going for the gritty and morbid. During the past few decades this trend has resulted in fantasy going dark: Evil often wins. Heroes don't exist.

This happened before.

The motion-picture industry turned out happy endings for decades, then in the sixties things began to change. Gritty, realistic films began to pop up, and antiheroes like The Man with No Name arrived in the Italian Western. The trend solidified in the seventies, with moviemakers like Scorsese, De Laurentiis, Coppola, and Kubrick, who often focused on complex and unpleasant themes. It was theorized that the public was tired of the old good-triumphs-over-evil stories because it was so out of sync with the realities of the American experience during the age of Watergate, the Vietnam War, the Civil Rights movement, and the Sexual Revolution.

Then *Star Wars* debuted in 1977 and everything began to change again.

I remember seeing *Star Wars* the weekend it opened. I wasn't expecting anything, and I was debating between it and the cartoon movie *Wizards*. Only one early review for *Star Wars* was out, a small block article in the *Detroit News* that slammed it for being unoriginal and using just about every movie cliché that existed, but the review did add that it was surprisingly entertaining. It was the comment about movie clichés that tipped the scales for me. I never cared for the gritty realism of *Midnight Cowboy* and *Taxi Driver*. I liked the old films, the ones I saw on television that I was too young to have seen at a theater. When the movie ended and the credits were rolling, I had one thought — so that's a movie.

I saw the same scenario play out to some degree in the fantasy book world. This time it was a novel series by a new author who made the unforgivable mistake of writing a hero story using every clichéd trapping available. It was actually the tale of a young boy destined to defeat an evil dark lord and save the world from destruction. It even had an old mentor wizard guiding him as well as a motley crew of humorous sidekicks (not unlike *Star Wars*). According to the professed mentality of the consumer, the books should have been laughable. In serious times, people don't want trite tales of do-gooders with happy endings. They should have been panned as the worst kind of old-fashioned echo. Instead, there is a Harry Potter theme park in Florida now.

So I have to wonder — what's the deal?

An aspiring writer friend of mine was working on a book in which a talking cat plays an important role. He presented part of his story to a writers' workshop and the overwhelming response was that the talking cat was cliché — a tired device as old as *Alice in Wonderland*. He was depressed afterward, and over drinks he asked me if his story was even worth pursuing anymore, as it wouldn't work without the cat. I told him that the cat doesn't matter. All that matters is if the story is good and if it is well written.

You see, I don't think people so much hate to read the same type of story, they just hate to read bad stories. There are an infinite number of ways to combine old ideas to create new books. If the plot is good, if the reader cares for the characters, if the setting feels real, then it doesn't matter if it's about talking cats or boys destined to defeat an evil dark lord. And trying to write a completely original story is sort of like trying to compose music with all original notes. It's not necessary, and I'm not even certain it's possible.

Some people have told me that I should alter the names of things to make the world more unique, less generic, but I chose to use elves and dwarves, kings and queens, castles and churches, precisely because everyone knows what they are — I don't have to explain them. The less time I have to take explaining the basics of my world, the more time I have to tell a great story and the less work readers have to go through to imagine themselves in the world.

How did you get published?

Well, as I mentioned, I wasn't planning on publishing. I had put that aspect behind me. But I did want my books to be read . . . Heck, all authors do. Originally I gave it to a few friends and they, not surprisingly, expressed their enjoyment . . . but, hey, they are my friends so I wouldn't expect less.

I mentioned that my daughter is dyslexic. This means she has a few strange quirks. She is easily distracted by the color of the background on a computer screen, whether a door is left ajar or a light is on in another room. When I finished *The Crown Conspiracy* I presented her with a stack of double-spaced 8½" × 11" pages, and she looked at me as if I were crazy.

"I can't read it this way . . . you said you were writing me a book . . . I need binding; I need a smaller page size."

I just sighed.

For anyone who has read my blog, or read or listened to any of my other interviews, you know that my wife is the engine behind my writing. She is an extremely competent person who will break any door and rise over any challenge — even something as daunting as publishing. And she is a great businessperson. So when I finally resigned myself that I should give publishing one more chance, I laid my plan well. I wrote a terrible query letter and presented it to my wife, along with my inept plan of mailing it to one agent a month for the next twelve months.

"Seriously?" she told me with a raised eyebrow. "Send me a copy to rewrite and go back to your editing . . . I'll take care of this."

Yes! I thought. Now I just might have a chance.

Robin was the one who, after a hundred or so rejections, got Aspirations Media (a small independent press based in Minnesota) to publish my first book. They had planned on putting out the second book in April 2008, but in March they informed us they really didn't have the cash for the printing. We negotiated the rights back and published the next four ourselves under the Ridan Label, a publishing company Robin set up. When the original print run of *The Crown Conspiracy* sold out, that reverted to us as well. By October 2010 we had kept up the breakneck pace of releasing one book every six months and saw a nice following both from readers and book bloggers.

With the release of book five the sales went up exponentially. For the first time in my writing career I was actually contributing some money to the household. And I was even able to pay off some pretty high credit card debt we had built when my single-income wife had been laid off not once but three times over a two-year period — OUCH!

A few months earlier, we had several publishers in the Czech Republic asking for foreign rights. Knowing that there was no way she could handle this on her own, Robin went in search of an agent to broker this deal. And landed Teri Tobias (who had sold foreign rights for Dan Brown and Patrick Rothfuss). She had left her position as foreign rights director at Sanford J.

Greenburger Associates to start her own agency.

The books were doing so well by the fall of 2010 that Robin got thinking there might be an opportunity to try New York again. Neither of us thought it would happen, or so fast, but to our amazement we received an offer from Orbit in just a couple of weeks. So Riyria has taken a strange path. It has been published through a traditional small press, self-published (primarily as e-books), and now through a big-six publisher.

if you enjoyed
THEFT OF SWORDS
look out for
RISE OF EMPIRE
Volume two of the Riyria Revelations

also by

Michael J. Sullivan

Amilia made the mistake of looking back into Edith Mon's eyes. She had never meant to — she had never planned on raising her stare from the floor — but Edith startled her and she looked up without thinking. The head maid would consider her action defiance, a sign of rebellion in the ranks of the scullery. Amilia had never looked into Edith's eyes before, and doing so now, she wondered if a soul lurked behind them. If so, it must be cowering or dead, rotting like a late-autumn apple; that would explain her smell. Edith had a sour scent, vaguely rancid, as if something had gone bad.

"This will be another tenent withheld from yer pay," the rotund woman said. "Yer digging quite a hole, ain't you?"

Edith was big and broad and missing any sign of a neck. Her

huge anvil of a head sat squarely on her shoulders. By contrast, Amilia barely existed. Small and pear-shaped, with a plain face and long, lifeless hair, she was part of the crowd, one of the faces no one paused to consider — neither pretty nor grotesque enough to warrant a second glance. Unfortunately, her invisibility failed when it came to the palace's head maid, Edith Mon.

"I didn't break it." *Mistake number two*, Amilia thought.

A meaty hand slapped her across the face, ringing her ears and making her eyes water. "Go on," Edith enticed her with a sweet tone, and then whispered in her ear, "lie to me again."

Gripping the washbasin to steady herself, Amilia felt heat blossom on her cheek. Her gaze now followed Edith's hand, and when it rose again, Amilia flinched. With a snicker, Edith ran her plump fingers through Amilia's hair.

"No tangles," Edith observed. "I can see how ya spend yer time, instead of doing yer work. Ya hoping to catch the eye of the butcher? Maybe that saucy little man who delivers the wood? I saw ya talking to him. Know what they sees when they looks at ya? They sees an ugly scullery maid is what. A wretched filthy guttersnipe who smells of lye and grease. They would rather pay for a whore than get ya for nothing. You'd be better off spending more time on yer tasks. If ya did, I wouldn't have to beat ya so often."

Amilia felt Edith winding her hair, twisting and tightening it around her fist. "It's not like I enjoy hurting ya." She pulled until Amilia winced. "But ya have to learn." Edith continued pulling Amilia's hair, forcing her head back until only the ceiling was visible. "Yer slow, stupid, and ugly. That's why yer still in the scullery. I can't make ya a laundry maid, much less a parlor or chambermaid. You'd embarrass me, understand?"

Amilia remained quiet.

"I said, do ya understand?"

"Yes."

"Say yer sorry for chipping the plate."

"I'm sorry for chipping the plate."

"And yer sorry for lying about it?"

"Yes."

Edith roughly patted Amilia's burning cheek. "That's a good girl. I'll add the cost to yer tally. Now as for punishment . . ." She let go of Amilia's hair and tore the scrub brush from her hand, measuring its weight. She usually used a belt; the brush would hurt more. Edith would drag her to the laundry, where the big cook could not see. The head cook had taken a liking to Amilia, and while Edith had every right to discipline her girls, Ibis would not stand for it in his kitchen. Amilia waited for a fat hand to grab her wrist, but instead Edith stroked her head. "Such long hair," she said at length. "It's yer hair that's getting in the way, isn't it? It's making ya think too much of yerself. Well, I know just how to fix both problems. Yer gonna look real pretty when I —"

The kitchen fell silent. Cora, who had been incessantly plunging her butter churn, paused in mid-stroke. The cooks stopped chopping and even Nipper, who was stacking wood near the stoves, froze. Amilia followed their gaze to the stairs.

A noblewoman adorned in white velvet and satin glided down the steps and entered the steamy stench of the scullery. Piercing eyes and razor-thin lips stood out against a powdered face. The woman was tall and — unlike Amilia, who had a hunched posture — stood straight and proud. She moved immediately to the small table along the wall, where the baker was preparing bread.

"Clear this," she ordered with a wave of her hand, speaking to no one in particular. The baker immediately scooped his utensils and dough into his apron and hurried away. "Scrub it clean," the lady insisted.

Amilia felt the brush thrust back into her hand, and a push sent her stumbling forward. She did not look up and went right to work making large swirls of flour-soaked film. Nipper was beside her in an instant with a bucket, and Vella arrived with a towel. Together they cleared the mess while the woman watched with disdain.

"Two chairs," the lady barked, and Nipper ran off to fetch them.

Uncertain what to do next, Amilia stood in place watching the lady, holding the dripping brush at her side. When the noblewoman caught her staring, Amilia quickly looked down and movement caught her eye. A small gray mouse froze beneath the baker's table, trying to conceal itself in the shadows. Taking a chance, it snatched a morsel of bread and disappeared through a small crack.

"What a miserable creature," she heard the lady say. Amilia thought she was referring to the mouse until she added, "You're making a filthy puddle on the floor. Go away."

Before retreating to her washbasin, Amilia attempted a pathetic curtsy. A flurry of orders erupted from the woman, each announced with perfect diction. Vella, Cora, and even Edith went about setting the table as if for a royal banquet. Vella draped a white tablecloth, and Edith started setting out silverware only to be shooed away as the woman carefully placed each piece herself. Soon the table was elegantly set for two, complete with multiple goblets and linen napkins.

Amilia could not imagine who could be dining there. No one would set a table for the servants, and why would a noble come to the kitchen to eat?

"Here now, what's all this about?" Amilia heard the deep familiar voice of Ibis Thinly. The old sea cook was a large barrel-chested man with bright blue eyes and a thin beard that wreathed the line of his chin. He had spent the morning meeting with farmers, yet he still wore his ever-present apron. The grease-stained wrap was his uniform, his mark of office. He barged into the kitchen like a bear returning to his cave to find mischief afoot. When he spotted the lady, he stopped.

"I am Lady Constance," the noblewoman informed him. "In a moment I will be bringing Empress Modina here. If you are the cook, then prepare food." The lady paused a moment to study the table critically. She adjusted the position of a few items, then turned and left.

"Leif, get a knife on that roasted lamb," Ibis shouted. "Cora, fetch cheese. Vella, get bread. Nipper, straighten that woodpile!"

"The empress!" Cora exclaimed as she raced for the pantry.

"What's she doing coming here?" Leif asked. There was anger in his voice, as if an unwelcome, no-account relative was dropping by and he was the inconvenienced lord of the manor.

Amilia had heard of the empress but had never seen her — not even from a distance. Few had. She had been coronated in a private ceremony over half a year earlier on Wintertide, and her arrival in Aquesta had changed everything.

King Ethelred no longer wore his crown, and was addressed as "Regent" instead of "Your Majesty." He still ruled over the castle, only now it was referred to as the imperial palace. The other one, Regent Saldur, had made all the changes. Originally from Melengar, the former bishop had taken up residence and set builders working day and night on the great hall and throne room. Saldur had also declared new rules that all the servants had to follow.

The palace staff could no longer leave the grounds unless escorted by one of the new guards, and all outgoing letters were read and needed to be approved. The latter edict was hardly an issue, as few servants could write. The restriction on going outside the palace, however, was a hardship to almost everyone.

Many with families in the city or surrounding farms chose to resign, because they could no longer return home each night. Those remaining at the castle never heard from them again. Regent Saldur had successfully isolated the palace from the outside world, but inside, rumors and gossip ran wild. Speculations flourished in out-of-the-way corridors that giving notice was as unhealthy as attempting to sneak away.

The fact that no one ever saw the empress ignited its own set of speculations. Everyone knew she was the heir of the original, legendary emperor, Novron, and therefore a child of the god Maribor. This had been proven when she had been the only one capable of slaying the beast that had slaughtered dozens of Elan's greatest knights. That she had previously been a farm girl from a small village confirmed that in the eyes of Maribor, all were equal. Rumors concluded that she had ascended to the state of a spiritual being, and only the regents and her personal secretary ever stood in her divine presence.

That must be who the noblewoman is, Amilia thought. The lady with the sour face and perfect speech was the imperial secretary to the empress.

They soon had an array of the best food they could muster in a short time laid out on the table. Knob, the baker, and Leif, the butcher, disputed the placement of dishes, each wanting his wares in the center. "Cora," Ibis said, "put your pretty cake of cheese in the middle." This brought a smile and blush to the dairymaid's face and scowls from Leif and Knob.

Being a scullion, Amilia had no more part to play and returned to her dishes. Edith was chatting excitedly in the corner near the stack of oak kegs with the tapster and the cupbearer, and all the servants were straightening their outfits and running fingers through their hair. Nipper was still sweeping when the lady returned. Once more everyone stopped and watched as the lady led a thin young girl by the wrist.

"Sit down," Lady Constance ordered in her brisk tone.

Everyone peered past the two women, trying to catch the first glimpse of the god-queen. Two well-armored guards emerged and took up positions on either side of the table. But no one else appeared.

Where is the empress?

"Modina, I said sit down," Lady Constance repeated.

Shock rippled through Amilia.

Modina? This waif of a child is the empress?

The girl did not appear to hear Lady Constance and stood limp with a blank expression. She looked to be a teenager, delicate and deathly thin. Once she might have been pretty, but what remained was an appalling sight. The girl's face was white as bone, her skin thin and stretched, revealing the detailed outline of her skull beneath. Her ragged blonde hair fell across her face. She wore only a thin white smock, which added to the girl's ghostly appearance.

Lady Constance sighed and forced the girl into one of the chairs at the baker's table. Like a doll, the girl allowed herself to be moved. She said nothing and her eyes stared blankly.

"Place the napkin in your lap this way." Lady Constance carefully opened and laid the linen with deliberate movements. She waited, glaring at the empress, who sat, oblivious. "As empress, you will never serve yourself," Lady Constance went on. "You will wait as your servants fill your plate." She was looking around with irritation when her eyes found Amilia. "You — come here," she ordered. "Serve Her Eminence."

Amilia dropped the brush in the basin and, wiping her hands on her smock, rushed forward. She lacked experience with serving but said nothing. Instead, she focused on recalling the times she had watched Leif cutting meat. Taking up the tongs and a knife, she tried her best to imitate him. Leif always made it look effortless, but Amilia's fingers betrayed her and she fumbled miserably, managing to place only a few shredded bits of lamb on the girl's plate.

"Bread." Lady Constance snapped the word like a whip and Amilia sliced into the long twisted loaf, nearly cutting herself in the process.

"Now eat."

For a brief moment, Amilia thought this was another order for her and reached out in response. She caught herself and stood motionless, uncertain if she was free to return to her dishes.

"Eat, I said." The imperial secretary glared at the girl, who continued to stare blankly at the far wall.

"*Eat, damn you!*" Lady Constance bellowed, and everyone in the kitchen, including Edith Mon and Ibis Thinly, jumped. She pounded the baker's table with her fist, knocking over the stemware and bouncing the knives against the plates. "*Eat!*" Lady Constance repeated, and slapped the girl across the face. Her skin-wrapped skull rocked with the blow and came to rest on its own. The girl did not wince. She merely continued her stare, this time at a new wall.

In a fit of rage, the imperial secretary rose, knocking over her chair. She took one of the pieces of meat and tried to force it into the girl's mouth.

"What's going on?"

Lady Constance froze at the sound of the voice. An old white-haired man descended the steps into the scullery. His elegant purple robe and black cape looked out of place in the hot, messy kitchen. Amilia recognized Regent Saldur immediately.

"What in the world . . ." Saldur began as he approached the

table. He looked at the girl, then at the kitchen staff, and finally at Lady Constance, who at some point had dropped the meat.

"What were you thinking . . . bringing her down here?"

"I — I thought if—"

Saldur held up his hand, silencing her, then slowly squeezed it into a fist. He clenched his jaw and drew a deep breath through his sharp nose. Once more he focused on the girl. "Look at her. You were supposed to educate and train her. She's worse than ever!"

"I — I tried, but —"

"Shut up!" the regent snapped, still holding up his fist. No one in the kitchen moved. The only sounds were the faint crackle of the fire in the ovens and the bubbling of broth in a pot. "If this is the result of a professional, we may as well try an amateur. They couldn't possibly do worse." The regent pointed at Amilia. "You! Congratulations, you are now the imperial secretary to the empress." Turning his attention back to Lady Constance, he said, "And as for you – your services are no longer required. Guards, remove her."

Amilia saw Lady Constance falter. Her perfect posture evaporated as she cowered and stepped backward, nearly falling over the upended chair. "No! Please, no," she cried as a palace guard gripped her arm and pulled her toward the back door. Another guard took her other arm. She grew frantic, pleading and struggling as they dragged her out.

Amilia stood frozen in place, holding the meat tongs and carving knife, trying to remember how to breathe. Once the pleas of Lady Constance faded, Regent Saldur turned to her, his face flushed red, his teeth revealed behind taunt lips. "Don't fail me," he told her, and returned up the stairs, his cape whirling behind him.

Amilia looked back at the girl, who continued to stare at the wall.